His Wicked Kiss

Gaelen Foley

piatkus

PIATKUS

First published in the US in 2006 by Ballantine Books,
First published in Great Britain in 2006 by Piatkus Books
This paperback edition published 2011 by Piatkus
Reprinted 2011

A CIP catalogue record for this book
is available from the British Library.

ISBN 978-0-7499-5605-9

Typeset by Phoenix Photosetting, Chatham, Kent
Printed and bound by CPI Group (UK) Ltd, Croydon, CR0 4YY

Papers used by Piatkus are from well-managed forests
and other responsible sources.

www.piatkus.co.uk

Gaelen Foley is the *New York Times* bestselling author of rich, bold his*t*rical romances set in the glittering world of R*e*gency Eng... ...le in tw... ...erous awards, including the Romantic Times Reviewers' Choice Award for Best Historical Adventure.

Gaelen holds a BA in English literature with a minor in philosophy and it was while studying the Romantic poets, such as Wordsworth, Byron and Keats that she first fell in love with the Regency period in which her novels are set. After college, she dedicated herself completely to her artistic pursuits, spending five and a half years moonlighting as a waitress to keep her days free for writing and honing her craft.

Gaelen lives near Pittsburgh with her college-sweetheart husband, Eric, and a mischievous bichon frise called Bingley. She is hard at work on her next book.

To find out more about Gaelen's books visit her website at www.gaelenfoley.com

C 03 0237026

Everything that lives,
Lives not alone, nor for itself.

—WILLIAM BLAKE
From "The Book of Thel," 1789, Plate 3, Line 26

Georgiana's Brood: THE KNIGHT MISCELLANY

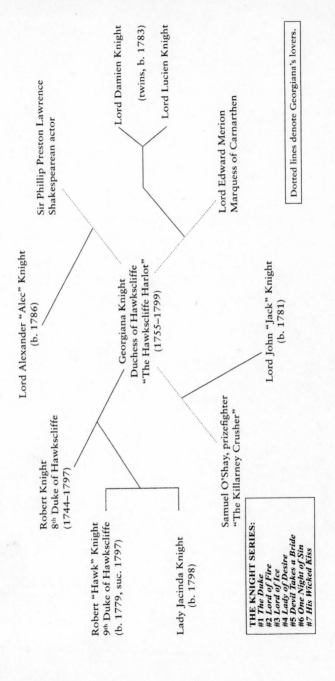

Sir Phillip Preston Lawrence
Shakespearean actor

Lord Alexander "Alec" Knight
(b. 1786)

Lord Damien Knight
(twins, b. 1783)
Lord Lucien Knight

Georgiana Knight
Duchess of Hawkscliffe
"The Hawkscliffe Harlot"
(1755–1799)

Lord Edward Merion
Marquess of Carnarthen

Robert Knight
8ᵗʰ Duke of Hawkscliffe
(1744–1797)

Lord John "Jack" Knight
(b. 1781)

Samuel O'Shay, prizefighter
"The Killarney Crusher"

Robert "Hawk" Knight
9ᵗʰ Duke of Hawkscliffe
(b. 1779, suc. 1797)

Lady Jacinda Knight
(b. 1798)

Dotted lines denote Georgiana's lovers.

THE KNIGHT SERIES:
#1 *The Duke*
#2 *Lord of Fire*
#3 *Lord of Ice*
#4 *Lady of Desire*
#5 *Devil Takes a Bride*
#6 *One Night of Sin*
#7 *His Wicked Kiss*

CHAPTER
∽ ONE ∾

February, 1818

S*he wanted to dance.*

Her toes in silken slippers tapped beneath the hem of her white—no, blue—no, her green *silk gown, in time with the elegant strains from the orchestra.*

Innumerable twinkling candles on the crystal chandeliers cast a golden haze over the ballroom, where pairs of gliding dancers whirled through the steps of the new, daring waltz: ladies in rich, pale, luminous silks, gentlemen in stately black and white.

Suddenly, through the crowd, she sensed someone staring at her. Peeking over her painted fan, she caught only a glimpse of a tall, imposing figure before the swirling motion of the dancers hid him from her view again.

Her pulse leaped. A thrill rushed through her, for she could sense him, feel him coming to ask her to stand up with him for the next quadrille.

Wide-eyed, her heart pounding, she waited, yearning for a clearer look at the face of her mystery man, her destined hero—

At that moment, a prickle of instinctual warning on her nape summoned Eden Farraday back from her lovely reverie.

Her rapt gaze focused slowly as reality pressed back in on her reluctant senses, bringing with it all the ceaseless sounds and pungent smells of another black, humid night in the tropical forest.

Instead of crystal chandeliers, a lone, rusty lantern gleamed on the bamboo table beside her hammock, which was draped beneath a cloud of filmy white mosquito netting. In place of lords and ladies, pale moths danced and flittered against the lantern's glass, and beyond the palm-thatched roof of the naturalists' jungle stilt-house, the darkness throbbed with teeming life.

1

Insects sang in deafening cadence. Monkeys bickered for the most comfortable branches to sleep on in the trees, but at least the raucous parrots had quit their noisy squabbling. Far off in the distance, a jaguar roared to warn a rival off its territory, for the great stealthy beasts' hunting hour had come.

Its fierce echo chased away her shining vision of London glamour, leaving nothing but the artifact that had inspired it—a yellowed, crinkled, year-old copy of a fashion magazine, *La Belle Assemblée,* sent by her dear cousin Amelia all the way from England.

The sense of danger, however, still remained.

She glanced around uneasily, her jungle-honed instincts on alert; her hand crept toward the pistol that was always by her side.

And then she heard it. A faint and subtle *hiss* from much too close overhead.

Lifting her gaze, she found herself eye to cold, beady eye with a monstrous eight-foot fer-de-lance. Fangs gleaming, the deadly serpent flicked its forked tongue in her direction. She shrank back slowly, not daring to move too fast.

Seeking warm-blooded prey, the big snake seemed to sense the vibrations of her pounding heart. The species invaded many a human dwelling in the torrid zone: humans left crumbs; crumbs brought mice; and the mice brought the fer-de-lance, a notoriously ill-tempered viper with a reputation for attacking with the slightest provocation.

Its bite spelled doom.

Slim and sinuous, it had slithered up into the weathered crossbeams of their shelter. It must have gone silently exploring then in search of a plump rodent entrée, for at present it was coiled around the post from which her hammock hung, and was studying her like it wondered how she'd taste.

To her amazement, it had sliced through the mosquito netting with those daggered fangs that dispensed a venom capable of killing a large man in under half an hour. Eden had seen it happen, and it was not a pleasant death.

When the fer-de-lance arched its scaly neck into that ominous S shape, she had a fleeting fraction of a second to see the attack coming, then it struck—angry reptile snapping out like a whip, a flash of fangs.

She flung herself onto her back on her hammock, brought up her pistol, and fired.

2

A disgusted yelp escaped her as the snake's severed head plopped right onto the center of her treasured magazine.

"Bloody—!" she started, then stopped herself from uttering the rest, only mouthing the epithet, for refined London ladies did not curse aloud. Still!

That dashed magazine had taken a blasted year to reach her, coming via courier by way of Jamaica. Rolling nimbly out of her hammock, Eden scowled at the wide-mouthed snake head that now marred the elegant publication. She flipped her long plait of auburn hair over her shoulder, brushed the mosquito netting aside and stepped away, shaking off her latest brush with death.

"Everything all right, dear?" her father, Dr. Victor Farraday, called in a casual tone from his work tent across the naturalists' camp, located deep in the heart of Venezuela's green, steaming Orinoco Delta.

She shot a distracted glance in his direction. "Fine, Father!" she yelled back and, with shaking hands, put her gun away. *Lord, I can't wait to get out of here.*

With a grimace, she picked up the magazine like a tray, balancing the dead snake's head on it, and marched stoically to the rustic railing that overlooked the wide, onyx river. She flung the head into the current without ceremony, and heard it plop down into the Orinoco with a small splash.

Well, no doubt something would eat it in minutes, she thought. That was the law of the jungle: Eat or be eaten. Sending a wary glance out across the inky river, she saw a number of red eyes gleaming by the lantern's glow, and then a large thing submerged with barely a ripple in the silver moonlight.

Eden shook her head. Man-eating crocodiles, poisonous snakes, bloodsucking bats—and Papa said London was dangerous. *Patience,* she told herself, doing her best to keep her hunger for civilization in check. It wouldn't be much longer now. They would soon be going home to England whether Papa liked it or not.

Turning to gaze in the direction of her father's work tent, her face filled with determination. She gave herself a small nod. *Yes.* The suspense was torture. She had to hear Papa's decision—now. She tore off the pages of her magazine that could not be saved and put them aside as fuel for the cooking fires, then strode out of their native-style dwelling, known as a *palafito.* She fixed her sights on the naturalists' main work tent across the camp.

3

A ring of torches burned around the perimeter of the clearing to keep the beasts at bay, but there was little help for the mosquitoes. She swatted one away as she passed the fire pit in the center of camp, where she greeted their three black servants with affection. Their bright grins flashed in the darkness. Now that the heat of day had passed, the servants, dressed in flowing, light, tropical garb, were cooking dinner for themselves.

Eden exchanged a few teasing remarks with them and forged on. The skirts of her cotton walking dress swirled around her legs and her thick leather boots sunk firmly into the soft turf with every stride. Her forward stare was confident, but in truth, her heart was pounding as she waited for the verdict.

Ahead, beneath the three-sided military-style tent, Dr. Victor Farraday and his brawny Australian assistant, Connor O'Keefe, bent their heads together in close discussion, poring over a weathered map. The field table was strewn with the latest specimens they had collected today on their trek, led by the local Waroa shaman to where the medicine plants grew. For now, however, their new finds were forgotten. Their faces were tense and serious by the dim orange glow of the lantern.

It was no wonder why. Her treasured magazine was not the only item the courier had brought today from the outer world, smuggling their mail and a few supplies in past the Spanish fleet trolling the coast.

There had also been a letter, equally out of date, from the solicitor representing Papa's aristocratic patron back in England. The letter announced the sad tidings that the old, philanthropic fourth Earl of Pembrooke, alas, had gone on to his eternal reward some months ago.

His Lordship's heir, the fifth earl, was young and dashing, rumored to be quite handsome and, if the Society pages of *La Belle Assemblée* could be believed, he was also known as a gambler and a bit of a rakehell. The new Lord Pembrooke was building himself a fine new country house, and as far as he was concerned, all the artists and scholars, musicians and sculptors and scientists that his grandfather had for so long commissioned could go hang. So he had instructed his solicitor to say.

In short, the famed Dr. Farraday had lost the funding for his research, and Eden had nearly cheered aloud to hear it.

She had bitten her tongue, however, and suppressed her joy, for

4

Papa had turned pale at the news, committed as any obsessed genius to his work. Oh, but it wasn't as though they would starve once they reached England, she reasoned with a hardheaded practicality that usually balanced out her dreamy side.

A trained physician and now a prestigious author as well, Dr. Farraday had a standing offer of a highly respectable teaching post at the Royal College of Medicine in London. When he accepted it, as he surely must, it wouldn't be long before she and Cousin Amelia would be promenading in Hyde Park among the other *elegantes,* causing the young bucks to wreck their stylish phaetons for turning to stare at them.

Soon—who could say?—she might actually have a normal life.

Clasping her hands behind her back, Eden cleared her throat politely to get the gentlemen's attention.

The two scientists had been so absorbed in their discussion they had not noticed her standing there. At once, they fell silent, halting their low-toned discussion.

"Well, boys," she said with a jaunty smile, trying with a touch of humor to lighten some of the tension they all were feeling about the sudden change in their situation. "When are we finally going to leave?"

Alas, her jest fell flat. The pair exchanged a guarded glance. Belatedly, Connor stood in the presence of a lady, knowing how she loved these small gestures of civility.

Connor O'Keefe was a tanned, blond, towering Australian, over six feet tall and twice as broad as the tribal warriors of the Delta. He was a strong man of few words and a specialist in zoology; his sensitivity to the forest animals was endearing to Eden, but more and more frequently of late, his unbroken stares made her uneasy.

"Everything all right?" he asked, resting his hands on his waist with a concerned frown. "Why did you fire?"

"A fer-de-lance got into the house. Sorry, Con. It was either your snaky friend or me."

"Good God, are you all right?" her father exclaimed, whipping off his spectacles and starting forward in his chair.

"I'm fine, Father," she assured him. "I wondered if Connor would take the vile thing away. Most of it's still stuck in the rafters," she said with a wince.

The Australian nodded firmly, then glanced at her father. "I'll be right back, sir."

"Yes, er, give us a moment, my boy. I should like to have a word with my daughter."

"Of course." Connor paused to give Eden's shoulder a gentle squeeze. "You're sure you're all right?" he murmured.

She nodded and folded her arms across her middle, forcing a smile as she struggled to ignore the subtle possessiveness in his touch. Somehow, she could not bring herself to mention her uncomfortable feeling around him to Papa, who loved Connor like the son he'd never had.

Besides, it would not do to make a fuss when she knew perfectly well that they depended on Connor for their survival. He caught their food, he built their shelters, he warded off hostile Indians and the occasional stray jaguar alike.

But sometimes, when she looked into his eyes, as now, she got the feeling that, in Connor's mind, he owned her.

Satisfied that she was safe, he nodded once and then prowled off into the darkness to do her bidding. Her gaze trailed after him warily.

"Sit down, dear," her father ordered, gesturing toward his assistant's empty field chair. She noted absently that his salt-and-pepper beard was in need of a trim. "We have much to discuss."

"Indeed." Taking the seat across from him, she launched cheerfully into her assumed role in coordinating their withdrawal from the jungle. She was her father's nominal housekeeper, after all, in charge of the smooth running of their camp. "I figure with the servants' help, it will take about a week to pack everything up properly. We'll have to make special provisions to ensure that your botanical samples will stay fully preserved in the sea air, but if we can figure out some way to get across the straits to Trinidad, we shouldn't have too long a wait before some British ship appears that can take us home—"

"Eden," he interrupted gently, but with a tone of finality. "We're staying."

She stared at him for a long moment, then shut her eyes tightly and shuddered. "Oh, Father, no."

"Now, Edie, I realize this may come as a bit of a shock, but we're making such great strides—sweeting, you like it here! I know you do. Look at the adventures we've had! Rising up into the trees to explore the endless canopy! Finding birds and animals

6

completely unknown to science!" He took her hand soothingly. "There, there, dear, don't look at me that way," he protested when she opened her eyes again with a crushed expression. "Think of the medicines we will bring back one day, the lives we'll save! We can't quit now. We simply can't."

She struggled to find her voice. "I thought we lost our funding. Lord Pembrooke—"

"Is a scoundrel!" he averred. "But no matter. That young cad will not impede our progress. True, we shall have to conserve on paper and other supplies, but we've learned perfectly well from the Indians how to live off the land. And, after all, we are British, by God! We must and shall press on."

"Press . . . on."

"Oh, yes, my dear! For, you see—" He leaned nearer, all middle-aged, boyish excitement. "I have a plan."

Oh, no. "A plan?"

He nodded eagerly. "We're going deeper, Edie. Into the interior."

Her eyes widened. "You don't mean . . . ?"

"Yes," he whispered, barely able to contain his glee. "Into the Amazon!"

Her jaw dropped.

He mistook her horror for awe. "Think of it, daughter! Our grandest adventure yet—an even more complex habitat than these Orinoco jungles! The Delta has been our mother and our tutor, preparing us, it is true. Ah, but the Amazon, that is our destiny!" He squeezed her hand, trying to pass on his excitement, but she yanked her fingers out of his light hold and shot to her feet.

"You're *mad*!"

"Oh, Edie—"

"I knew it! It's finally happened, just as I always feared! Too much time in the wilderness has finally addled your wits, Papa! Good God, I'm probably next!" She clapped her hand to her forehead, but he merely laughed. "I'm not jesting—and I am *not* going there! Well, somebody has to put their foot down! Be sensible! There are headhunters there, cannibals, not peaceful natives like the Waroa—and God knows what all else!"

"Nonsense, Connor will protect us. I need you by my side in this, Edie. You know I cannot do without you. As long as we're together, you will be perfectly safe. By Jove, once we've conquered the Amazon, we'll return to England, I'll give lectures on our journeys. I'll write another book! A new narrative to rival von Humboldt's. We'll never need to rely on another rich patron again."

She threw up her hands, exasperated beyond words.

He knitted his gray eyebrows together. "What?"

She had promised Mama on her deathbed that she would take care of him, but how was she to do it when the man had no care for his life?

"Father," she said sternly, folding her arms across her chest, "you are fifty-five years old. Your hero von Humboldt was in his prime when he made that trip, and it nearly killed *him*." This point earned her nothing but a snort and low mutter of offended male vanity, so she tried another tack and sat down again, staring earnestly at him. "Have you forgotten that outside these jungles, Venezuela is at war?"

"Of course I haven't forgotten," he grumbled, scowling at the reminder. "I'm not quite senile yet. What of it?"

"To reach the Amazon, we'd have to cross the plains. The *llanos* are the main battlefields between the forces of the Spanish Crown and the rebel colonists."

"So? We still have time. There's a lull in the hostilities now. The rebels up at Angostura have firm control of the interior, while the Spanish keep to their ships on the coast. What's the problem?"

"The problem?" She nearly laughed, barely knowing where to start. "To begin with, each side thinks you're a spy for the other! The Spanish suspect you're in league with the revolutionaries, and the colonists think that you're working for Spain."

"If they really thought that, I would have been expelled from the country by now. Dash it, Edie, as I told those blasted bureaucrats from Caracas, science is neutral! I am here for the good of all mankind."

"Ugh!" She buried her face in her hands for a second, which muffled her retort: "You're here because you're hiding from the world."

"What did you say?" he asked sharply.

With a sigh, she checked her vexation and lowered her hands to her lap. "Nothing, Father."

"I daresay. You had better mind your tongue, my girl," he advised, settling back onto his rough wooden stool and giving his waistcoat a dignified tug. "I grant you a long leash, it's true, but I am still your father."

"Yes, sir," she answered, head down. "But . . ."

"But what, child?"

She held him in a searching stare for a moment. "You promised me last year that we'd be going back to England."

This was, it seemed, precisely what he did not want to hear.

He immediately scowled and looked away, busying himself with his botanical finds. "England, England, why are you always on about that wretched place? You really think the world out there is all so wonderful? How would you know? I've kept you sheltered from it here. If you remembered it better, you'd thank me. It's not all fine carriages and fancy balls, my girl. That world out there has a dark side, too." He sent her a glance from over the rim of his spectacles. "Disease, crime, filth, poverty, corruption. There's none of that here."

"There's no one to talk to!" she cried with a sudden threat of tears leaping into her eyes.

With a compassionate wince, Papa plopped down onto his stool again. "Nonsense, there's me! I am exceedingly good company— and there's Connor, too. Well, he doesn't say much, I'll give you that, but when he does, it is worth listening to. There, there, my pretty child," he said, patting her hand with a worried look. "I assure you, we are far more intelligent conversation than you will ever find in the drawing rooms of London."

"Just once, I'd like to know what normal people talk about," she said barely audibly.

"Normal? 'Tis but another word for mediocrity!" he scoffed. "Oh, Edie, for heaven's sake, those London chits you so admire are the silliest, most trivial creatures on God's earth, not a thought in their heads beyond ribbons and bonnets and shoes. Why the devil should you want to be like them, anyway?"

She stifled a groan. *Here comes the lecture.*

"Look at the advantages you enjoy here! You dress how you want, say what you want, do as you please. You have no idea how those Society girls are forever dogged by chaperones whose sole purpose in life is to regulate their every movement. You'd go mad if you had to endure it for a day. Look at the freedoms I've given you—the education, for heaven's sake!"

Freedom? she wondered. *Then why do I feel like a prisoner?*

9

"I trained you up more like a son than a daughter," he went on, traveling well-worn paths. She nearly had it by heart. "By Jove, do you think your fine London ladies can recite every known genus in the *Aracaceae* family? Make a bush tea to cure yellow fever? Set a broken bone? I think not," he declared proudly. "You, my dearest Eden, are utterly unique!"

"I don't want to be unique, Papa," she said wearily. "I just want to be a part of the world again. I want to belong."

"You do belong, darling. With me!"

She looked away, suddenly feeling trapped. He understood perfectly well; he just pretended not to. "Have I not been a dutiful daughter? Have I not stuck by your side through thick and thin, and looked after you, and aided in your work, and done everything you asked of me?"

"Yes," he admitted uncomfortably.

"Papa, they say in England that a lady is a spinster by the age of twenty-five. I know you have no head for such things, but just last month, I turned twenty-three." He started to scoff, but she lowered her head. "Please, don't laugh at me for once. It's not just the ballrooms and fancy carriages that interest me. I admit, I like those things—what girl would not?—but that's only a small part of it, and I should hope that you know me better than that by now."

"Well, what then, Edie, my dearest?" he asked kindly. "What is eating at you so?"

She looked into his eyes, feeling so hesitantly vulnerable. "Can't you understand? I . . . I want to find someone, Papa."

"Who?" he cried impatiently.

"I don't know yet who! Someone—someone to love."

He sat back and looked at her in pure astonishment. "So, that's what all of this is about!"

She lowered her head again, her cheeks aflame. Having admitted her heart's loneliness, she now rather wished the earth would open up and swallow her.

Papa slapped his thighs with both hands in sudden enthusiasm. "Well, I daresay the perfect solution has been right under our noses all along!"

When she looked at him hopefully, he jerked a not-so-subtle nod in the direction Connor had gone.

Eden turned scarlet. "Oh, Papa, please don't start with that again!" she whispered fiercely.

10

"Well, why not? If all this fuss boils down to your hankering for a husband, you needn't look far. If it's time for you to take a man, have Connor."

"Father!" she cried, scandalized.

"The man worships you, if you haven't noticed." A smile of mingled pride and amusement tugged at his lips, as if she were still a four-year-old learning the Greek alphabet. "He has my blessing and then we could all remain together just as we are, continuing on with our work. It is the most convenient situation. Well, why not, what's wrong with him?"

Clearly, Papa had forgotten the incident in the forest when she was sixteen.

She lowered her head, not bothering to remind him, for she was loath to speak of it herself.

"Connor cares for you, Eden. There's no arguing that. He's proved himself a hundred times over. Well, he's a fine, strapping specimen for you, ain't he? Fearless, capable, as the male of the species should be. Strong, robust bloodlines. Good instincts. Sharp mind," Papa said, ticking off his protégé's many virtues as Eden lifted her head again, folded her arms across her chest, and held her father in a quelling stare. "Of course, there's no vicar in residence, but what's a bit of paper in a place like this? You could be married by the local shaman—or have a hand-fasting like the Scots. Don't fuss, girl. There's no shame in it. It is but Nature's course, my dear. All creatures take a mate upon reaching reproductive age."

"Really, Father!" she exclaimed, finally mortified past bearing by his blunt scientist's speech. "Is there not one atom of romance in your soul? The propagation of the species might very well serve for a frog or a monkey or a-a fish, but I, Father, am an intelligent, beautiful—well, reasonably attractive—young lady. I want roses a-and poetry before I'm past my prime, and boxes of candy, and drives in the park! Is that so much to ask? I want to be wooed by Town Corinthians in coats from Savile Row! I want courtship, Papa, and suitors—even one will do. Maybe I *can* recite every genus name in the *Aracaceae* family, but that only goes to show what sort of oddball I've become in this place!"

"Well, so's Connor! A perfect match."

"Will you please be serious?" She sat down again with a huff. "It won't do, Father. I mean to rejoin the world someday, but Connor cares for civilization even less than you do. It's torture for him when we visit your friends in Kingston Society. He won't talk to anyone. He sits in a corner brooding and doesn't even try to fit in."

"Well, Eden, he's shy."

"I *know*. And I feel sorry for him—but I don't want to marry someone just because I feel sorry for them," she whispered so Connor, with his sharp senses, would not hear and be hurt.

"Well, suit yourself," Papa concluded with a sigh. "But I'm afraid there is nothing to be done for it, in any case. We cannot afford passage now that our grant's been cut. The voyage is too expensive."

"Couldn't you buy it on credit?"

"Put myself in debt for something I don't even want? You would have me as profligate as Lord Pembrooke!"

"We can pay it back once you're settled in your post at the college."

"No! I am not taking the post, Eden. Ever." He stood abruptly, turned away, and avoided her gaze as she stared at him in shock. "I've given the matter a great deal of thought," he said brusquely. "I probably should have told you sooner, but I shall not be able to fulfill the promise that you wrenched out of me last year. We're not going back to England, and as for London Town, I'd sooner visit Hell."

"What?" she breathed, paling.

"I'm sorry to break my oath to you, daughter, but you're all I have left, and I'll be damned before I'll ever expose you again to that vile, stinking cesspool of a city that killed your mother," he finished with a bitter vehemence that stunned her almost as much as his shocking revelation.

Dr. Farraday threw down his pen with an air of weariness, looking slightly haggard in the lantern's glow.

Her mind reeling with disbelief, Eden told herself he didn't really mean it. He was just so shattered, still, from Mama's death. Tears filled her eyes for the pain that still haunted him and had set both their lives on this strange course. She rose and moved closer, laying her head on his shoulder. "Papa," she whispered, "it wasn't your fault you couldn't save her."

"I was her husband and her doctor, Edie. Who else am I to blame? God?" He sounded calmer now. Defeated. He put his hand atop hers on his shoulder, but did not look at her. "There, there, child. I shall be fine in a moment."

No, you won't. It had already been twelve years. She hugged him for a long moment around his trim middle with an ache in her heart. "Papa, we can't stay out here forever."

He said nothing.

"I know you're only trying to protect me, but do you really think Mama would have wanted this—for either of us?"

"Your mother, lest you forget, is the reason we are here." He took a deep breath to steady himself. "Every cure we find exists in honor of her memory—"

"Stop punishing yourself," she whispered, hugging him again about his shoulders. "She wouldn't have wanted you to cut yourself off from the world this way." She didn't bother mentioning that he was cutting *her* off from the world, too. She leaned her head against the side of his, feeling so helpless to heal his hurt. "I know you seek to honor her with your work, Papa, but if you ask me, what she really would've wanted . . . was grandchildren."

She shouldn't have said it, she realized a second too late. Papa stiffened, shook his head, and then simply closed down as emotion threatened to overwhelm his logical brain.

He withdrew before her eyes, turned his back on her, and peered into his microscope, escaping the pain and dreadful loss inside the orderly circumference of that tiny world, just as he had for years.

"The expedition to the Amazon goes forward," he said in a monotone. "I am sorry you are unhappy, but we must all make sacrifices, and the desires of one individual are of no consequence beside the greater good. You will accompany me just as you always have; I am your father and that is my answer. Now, if you'll excuse me, I have work to do."

His bristling posture made it clear she was dismissed. Eden studied his tense profile, at a loss. She did not know what else to say, what to do. There was no reasoning with him when he fell into this black and distant mood. Any significant talk of her mother was always the catalyst for his stony withdrawal, most of all the future together that he and his wife would never have.

Eden blinked back tears and turned around without another word, walking back numbly to the *palafito.*

Connor looked at her in silence when she came in. He was leaning against the post from which he had removed the dead viper.

Eden glanced in his direction, but could not meet his probing stare, wondering if he'd overheard Papa's mortifying suggestion that they mate.

The Australian folded his brawny arms across his chest, watching her with a hunter's patient, somber gaze.

Shaking her head, she went past him. "He's mad. He's going to kill himself and both of us in his quest to save mankind. The Amazon!"

But of course Connor was already aware of her father's plans. For all she knew, it might have been his idea. "Whatever your father might have said, you know he'd never mean to hurt you."

"I know." Feeling trapped, Eden went to the railing and stood for a long moment gazing at the night-black river.

She heard Connor's heavy footfalls approaching behind her. He came and leaned beside her at the railing. From the corner of her eye, she saw him staring at her. "It's going to be all right, Eden. I'm not going to let anything happen to the two of you."

"I want to go home."

"This is your home."

"No, Connor, it's not. You belong here—I don't!" she exclaimed angrily, turning to him.

His broad, strong face darkened. Did he understand at last what she was trying to tell him? He lowered his gaze and turned away in stony anger, swiftly stalking off to leave her alone again. Eden closed her eyes for a second and let out a measured exhalation. When she flicked them open again, her desperate gaze tracked the Orinoco's inky course that led for many miles down to the sea. The great and deadly river. It was the only way into these impenetrable jungles. And the only way out.

Tall and hard, dressed all in black, Lord Jack Knight lit his cigarillo off the torch in his hand, then leaned down with an easy motion and ignited the cannon's fuse.

One . . . two . . . three . . .

"Boom," he murmured, the cheroot dangling from his unsmiling lips as the big gun's thunder crashed across the valley. Screaming out of the iron barrel, the cannonball flew through the night like a comet, its fiery reflection flashing across the black glassy surface of the Orinoco.

It streaked down from the dark skies to slam into the giant rock that jutted up from the middle of the river, the famous Piedra Media, used as a marker to record the depth of the seasonal floods—a serviceable target.

Direct hit.

On the flower-laden terrace behind him, his Creole audience burst into applause, hailing their new cannon with the same hearty zest that they applied to every area of life.

"Bravo, *Capitan*!"

"Well done!"

Jack ignored them.

The leading citizens of Angostura had built their elegant stuccoed villas along a well-situated ridge overlooking the river; and so, from the terrace of the Montoya home, the wealthy Creole leaders of the revolution had a fine view of the accuracy and power of the weapons he had obtained for them.

"This is a wonderful piece of artillery you have given us, Lord Jack!"

"Should help you ward off the Spanish if they come up the river," he muttered. "So should these." He snapped his fingers at his assistant and pointed to the several dozen crates of fine Baker rifles that he had also brought them.

It was a pity Bolivar could not be present for the demonstration, but the rebel leader was off trying to turn his rather pitiful band of half-breed peasants and illiterate farmboys into an army.

God help 'em, Jack thought, for at this very moment, fifteen thousand royal troops waited on their ships for the order to attack.

King Ferdinand of Spain, Bourbon puppet of the Hapsburgs, an all-around unpleasant fellow by most accounts, newly returned to his throne now that Welly and the boys had beat Napoleon, had decided to flex his half-forgotten power, and had sent the largest force ever to cross the Atlantic to crush the colonials' hopes of liberty.

Jack had his reasons for getting involved. He was more cynic than idealist, but he never could tolerate a bully, and it was plain to see that if somebody didn't help the poor sods, there was going to be a slaughter.

"Here you are, sir." His trusty lieutenant, Christopher Trahern, handed him one of the precision rifles, already loaded.

Jack lifted the weapon to his shoulder, drawing a bead on one of the unpleasant vampire bats that flapped up and down the inky river in a swooping zigzag.

"What's the range on that thing?" inquired Don Eduardo Montoya, the owner of the villa, and one of the rebels' top financiers.

"Two hundred yards. Accurate if you are."

Crack!

The crisp report of the rifle echoed down the hillside of the town as he shot the blood-sucking bat right out of the night sky. Pleased, he handed the Baker back to Trahern. "Reload for Mr. Montoya."

"Aye, Captain."

Down on the docks at the foot of the hill, his men were still unloading goods from the riverboat in which Jack had arrived less than an hour ago. Hardened as they were to close fire, even his stalwart crew looked a little nervous with all the hotheaded revolutionaries firing off their new British guns.

"Let me try one of those!" exclaimed Carlos, Montoya's son of twenty summers.

Tearing himself away from the trio of young beauties who had been fawning on him, the handsome young hidalgo strode over to the stone balustrade that girded the pleasant, flagged terrace.

Jack sent the lad a wry, assessing glance, having already pegged the Casanova as an incorrigible seducer of the servant girls. Not that he could blame the lad. *Damn,* he thought with a surreptitious glance in the young beauties' direction. *South American women.* Even the servant girls looked like Helen of Troy.

Jack noticed one of them watching him with wary interest. Delicious creature, with caramel skin and a veil of smooth, black hair that hung to her waist.

When his stare homed in on her, her dark eyes widened. She dropped her gaze with a wildly unsettled look and fled, disappearing back into the house, ostensibly returning to her duties.

He let out a low sigh, pursed his lips, and looked away. Ah, well. *Terrified another one.*

His ruthless reputation must have gone before him, as usual.

Carlos grabbed the reloaded Baker out of Trahern's able hands and put the rifle to his shoulder, giving it a feel. "Ah, I'll kill a hundred Spaniards with this little beauty!"

Jack snorted, resting his hands on his holstered waist as the boy took aim. "Just try not to get yourself killed."

Carlos squeezed the trigger, hitting his target. "Ha!" With a cocky grin, he tossed the Baker to Jack and sauntered back to his harem to be admired.

Jack eyed the youth in sardonic amusement as he set the gun aside; he, too, had thought himself invincible at that age. "Word of advice," he offered Don Eduardo. "Keep that pup of yours away from the battlefield. He's much too green and bent on glory."

"Easier said than done, my friend." With a cordial chuckle, Don Eduardo clapped him on the shoulder. "Come inside and have a drink."

They strolled into the luxurious villa, where floor-to-ceiling windows overlooked the terrace. Filmy curtains wafted in the night breeze, cooling the stately drawing room. The elegant furnishings and gilt-framed oil paintings might have easily placed the home in London, Paris, or Madrid, but they were many miles from any such civilization now. The capital of Caracas, a couple hundred miles away, was the nearest city, but situated on the coast, it had fallen back under the control of the Spanish empire. The rebels held control of the interior, however, and had made the hot colonial settlement of Angostura their stronghold.

The town reminded Jack a bit of New Orleans—another place where he had gotten into more than his share of trouble. Beyond its low hills, abundant flowers, and shady live oaks covered in Spanish moss, stretched endless miles of flat tidal plains called the *llanos;* until finally, the mighty Orinoco, Venezuela's watery highway, slipped into shadowed jungle, before emptying into the sea.

"How long will it take you to reach England, Lord Jack?"

"Four to six weeks, depending on the winds."

"You will be pleased to hear that Bolivar means to award you with ten thousand acres in rich cattle land as a token of his thanks when the war is won." Montoya cast him a shrewd glance, as he checked the label on a bottle of port by the flickering light of the pewter candelabra.

Jack stared at him. "That isn't necessary."

"Ah, but we are very grateful for the help you have promised our cause, my lord. See for yourself." Finished pouring the port, Montoya took out a map, unfurled it on the table, and leaned closer to inspect it, nodding at Bolivar's signature. "The Liberator has etched the boundaries of your holdings here. We wish you to accept it—as a gift."

"Let me see that." Jack narrowed his eyes. With the flat of his

17

dagger, he traced the outlines of the land he was to be given at their leader's behest, but his lips twisted in a cynical half smile.

A bribe.

So. They didn't trust him. He was a little offended but not altogether surprised. His lashes flicked downward as he glanced over the map, but he mentally shrugged off the insult. He did not need their money or their land, but if it put their minds at ease, he could pretend to take the bait. Far be it from Black-Jack Knight, after all, to do anything out of the goodness of his nonexistent heart.

Besides, there were vast profits to be gained if this brash plot succeeded, opening up the continent to trade.

For centuries, Spain had had a chokehold over South America, jealously guarding her rich colonies with ironclad monopolies.

If Bolivar managed to cut South America free of her chains, then the risks that Jack was now taking to come to their aid would ensure that Knight Enterprises would be among the first outside companies to establish favorable trading agreements with the newly independent nations.

Unfortunately, the colonists hadn't a prayer of winning this fight unless they received reinforcements—and soon.

The rebels had plenty of silver. What they lacked was men. Jack, however, based in neighboring Jamaica, knew exactly where to find this commodity in abundant supply, namely, the half-pay heroes of Waterloo.

Pouring back into England after winning the war against Napoleon, countless thousands of British soldiers were arriving home only to find there was no work for them, no way to feed their families. Throughout England, Scotland, and Ireland, there was a surplus of skilled and battle-hardened warriors, many of whom would be willing to fight as mercenaries in South America, especially since Bolivar's cause could be called noble, if a man cared for such things.

There was only one small snag. Parliament had just issued a decree forbidding British soldiers from going and joining the fight. Obviously, Englishmen fighting alongside Venezuelan rebels to divest Spain of her colonies would have raised many an eyebrow in Madrid.

Having just extricated the nation from twenty years of war against France, the last thing the Foreign Office wanted was fresh trouble with the Continental neighbors—this time, Spain.

18

But if Jack knew one thing about soldiers—which he did, having a bona fide war-hero amongst his brood of brothers—it was that they were practical men. Loyalty to king and country only went so far; you could take a soldier's arms and legs and blow his bosom friends to smithereens, but you did not trifle with his family.

No self-respecting warrior who had helped to thrash the *Grande Armée* was going to stand by and let his children starve, not when he could take up his musket and sword and earn excellent pay in South America.

All it took was someone with the right connections, high and low, the nerve, the discretion to recruit said mercenaries without attracting the notice of the British government, the ships to bring the two parties together, and the ability to slip a few thousand troops past the Spanish blockade.

That was where Jack came in, but nobody had to know that he actually cared.

He looked up from the map, nodded his acceptance of their offering, and took a large swallow of port.

Montoya's face flooded with relief. "We have a deal, then? You will bring us men?"

He let out an appropriately mercenary laugh. "Men?" He slapped Montoya's shoulder with a wolfish glint in his eyes. "Tell Bolivar that I will bring you devils."

Some time later, Jack walked through the darkened guest apartment he'd been assigned for the night, wearily unbuckling his pistol holster and tossing aside his knife belt in turn.

He pulled off his black jacket and dropped it on the large bed as he sauntered out onto the balcony, feeling restless.

Resting his hands on the black wrought-iron rail, he stared out over the river, trying not to think about all he stood to lose if things went badly. His freedom. His company. Possibly his neck. None of that bothered him, though, as much as the prospect of facing a world again that he had walked away from a long time ago. A world that had not wanted him.

His mind drifted off across the darkened landscape, far away, toward his destination over the sea . . . to the green, rolling, patchwork fields of his native England.

Every muscle in his body clenched. A steadying exhalation escaped him quietly. It was hard to believe that in a few weeks' time, he would set foot on English soil again, after his long, long exile. Nothing but the threat of this slaughter practically in his back garden could have induced him to return.

He'd have to see his brothers again, he supposed, and of course, one could not forget Maura.

His face hardened. Perhaps when he saw her again after all these years, he could ask her if marrying the marquess had been worth it.

Turning away from the railing, Jack prowled back into the unfamiliar chamber and shrugged off his waistcoat, tossing it willfully aside, along with his troubled thoughts. *Hot bloody night.* How was a man supposed to sleep? He was spoiled, he guessed, by the cool ocean breezes at his elegant white-stuccoed villa in Jamaica.

His principal home sat high on a cliff overlooking the sea. It was a short drive into Port Royal, where his company, Knight Enterprises, was headquartered. *This* was the home he had made for himself, he thought, though a part of him had yet to be convinced that he actually belonged anywhere on earth.

As he lifted his loose linen shirt off over his head, a timid knock sounded at the door.

"Aye?"

Jack waited, expecting some last-minute reminder from Trahern on the shipment of tropical hardwoods they'd be collecting in the morning before they set out—the rare zebrawoods in particular were going to fetch a steep price on the London markets—but when the chamber door opened, his eyebrow lifted.

The pretty señorita from the terrace peeked in, carrying a water pitcher in one hand and a stack of freshly folded towels in the other. "I-I have these things for you, sir," she said in the sweetest little accent.

It turned his blood to honey. A narrow smile crept over his face. "Come on in, darlin.'" He stared hungrily at her, stunned all over again by these local goddesses. In brooding speculation, he watched her carry the items over to the mahogany washstand. She sent him a shy but sultry smile.

Four to six weeks at sea . . . no woman to warm his bed.

Jack reached into the pocket of his discarded coat for a few gold coins, fully prepared to make it worth her while.

She must have felt his study, for she glanced over her shoulder at him, her curious gaze flicking down his bare chest, over the thick muscles, work-hardened contours, and assorted scars on his body.

He lifted his chin, offering himself for her pleasure without a word. The girl swallowed hard, clearly interested, but perhaps also intimidated by his size and the bruiser's build that he had inherited from his real father, a champion prizefighter; she was, he guessed, more accustomed to the wiry body of that no doubt overeager boy.

"I don't bite," he whispered with a shadowed smile.

But perhaps she liked what she saw, for when he crooked his finger at her slowly, she approached with cautious steps.

"Will there be—anything else, my lord?" she asked a trifle breathlessly.

He nodded, staring, and pressed the gold into her hand. The girl trembled but uttered no protest as he began gently unlacing her bodice.

CHAPTER
∽ TWO ∽

*T*he next morning, Papa and Connor set out early to visit the Waroa settlement a few miles away in hope of finding an Indian guide who might be willing to take them into the Amazon.

Eden prayed the Waroas had more sense than her genius father. Perhaps Papa's friend, the shaman, might even talk him out of this mad plan, for most tribes in the region dreaded as much as the whites did the fierce Yanomami who ruled the Amazon forest. They were said to make a soup out of the enemies they killed.

The more she thought about it, the more she feared her sire was truly fixed on his own destruction, perhaps without even realizing it. Perhaps death really was his underlying plan—to be all the sooner reunited with Mama. She worried over this morbid possibility all morning as she went about her usual list of chores: managing breakfast, giving the servants their daily instructions, checking supplies, taking down the instrument readings and recording them in the logbook: temperature, barometric pressure, and lastly, the river's current depth.

For this final item, she followed the plank-and-hemp boardwalk from their camp down to the little rickety dock that the men had constructed. Along the way, she found solace in the morning breeze that rustled gracefully through the palm fronds, and swayed the hanging vines and lianas.

Tilting her head back, she watched blue and gold and scarlet macaws swoop overhead, spiraling through the canopy like living fireworks. Three stories overhead, a spider monkey swung from branch to branch with its baby clinging to its back. Closer to earth, a large, sleek aguti dug in the soil with its long front claws, trying to pull up a root for its breakfast, and snuffling in the dirt with rodent pleasure. Eden watched it for a moment, rather amused, then continued on her way.

A big blue dragonfly zoomed across her path as the boardwalk rounded the giant buttressed roots of a native mahogany tree. Nearing the riverbank, she paused to scan the surrounding area before walking out onto their shaky private dock: She had no intention of becoming anything's breakfast.

Finding the way clear, she proceeded out to where three dugout canoes were tied, bobbing in the lazy current.

Making her notations, she squinted at the marker-pole that Connor had sunk into the river mud some ten feet from the bank. It served as a huge ruler. *Twenty-five feet.* Low today, even for the dry season.

She marked the reading with her pencil in the logbook.

A sudden spray of water nearby startled her, but then she smiled, alerted to this visit from one of the mysterious pink dolphins that inhabited the river. Magical creatures, invisible in the *aqua negra.* She crouched down, scanning the murky shallows. Her smile broadened as she caught a glimpse of a coral-pink tail fin.

The Indians called these animals *Buoto* and believed they were really sorcerers in dolphin form, who dwelled in a golden kingdom that existed underneath the river. Whenever a baby was born in the village to a girl with no husband, the elders proclaimed it the work of a *Buoto* who had changed himself by enchantment into a handsome young warrior and had sneaked into the village to find a wife. The *Buoto* were infamous for their amorous ways when they transformed themselves into men. Fortunately for Eden's virtue, the pink dolphin was gone again as swiftly as it had appeared.

Satisfied with her notations, she returned to camp to finish with her list of morning chores.

Upriver at Angostura, Jack received his delivery of rare tropical hardwoods from the local timber dealer and personally oversaw the laborious process of attaching the barge piled with felled trees to the wide, flat-bottomed river craft he had hired.

When all twenty crewmen from his gunship were accounted for, he shook hands on the dock with Don Eduardo.

"Safe journeys, Knight." Montoya followed Jack's upward stare to the balcony of the guest apartment, where the dark-haired girl, wrapped in a bedsheet, languidly waved farewell from the wrought-iron railing.

Jack blew her a kiss.

"You may take her with you if you like," his host said in discreet amusement. "At least it would keep her out of my son's clutches."

"God, no." Jack flicked him a wry look. "A woman at sea? Nothing but headaches." With that, he jumped into the sturdy riverboat, an odd-looking hybrid of steam and sail, but serviceable.

Don Eduardo sauntered to the edge of the dock as Jack's men tugged the ropes free from their mooring posts. He sent them a final salute as Jack gave the order to set sail.

When his men poled the craft away from the docks and out into the middle of the river's slow but powerful current, Jack set his gaze straight ahead, not sparing one look back at the woman he had ravished so thoroughly last night.

Such was a sailor's fate. The trick, of course, was never to stay in one place long enough to get attached. And that was just the way that Jack preferred it.

He spent the first hour of their journey keeping an eye on the local pilot he had hired to navigate them down the unfamiliar river. He knew enough about the sea to realize that a wise man treated a great river like the Orinoco with extreme respect. He always preferred local guides in his travels, and as the swarthy mestizo captain of the riverboat got them off to a smooth start, Jack went to check on the lumber, and got a splinter for his pains. Finally, with their downriver voyage well underway, he decided that he could relax for a while.

With Trahern leaning nearby, gazing at the wide, sun-drenched river ahead, Jack settled in for the day-long ride with a copy of Angostura's first official newspaper, recently established by Bolivar. Reclining in a battered wooden chair inside the cramped pilothouse, he put his feet up, crossed his booted heels, and chewed on an unlit cheroot.

"I still don't see why you didn't insist that they pay you silver," Trahern said to him at length in English, which their pilot did not understand. "You could sell it on the currency market in China, and your profit is fifty percent."

"Chris, relax. We're already running a perfectly adequate silver trade out of Buenos Aires." It was smuggled silver, of course, but why split hairs? The English Crown turned a blind eye to the flourishing business of British smugglers in South America; after all, John Bull was painfully light in the pockets these days. "You have to be patient if you want to get rich," he advised, turning the page of the newspaper before abruptly tossing it aside. "Utter tripe. Liberty this, liberty that. Naught but the usual propaganda."

"But you love propaganda, Jack," Trahern said in amusement.

"Only when I'm the one using it. Bloody God, it's hot. Open that window wider."

Trahern obeyed. "Look!" He pointed to a group of colorful riders storming across the flat golden plains. "A band of *llaneros*."

"Thank God Bolivar finally got them on his side, at least."

"Something like a cavalry," Trahern agreed with a shrug.

"At least they know how to fight," Jack murmured. "They won't run. And they know the territory." He watched the rugged cattlemen of the plains driving their herds to fresh grazing.

After the impressive cavalcade had passed, he leaned back thoughtfully in his chair. "Think I'll catch a bit of sleep for now. That girl wore me out."

Trahern laughed. "Poor fellow."

Jack grinned and tugged the brim of his straw hat down lower over his eyes; folding his arms across his chest, he stretched his long legs out before him and dozed. He hadn't gotten much sleep last night—not that he was complaining—but he knew he'd need to be sharp when it came time to slip past the Spanish at the coast and rendezvous with his ship. *The Winds of Fortune* was hiding now in a cove near Icacos Point, a rocky peninsula that jutted southward off the island of Trinidad in the straits known as the Serpent's Mouth.

He'd left his third-in-command, Lieutenant Peabody, in charge of the vessel, with Brody, the stalwart master-at-arms, to lend a bit of added steel to his orders. Nevertheless, being parted from his beloved vessel with the Spanish flotilla so nearby made him a tad nervous.

As soon as the *Winds* picked up Jack and his men, along with this small fortune in timber, they would set sail across the Atlantic, and ride the trade winds back to the British Isles.

It was midmorning by the time Eden was finished cataloguing the latest editions to her father's ever-growing herbarium and making sure that all their recently pressed and dried botanical samples remained undamaged by the relentless humidity.

At last, finding herself at her leisure, she wasted no time in escaping up into the green Gothic cathedrals of the canopy.

From the age of ten, Eden had mastered the art of climbing trees using an ancient invention from the Indians called a foot-belt. Ascended to some five stories over the forest floor, she stood in the elbow of a towering mahogany for a while, staring out at the beckoning distance.

Not even Father liked climbing this high, but Eden did. She could see forever from up there; somehow, from that higher vantage point, it was easier to think.

Things seemed clearer, simpler. Miles upon endless miles of jungle opened up on every side around her, sprawling horizons, with a misty blue glimmer of the sea beckoning from the great beyond. As she stared into the hazy distance, restlessness churned in her veins, born of too much isolation.

Here in her fierce paradise, the loneliness whispered its ever more urgent question: *Will I always be alone?*

Jack was not sure how long he had dozed when Trahern spoke his name in an odd tone.

He opened his eyes and looked around, and could have sworn they'd traveled back in time a thousand years.

Leaving behind the golden savannahs with their blue skies and vast horizons, they had entered a mysterious, dripping, emerald world of green light and moss-colored shadows.

The miles-wide river had split into a thousand narrow fingers at the Delta, a complex maze of smaller natural canals, called *caños,* all of which led to the sea.

Jack saw that their swarthy mestizo pilot was taking them down one of these quiet arteries through dense jungle. The lush vegetation formed a tunnel over the waterway, sealing in the hothouse environment. The air was thick and moist, without a breeze.

As the boat glided deeper into pristine tropical forest, the constant birdsong and animal noises somehow did not disrupt the profound stillness of this place. Jack stared in wonder.

Even his raucous crew had gone silent.

Countless long-legged insects skated on water whose surface looked like olive-colored glass. Suddenly, an aggressive, throaty roar shattered the stillness from somewhere up in the trees. His men jumped then looked around uneasily as the roar turned into a series of staccato screams.

"What the hell was that, Cap'n?" Higgins, the foretop man, muttered, blessing himself with a hasty sign of the cross.

"Howler monkey," Jack murmured, recalling descriptions he had read. Searching the boughs overhead for the large monkey, instead he spotted the magnificent white plumage of a harpy eagle with the noble bearing of a mythical griffon. He pointed, showing it to his men. "Look at that!"

Green parrots, orange-billed toucans, and riotous macaws fled out of the harpy eagle's path as it pushed off the branch it had been perching on and swooped off down the clear path of the *caño,* its six-foot wingspan carrying it along at an astonishing speed. Jack stared down the river as the great eagle swooped upward again with an easy flap of its giant wings and disappeared into the canopy, but then a flash of bright motion in the dark water drew his attention lower.

"What was that?" Trahern murmured, scanning the waterway ahead alongside Jack. "Crocodile?"

"But I could swear it was . . . pink?"

They looked at each other in consternation, but then the creature swam by the boat and all of the men exclaimed in wonderment as the thing proved to be a pink dolphin.

"Buoto," said their local pilot sagely, then he pointed over the wheel. *"Mira aquí!"*

On the right bank of the river sat a primordial monster that could have been descended from fire-breathing dragons of legend.

"Holy Mother," Higgins breathed, staring at the enormous beast.

The Orinoco crocodile was longer than the boat. Jack stared at the magnificent monster in awe, but Trahern took one look at it and picked up the nearest Baker rifle.

"No." Jack stopped him, but the beast's instincts were equally defensive, and with a wicked speed that sent a chill down all their spines, the crocodile launched into the water with silent power, barely making a splash.

How something that big disappeared so completely was impossible to say, but its leathery hide was superbly matched to blend in with the olive-drab river. The crewmen looked around at one other, the unspoken question on everyone's minds.

27

Trahern cleared his throat. "Are those things, er, ever known to attack boats?" he asked their pilot somewhat nervously in Spanish.

"*Sí, a veces.*"

"Sometimes? I see. Well, that is most reassuring," Tra-hern muttered to Jack, who grinned. "You should've let me shoot it."

Trahern huffed off to check the other side of the boat.

With the lieutenant gone, Jack stood alone at the railing on the blunt prow of the boat, lost in a rare sense of wonder at the strange and beautiful yet fearsome world unfurling all around him. The bright blooms of a passion flower caught his eye on the banks, and as he stared, a zooming flash of blue appeared as if by magic at the flower's lip and hovered there, a delicate miracle.

For the space of only a few heartbeats, the hummingbird fed on the blossom's sweet nectar; when thunder rumbled in the distance, it was gone. A breeze moved through the thick, rubbery palm fronds like the subtle stirring deep within him of a hunger for something all his gold could not buy nor all his power command . . . something he had long since ceased to believe in.

But the warm wind brought with it a baptism of soft, silver rain: Jack tilted his head back and welcomed its caress.

High in the treetops, Eden always had her best ideas, and today was no exception. Gazing out over the jungle, she had been inspired with one last-ditch scheme to save her father from himself. The solution was simple.

Perhaps they did not have the money for all three of them to travel back to England, but she could go alone, taking with her a sampling of her father's most important discoveries; in London, she could meet with the new Lord Pembrooke, their former patron's heir, and personally present to him the wonderful cures that Papa had found.

If she could convince the rakehell earl of the importance of her father's work for the good of all mankind, then perhaps His Lordship would see fit to reinstate their grant. But even if the thoughtless rake refused, there were many rich philanthropists in London. Surely, she reasoned, given her father's fame and the strength of his work, she could find *someone* willing to fund his research.

That way, Papa could remain here, in the relative safety of the Orinoco jungles, rather than chasing certain doom into the Amazon. As for her, she could stay with Aunt Cecily and Cousin Amelia as soon as she arrived in England, so there would be no worries over her being chaperoned. All in all, it sounded to her like the perfect answer: Everyone would win.

Of course, knowing Papa, he'd probably find some fault with it; nevertheless, the mere possibility lifted her spirits. For now, there was nothing to do but wait until he got back so she could ask what he thought of her plan. Pleased with her inspiration, she climbed down to a lower branch and got to work on her orchids.

With her shin-length cotton walking dress hitched up a bit, she settled herself astride a thick, mossy bough that arched over the river; her booted feet swung idly as she became absorbed in her scientific studies.

Eager as she was to return to civilization, she was honest enough to admit that her life in the Delta could not be described as unpleasant. There was contentment in such days. In spite of everything, the peace that she always felt high in the canopy soon settled over her.

Within an hour, she had not only made a discovery that was going to astound Papa, she had also made a friend in the form of a curious little capuchin monkey that had taken an interest in her. It watched her every move, nestled in the crook of the branch just above her.

The capuchin's markings gave the animal its name, after the order of brown-robed monks who had come to the New World as missionaries with the conquistadors. The little imp had a white face with big, round eyes, a brown body with a black beanie cap, and black sleeves.

"Look at this," she murmured to it. "Isn't that . . . remarkable?" Adjusting her thick leather gardening gloves, Eden gripped her small knife harder and cut carefully into the carpet of moss that had made its home on the broad branch of the tree, examining the air-feeding tendrils that helped it attach there.

Meanwhile, seeds from the upper canopy pinwheeled past her, falling earthward like nature's confetti.

Continuing her examination of the little world living on the branch, she noted scratches in the tree bark left by birds pecking for insects, then discovered a bulgy-eyed baby tree frog floating in the rain-filled cup of a bromeliad.

Though it was tiny, she dared not touch the creature, for most jungle frogs were extremely poisonous. The secretions from their skins supplied the natives with a key ingredient in the lethal curare with which they tipped their blow-darts.

She returned her attention to the latest species of orchids she had found, a gorgeous cluster of purple-and-white blooms growing quite comfortably on the thinning bough, nearly over the center of the river. Inching ahead and balancing with intense concentration, she managed to take a few clippings for further study, and then indulged in the glorious fragrance. She inhaled the flower's delicious vanilla scent, so luxuriously enhanced by the nourishing daily shower that now misted the jungle.

The rain had been soaking her to the skin for some time, but Eden quite enjoyed it. Having captured her orchids, Eden made a note of where she had found them, doing her best to shield her paper from the rain, when her monkey friend swiveled his head and went motionless, peering upriver for a second.

Suddenly, the capuchin let out a warning screech and fled up into his leafy towers. Eden froze, scanning the branches around her and praying she did not see an early-waking jaguar.

Her heart pounding, she listened in fright for any sound above the soft, steady patter of the rain on the leaves and searched the surrounding canopy, knowing full well the animal's spotted coat made it almost impossible to see until it was too late.

She was trying to decide if it was better to be eaten there on the branch or to tumble into the river below, when suddenly she heard voices.

Male voices—many in number.

And they were speaking English!

Turning to stare in the direction the capuchin had first looked, she now beheld a most astonishing sight.

People!

A squat, tubby riverboat pulling a barge piled with timber was emerging slowly from around the river bend.

Whatever are they doing here? she wondered as she stared with excitement bubbling up in her veins. *Never mind that!* This could be just the opportunity she had been praying for.

As the boat drifted closer, she studied the rough-looking men at the rails and lounging under the canvas shade on deck.

Admittedly, they did not look like a promising lot, resembling so many pirates. Many were shirtless in the heat, their swarthy hides tattooed and sinewy. Hope rose, however, when she noticed a young blond man striding toward the prow.

Unlike the others, he was quite fully dressed, though perhaps slightly wilted in the damp jungle heat. He seemed unwilling to be daunted by it. With his gentlemanly cravat in good order, cuffed white shirtsleeves neatly fashioned in self-conscious propriety, and ebony knee-boots, he looked like a proud and very correct young officer.

Her heart fluttered. Gracious, he was the handsomest creature she had seen in ages . . . until, following his progress, her gaze came to rest on the dark, magnificent man that the younger fellow now joined at the rails.

An indescribable awe—or fascination—came over her as she stared at their kingly leader. She had studied animals long enough to be able to pick out in an instant the dominant male, and there was no question whatsoever that he was it.

He appeared to be in his late thirties, and good Lord, he was big. He even had an inch or two on Connor, she reckoned, with several stone in pure muscle over Papa. The imposing stranger looked surprisingly at home in the jungle setting. A knotted red bandana hung around his neck in the Spanish style; he wore a loose white shirt, having apparently discarded his coat and waistcoat in the heat. His shirt fell open in a V down to his breastbone, baring his glistening, muscular chest.

The fine white linen had turned translucent in the rain and clung to his massive shoulders. Below, he wore dun-colored breeches that disappeared into shiny black boots.

Eden realized something all of a sudden.

I know who this man is.

Lord Jack Knight, the mysterious merchant-adventurer who had turned himself into a shipping magnate worth millions—one of the most feared and powerful men in the West Indies.

Black-Jack Knight, some called him.

Kingston Society had swarmed with stories about the enigmatic adventurer, but despite his whispered reputation as a very bad man, the local Quality complained that he was too much of a loner and rarely made appearances at their genteel gatherings. He was the second son of a duke, according to their tales, but he had turned his back on his native England years ago to make his own way in the world. By all accounts, he had succeeded on a grand scale.

31

It was said he owned large portions of Jamaica, and had a fleet of eighty ships, with warehouses on every continent. No region of the globe was beyond his reach: furs from the northern wilds of Canada, silks and spices from the East, sugarcane from the torrid zone, and amazing new industrial machines from the north of England. His company, Knight Enterprises, was headquartered in Port Royal, but she had heard he lived outside the town in an elegant, white-stuccoed villa on a cliff above the sea. It had over a hundred rooms, but he lived alone there, except for his servants.

Some people claimed he had ill dealings with the smugglers who plagued Buenos Aires. Others whispered he had actually helped the Americans during the War of 1812, and since he was British-born himself, that would have made him all but a traitor if it was true. There were darker tales still, rumors of piracy in his shadowed past, but as far as Eden knew, no one had ever dared confront him to find out if all of this was fact or legend.

Well, blazes, she thought with a slight gulp, though her stare intensified. *I don't care if he's Blackbeard himself if he can get me out of here.*

Seeing the way he carried himself, it was easy to believe that such a man could wrest his fortune from the untamed sea.

Power, danger, and bold vitality emanated from every line of his towering physique; he held his head high with an air of intelligent command. His square face was framed by dark sideburns, his tousled hair the same dark, warm brown as the toppled mahoganies his boat was pulling.

"Look!" the blond young officer suddenly cried. "There's—" He squinted in disbelief. "There's a lady in that tree!"

Oh, dear. She had been spotted. It was too late now to lose her nerve.

The crew let out with marveling oaths and exclamations, following the direction of the young man's pointing finger. The sight of her there, sitting on the branch that over-arched the river, must have been so unlikely that most of them seemed to find it quite hilarious.

She clenched her jaw and colored a bit, but refused to be nonplused. She rested one hand behind her on the bough and leaned back idly, trying to look nonchalant.

One sailor slapped his thigh as he guffawed. "If them grow on trees in these parts, Cap, you can drop me off 'ere!"

She forced a long-suffering smile as a few of them bellowed with laughter, but Lord Jack, with a mystified look, walked toward the bow as the boat drifted closer, coming within a few feet of Eden's perch.

The light rain trickled down his broad forehead to his thick, dark eyebrows. He had deep-set, hooded eyes and a large but aquiline nose. A day's beard shadowed his rugged jaw, adding to his dangerous aura. His lips, she thought, looked a little chapped. *And altogether kissable.*

The unbidden thought quite startled her.

"What species of bird is that, do ye reckon?" one of his men persisted, rousing more laughter from his mates.

Turning redder by the second, Eden frowned, thinking their master just a little wanting in manners for not silencing their sport. Maybe he was a pirate, after all.

For her part, Eden was beginning to feel a tad foolish, knowing full well that tree-climbing was hardly how *La Belle Assemblée* advised young ladies to behave.

Alas, here she was being stared at by a magnetic, thoroughly compelling man, whose fleet of ships might be her only ticket out of here—a man whose direct and confident gaze made her heart beat faster—though that, in small part, might have been due to dread.

As she held his stare, however, unable to look away, she marveled at what fascinating eyes he had. In contrast to his sun-bronzed complexion, they were the turquoise blue of Caribbean waters. She detected a sparkle of amusement in their depths as he perused her, not quite successful in masking his roguish astonishment.

"You do see her, my lord?" the young officer asked. "Please tell me I have not gone mad in the heat."

"Trahern," he ordered in a calm, authoritative tone, not taking his eyes off her. "Stop the boat."

No, indeed, the tropical sun had not addled his assistant's wits unless it had cooked Jack's, also, for he, too, saw the luscious young redhead in the tree. Straddling the thick bough, she swung her feet a bit self-consciously right above the spot where the pilot now managed to bring the boat to a halt.

Finding any sort of female on a branch above the Orinoco a hundred miles from any human settlement might have been rather a shock, let alone a stunning beauty with big emerald eyes and, from his quick assessment, perfect proportions.

Her long chestnut mane hung unbound. Wet with rain, she slicked it back from her face as he watched her, his stare following the auburn tendrils that twined over her delicate shoulders. She wore a light green walking dress with frilly pantalets peeking out from underneath before they disappeared into thick brown boots. Jack could not help staring.

Her face, a softly rounded oval with a light speckling of freckles, glowed with rain; she had high cheekbones with a peachy complexion and a straight, perfect nose.

Though not normally given to damsel rescues and other good deeds, he shook off his momentary daze, more than happy to make an exception and play the hero in this case. "Good day, miss," he greeted her, prepared to offer his assistance. "I see you've gotten yourself into a spot of trouble up there."

"I have?" she asked warily, tilting her head. "How's that?"

Jack furrowed his brow. Her self-possessed response startled him; he had expected more of a cry for help. He glanced discreetly at his men; they shrugged, as perplexed as he.

He turned to the girl once more as she drew off her leather work gloves and then picked a leaf out of her hair with a small scowl. "Is everything, er, quite all right?"

"I think so," she said warily, eyeing him as though he were the oddball. "Is everything all right with you?"

"Of course." Jack was nonplused and beginning to wonder if they were speaking the same language. "That doesn't look very safe," he pointed out. "Do you need help getting down?"

"Oh!" she answered with a sudden, startled laugh. "No, I don't need any help getting down. But I'm sure you're very kind," she added indulgently.

Jack stared at her in perplexity. "What the blazes are you doing in that tree?"

"Studying epiphytes."

"Epi-whats?" Higgins muttered.

"Orchids," she clarified.

"Those parasitic flowers growing all over the trees," Jack told him in a rather jaundiced aside, folding his arms across his chest. A comparison to most of the women he knew came to mind, but he kept it to himself.

34

"Orchids are not parasites!" the young lady informed him with great indignation.

Jack cocked an eyebrow. *Hmm.* Not only had the chit not fled in terror of him, but now she dared contradict him to his face.

Obviously, she had no idea who he was.

"Quite the contrary," she continued, "and I can prove it if you like, for I have just made a most astonishing discovery!"

"Have you?" he echoed, certain that her discovery could not be any more astonishing than his present one—namely, her.

She nodded emphatically. "I have just learned that the symbiosis between the epiphytes and these canopy giants goes even deeper than we ever previously suspected!" She looked irked with herself the moment she had blurted it out, as though she realized after the fact how tedious scientific conversation might be deemed in some circles.

Jack was secretly amused and gave her the slightest encouragement. "You don't say."

"Shall I explain?" she offered, lighting up.

"I don't think she gets out much," Trahern murmured under his breath.

"By all means," Jack invited her, masking his amusement. He silenced his chuckling men with a curt order.

Visibly pleased by his interest, the little oddball warmed to her topic. "Oh, it's very exciting! These orchids, you see, have flourished on this tree branch for many generations, lived and died and then decayed right here on this thick bough, until eventually, over a number of years, they've created their own little bed of soil and mulch, right here on the branch. They don't need any soil of their own to grow in, of course—far from being parasites, they have special roots that allow them to suck the water right out of the air, you see, like this rain." She held out her cupped hand to catch a few raindrops as she looked up into the drizzling canopy.

When she tilted her head back, his stare homed in on the damp white fichu tucked into the neckline of her gown, a gauzy covering that clung to her demure cleavage.

"Is that . . . right?" he murmured faintly, struck by a jolt of unexpected lust.

"Quite. Here!" Leaning down to toss a purple flower to him, she nearly gave Jack a fit of apoplexy in his certainty that she was going to fall out of the tree and straight into the mouth of a crocodile. But she was blithely unconcerned for her own safety. "Today I discovered that these little orchids give back to the tree that shelters them in the most wonderful manner."

"How?" he asked, drawn in to her little mystery in spite of himself, and perhaps just a wee bit enchanted.

"They feed it. Look." She lifted up a cross-section of what appeared to him to be mere grubby turf. "When I cut into the orchids' bed of soil here for closer study, I discovered that the tree had actually begun sending these little rootlike structures right out of the *branch* so that it could take in nutrients from the mulch that generations of decaying orchids had created here. Don't you see what this means?"

Jack attempted to answer, but thought better of it. He just shook his head.

She laid her hand on the massive branch that she was sitting on and gazed up wistfully into the canopy. "They give to each other, neither harming the other. This great big mahogany gives this tiny, delicate flower shelter and solid support, while the orchid, in turn, creates nourishment to help feed the tree and keep it strong. They live together in perfect harmony, and isn't it just so . . . beautiful?"

Jack stared, mute with a very male sense of admiration.

He wasn't much for botany, and though miraculous, the arrangement between the flower and the tree did not seem half as rare and beautiful to him as this dainty, eccentric little bluestocking.

He knew now who she was.

His acquaintance with Victor Farraday and his younger sister, Cecily, went back to their days in England twenty years ago, though both he and Victor were expatriates now. The last he had heard, the famed naturalist had disappeared into the Orinoco Delta and had not been heard from since.

"You're Dr. Farraday's daughter," he informed her.

She straightened up proudly with a nod. "And you are Lord Jack Knight—though Jack is really just a nickname for John. So I'm told."

If he had been astonished before, he was now thrown completely off kilter. "You know me?"

She laughed. "I saw you before. At an assembly ball in Kingston."

"Really?" he echoed again, even more faintly this time. The world was feeling more than a little topsy-turvy.

"Yes," she declared with great certainty. "I believe you had on a black coat."

"You were at a ball I was attending and I did not notice you? Highly unlikely—ah, unless your father made a point of keeping you out of my sight."

"Perhaps," she admitted with a slight hint of flirtation sparkling in her eyes.

Jack was not quite sure what to make of it, but he gazed at her with a cautious half smile. Either she had not heard, isolated in this wild place, that he was the Devil incarnate, or was too starved for human company to care.

As someone who had little use for the human race in general, Jack found himself strangely moved by her shy but eager smile.

Fancifully, he thought her like a beautiful half-wild princess of this mysterious emerald realm—or a wondrous rare forest animal that had never seen Man before and did not know enough to be afraid.

Total innocence.

But noting the pistol and machete that she wore strapped to her slim waist, he gathered in deepening respect that the lady knew how to take care of herself. No doubt Victor had trained his daughter well in survival skills. To be sure, one look in her green eyes, with their forthright expression of confident determination, warned Jack that she had also inherited her father's brains.

Epiphytes, indeed.

He cleared his throat. "Is your father, er, at home, Miss Farraday?"

"No, he went to visit the Indians—oh, but don't go! He should be back soon. Would you like to wait for him? Come and see our camp. I could make tea!"

"Tea? Well—that's very kind, Miss Farraday, but, ah, it's ninety degrees."

"No, it's only eighty-seven! Oh, do come and have some pineapple, then. Please?" she begged him prettily. "We *never* have any visitors or news from the outside world. Come and visit for a while—just to be sociable? Papa will be back soon, I promise!"

Jack and Trahern exchanged a guarded glance.

Sociability had never been Jack's forte, but his chivalrous assistant shrugged and gave him a discreet nod expressing his sympathy for the young beauty, who was clearly starved for human company.

"Is that a yes?" she prompted with abundant optimism.

Trahern elbowed Jack covertly.

"Oh, all right," he grumbled at the lieutenant under his breath, resigned to it, for in truth, he hadn't the heart to deny the chit. Besides, he knew better than anyone that the war would be heating up over the next few months. Dr. Farraday deserved a private warning to get out of Venezuela while he still could.

Jack lifted his chin and met her eager stare. "We would be pleased to visit with you, Miss Farraday, but only for a little while. I'm afraid we're on a very tight schedule—"

"Hooray!" she cried, rousing a gasp of fright from Jack as she stood up blithely on the branch with catlike balance. "Bring your boat just around the bend, there's a dock there—oh, but do be careful, please. It's a bit rickety and you wouldn't want to fall into the water."

"Uh, crocodiles?" Trahern ventured.

"Piranha," she said sweetly.

"Do you need help getting down from there?" Jack started, certain she would stop his heart with her acrobatics, but she just laughed.

"Hardly," she said with a chuckle, seizing hold of a sturdy hanging vine. "I'll meet you below."

And then, grasping the rope-like liana in both hands and, twining it around one trim, shapely leg like the deuced trapeze artist at Vauxhall, Eden Farraday went whooshing off the branch and swung away into the leafy obscurity of the jungle, her red hair flying.

CHAPTER
∞ THREE ∞

*T*he rain stopped as suddenly as it had begun, as though some master gardener had turned off the mechanical waterworks in a huge, glassed hothouse.

As the riverboat maneuvered around the bend to the Farradays' bush camp, Jack and Trahern had barely recovered from their amazement at their intrepid young hostess's display of jungle prowess, but they found the small dock awaiting them ahead, just as she had specified.

Three dugout canoes bobbed in the *caño*'s gentle current. As their pilot steered the boat closer to the dock, Jack stared in fascination at the primitive-looking stilt-house alongside the river.

"Remarkable," Trahern murmured, sounding as fascinated as he was. "It's like a scene out of *Robinson Crusoe*."

Jack leaned with hands braced on the boat's railing, musing as he stared. "A man could live his whole life here without tuppence to his name," he said quietly, and the thought sparked an even more intriguing question in his mind.

Was it possible that, being raised in this place, so far from the corrupting influences of civilization, Miss Farraday had grown into that rarest of species—a woman who did not care for a man's worldly possessions or social standing—a woman who could not be bought?

Noise from his crew stirred Jack from his thoughts. The men guffawed and wolf-whistled, seeing the frilly ladies' underthings hanging on a makeshift laundry line. The frown he shot over his shoulder silenced them, but privately, Jack was rather entertained by it himself.

She was going to turn five shades of scarlet over this.

Fixing his gaze on the shore, Jack pulled on his brown jacket in spite of the heat. Their hostess deserved at least that much courtesy from him, but there was no way in hell he was donning a waistcoat.

The boat's gangplank banged down onto the precarious little dock, and he strode toward it across the deck.

Trahern hurried after him.

Jack stopped the rest, holding up his hand. "Stay aboard," he ordered. "The slightest sniffle or cough from you all could spread to the Indians here and they'll die. We'll be underway again in a quarter hour."

"How did you know that?" Trahern murmured as the two of them marched down the gangplank to the dock.

"I've been reading Victor's book."

"Oh!" Trahern was visibly surprised.

Jack led the way, stalking down the rustic hemp-and-plank boardwalk, which was raised some inches over the forest floor.

Behind them, the blazing tropical sun came back out over the river, burning off the temporary coolness from the rain. The broad leaves above still dripped, however, as they entered the netherworld gloom of the emerald jungle.

The plants and young trees on either side of the walk-way threatened to take it over, while countless lianas hung down from the branches above. Ahead, he saw a flicker of movement, pale swishing skirts. His male senses pricked up.

Light footfalls pattered closer, their rhythm vibrating toward him down the planks. A shy silence followed. He searched the greenery. Where was the little imp? Stopping at the lattice of a chest-high fan palm that arced across the path, he saw curious green eyes peeking at him through the pinnate fingers of the palm frond.

His heart beat faster. With a gentle motion, he slowly pushed the broad, flat leaf aside—and there she stood.

He held her wary gaze with a strange sense of soft delight. The girl was even lovelier up close. She gave him a guileless smile, then her glance flicked past him.

"Miss Farraday, allow me to present my assistant, Lieutenant Christopher Trahern."

The younger man bowed to her. "Miss Farraday."

"Eden, please," she corrected them both with a warm, rather

bashful smile. "We are not so formal here. Welcome. This way."

She showed them up the walkway until they reached her scientist father's elaborate camp ringed by unlit torches on bamboo stakes set every few feet apart. The thirty-foot clearing had a fire-pit in the center; across from the stilt-house were two large military-style tents, one closed, the other open on three sides.

The open tent contained a large work table with two microscopes, several compasses, a small scale, and an array of more obscure scientific instruments. A few black servants went about various tasks, but stopped and gaped at the strangers, then grinned and waved.

Eden introduced them all. She showed them into the stilt-house, informing them it was called a *palafito*. Inside, there were a few hammocks slung here and there, and makeshift pieces of furniture that led Jack to suspect they were standing in the young lady's bedroom.

One bamboo table held three stacks of old books that were moldering in the unwavering humidity. Shakespeare, Aristotle, Rousseau, and the poetry of Scott.

"I see you like to read," Trahern observed while Jack examined a long, native blowgun hanging on the wall.

"Oh, yes. Well, there's not much else to do around here." She cast him a demure smile over her shoulder and then whacked the top off a pineapple with her machete—deadly aim with barely a glance.

Jack marveled privately and shook his head. Eden Farraday was surely the strangest female he had ever met in his life. She proceeded to carve the pineapple into flat, neat slices with a series of unhesitating blows. He watched her warily, hands on hips. "You're pretty good with that knife."

"You should see me with a blowgun," she replied with a saucy smile, turning to offer him a piece of the sweet, juicy fruit.

He took it with a guarded nod of thanks. Trahern accepted a slice, too, then Miss Farraday helped herself to a piece and invited her servants to have the rest if they desired it.

Meanwhile, Jack inspected a dainty music box that sat on a shelf next to a few other small tokens of civilization: a foggy hand mirror, a hairbrush with a rusty pewter handle.

"Isn't that pretty? It plays Mozart." She came over to Jack and opened the lid of the music box. A few lingering notes rose out of it before dwindling into silence. "It needs to be wound up again." She glanced at him with somber eyes. "This once belonged to my mother."

He looked askance at her, reminded anew after these many years that Victor's wife was dead from a fever outbreak that had hit portions of London some twelve years ago. A sad fate for a physician, failing to save his own wife. No wonder Farraday had turned his back on the medical profession. None of his art could save her.

Dr. Farraday had explained in the introduction to his book that, after his wife's death, he and his only child, a daughter, had moved to the West Indies. Some Creole friends trying to cheer him from his despair had suggested a short visit to the Orinoco jungles, knowing his long-standing interest in natural philosophy and the sciences. He had thought it might be good for his soul, so he had agreed to the trip. In the forest, however, the bereaved doctor had caught a fever that ought to have killed him, but his life had been saved by the application of unknown herbal remedies from an Indian witch doctor.

According to his book, Dr. Farraday had known then that his life's purpose was to discover the secrets of the ancient Indian cures and the jungle plants from which they were made; this knowledge he intended to bring to the civilized world one day so that more lives could be saved.

His book failed to mention that the good doctor had dragged his daughter into his dangerous quest along with him. Now that Jack knew the truth, it made him rather angry, though he did not show it. This was no place for a young girl. "I am sorry about your mother," he offered in a brusque tone.

"It's all right." She smiled wistfully and set the music box back on the shelf, refusing to dwell on her loss. "So, what brings you gentlemen to Venezuela?" Withdrawing to lean against the post behind her, she took a bite of pineapple.

"We were just, ah—" Trahern started.

"Visiting friends," Jack said smoothly.

"I see," she murmured with a shrewd nod. "Friends up at Angostura?"

Jack and Trahern exchanged a discreetly startled glance, both rather taken off guard, for neither could miss the knowing tone of her voice. For his part, Jack was mystified.

Most females of their acquaintance at least pretended not to have a thought in their heads aside from dancing and soirees and the latest style of gowns, but this girl had practically asked point-blank if their visit was political in nature.

"No matter," she said with an airy wave of her hand, dismissing the topic as though she did not wish to make her guests uncomfortable. "It's of no concern to me if you help the rebels. Frankly, I hope they win, though Papa insists that science is neutral."

"Nobody said anything about helping the rebels, Miss Farraday. We're here on business," Trahern corrected her with a charming smile, still mistaking her, Jack suspected, for a female who could be managed. "We do a large trade in tropical hardwoods, you see. We merely came to collect those trees you might have noticed on the barge."

"Ah, yes. About those trees." She sent Jack a questioning glance that expressed her well-founded skepticism that the head of Knight Enterprises should have come in person to collect a mere haul of timber, but she did not press the matter, shrugging it off with the noblesse of a Town hostess. Jack watched her, fascinated. But as she wiped the corners of her mouth daintily with her fingertips, he realized this new subject proved no safer.

"I saw they're mostly rosewoods and mahoganies," she said, "but I noticed a few zebrawoods among them, and I do hope you didn't cut too many of them down."

"*We* didn't cut down any of the trees, Miss Farraday," Trahern said. "We bought them from a local dealer."

"Yes, but they are so very rare, you know. The zebrawood takes fifty years to reach maturity. If too many are cut at one time, the groves cannot replenish themselves."

"Their rarity is what makes them so valuable, Miss Farraday," Jack spoke up in a cynical tone, irked by a fraction at her chiding. "The fine furniture-makers of London will pay handsomely for them."

"London?" she breathed, coming away from the post all of a sudden. Her eyes widened as she took a step closer. "Is that where you're headed to next?"

He nodded. "Why do you ask?"

She stared at him intensely, then bent her head, as though growing tongue-tied all of a sudden.

He lifted his eyebrow. "Is something wrong, Miss Farraday?"

43

"Oh—no. I-it's nothing, it's just I—have so often wished that I could go there."

"To London?" he drawled. "Whatever for? The weather is cold and so are the people."

She lifted her astonished gaze to his. "No, they're not!"

"Of course they are. 'Tis a miserable place. I'm only going 'cos I have to." His tone was idle, but he was speaking more candidly than she might have known.

"Why do you have to?" she demanded.

"Got to get rid of those trees, o' course." He could not resist teasing her a little. It wasn't as though he could tell her the truth. "God knows, if Prinny gets a zebrawood table, so must every hostess in the ton have one to grace the entrance hall."

His jaded words roused a chuckle from Trahern, but Miss Farraday did not look at all amused.

"I'm sure they're not as bad as you say."

"No, indeed, they're worse," Jack murmured, his eyes dancing with his newfound sport of baiting her. "Pompous, idle. Trust me, love. I know that lot like the back of my hand. My elder brother is a duke, after all. Trahern, maybe Hawkscliffe's duchess would like a zebrawood table, what do you think?"

"Charge him double."

Jack laughed, then winced as pineapple juice dripped into his splinter. "Ow."

Miss Farraday frowned at him, looking a little unsure about whether it had been a good idea to invite him for a visit, after all. "What is the matter?"

He mumbled it was nothing.

"Did you hurt yourself?"

"Just a splinter from loading up the wood."

"Let me see that." She marched over to him and seized his hand, prying his closed fist open. She inspected the pinlike fragment of wood buried beneath his skin, then sent him an arch look. "Zebra-wood, I warrant."

"Well, I do try to keep in the fashion."

"You deserve this splinter, I daresay. Nevertheless, I am going to help you, Lord Jack. Sit down, please."

"No, thanks. It's nothing. I'll attend to it on my ship—"

"Sit!"

Jack lifted his eyebrows at her tone that brooked no argument.

44

"No open wounds in the jungle," she stated. "That is a rule."

"Open wounds?" He scoffed. "It's barely a scratch."

"It's a large scratch, and it's deep. Trust me. If you don't take care of it right away—well, you don't want to know what can happen."

"What can happen?" Trahern asked, blanching.

"I'm sure you don't want me to tell you. Gentlemen, trust me, it's very disgusting."

They stared at her expectantly.

She relented with a sigh. "Even small scratches can become infected quickly in the jungle. If you must know, there's a tiny insect that likes to lay its eggs in any open wound it finds. After that, the only remedy is amputation."

Jack sat down at once on the stool she had indicated and gave her his hand. "I'm all yours, my dear. Just tell me this doesn't involve your machete."

She shot him a chiding smile and went to fetch her sewing basket.

Eden could feel him watching her with his predatory stare, but her heart still pounded at the news that he and his crew were heading next to England.

Surely this was the miracle she had been praying for. Now all she had to do was to find the nerve to ask the notorious Black-Jack Knight if he'd take her along for the ride.

He had no reason to oblige her, she knew, and if he was as wicked as the rumors claimed, she might be safer accompanying Papa into the Amazon. Even if he was an ex-pirate, she did not wish to seem pushy or rude, imposing on him.

Oh, it was so very lowering to know he had millions and she hadn't pennies for the trip. She had her pride. Nevertheless, she was determined to show him that she could be useful. Perhaps her skills would help to gain her the favor she so desperately needed. Bolstered by that hope, she returned and sat across from him while Mr. Trahern anxiously searched himself for any small open wounds or odd insect bites that he might have overlooked.

Eden dragged her stool closer to her patient's and pulled his large, warm hand onto her lap, turning his palm upward; his knuckles rested on her thigh.

His smoky stare homed in on her, as though he, too, had felt the shock of electricity that jolted through her when they touched. Eden's heart skipped a beat. Her cheeks colored as she bent her head to assess his splinter, her sewing needle poised between her fingers.

Lord Jack frowned when she used it to poke the heel of his hand. "I do hope you know what you're doing."

"Of course I do. I'm a physician's daughter. And do you know what you are?" she murmured with a cautious smile, brushing a stray lock of her hair behind her ear.

"Do tell," he purred, watching her.

"Just a big, grumpy lion with a thorn in his paw."

A rueful smile spread across his face. "Yes, Miss Farraday, I'm afraid you've summed me up rather neatly."

They exchanged a smile that lasted just a moment too long, then she turned her attention back to her task, trying to ignore the girlish flutter of her heart.

The little sliver of wood had worked its way in deep. It looked like it hurt. As Eden ran her thumb across his palm, marveling privately at how big and full of strength his callused hands were, again she sensed him staring at her. The potent male interest in his gaze was a bit unsettling; she did her best to ignore it and willed her hands not to shake. With a murmured warning, she pricked his skin gently, and widened the incision a bit to go after the splinter.

"So, Lord Jack—" She cleared her throat. Papa always said it was best to distract the patient during such proceedings. "You don't plan to cross the ocean in that steamer?"

"In the steamer? No, Miss Farraday—"

"Eden," she interrupted softly, glancing up to meet his gaze.

A speculative look filled his aquamarine eyes. "Eden," he corrected himself barely audibly. He paused before continuing in a more casual tone: "My ship is waiting for me off Trinidad. We're to rendezvous at the coast."

"Is it a big ship?" she asked, wondering if there might be room for her.

"Very big," he replied in silken innuendo, and gave her a wicked smile.

She felt her face heat. "What's it called?"

"The Winds of Fortune."

"That's—a nice name," she said a bit breathlessly.

"Thank you."

Exchanging the needle for the tweezers, she sent another wary glance his way and this time caught him staring point-blank at her mouth, the drift of his thoughts perfectly plain on his handsome face.

Her heart pounded. "I thought most ships were named for ladies."

"Not my ships."

"Why is that?"

"My ships are reliable."

"I see. And your ladies are not?"

His only answer was a world-weary flick of one eyebrow, along with a dry half smile.

Eden laughed quietly and lowered her head again. "I fear, Lord Jack, that you are a cynic."

"Born that way."

Spurred on by an almost scientific curiosity, she leaned closer and asked the supposedly forbidden question of Jack Knight. "You know," she confided in a daring murmur, "they say you used to be a pirate."

"Do they?" he whispered.

Her naughty smile widened. "Is it true?"

His eyes danced as he considered for a moment. "It is, my dear, shall we say, a matter of perspective."

"Ah." She nodded sagely, only realizing after a moment that he hadn't told her anything. His evasive answer only whetted her interest.

Meanwhile, his dark, longish hair was already drying from the rain; gazing at him, she was filled with the impulse to run her fingers through its soft, tousled waves. She fought the urge to touch his face, as well, his skin so deeply tanned from an adventuring life lived outdoors, on the deck of a ship.

No, she conceded, still studying him at close range, he was no elegant Town dandy like the ones who went strolling through her daydreams, but there was something positively thrilling about this man.

She remembered the ball in Jamaica where she had first seen him; he had been the most riveting man in the room, drawing the stares of every woman present, while most of the men simply stepped out of his way.

Gazing openly at him a moment longer, Eden decided that what

47

she liked best were the faint, smiley crinkles at the outer corners of his deep-set eyes. He had kind eyes, she thought, and wondered if he knew it.

"Eden," he said softly. Her name sounded delicious on his tongue. "You're staring at me."

Caught. She bit her lower lip and blushed. "But, Lord Jack," she replied just as gently, "you're staring, too."

He knew, of course; his slow grin was decidedly sly.

A hot wave of pure, visceral attraction rushed through her, a fevered contagion that she caught directly from him.

Fighting to maintain her wits, she cast about for a neutral topic. "How do you intend to get past the Spanish?"

"Oh, I have my ways."

"I'll bet you do," she murmured.

He leaned closer. "You've got very good hands."

Eden held her breath, her pulse racing. As he stared into her eyes, she thought he was actually going to kiss her.

She was motionless, dazzled—waiting—but then, with a look of regret, he eased back in his seat again.

It was another moment before she could breathe, let alone continue. She scoffed privately at the foolish staccato of her pulse, and the twinge of disappointment that the notoriously bad ex-pirate had decided to be good.

Of course, a real lady should have considered his attentions outrageously rude. Cousin Amelia, a proper young miss of the Quality, would have fainted by now. Dismayed that she could not even manage to feel properly offended, Eden lowered her head with renewed concentration and finished removing his splinter.

She caught the tiny shard of wood between her tweezers, and, maneuvering with gentle precision, finally got it out.

"Good news," she announced, looking at him again with well-recovered poise. "You're going to live."

"More's the pity. Eden?" he said abruptly. "Why does he keep you hidden away like this?"

"You mean Papa? Oh, he thinks he is protecting me." She tidied up the small incision with a splash of brandy on a cloth. "He isn't a genius in all things, Lord Jack, especially matters of the heart." Saddened by the admission, she stood up to put her things away.

"But it's a crime, his stranding you here like this." His stare tracked her with an intensity that she could feel from across the room. "You should be in Kingston, being worshiped by the sons of wealthy planters."

She turned around abruptly, shocked and flattered and above all thrilled to think that, at last, somebody understood. Why, she had just met the man and somehow he knew her heart better than Papa did.

She stared at him in amazement.

Folding her arms across her chest and leaning her hip against the table, Eden was wildly encouraged all of a sudden to think that if he liked her so well, then surely he would help her.

There could be no doubt that lordly male chivalry would compel him to escort her safely home to England, if she only asked. He was obviously a gentleman, no matter what the rumors said; he could have kissed her moments ago, after all, but had done the decent thing and refrained. Besides, she had just done him a favor, hadn't she, removing his splinter and possibly saving his hand? Surely he would be happy to do a good deed for her in return.

Yes, she thought, she could ask him now. Pirate or no, her excellent instincts told her that she could trust this man.

She bit her lip and summoned up all her nerve. "What would you say," she began slowly, "if I asked you for a favor?"

"A favor?" His eyes narrowed in sudden wariness. "What sort of favor, exactly?"

Her confident smile did not waver, though her heart was in her throat. Eden lifted her chin and squared her shoulders: "Take me with you to England."

CHAPTER
∽ FOUR ∽

Take her . . . ?

Jack stared into her hope-filled, emerald eyes, thought of his vital secret mission—his highly illegal secret mission—and let out a curse.

"No." He shook his head and rose with a shudder. "Absolutely not."

"But why?"

"Because it's a mad idea!"

"No, it's not!" She took a step toward him and seemed to force her coaxing smile. "You're going there anyway, aren't you?"

Bloody hell. "Is that why you asked me here for a visit?" he asked crisply. "To butter me up so you could get what you wanted?"

She lowered her head at the question; Jack scowled.

He glanced at Trahern. "Ready?"

"Aye, sir."

"Oh, please don't go—you only just got here!" Miss Farraday jumped in front of Jack, blocking his path. She seemed undaunted by his famous glower, though she only came up to his chest and had to tilt her head back to meet his irked gaze.

Her anxious smile refused the quashing effect of his glare. "You said your ship is big—very big. There must be room on board for me!"

"There's not."

"I don't take up much space, as you can see."

"Thank you for the pineapple, Miss Farraday—"

"Eden," she insisted, trying to drag him into a familiarity that he did not desire, the better to make him do her will. Aye, that was how they got their claws into a man.

She was a most determined creature, darting left and right to block his path as he tried to step past her.

"I'm sorry, Miss Farraday," he said through clenched teeth, "but my ship is not equipped to take passengers. It is a merchant vessel, a cargo ship. I have no place to put a young lady—"

"I don't require any special accommodations. I could sling my hammock anyplace! In fact—" She gulped with an air of desperation behind her dwindling smile. "That, er, brings me to my next point."

Jack set his hands on his waist. "Oh, there's more, is there?"

"Um, yes, well, you see, I-I have no money, actually. Terribly embarrassing. I'm afraid I can't pay for my passage. But I will work," she added stoutly. "I could help in the sickbay or the galley. I'm a hard worker, just tell me what to do. I won't complain. I'm quite cheerful."

"Yes, I can see that," Jack said through gritted teeth.

Trahern stifled a cough.

Jack shot him a fierce look.

"I've heard about press gangs, so I know that every ship can always use an extra pair of hands—"

"Not yours, my dear." A quiver of lust shot through him only to imagine where he'd like those skillful, pretty hands to work on him.

"But why?" she asked with a sorrowful, doe-eyed blink.

"Because I said so," he growled. "Now will you please get out of my way?"

"No! I don't mean to be a pest, but it's just that I need so badly to get back to England."

"Why is that?" Jack demanded, though he swore to himself he did not care and didn't really want to know. He was not taking her to England, and that was that. There was too much at stake to risk adding a feckless young beauty underfoot.

"Father's patron died," she exclaimed. "His heir has cut the funding for our research." This instantly flared Jack's instinct for lucrative opportunity as Eden continued: "I intend to return to England so I can speak to the new earl and convince him to reinstate our grant."

He raised an eyebrow. "*You're* going to speak to the earl?"

"Yes," she declared with a firm nod.

He stared at her. "Nobody's going to listen to you, a mere slip of a girl."

51

"Oh, yes, they will." She planted her fists on her waist. "I'll *make* them listen."

He found himself fighting a wry smile, damn her. Jack eyed the redhead warily, a trifle amused in spite of himself as he realized that, indeed, the chit had made *him* listen.

Somehow it was easy to picture the intrepid little epiphyte lady taking this earl by the ear like an errant schoolboy and making him pay attention to her scientific lecture. Jack couldn't help but wonder how she'd set London on its ear if she had half a chance—or rather, knock it on its pompous arse.

That thought nearly persuaded him to take her there just for the pleasure of watching it happen, but of course, he couldn't risk it. He shook his head with the faint, reluctant smile.

The girl had pluck, he'd give her that, brains, too, but on top of all the usual perils of a sea journey, his secret mission was already complicated and dangerous enough. The rumor mills of London would be churning when he reappeared after such a long absence, and his many enemies would be watching for any opportunity to pounce. He had yet to meet a female who could keep her mouth shut when she had a secret to tell, and this one already knew too much—whether she realized it or not.

"I am sorry," he said in a kinder tone, but with finality, "I honestly cannot help you." With that, he stepped past her and strode out of the *palafito*.

Miss Farraday whirled around and came scrambling after him. He could hear her, though he didn't look back.

"But I'll tell you what I will do," he continued before she could argue, her pattering footfalls dogging his long strides. "Have your father write to my offices in Port Royal. Send me a proposal. I'll fund his research for . . ." He ran a quick mental calculation. "Eighty percent of the profits from any medicines he develops."

She stopped following him, apparently in shock. "Eighty percent!" she cried. "Don't you think that's a bit high?"

"Of course it's high." He stepped up onto the boardwalk and sent her a knowing smile over his shoulder. "Ever heard of negotiation?"

"Negotiation," she echoed under her breath. "Right!"

As he walked on, he heard her rushing after him again.

"So, maybe you *would* be willing to bring me to England if we could reach some sort of deal—"

52

"Now, wait one minute, that's not what I meant." He shot her an impatient look askance. "I was speaking in general terms."

"Infuriating man," she muttered under her breath as he continued down the boardwalk. "Would you stop walking away? Lord Jack? Will you please just wait?" A fair hand grabbed the crook of his arm and held on with a tenacity that would have impressed his bull-terrier, Rudy, the only living thing aside from Trahern that Jack really trusted.

"What do you want from me?" he asked wearily, turning around to face her. "You need to talk this over with your father."

"You don't understand."

"I'd help you if I could, but it simply isn't safe."

"Yes, I know, the sea is perilous, but I . . . I trust you."

Her innocent gaze was nearly his undoing, a fact that vexed Jack in the extreme. "You trust me. Girl—" He scoffed, shaking his head. "You don't even know me!" He pivoted and marched down the walkway in something of a daze, his heart pounding in time with the rhythm of his forceful strides. Lord, she had no business "trusting" him.

He certainly didn't trust her. The chit was dangerous, aye, deadly, and he was getting the hell out of here. Before she found a way to twist him 'round her little finger.

Eden fumed as he walked away from her yet again. Was there no reasoning with the man? He simply laid down the law and expected everyone to—

Suddenly, she heard Papa and Connor hailing the servants from the far edge of camp, returning from their day's journey just in time, naturally, to complicate matters.

Blazes!

"Edie! I say, do we have visitors? Who is that?" her father called, but she did not answer, for every second now was precious.

There was no time to explain to her obdurate papa.

She picked up her skirts and dashed after Lord Jack again, her footsteps pounding on the planks. "Papa's come. Why don't you stay and talk to him?"

"Jack Knight, you blackguard!" her father bellowed at that very moment from the head of the boardwalk some yards behind them. "Get the hell away from my daughter, sir, this *instant*!"

"Thanks, but I'll pass," Lord Jack muttered sarcastically to her.

"Eden, step away from that scoundrel! That is a dangerous man!"

"Nice to see you again, too, Victor!" he called drily. "Don't worry, I'm on my way out."

Eden paused only long enough to shoot her father a quelling look, gesturing at him to remember his manners, and then she scrambled after her escaping guest again.

Ahead, Lord Jack smacked the palm fronds aside and marched past them. They sprang back into place like a green door swinging shut behind him.

Eden refused to be brushed off, though her hope was running thin. "So, it's true, then," she flung at his retreating back while his crewmen stared. "All you *do* care about is gold! You won't help me simply because I can't pay!"

"Sweetheart." He swung around to face her with a frank leer that raked down over her body. "If you were on my ship, believe me, you *would* pay me back. You'd work it off, every penny. Only I don't much think you'd like the price."

Shocked to the core, she drew herself up in grand indignation. "You, sir, are not a gentleman."

"You finally just figured that out?"

"Eden Farraday, get over here this instant!" her father bellowed. She glanced over angrily and saw Papa marching toward them, red-faced. "A word with you, sir!" He pointed to the barge. "What is that timber you're hauling?"

"Uh-oh," Eden taunted softly. "Now you're in for it."

Lord Jack glanced at her, sufficiently warned to brace for her father's explosion.

Dr. Farraday took a closer look at the pile of wood. "*Zebra-woods?* Zebrawoods, you bloody plunderer! How dare you? Fifty years of growth, and you chop it down for a bit of filthy lucre? Damn you, sir—get *away* from my daughter!"

Instead of telling Papa that escaping Eden was precisely what he had been trying to do, Lord Jack took what appeared to be an intense personal insult at Papa's order; she glanced over at him just in time to see the look of pure, bloody-minded rebellion that darkened his face.

"Get away from her, eh?" he growled under his breath. "Oh, so I'm not good enough for your daughter, is that it?" He sent her father a pirate grin and suddenly seized Eden around the waist,

54

yanking her forward so that she crashed into his steely warm chest.

Before she could even react, his mouth swooped down on hers, hot and hard; in front of everyone, Papa and all, he plundered her lips in a brigand's kiss.

Cousin Amelia would surely have expired on the spot. But Eden, alas, was not Cousin Amelia.

He started rough, bruising her lower lip in his unyielding haste, his scruffy jaw scraping her tender chin, but the instant she whimpered, trapped in his iron arms, his kiss softened.

Then she forgot entirely to fight. Her eyes fluttered closed, and for a few seconds, time floated on the wavering path of a butterfly.

His kiss deepened, widening her lips for the slow, exploratory stroke of his tongue in her mouth.

In the foggy distance, men were shouting, but she had traveled a thousand miles away from the chaos as Jack's hand tangled sensuously in her hair. He gripped her nape as his mouth slanted over hers in hungry demand; her hands clung weakly to his broad shoulders. His tightening embrace crushed her breasts against his chest. But though he held her firmly, inwardly Eden was falling, falling from the highest treetop, pinwheeling weightlessly to earth like a winged seed. She was totally in his power and the pleasure in this sudden helplessness alarmed her.

He went on kissing her for several delicious seconds more, as though he had forgotten this was merely an act of defiance; she felt his earlier anger melting away. He tore his mouth away from hers all of a sudden with a breathy curse. When he released her, she stumbled, dizzy and disoriented, and would have fallen off the dock straight into the river if he had not immediately reached for her and steadied her again.

They exchanged a shocked glance as he gripped her elbow and pulled her to safety. His eyes had darkened to a stormy slate blue. Then a rueful half smile curved his lips.

"You almost make me change my mind," he whispered low, so only she could hear.

She noticed, then, with an appalled jolt, that they were caught up in the middle of a standoff.

Connor had arrived.

He had stopped in his tracks farther up the boardwalk and, upon seeing Jack grab her, he had reached for the rifle strapped across his back.

But when the Australian had pointed his weapon at Jack, a dozen sailors on the riverboat had instantly seized their Baker rifles and had taken aim at him in return. Papa had stepped in front of Connor, his arms spread, while Mr. Trahern screamed at his men to hold their fire.

"Good God!" Eden breathed, but Jack took control with a kingly roar: *"Lower your weapons!"*

His men obeyed without hesitation, but Connor kept his rifle trained expertly on Jack.

The look on Connor's face told her that he wanted blood.

She had seen that look before, that terrible day in the forest. It was a memory she loathed more than anything.

Barely aware that she had moved in front of Jack, Eden lifted her hands in a calming gesture. "Connor, please. Put the rifle down."

He stared at her in icy stillness: silent accusation.

Fear spiked through her when she read the fury in his eyes—as though he saw and understood just how much she had enjoyed Lord Jack's outrageous kiss.

"Do as she says, man!" her father snapped. "Put the gun down! Are you mad?" *Yes, Papa, he is, a little. Hadn't you noticed?* Eden thought.

Still poised to kill, Connor flicked a guarded glance in Dr. Farraday's direction.

He suddenly swung the rifle back over his shoulder and sent Eden an icy stare that promised there'd be consequences later. He pivoted on his heel and left the scene without a word, but Eden had turned pale.

A knot formed in the pit of her stomach, for she knew that she would have to face him alone soon, and it appeared their protector's patience with her had just run out.

Jack had no idea who the tedious fellow was who had aimed the rifle at his head, but he was used to people wanting to kill him, and at the moment, he was too drunk off her sweet mouth to care.

Her father was screaming at him, but Jack just stared at Eden, reeling with the unexpected bounty of her kiss, his senses thickened with desire. Those plump, silky lips were every bit as luscious as he'd briefly fantasized, and Jack wanted more, kisses down her neck and arms, kisses up her legs.

He thought of her story of orchids and trees, their sweet symbiosis, and felt the power of this woman shake him. Her unsullied,
inward beauty somehow fed his soul.

True, he had wanted to taste her from the start, but he had only
succumbed to the impulse to shove it in her father's face. Victor's
words—*"Get away from my daughter!"*—were ones that Jack had
heard before. They had flung him back to another place, another
time, another girl.

The Irish bastard.

Never good enough.

"Stay away from our daughter." Ah, that foolish chit he once
had thought he loved. What would he not have done for her at
seventeen? He'd have drunk hemlock to prove his love if Maura
Prescott had asked him to, but she had thrown him over for a
title.

It was a lesson Jack refused to forget, a mistake he would sure
as hell never repeat—caring all out of proportion—but admittedly,
he'd gotten more than he'd bargained for when he had taken Eden
Farraday into his arms.

Her father marched over and grabbed her by her wrist, pulling
her away from Jack and planting himself between them. "How
dare you make a move like that on my daughter, you barbaric
fiend?"

"Me?" Jack's desire to protect her came out of nowhere, but
somebody had to speak up for the girl. "What about you, keeping
her here like a prisoner?" he boomed right back at him. "Jesus,
man, look around you! Crocodiles, poison spiders, vampire bats!
This is no place for a lady!"

"Don't you tell me how to manage my daughter! She could survive in this jungle better than you!"

"Survival? Is that the best you aspire to provide for your child?
Eyes down, you lot!" he roared at his crew when he noticed them
watching as though it were a stage play. "What are you staring at?
Look lively! Trahern!" he bellowed. "Get the damned boat started!
We've got a schedule to keep!"

"Aye, sir."

Jack turned back to Dr. Farraday, while Eden stared dazedly at
him. "The girl wants out of here, and who can blame her? I can't
think how you mean to proceed, in any case, now that you've lost
your funding."

Victor froze, then looked at his daughter as though she were a traitor. "You told him?"

Eden faltered, apparently caught off guard, then she offered up a hapless shrug.

Her father glowered.

"Well, don't get angry at her for it!" Jack said impatiently. "She's the only one around here who's got any damned sense! Victor, if you were half the genius you're supposed to be, you would see that getting out of the Delta now is the only intelligent thing to do! Bloody hell." Jack did not have time for this. He was irked and sweaty and insulted, himself, from Victor's tirade, but the sweet thing looked so lost standing there that he at least had to try one possible way to help her—though nothing so foolhardy as taking her with him to England.

"Look," Jack said gruffly, "the coast is very hot right now. I can take you all to Trinidad if you can be ready to go in three hours."

"What are you talking about?"

"Much more than that, and we risk running into the Spanish patrol boats. I would like to avoid an altercation—"

"Since when?" Victor retorted. "You're rather famous for fighting."

Jack gave him a stony look. "You'll take my offer if you're wise. Within six months, this war will be heating up in earnest. This could be your last chance to get out."

Eden sent him a probing look.

"Never mind how I know," he warned her before she could ask.

"For your information, we have no intention of leaving," her father clipped out. "*We* do not run away from difficult situations, unlike some people."

Jack narrowed his eyes, taking her father's point like the tip of a dagger.

Victor kept on ranting, but Jack just shook his head and lowered his gaze. God's bones, why was he wasting his time here? Pretty or no, Eden Farraday wasn't his problem. If he wanted a beautiful girl of his own, he would buy one.

He gave her a hard look, but did not know what else to say. God knew, the whole picture was becoming very clear: the stubborn father who wanted his daughter by his side to look after him, and that other fellow who'd tried to blow his head off.

The blond man's belligerent stance had announced in no uncertain terms that he had staked some kind of claim on Eden Farraday, whether she liked it or not.

Jack shook his head at her father. "You're a damned fool," he said pointedly to Victor, then jumped back onto the steamer and gave the order to move out.

He was instantly obeyed. His outbursts were rare, but they still left his crew walking on eggshells.

As the boat trundled away from the Farradays' rickety jungle dock, he tried to follow his standard policy of never looking back where females were concerned, but unlike his delectable plaything from last night, Eden Farraday was not so easily forgotten.

In spite of himself, he cast a brooding glance over his shoulder and saw her still standing there, staring after him, her lovely face forlorn.

Though he looked at her without expression, he could not escape the guilty sense that he was abandoning one of his own in this place, very like a pirate captain marooning one of his crew on a desert isle for some nefarious misdeed.

Too bad, girl. Life's tough.

He knew that better than most.

She *trusted* him? He scoffed inwardly, shaken by the words. Nobody trusted him. Nobody should. He was an all-around bastard and damn proud of it.

Hardening his mutinous heart with a will, he looked ahead again toward the unforgiving sea.

"How dare you discuss our private business with him?" Papa demanded, turning to Eden as the riverboat and its burden of lumber receded into the distance. "You have no idea what manner of man he is! Jack Knight is a scoundrel and a blackguard, and whatever he's doing here, stirring up trouble, I guarantee you he's up to no good!"

"What, you don't want me to mate with him, too, Father?" she answered under her breath.

"Mind your tongue!" he thundered, hearing in spite of her low tone. "His behavior here was unforgivable, and as for you, I have had quite enough of your impertinence! You are staying here with us, and that is final!"

Having laid down the law, Papa began marching away, shaking

59

his head and muttering to himself about her mischief, his chest puffed out with parental indignance.

Tamping down her frustration, Eden called after her sire before he was out of earshot. "How did he get past the Spanish, do you suppose?"

"I'll tell you how!" He stopped with a snort and turned around to face her. "Jack Knight cut his eyeteeth running guns and black-market brandy past Napoleon's Continental Blockade. He's nothing but a glorified criminal—which is why you are to forget you ever laid eyes on him! Why do you think he's the bloody king of Port Royal? You've heard the stories about that town—a city of pirates and thieves!"

"If he's so bad, then how do you know him?"

Papa gave her a dubious look, shook his head as he debated with himself, then wiped the sweat wearily off his brow. "Your aunt Cecily, in her girlhood, was a companion to Lady Maura Prescott, the young daughter of the Marquess of Griffith—Prescott is the family name. I was mildly acquainted with the girl, since my sister was constantly in attendance upon her. Arrogant chit, I always thought. At any rate, that is how I met Lord Jack. He was devoted to Lady Maura, but the two were not allowed to wed. They were very young and," he admitted reluctantly, "they were in love."

Her father paused, reflecting on those long-gone days.

"My sister told me that when Lord and Lady Griffith ordered their daughter to tell her beau she could never see him again, Jack tried to get her to elope with him. Maura refused," he said with a shrug. "Jack left England in a fury and to the best of my knowledge has not been back since."

Just like you, Papa, she thought. *An exile.*

"Now, if you will excuse me, I am in dire need of refreshment after this long and tiring day we have had. I shall want my supper within the hour. Oh, and by the way—" he added, already marching back up the boardwalk toward camp. "The shaman's nephew has agreed to take us to the Amazon. We're leaving in three days."

Eden's jaw dropped, but Papa did not look back. She stared after him in horror, the reality of his mad quest dawning on her with a kind of delayed amazement.

It could not be! Reeling, she turned and stared hopelessly after the riverboat dwindling into the distance.

Shading her eyes against the blazing sun, she realized her only hope of ever attaining a normal life was drifting away down the Orinoco. Oh, this was a disaster. She could hardly believe Papa truly meant to go through with it.

Dropping her gaze to the rough planks of the dock, she dragged her hand through her hair and tried to think what to do.

It was then that her downcast gaze suddenly happened across the familiar sight of the dugout canoes hitched to the dock. Her churning thoughts halted abruptly.

She stared down at her canoe for a second—and then the idea rolled through her mind like thunder.

Yes.

Papa and Connor both had driven her to this. It was the only solution that remained.

All in one reckless, thrilling flash, she knew what she had to do.

Her pulse pounding, Eden lifted her gaze and stared down the river at the shrinking steamboat. It really seemed she had no choice. Leaving was the only way to stop Papa from carrying out his suicidal quest into the Amazon.

She knew deep in her heart that he would drop everything to follow her, even if it meant facing civilization again. Perhaps if he could just see England for himself after all this time, he would realize the world out there wasn't nearly as bad as he had come to believe. Indeed, her running off now might be the only way to save his stubborn hide.

And then there was Connor. Leaving would also put some distance between the two of them. God willing, it would help him to see and to accept at last that she *did not want* to spend the rest of her life out here as his mate. After her kiss with Jack, it seemed he had finally taken the hint, but she knew he was angry.

She did not want to risk a confrontation with him out here in the wild, where there was no code, no rule of law to stop him from overpowering her. Out here, might made right, and Connor was the strongest of them all.

All these years, he had held back his passion out of reverence for her, waiting until she was ready, but after today, seeing her return Jack Knight's kiss, she knew that only his fury awaited her now, and she was afraid. She had seen long ago what he was capable of; if his rage broke free, there would be no choice but to give in. Then she'd be his prisoner here for the rest of her life.

61

She was already in motion, striding up the boardwalk and checking off a mental list of supplies that she would need.

Connor had headed out of camp with his rifle over his shoulder to vent his frustration with work, but she knew she'd have to go quickly before he came back.

Jack had warned her what would happen if she came aboard his ship; ah, but what the captain didn't know wouldn't hurt him. She was stowing away and no one was going to stop her. She could take care of herself, and besides, she planned on staying out of sight until they reached England. A hundred forest animals had taught her how to hide.

Crossing the camp, she slipped into her father's research tent and with trembling hands gathered up the strongest examples of her father's work to show to the new Earl of Pembrooke, just as she had told Lord Jack she'd do. She tucked them covertly into a canvas haversack. Glancing over her shoulder to make sure no one saw, she strode next to the *palafito* to collect her things.

She knew she had to hurry or *The Winds of Fortune* would soon set off across the sea without her.

Back inside the stilt-house, she changed into breeches, shirt, and Papa's old brown leather jacket, which she sometimes wore for practicality's sake when she joined the men on their most untamed expeditions to the deepest reaches of the jungle.

Tying a dark blue neckerchief over her hair also helped to disguise her sex in case any of Jack's crewmen should spot her. Moving as swiftly as possible, she threw as many supplies into her haversack as she could carry—including Cousin Amelia's last letter with her Bedfordshire address on it, and a few issues of *La Belle Assemblée.*

All that was left to do was to say her farewells, but she dared not risk it. Staring across the camp, she watched her father explaining his plans to the servants, and wavered, sorrowfully torn. But then she shook her head.

Go. A chance like this only comes along once in a lifetime. It was what Mama would have said. Pausing at the bamboo table, she quickly jotted a note to Papa and Connor, telling them what she was doing so that they would not worry too much. She signed with all her love and then, without further ado, slipped out the side of the *palafito* and took the muddy shortcut down to the dock.

After briskly tossing her haversack into her trusty dugout canoe, she sat down in the little vessel and took up the familiar oars, giving herself no time to lose her courage. She freed her little boat from the dock and shoved off with an oar.

Within moments, she was gliding silently down the *caño,* pulling on the oars with all her might.

She rowed swiftly, rowed until her shoulders hurt; she spotted terrifying, ridged silhouettes cutting sinuously through the water here and there, vast, dark shapes in the shallows, but she refused to turn back.

And then, about a half hour into her perilous journey, she spotted the lazy riverboat, slowed by its barge piled with lumber. The steamer traveled on the main river, but Eden took the smaller *caños* that ran parallel to it; thus, she managed to stay hidden by the jungle brush while keeping abreast of the larger vessel.

She made swift progress thanks to the strengthening current as they neared the Gulf of Paria. Soon, mangroves began to appear, and she could taste salt in the air.

She grinned with hearty enthusiasm when she noticed she was actually pulling ahead of the steamer. It had run into a spot of trouble on a sandbar. Though it wasn't a race, arriving before Lord Jack did could only work to her advantage.

She rowed harder.

Before long, she came to powdery white beaches lined with graceful palm trees. Windy white-tops broke against the shore, while farther up the beach, fat iguanas sunned themselves on the rocks. Ahead lay the wide blue ocean, with the island of Trinidad slightly to the north.

In the narrow strait called the Serpent's Mouth that flowed between the island's southern edge and the mainland, a magnificent seventy-four-gun ship rode at anchor on bare poles, revealing the intricate webwork of rigging that supported the three towering masts.

No room? she thought with a snort. Lifting her telescope to her eye, she read the ship's name painted near the jib. *The Winds of Fortune.* It was his vessel, all right—as big as a floating castle and bristling with deadly armaments.

Awed by the majesty of the great vessel, she studied the colorfully painted figurehead for a moment, while the ship's attendant cutters scurried about the copper-clad hull like drone ants around the queen. Her gaze ran the length of the two-hundred-foot hull with its double gun decks, all the way back to the carved and gilded stern.

How in blazes am I going to get on that thing? she wondered, peering through her spyglass. She considered her options. *Climb up one of those ropes?* She was a skilled climber, after all. *No, they'll see me. What about those big crates they're loading aboard? Perhaps I could stow away in one of those.*

It seemed as good a plan as any.

Taking one, long, last look back at the jungle and wondering if she would ever see it again, she faced forward once more, steeled her nerve, and then darted out of her hiding place, running stealthily from rock to rock toward the great pile of wooden crates being loaded onto the ship.

With the sailors distracted by the steamer's late arrival, finally free of the sandbar, Eden stole over to the pile of crates variously labeled PINEAPPLES, LIMES, COCONUTS, MANGOES, and BANANAS. She wrenched the top off one and dove inside, hastily pulling the lid back on over her head.

From the inside, the big crate was about the size of a jaguar trap. Again she thought of Connor and wondered how he might react when he discovered she had fled.

She waited, heart pounding, then she held her breath as more of Lord Jack's sweaty sailors returned, trudging back through the sand to continue their task of loading the crates onto the longboats for transport to the huge gunship.

"Boney's balls, these limes is heavy!" a man in a red shirt exclaimed as he picked up the crate Eden was hiding in.

"At least we won't get scurvied, eh?"

"Give me a hand with this one, Sharky! I'll break me damn back," the first said, but thankfully, nobody noticed her presence as they carried her crate over to the longboat and stacked her in with all the others.

Before long, the cutter took to the waves, the seamen rowing out to the ship and complaining all the way about the heat.

Rolling a few limes out of her way, Eden peered out through the slats of her crate, wide-eyed. She couldn't believe how big the vessel was as the Englishmen rowed closer. With her sails furled, her bare masts scraped the very sky.

They must have chopped down a hundred acres of oak to make that ship, she thought. Then suddenly, from out of the blue sky, a giant crane descended with a cargo platform hanging from its huge metal hook. When it came down low enough, the sailors began transferring the crates of fruit onto the platform.

" 'Hoy, Bob, think Cap would notice if we took a few o' these 'ere limes?" a large fellow with an earring asked the others as he lifted Eden's crate onto the platform.

She balled up as small as she could make herself and prayed no one would see her.

"Course he'd notice, knowin' 'im, you tit. Tie 'er up tight there!" Sharky ordered the others, then they secured the stack of crates with rope. "Himself'll have a fit if we drop 'em in the brine."

"Right, take 'er up!" the one in the red shirt yelled, gesturing to the men operating the davit.

Up on the ship's deck, another team of sailors lurched into motion, pushing the mighty winch around in a circle, and drawing the great pulley upward. Meanwhile, another pair of seamen posted at the taffrail kept a weather eye out for the Spanish fleet.

Eden stared out over water and land, barely daring to breathe as the cargo platform ascended, up and up and up so high, until she could see for miles over the jungle's treetops.

The forest was afire with a blazing fuschia sunset behind it, silhouetting towering spiky moriche palms and the leafy giants of the canopy that had been her playground, while the Orinoco ran like liquid gold. She could see the Delta's labyrinth of meandering *caños* and could almost make out the flat-topped mountains called *tepuys* in the distance.

Somewhere in his green paradise, Papa believed she was preparing to cook his dinner. She felt a twinge of conscience, but heavens—England!

She clung to her dream for all she was worth and refused to look back. She swore to herself that this was for the best.

As the cargo platform floated over the ship's bustling main deck, she caught a glimpse of the river steamboat now sputtering to a halt at the beach.

Lord Jack jumped down onto the sand, waded through the shallows and paused to splash himself. She could still taste his kiss. She watched him flinging water over his dark, tousled hair and then striding up onto the beach to take control of the operation. The men were already working hard, but visibly doubled their efforts when their captain arrived.

65

Better not let him catch you, her feminine instincts advised as the sun burned his tanned, powerful image into her brain.

Then she was plunged in darkness as the crane descended through the large square hatch, going down ever deeper into the bowels of his great ship, until, at last, she was swallowed up in the deep, dark recess of the cargo hold.

CHAPTER
∾ FIVE ∾

*T*hat night, *The Winds of Fortune* slipped away under cover of darkness, evading the Spanish patrol boats by stealing around Galeoto Point at the lower corner of Trinidad, and then breaking sharply northeast at the twelfth parallel.

Jack had ordered the crew to be silent and the ship's lanterns doused. The mood on board was tense until they could be sure they had not been spotted by the Spanish. Nevertheless, a fair wind out of the south drove them along.

It was a fine night to make sail, cool and partly clear, but though tranquil, there was an eeriness to the silence and the way the bright half moon lit up the cloud clusters here and there.

Luminescent algae, famous in the torrid zone, glowed atop the waves.

"Lieutenant, what is our speed?" he asked the officer in charge of the watch.

"Five knots, sir."

Not bad, for all our cargo, he thought. Because they were still in coral reef areas, caution dictated a moderate pace.

They glided along under partial sail while the quartermaster made his patient soundings off the bow, on constant watch for rocks beneath the surface.

A smattering of some twenty small islands dotted the seas around Trinidad and Tobago; shallows and reefs surrounded most of them. Only when the *Winds* reached the edge of the continental border, where the shallow coastal waters dropped away into the abyss, would Jack give the order for full sail and full speed ahead.

For now, standing arms akimbo near the helmsman, smoking a

cheroot, he passed a glance across the starry sky. "How reads the barometer, Mr. Clark?"

"Stable, Captain," the ship's master replied.

Jack nodded. "Steady as she goes, boys," he murmured to the crew, strolling restlessly from the quarterdeck toward the bow. Canine claws ticked along right behind him over the spotlessly clean planks, as his faithful mutt, Rudy, shadowed his steps.

The product of a bulldog's illicit liaison with an English White terrier, Rudy was stocky and thick-set and low to the ground, fearless despite being only as high as Jack's knee.

He trotted across the decks as if he owned the ship, or rather the whole of the sea. Rudy had a short white coat, a black circle around one eye as though he had been in a brawl, a very silly-looking Roman nose, and the soul of a clown. The dog, in short, was the best friend he'd ever had, but Jack Knight was not the sort of man to admit such things.

"Sir, we've just reached a hundred feet of depth," the quartermaster confirmed from his post on the bow, having just pulled up his sounding lines.

"Excellent." Jack's smile broadened. "Make sail, boys. Let's head for the middle latitudes and rope ourselves a westerly."

The crew muffled their answering cheer and eagerly ascended the stiff rope ladders of the rigging.

Exhaling smoke, Jack tilted his head back and watched them climb out onto the yards with unflinching bravery despite the ship's constant wide rocking and the action of the wind.

In four minutes flat, they unfurled the rest of the magnificent vessel's full two acres of pearly canvas, gleaming and magical in the moonlight.

It always took Jack's breath away to see her come to life with the breath of the wind filling her sails. "She's a beauty, is she not, Lieutenant?"

Peabody smiled at him in perfect understanding of his sentiments. "Aye, Captain."

"Carry on," he said at length, leaving the watch in the second lieutenant's able hands.

Drifting to the rails, Jack gazed down rather broodingly into the foaming wake off the bow, easy with the *Winds'* familiar rocking as she ploughed on through the waves and sent up plumes of brisk spray.

Far below, a few dolphins plunged merrily alongside them, their slick hides gleaming in the moonlight. It was a good omen and all had gone smoothly, yet Jack's mood was a little pensive.

Regret gnawed him. The forlorn image of Eden Farraday left standing alone on the dock stayed vivid in his mind. He wished he could have helped her, but, no. As usual, Jack Knight had been cast in the role of villain. He let out a sigh and shook his head. He decided he would go back and check on her again when he came back to deliver his mercenaries to Bolivar. Next time, he would get her out of there whether her father liked it or not.

And if that blond chap tried pointing a gun in his direction again, Jack thought grimly, he would deal with him, too.

An insistent whine from below drew his distracted attention just then. When he glanced down, he saw Rudy standing beside him with his favorite stick clamped between his jaws, his tail wagging eagerly.

With a rueful smile, Jack took the stick out of the dog's mouth and heaved it toward the stern in a long throw.

"Fetch," he muttered, but Rudy needed no such instruction, already scampering after his prize as though the bit of timber were worth its weight in gold.

For a week, Eden had endured the inky cargo hold. She hid in total darkness, longing for light, for fresh air, and most of all, for any human company besides her own.

The temperature had dropped as the ship traveled north inexorably, leaving the land of summer and the tropical temperatures she was used to for climes reminiscent of faintly remembered autumns—a brisk, sunny coolness by day giving way to colder temperatures at night. Of course, where they were headed, February meant the dead of winter, though they wouldn't arrive, she presumed, until the end of March.

In the meantime, the unrelenting blackness had begun playing tricks on her mind. There was too much time to worry about the rats she heard scratching about in the darkness. She hoped they did not grow bold enough to bite her.

Above all, there was too much time to think . . . about everything that could go wrong with her adventure now that she had flung herself into it. Time, as well, to contemplate the mighty captain of this ship.

69

Since this was a far more interesting subject, she spent countless hours pondering what Papa had told her about Jack Knight—yet somehow she only arrived at more questions.

Why, for example, had he been forbidden to marry the girl he had loved, Lady Maura? If he was the second son of a duke, why had her parents deemed Lord Jack unsuitable? Was that the reason he had not returned to England all this time? Had he no family there to draw him back for a visit?

And what was he *really* doing in the jungle that day in the first place? She remembered the mysterious look in his eyes when she had asked about his visit to the rebel town of Angostura. Papa had claimed that his mere presence in Venezuela meant that Lord Jack was up to no good. Collecting timber . . . ? No. They were hiding something, he and his men. Whatever the rogue was involved in, he obviously didn't want her to know.

Alas, the spirit of inquiry had been nurtured in Eden from too young an age to leave the mystery alone. There was nothing else to do, hour after hour, so she decided to look around and see if she could find some answers.

Taking the tinderbox out of her satchel of supplies, she lit her candle with a few clicks of the flint. She knew she had to conserve her candle, but the light was such a blessing. With the small flame to guide her, she went exploring a bit.

The great rocking warehouse of the cargo hold contained no clues about Jack's secrets, but was piled with orderly mountains of supplies. Barrels of water and wine. Various tools and spare sails. Black powder stores and cannonballs. There was plenty of food and water to see her through the long journey, but the air was fetid just above the bilge.

She did not need her physician-father to tell her that amid such ill vapors, fevers lurked. Indeed, she doubted she had another two days' worth of breathable air down here. She realized grimly that she would have to ascend to the next level and find a new hiding place.

This she did the next afternoon, sneaking up onto the orlop deck, and here she had passed another several days in hiding. There was still no daylight to be had, for the creaking orlop, like the cargo hold, sat below the waterline, but at least there were lanterns in the cramped, narrow passageways and better ventilation. The sea air filtered down through wooden grates placed over the hatches far above, on the main deck.

The orlop also housed supplies, including the vast tonnage of goods that Lord Jack was transporting to market in England. The mahoganies and other tropical hardwoods took up much of the space, but there were also great quantities of sugar, rum, cotton, tobacco, and indigo. Useful items all, but nothing yielding information about the captain's jaunt to Angostura.

In her wary explorations, ever dodging the crewmen who passed by going about their business, she had found the bread and cheese room, where the ship's cats were on constant duty stalking rats. She found the wood shop of the ship's carpenter, and the office of the purser, the frugal fellow in charge of accounting for all the supplies—who used what and how much.

Though she often heard the easygoing carpenter singing in the wood shop as he banged away with his hammer, and smiled in secret at the purser's constant muttering to himself as he scribbled away in his office, balancing his ledger books and grousing about how nobody appreciated him, Eden stayed out of sight and made friends with the ships' cats to pass the time.

Now and then, as the days passed, she sought to comfort herself by summoning up those familiar, shining images of brilliant ballrooms, elegant music, lords and ladies dancing—but it was then that she discovered there was something wrong with her pretty fantasy.

Each time she imagined herself at the ball, the man who now stepped forward from amid the swirling dancers to claim her was none other than that blackguard ex-pirate, Lord Jack.

A fortnight out from the Spanish Main, *The Winds of Fortune* had traversed over a thousand miles of ocean, traveling at eight knots on a steep northeasterly angle. They had cleared the warm Sargasso Sea and were now in the middle of the cold Atlantic.

Taking current wind conditions into account, Jack gave orders to change the set of the sails slightly and advised the helmsman to adjust his steerage on the wheel.

All was in order, and the captain was pleased.

The sails were in fine trim, the men cheerful in the rigging, the lookout posted in the crow's nest. A dozen crewmen mopped the decks, while another group received their weekly training with pistols and cutlasses from gruff, tough Mr. Brody, the master-at-arms. Old Brody also served as Jack's fencing coach and occasional sparring partner at his daily practice in fisticuffs and the other manly arts of self-defense.

The sailors stood at attention and saluted their captain as he strode past, inspecting them and their efforts, asking questions here, giving orders there, granting a few approving nods to men who had done good work.

Indeed, as he strolled the decks with Rudy at his heels, the smooth running of his prize vessel—and his worldwide company, for that matter—inspired Jack with a most gratifying sense of solid order, security, and accomplishment. And yet . . .

He was plagued by a deepening awareness of a large hole in his life. An emptiness. He had sensed it vaguely and ignored it for a very long time now, but it had sharpened since they'd left Venezuela into a nameless hunger, a gnawing urgency.

Yes, he had built up an empire and possessed a fortune to rival his ducal brother's, but he had no one to share it with, and worse, no one to leave it to. If he died unexpectedly—and there was always a chance of that, the way he lived—everything he'd worked for, the company he'd spent his life creating, would die with him.

The solution was plain, of course: He needed sons. And if his father had had five, Jack wanted six. But getting heirs meant finding a wife, a prospect he so little relished that he had been putting it off for years.

Where could a man find a woman who would bear his children and otherwise leave him alone? As he prowled the decks of his ship, irked with the whole uneasy subject, only one tolerable candidate came to mind—Eden Farraday.

Now, there was a girl who could take care of herself. Hell, if he was smart, Jack thought, he'd marry her. Look at the conditions she was used to, he reasoned. For the kind of luxury that he could give her, she would probably do whatever he said. Her capacity for loyalty was unquestioned, having stayed with her father through his quest. By now, it was clear she'd be happy just to get out of the jungle—but Jack could give her so much more than that, if they could come to a reasonable agreement. A life of privilege, social position. A life of ease.

She deserved it more than most of the women he knew.

Certainly, in their brief meeting, she had displayed qualities that suggested she could breed him first-rate sons: strength, confi-

72

dence, robust health, keen intelligence, courage, resourcefulness. Observation had also told him that she would be a good mother, for she had shown her nurturing side even to him in removing his splinter.

Considering *his* dam's selfish ways, his future wife's ability to love his children was of paramount importance to Jack.

Oh, all of this sounded like madness, he thought, scowling—but in practical terms perhaps it wasn't such a bad idea. By all visible measures, the redhead seemed to fit the bill.

She was caring, capable, deliciously beautiful, and, best of all, not some ninny-headed Society miss whose response to danger would be to faint gracefully into a chaise longue.

Indeed, she was still quite young, but as a few years passed and she came into her own, she would further mature into a formidable queen who could hold down the fort when he was on the other side of the world for long periods of time, attending to the far-flung reaches of his empire.

If Victor trusted her to help in his complex scientific work, then Jack saw no reason why she could not be trained to keep an eye on the company for him.

The ideal wife—one with sense, one he could trust, one who could stand on her own two feet—would almost be, he mused, a kind of partner in the firm.

He just never thought that he could find one.

But now there was Eden Farraday, hidden away in the trees, where more deserving fellows could not find her. Not to mention the fact that the memory of her kiss still made his body burn with agitated lust.

Hell, he wondered if she'd even have him after he had let her down by refusing to take her to England. What choice had he had? His mood gone restless, Jack joined Trahern at the rails.

"No sign of the *Valiant* yet," his top lieutenant informed him, peering through a spyglass.

"No, I don't expect to see the old man 'til above the fortieth parallel," Jack muttered, though the thought of his uncle, Lord Arthur Knight, made him smile wryly.

It was comforting to know there was at least one family member he could relate to, probably because his distinguished old nabob of an uncle had been, in his day, as much a black sheep of the family as Jack was.

73

Decades ago, after a spat with his elder brother, the previous Duke of Hawkscliffe, the second-born, Lord Arthur Knight, had scorned the family empire, packed his trunks, and sailed off to India to make his own fortune. He had flourished there by his wits and the sweat of his brow, had found a wife and raised a family, two fine sons and a beautiful daughter; he had risen through the ranks of the East India Company, and then, upon retiring, had used everything he knew from three decades of cutthroat business in the Orient to help Jack grow his firm into a force to be reckoned with.

He was the closest thing to a true father Jack had ever had.

Arthur and he had made a deal to return to the shores of their homeland together—for moral support, as it were. It was hard to say which one of them the rest of the clan would be more shocked to see.

Trahern snapped his spyglass shut and looked at Jack hopefully. "Do you think your uncle might bring Miss Georgie with him?"

Jack laughed. "What, the belle of the Spice Islands? Queen of Bombay? Do you think she'd really tear herself away from her social life just to see you?"

"No." Trahern sighed. "But a chap can dream, can't he? The woman's a goddess."

Jack shook his head at him sardonically. "Forget her, man. She'd eat you alive."

"Yes, but I don't think I'd mind it."

"Hey." He arched an eyebrow, frowning at him. "That's my little cousin you're talking about."

Rudy interrupted with a sudden storm of barking, once again at his favorite hobby of trying to get to the chickens and ducks that lived in crates inside the lifeboats. The live poultry were kept on hand to supply the galley with fresh eggs.

A clamor of alarmed clucking and quacking arose from inside the jolly boats, and though the sailors on hand tried to deter the bull-terrier from his game, Jack sighed and went to collect his errant pet.

He grabbed Rudy's leather collar, hauled his panting dog away with a halfhearted scolding, and returned to his luxurious day cabin. When he walked into the spacious wood-paneled chamber, Rudy scrambled ahead of him, greeting Phineas Patrick Moynahan, Jack's grubby, nine-year-old cabin boy, otherwise known as

74

the Nipper. The little tyke was shining Jack's boots, but Rudy's joyous greeting shoved him right off his low stool.

The Nipper landed on the floor with a peal of half-vexed laughter. "Get off o' me, ye daft mutt!"

Rudy licked his cheek in answer, then waited for the boy to play with him, his tail wagging wildly.

Jack was all business, however, and gave the lad his next errand. "Mr. Moynahan, I require my clerk. Go and fetch Mr. Stockwell for me. I wish to dictate a letter."

"Sorry, Cap, can't." He climbed back onto his stool. "He's gone down to sickbay with one o' them tropical fevers."

"Really?" Jack asked in surprise.

The Nipper nodded and picked up the other boot.

Yesterday, Stockwell had complained that he wasn't feeling well during their work, but Jack had not suspected it was serious. "Mr. Moynahan," he said abruptly, "you have boot-black on your forehead."

With a scowl, the Nipper reached up to wipe it off and only succeeded in smearing more sooty polish across his face.

Jack fought a smile. "Martin!" he called, summoning his valet to fill in for his clerk.

The neat, fussy, little man instantly came hurrying in answer to his call. While Martin fretted over the assignment outside his usual duties and hurried about getting paper and ink, Jack took a seat and propped his feet up on the corner of his large, baronial desk, leaning back and musing on how to start the letter.

A knock sounded on the cabin door as he was mentally composing a terse greeting. "Come."

Jack looked up as the grizzled master-at-arms entered.

"Problem, Brody?" Jack glanced at his fob watch. "Our training session's not 'til four."

"If I could have a word with ye, Cap'n," he said, his hat in his hands.

"Of course. Speak freely."

Brody eyed Martin with his usual warrior's wariness. "Thought you should know, Cap, there's a rumor goin' around among the men, quietlike, says we picked up a stowaway off o' Trinidad."

Jack steepled his fingers in thought. "Really?"

"Aye. One o' the carpenter's mates thought he caught sight of a young lad hidin' on the orlop deck."

"Is that right?" he murmured, taking no heed of how the Nipper had perked up at the news.

He considered for a moment; Brody waited.

Jack brought his feet down off his desk with a clomp. "Take a couple of the men below and have a look around. If you find anyone hiding out down there who's not on our roster, put him to work. Everybody pays their way on my ship," he reiterated, shoving away another taunting memory of a redhead with emerald green eyes.

No, it couldn't be.

Eden Farraday was bold, not insane.

Besides, no one could mistake that luscious beauty for a lad, even in the dim half-light of the orlop. No doubt it was just some poor orphan runaway from one of the Caribbean islands looking for a better life. His merchant fleet picked up strays all over the globe. If they refused to work, his firm policy was to turn them in as thieves. He wasn't running a charity, after all.

"Remind the crew there are consequences to be paid for anyone who helps conceal a stowaway," he ordered. "I won't tolerate anyone stealing from me."

"Aye-aye, Cap'n," Brody answered stoutly and went to do his bidding.

"Where are you going?" Jack asked as the Nipper popped up from his stool and ran across the cabin.

Rudy's ears pricked up at the boy's movement, but the dog remained lying near Jack's desk.

"Oh, um, gotta refill the scuttlebutt, Cap."

"You've finished with my boots?"

"Almost, sir. They need a final buffin,' but the polish ain't dry yet—"

"Isn't," Jack corrected gently.

"Aye, sir—*isn't* dry yet—and since you're always sayin' as how I should use me time wiser . . . ?"

"Ah, right. Of course. Very good, Mr. Moynahan. Run along, then," he said, eyeing the little imp with a twinge of suspicion.

The Nipper, dismissed, went tearing out of the day cabin. Jack could not recall the child ever having been half so eager to complete his chores, but he shrugged it off and began his dictation: "My dear Abraham," he clipped out while Martin quickly began writing, "it is with great regret that I have watched the friendly relations between our two companies dissolve over the course of the past few years. Despite my efforts to maintain fair, indeed, preferential policies toward your firm . . ." His voice trailed off, his train of thought dissolving.

"Sir?"

It *couldn't* be Eden Farraday.

She wouldn't.

Would she?

Don't forget who you're dealing with here. She was no ordinary female, the little wild woman.

Which was, of course, exactly why he wanted her. She had gotten under his skin like that damned splinter. . . .

Staring at nothing as he tapped his pen on this desk, Jack recalled her fearless plunge off the tree branch, swinging on that blasted vine, the cheerful ease with which she had hacked the pineapple into neat slices with that razor-sharp machete.

Aye, the way she had stood up to him, Black-Jack Knight, the so-called terror of the seas. She had looked him in the eye and spoken her mind with a frankness most men wouldn't dare.

But was she foolhardy enough to stow away after he had denied her request for passage?

Of course she was, he realized, though he was barely able to wrap his mind around the notion that all this time that he'd been lusting for her, she might have been here on his ship, right under his very nose, and now could be in arm's reach.

The terror of the seas suddenly found himself with butterflies in his stomach.

Jack scowled. *Ridiculous.*

"My lord?"

"Dismissed." In state of mystified incredulity, he got up from his desk abruptly and tossed the pen down. "We'll finish later, Martin. I have to go, ah, check on something."

His valet looked startled. "Your letter, sir?"

"It can wait." Jack strode out of the day cabin and headed for the orlop deck.

He had to see this stowaway for himself.

Reclining in the orlop deck with her head resting on a sack of sugar, Eden was thumbing through *La Belle Assemblée* in a state of extreme boredom, having already memorized every page, when suddenly, her jungle-honed senses registered an unfamiliar presence somewhere very nearby.

She froze for a second, then rolled onto her side and crouched down behind the fruit crates. Someone was coming—or already here?

She held her breath, listening for all she was worth. Her straining ears pinpointed the faint patter of bare footsteps on wooden planks.

"Come out, come out, wherever you are," called a soft, rather high-pitched voice. She furrowed her brow. Why, that sounded like a child's voice. "I know you're 'ere. You can't hide forever, can you? Nobody's invisible."

It *was* a child, she thought, startled. But, of course, youngsters served various roles at sea, from cabin boys to powder monkeys.

Starved as she was for human company—and greatly relieved, as well—for really, how much trouble could one small boy be?— she could not resist stepping up silently onto the edge of the bottom crate and peering over the stack at her pint-sized pursuer.

She smiled to herself upon spotting a barefooted urchin creeping with kittenish stealth through the crowded cargo bay, peeking around a mound of sugar sacks and barrels of gunpowder, as though playing hide-and-seek.

The wee lad was adorable, searching eagerly for someone on his own eye level, while she peered down at him from above.

He had a wild thatch of bright blond hair in dire need of a trimming and was dressed in a neat, short jacket like a miniature officer, with loose, wide matelots up to his ankles.

"Are you running away, then? We get stowaways all o' the time who are running away, but not me. My Auntie Moynahan sent me to be a 'prentice on Lord Jack's ship. Maybe you could be a 'prentice, too. I could ask the captain for you, if you want. Cap'n Jack listens to me," he added with an air of great importance. "You should come out now and take my help if you're smart, 'cos Mr. Brody and a few of the mates are on their way down 'ere to find you. They know you're here."

Good God! Eden's heart skipped a beat at this terrifying news. She wasted no time wondering who Mr. Brody was, but was already pulling her satchel of Papa's botanical specimens over her shoulder and slipping silently toward the door.

She had to get out of here—now. Stealing up the narrow ladder of the companionway with her bag over her shoulder, she arrived on the lower gun-deck and dodged down the cramped passageway at the top of the steps.

When she came to the corner, she looked left and right, advanced cautiously, hearing noises ahead, then nearly stepped out into the sailors' mess hall. Hundreds of hammocks hung from the ceiling amid the bustling chaos of half the crew having a meal. Most of the men were too busy devouring their food to notice her; others were swigging their grog or cheering on an arm-wrestling match in progress on the far end of the large open space. She darted out of sight again, backing into the dim passageway.

Hearing voices in the other direction, she glanced over and drew in her breath. Five rough-looking sailors were trudging down the companionway, heading for the orlop deck. She pressed back deeper into the shadows and surmised that these were Mr. Brody and his mates. Blending into the perpetual twilight belowdecks, she stepped into another companionway and ascended to the middle gun-deck, creeping silently down the passage.

Steadying herself against the rocking of the ship, she could smell the galley stoves cooking and hear the men relaying orders through the hatch. On this level, the flanks of *The Winds of Fortune* were also lined with long rows of bristling cannons, but here, the wooden gun ports were open on both sides, creating a delicious cross-breeze.

Glorious golden sunshine filtered down through the grate over the hatch some yards away. Eden stopped to stare at it for a moment. Lured like one mesmerized, she crept toward it, blinking against the light.

For a brief moment, alone in the companionway, she allowed herself to absorb it, stepping into the stray shaft of dusty sunlight. She tilted her head back, basking in its nourishing glow. Closing her eyes only for a second, letting the beam of sunlight warm her face, she suddenly sensed someone watching her.

She had heard no one, but when she flicked her eyes open and looked down the dark passageway, she saw him—a formidable silhouette at the far end of the corridor.

He had just stepped down from the companionway and stood motionless, staring at her. The light from above fell upon his head and across his broad shoulders, haloing his tall, powerfully muscled form with its brilliance, though his face was in shadow.

79

Looming and darkly beautiful, he said not a word as their stares clashed from across the passageway.

Jack.

Like the prey entranced by the predator, she was momentarily transfixed by the way his aquamarine eyes glowed in the half-light; his stare stayed fixed on her, just like in her ballroom fantasy.

She remembered then that she was a trespasser on his property; this ship was his floating fortress, and he its feudal lord. He did not call out to her, but the second he moved—began striding toward her—Eden whirled around and fled.

She raced aft with all the jungle stealth at her command, but when the ship rocked, she nearly tumbled headlong into the officers' wardroom, lieutenants and midshipmen preparing to dine.

Recovering her balance, she rushed on, not stopping to heed one of the officers who yelled after her, "Look lively, sailor! Man your post!"

She could sense Jack coming after her, feel him gaining on her. She flung around another dim corner of the passageway, but all that was ahead of her was the open deck.

Casting about in desperation for any place to hide, she spotted a closet marked LIFE BUOYS and dove into it. She wedged herself in among the piles of hard cork life rings and pulled the door shut silently. She held her breath, her heart pounding.

Listening hard over the din of her own thundering heartbeat, she heard sharp, forceful strides approaching over the wooden planks.

"Captain, is something amiss?"

"Did anyone come this way just now?" a deep, commanding baritone rumbled.

"Why, yes, sir. One of the quartermaster's lads, I think. He ran up on deck a moment ago."

Lord Jack growled, just outside the door of the closet.

Eden waited with her heart in her throat.

After another nerve-racking moment, he prowled on.

Just when she started to exhale, a light, swift tapping sound scampered after the captain—was that a dog? The animal stopped suddenly. Along the crack at the bottom of the closet, an eager, rapid snuffling sound arose. Eden's eyes widened in the darkness. She could just make out the tip of a black canine snout. *Oh, no . .*

*

An explosion of wild barking erupted from the other side of the closet door. She gasped and fell backward against a pile of hard cork life buoys. Panic rose up swiftly, instinct readying her to fight or flee.

"Rudy! Here, boy! Enough o' that!" the officer scolded. "What mischief are you into now?"

Slowly, the hard, firm footsteps returned.

"I think he's cornered one of the ship's cats, my lord."

Their ominous rhythm stopped on the other side of the door. "We'll see."

Jack grabbed Rudy's collar and handed the dog off to Peabody with a nod silently instructing him to take the animal away. He paid no mind to the other officers who had come out of the wardroom and crowded into the passageway to see what had caused the commotion.

Turning once more to the closet with narrowed eyes, Jack waved the men back and drew his cutlass in case he was wrong about their stowaway's identity. God's truth, he still wasn't sure if he believed his eyes after the vision of that lithe figure he had spotted in the corridor, standing in a sunbeam.

Warily, he gripped the latch and suddenly threw the door open, thrusting his free hand blindly into the closet. As his questing hand grasped the front of the miscreant's clothing, a small yelp rose from the darkness.

"Come out of there!" he boomed, hauling the stowaway out into the open.

Despite the fact that he'd already guessed it, seeing her again, eye to eye, shocked him to the core. It was Eden Farraday, all right—looking a mess, trapped, and terrified of his wrath.

Jack released her as though he had been burned.

His flabbergasted stare traveled over her, from the soiled bandana tied around her head to the dirty shirt, men's waistcoat, and oversized breeches she wore held up by a length of knotted cord, all the way down to her scuffed, dusty knee boots.

He could hardly find his tongue. "You're going to show up in London looking like that?" he blurted out, still dazed.

She let out a war cry at his cynical greeting, and perhaps he should have known better than to corner the little wild thing, for even as he stood there in astonishment, she attacked, flying at him.

81

She shoved him aside with what he guessed was all her might, though he barely budged, then she launched past him.

He reached for her, but in the blink of an eye, she ducked under his arm and fled. He pivoted and grabbed her, but only got the canvas knapsack on her shoulder. The girl herself kept running.

Jack suddenly looked down and realized she had nicked his pistol right out of its holster on his hip. Now he glowered.

"After her!" he bellowed at his men.

"*Her,* Captain?" one echoed in surprise.

The young midshipman blanched at Jack's hellish glance.

They scrambled to obey.

Damn her, the maddening minx!

He was right behind the pack of his men, stalking with heavy footfalls down the dim companionway. He'd ring her bloody neck for that stunt. How dare she take his weapon—with so many of his men there to witness it? How could he have let her?

Ah, but a beauty like Eden Farraday was made for making fools out of men.

"Where do you think you're going to go?" he roared as she went pounding up the gangway like the fox with the hounds at her heels. "We're in the middle of the damned ocean!"

In her panic, she dashed out onto the upper gun-deck, no doubt blinded by the blaring sunshine after so many days belowdecks.

The baying of his men had roused the crew on duty topside, and by the time Jack reached the top of the gangway, his horde of lusty tars had their stowaway surrounded.

"Easy, now, there's a bold lad," good old Higgins was saying, trying to contain the situation.

"Lad or lass?" another sailor yelled. "Cap said it's a her!"

Shocked murmurs rippled through the crew as the rumor traveled across the decks.

Jack saw that although she was ringed in on all sides, the girl struggled to keep them all at bay with her jungle machete in one hand, his stolen pistol in the other.

"A her?" the men were murmuring.

"It can't be," others scoffed.

"He's wearing breeches, ain't he?"

"So? You never heard o' them Queer Moll clubs where the gents prance around wearing ladies' gowns? She could be the opposite of their sort."

"Or a lady pirate, like Mary Read or Anne Bonny!" another helpful soul chimed in.

"I'm not a lady pirate, you mongrels!" Eden hollered at them, but this did nothing to resolve the question. "Stay back!"

Hearty laughter spread across the decks, but Jack frowned, squinting against the sun. This was hardly the sort of thing he cared for his sailors to discuss in front of a young girl, but a dose of male crudity might be exactly what she needed to illustrate the fact that the world beyond her green paradise was a dark and strange and frequently dangerous place.

Maybe then the chit would learn she could simply not carry out whatever mad adventure popped into her head. God, she was as bad as her daft father, he thought as he restrained the surge of protective instinct that coursed through him. Folding his arms across his chest, he let the lads taunt her for a moment while he remained in the shadow of the ship's waist, close enough to intervene if need be. For now, he decided to give her a minute or two to test her mettle. *The minx got herself into this. Let's see how well she can get herself out of it.*

With raucous humor, the crew continued debating the mystery of their stowaway's gender. Their confusion was understandable, given her boyish clothes and the nimble way she wielded two weapons at once—a fact that infused Jack with an absurd sense of pride in the little tigress.

She had lost weight since their jungle encounter; with her hair tied back beneath the kerchief, her delicate features had been sharpened by hunger. Her athletic leanness had dwindled to a wiry, waiflike fragility, and she was looking decidedly bony, the loose, masculine clothing hanging off her thin frame. But although her smudged, pale face bespoke youthful strength, fierceness, and grim resolve that might have belonged to either sex, for all that, she was just a girl.

Nervously scanning the wall of dirty, sweaty, rough men that ringed her in, her gaze stopped on Jack, her green eyes flashing out a heart-tugging plea for help.

Finally, she seemed to have gotten a good look at his crew and had apparently realized that, aside from her knife and the two bullets in Jack's double-barreled pistol, he was her only possible protection.

He merely lifted his eyebrows and sent her an attentive smile, waiting to see her next move.

At his show of amused indifference, her pleading gaze of a moment ago hardened to one of defiance. A stubborn gleam came into her eyes as if to say, *To hell with you, Jack Knight. I don't need you, anyway!*

Hmm, he thought. Having dealt with innumerable unruly and cocky youths before, indeed having been one himself ages ago, he had long since learned how to manage such creatures. They usually made fine sailors after a few months of his pounding them into submission. Eventually they realized that one of them was going to break and it wasn't going to be Jack. Some navy-style discipline was all it took; their juvenile aversion to authority merely required a bit of taming.

But all those countless young sailors he'd subdued had been males, he realized a tad uneasily, and though his crew might still be in the dark on the matter, Jack was acutely aware that their little stowaway was very much a woman—a species, God knew, that operated under an entirely different set of nature's laws.

Trahern, in charge of the watch, now marched onto the scene. "Leave off! Back to your posts! The captain will deal with the lad! Leave the boy alone, all of you!"

Jack arched a brow sardonically to find Trahern still innocent of their stowaway's true identity.

One of the sailors tried to educate him on the matter. "I'm tellin' ye, Mr. Trahern, that there ain't no lad!"

"Aye, it is!" another argued.

"You're blind! I'll bet ye grog rations."

"I'll take that wager! Look at the eyes, aye, you can tell by the mouth of 'er!"

The sailor rolled his eyes. "Pretty little girlies don't use guns!"

"So, what *are* you, then?" big Ballast the gunner demanded, sauntering up to her without fear of her weapons, his gold tooth flashing, his bald head gleaming in the sun.

Jack tensed a bit, looking on. Every ship had its chief troublemaker, and on *The Winds of Fortune,* that distinction belonged to Ballast, the surly gunner who fancied himself first among the crew and obeyed only two people on the ship: Mr. Brody and Cap'n Jack.

"Lass or lad?" he taunted her. "Show us your bait-'n'-tackle and settle the wager!"

"Stay back!" she warned as Ballast, laughing, made a swipe to grab her arm and missed.

Eden nimbly twisted clear of him.

"Aw, don't be like that," he persisted, circling her, while most of the crew laughed at their sport. "We want to see what you got!"

"Leave the kid be, Ballast," Higgins spoke up, taking a brave step toward the much larger man.

Ballast shoved Higgins and sent him falling back against another cluster of sailors, who caught him. "Why don't you go lick Cap's boots for a while? That's all you're good for!"

Jack was already in motion, marching forward to break it up, but at the last moment, Ballast reached out with a bold laugh, trying to grab her again, and Eden reacted in self-defense, her blade flashing in the sun; Ballast fell back with a garbled curse, a nasty slice across his tattooed forearm.

The crew's raucous laughter turned to shocked gasps.

"Why, you little maggot." Ballast drew his knife. "I'll gut you for that!"

"Try it if you want a bullet in your brain," the girl replied with admirable self-possession. "But I overestimate you, sir. It's clear you haven't got a brain at all!"

At that moment, a gust of wind whipped away the handkerchief tied around her head, and her gorgeous mane of coppery locks came tumbling down around her shoulders, blowing in the breeze.

Every man present gasped aloud—and stared.

"Enough!" Jack jumped down off the quarterdeck into their midst with his cutlass drawn. "This girl is under my protection," he announced as he passed a brutal glance across the crowded decks. "If any man lays a hand on her, I will personally hang him from the bowsprit. Understood?"

There were a few sheepish "Aye-aye, sirs," as the men cleared out of his way.

Ballast repented of his rash behavior now that his captain was on deck. He lowered his shaved head as he gripped his bleeding wound. "We, uh, found the stowaway for ye, Cap," he mumbled.

"So I see," Jack said crisply. "Get to the sickbay. You are bleeding all over my deck."

"Aye, Cap." Ballast sent Eden a look of lingering disbelief as he went slinking off to seek the surgeon's care. Jack would deal with him later, and the gunner surely knew it.

"Back to work, men!" Trahern commanded.

"You heard him, ye malingerin' rotters!" Brody barked, reappearing on deck at that moment after his fruitless search of the orlop deck. The men looked lively at the master-at-arms' gravelly bellow.

Jack sent Eden a wrathful glance. It was nice to know the chit could take care of herself, but bloody hell!

He turned to her, read the belated terror in her eyes, and suffered a sharp pang of self-reproach for letting them make sport of her. Still, he trusted he had made his point.

Jack held out his hand. "Give me back my gun."

Her green eyes were wide, still filled with fright. She swept the surrounding crew with a rattled glance. "Not on your life," she said with a gulp.

"Eden, you're already a stowaway, and you stole my weapon in front of my men," he said softly. "Don't make this any worse for us both than it already is."

She wetted her lips with a nervous flick of her tongue and again eyed the crew. "But, Jack—"

"I'm the one you'd better worry about now," he warned in a low voice. "Give me back my damned pistol."

He waited immovably; the crew paused in returning to their tasks and looked on in palpable tension as the fierce little female stowaway dared refuse the captain's order.

Jack flicked his fingers impatiently, beckoning her to hand the gun over; he stretched out his waiting palm.

The same hand from which she had dug out the splinter. In the old parable, the lion never forgot the kind deed, and spared the youth who had helped him.

Jack stared at her intensely.

She agonized over the decision, the war of emotions transparent on her lovely face, but after a long moment, she slowly yielded, handing it over.

Jack clasped his weapon and thrust it back into its holster. "There. Wasn't so hard, was it? Now the knife."

"No!"

He flicked his fingers again.

"It's mine! You can't have it!"

He stared at her.

"No, Jack, please," she begged him in a pitiful whisper.

"Hand it over," he answered in a hard tone. "You've got no choice."

"You're a bully!" she yelled with a flash of renewed temper.

He raised an eyebrow. But he had ways of getting her compliance. "Hand me that knapsack," he said to Trahern, who had taken hold of it. The lieutenant handed him the canvas knapsack that Jack had pulled off Eden's shoulder. "What's in here, my dear?" he asked her, for the bag was very light.

When she failed to answer, he opened it and glanced inside.

Aside from an orange in the side pocket, stolen from his cargo hold, the knapsack contained nothing but some pressed leaves in waxed paper.

He knew what it was, but eyed her sardonically, trying to prod her into giving up her weapon. "Weeds?"

He took the orange, tossed it to the Nipper, and then handed the bag back to Trahern. "Throw it overboard."

"Yes, sir."

"No!" she cried. "Mr. Trahern, please, you can't!"

"Why?" Jack demanded.

Trahern hesitated, looking from his idolized captain to the lady stowaway and back again, torn between duty and chivalry.

Eden lifted her chin and pointed to the bits of pressed plants. "Those are not *weeds,* as you know well. They are botanical samples from my father's research—plants with healing powers. I am taking them to London to show to Lord Pembrooke."

"Oh, really?"

"Yes, Jack. Really."

"Captain," he corrected her, putting her in her place, given the circumstances. He would not be addressed with such insolence in front of his men.

She lifted her chin. "*Captain,* they are rare and precious plants that the scientists at the Royal Botanical Gardens will want to seed for their greenhouses!"

"Fascinating. Trahern, throw it in the ocean."

"Yes, sir." Crestfallen, his lieutenant continued toward the rails.

"No!" Eden cried.

"Wait," Jack ordered.

"Please." She gazed at him in exasperation.

"Very well, Miss Farraday," he resumed in a consummately reasonable tone. "Give me your knife, and I will spare your weeds."

His offer only got him her glare. Then she muttered, "You want it? Fine. Here it is!"

Without warning, she hurled her machete—it flew through the air and plunged into the mast quite near Jack's head.

The crew let out amazed exclamations at her defiant display of prowess, no doubt impressed by her aim.

Jack's eyes glowed with pride as he gazed at her for a second. He glanced drily at the large knife still shuddering from the impact, the blade sunk about two inches into the wood.

The wild woman, his future wife, folded her arms across her chest and lifted her chin, still furious, but looking decidedly pleased with herself.

"Miss Farraday," he reproached her with an indulgent *tsk, tsk.* "You stabbed my ship."

CHAPTER
∽ SIX ∽

*T*hough she held her chin high in a show of grand defiance, Eden knew she was defenseless after having been disarmed. But when Lord Jack started toward her with that strange, murderously tranquil smile on his face, she blanched and spun around, seeking any escape route.

There was nowhere to flee. Her heart pounded. Her frantic gaze scanned the sun-splashed decks and homed in on the rigging.

"Oh, no, you don't," he chided, grabbing her around her waist as she tried to scamper up the nearest sturdy rope ladder.

He pulled her bodily off the rungs of the mainmast shrouds and slung her over his shoulder, plopping her into place with a hearty clap on the rump.

She let out a small shriek at the indignity and fought him as best she could, but Jack was undeterred, easily restraining her flailing arms and legs. He had the nerve to laugh at her struggles.

"Put me down, you blackguard—pirate—beast!" she yelled, even as it became very clear which one of them was in charge; but that didn't stop her from fighting, never mind the fact that all that stood between her and one very large, very powerful, very annoyed ex-pirate was whatever shred of chivalry still dwelled within his breast.

A dubious hope.

"Don't do anything I wouldn't do, Cap," a cheeky sailor said with a wink as they passed by.

Jack shot him a scowl. "Roll a barrel of fresh water into my day cabin. Chit smells like the bilge."

"I do not!"

"Aye, sir." The sailor snapped to it.

"Yes, you do."

"Food and drink, post-haste," he ordered another. "Stop kicking me, Eden."

"You deserve it!"

"I'm not the one who stowed away," he reminded her as he carried her past the great steering wheel of the ship, past a group of gaping, wide-eyed young sailors. Lord Jack maneuvered her in through a door on the quarterdeck.

"Put me down, damn you!"

"Such language!" he exclaimed mildly. "You won't make many fine friends in *London* talking like that."

"You," she informed him, dangling precariously off the cliff of his huge shoulder, "are an ogre."

He set her down on her feet with a plunk, smirked at her in the most deliberately provoking way, and then went back to the door to accept the delivery of the barrel of fresh water.

Dry-mouthed upon finding herself alone with him, she tugged her father's borrowed jacket back into place and stole a nervous glance around at the room into which he had absconded with her.

After so many days in the dim, utilitarian storage areas, she was admittedly impressed by the sprawling stateroom's smart, masculine style. To be sure, she had come quite a few steps closer to civilization.

The captain's day cabin was a handsomely appointed business office with dark wood paneling, brass wall sconces, and a few oil paintings in gilded frames. It had a curious floor covering of stretched canvas that had been painted with black and white squares to resemble marble tiles; from the low, beamed ceiling above hung a pewter chandelier centered over the round worktable in the middle of the room.

The heavy, claw-foot table, strewn with charts and maps, was part of a suite of mahogany furniture with chairs in red leather upholstery; the main piece, however, dominating the stateroom, was the grand baronial desk. But although the room's furnishings suggested the establishment of a prestigious London merchant, there was no forgetting they were on a ship in the middle of the sea, for along the back wall, a row of sparkling stern windows revealed an endless horizon of deep sapphire ocean.

Built-in storage benches below the windows were cushioned with the same red leather upholstery as the chairs. Beyond the stern windows, a narrow jib door led to a private, open-air balcony with a carved, gilded railing and a few low-slung chairs here and there. It was shady and cool out on the stern gallery, sheltered by the overhang of the poop deck above.

Turning to Jack again, she watched him roll the barrel of water into the room before closing the door in the cheeky sailor's eager face. He locked the door then turned to her.

She took a wary step backward.

"You, Miss Farraday, are one bloody-minded individual," he informed her, resting his hands on his hips for a moment. "I could almost admire that, if you weren't so damned much trouble. But— you're here now, aren't you? So I'm just going to have to deal with you." He trailed a brooding glance over her from head to toe.

Eden shifted her weight uncomfortably.

"Right," he said with a businesslike nod. "Take off your clothes."

Her eyes shot open wide. "What?"

"Take them off and throw them in the ocean," he instructed, nodding toward the balcony as he prowled across the room.

"I shall do nothing of the kind!"

He paused and looked at her, one eyebrow arched. "Pardon?"

"No!"

"I gave you an order." His dark stare sharpened. "Or would you rather I do it for you?"

"You stay away from me!" she cried, darting around the work-table.

"Then do as you are told," he warned, but instead of coming around the table to forcibly disrobe her as threatened, he disappeared through a small door into a roomy storage closet that adjoined the cabin.

Eden made no move to obey his scandalous order, instead only peering after him as he reached up and brought down a large wooden bathing tub that had been securely stored out of the way on hooks sunk into the bulkhead.

He backed out of the little room, angling the big tub carefully through the narrow doorway. "What are you waiting for?" he asked when he saw her. "Strip."

"You can't be serious."

He just looked at her, and it was obvious he wasn't jesting.

"Really, my lord! Is this how you treat all your passengers?"

91

"You are not a passenger, Eden, you are a thief," he replied matter-of-factly. "Now, if you would rather not be treated like one and spend the duration of our voyage in the brig, to be turned over to the authorities when we arrive, I suggest you comply."

"You wouldn't!"

"Quarantine you for the safety of my men? You're damned right I would. Come, Miss Farraday, you are a physician's daughter." He rolled the bathing tub over to a large rectangle of sunlight streaming in through the stern windows. "You know fevers brew down in the hold where you've been hiding. Illness kills more men than battle out at sea, and I will not have you spreading disease among my crew. You must wash, and those clothes must be destroyed. Let's just hope you haven't picked up any lice, as well, or we may have to cut off all those pretty auburn tresses."

She gasped, her hand flying up to protect her long hair, but she remained rooted in place, clutching her jacket closed despite the heat.

Lifting the seat of one of the red leather window benches, Lord Jack pulled out a fresh white bedsheet, shook out the folds, and then used it to line the bottom of the bathing tub.

"There," he said with a devilish gleam in his eyes. "Now you won't get a splinter in your lovely bottom. Though if you did, I would be glad to get it out for you. Return the favor, don't you know."

Eden narrowed her eyes at him in warning as her cheeks turned scarlet. Her pulse was pounding.

With some chagrin, she recognized the truth of what he said about observing proper hygiene at sea to avoid any outbreak of disease.

On the other hand, she also remembered his lascivious threat about how she would pay for her passage if she came aboard his ship, and here he was telling her to get naked.

It did not bode well.

Lifting the heavy water barrel easily onto one mighty shoulder—the one she had lately occupied—Jack carried it over to the tub and set it down again. He popped the seal off the barrel's lid and removed it. "Go on," he said, glancing at her as he picked up the water barrel again, pouring half its contents into the bathing tub. "I don't have all day."

Eden just stood there, at a loss. Lord Jack had turned this into a battle of wills, but everything was so far stacked in his favor that how could she possibly win?

When he set the barrel down again, the masterful nod that he jerked in her direction needed no words to order her into the water.

Yes, she had stowed away, but was she really a *thief*? She had never thought of it like that; she had known it was naughty but hardly an actual crime. Yet he had threatened to hand her over to the law if she did not do as he said. She glanced in distress from the bathing tub to her captor, realizing that her insubordination so far had only been tolerated because of her sex.

But if that thought inspired a fleeting sense of gratitude, he ruined it when he dropped casually into the armchair across from the tub.

Her eyes widened. "Aren't you going to leave?"

"Hell, no. Why should I?"

"But—you don't mean to sit there gawking at me?" she cried.

"Oh, my dear, I think I am entitled to it." He stretched his arms upward and then linked his fingers behind his head, regarding her with a diabolical smile. "Looking at naked women, after all, is one of a man's few great joys in life, a pleasure sadly lacking at sea. But don't worry, my dear. You haven't got anything I haven't seen before. Proceed," he commanded with a kingly wave of his hand. He sat back again and waited for the show.

Eden glared at him.

His eyes danced; his stare caressed her.

She looked at him imploringly.

"I told you this was how you would repay me," he reminded her softly, reckless charm edging his faint smile. "You brought this on yourself, my wild little jungle flower. Go on. It's just you and me," he said in a silky tone that had probably bewitched young ladies on several continents.

Eden was trembling. *Horrible, wicked blackguard.* Fortunately for her own sake, she bit her tongue instead of uttering her sentiments aloud. Her chin came up a notch. "What then, am I, your entertainment for the journey?"

"Yes. Something like that."

He enjoyed toying with her, she realized. It was written all over his handsome face.

"Is it so hard for you to obey one simple order?" he inquired, then he reached over and picked up a quill pen off his desk. "Must

I flog you into submission?" he murmured, waving the feathery plume back and forth suggestively.

Eden shivered as she scowled. "You are despicable."

"I just saved your arse," he reminded her with a pointed smile.

It was clear the captain wasn't budging; she might as well have argued with the rock of Gibraltar. Her heart was pounding fiercely as she cursed him in her mind. She bit her lip, turning toward the waiting bathtub. If only it did not look so wonderfully inviting. She eyed it longingly.

Truly, she might have found the strength to make a stand against the barbarian, but she yearned to wash and was too practical to refuse the creature comforts of which she was in such dire need.

A fact the scoundrel knew full well, she thought, abruptly recalling the many times she had gone swimming *au naturel* in the jungle with her sweet friends among the Waroa maidens.

The young Indian girls had known all the hidden places where it was safe to play in the crystal waters. Many a day she had gone with them to escape the heat, splashing about and collecting the gorgeous blooms of water lilies, softening their skin with mud and clay mixtures, and adorning themselves with pearls that they harvested from the oysters that grew in the river.

Nudity had never bothered her then any more than it had bothered the native girls. Yes, she must think of it like that. She'd just pretend he wasn't even there.

Sending him one final look of reproach, Eden turned away, fingering the hem of her long white shirt.

"Ahem."

She glanced at him over her shoulder.

He swirled the feathery plume in a little circle in the air, instructing her to turn around again. "Don't try to hide, my sweet. I've paid for this, remember?"

Eden looked at him in loathing.

Lord Jack smiled.

Fine. If he wanted to be so abominably rude, she'd do her best to shock him right back without letting one iota of modesty get in her way.

Gathering up the remains of her still-defiant courage, she pulled off her boots and stockings and kicked them aside, sending him a withering glance as she did so, then untied the length of cord holding up her breeches.

Veiling her gaze behind lowered lashes, she took them off. Lastly, she lifted her damp, tattered shirt off over her head.

She quickly bent and scooped up the whole pile of her clothes, leaving behind only her boots.

Naked as the day she was born, she walked past him, shooting him a go-to-hell smile as she proceeded out onto the stern gallery, where she dropped all her dirty and allegedly disease-ridden clothing over the rail.

She watched them fall into the waves far below and for a moment let the wind ripple through her hair and enjoyed the warm kiss of the sun on her bare skin. This, at least, was a good deal better than the cargo hold. The sun, like the very source of her strength, restored her to feeling some small semblance of control over this frightening situation. Taking a deep breath, Eden pivoted away from the railing and strolled back languidly inside.

Lord Jack's turquoise eyes had glazed over as she walked toward him. His stare traveled down every inch of her body, consuming her with unnerving intensity.

Frank, open lust.

It rather terrified her, but she was too angry to let her fear show. She didn't grovel to anyone and certainly not to a blackguard like him.

She stepped into the bath with an expression of cool pride and lowered herself into the water. When she sat, she drew her knees up against her breasts, finally hiding herself from him as best she could.

With a ragged inhalation, it seemed Lord Jack remembered then to breathe.

He looked away for a moment as though to collect himself, his hand obscuring his mouth.

"Are you entertained n-now, my lord?" Eden asked resentfully, her teeth chattering a bit, though the day was warm.

He did not answer at first. He looked at her again, dragged his gaze up from her body and leaned forward in his chair, resting his elbows on his knees. It seemed as though there was something he wanted to say, but no words came.

He locked his fingers loosely before him and just looked at her.

"Stop staring at me," she said with a plaintive note in her voice.

"Forgive me, Eden." His voice was husky. "Your body is sublime."

Truly, she wanted to die of mortification. "Could you at least pass the soap?"

Amusement registered in his eyes at her request, chasing off some of that intimidating, dark intensity. He rose and went to get it for her. When he returned, he handed her an oval of fine, transparent amber soap wrapped in waxed paper.

Eden cautiously took the soap, then dunked herself under the water, holding her nose. Her hair floated around her, but she refused to resurface until she was confident she could simply ignore him. She must try harder to pretend he wasn't there.

How horrid he was, tormenting her like this.

Coming up again from beneath the water, she rested her head back against the tub's rim, determined to relax and enjoy her long-needed bath. The tepid, silky water soothed her agitated skin and aching muscles. At length, she began washing with the expensive soap, doing her dead-level best to ignore the hulking, six-foot, muscle-bound pirate sitting less than two feet away, devouring her with his gaze.

"I need to wash my hair," she announced after several moments. "Do you have any shampoo?"

With a grunt of assent, he got up again, went back into the side closet, and returned to present her with a small bottle containing a luxurious concoction of French shampooing.

Eden accepted it while he stood by the tub; he picked up the barrel and lifted it, nodding at her to indicate he would help her wet her hair. She tilted her head back and waited for the water to descend on her, a man-powered waterfall.

At least there was one good use for all those muscles.

"So," he said slowly after a time as he poured some water gently on her hair, "you thought you'd stow away. Ignore everything I said."

"I can explain—"

"Don't talk to me. I don't want to hear your excuses." He doused her, dumping an extra half gallon of water on her head.

She sputtered and glared at him the moment she had wiped the water out of her eyes.

But her thick hair was well soaked through now, so she took a large dollop of the shampoo and began working it into a lather, muttering, "You don't have to drown a person."

"You'll live. Close your eyes before you get soap in 'em."

"My lord, I know you're angry—"

"You know nothing. Stop talking," he grumbled. "I'm trying to think."

Eden sealed her lips in simmering obedience and looked away while Jack went and sat down again, his expression unreadable.

"Ah, what am I to do with you, girl? Feed you to the fishes? Put you in a lifeboat and let you row the thousand miles back to your father?"

She shot him a worried glance. Suddenly it seemed like a bad idea to irk him in any way. Eden gave up trying to reason with him, at least for the moment. There was no telling what new scheme might be percolating in his inscrutable brain, but arguing would only provoke him and would probably make things worse.

Shrugging off his displeasure with a low huff of indignation, she turned her attention willfully to the pleasanter task of washing her hair.

When a knock sounded on the cabin door, her captor went to answer it. He opened the door only narrowly and returned with a tray of food, which he set on the table. Then he went into the adjoining chamber and came back out with one of his own large white shirts, neatly folded. He set it over the nearby chair back for her to wear when her bath was through.

Seeing that she was done washing her hair, he returned without a word and lifted the barrel again to help her rinse the suds away. He made no attempt to dunk her this time, but carefully doled out more of the water, letting it wash in a steady stream over her hair.

"You were going to England anyway," she tried again in a calmer tone a few minutes later. "Your refusal was ungallant and completely arbitrary—"

"That's not true. I offered to take you and the others to Trinidad. Not total obedience to your wishes, but better than nothing." He set the empty barrel aside. "At least it would've gotten you out of there. It was your father who refused."

"I know." When she looked up at him, she was suddenly struck by the way the golden sunlight slanting in from the stern windows played along the rugged line of his iron jaw, softening all the harsh planes and angles of his tanned face. She held his stare for a moment, then let out a sigh and leaned back, resting her head against the rim of the tub. "I'm sorry."

"No, you're not," he replied, startling her with his frank tone.

"You got what you wanted. I think you know exactly what you're doing. Fortunately," he added as he picked up the soap and began to wash her arm with the utmost care, "so do I."

She pulled away with a belated flash of angry shock. "Don't touch me!"

"Easy," he whispered.

"Stop it!" she cried as his large, deft hand smoothed the oval of soap across her damp chest.

"Relax, Eden—"

"Leave me alone!" She splashed him in her effort to escape his beguiling hands, getting water all over his shirt.

The cloth darkened in big wet spots across his chest and flat belly and on one shoulder. He glanced down at himself, and her fear escalated when he looked at her again with a feverish gleam in his eyes. "You want to play rough, eh?"

Her voice vanished as he lifted his shirt off over his head. The scandalized protest died on her lips as her gaze trailed over his stone-carved body. *Oh, God,* she thought with a large gulp. For one moment, simply from shock, she allowed herself to look at him—really look at Jack Knight.

His pink, narrow lips were pliant and sensitive in contrast to the dark scruff on his chin—in need, again, of a shave. Her stare descended below the hard, square angle of his jaw to the forward jut of his Adam's apple, and down his thick neck, to the manly architecture of his collarbones. How solidly he was made, she thought.

How beautifully.

All of a sudden, she wanted to touch him—to trace those strong bones. To stroke the broad, muscled swells of his chest.

His flat, tiny nipples were a brownish pink in color, and a sprinkling of dark hair lightly furred the valley between his chest muscles; this beguiling region narrowed to a sleek groove that continued down the center of his sculpted abdomen.

No, she thought with a shiver of thrill, she *dared* not touch him or do anything to provoke him. Staring like this was dangerous enough. He was too formidable in size, his massive chest and shoulders forming a veritable wall of muscle before her. His Herculean arms were veined like the sleek, glossy hide of a race-horse, and his smooth, bronzed skin bore an array of battle scars.

Once more, he picked up the soap and came after her again,

staring into her eyes in sensuous challenge sharpened by a trace of insolence, as though he would prove to her now who was in charge. She held stock-still, keenly recalling the desperate longing that had kept her awake for so many nights, alone in the jungle.

Instinct, deeper than reason, told her to wait.

This time when he touched her, she jumped a bit, but by choice did not fight him. She was not sure it was wise, in any case, to argue with all that muscle: she was intimidated by it, amazed by it, and ever so slightly . . . aroused.

Closing her eyes, she waited passively, allowing him, just for a moment, to explore her—but ready to battle him again if she felt in any way threatened.

"There," he breathed, his slow, steady hands warm and gentle as he smoothed small circles across her chest and up over her shoulders. "That's better, isn't it?"

She swallowed hard.

Her heart was slamming about so hard behind her ribs that she was sure he must have felt its wild rhythm, his fingertips gliding over her skin.

After a moment, Lord Jack eased behind her and washed her back, drawing the soap between his fingertips in a sensuous line down her spine. His big hands massaged the lather across her shoulder blades and, slick with soap, molded the curves of her waist. Eden was breathless as he bathed her.

He washed her arms, all the way down to her fingertips, slippery soap between each of her fingers. She could hear his deepened breathing by her ear. He stroked her underarms as though there was no part of her he could not enjoy, and she drew in her breath as his roaming hands brushed the outer curves of her breasts.

Reaching around her, he lathered up her midriff in slow, languid circles until she was shaking. *This is madness.* But what could she do? There was nowhere on this ship to hide from him; now that she had been discovered, she was completely in his power.

"What are you going to do to me, Jack?" she breathed after a moment, a catch in her voice.

He touched her cheek, his gaze following his hand. "Exactly what I said I'd do, lovely. I'm going to collect."

"Collect?" Her mouth went dry as she remembered how he'd warned her she'd have to pay with her body if she came aboard his ship. "You would force yourself on me?"

99

"No, sweet. Never that," he whispered, quite near her ear. "You'll be willing when I take you."

She shuddered. "So, you will seduce me."

"Mm."

"I am a virgin, Jack."

"I know, my love."

"I-I'm saving myself for my husband."

"Excellent," he said hoarsely and then he touched her face again, drawing her head back gently as he sought her lips. "That is excellent news."

She yielded helplessly.

Having dreamed of his mouth on hers from that day in the jungle, it was beyond her power to deny them both another taste of this reeling heaven.

The memory of his kiss had preoccupied her since she had first tasted it. He claimed her lips now, again, in hungry greed, while his soapy fingertips glided over her hairline and down her cheek.

His light touch eased her head back until it rested on the broad muscle of his arm. She tensed as his other hand slid slowly up her belly and cupped her breast. He let her pause but did not release her from his kiss; he squeezed her nipple between his thumb and finger, rolling it with the most beguiling pressure, both firm and tender. She quivered and let out a restless moan.

He licked her parted lips in time with the rhythm of his fingertip flicking back and forth over her nipple, and her body reacted of its own accord, her back arching, thrusting her breast more fully into his large, warm palm.

His kiss deepened while he rinsed her body with trickling handfuls of water; as he moved smoothly to the side of her, his mouth only left her lips to travel down her chin, her neck, and down into the valley between her breasts, until he claimed her nipple in a kiss as deep as the one he'd drunk from her lips.

Overwhelmed by his passion, she lay back against the tub's edge and ran her fingers through his dark hair as he suckled her.

The taste of her plump, swollen nipple in his mouth—the feel of her fingers in his hair—had him rock-hard, his blood pumping. He wanted nothing so much as to lay her down atop his nearby desk and take her. He could feel her willingness as she melted under him, but the whole thing was getting out of control.

Jack could hardly believe the ferocity of his desire for her. He knew this had to stop. It was too intense, escalating too swiftly. The girl was a virgin. She was at his mercy, and although she had trusted him enough to let him touch her, she really did not know what she was doing.

He was by no means settled upon marrying her, and if she let him have his way without that vital promise, it meant nothing for her but permanent and total ruin, and maybe a bastard son who would only grow up suffering the cruel slings and arrows of the world's scorn. He thought of her loneliness back in the jungle, her yearning for any human contact; and, terror of the seas or not, her vulnerability got to him. For all his threats to make her pay her way, he refused to take advantage of this naive, exquisite creature. The only thing he knew for sure was that he had to protect her.

Even from himself.

Through the haze of lust, he released her pert breast from his savoring kiss and trailed his lips back up her throat, grazing her mouth. He was panting.

She wrapped her arms around his neck and caressed his mouth slowly, so sensually with her own. She wanted more, and Jack did, too, agonized by her ardent response.

But he held himself back.

No, he thought, the only way that this could happen was if he married her, and he suddenly wasn't sure that he wanted to do that.

Her impact on him was too powerful. Eden Farraday was not like other girls. The sheer courage of her stowing away had proved she had the will, strength, and determination to go after what she wanted in life, just like Jack did. By God, this bold young tigress could birth heroic sons for him—but that was just the point.

Everything he had seen of the naturalist's daughter made him rather sure that she would never be content simply to have his babies and let him carry on about his business in his usual, nomadic, fairly solitary way.

She'd make demands, not the material sort that were so very easy to grant—but the hard kind, demands meant to drag his heart out of hiding. She'd try to change the way he was—they always tried, these women. Try to turn him into someone that he did not want to be.

Problem was, for a girl like her, Jack thought he might actually try it. There was the rub precisely.

She might just be the one who could finally make him stay, and for that reason, he knew he had to be extremely wary. His body burned to possess her, but he had to think this through.

Rational thought, alas, was impossible as she kneaded his shoulders and petted his face, his neck. He stroked her hair and fed off her kisses like the sweetest ambrosial nectar. God, he wanted her. They were both on the verge of getting entirely carried away, but if he didn't put an end to this, it would soon be too late for regrets.

With a breathy gasp, he found the strength at last to tear his mouth away from hers. He heard her whisper his name as he pressed a gentle kiss to her forehead.

He closed his eyes, trying to bring his thundering pulse under control.

Her eyes were wide, searching his, as he pulled away without a word. He read uncertainty in their depths, a flicker of hurt at what she took as a possible rejection. She did not understand, of course, why he was stopping; mute with hunger for her, he was unable to explain. He dropped his gaze.

Shaken by the power of what had just passed between them, he rose to his feet and withdrew to the stern gallery, removing himself from the nearness of severe temptation.

When he walked outside, the cool ocean breeze fanned his fevered skin. He braced his hands on the carved railing and stared down blindly at the frothy wake; he ordered his heartbeat to slow back to normal.

Keen for a smoke, he tried to light a cheroot, but gave up with a curse after a moment, his hands still trembling too much to make the task achievable. What the hell was the matter with him? He raked his hand through his hair and spent a few more minutes willing his body into submission.

At length, he took a deep breath and let it out slowly as sanity finally began to trickle back in. Very well, then. He would resist her allure for the sake of self-preservation—but *she* didn't have to know that his threat to bed her was an empty one. A shade of sensual intimidation would help to make the unruly creature mind. When he was satisfied that he had brought his raging want of her under control, he turned around and prowled back guardedly into the cabin.

Upon his return, he saw that she had used his brief absence to get out of the tub and dry off, and had donned the clean white shirt he had left on the chair for her. It hung nearly to her knees, and though she had rolled up the voluminous sleeves, the V of the neckline plunged almost to her navel. It did not fit her properly at all, but Jack found himself savoring the sight of her wrapped in his garment; it filled him with a most peculiar glow of possessive satisfaction.

Holding the oversized shirt closed with one hand, she was roughly combing the tangles out of her wet hair with the other. The process looked painful, but as he watched, she averted her gaze, obviously embarrassed after their little adventure together just now. The chit was bright pink beneath her freckles.

Her virginal blush pleased him, too, but he hid his delight behind a stern exterior, lest they get caught up again. "Does your father know where you are?"

"I left him a letter." She bit her lip and eyed him uncertainly, filial guilt written all over her face.

"Don't worry," Jack advised in a gentle murmur. "He's a grown man. He'll be fine."

Her quick, shy glance bespoke thanks for his reassurance. As she finished combing out her hair, Jack swept an inviting gesture toward the waiting food on the table. Eden nodded and approached it cautiously, like some wary forest doe.

"Who was that other fellow that day in the jungle? The one with the rifle?"

"Oh—my father's assistant. Connor O'Keefe." She picked up a small plate and surveyed the selection while Jack filed the name away in the back of his mind. "Why do you ask?"

"I don't like him."

"I don't think he likes you, either, Jack."

"But he certainly seems to like you."

She dropped her gaze and fell silent for a moment. "Is it my turn to ask you a question now?"

"Depends on what it is."

She finished arranging her plate with a meditative look, then sat down slowly, watching him. "Are you on the rebels' side or were you up at Angostura plotting against them?"

He arched one eyebrow, admittedly taken aback by her choice of subjects.

"I know something's going on, Jack. I may be a female, but that doesn't mean I haven't got a brain." She put the linen napkin on her lap. "I told you where my loyalties lie. I'd rather see Bolivar win."

"Well, he can't," Jack murmured. "Not unless he gets some help."

Her eyes narrowed in satisfaction. "So, you *are* on their side?"

"What do you think, Miss Farraday?"

She gazed at him intently. "Papa says there isn't really going to be a war. Because the rebels are too drastically outnumbered."

"Even a genius is occasionally wrong. After all, situations change."

She tilted her head. "Isn't it your company's claim to fame that you can get anything that anybody needs, from nearly any corner of the world?"

He knew he should put a stop to this, but it was fascinating watching her work it all out in her mind. "That is true. Yes."

"And the rebels need men." She leaned forward in her chair. "You're going to find them extra soldiers, aren't you?" she whispered. "But where?" she persisted before he could silence her. "England? Oh . . . but of course! All those soldiers back from the Peninsula—"

He rolled his eyes and let out a sigh. "Eden."

"But England would never dare step between Spain and her colonies."

"No. Not in any official capacity. However," he conceded, giving in to her against his better judgment, "a soldier can change his uniform, can he not?"

"Ohhh." Her eyes wide, she sat back slowly, lowering her gaze. For a long moment, she said nothing as she tried to absorb it all, then she lifted her gaze to his. "Couldn't you get into trouble for this?"

"Not if they don't find out." He gave her an innocent smile and popped a grape from the silver tray into his mouth.

"I see! So—bringing all these products to market in London is only a-a sort of pretense, isn't it?"

"Enough. We must not discuss this any further."

"But why? I've already figured it out, Jack. I was *there*!" She searched his face, shaking her head. "How did you get involved in all this?"

He hesitated for a moment, then shrugged it off. Ah, hell. What did it matter now if he told her? It was easy enough to ensure that one young girl didn't get in the way.

"Do you remember the earthquake that devastated Caracas a couple of years ago?" He bent down, leaning his elbows on the back of the chair across from her at the table.

She nodded. "That was right on the heels of Bolivar's last attempt to free his country."

"Exactly. After a series of victories, the rebels had just chased the Spanish out of many parts of Venezuela. They were in Caracas setting up the new government when the earthquake hit. Hate to say it, but their luck is worse than mine," he added drily.

She smiled with a thoughtful gaze. "Didn't the Catholic church declare that earthquake an act of God?"

"Aye, condemning the revolution. The *royalist* church. The bishops always side with the king. Naturally, they proclaimed the quake a sign of God's judgment against the revolution. Hearing that, a lot of Venezuelans thought the bishops might be right. Morale eroded. People lost their nerve. Well, it was the perfect opportunity for Spain to take back the ground they had lost. When they launched another attack, the resistance fell apart."

She nodded. "Yes, I heard."

"What you may not know is that, after that defeat, Bolivar and his entourage had to flee for their lives, with some of Spain's top assassins at their heels."

"Really?"

He nodded. "They were marked men. Considered traitors to Spain. Now, I had sent a dozen of my ships to take food and medical supplies to Caracas after the earthquake. Apparently, Bolivar and his aides sailed out amid my ships' formation on their return journey to Port Royal. They wound up in Jamaica—nearly on my doorstep. Well, I have a policy, you see. Nobody kills anybody on my turf, at least not without consulting me first. When I heard about their plight, I gave them my protection. Mr. Brody, my head of security—who I think you may have met—"

"Indeed."

"On my orders, Mr. Brody set up a ring of armed men around the perimeter of my property for the duration of Bolivar's visit. As a result, we intercepted the Spanish assassins and sent them packing."

She stared at him, her eyes round. "You saved Bolivar's life? You had the Liberator and his council as guests in your home?"

"For a short while—and let me tell you, far from acknowledging defeat, he and his advisers were already planning their next attempt to free their country. That's when I first got involved. You have to admire a man who gets up every time they knock him down—who keeps on going even despite the supposed wrath of God."

Eden shook her head; Jack was absurdly pleased that his actions had impressed her. "I don't suppose the Spanish like you very much after that."

"Nobody does, Miss Farraday, hadn't you heard?"

She smiled, blushing a little. "Well, I think it's entirely noble, what you're doing."

He snorted. "Don't be too sure. I stand to triple my fortune if all goes well."

"You wouldn't risk angering two of the most powerful nations on earth just to make money, I think. Besides, you had nothing to gain by sending Caracas humanitarian aid after the earth-quake."

"Maybe I was merely paying off my many sins," he drawled, growing uncomfortable with her admiring gaze. He rose and went around the table. "Now, my dear, I hope I've satisfied your curios-ity."

"I want you to know that I won't tell a soul about what you're doing," she said solemnly, turning to face him as he approached her. "Not even Cousin Amelia."

"Oh, I'm not worried about that," he murmured, cupping her face. He gazed at her fondly for a moment, stroking her silken cheek with the pad of his thumb.

What a funny little thing she was, he thought in tender amuse-ment. So serious and true. He gathered by her blushing smile that Eden thought he wasn't worried about her keeping silent because he trusted her, but she was mistaken.

The reason he wasn't worried was because the minute she had guessed the truth, he had already decided that he wasn't letting her anywhere near London until his mission was complete.

The risks were too great. He owned a splendid castle on the coast of Ireland; she could wait there until the job was done, safely tucked away in medieval splendor, far from London, where she could not cause him any trouble with a careless word or a naive admission.

She was going to hate him for it, naturally, but if she had waited all these years to visit London, another six months wouldn't kill her.

"Come," he murmured, pulling her chair out for her. "Bring your plate."

"Where are we going?"

"You can finish eating in my sleeping cabin. The officers need this stateroom to do their work—and you'll be safest in there, anyway. Mind you are not to leave these chambers unless you are accompanied either by me, Mr. Brody, or Lieutenant Trahern." Eden grabbed her plate as he tucked her under his arm and steered her over to his private quarters. Opening the door, he shooed her in. "There you are, then. Make yourself at home."

"Jack," she said, stealing a brief glance into his cabin. "There's a cannon in there." She turned to him, her brow furrowed.

"Yes, a twelve-pounder. It won't bite you. Run along now." He nodded toward the room. "Some of us have work to do."

Stepping past him in wary uncertainty, she entered his spartan cabin. His wood-framed berth was built into the bulkhead, draped with curtains to block out the light and to keep in the heat.

Although there was a washstand in the corner and a large leather sea chest by the foot of the bed, the waist-high cannon did rather dominate the room. Its muzzle thrust out belligerently from the open gun port, as if to keep the world at bay. He folded his arms across his chest.

"I hope you find everything to your liking," he said sardonically, not deigning to point out that she was, after all, a stowaway.

Beggars could hardly be choosers.

She sent him a contrite nod. "Thank you."

"There's a series of locks on this door." He pointed them out and looked meaningfully into her eyes. "I suggest you use them to keep out the men."

"Will they keep you out?" she asked in a saucy tone.

"No, my dear, I have the keys." Fighting a smile, he gave her a nod of farewell and turned to go.

"Jack?" He turned around in question at her soft call. She leaned in the doorway and gave him a frisky half smile. "Don't you want to kiss me good-bye?"

The invitation stunned him, but that just went to prove how dangerous she was.

"No," he replied in a pleasant tone, hiding his amusement.

107

She frowned.

He turned away with a low chuckle and grabbed his discarded shirt from the chair back where he'd left it. He pulled it on again as he walked away.

"Captain," she called after him, her tone not quite so sweet as a moment ago.

"Yes, my dear?" he asked indulgently, tucking his shirt into his snug breeches.

"I want to know, honestly—is it true? Were you really a pirate?"

"Now, Miss Farraday," he chided as a devilish sparkle crept into his eyes. "You mustn't believe every idle rumor you hear."

He gave her a wink. "I'm sure I had those letters of marque lying around somewhere."

She gasped.

He nodded his command to her to lock herself up in the cabin.

With a scandalized grin, she obeyed, and when he heard the locks turning, he smiled. Maybe now his officers could get back to work—and Jack could at least pretend that life on board *The Winds of Fortune* would now get back to normal.

CHAPTER
⤳ SEVEN ⤳

Aha, so, he was once a privateer! Eden thought as she closed the door. Well, why hadn't the rogue simply said so in the first place? At least that was reasonably legal, unlike piracy. She had a sneaking suspicion, as she turned each of the seven locks, that he enjoyed letting people fear the worst about him.

As an afterthought, she wondered what sort of paranoia led a man to put seven iron locks on his door, anyway—as if he feared a mutiny. But clearly, there was no danger of that. From all that she had seen up on deck, his men held him in the deepest awe.

Eden was rather awed herself.

Ambling over to his built-in berth, which was more than six feet long and nearly as deep, she sat down warily on the sturdy mattress. Well, she thought as she looked around at the stark simplicity of his quarters, the head of Knight Enterprises certainly didn't live like a millionaire.

All his ambition was obviously not aimed at acquiring a life of luxury, for she saw no evidence that he had taken to spoiling himself. She picked up her plate again, and slowly finished eating, half listening all the while to the busy officers on the other side of the door.

She heard muffled talk of winds and currents, degrees of latitude and schedules for the crew. Finished eating, she put her ear to the door when she heard Jack's kingly baritone. The captain was apparently dictating a letter to a business associate.

Hanging on his every word, she found herself wishing she could have gone out there and participated somehow, but she was quite indecent, wearing only his shirt, and besides, she had not been invited.

No doubt Jack felt she would only be a distraction to his men. Even she could admit she had caused enough trouble for one day. With a sigh, she leaned against the door.

Boredom quickly crept in.

"What to do, what to do." Her gaze traveled around the cabin.

Jack had ordered her to rest, but she was wide awake, indeed, jittery after the scandalous way he had touched her in the bathing tub. She closed her eyes, a hot shiver coursing through her body at the all too vivid memory. She could almost still feel his warm, wet mouth at her breast.

Blowing out a frustrated breath, she thrust off the sensation with a will and pushed away from the door. Pacing across the cabin, she examined the great iron cannon a bit, then grazed her hand along the drapes that framed his oversized berth.

Gazing somberly at the captain's huge bed, she could only wonder what might happen there when he came back tonight, as promised. He had threatened from the start to make her pay her way with her body; earlier, he had sworn that she'd be willing when he came to collect his price.

Today's little demonstration proved he did not lack the power to rob her of her wits and her better judgment.

What had made him stop, she did not know.

Maybe she was just too much of an eccentric jungle oddball for him, she thought. But, no. She lowered her gaze. That was just insecurity talking. She had seen his lust for her burning in his turquoise eyes—thrilling, a little scary. Something else had made him pull away and spare her virtue today.

But for how long would his self-restraint hold?

Wrapping her arms around her waist, Eden turned and gazed in the direction of the stateroom, where she could still hear him handing down commands. Her cheeks heated merely to ponder what the night might hold, for she had a feeling that when he came through that barricaded door after dark, he was going to do things to her, delicious things, that would make it impossible for her to resist. And then the freedom she had enjoyed for so long would be lost in the blink of an eye.

If things went too far, she'd have no choice but to marry him, and marriage, of course, gave a husband total legal control over his wife. She trembled at the thought of the mighty Lord Jack for her lord and master, with his iron will and countless secrets. She'd be no more than a thrall to him.

She had to resist. *But how?*

Given his reputation, he might not even *offer* marriage once he had his way with her. He might simply prefer to leave her ruined.

No, she thought with a chill, Papa would never let him get away with that. Connor would kill him if he disgraced her.

At any rate, she could not bring herself to believe that Jack would ever do something that cruel.

Still, the train of her thoughts had begun to unnerve her. She padded silently across the cabin, desperate for some means of distracting herself, but try as she might, she could not stop thinking about Black-Jack Knight.

The man fascinated her. Well, she had never met anyone on a secret mission before.

Of course she forgave him now for refusing that day in the jungle to escort her back to England. It was obvious in hindsight that he couldn't have told her the real reason why he had declined her request, even at the risk of looking utterly ungallant.

Indeed, now that he had told her how dangerous his true goal was, she was already worried about what could happen to him once they reached England. Most of the countries of Europe had embassies in London, and that included Spain. They would be watching him, she realized. They would all be watching him.

It was hard to decide in that moment which of them was madder: Papa or Jack. Papa, with his quest into the deadly Amazon to find medicines for the good of all mankind, or Lord Jack, risking everything to back a cause he believed in, freeing a nation.

Thinking of her sire, she hoped that by now Papa, too, was at sea. She had to believe that upon finding her missing, he would have abandoned his lunatic quest in order to come after her instead. Guilt gnawed at her, and filial anxiety, as she pondered his certain wrath at her when they next met.

She had dashed well better find a new patron in London or he might never speak to her again, once he realized she was safe.

The important thing was that he'd be alive—not that he would ever thank her for it. As for Connor . . . well, she was happy to conclude that the big Australian wasn't her problem anymore. Surely by now he had taken the hint.

111

Drifting over toward the mahogany washstand in the corner, she glanced at herself in the mirror and frowned at her bony reflection. Then, with a sudden surge of curiosity—why not?—she opened the top drawer of the washstand to see what it might hold.

Inside lay a slim silver case of cigarillos along with an array of grooming items: a comb, a bristly toothbrush, a shaving razor with a stropping stone, small scissors for his nails. She found a tiny bottle of cologne shoved into disuse in the back of the drawer; she took it out and sniffed it, smiling. *Very nice.* Putting it away, she closed the drawer again.

All right, bored again. Now what? Glancing over her shoulder, she eyed the sturdy leather sea chest over by the bulkhead, then sent a surreptitious glance toward the door.

Hmm. The captain hadn't said anything about her not being allowed to look around, she reasoned. Scientific curiosity drew her over to the great leather trunk.

She crouched down before it silently and, much to her surprise, found the brass closure unlocked. She inched the lid open and peered inside. Nothing too exciting at first glance.

On the top lay an extra greatcoat of black wool, unneeded in the tropics. Beneath it she found a pair of pistols holstered in a belt and a large knife in an ornate sheath. These sprawled atop messy piles of papers and books, one of which proved to be a copy of *Travels in the Orinoco Delta,* by one Dr. Victor Farraday. With a startled but tender smile, Eden lifted her father's book out of the trunk, absurdly pleased that Lord Jack had read it.

Just holding it in her hands made her feel closer to Papa. In truth, this past fortnight had been the longest they had ever been parted. She thumbed through the pages fondly. Reading a paragraph here and there was almost like having Papa here, talking to her.

It is but Nature's way, my dear. All creatures take a mate upon reaching reproductive age. . . .

Shaking her head quickly, she set Papa's famous narrative aside and dug around in the trunk to see what else she might find. A bulky lump beneath some letters turned out to be a silver-plated winner's cup mounted on a small polished block of white marble. *How very curious.* It was heavy as she rolled it onto its side and read the inscription:

SAM O'SHAY
"THE KILLARNEY CRUSHER."
BARE-KNUCKLE CHAMPION OF THE EPSOM DOWNS MATCHES
MAY 10, 1792
HEIGHT: 6'4", WEIGHT: 15 STONE.

Goodness, the man had been a giant. Though, on second thought, the captain himself was probably about that size.

Of course, so many years ago, Jack would only have been a young boy, maybe ten years old. She let out a soft "Hmm," and furrowed her brow, pondering the prize, but could arrive at no explanation for why Lord Jack might have this. Perhaps some revered male figure in his youth had taken him to the boxing match. Perhaps he had bought it more recently, as an admirer of the Irish pugilist.

Shrugging off the question, she picked up one of the letters that had lain over it. She bit her lip, fingering the letter in temptation. *No, I can't possibly read this,* she thought, but when she noticed that it was in a woman's round, frilly handwriting, curiosity got the best of her. *It could be from that girl he loved when he was a young lad—Lady Maura? The one who wouldn't marry him . . .*

Seized with a desire to find out if Lady Maura had lived to regret her choice, given the magnificent specimen that Lord Jack had become, she turned the letter over furtively only to learn that it wasn't from Lady Maura at all.

Ah, it seemed Lord Jack had a sister!

Wide-eyed, Eden could not help herself. She spent the rest of the afternoon reading. His sister's name was Jacinda, and she had written her errant brother volumes about their family, their ever-growing ranks of new babies and little children, and all their glittering adventures in Society. Though scarcely older than herself, the picture that emerged informed Eden that Lady Jacinda was nothing less than a leading hostess of the London ton. Tea in the Queen's drawing room! A private ball at Devonshire House! The races at Ascot!

Jacinda's accounts were far more authentic than the journalists' secondhand reports about Society's world in *La Belle Assemblée.* She sounded like an entirely warm, charming, and elegant personage—exactly the sort of lady Eden only wished she could become.

113

It became clear that Jack's whole family moved in the first circles of Society.

She could hardly believe it.

Indeed, she was in raptures reading about their amazing lives. Jacinda's sparkling descriptions brought each of Jack's siblings to life in her imagination. The proud lords did not sound quite so intimidating through the eyes of their little sister: Robert, the impeccable Duke of Hawkscliffe, champion of noble causes in the House of Lords and musical collector of fine pianos. His Grace lived in splendor in the heart of London with his beautiful and, by the sound of it, saintly duchess, Bel.

Next came the brave twins, Damien and Lucien—one raising thoroughbred racehorses for a hobby, the other raising eyebrows with all his controversial opinions. Damien, "our Colonel," as Jacinda called him, proved to be a distinguished war-hero, while the mysterious Lucien worked in some vague capacity for the government. Jacinda told Jack that no one was quite sure what Lucien did, nor was he allowed to talk about it.

Then there was the charming Lord Alec, man about Town, who had just won the girl of his dreams along with an enormous fortune at the gaming tables. Jacinda also wrote about her best friend Lizzie, who seemed to be as close to them as any family member; newly married to a viscount, Lizzie, whoever she was, was expecting her first child. Noting the date of the letter, which was a few months old, Eden wondered if Lizzie had birthed the babe yet, and if it had been a boy or a girl.

As for Jacinda herself, Eden learned that she was married to a marquess she called Billy and who she swore was the dearest, handsomest, most wonderful being on the face of the earth; Jacinda said she was sure Jack would approve of him for reasons she would not commit to paper. Above all, she wrote paeans of love about her wee son, Beauregard. Beau's first solid food. Beau's first step. Beau's first puppy. Beau escaping up the aisle in the middle of church, and everybody at the service vowing the golden-haired tot was the most beautiful child they'd ever seen. Beau was the apple of his papa Billy's eye. . . .

Through a mist of sentimental tears, Eden shook her head and slowly let the final sheet of thick linen paper drop to her lap.

Every letter from Lady Jacinda had ended the same way:

Thank you for the gifts you sent, my dear brother. Please come home soon. We'd love to see you anytime. Your devoted sister, Jas.

Jacinda had not come out and said it, but the young woman clearly wondered why little Beau's Uncle Jack did not wish to be part of the toddler's life—of all their lives.

If I had a family like this, Eden thought, *I'd never leave.*

It was obvious Jack felt differently. Even in Jamaica, he had a reputation as a notorious loner. By the sound of it, the second-born Knight brother was as much of an exile from the mainstream of humanity as Eden's own papa. But why?

She shook her head, troubled by the question as she put the letters away again and replaced the weapons, the boxing cup, and the black wool greatcoat over all. But after reading those letters, one fact had become very clear.

Tempting as he was, she could not let Jack kiss away her senses with seduction, for if things went too far and she ended up having to marry him, she saw now that she would only wind up sharing in his isolation, just the way she had endured Papa's.

Like her father, he was too strong a man for her to harbor any illusions about changing his ways. You had to take or leave a man for what he was.

Eden knew what she wanted. She wanted life—normal life. Everyday things. She wanted people. She wanted crowded streets and chaos and grime and laughter and gossip and news. She'd had enough of pristine solitude; she was positively bursting with enthusiasm to rejoin the world again.

She felt drawn to Jack—she could admit that—but she had to protect herself. If she wound up in a situation where she had to marry him, to cast in her lot with another exile, then she might as well have stayed in the jungle and agreed to marry Connor.

The only difference was she felt safe around Jack, while Connor left her cold.

The sharp crack of a fowling piece and a burst of brutish laughter from the taffrail broke Dr. Farraday's concentration.

Seated in the shade of the quarterdeck atop a mound of old netting, he looked up from his book of Wordsworth's poetry, which he'd been reading to try to distract himself from wild worry over his daughter.

Squinting through his spectacles against the sun, he glanced toward the stern only to discover they were using frigate birds for target practice again. Victor pursed his mouth and fumed, feeling impotent, but he dared not stop them.

Connor and he exchanged a guarded look. Fortunately, he had already lectured his assistant on minding his bad temper lest he get them both killed.

It was just their luck that they had wound up procuring passage to England on the very ship of the damned.

Another frigate bird exploded in midair and rained a burst of blood into the sea, and Victor looked away, heartsick. Yes, the creatures were common enough and a nuisance, to boot, ever lighting on the spars and swirling about the masts, but they couldn't be eaten and there was no reason whatever to kill them.

No reason but that doing so helped their drunken captain stave off boredom.

He searched his considerable intellect for some means of distracting the man, but God knew self-preservation forbade him from uttering a protest. He was quite sure that any complaint would have gotten him promptly thrown overboard, aye, and then the crew of lost souls should have had more sport laying wagers on how long it would take him to drown.

With a disheartened sigh, he closed his book of poetry and shook his head, wondering if humanity had improved one iota in the twelve years since he had fled it. For his daughter's sake, he now had no choice but to face the harsh and grating noise of humanity again, as Wordsworth put it.

Certainly, if this ship was a fair sample of the ways of men, he still had no use for civilization.

The vessel was a very bad business all around, and Victor was almost ready to admit that it would have been better to have gone with Jack Knight.

They had found Eden's farewell note some hours after she had run away. By that time, it had been too dark to follow her; to embark on the river at night in their low-slung canoes would have been suicide, with the crocodiles in season. So they had been forced to wait 'til morning to go after her, and had spent the whole night hastily packing up their camp. That was to have been her job.

Connor, of course, had been beside himself, but Victor had

116

somehow staved off panic. He had wanted to wring her neck, but somehow he could not escape the sense that he'd had this coming.

Besides, he possessed great faith in his daughter's survival skills and her adventuring spirit. He held onto hope that she perhaps had changed her mind, that after a good cry and a few hours to sulk, they might still find her on the coast, lounging on the beach, perhaps, and begrudgingly ready at last to journey with them into the Amazon.

No such luck.

They had found her abandoned canoe hidden amongst the mangroves, but there was no sign of Eden nor *The Winds of Fortune*. Trudging along the sand in search of her, shouting her name, they had almost immediately run afoul of the Spanish forces patrolling the coast.

They had been stopped and in short order found themselves detained by officials of the Spanish navy. Taken into custody, they were put in separate cells for three days and interviewed at length by various mid-ranking officers in the service of King Ferdinand.

After a sennight, their identities and the purpose of their expedition into the Delta were finally verified when their papers were found, documenting their right to be there by the express permission of Spain's designated Viceroy in Caracas.

By that time, many of their carefully preserved scientific samples had been compromised by the soldiers rummaging through their traveling chests, searching for any signs of criminality, but at last they were released and politely advised not to come back.

This was precisely what Victor had feared, but expulsion from his paradise no longer signified when his sweet child was out there somewhere without him, at large. The days to brood alone in his cell had awakened every fatherly instinct within him. He had lost his wife and would not, by God, lose his child as well. He blamed himself for her running off, as well he might.

More than anything else, he was glad that in those tense, hair-raising moments just before their capture, as the Spanish soldiers had closed in on them, surrounding them on the beach with guns drawn and bayonets bristling, he had managed to make Connor listen. Speaking swiftly under his breath to the outraged Australian, he had succeeded in convincing Connor to deny any knowledge of Jack Knight's visit to the jungle, or rebel activity up at Angostura, or anything at all besides insects and reptiles and plants. *"We know nothing, do you hear me?"*

Connor had merely growled in thwarted fury, leaving Victor to wonder in their separate cells if his assistant had told the Inquisition anything or not. It had not gone well for Connor on the beach, and frankly, Victor marveled that they had not shot him on the spot.

Connor had gone a bit mad when they came to put him in shackles—rather like a wild animal backed into a corner, Victor thought uncomfortably. The Australian had even thrown a punch, but the Spaniards had held their fire.

Instead, half a dozen of them had leaped on the big man and had pummeled him down into the sand.

Now, four days later, Connor still had bruised ribs, a black eye, and a jaw that clicked when he moved it, but he informed Victor that he had said nothing of Jack. Thankfully, he understood as well as Victor did that the Spanish would have immediately sent a few of their galleons after Jack to investigate his suspicious visit to Angostura, and the sea battle that would have no doubt ensued would have put Eden in unacceptable danger.

Their terrifying ordeal behind them—so they thought—they had hastened to British-held Trinidad and had sought passage on the first boat they could find heading for England.

The one-eyed, one-legged captain, more than happy to take advantage of their desperation, had accepted in lieu of gold coins the naturalists' expensive scientific equipment, which he could later pawn. As *The Sea-Witch* was the only vessel to leave Trinidad for some weeks, Connor and he had taken their chances.

At first glance it had been obvious that all was not well aboard *The Sea-Witch,* a leaky, squalid twenty-gun frigate with filthy decks and tattered sails. Her ostensible line of work was running sugar and tobacco to England from the West Indies, but Victor had a feeling that darker business was afoot somewhere out of sight. If this was so, he did not want to know it.

His only interest was to find his daughter safe. Until he held her tightly in his arms once more, the good of all mankind could go hang. He asked no questions, and this pleased the captain, too.

He and Connor had been prepared to endure dreadful accommodations, musty cots, tainted water, awful food—the only ones who ate well were the ship's cats, thanks to a large supply of rats—but they had only sailed a few days out from port when it became apparent that the situation was even worse than they had feared.

118

The captain was every bit the crude, abusive ruffian they had suspected, but the crew eyed their master in surging hatred and Victor could already smell a mutiny brewing.

Perhaps the captain feared it, too, for he spared no man for even minuscule infractions.

One sailor had already been keel-hauled and another two flogged, but the captain, ever clunking up and down the decks on his wooden peg, spewing abuses, relied on his first mate to protect him, a man with the face of a rapist.

Even during more tranquil hours, the mood of cruelty was palpable aboard the ship—dark, untempered passions—violence that might flare out at any time. Connor and he had been appalled to watch the men beat to death a rat that had scampered across the fo'c'sle. The crewmen's jovial laughter at the game was still ringing in Victor's ears a few days later, when the first mate climbed out onto the bowsprit and shot the pair of dolphins swimming alongside the ship for the spectacle of watching the great sharks come and feed.

More disturbing or, rather, threatening even than this, however, was the change that Victor sensed coming over Connor with each day that passed.

He was keenly aware that the brawny Australian was all that stood between the vicious crew and himself, a small-framed, weaker man of poor vision and advanced years. Victor knew he was at risk, though had more brains than the whole of the crew put together.

Moreover, he could smell the mutiny coming and when violence broke out, he feared that his weakness would make him a natural target. He needed Connor's protection now more than ever, but these days, he thought uneasily, his fellow naturalist did not seem entirely right in the head.

Trying to get the man to speak of what ailed him was as useless as ever, especially in their current situation. Victor could do nothing but watch his young friend with a scientist's keen powers of observation in an effort to discover what was wrong, but he still could not quite put his finger on the nature of the problem. He had a terrible foreboding sense that something was . . . *building* in Connor.

Something that must eventually explode, like the crew's churning hatred.

Perhaps with her woman's intuition Eden had sensed the shadow in him, too; perhaps, Victor thought with a pang of regret, that was why she had refused the match.

In any case, he vowed to himself that from now on, he would *listen* to his daughter in a far more serious way than had been his habit in the past.

"Victor?"

Connor's low query stirred him from his musings.

"Yes, my boy?"

Connor was staring down at the deck before him as though the answers he sought might be written there, if he could only make them out.

Victor took off his spectacles and turned to him with a worried frown. "What is it?"

"It's . . . my fault she's gone," he forced out in a struggling tone.

"Now, now, my lad, we are both to blame—"

"No." Connor sent him a tortured glance and shook his head slowly. "If I were different—better—but she did not want me and that is why she left."

Victor looked at him sadly. He did not know what to say. Emotions had never been his strong suit, after all.

"You know this man, Jack Knight." Connor sent him a penetrating look. "Will he hurt her?"

Victor knew the answer at once and shook his head, easily recalling the worshipful protectiveness with which the young Lord Jack had shielded Lady Maura's every step. "No. Not if there's the merest remnant of the lad I once knew beneath that hard outer shell. Not a chance."

"I pray you're right," Connor said, staring forward. "Because if he harms one hair on her head, Jack Knight is a dead man."

By evening, the whole ship buzzed with the sailors' high-spirited but raunchy discussions of how Cap'n Jack would have his fun tonight with the tasty morsel locked up in his cabin. There were no wagers on *if* he would bed the wild redhead, only on how many times, and whether or not there'd be any girlish screaming.

Given their fair stowaway's fierce display on deck this afternoon, the men hoped he'd stay on his toes with the wench, for she'd surely try to slit his throat if he laid a hand on her. If he was wise, a few thought, he'd tie her up before he climbed aboard.

Yes, they were princes, the lot of them, Jack thought wryly, ignoring their ribaldry with an occasional scowl here and there to silence them. God knew, the lusty images they concocted did nothing to help the underlying level of arousal that had gnawed at him all day after Miss Farraday's lovely bath.

How he was going to keep his hands off her, he did not know, but Jack clung to his earlier decision to resist temptation. She was luscious, yes, and could breed him strapping sons, but lust aside, she was not at all what he had in mind.

When it came time for him to take a wife, he would choose someone docile. Someone tame. Someone who'd never dare question him, but would follow his orders as assiduously as if she were but an extension of himself.

Eden Farraday was altogether her own person. Her own delightful, artlessly innocent, sensuous nymph . . .

Bloody hell.

It was most irksome, his constant awareness of her, cloistered away in his cabin. Her presence somehow permeated the ship: a change in the air. It all felt so odd.

Annoyed at himself for his failure to maintain his policy of cool indifference, he huffed and scowled and did his best to work off his preoccupation with the tantalizing female by hard physical labor on deck, and when that didn't do the trick, by exhaustive practice with his fists, pounding his thick leather punching bag into oblivion—but it was no use.

It was almost as if he could smell her, so near, her dewy-fresh, vanilla-orchid scent. It was driving him mad.

What was this ridiculous reaction? She was just a girl, like any other. Well, except for her eccentric ways, all those wonderfully odd little quirks. . . . *Oh, God. What the hell is wrong with me?* He had left a dozen more beautiful women than her without a backward glance.

But that was just the point.

Stuck out at sea and sworn to protect her—as if he didn't have enough already to worry about!—there was no escape from Eden Farraday.

They were in the middle of the bloody ocean; it was not as though he could carry out his usual tactic of moving on in his nomadic way before anybody got too close.

On the contrary, for the next few weeks, he'd be sharing very close quarters with her, forced into intimate contact.

The worst part of all was that he could not even manage to feel properly angry about the way she had invaded his space and installed herself in his inner sanctum. He was baffled, but the region of his solar plexus tingled even now with eagerness to get back to her. This was insane.

He had not experienced such absurd reactions to a female since he was a witless lad of seventeen, agog over stupid Maura Prescott. No one had gotten to him since.

Thrusting the stowaway out of his mind for the umpteenth time, he went to put the fear of God in Ballast.

He found the unruly gun captain in the sickbay, where the surgeon had just finished putting ten stitches in his tattooed forearm, which Eden had sliced. When he was satisfied that the gunner was cowed by his threats and promises of doom if he even looked at Eden, Jack returned to the main deck to ask around for any articles of ladies' clothing on board for her to wear.

He was hoping one of the officers might have bought a dress for a wife or sweetheart back home, but no such luck. The only gown anyone could find for her was a glittery bluish-green thing that the crew always made the newest midshipman wear as a joke during the bacchanalia of King Neptune's Court that occurred at each equator crossing.

It was more a Carnavale costume than a proper lady's gown, but it would have to do for now.

"This trip just keeps getting stranger," Trahern mumbled, shaking his head as he eyed the dress.

"I'll have Martin sew her some decent clothes in the days to come," Jack mused aloud. "We've got several bolts of fine cloth in the hold. Can't have her freeze to death. Getting colder as we move north."

Trahern nodded. "Jack?"

"Hm?" he asked, distracted from hazy images that had begun to dance inexplicably in his brain—visions of himself doing all the sorts of things with his little future sons that no one had ever bothered to do with him.

He blinked them away, irked with himself anew. "What?"

"You won't . . . hurt her, will you?"

He lifted his eyebrows. "Christopher."

"I know you want her. It's just that she's been so sheltered, Jack—"

"Don't worry, man! As I said, she's under my protection. The crew can think what they please, but you know me better than that."

"Just checking."

"Hell, I'm the one you should fear for," he added in sardonic reproach. "I'm putting my life in her hands."

"What do you mean?"

"I left her in there with my sidearms and my knife."

"You did?" he exclaimed. "How could you of all people forget a thing like that?"

"Who says I forgot?" He flashed a wan smile. "If she feels at all threatened, you cannot doubt she'll use them. You saw what she did to Ballast."

Trahern snorted. "He deserved it."

"Aye. Which is why I shall give the lady no cause to shoot, stab, disembowel, castrate, or otherwise maim me."

"Well, you always liked living dangerously. By the way, I noticed you didn't flog Ballast for his offenses," Trahern said after a brief pause. "I was wondering why."

Jack had a strong stomach, but any man of feeling regarded with deep distaste if not repugnance the occasional necessity of doling out harsh justice at sea. On the other hand, Trahern was right. Flogging was standard procedure. The men knew the consequences of insubordination, and so, by now, the whole crew knew that Cap'n Jack had let Ballast off light—this time.

Jack looked at him ruefully. "I didn't want the girl to hear the screams. She'd only blame herself."

"Maybe she should."

He frowned, shaking his head. "She's an innocent. She's been through a hard enough ordeal."

Trahern stared at him.

Jack shrugged, abashed after his heartfelt assertion. "Anyway, she taught Ballast a lesson, herself, I'd say. He needed ten stitches, did you hear?"

"Yes, I heard." Trahern studied him with a faint smile of amusement tugging at his mouth.

"I'm going to bed," he announced.

"Good night, Captain. May God keep you safe in there."

Jack laughed idly, gave him a farewell nod in answer, and headed for the quarterdeck, tossing the glittery gown for Eden over his shoulder.

He prowled into the moonlit day cabin, savoring the light breeze coming in off the stern gallery. As he approached the locked door to his sleeping cabin, he paused, wondering if he really should sleep elsewhere.

He could, he supposed, sling a hammock here in the day cabin. He turned to peruse the sturdy hooks sunk into the beams overhead. *Hm.* Privacy was always in very short supply at sea. If he did not share a bed with her, word would soon get around. What would the crew have to say about that? He could practically hear them already.

If Cap'n Jack hadn't bedded his little jungle flower, then maybe he wasn't staking a serious claim on her for himself. That could lead some to believe the wench might be fair game, after all. No, the only way to stave off such dangerous murmurings was by the two of them sharing his bed.

Besides, why should he be inconvenienced and have to change his habits just because the girl had stowed away? His adventurous mode of life had taught Jack to sleep, as they said, with one eye open; the only place he felt truly comfortable enough to close his eyes in deep rest was behind that barricaded door.

Most of all, he'd already decided that nothing was going to happen between Eden and him. He was not Ballast. He could control himself. Besides, he still had many questions—

Admit it. You just want to be with her, his thoughts interrupted, mocking him. *You big fool. You like her company.*

So what, anyway, if he felt drawn to her? he thought, bristling defensively. Anyway, it was probably due to the respect he had for her father, nothing more.

Or perhaps it was due to the fact that she was one of the few people Jack had ever seen who knew as much as he did about loneliness.

That was when he realized that he couldn't leave her in there all by herself, day and night. She'd lose her mind. She had already been starved for companionship when he had found her in the jungle. His nonexistent heart clenched, recalling how she had been too vulnerable even to hide it.

Hurt that innocent?

Why, if she thought him capable of it—if Black-Jack Knight was indeed that far gone, a damned soul, lost to honor—then he'd rather she shot him when he walked through that door.

His expression stoic, Jack took out his keys and began the great unlocking.

In the silence, every iron bolt with which he'd protected himself for so long seemed to slam back into its housing with an echoing, fateful *boom.*

As he gripped the doorknob and took a deep breath, he almost wished she'd hit him in the head with some hard object the moment that he stepped into the room.

Knock him out cold.

Unconscious, he couldn't possibly give in to the urge to ravish her.

He needed a wife, yes, but Eden Farraday was too much of a threat.

CHAPTER
∞ EIGHT ∞

Alone in Jack's berth, Eden huddled close to the wall, her eyes wide, her heart pounding with violent force as she watched the seven locks slowly turning all down the barricaded door.

A little moonlight shimmered into the dark space of the sleeping cabin. It gleamed on the wicked iron cannon and danced tauntingly on each metal bolt as it came undone.

Eden clutched the covers to her chest and swallowed hard.

She did not know what was going to happen to her tonight, but wearing nothing but the captain's shirt, wrapped in the sheets that still bore his scent, her fate already seemed sealed: deflowerment at the hands of that very dangerous ex-privateer.

Earlier, in the afternoon, she had managed to get some sleep, but by nightfall, with the expected hour of her captor's return drawing near, she had come wide awake again. There was nothing to do except wait and listen with growing anxiety for any sign of his approach.

The ship was full of strange noises: creaks and pounding footfalls across the decks above, ceaseless waves slapping the hull. She thought she'd heard the mournful singing of a whale echoing through the night some time ago.

Then she had heard it—and her seething thoughts broke off abruptly—firm, steady footfalls coming closer.

Closer.

Anxiety had turned to virginal dread at the low, metallic jangling of keys on the other side of the door. Then the locks had begun to free themselves, one by one.

What if she couldn't resist him? What if he got rough?

Somehow London seemed farther away than ever. . . .

At the last minute, cowardlike, she decided to feign sleep. She shut her eyes and held stock-still as the door inched open. She heard his by now familiar baritone as he mumbled a command to his dog to stay in the other room, that hell hound who had betrayed her hiding place earlier today. If it weren't for that blasted dog, she might still be safely secreted away on the orlop deck.

With the slow creak of the door inching open, she sensed a warm glow of light from behind her closed eyelids. Determined to convince her captor that she was fast asleep, she opened her eyes to the merest slits, trying to peek at him through her lashes.

She saw him hesitate in the doorway, looking as unthreatening as was possible for a giant, rugged male with a scruffy dark jaw, a bronzed tan like a heathen, and eyes like the wild sea. He stopped, as though unsure whether or not he should come in; he looked at her by the light of the lone candle in his hand, but not in lust. He seemed to be making sure she did not have a weapon.

What the devil?

The bristling tension in his vast shoulders relaxed by a fraction as he eased into the room, moving like a man who had half expected to be walking into an ambush.

Watching him through her lashes, Eden wondered what the swathe of blue fabric was draped over his arm. Turning around, Jack closed the door behind him, trying to stop it from squeaking as it swung; then he began resetting all those blasted locks, visibly taking pains to be quiet.

This was not the behavior of a man with rape in mind, she thought. Feeling rather silly, Eden pretended to wake up when he turned around again, once the door was sealed.

"Oh—sorry. Did I wake you?" he mumbled.

She sat up with the cover still clutched to her chest and managed a not very convincing yawn. "It's all right. I had just dozed off."

He shifted his weight, glancing around uncertainly. "Do you, uh, need anything?"

Startled by his politeness, she shook her head.

"Good," he answered. He nodded at her and then crossed abruptly toward the washstand. "Oh, I brought you something to wear." She perked up as he tossed the blue thing across the cannon. "I'll put the candle out in a moment. Just want to wash up before bed."

She nodded, mystified. Goodness, who was this gentleman?

Was he the same man who had ordered her to strip for his pleasure this afternoon? The same callous rogue who had rammed his tongue down her throat that day in the jungle? Why the sudden change of tactics? Eden regarded him in suspicion.

She had already learned that Jack Knight didn't do anything without a reason.

He lifted the hinged top of the mahogany washstand to reveal the built-in sink. It even had a little silver-handled spigot that let water out of the concealed reservoir in the back of the commode. She watched him insert his beeswax taper into one of the symmetrical candle holders on either side of the washstand for light; then he took a washcloth out of the lower drawer. But when he lifted his shirt off over his head, she ducked back behind the curtains of his berth again, her heart racing.

After a moment, the temptation was too great. She leaned out ever so slightly to watch what he was doing.

Unaware of her study, he stood in profile to her. Her eyes widened as he reached for the falls of his breeches and started to unfasten them. He seemed to think better of it, however, let out a low sigh as he buttoned them again, leaving them on.

Eden was relieved, yet the longer she watched him, the more his rock-hard body entranced her.

So beautiful.

He caught her staring as he turned to lean his back against the bulkhead, pulling off his boots. He met her gaze warily, but said nothing as he dropped his black boots on the floor with one heavy clunk after another.

Her cheeks reddened. She cleared her throat, in need of a brisk change of subject. "What did you find for me to wear?" Not waiting for his answer, she climbed out of the bed and went over to the cannon, picking up the blue cloth. She held up the whimsical, low-cut gown by its shoulder seams, and stared at it for a long moment, not quite sure what to make of it.

Jack glanced over as Eden burst out laughing.

"What on earth is it? A costume for a mask ball?"

"Something like that." He grinned. "I believe the wearer of that dress is meant to play the part of the Princess in King Neptune's Court."

"Oh, it's wonderful! I love it!" Pressing it to her, she twirled, adoring its liquid motion. "It's so shimmery! What fabric is this, lamé?"

128

"I haven't the slightest idea." He turned to her with his eyebrow cocked and one hand propped on his lean waist. "You do realize that is not a proper gown, Miss Farraday?"

"I think it's lovely!"

He shook his head at her in sardonic amusement. "All the same, I've arranged for my valet, Martin, to begin working with you tomorrow. It'll be bitter cold soon. I've told him to sew a few things so you'll be warm as we travel north."

At his words, she was humbled by his generosity, yet her heart sank. She stared soberly at him as he leaned closer to the mirror and trailed his fingertips along his scruffy jaw with a frown. "Damn, I need a shave."

"Jack?"

"Yes?"

"I don't wish to be any trouble."

"Oh, really?" he countered, shooting her a twinkling glance. "Since when?"

She frowned as he leaned down and began splashing his face.

"I don't know how I'll ever pay you back."

"Hmm." He sent her a dubious smile as the water trickled down his face. Droplets coursed down his chest as he straightened up again, rubbing the back of his neck with the wet washcloth. If some lewd joke was on the tip of his tongue, he kept it to himself.

After a moment, he ran the wet washcloth down his muscled arm. Eden watched him for a long moment, but when she saw he could not reach the center of his broad back, she put the dress down and walked toward him bravely.

Taking the washcloth out of his hand without waiting for him to argue, she brushed past him to rinse it out in the basin, put a little soap on it, and then circled around behind him again. Jack watched her from the corner of his eye.

Slowly, she touched the damp cloth to his smooth, sun-browned back. He tensed at first, as though wary of her touch, but as she cleaned him in long, careful strokes, his supple flesh relaxed beneath her touch. As she washed off sea salt and dried sweat, his skin took on a velvety sheen in the candlelight.

When she moved forward again, reaching past him to rinse off the cloth, his gaze tracked her, full of smoldering heat.

A blush suffused her cheeks; she could suddenly think of

nothing but his powerful arms around her, his mouth claiming hers like that day on the dock.

She swallowed hard and dropped her gaze. Ready once again, she continued her task; Jack braced his hands on the corners of the washstand, leaning down a bit to let her reach his shoulders. He put his head down and closed his eyes as she complied, washing his wide shoulders, dabbing at his neck as well, and smoothing his thick, wavy hair out of the way with her other hand. Then she ran the cloth across his muscled chest, caressing him. He sighed as she bathed his sculpted sides.

"So many scars," she observed in a soft whisper, tracing one of the many pale, angry lines that marred his otherwise beautifully chiseled torso, like fine cracks in a marble Hercules.

"A few," he conceded, his eyes still closed.

"Where did you get this one?" Her fingertip followed a long slash mark along his right ribs.

He dragged his eyes open and glanced down at the one she had asked about, then smiled ruefully. "Gibraltar. Tavern fight with some Royal Marines."

"And this?" An awful-looking gash, long healed over, on the right side of his waist.

"Oh, that. Sea battle against Asian pirates on the Indian Ocean."

"Really?"

"They hit us with a broadside, and I was pierced with a flying shard of splintered wood half a foot long."

"That's inches from your liver. You could have died."

"Aye, so they said." He shrugged. "I was lucky."

"What about this one?" she murmured, touching the jagged, star-shaped outline of a hole on his right shoulder that she knew on sight had been made by a bullet.

"That one, my dear—" He grasped her wrist gently and plucked her hand away, "is a very long story." He kissed her hand and gave it back to her. "I'll take it from here."

She did not argue, for the searing hunger in his eyes warned that her touch was tormenting him. Instead, she leaned her elbow on the edge of the washstand and searched his face intently.

"What?"

"I would so hate for you to come by any new scars."

He smiled mildly. "Thanks, but it's probably inevitable."

"You're really putting yourself on the line for the rebels, aren't you?" She let her troubled gaze travel down over all the marks of pain on his body. "Why risk it?"

"I thought we already talked about this."

"Yes, but I don't understand. It isn't even your country. You can't need the money. You're already rich. Is it just for the thrill?"

"Hell, no. I am not a reckless man." He moved past her. "I have my reasons."

"Nothing you feel you can tell me?" She turned to watch him.

He went to the door again, apparently to check the locks one last time before sleep. There, he paused with his back to her, barely glancing over his shoulder. "It's a very satisfying thing in life when you're able to do something no one else can," he said in a low voice. "Not even people who think they're better than you. Not even a duke," he added under his breath.

Eden gazed at him in wary tenderness as he turned around slowly and leaned back against the door. He returned her stare but made no move to come any closer.

"Are you talking about your brother, Hawkscliffe?"

He shook his head. "The dead one, before him."

"Your father?"

He folded his arms across his chest and dropped his gaze. "Yes. My *father*," he said in a low, scornful sort of growl.

"You didn't get along with him?" she asked softly.

"Couldn't do anything right for him." He shrugged. "It doesn't matter."

She gazed at him, not knowing what to say; it obviously mattered a great deal.

"I'm helping Bolivar because I *can*. Come on." He nodded toward his berth. "Let's go to bed."

Following his glance at the sleeping quarters they were to share, she bit her lip. All of a sudden, his six-foot berth didn't look so big.

"After you," he ordered.

"Which side do you want?"

He looked at his bed. "You take the wall."

She nodded, drew a deep breath, and then climbed into his berth while Jack crossed back to the washstand to blow out the candle.

He doused it with a puff of breath. Immediately, they were plunged in silver moonlight just as Eden slid beneath the light coverlet and sheet.

131

Jack approached, pewter moonlight sliding along the sleek contours of his mighty shoulders and powerful chest—as though he were forged of polished steel, or as if his very skin were a kind of supple armor. Taut silver ridges and blue shadows contoured every compact muscle of his sculpted abdomen. The scars were invisible now.

Eden held her breath at his beauty as he sat down on the edge of the bed, punched his goose-down pillow into the desired shape, then reclined slowly beside her, folding his arms behind his head. It was not lost on her that he kept the covers between them, lying atop them rather than joining her beneath their light warmth.

God. She was positive he could hear her pulse thumping in the awkward silence.

When he changed position after a few minutes, lowering his hands to his sides, he bumped her thigh with his left hand—a fleeting, accidental touch—but even as he mumbled an apology, she fairly quivered in response. This was insane, but her body was throbbing.

Right, she told her fevered flesh, closing her eyes resolutely. *Go to sleep now.*

Silence.

She could tell by his shallow breathing that he was wide awake, too. Indeed, she could feel the pull of his masculinity, almost hear his body begging for her touch, but she didn't dare.

The silence stretched.

"Eden?"

"Y-yes?" she asked at once, swallowing hard. Her chest rose and fell in abrupt pulls of breath, all but panting.

"Is it my turn to ask you a question?" he whispered.

She licked her lips, prepared to say yes to nearly anything. "All right." She rolled onto her side and braced her elbow on the pillow, resting her cheek in her hand. "What do you want to know?"

He rested his hands on his stomach but turned his head to gaze at her. His eyes glittered in the dark. "Why'd you do it?"

"Do what?"

"Stow away."

Somehow the question took her off guard. But at least it turned the subject away from her growing desire to pounce on him. "I told you. I have to find a new patron for Father's work."

"Ah, right." He looked at the ceiling again. She could just make out his wry smile. "My money wasn't good enough for you."

She poked his shoulder in playful reproach. "That's not true. You wanted the lion's share of the profits."

"We were negotiating," he reminded her in a reasonable tone. "Besides, what else would you expect than for me to want the lion's share? You're the one who said I'm just a big grumpy lion with a thorn in his paw."

She smiled. "Well, you are."

"You got the thorn out."

"I think," she said slowly, "there may still be a few more buried inside you."

He turned his head and looked at her.

For a long moment, they stared at each other in silence.

"Maybe," he admitted barely audibly. "But you haven't answered my question. If it was just to find a patron, you'd have accepted me. But there's more to it, isn't there?"

Eden laid her head down on her pillow, still holding his gaze.

He reached over and caressed her cheek with one knuckle. "What is it that made you run away? The snakes and spiders? Couldn't take it anymore?"

"I wasn't made for solitude, Jack." *I was made for love,* she thought, but she didn't say it aloud.

She didn't have to. The look in his eyes told her he already knew. He rolled onto his elbow and captured her face in his other hand. Her pulse climbed. Gazing into her eyes, he bent his head toward her lips, giving her plenty of time to protest.

Instead, Eden wound her arms around his neck and pulled him closer, melting under him as his warm, fine mouth descended on hers. She stroked his face, raked her fingers through his hair, and lost herself in his wondrous kiss, so deep and drugging and slow.

He eased partly atop her, cupping her waist through the light bedding, and then, more sensuously still, kneading her hip through the coverlet in the most provocative fashion. With his chest flush against her breasts, Eden could feel his heart pounding. The might of his body, the power of his passion, though leashed, nearly threatened to overwhelm her. She had never experienced such potent desire, when all of a sudden her prior decision to resist shone out through the haze.

"Jack!" she gasped, pressing up on his shoulder. She tore her lips away from his kiss with a groan of denial.

"Eden," he panted. "What's wrong?"

"Jack—stop. Please."

He lifted his head and gazed down at her, his chest heaving, his lips bee-stung with her kisses. Slowly, he seemed to come back to his senses. He looked away and, a second later, lifted his weight off her, withdrawing to his side of the bed.

"Good night, Miss Farraday," he said after a long moment.

Relief flooded through her to find that the terror of the West Indies had actually obeyed her. She gave him a tremulous smile. "Good night, Lord Jack."

The next morning, Eden donned the sparkly sea-princess gown, then made friends with the dog while Jack went and rang a bell to summon his valet. He unfolded a painted wooden screen that had been leaning against the wall, then he set it up, blocking off a portion of the day cabin.

"You and Martin can work on your sewing over here."

She smiled at him, wholly grateful to have been allowed out of the cramped sleeping cabin. Despite their cordiality, both she and Jack were feeling a little self-conscious this morning after waking up entangled in each other's arms. Neither was quite sure how it had happened.

"Halloo!" His valet made an entrance at that moment, arriving promptly in answer to Jack's summons.

A neat, prim, rather dandyish little eccentric, Martin made an entrance with his sewing basket draped over his arm and his nose in the air. Impatiently he waved in one of the sailors, who teetered along under the huge pile of fabric bolts that the valet had apparently loaded into his helper's arms.

"Oh, there she is! What an angel!" Martin sailed toward Eden, his hands in the air. "Ah, you precious thing! Let me have a look at you, darling!"

Jack leaned his hip on the corner of his desk and looked on with an expression of bemusement as Martin spun Eden in a circle and then stood back to pass an assessing stare over her, one fist cocked on his waist. "Yes, hm," he murmured to himself, warming to his project. "I think I may be able to work with this."

Eden cast Jack a worried glance.

He grinned, his blue eyes dancing. "Then I shall leave you to it." He heaved up, pushing away from his desk.

"Where are you off to?" she asked.

"Got to get dressed. Work to do. Nothing too daring, Martin," he ordered as he strode toward the sleeping cabin. "Try to be at least a little practical. I know the fashionable ladies deem it very smart to go around half-naked, but I don't want Miss Farraday catching her death as we move north. She's used to the tropics, remember."

"No worries on that point, my lord," he answered, frowning at their choices of fabric. "I fear we shall have little choice. We'll do a walking dress in the sprigged muslin, I should think. A spencer in the blue broadcloth. A pelisse, perhaps, in the green merino wool." Martin was talking more to himself than to Eden, and Jack had already left them, clearly having no interest whatsoever in such things. "Oh, but it's all so dreadfully plain!" he fretted.

"It's all right," she hastened to assure him. "I'm not half bad with a needle myself. When I reach London, I can get some lace to sew along the bottom of the skirts, or trim the pelisse with ribbon or even gold frogging."

"Well, not frogging, my dear. It's all exploded this year."

"Is it?" she asked in surprise.

"La, child! It's a wonder you know anything of fashion where you've been. I imagine you mostly wear fig leaves!"

"Only in the latest styles," she replied with a grin. "My cousin has been my salvation sending me the ladies' magazines. I devour them, but with our camp being so remote, they're always nearly a year out of date by the time they get to me."

Martin said nothing, but with a sly look, reached under the lid of his sewing basket and pulled out a copy of *La Belle Assemblée,* which he placed in her hands.

"January?" she gasped, looking at it. Her jaw dropped and she gaped at him. "It's practically new!"

She let out a small shriek of delight and hugged him without warning. He laughed and blushed a bit at her enthusiastic thanks, and Eden realized her spontaneous reaction had shocked the little man, but from that moment, she and Martin were fast friends.

They measured and draped, compared colors against her complexion in front of the mirror and discussed all the intricacies of achieving an elegance that must always, he assured her, appear effortless.

"I admit I've been looking forward to this ever since the captain mentioned it. Secretly," Martin confessed, "I have always wanted to try my hand at designing for ladies."

"I didn't hear that," Jack muttered as he came back out, clean-shaved and smartly dressed in a dark blue, single-breasted waistcoat buttoned down snugly over a fresh white shirt with loose sleeves, and nankeen breeches over shiny black boots. He adjusted the neat, square knot of his ebony neckcloth as he crossed to the center table to retrieve a few nautical maps.

Eden watched him pass, her eyes wide.

Good Lord, if she could barely resist him last night as a rough, sweaty, half-naked barbarian, how was she supposed to prevail when he looked like this, all fine and clean and elegant?

When he glanced at her a trifle self-consciously, she snapped her jaw shut, but privately, she was still agog.

The blue waistcoat turned his eyes to a deep sapphire shade, and his bronzed skin looked wonderful, his erstwhile scruffy jaw bare and fresh and touchable. The smooth shave had merely revealed the manly precision of his chiseled bone structure, the cleaner look transforming him from a pirate into a prince. Good God, he wasn't just handsome, the man was magnificent.

Before he went out to take the helm of his ship, Jack sent her a very slight but gentlemanly bow, with a faint whiff of his nice cologne trailing in his wake.

Martin turned to her with a knowing glint of mischief in his eyes. "Oh, I see you've had an influence on *somebody,* my dear."

She bit her lip and smiled at him, still dazed, as her cheeks turned pink.

Up on deck some time later, Jack received a report from Lieutenant Peabody that his clerk's condition had worsened through the night.

Poor Peter Stockwell now had gone beyond the surgeon's art. Mulling this over, he found himself drawn back to the day cabin, where Martin had Eden draped in pale green muslin with her arms held out to her sides.

"Now with that gorgeous red hair of yours, you're going to have to be careful of the colors you choose for your wardrobe—"

"Jack!" Her lovely face lit up, more from her enthusiasm over the creation of her pretty new clothes rather than from seeing him,

136

he was sure, but she immediately noticed his brooding expression and frowned at him in concern. "What's wrong?"

"Sorry to interrupt. Miss Farraday—one of my men is very ill. It looks like yellow fever. The surgeon thinks he might not make it. I was wondering if there might be anything in your bag of jungle weeds—"

"I'm on my way." She was already extricating herself from her muslin drapery, revealing her sea-princess costume once more.

She grabbed the haversack of her father's botanical samples and strode toward Jack, leaving Martin startled, his needle poised in midstitch.

"This way," Jack murmured, leading Eden to the main hatch, where wide stairs led down into the lower decks.

"How long has he been ill?"

"A few days."

They marched down to the sickbay, fore on the middle gun deck, and Jack wrinkled his nose briefly at the strong scent of vinegar used to clean the place. He showed her over to the patient, who lay shivering in his berth in the grip of a fevered delirium.

The surgeon, Mr. Palliser, was standing beside Stockwell's bed. When he saw Jack, he shook his head regretfully. It seemed the doctor had simply given up.

Jack and Eden went to Stockwell's bedside, and he tensed as he read the suffering in his loyal clerk's face. The pallid man streamed with sweat, shaking in his cot. Though barely conscious, he spotted Eden with a glazed stare.

She looked tenderly at him, compassion spilling from her emerald eyes as she took his hand like a very angel of mercy. "What's his name?"

"Stockwell. Peter Stockwell."

"Peter, how are you feeling?" she asked softly. "Can you hear me? I'm here to help you." She picked up the damp washcloth nearby and blotted his face with it. "You're going to be all right, do you hear? It's just going to take a little time."

Her gaze wandered to Stockwell's arm, which, when she turned it wrist up, revealed the marks of having been recently bled.

Jack saw her expression harden slightly.

"Right, we're not going to be bleeding him anymore," she ordered in a startling tone of pure feminine steel.

"I beg your—my dear young lady!" the surgeon sputtered, then

137

harrumphed. "Bleeding is the customary treatment in such cases," he informed her with great condescension, not at all happy to be told by the stowaway how to do his job. He had been saving lives, after all, since before the girl was born. "The foul humors must be released—"

"Let's try something else," she said sharply, ready to fight for Stockwell's life, it appeared.

"Captain?" Mr. Palliser turned to Jack with a long-suffering look.

Jack considered the matter. A man's life hung in the balance. Palliser's way had already failed, so Jack decided to trust her. After all, she was the great Dr. Farraday's daughter. She had to know a thing or two about these tropical ailments. He nodded. "Do as she says."

Palliser gasped at the order, but Eden sent Jack a passing glance of gratification as she took the satchel off her shoulder.

"I'll need a mortar and pestle and a quart of boiling water," she said to the surgeon's mate. "Let's try to get him to take some juice. He needs liquids. Is there any ice on board?"

"Not much," Jack said.

"Bring me whatever you can spare. We've got to get his fever down. If nothing else will serve, we may have to lower him into the water."

Jack's curt nod sent the second mate scurrying to do her bidding, then Eden turned to him and shoved him gently toward the door. "Go. Stay away from here. Whatever it is, I don't want you catching it."

"I don't get sick. What about you?"

"Don't worry about me, I'm used to these things. Go."

"Eden, I'm the captain. Every man on this ship is my responsibility—and every woman," he added pointedly.

She gave him a private smile. "Very well. Make yourself useful, then, Captain. I'll stay with Mr. Stockwell. Go and ask around among the crew to see if anyone else is showing the same symptoms. Send them here and that will help contain the danger."

"Aye-aye, ma'am," he murmured wryly, sketching a salute.

To his relief, his investigation yielded no results. The disease had not progressed yet to any other crewmen. Jack returned to see if she had all she needed, but the running of the ship required his attention, and so he had to make do with checking in frequently throughout the day.

By the next evening, he was not the only one who was impressed with the intrepid Miss Farraday. For two days, she had tended her patient constantly, barely taking ten minutes for herself.

When Jack arrived at the sickbay for a progress report, he heard her in conversation with the surgeon's staff and paused outside the door, eavesdropping on the great Dr. Farraday's daughter from sheer curiosity.

She was taking the medics' questions about the tea of bark and herbs that she and her father had learned from the Waroa shaman. The surgeon and his mates had many questions about the other dried plant samples in her bag, asking about the apothecary uses of each.

"And this?"

"Ah, yes, one of my father's best discoveries. It's from the cassia plant, a large shrub that grows on river banks. The crushed leaves make a fine cure for skin infections. Made into a poultice, it can speed up the healing of flesh wounds." She showed them another. "This is the agrobigi, from the legume family. A tea made of it will cure dysentery."

"Here?"

"A powerful painkiller. The natives call it *Al-lah-wah-tah-wah-ku*. It's in the black pepper family."

They attempted to parrot the name, to little avail.

Jack put his head down in amusement and listened to her with tickled pride in her skills.

"This one's the bergibita, for stomachache," she went on. "Here is the jarakopi, for bringing down fevers. We may resort to this for Mr. Stockwell if the chinchonna bark does not suffice. And this one, konsaka wiwiri, is useful for healing diseases of the gums."

They marveled.

"What does this one do, Miss?" one of the surgeon's mates asked.

"Careful with that!" She took it out of his hands with a knowing smile. "That's the caapi plant, known as the vine of the gods. It's a powerful sedative and hallucinogen. You'll be off in dreamland swimming with the mermaids if you get any of that in your mouth."

They laughed at her charming warning, but Jack heard someone coming just then and glanced down the dim passageway.

"What are you doing here?" he demanded as Ballast came trudging out of the dim half-light.

"Captain, sir." The man bowed. "Surgeon said I should have me stitches checked today to see if I was fit enough for duty." Glancing through the open door of the sickbay, Ballast saw Eden and blanched.

Jack snorted, then nodded his permission for the gunner to proceed, but the piercing look he gave Ballast needed no words to warn him that he had best mind his manners.

The big, bald sailor went slouching in. Jack remained in the doorway, curious to see Eden's reaction to her nemesis.

She froze at the sight of the towering gunner, but Ballast knew his captain was watching; his humble manner made it clear he was now more afraid of Eden than she had any cause to be of him.

She kept her distance, remaining near Stockwell's cot while Mr. Palliser checked the gunner's stitches. But when the surgeon was through with him, she did something that stunned Jack.

Squaring her shoulders bravely, she strode toward Ballast with her knapsack hooked over her shoulder.

Palliser glanced at her in surprise as she stopped before Ballast, who was now seated on the bench by the wall.

"Pardon me," she addressed him in a formal tone. "They say your name is Ballast."

The gunner looked up, on his guard. "Aye, ma'am. That's what they call me." He regarded her with a surly, sideways look, no doubt dreading the fact that Jack was right there to see her talking to him and would pound him to a pulp.

"I am Eden Farraday. I just wanted to say, well, that I'm very sorry that I cut you. I reacted out of instinct. I hope you understand."

Astonishment spread across Ballast's craggy face. "You're apologizing, Miss—to me?"

Her nod was firm. "I'm afraid we both acted badly, but I am sorry for your pain, and I hope there will be no hard feelings."

Bravely, she thrust out her hand.

Jack knew the gunner dared not shake it. Not after his captain had sworn to hang any man who touched her.

"It don't matter none." Ballast looked away with an uneasy snort, but he still watched her warily out of the corner of his eye.

Eden's face stiffened at his refusal of her peace offering, but she was undaunted. She reached into her knapsack and pulled out one of her mysterious potions. "Here. Try this salve. It'll help the wound to heal faster."

"I don't think I will, Miss, if it's all the same to you."

She lowered her head. "I understand, You have no reason to trust me. Well, I'll leave it here in the sickbay for you, if you should change your mind, Mr. Ballast."

The gunner mumbled a vague thanks as he rose. Eyeing her suspiciously, he went to the doorway. He paused on his way out, giving Jack a perplexed look.

Jack could not suppress a smile in answer, and shrugged.

Ballast bowed his head again and returned to his duties.

At last, Jack sauntered into the sickbay, gazing at his little stowaway in admiring fascination.

"What are you smiling at?" she whispered, hushing him as he approached, for her patient was sleeping.

Jack grasped her shoulders lightly, leaned down, and pressed a kiss to her cheek. "Nothing. How are you holding up?"

She rubbed the back of her neck, wrinkling up her nose with a weary little smile. "A bit hungry, I suppose."

"Go take a break for a while. Martin or Trahern will see that the galley sends food for you up to the cabin."

"I couldn't leave him—"

"I'll keep watch if it makes you feel better. Go on. You've been here all day."

"You're sure you don't mind?"

He nudged her gently in the direction of the exit, felt his heart clench at her grateful smile, and sat down in the chair she had pulled next to Stockwell's cot.

She returned about an hour later, bringing tea for them both. The day's end half-light had turned to full darkness, so Jack had lit a lantern on the table next to his chair. He stood up as she returned, offered her his seat, and gave her his uneventful report on the patient. Soon, they were both seated with the tea tray on the table between them, and the lantern turned down low.

Stockwell slept on.

"You didn't have to apologize to Ballast, you know," Jack murmured, watching her savor the steam rising from her cup. "The man is a bit of a brute."

"Even a brute deserves to be treated with dignity," she answered

141

with a smile. "Besides, I figured a little diplomacy on my part would make your life easier—help to keep the peace aboard the ship. I never wanted to cause any trouble, Jack." She shook her head. "I'm just happy I was off in my aim when I cut Ballast, or I might have killed him. It was only luck that I missed a major artery in his arm. If I'd hit it, he'd have bled to death."

"You do recall his threat to gut you, I presume? He could have done it easily, you know."

She smiled at him with a knowing twinkle in her eyes. "Not with you standing there."

Pleased by her faith in him, he sighed, and sat back slowly, holding her gaze. "Maybe you and I should talk again about your father's project. Those medicines. They're pretty impressive."

"I know. It's all down to the fact that Papa managed to win the shaman's trust. The tribes don't share their knowledge with outsiders unless they are convinced of their integrity. And that," she added, "is Papa's forte."

"The implications for these cures are fantastic. Take the military use just to start. England's got thousands of troops all over the torrid regions of the earth. India, for example. I have two cousins in the cavalry there, and the tropical fevers that sweep through the ranks devastate their forces after each monsoon. There's the West Indies, the Mediterranean, the tropical regions of the Australian continent. Even the southern parts of America are ridden with swamp fever. Do you know how much nations would pay for a means to keep their troops alive?"

"Jack, the point of the medicines isn't to improve the odds in warfare. They're for saving lives, not taking them. Besides, they're not for sale."

"What?"

"It would be wrong to horde them when people are dying. These cures belong to the whole of humanity. Lord, I sound like Papa."

"Eden," Jack whispered, studying her face pensively. "This world is a very bad place to be an idealist. You have to watch out for your own interests, because nobody else is going to do it for you."

Her face was somber as she digested his words, then she looked at Peter Stockwell.

Jack took another swallow of tea. "Tell me what else your father is working on."

142

She let out a low, sardonic laugh at his question. "The last I spoke to him, he wanted to go to the Amazon. That's why I knew I couldn't stay."

"The Amazon?" Jack echoed in amazement. He stared at her in shock. "What, just the three of you?"

"And our servants, plus a few Indians."

"Good Lord, that's pure lunacy."

"Yes, I know!" she exclaimed, turning in her chair to face him. "You agree with me, then? Really, Jack?"

"Damned right I do. It'd be madness to undertake such a thing without a proper expedition. It takes funding, planning." He furrowed his brow as he considered the scheme. "He'd need a team of twenty or thirty armed men just to survive it. A year's supplies, at least. Pack animals. Boats. A couple of surgeons in case of accidents. Half a dozen more assistants. A survey team, illustrators, engineers, sharp-shooters for protection. A large supply of trading goods to help smooth the way with those deadly tribes of the interior. My God, and to take a woman with him? Did it not occur to your father what could happen to *you* out there?"

Eden sighed. "He thinks, no matter what, that I'm always safest by his side. It's only 'corrupt civilization' that ever scares my father. Oh, I can't tell you how relieved I am that you agree with me, Jack," she said, laying her hand on his arm with a most heartfelt touch. "I was so afraid I was only being . . . selfish."

"Selfish?" He scoffed. "Sensible is more like it." He shook his head. "I don't even know what to say about this. I think your father has been in the wild too long. He was obviously not thinking clearly."

She gazed at him for a long moment in silent appreciation, her gratitude for his words written all over her lovely face. "Do you know what he said when I begged him to leave the jungle? The desires of the individual are of no concern beside the greater good. That sometimes we have to sacrifice ourselves, no matter what."

Jack looked into her eyes. "Isn't that what you had been doing for the past ten years?"

"Twelve," she whispered.

"How could he say that to you after the way you devoted yourself to him? That must have hurt you terribly."

She lowered her head. "Sometimes he just doesn't *think*."

Jack watched her in tender concern. "What about your father's

143

assistant, O'Keefe? Didn't he try at all to talk Victor out of his Amazon scheme?"

"Oh, of course not. Connor thought it was a grand idea."

"Even to bring you?"

"Especially to bring me." She withdrew her hand and clasped her fingers upon her lap.

Jack raised his eyebrow. "I see. So . . . there is something going on between the two of you?"

"He wishes there were," she said in a low tone, staring down at her hands.

"Eden."

"Papa suggested that—" She sighed. "If I was lonesome in the wilderness, that I should marry Connor."

He scanned her face. "This plan found no favor with you?"

"I don't love him," she answered with vehemence, then shook her head. "I've tried. But I can't."

"Why not?"

She glanced at him warily. "Connor lost my trust."

"How?"

She let out a slow exhalation, and then decided to share the grim tale. "When I was sixteen, a young Indian warrior, perhaps twenty years old, followed me into the forest. I had gone off alone to sketch my orchids. I was startled when he made his presence known. He started flirting with me. At first, I was merely nervous, but he wouldn't leave me alone. Then I got scared."

Every muscle in his body had tensed as he listened. "Go on," he said quietly.

"Connor heard me when I screamed. He was there in the blink of an eye, I scarcely know how he found me so fast. But he pulled the boy off me and then—beat him senseless, right in front of me. It was horrible to watch. He just—tore him apart. He beat him so viciously the boy died a few days later." She hesitated, shaking her head at the memory, her eyes glazed. "Connor was covered in blood. I'll never forget the way he looked at me."

Jack was silent.

She lifted her gaze to his once more. "Ever since then, he seems to think that I am his possession. I guess he felt that way all along, which is why he reacted to you as he did."

"Come here." He pulled her closer and put his arm around her shoulders. She leaned against him; Jack pressed a kiss to her temple. "Nobody could ever own you, Eden Farraday. If that's the situation, you were right to get out of there."

She was silent for a long moment. He could sense there was something she wanted to say.

"What is it?" he murmured, brushing his lips against the corner of her forehead.

"He may come after you, Jack. I do rather doubt he'll leave the jungle just to follow me—he hates the world and can't get on at all in civilization—but you deserve to know the possibility exists. He was in a rage, you see, that day he saw you kiss me."

"Oh, hell." He sighed. "So, I put you in danger by doing that."

"I didn't mind," she said hastily, giving him a shy smile. "Besides, it wasn't just you kissing me that made him angry. What made it far worse in his view, I'm sure, was to see me kissing you back."

"Yes, you did, didn't you?" Jack murmured in a husky tone, reaching over to tug a long lock of her hair in teasing affection.

"How could I not?" she retorted as a blush crept into her cheeks. "You didn't give me much choice."

"Oh, come, it wasn't so bad, was it? Besides, it had to be done."

"Why, because my father annoyed you?"

He shook his head and grazed his thumb along her plump, sensitive lips. "There was no way I was leaving that place without kissing you. I needed at least a taste."

She blushed and lowered her gaze.

Jack watched her ravenously.

"The point is," she resumed, "if he got the chance, I wouldn't put it past Connor to try to strike back at you somehow."

"Don't worry, sweeting. I'm not afraid of him."

"I am," she said in a small voice.

Overwhelmed by the urge to protect her, Jack pulled her onto his lap. "Come to me. It's all right," he whispered. He pressed her head down gently onto his shoulder; she wrapped her arms around him and nestled her face against the crook of his neck. "Nobody's going to hurt you. Not while I'm around."

She hugged him more tightly, pressing a tender kiss to his cheek. After a moment, she mumbled absently, "I like you all clean shaved."

He paid little mind. "Remember everything I said earlier, about funding your father's research?"

She nodded.

"I take it all back," he declared. "A new patron is the last thing that you and your father need. That's not what you really want anyway, is it? Funding his project would only give him the means to return to the middle of nowhere, and drag you back with him. It's time to be honest with yourself, Eden. This isn't what you really want."

"No," she admitted in a reluctant whisper.

"You both need a break from the jungle before it turns the lot of you into, what, noble savages."

"Yes." She hugged him harder, almost fervently. "Oh, Jack. I'm praying Papa followed me out of the jungle—"

"I'm sure he did. He'd have to be worried sick. This may be just the thing to jar him back to his senses."

"When he sees London again, and Aunt Cecily, and all my cousins, I'm sure he'll realize that it isn't as bad as he's come to believe. It was Mother's death that changed him. He's been hiding out there in the forest."

"And keeping you with him. Listen to me." He took her face between his hands and gave her a sober look. "You have nothing to feel guilty for in leaving. Your father's the one who's been self-ish—and the next time we meet, I shall make a point to tell him so."

She smiled ruefully. "Not that he'll listen."

"You haven't heard me roar," he explained in a teasing whisper, then he chucked her gently under the chin. "No more talk of patronage, now, or what your Papa wants. The important question from here on in is what do you want, Eden?"

She relaxed in his arms again, laying her head on his shoulder. "I want what I've always wanted," she said after a moment's consideration, then reached up to play with his hair, a faraway smile curving her lips. "I want to go to London and join in all the pleasures of the Season."

"Hm." He wrapped his arms around her waist. "And why do you want that?"

"Oh, I don't know, you'll think it sounds silly—but it just—it seems to me like London is the place where life is *really* happening. Everywhere else is just . . . pale imitations." She shook her head, seeing visions he could only guess at, by her dreamy look. "So many people. So much to do. The elegant shops and houses.

146

All the beautiful lords and ladies . . . just like in the magazines." She leaned her cheek wistfully against his. "How I wish that I could be like them."

Jack held her in silence, not knowing what to say.

He got the feeling there was something she still wasn't telling him, but from what she *had* said, there were so many wrong assumptions built into her innocent words that he didn't know where to begin to correct her.

Besides, it wasn't his place. Who was he to dash her little-girl illusions about the glittering delights of London Town? He had no desire to nay-say her, especially now, after she had opened up to him.

Maybe she needed to hold onto that illusory dream right now, anyway, to keep her courage up for the unknown road ahead. He merely worried what would happen to her when she got there and found out there was another side to that world, as well. A dark side. A cruelty. An emptiness one had to guard against.

Those who had been exposed to it, as Jack had in his early years, quickly came to realize that the one thing a life of opulence lacked was meaning; that lack had nearly destroyed his youngest brother, Alec, as his sister's letters had described.

No, Eden didn't know that side of London life at all, but Jack did. He had survived firsthand the particular cruelty of the ton.

Considering that Eden was as much of an outsider as he was, he feared what could become of her in Society. At least in the jungle, she understood the dangers. In London, she would walk right into any number of traps. Chances were, she'd have to learn the hard way. And what then? Pain and disappointment could quickly leave her jaded.

A few years of trying to be what Society required would turn her into someone as cynical as he—or worse, a mercenary woman like Maura and her ilk, those title-chasing females who sold themselves on the marriage mart for a country house and a coronet.

Having already developed a certain fondness for the little jungle oddball and all her charming quirks, he didn't want to see her hurt or changed by her efforts to fit in. Indeed, the whole prospect only made him want to protect her all the more.

Well, she still had time, he mused. He hadn't told her yet that, in fact, he was not taking her directly to London. She'd be staying in Ireland for six months, until his mission was completed.

As a result, she would actually miss the whole Season. Maybe by next year, she might have a better idea of what she was getting herself into. She could better prepare herself that way and learn ahead of time where Society's worst traps were buried.

For now, Jack dared not tell her of his decision to leave her safely ensconced at his castle in Ireland. Informing her now would only lead to feminine fury and tears—and they were getting along so well, he thought as he held her on his lap and gently stroked her hair.

A few more hours into their vigil, Eden fell asleep.

Since she had worked for two days straight tending her patient, earning, in all, the greatest measure of respect that he had ever had for a female, Jack lifted her in his arms and carried her up to his cabin, where he laid her in his bed.

He pulled the coverlet over her slender body to make sure she stayed warm. He smiled as his gaze trailed over her in the sparkly sea-princess gown, her auburn tresses spilling gracefully across his extra pillow. *You want to be one of the beautiful people?* He shook his head. *Eden. Don't you know that you already are?* Aye, she was more beautiful than most of them could ever hope to be, and this kind of beauty had nothing to do with her fairness of face.

He leaned down and placed a whisper-soft kiss on her pale, smooth forehead, then straightened up slowly and withdrew from the room without a sound.

CHAPTER
∽ NINE ∾

*E*den dreamed of orchids.

A weightless rain of petals, so delicate and pale, floating down on her, and Jack was there, smiling, brown, solid as an oak in the mossy jungle shadows. But somehow, instead of their usual vanilla scent, the orchids smelled like cinnamon. . . .

"Oh, Miss Farraday," murmured a deep, playful singsong, beguiling her to awaken. "Milady, your breakfast is served."

Reality pirouetted its way into her magical dream. The morning sunlight filtered through the cotton sheet that veiled her eyes.

That husky whisper came again: "There's chocolate here."

Her stomach growled in answer to the lovely smells floating through the thin layer of cloth.

Chocolate . . . and cinnamon?

Ahhh . . .

She was already smiling before she was even quite awake.

Drowsily inching the sheet down from her face, she peeked over the edge of it, and saw Jack sitting beside her on the edge of the bed, his arm braced possessively across her body.

By the soft, gold, rosy light of morning, the terror of the West Indies was watching her with a tender, slightly doting smile on his ruggedly handsome face.

"Jack!" she said softly, and sat up, clutching the bedsheet to her bosom.

He leaned near and kissed her cheek. "Good morning, sweet." He swept a gesture to the legged tray waiting on the bed. "May I present this celebratory breakfast in your honor."

"Goodness, I accept, but what are we celebrating?" she asked with a large yawn.

149

"The fever's broken. Peter Stockwell is awake, and more importantly, alive."

Her eyes widened. "Oh, thank God."

"Thanks, also, to you, my intrepid little doctor." He handed her a mug of hot chocolate without further ado.

She was thrilled by this rare luxury, glancing down into the cup, then at him again. "Is there sugar in it?"

"Lots."

She sipped of its sweet, dark comfort and let out an appreciative sigh.

"Let's see, what else have we got for you here?" he mused aloud. He reached toward the breakfast tray and lifted off the silver lid, revealing a glass of juice and a beautifully arranged plate of sliced ham, fresh grapefruit, and cinnamon rolls, still steaming warm, with raisins peeking out from underneath the white glaze that dripped down the flaky sides.

Tempted, Eden set her chocolate down, licked her lips, and picked up the cinnamon roll, taking a large bite. Jack's smile broadened at her amazed exclamations of delight. After years of taking care of Papa and Connor in the jungle, she could not remember anyone ever having made such a fuss over her.

She pushed the plate toward him. "You don't mean to make me eat all of this by myself?"

"Yes." He grinned with a flash of even, white teeth. "Every crumb."

She gave him a look of playful scolding and held up a cinnamon roll to his lips. He took a huge bite, and Eden ate the other half, then leaned forward, giggling as she chewed, and kissed him on the mouth.

"Mm." Jack swallowed, returning her playful peck as he reached for a sip of her chocolate. "That's good."

"I told you so."

"I meant your kiss." He set the cup aside and lifted the glass of juice out of her hand. Setting it on the tray, he gave her a hungry stare. "I want another."

Her pulse leaped with anticipation as he cupped his hand around her nape and gently drew her closer. She sighed softly as his lips caressed hers, melting into his embrace.

She had not realized how much she had been craving him and counting the hours since he had last reached for her. It seemed ages since she had last felt his arms around her, but it had only been two nights ago when he'd kissed her in his bed.

As she wrapped her arms around his neck and returned his kisses eagerly, he pulled her closer with an arm around her waist; his fingertips glided down her neck, the light touch causing her to shiver.

She knew she shouldn't want this, but she did.

She knew that it was dangerous, but she wasn't afraid.

As she stroked his smoothly shaved cheeks and the dark silk waves of hair, her world turned giddy spirals. She wasn't sure what was happening to them, but the exquisite pleasure they took in each other was something that neither of them had expected to find. It was a pleasure that was much more than physical.

"Good morning, Eden," he whispered, after a long moment of reveling in her response.

"Good morning, Jack." Her voice was a breathless purr.

Taking hold of the lapels of his unbuttoned waistcoat, she pulled him closer, smiling, and demanded more kisses.

He gave them happily, letting her hair tumble through his splayed fingers. His breathing was deepening; her whole body tingled as she ran her hand hungrily down his waist.

"I have to stop this," he ground out, dragging his lips away from hers.

"Why?" she breathed.

"Because I want you."

"Well?"

He shuddered and closed his eyes at her urgent whisper, leaning his forehead against hers. "Eden."

"Jack."

"You don't know what you're asking."

"Then why don't you show me?" She traced the curve of his ear with her lips. "I trust you, Jack. I've trusted you from the start."

"Aye, that's the problem."

Sitting back, she lifted his hand to her lips and kissed his fingertips. His face was taut, and the aqua hue of his eyes promptly darkened to the deepest blue. He watched her, fascinated, as she took the end of his middle finger into her mouth.

All of a sudden, he leaned in and captured her face between his hands, replacing his finger with the urgent stroke of his tongue. Her heart thundered. His fine mouth slid back and forth across

151

hers, coaxing her lips open wider. She knew the fundamentals of the mating dance, at least in theory, and he mimicked it now, with his tongue delving deep in her mouth.

Her chest was heaving when he finally ended the searing kiss.

"Lie back," he ordered in a husky murmur.

Without hesitation, holding his fevered stare, she obeyed.

He set the tray aside and moved onto the bed beside her, his every motion full of smooth control. He traced his middle finger slowly down the center of her body, letting it snag on the low-cut V of her shimmery sea-princess gown.

She looked at him in nervous curiosity as he slipped his hand inside her dress; but she closed her eyes and moaned when he squeezed her nipple. He kissed her chin while she reveled in the sensation, then flicked the corner of her lips with the tip of his tongue. She turned her head and devoured his offering of fresh kisses. Meanwhile, his hand left her bodice and traveled lower, down to her waist.

She wound her arms around his neck in wild anticipation when she sensed him discreetly inching her skirt up her thigh.

"Oh, Jack." She hugged him harder, her body on fire.

"May I?" he whispered, skimming his hand up beneath the gauzy blue fabric, his deft touch running slowly along her inner thigh.

Panting, Eden stared at him, unable to give her reckless yearning voice. *Touch me.*

He gave her a knowing half smile then bent his head to her throat, letting her frantic pulse beat against his lips. His questing fingers glided deep between her legs, exploring, caressing her, pleasuring her. She groaned, accepting his incursion in helpless yielding. Her limbs went lax, her knees weakened, and she let her thighs part in uncertain welcome.

"Tell me what you like," he whispered, but the power of speech was beyond her.

She liked it all. He kissed her shoulder like a man in a trance as he penetrated her with one and then two fingers, making her so hot and so wet she feared she was melting. She groaned, soon given over entirely to hot, craven lust.

Oh, *God,* yes, this was what she had burned for without even knowing it. She was entranced, could think of nothing but the power of his strong body enfolding her, and his clever hands taking her to places she had never been, had never dreamed existed. She wanted to visit all of those places with Jack.

He cradled her head with his other hand and teethed her earlobe lightly, his heavy breathing raspy by her ear. "Just let it happen, my love."

"Let what happen?"

"You'll see."

She moaned in helpless bliss as she held him close, one arm draped around his neck, the other hand clutching the covers. The fervent pleasure of his touch dazzled her, coaxed her ever closer toward some unknown cataclysm. She could do naught but trust him to take her there safely.

She wondered what was going to happen, like he said—and then all of a sudden, she knew.

"Jack!" she wrenched out as the blinding wave hit her, washing through her core with shattering power. She shuddered and arched and clung to him like a drowning woman, gasping in the rush of wild release.

Panting by her ear, he growled her name as her pleasure spilled over into deep, sweet currents of panting joy. He kissed her temple while the throes of bliss gradually eased.

For a moment, eyes closed, she brushed her cheek tenderly against his. "Oh, ... Jack."

Her ability to reason had returned—enough, at least, to deduce that he, too, had needs, and how fascinating it would be, she thought, to fulfill them.

All of her limbs felt like jelly, but she rallied the strength and the courage to reach down to offer him the same.

He flinched and stopped her before she could caress him through his black trousers. "Don't, sweet. It would be more than I could bear."

"But I want—"

"No, angel." He laughed softly, though his wince seemed pained. "Just relax. Trust me."

"I do," she whispered.

He let out a rueful sigh. "So it seems."

With a wide smile, she flung herself into his arms. They lay abed together for some time after that, Jack cradling her head on his chest, while his other hand, still trembling a little, trailed light caresses over her hair.

153

She sighed, smiling dreamily. Lord, if this was breakfast, she could barely wait to see what was for lunch.

At his desk later that afternoon, Jack was supposed to be going over the quarterly reports from the heads of each of his company's main divisions, making sure they all were following his orders properly, executing his decisions promptly, and not letting any of the details fall to the wayside, but his mood was restless.

It had turned into a fairly ordinary day, Trahern on deck in charge of the watch, the Nipper brushing Rudy in the corner. Peter Stockwell was still in recovery.

But Jack was distracted by his awareness of Eden hard at work on her sewing with Martin behind the painted screen in the corner. No, not so much distracted, he mused. Painfully randy. Completely frustrated. Bluntly speaking, in dire need of sex.

It was no longer a question of *should* he hold back, but *could* he?

This was torture.

Of course, he realized in hindsight that he had brought it on himself, from the first day he'd kissed her fifteen hundred miles ago, back in the jungle. Then he had sealed his fate by making her strip and take a bath in front of him. He supposed he deserved this torment now for underestimating her.

Her innocence was a weapon against which he had no defense, not for all his cannons, swords, nor all his Baker rifles.

But if he had to sleep beside her one more night without making love to her, he sincerely feared he was going to lose his mind. Yes, his control was slipping, but the most alarming part was that it wasn't just lust anymore; a very warm and simple affection for her was gathering strength in his heart.

Devil take her, all of this was utterly foreign to him. It was a most unsettling sensation. He was still in the dark, anyway, as to how a young stowaway from the cargo hold had become the queen of his ship.

The men were enchanted with her, Mr. Palliser spoke of her in tones of awe, and even Ballast had been won over. The surly gunner had whittled her a little porpoise out of a scrap of wood to show in his gruff way there were no hard feelings between them. The Nipper was now no more than twenty feet away from her at any given time, and even the dog seemed to prefer her to him.

As for Jack, he did not have a name for what he felt.

All of his sane, logical reasons not to bed her, when it was obviously what they both wanted, seemed to be wearing rather thin. It all seemed so simple: Bed her, marry her. He still needed heirs, of course, so that only left his fears to contend with.

The ones he liked to pretend did not exist.

There was so much she didn't know about him. So much that he couldn't tell her. But the more she came to matter to him, the less inclined he was to explain to her all of the ways in which he was unworthy.

No matter, he thought grimly. When she finally got to London, she'd hear.

On the other hand, when he thought of all she had been through, well, he could only wonder what all his strength and efficacy were for, if not for taking care of someone else? Someone exactly like her.

But she was not the kind of woman he'd ever had in mind for a wife. He had planned on some docile female who would not dare to venture anywhere near the locked doors inside him.

That in no way described Eden Farraday.

And yet, for all her courage and all her brains, and all her damned persistence, who knew better than he how vulnerable she was? How sheltered and naive? Who besides him could take care of her properly?

Aye, he was beginning to think this girl might need him, whether she knew it or not. Jack enjoyed being needed: It not only made him happy, it gave him a sense of control. What was a great deal more threatening, however, was considering the stark possibility that he might bloody well need her, too.

Now, *that* was a very dangerous state of affairs.

"Psst—Captain!" A playful whisper beguiled his attention over to the sewing corner.

He glanced over to find Eden peeking around the edge of the screen, her eyes sparkling. She held up two fabrics. "Which do you like better? The red wool or the dark green velvet?"

They had found more bolts of cloth that were supposed to have been sold in London.

A smile tugged at his lips, for it was plain to see she was having a marvelous time. "I have absolutely no idea."

"Oh, come. It's for a little spencer jacket," she explained eagerly. "What do you think?"

He shrugged, shaking his head. "Either one."

Her smile turned to a mild pout. "You must have a preference, Jack! You're the deciding vote. Martin and I can't agree."

His valet stood behind her, out of Eden's sight, pointing emphatically to the green. Well, it would match her eyes. Jack hid his smile and seconded the choice.

At once, Eden glanced suspiciously at Martin. His brief pantomime done, the valet looked at her, all innocence. Jack bent his head, suppressing a small laugh. His preference, in truth, was for her to wear nothing at all. . . .

The delectable image that bloomed in his mind at that thought was the final straw. He stifled a groan and pushed up from his desk, going out with a long-suffering growl to practice his fencing. The mental work was beyond his powers of concentration at the moment.

A bout of rigorous exercise ought to help him work off the frustration.

After Jack left, Eden remained in the day cabin working on the sleeve of her new walking dress. Martin was the next to hurry off to see to his regular duties, namely, ironing the captain's linen shirts down at the laundry. Eden did not mind the time alone, however, for her mind was much preoccupied.

Ever since their interlude this morning, strange thoughts about Jack had begun flitting through her brain. Though they had only known each other a short time, having had the chance to observe him in his natural habitat, as it were, she had noted much about the big fellow to love.

She was awed by the noble courage of his mission on behalf of the colonists battling for freedom—something not even his ducal father could do, as he had pointed out. Too, she was moved by the pain that she sensed in his silence on the subject of his family.

After watching him for a few days now, she was all the more impressed by his leadership, his care for his men, and his shrewd abilities, running his empire from that grand mahogany desk in the day cabin.

Given his ruthless reputation, she was shocked at how kind, even indulgent he had been to her, and she got the feeling he was a little shocked by it himself. Clearly, he didn't have to do any of this—feeding her, clothing her, sharing his cabin, protecting her from any possible threat from the crew.

Most of all, she was amazed at how easy it was to tell him her innermost thoughts, desires, and fears. His manner that night down in the sickbay had been so caring that she had even found the strength to relate to him the whole, upsetting tale of the Indian boy in the woods. He had been the very soul of kindness about it.

In sharp contrast to Connor, Jack made her feel so safe; and in contrast even to Papa, he *listened* to her. And so these unsettling questions had begun to revolve in her mind like so many seagulls circling the masts of an anchored ship.

She had set her sights long ago on dashing Town Corinthians in coats from Savile Row, but ever since Jack Knight had come sailing into her life, her shining visions had begun to feel a bit like gaudy childish fantasies. What if this man was her destiny? The true love that she'd have crossed the world to find?

She had stowed away to get to London, yes, but what if the journey turned out to be more important than the arrival at her destination?

Restless with her questions, she got up to take a break from her sewing, and stretched a bit. Rubbing her neck in mild fatigue, she glanced out through the weather-eye window and promptly spotted the captain engaged in fencing practice with tough old Mr. Brody and a few of the other officers.

Eden held her breath and stared.

Shirtless, his bronzed body rippling with muscle and gleaming with sweat in the golden daylight, Jack was taking on several opponents at once, while the sun sent blinding flashes off his wheeling sword.

She stood there motionless, awed by the sheer magnificence of the man and by the beauty of his deadly skill; riveted, she watched him deliver blows of massive power, swift, precise—and ruthless.

Mr. Brody called a halt and barked more instructions to the men arrayed against Jack. Unaware that he was being watched, Jack took a short break from his exertions, spilling water over his head, and taking a few swigs from his canteen.

Her gaze slipped down his glistening chest and abdomen, his regal physique inspiring her to wonder if and when she'd get the chance to pleasure him the way he'd done to her. She was certainly happy to try.

157

The Nipper marched toward him all of a sudden, wielding a play wooden sword. She could not hear what the wee cabin boy said, but he apparently felt it was his turn to practice with the captain.

Jack flashed the child a grin and picked up a nearby mop that one of the sailors had been using to swab the decks. He used the blunt wooden handle to parry the Nipper's blows.

Little Phineas Moynahan looked positively minuscule battling Jack for all he was worth, a merry David and Goliath match. After playing swords with the boy for several minutes, the big captain let the Nipper get a hit in and dropped his weapon, clutched his body, and pretended to die.

Down onto the decks he fell, playacting his demise.

A soft smile touched her lips as Eden watched the pair, transfixed.

Phineas cheered his own victory over the fallen giant, but when Rudy pounced on his master, licking his cheek, Jack shoved the dog away affectionately. He jumped up again, rumpled the boy's hair, and returned to his real practice.

Eden feared she had just fallen in love.

As a result, when Jack came marching in, his practice done, she couldn't stop blushing or gawking at the man. She tore her gaze away, her heart racing, and tried to focus on her work, but when she pricked herself with her sewing needle on account of the trembling in her hands, she could only wonder what in blazes was wrong with her. Why could she not act naturally around him all of a sudden? She had not had this problem before. She felt awkward and shy, transparent and smitten. If Jack noticed the change, he gave no sign. Oh, *stop* it, she ordered herself, clearing her throat.

"How was your practice?" she asked in what she hoped sounded like a nonchalant tone.

"Good, except I think I strained a hamstring."

She lit up. "I could make a poultice for you!"

Heading for the storage closet, he sent her a startled glance over his shoulder. "That's all right. Bit of a soak in the tub should cure me just fine."

The tub.

As he stepped into the closet to retrieve the bathing tub, her face turned scarlet with wildly improper notions.

But since it seemed plain that he wished to avoid temptation, she realized she had better go. Indeed, it suddenly occurred to her that after days of having her underfoot, the man might actually like some time alone. Cringing at the thought of how she had imposed on him, she put down her sewing at once, pulled on her light, newly made pelisse to ward off the wind, and headed for the door.

Jack looked at her in question.

"I'm sure you'd like to relax," she explained in a halting tone.

He looked a bit relieved that she did not intend to stay to help him bathe. Clearly, the man could not hold himself responsible for what might happen if she attempted such a thing.

"Remember to stay near Brody or Trahern."

"Aye-aye, Captain." She gave him a jaunty salute and then managed to walk into the wall as she realized her feelings for him were probably written all over her face. "Blast."

He furrowed his brow. "Are you all right?"

"Er, fine, thank you," she mumbled, flustered. "Well—good-bye, then."

"Good-bye, Eden," he murmured in a tone of bemusement.

As soon as she pulled the door closed behind her, she cursed herself for acting like a dolt, but at least she managed to compose herself again before stepping out onto the quarterdeck.

Outside, she spotted Mr. Trahern caught up in a chaotic bit of wrangling. One of the young sailors up on the mainsail yardarm had managed to make a tangle of some ropes, or rather, sheets, as the crew preferred to call them.

The lieutenant was in the midst of getting it all sorted out, so she turned aft to look for her other authorized guardian. On the elevated poop deck at the stern of the ship, she saw old Brody checking, cleaning, and putting away the array of weapons that Jack and the others had been using in their practice.

The fierce Mr. Brody, she mused, watching the leather-tough old warrior at his work for a moment. The master-at-arms was an intimidating hunk of gristle, but she had her orders, and besides, he seemed to be a favorite with Jack. She was curious to find out why.

With her mind made up to brave *The Winds of Fortune*'s renowned curmudgeon, she squared her shoulders, put on her best smile, and climbed the short ladder up to the poop deck, in the shadow of the mizzen-mast.

He eyed her suspiciously as he inspected the blade of one of the sabers. He gave the sharp steel an idle polish as she approached, tucking her blowing tresses behind her ear.

"Good day, sir. The captain is preoccupied in the day cabin. He told me to stay near you or the lieutenant if I walked out, and since Mr. Trahern appears to be busy, I thought I'd pester you." She beamed prettily at him, clasping her hands behind her back.

Brody scowled, squinted in Trahern's direction, and began grumbling under his breath. "Oh, busy, is he? Our fine lieutenant." A snort emitted from his half-flattened nose. "That young lie-about. Don't look busy to me. . . ."

Eden lifted her eyebrows at his querulous commentary. *Oh, dear.* No wonder the whole crew feared him. Not daring to venture another remark, she lowered her gaze and then made herself use-ful, helping him to put away the weapons.

"So," he muttered, "you're the stowaway."

"Guilty as charged," she admitted with friendly caution as she wiped one of the blades with the nearby cloth, sheathed the weapon, and handed it to him.

He harrumphed as he put it in the long wooden case. "Ain't a decent thing for a young lady to do, stowin' away."

Eden was taken aback. "Well, no. I suppose not. Still, I had my reasons."

"Aye, I'll bet you did." He thrust the button-shaped safety guard onto the point of the epee and tossed it, too, into the case. "Think you're mighty clever, don't you? Trickin' the lot of us. Stowin' away. And now ye got him eatin' out o' the palm o' your hand, don't ye? A pretty bit of business, in all, and very neatly done."

"Neatly done? Whatever do you mean, sir?"

"He's got a lot of money."

"So?" she retorted.

"Ye don't like shiny baubles? Fancy gowns? Fine houses? None o' that?"

She stopped and turned to him, propping her fist on her waist. "Exactly what are you implying?"

"Ha! Cap'n thinks ye wanted to get to England, see, but I think it was *him* ye wanted all along."

Her jaw dropped. "Mr. Brody. If you are actually suggesting that I did all this for the express purpose of trying to snare Lord Jack in matrimony, then I fear you are going quite senile and should not be handling weapons." She turned away in cold fury, her pride stung.

"Forgive my intrusion. I don't wish to trouble you further. If you'll pardon me, I will seek out Mr. Trahern."

"Bah." A low, gruff cackle rose behind her as she pivoted and began marching away. "Go have yourself a fine sulk, lassie. No matter. You ain't the first to try to catch him in your noose, and I sincerely doubt you'll be the last."

"I don't sulk," she said crisply, turning around with a warning glare.

But he wasn't through with her yet, taking her measure with a canny stare. "All you wicked women just want to get your claws in the lad, on account of his gold."

Eden narrowed her eyes. A hundred stinging retorts shot into her mind, but suddenly, through her outrage at his baiting insults, Eden realized Mr. Brody was merely trying in his own, hard-headed way, to protect Jack.

Loyalty was behind all this.

It dawned on her then that the old cudgel was testing her—trying to see, perhaps, if she was good enough for the captain.

Aha.

Though still offended, she decided to hold her ground. Retreat was surely the fastest way to fail in Mr. Brody's estimation. And for whatever reason, the old man obviously mattered to Jack.

She took a step toward him, refusing to be chased off. "He's a good fighter," she remarked, then tossed him a challenging look. "I suppose you're going to say you taught him everything he knows?"

Brody's leathery face cracked at last in a wary grimace of a smile, as though she had finally won a glimmer of approval from the old cuss by standing up to him. "Nay, Miss," he said. "I only train the lad. The natural talent he gets from his sire."

Well, this was much more like it.

"You knew his father, Mr. Brody?" she inquired in a civil tone.

"Knew him?" He snorted. "Went twenty-five rounds in the ring with him at the Oxfordshire matches of seventy-eight. Can't say I remember it much, though, on account o' the blows to the head." He let out a low chortle. "After that, though, the Killarney Crusher and I were the best o' mates."

"The Killarney Crusher?" Eden tilted her head and furrowed her brow in total confusion. Wasn't that the title of the boxing champion whose name was engraved on the trophy cup hidden away in

Jack's sea chest? "I thought his father was the Duke of Hawkscliffe."

Brody's deep-set eyes widened. He suddenly turned away with a stricken look. "Oh, bloody 'ell!" he muttered under his breath. "I've gone and done it now."

The next day, after yet another torturous night's denial in their shared bunk, Jack sauntered out onto the stern gallery in search of Eden. A part of him felt a bit silly seeking her out—wasn't he the man who claimed the favors of the women he wanted, then sailed on without a backward glance?

Ah, well. He was past trying to rationalize this to himself. He simply liked being near her, aye, and it made him feel all warm and peculiar inside to gather that she also liked being near him. Certainly, her innocence was new to him. All lust aside, it made a man feel whole and clean.

Some dark, guarded region of his innermost self was opening ever so slowly, like a clenched fist gradually being relaxed. He wasn't sure how it all worked, but he knew it was all her doing: the stowaway who had become his fair companion.

In truth, the strangeness of the changes she had wrought in him felt a bit shaky, but Jack had an instinct for survival, and he sensed that this was good for him.

She was good for him.

Stepping into the doorway that led out onto the shady gallery, he spotted her giving the Nipper a reading lesson.

Eden was seated on one of the outdoor chairs with the boy nestled close beside her, her arm around his skinny shoulders. They were using the Bible for their text. Jack realized abruptly it had never occurred to him to put any children's books on his shelves.

Charmed by the scene before him, Jack paused to lean in the doorway and watched for a moment, unobserved. A wry smile softened the lines of his face as he listened in on their lesson.

The teacher was a lovely thing in her new walking dress. It was long-sleeved and demure, made from the good sprigged muslin he had intended to bring to his sister. Her auburn hair was pinned up in a loose chignon with an array of little tendrils escaping around her face and her nape. It was very pretty, indeed, Jack thought. He had only seen her hair long and flowing until now; the coif made her look more mature and not so wild.

As for the Nipper, Jack noticed the kid looked tidier than normal. His hair was combed. His face was clean. He was actually wearing shoes. Why, he had never seen the little rapscallion behaving himself with such docile sweetness.

The wee pupil was trying very hard to please "Miss Edie" with his efforts; never having had a mother of his own, Jack could well imagine that the child was in raptures just to have her attention. Perhaps sensing this need in him, Eden praised him lavishly for every word he got right, doling out encouragement in equally generous doses.

Jack stared at them intensely, his arms folded across his chest.

"Reev . . . rev . . . ell . . ."

"That's good. You can do it. Sound it out."

"Revel . . . ations," the Nipper said slowly, then looked up at her with a grin.

"Excellent, Phinney!" She tousled his hair and gave him a little congratulatory hug. "My goodness, you learn fast!"

Her praise fired his enthusiasm to take on the next paragraph. Jack watched her watching Phineas and listening to his efforts with a fond, tender smile, stroking his hair now and then and murmuring to him to take it slowly, concentrate; the boy struggled along as best he could, following the lines of text with his grubby finger.

The whole of this scene turned Jack's reflections inevitably back to his longstanding need for an heir.

He had always wanted sons, but as he watched Eden and recalled her devotion to her father, he thought it would be a fine thing to have daughters, too. Sons could run his company, keep it solid, expand it to the ends of the earth, ah, but daughters would take care of him when he was weak and forgetful in his dotage.

Truly, watching the woman and child now, Jack had to admit that maybe his separate way of life for all these years was not for the best. He could look in through the window, as it were, and *see* there was a warmth in being associated with others in a deeper way. But a lifetime of wary isolation could not be undone in a day.

On the other hand, he thought slowly, these children of his were not simply going to appear out of thin air.

His lust for Eden returned all of a sudden with shocking ferocity.

Just marry the chit and get her with child. You can worry about the rest later.

163

She glanced over at that moment, as though she felt his predatory stare; she looked into his eyes and sent him an intimate smile.

The boy now noticed him standing there, leaped up from his seat, and ran to him. "Cap'n Jack!"

"Fair weather, Mr. Moynahan. I see you're getting practice with your reading."

"I better go check on Rudy!" the Nipper blurted out, as though suddenly struck shy.

Eden peered after her pupil in amusement as he went tearing off through the day cabin in search of his canine playmate.

Jack looked at her and smiled. "Lesson's over?"

"It appears so." She chuckled, closing the Good Book and setting it on the low table. Then she rose and walked toward him. "Frankly, I'm surprised he lasted as long as he did. It's not easy for a little fellow his age to pay attention."

Jack gazed into her eyes as she came and leaned in the doorway opposite him. "It's kind of you to look after him."

"Pish. One's got to pass the time somehow."

"What do you make of his abilities?" he inquired. "Stockwell tutors the boy from time to time, but on the whole, his education is sadly neglected."

She shrugged. "He seems very clever to me. You *do* realize, by the way, that this child idolizes you?"

"Well, everyone does, hadn't you noticed?"

She laughed at his droll remark.

Jack smiled, scoring himself one point for the old Irish charm. "I try to be a good example for him," he admitted in a more serious tone. "Give a little guidance now and then. Teach him how to be a man."

"Where's his real father?"

"Nobody knows, poor little mite. He was abandoned as an infant. Left on the front steps of a church with nothing but the blanket he was wrapped in. Not even a name. An older lady I employ, the housekeeper at my property in Ireland, Mrs. Moynahan, she took him in," he explained. "But the boy's rambunctious, as you've no doubt noticed, and as he got bigger, he became too much for her. The lady likes things orderly."

"Ah. So, you took him next?"

He nodded. "At least he knew who I was from my occasional visits to the property. I made him my cabin boy so I could keep an eye on him and make sure he was learning a trade. He'll make a fine sailor one day. Still, it's a damned hard thing for a helpless youngster, being abandoned like that. Not wanted." Jack frowned in the direction the Nipper had gone. "Honestly, in your . . . feminine opinion, do you think he's all right?"

A softness crept into her green eyes, a tender smile for his worry. "I think he's just fine. But—a little lonely, perhaps. Contact with other children would do the boy a world of good."

"Yes, but—" He looked out to sea in vague distress. "Don't you think they'd be cruel to him, push him away, on account of his having no father? No name?"

She stared at him for a long moment with a compassionate gaze that seemed to see right into his soul. "I suppose a few might. But why would he want to be friends with those children anyway, when others will be happy to accept him for exactly who he is? It isn't as though his origins are the boy's fault," she added. "He has nothing to be ashamed of."

"No." Jack fell silent, lowering his gaze. "What about you, Miss Farraday?" he murmured after a moment. "Do you want to have children?"

"What, with you?"

He looked at her in surprise and found a teasing twinkle in her eyes and a saucy smile on her lips.

He arched an eyebrow, shooting her a droll look. "Yes, actually. Right now. Shall we get started?"

"Jack!" she scolded, blushing crimson.

"I'm jesting," he lied in a husky murmur, gazing at her with a heated glow in his eyes and a pulsing in his groin. "You are good with him, though."

"So are you," she said softly.

"You didn't answer my question. Do you ever intend to have children someday?"

"Oh, loads!" she exclaimed, lightening the mood again with her airy manner. "A dozen, at least."

"Really? A litter?"

"My aunt Cecily has eleven. One of her friends has got sixteen." He let out a low whistle.

"The more the merrier, I say."

"Sounds painful for the ladies."

"Not if you're healthy. Besides, it's what my mother would have wanted. A brood of grandchildren. She was always so disappointed she could have only one child—me—though she swore on her life that I was so wonderful in every imaginable way that no other child in the world could ever have compared, so it was just as well, or she'd have forgotten to feed it."

He grinned, wondering what it was like to be adored like that by one's parents.

"For all that," she added, "I can't help but feel that if Papa had a few grandchildren, it might draw him back out into the world again instead of hiding away like a hermit."

"*Or* he might try to drag the lot of you into the jungle. Ever think of that?"

"Won't work. I survived, and it wasn't all bad, but I would never allow my child to be raised the way I was."

"Nor would I," he agreed quietly. As her probing gaze homed in on him much too shrewdly, Jack felt the sudden need for a change of subject. "You look very pretty today, Miss Farraday." He lifted her hands to his lips and kissed them both.

"You like my new gown?"

"Indeed, I'm entirely pleased with my investment. However—" Still holding her hands, he tugged her toward him gently. "I should like to collect my dividends, if you don't mind. Whatever small sum you see fit to return to me at this time."

"Hmm," she purred as he took her gently into his arms. "I suppose the board could agree to a modest dispensation." She slid her hands up his chest and clasped them behind his neck with an arch and slightly flirtatious smile.

"Ah, Eden," he murmured as she tilted her head back, offering her lips. "You captivate me." The words escaped him before he could stop them.

"Why, Jack!" she whispered in a breathy tone full of pleasure. "For that, I shall pay you back with interest."

And she did, cupping the back of his head as she kissed him for all she was worth. Her artless passion took his breath away. It was a kiss that a fortune in gold could not buy, a kiss like those in the fairy stories with the power to break curses. Jack did not think he had ever been kissed like this before, with her whole heart in it. All the women before her faded into mere phantoms, so many dissolving wisps of smoke.

Ah, heaven. Gathering her closer, it would have been absurd to

166

deny that this girl was already connected to him more deeply than any previous involvement—even Maura, in the farthest reaches of his past.

The first love who had sold him down the river. No, this was nothing like that. And Eden was nothing like *her.*

On a sudden wild impulse, he was teetering—actually teetering on the verge of asking Eden to marry him—but ending her earth-shaking kiss, she spoke first.

"Jack?"

"Mmm?" he murmured, a little drunk from her sweetness.

She took his hands in hers and held them as she retreated a step and leaned back against the doorframe, mirroring his stance.

Gazing at her, he was amused to see her cheeks flushed and rosy, her moist, shiny lips still aglow. She spoke slowly, dreamily. "When we get to London . . ."

"Yes?" Her words jarred him a bit out of desire's haze with the guilty reminder that she still did not suspect his true plans for her.

"Do you expect to visit your family during your stay?"

"My family?" Ah, his favorite subject. His faint smile tensed.

"You *do* have family, don't you?"

"What makes you think that they'd like to see me?" He slipped his hands out of hers and put them in his pockets. "Did I mention I've got that ache in my knee that always means bad weather's on the way?"

"Jack, don't change the subject."

He rolled his eyes. "Eden—"

"There's something that I have to tell you." Her face was set; desire's blush had dimmed in her cheeks. "I read your sister's letters."

He froze. *"What?"*

"That first day you found me on the ship, when you locked me up in your cabin. I was bored, Jack. There was nothing to do. I found them and I-I got engrossed," she said with a penitent shrug.

He stared at her, appalled.

"I know it was wrong, and I'm sorry—but the point is this. From everything your sister wrote, I'm sure your family loves you. You should see them again when we reach London. Try to make things right."

"Make . . . things right?" he echoed in utter shock, which

167

promptly turned to fury. "You are *unbelievable!* And for your information, I am not the one who made things wrong!"

"I never assumed that you were!" she assured him. "Jack, I'm only trying to help. Whatever bad blood lies between you and your siblings, I don't want to see you let it ruin your life."

"Ruin my life? Don't be absurd!" He scoffed. "My life, it so happens, is better than most people's wildest fantasies. Do you know how much I'm worth?"

"I'm not talking about your money, I'm talking about *you.* I think I know what you're worth, Jack. The question is, do you?"

He turned away with a low curse, but she persisted, tenacious as ever.

"Is that why you work so hard, because you think you are worth nothing without all your wealth and power?"

"Leave me alone. This conversation is tedious." His tone was merely irked, but inside he was trembling. "I can't believe you read my private correspondence." He pinned her with an angry glance. "I trusted you."

"I wanted to know more about you, that's all. Jack, I could have concealed what I did, you know, but look how I told you flat out. You *can* trust me. I'm concerned about you. You have a problem and I want to help."

"I don't have a problem and I don't need your help. I don't need anybody's help. Never have." He glared at her. "Never will."

She took an impatient step toward him. "I want you to hear what I have to say: Stop wasting *time.*"

"What are you talking about?"

"They're your family, Jack. If I had one more day with my mother, I would pay a king's ransom for that, but I can't. She's gone. And someday, you're going to know how that feels."

"Well, I was never adored by my family as you were, and you're never going to know how *that* feels!"

She dropped her gaze and let out a low exhalation eloquent of a feminine struggle for patience. "I just don't want to see you end up alone."

He let out a rude bark of a laugh and turned away from her. "Why not? I'm used to it! Gets a little dull sometimes, perhaps, but at least this way no one can stab me in the back."

"Is that what happened?" she asked softly. "Did someone betray you?"

"Stay out of it, Eden. It's none of your affair."

"Maybe you're afraid that I'll betray you, too. But I won't, Jack, I promise. I can prove it, if you'll give me a chance. Talk to me."

No, he realized in reluctance, he did not feel that Eden would stab him in the back. But he still didn't want to tell her anything. *Did he?*

He swallowed hard, his heart pounding violently. He closed his eyes with a faint wince. He never explained himself to anyone. Certainly, he had never attempted to explicate how he had sacrificed himself for his brothers and his little sister. To this day, nobody even realized. *To hell with them.*

"Jack?"

"In a family at war," he said slowly, his back to her, "the rest can make peace if one becomes the scapegoat. A common enemy against whom the others can rally." His face was stony. "I became their villain. A damned lightning rod for all the wrath and anger under that roof—it all came down on me. I was the only one strong enough to bear it. But after a time, I got lost in the role." With his back to her, she could not see his taut grimace. She could never know how alone he had been in that house. Nay, in that world. Shunned by all. "Finally, I knew I had to leave." He thought of Maura. Her petty betrayal. "There was no reason left for me to stay."

He heard the rustle of her skirts as she edged closer. "But that's just it, Jack. You're not a villain. You may have convinced the world of that and even yourself by now, but you never fooled me. Not for a second." He felt her light touch on his back—so gentle it made him flinch. A blow would have been easier to take. "I felt drawn to you from the first moment I saw you at the ball in Jamaica. I think Papa sensed the way I noticed you. That's why he pulled me away. He didn't want to lose me to you. You see, Jack, I've got very good instincts. Maybe I don't know much about the way of the world, but I know my own heart. And it tells me that behind these dark fictions you've raised up around yourself, you are one of the . . . the kindest, noblest human beings I've ever known."

He pulled away and whirled around with a glower. "The hell I am!"

"It's true." Her eyes were huge and full of light; her youthful face was somber.

He backed away from her. "And you've met a total of, what—eight, nine human beings in your entire life, hidden away out there in the jungle?" he bit out sarcastically. "Don't tell me about instincts. It's experience that counts, and the more experience you gain, my love, the more you'll see the jungle's everywhere." He shook his head. "This life is nothing but a struggle to survive. Well, guess what? Surviving is the one damned thing I'm good at. And you, you don't know bad when you see it, because all you've got in you is good. That's all you're able to see because you're looking at everything through the crystal-clear prism of who you are, Eden. But all of your purity cannot make me good."

She was staring at him with tears in her eyes. "You learned to believe in a lie a long time ago, Jack, a lie you still believe to this day."

"Ah, so I am deceived?"

"In a sense, yes." She blinked her tears away. "Everything that you just said is rubbish. You are good. What kind of a man risks his freedom and his whole life's work to help the cause of freedom? A villain? Who sends twelve shiploads of food and water to a city ravaged by an earthquake? Who takes a naive stowaway under his wing and protects her instead of treating her as she deserves? You are no villain, and I will not tolerate you speaking about yourself that way again."

"Oh, well, pardon me."

"I know now why you steer clear of humanity—"

"Have you looked at humanity lately?"

"You sound like Papa."

"Except that I'm sane."

"I can only imagine what you were subjected to when you were the Nipper's age that made you believe these things, but I would never treat you that way. You must know that."

"I could comment if I had any idea what in Lucifer's name you were talking about."

"Jack—I know about your father."

His next sarcastic comment withered on his tongue.

He felt as though he had just been run through with a lancer's pike, but while his face drained of every drop of color, she charged on.

"I understand now why you think everyone's against you, why you're so angry. Why you keep to yourself and don't trust anyone. All those locks on your door, oh, my darling . . ."

He backed away from her, shocked and rather horrified that she'd heard of his mongrel origins. Reading the letters was one thing. But this was something else. He knew what came next.

170

He knew.

From experience.

"Don't be angry. I'm on your side, Jack. It doesn't matter to me, your parentage. Please, I only want to help. Is that the reason you weren't allowed to wed Lady Maura?"

At that traitor's name, the one person he had believed for a while had really cared about him back in those days, the past rushed back like a swarm of bats, flapping around him with tittering ghoulish laughter at all he'd accomplished for the past twenty years, reducing it to nothing. Negating in the blink of an eye all his efforts to show them he'd make something of himself, after all.

No, these memories could only remind him that he'd always be the Irish bastard, nothing more, not fit to associate with his own brothers. A bad influence. No good.

No good to the core.

"Jack?" Eden whispered, and through the wave of pain, he was dimly aware of her staring at him in alarm.

All of a sudden, he let out a deafening roar that shook the glass in the stern windows. With a violent motion, he swept the contents off his desk—charts and papers, pencils and ledger books crashed chaotically onto the floor.

Eden watched them fall, then looked at him in wide-eyed fright.

Her fear grounded him once more in what he was. Why should he fight it? The darkness in him was always there. It made him good at what he did.

The crew above must have heard his howl, too, for the usual beat of footsteps across the deck halted.

Jack prowled toward her, his expression black.

Eden looked terrified, but his little jungle redhead held her ground even when he leaned down to glare in her face.

"Who told you?"

She gulped, bending back a bit. "He didn't mean to, Jack. I—it just slipped out."

His eyes narrowed to angry slashes. "Brody."

"He spoke of you only in pride, I swear! Jack—" She touched his cheek, but he knocked her hand away.

"Don't touch me."

Without another word, he pulled away and walked out.

CHAPTER
∞ TEN ∞

More days passed.

If there was any way to make the ship go faster, Jack would have left Eden at his Irish estate and simply let her drop out of his life, sailing away on his mission.

But there was not.

He was stuck with her in a cramped cell in the middle of an endless ocean. There was nowhere to escape from her, and nowhere to escape from his bleak certainty that no one was ever going to love him, no matter how rich he got or how many companies he owned; and no matter how many times he told himself that he didn't give a damn, it was always going to hurt.

As *The Winds of Fortune* crept higher into the north latitudes, autumnal temperatures above the equator gave way to winter, cold and gray.

They'd be there soon.

Eden was having a terrible time with her sewing. As night descended, the winter's early twilight encroaching, she worked by candlelight in the stateroom, seated on the red leather window bench. Her hands were wobbly with the needle until she even pricked her finger.

"Ow!" She threw her work down, popped her finger in her mouth, and noticed herself feeling seasick.

She assumed at first that the ill, shaky feeling in her stomach was due entirely to being upset over her fight with Jack, who had barely spoken to her since his explosion. Without his friendship, the sea had become a very desolate place. He had taken to sleeping in a hammock in the stateroom, leaving Eden to lie awake alone in his berth, fearing to contemplate what could happen to her in this elemental shipboard world with her protector angry at her. But when she heard the low whistling of a draft blowing in through the cracks around the closed jib door, and noticed the fine brandy sloshing about in its crystal decanter atop the mahogany cabinet, she realized there might be another explanation for her touch of mal de mer.

Turning to gaze out the bank of stern windows, her breath formed steam on the glass; she saw that the wind had picked up and the sea had turned choppy. Whitecaps showed here and there atop the dark waves. Farther out, the indigo line of the horizon see-sawed a bit more distinctly. The ship was so big that its rocking most of the time was nominal, but now she could feel its motion. Perhaps they were in for a gale.

Wonderful. A storm brewing outside, and a human hurricane at the helm, cold and dark and unpredictable . . .

That man.

She considered going topside to ask the captain what was happening, but on second thought, that sounded like a recipe for more hurt, since he clearly wasn't speaking to her anymore—even though she had said she was sorry. Even though she had only been trying to help.

With a sigh, Eden leaned against the wooden bulkhead and drew her slippered feet up onto the leather bench, wrapping her arms around her bent knees.

She was a little angry at him for being angry at her. Perhaps it was time to revisit her visions of dashing Town dandies in coats from Savile Row. Elegant men. Cultured men.

Pirate-barbarian-beasts who yelled in her face had never been part of the plan.

Still, it was strange to think that under that façade of rock-hard invulnerability, Black-Jack Knight was exactly what she had said he was from the start: a big, howling lion beset by a nasty thorn in his sensitive paw pad.

Why, he's just a big baby, she thought in simmering mutiny, especially when she recalled the day he had first found her aboard his vessel and had forced her to strip. Oh, not for lascivious reasons, she understood now.

The man was, sadly, expert at controlling his lust. He had given the order because he had known it would symbolically reduce her to complete vulnerability—and why should he want that? she thought. Because he trusted no one. Not even a harmless stowaway.

He had wanted her naked before him in every sense of the word, not just physically, but mentally, emotionally, as well. He had wanted to stare into the deepest regions of her soul, and she had let him—*Why?* she thought again. *Because I have nothing to hide.*

Ah, but let her get a peek at *him* without his steely armor on, that tough, bad, need-nobody aura of his, and *this* was how he behaved. Thundering at her and slamming about like a huge, terrifying barbarian.

Just then, a pattering of footfalls reached her from beyond the stateroom's door. The Nipper burst in. "Miss Edie! Miss Edie! Up on deck! Quick, hurry!"

"Phineas, what is the matter?"

Barreling over to her, the boy grabbed her hand. "Come on, hurry, I'll show you!"

"Let me get my pelisse—"

"No, you'll miss it!" He was already pulling her out of her seat. "Come on!"

Befuddled by the child's clamor, she let the Nipper tug her outside, but the moment she stepped onto the quarterdeck, she stopped in her tracks.

"Look!" The boy pointed, but Eden was already staring up at the sails in amazement.

Against a black and moonless sky with a wisp of fog, an eerie blue light danced along the spars and coated all the ship's sails.

She stared at it, frightened yet mesmerized.

The ghostly illumination was as bright as lightning, but clung to the canvas, hanging stationary, only wafting on the night's haze.

With a glow like blue flame, its brilliance illumined the humble faces of the crewmen on deck who were virtually silent with awe, marveling at the phenomenon.

Some blessed themselves with the sign of the Cross while others took off their caps and clutched them to their chests in superstitious reverence.

Then she noticed something else. The strong wind of a mere quarter hour ago had stopped.

They were becalmed.

Looking around, she spotted Jack standing near the mizzen

174

mast, his head tilted back as he, too, gazed at the unearthly lights. He was very still, his angular features bathed in the strange blue glow.

For a moment, Eden stared at the rugged captain of *The Winds of Fortune,* looming a head taller than all of his devoted crew. Drawn to him, she climbed the ladder to the poop deck and walked toward him, ignoring the fact that he was angry at her. She had to be near him in this moment, she knew not why. Perhaps to share in the miracle with him. Perhaps fear of the unknown phenomenon drove her to his side, seeking him out for the instinctual sense of protection that she always felt when he was near.

As she strode toward him, she detected a strange charge of electricity fairly crackling in the air, like the change in atmosphere that came before a tempest. It made the hairs on her arms and nape rise, but the pounding of her heart was entirely due to Jack's presence.

He seemed unaware of her study. Warmly dressed to ward off the elements, he wore a thick brown corduroy coat with a woolen scarf wrapped around his neck, his hands encased in a pair of heavy work gloves. The dark scruff on his jaw was growing back in, giving him once again that rough edge that she secretly found irresistible.

Indeed, she hesitated, for at the moment he looked as large, remote, and forbidding as a rocky island in the middle of a cold, cold sea. He looked so hard, so tough, and so alone, she thought, though he stood in the middle of his crew. His expression was closed and guarded, his mouth a firm, unsmiling line. Then he looked over and noticed her there.

He stared at her as she approached with cautious steps; seeing the stony look in his eyes, a small corner of her heart despaired. Even if she gave him everything she had, she would probably never really reach this man, never make him stay.

In his own way, he had isolated himself from the world as thoroughly as Papa had. Papa had the jungle; Jack had the sea. Papa had science; Jack had work. Her father had turned his back on civilization because it had destroyed the woman he loved; Jack kept humanity at arm's length, coolly rejecting the world before it rejected him.

That had to be why he had gotten so angry, she concluded as she held his stare. He must have thought that she, too, would reject

175

him on account of his bastardy. Those scars clearly ran deep. Rejecting Jack, however, was the farthest thing from her mind.

Closing the distance between them with slow, measured paces, Eden faced facts: She wanted to be with this man. So badly that it shook her. But even if he would have her, after coming all this way in her journey, how could she even contemplate linking herself to a husband who would only drag her along into his lonely exile, just like Papa?

She could imagine it now—life as Lady Jack Knight. Sailing across the globe from port to port. Never settling down. No solid home. No normal life. They would be nomads.

Rootless.

But at least I would be with him, she thought bravely.

Jack Knight, in all his dark, flawed glory.

He said nothing as she joined him. He merely reached into his coat and took out a cheroot. Though he put it in his mouth, as usual, he didn't light it. Cap'n Jack loved his cigars, but he allowed no smoking on the ship—after all, her hull was made of wood.

She looked up once more at the strange floating illumination. "What is it?" she whispered.

"Saint Elmo's Fire."

"But what is it, where does it come from?"

"Nobody knows." Jack looked at her warily in the darkness.

"It's wondrous," she breathed. As she tilted her head back to study the weird blue light, she could feel him staring at her.

Then his voice reached her, low and deep. "They say the chance to experience it only comes along once in a lifetime."

She was afraid to look at him. "R-really?"

"Aye." He, too, stared up at the sails in guarded nonchalance. "Conditions have to be just right. Even then, it never lasts."

"Oh." Her heart was pounding, but his final words had left her slightly crushed. "I-it doesn't last?"

"Not for me."

A slight shift of the rocking deck set her slightly off balance; Jack steadied her, and the strange lightning seemed to leap between them.

She glanced up at him, mumbling her thanks as the spectral glow enshrouded them; she found him staring at her like a man who was stuck inside himself and didn't know how to get out.

176

She held his gaze with a lump in her throat, but she knew it was now or never. She had to let him know how much she cared.

"Jack," she whispered. "I realize you're embarrassed I found out about your father—"

"Embarrassed?" he echoed with a low, bitter laugh.

It stung her. "I thought it might help if I told you something embarrassing about me."

A skeptical pause. "Like what?"

"That night we tended Peter Stockwell together, and I told you about how I yearned for so long to go to London. Remember, I said I wanted to take part in all the pleasures of the Season?"

He nodded.

"I'm afraid I wasn't entirely honest with you about why."

He slanted her a piercing look of question. The sharp, cool suspicion on his face left no doubt that his immediate assumption was some unworthy ulterior motive on her part.

"I couldn't come out and say it that night when we were talking because I didn't want you to think me a fool. But, Jack, the real reason I was so desperate to take part in the Season is simply because I-I wanted to find a husband. But not just any husband. Oh—blazes, this isn't coming out right." Her cheeks flamed.

Jack watched her with a look of fascinated distrust.

"The true reason I wanted to go back to civilization was to find—someone to love," she forced out before she lost her nerve. "Only, I-I think I may have already found him."

He stared fiercely at her.

Eden held his gaze, her heart pounding. She shivered in the cold, more naked now in her walking dress than she had been when he had ordered her to strip.

He looked away almost angrily.

Why doesn't he say something? I practically told him I loved him. Oh, God, why couldn't I keep my mouth shut?

Unable to bear his damning silence, she scanned the sails, wishing any passing whale might leap up and swallow her. "So, er, why is it called Saint Elmo's Fire?"

"Patron saint of sailors," he mumbled, avoiding her gaze just as studiously as she avoided his.

She suddenly frowned. "Is it dangerous? Could it not set the sails on fire?"

"No. Nothing like that. It is an omen," he added in a low tone.

"Of what?" At last, she forced herself to turn to him.

His shrewd gaze scanned the dark skies. "Storm." Even as he uttered the ominous word, the blue glow began to fade, gone in another heartbeat.

The night sky turned to black.

"Barometer's been dropping all day," he added.

The reverent hush lingered all around the decks; the men watched the sky in silence, waiting to see if it might come back.

Instead, the wind returned, rising with eerie speed. With a burst of frigid air, it warned them all of its malicious intent, aggressively flapping the sails.

"Comin' up fast, Cap," the quartermaster called. "She'll be a gale soon."

Jack sent the man a terse nod, then turned cautiously to Eden. "You should get below. Take the boy and stay out of the wind. We have to make our storm preparations. If it gets bad—and it could, this time of year—Martin will show you down to the lubbers' hold. It's the safest spot on the ship."

"Where will you be?" she asked anxiously.

"Up here," he replied, looking around at the decks. Then he glanced at the sails. "Up there, too, if it comes to it."

"Jack—be careful."

"Don't worry. We face foul weather on every trip." He started to walk away. "Tell the Nipper to put the dog in his cage, too, will you? Rudy hates storms. We've got a crate for him. The boy knows where it is."

One of his men called to him.

"I'll be right there!" he yelled back. The wind ran through his hair as he angled his chin downward to meet her gaze intently.

They stared at each other for a long moment.

"Go on," he murmured, nodding toward the quarterdeck.

Eden lowered her gaze, abashed at being dismissed like this after her reckless confession. She had practically told him she was in love with him, and it had made no visible impact on the man whatsoever. Well, she didn't wish to get in the way. Feeling a very naive and hopeless fool, she pivoted and strode back belowdecks to collect the Nipper and the captain's dog.

Jack remained where he stood a moment longer, watching her walk away.

*

All through the onyx night, the storm had chased them, churning closer, bearing down until Jack decided they could not outrun this March lion and gave the order to drop anchor.

He had hoped the gale might blow itself out if he could stay ahead of it, but it was moving over the water at a wicked clip. They were going to have to stand and brace to take their lashes, battening down the hatches and taking in most of the sails.

Jack fought the storm even as he fought himself, the ugly weather mirroring the confused currents tossing and clashing inside of him. He knew he had a choice to make. Either he could go on fighting this—denying it—the ever strengthening bond between him and Eden. Or he could try to believe that someone could actually love him.

Him.

Not his money. Not his power. Not his flesh.

The man within.

God knew the chit was daft enough to brave it, too innocent to know any better, unsullied by the world. Eden did not look at things like other people did, so perhaps it was no wonder that she saw him in a different light.

All Jack knew was that she was the only woman on whom he could ever imagine risking his heart again, baring his soul.

A creature of such purity would not hurt him, surely.

But it was so hard to believe that, given the life he had led. All those years when he had been the Nipper's age and smaller, inexplicably rebuffed by the duke he had thought was his father.

Disregarded even by the servants who were supposed to be seeing to his needs—nurse, governess, tutor. They knew where their bread was buttered; his brother Robert had been treated like a little prince, while Jack might as well have bedded down in the stable.

The worst, though, was being treated by his mother as though he didn't exist. The scandalous duchess had been ashamed of her lewd dalliance with the Irish gladiator—at least for a while, until her next escapade. Her second son had been nothing but a constant reminder of her fall from grace.

That was to say nothing of the merciless way he had been treated by the boys at school, who had known of his true parentage before he did, thanks to their parents' gossip. It had been a hard way to find out that he was a bastard. But at least it had explained why the neighbors had looked down on him for what he was—including Maura's parents, Lord and Lady Griffith.

And so, from these many sources, it had been ingrained in him from an early age to expect cruelty and indifference from the human race, and to guard against it—always.

He relied on himself, no one else, accruing fortune and power as if these alone could ensure a secure place for him in the world. On those lonely nights now and then when he ached with the need merely to have somebody to hold, he looked around for a girl whose face and figure he liked, and he paid her well for her time.

It seemed insane even to think about actually trusting again. But he knew if he ever found the courage, his choice would be Eden Farraday. Aye, he could either turn back or go deeper.

He hadn't liked her prying into his past, but on the other hand, she didn't really understand what he had been through. How could she know how cruel Society could be, raised as she had been in the wilderness, so sheltered from man's inhumanity to man?

She had never been exposed to the ton's little cruelties and he sincerely hoped she never had to learn them firsthand. God only knew what she'd hear people saying about him if and when she ever got to London.

Even if he made her his own, she might be condemned to share his fate as an outcast. . . .

The storm raged on throughout the night, a dark, cold battle outside Jack and in him, too.

When dawn came, its hard pewter light revealed leaden skies and waves like mountains on all sides. But the fight, he saw, was far from over. Indeed, it was only then that the storm unleashed its full icy wrath, battering them from directly overhead—a beast of sixty knots with periods of even stronger gusts lasting up to five minutes each.

"Heave to!" Jack bellowed, his thick coat, hat, gloves, and scarf all soaked through, while his long, hooded oilskin flapped noisily in the gale.

His face was numb from the bitter cold. Driving rain had turned to wet, stinging snow, reducing visibility to nothing. Fury, however, kept him warm as whipping wind and towering seas tried to swallow his ship whole.

The Winds of Fortune groaned as she pitched and rolled heavily, facing the storm under shortened sail. A couple of reefed topsails

flew aloft to try to steady her, but soon her stay sails were shredded to ribbons. From there, they rode out the storm under bare
poles.

Her anchors dug into the depths like the fingers of a person
clawing for purchase on the edge of a cliff. He knew they had
already been driven off course. Tomorrow he could figure out
where the hell the wind had blown them to—if it was over by then.

Sheets of water sloshed across the deck, swells a few feet deep
splashing in through the forward gun port. Still more water poured
in over the leeward rail. He saw that some of the hawse holes had
come unplugged and roared at the men to plug them up again.

"This damned weather is getting the best of 'er pump, Cap'n!"
the quartermaster yelled over the storm's howling as he received
the report from belowdecks.

"Tell the carpenters to get down there and check for any leaks!"

"Aye, sir!"

"We got to get the spars down!" he ordered grimly. "They're
putting too much pressure on the masts. Strike the topgallant and
topsail spars!"

The quartermaster and the bosun exchanged a grim glance, but
they, too, knew it had to be done.

"Aye, sir!"

The bosun relayed the order, and the bravest of his tars got their
tools together and dutifully began climbing the shrouds.

Jack hated with all his heart to send any of his men aloft in this.
Disassembling the spars from the masts was backbreaking work,
even without the wind trying to peel a man off the rigging, and the
foot-lines he stood upon coated with ice.

But if they didn't take those huge, heavy yardarms down, they
risked being dismasted. The violent pitching of the ship was making all three of his masts bend. They had been massive trees once,
after all, and could give somewhat in the wind, but the mighty
crossbeams of the spars added so much weight to the top portions
of the masts that they could snap in half and come crashing down
on them. If that happened, they all would then be at the mercy of
the cold Atlantic.

Watching his sailors ascend slowly and carefully much in contrast to their usual carefree speed, Jack could not have been more
proud of his crew. He stared at them as the weather dripped down
his face.

181

Any captain's heart would have lifted to see his men working in splendid unison, neat as clockwork, stout-hearted and very well trained. They held their posts without flinching or complaint; if one got into trouble, the nearest few rushed to help. No man, after all, could stand alone against the weather and the sea.

As he watched them, Higgins lost his footing and dangled for a moment over the decks, but the two men near-est him grabbed him and pulled him back onto the slick shrouds.

Jack exhaled slowly, his heart pounding. By God, he would not lose a single man to this bloody storm.

Scowling at the tossing sea, he strode across the quarterdeck and took the wheel himself, relieving the helmsman. He threw his full weight against it, refusing to let the wild waters take control of the rudder.

Gritting his teeth, he held it steady 'til his arms shook. *Should've been a bloody lawyer.*

Belowdecks, deep in the lubbers' hold, Eden wasn't faring much better. Martin was violently seasick, Peter Stockwell, moved there from the sickbay, lay moaning in his cot, Rudy the dog was barking nonstop in his cage, while the Nipper complained continually.

"I can't take it anymore in here! It smells like puke!"

"Phineas, you are forbidden to leave here and that is final."

"Why can't I go see Cap'n?"

She had lost patience after the twentieth repeat of the question. "Because I said so."

"I ain't gotta listen to you!"

"Oh, yes, you do. Lord Jack put me in charge of you. You can take the matter up with him *after* the storm if you like. For now, you are absolutely staying here with me. Why don't you make yourself useful by calming Rudy down? If anyone can get him to be quiet, you can. Will you try?"

"Fine!" He snorted and scowled at her, but bent down with a sulky look and began talking softly to the bull-terrier, poking his fingers through the mesh cage in an effort to pet the dog.

She realized the Nipper's insistence on seeing Jack was simply due to the fact that he was scared—they all were—and being near Jack made the child feel safe. But right now Jack had a job to do, and all of their lives depended on him.

She turned away, satisfied that she had distracted her charge for the moment, and gave poor Martin a washrag soaked in diluted vinegar for the mal de mer. She winced as he retched again, but there was nothing left in him to throw up.

As he sat back against the bulkhead, she molded the vinegar-soaked cloth across his green-toned forehead. "You poor thing. Hang on, dear. It can't last forever."

Peter Stockwell groaned and she went to check on him next.

Because her back was turned for that brief moment, she did not see Phineas wedge Rudy's cage open a few nar-row inches. The boy reached one small hand in to pet the dog, determined to calm him, but just as Eden turned around, Rudy shot past the Nipper and ran straight for the door, which Eden had propped open with a chair because of the poor ventilation.

She gasped as the dog flashed out in a streak of white with Phineas right behind him.

"Rudy, come back here!" the boy shouted, chasing the animal.

"Phinney!" She flew to the doorway.

He was gone.

"Oh, I'll wring his neck," she breathed, then rushed down the dark passageway after the boy.

She berated herself with every step, awash in guilt and rising panic. Where had they gone? It was so dark belowdecks.

The companionway ahead of her pitched to and fro, spilling Eden into one wall and then the other as she hurried down the nar-row passage on a zigzag path. The lanterns above rocked from side to side, and any of the furniture that wasn't fastened down traveled back and forth across the planks.

She winced at the motion, her stomach protesting. She had to hold on tightly to the bannister of the gangway as she climbed up to the next deck. She could hear, feel the deep vibration of the sea battering the hull, the ship's creaking like a human utterance of pain.

The men hurried past her, back and forth, with barely a glance. She stopped one of the carpenter's mates. "Did you see the Nipper come this way?"

"No, ma'am. If you'll pardon—"

"Of course." She let go of him.

Finally making her way to the middle deck where the livestock was stowed, she found a good number of frightened animals— chickens, ducks, rabbits in their cages. In the central pen, goats and pigs huddled in the hay.

But no Nipper.

Once more, Eden was zigzagging up the companionway, climbing the gangway stairs and holding on for dear life as the ship bucked and rocked.

A blast of nature's sound and fury greeted her as she stepped outside, instantly wishing she had worn her new-made coat. Accustomed to tropical heat, she could barely catch her breath in the bone-chilling cold. She glanced up in wonder at *The Winds of Fortune* riding out the storm under bare poles, a few shredded sails flapping like pennants in the violent wind.

She spotted Jack on the distant forecastle, barking orders at his men. She followed his upward gaze and spied a number of sailors perched aloft, somehow wedged into place despite the pendulum-like rocking of the skeletal masts.

They were working one of the horizontal spars free from the masts, lowering it slowly by a system of ropes and pulleys. She had no idea what that was all about, but she had to find the Nipper—and the wayward dog.

"Phineas!" The bitter wind tried to rip her voice away. Searching the decks and praying the little boy had not been washed overboard already, she suddenly saw him. "Phineas!"

He had hunkered down under one of the sturdy wooden racks that secured the lifeboats in the ship's waist. He had managed to grab Rudy and was hugging the wriggling dog in his arms.

Eden waded toward him through ankle-deep water, snow clinging in her hair. She shouted for him to come out from under there, but again, the brutal wind snatched her words away.

She saw he was too petrified to move and realized grimly that she was going to have to make her way to his side, pry him bodily out of his hiding place, and bring him back belowdecks herself.

She brushed the stinging salt out of her eyes, braced herself, and went to collect her errant charge.

"What the 'ell are you doing here?" a deep voice barked at her.

She looked over and saw Mr. Brody draped in a black oilskin like the one Jack wore. The master-at-arms came trudging toward her.

Jack heard Trahern shout. He looked in question toward his lieutenant on the quarterdeck. Trahern pointed at the ship's waist.

Jack followed the gesture, saw Eden, and let out a curse. What in blazes was she doing on deck at a time like this? She was walking toward the lifeboats—then Jack spotted the boy and dog. Moving around the wheel, he narrowed his eyes against the lashing rain. He might have panicked with all three of them in such danger, but Brody was already on the scene.

The grizzled old master-at-arms took Eden by the elbow and hurried to help her collect the boy. Brody got a rope and looped it around the dog's neck, tugging the crazed bull-terrier toward the hatch that led back down to safety.

A step behind him, Eden pulled Phineas by his hand. The boy must have gotten away from her, but she appeared to have gotten the situation under control.

He waved his thanks to Brody, who was in the process of escorting woman and child back below, then shook his head with a harrumph.

Just as he moved back to take the wheel again, he heard a sickening crack from above.

The men aloft yelled.

They caught the spar, thank God, before it fell—but a thick, tangled knot of sheets and tackle came free without warning, swinging down across the decks.

Jack watched in horror, unable to stop it, as the loose rigging arced across the ship's waist and slammed into Eden, sweeping her over the bulwark.

He roared, already in motion.

For a second, she clung to the loosed shrouds, flapping free over the rail, a look of stunned terror on her face. The Nipper ran toward her.

Then a powerful swell rose up and engulfed her, greenish gray, stone-colored: Her face vanished under the wave.

When it receded, the wet, heavy rigging still remained, tangled over the side of the ship, but it was empty now.

She was gone, taken by the sea.

Jack gave the helmsman the wheel, threw off his oilskin and leaped off the fo'c'sle, running toward the leeward rail. He roared at the boy to get below and spotted Eden in the water, struggling to keep her face above the waves.

The chaotic surface currents were already drawing her further away from his ship, and the cold would claim her within minutes.

"Give me a rope!" he screamed.

"The boats, sir! Shall we lower 'em?"

"No time!"

Trahern handed him a rope, which Jack tied around his waist and knotted with swift expertise, jerking a nod at a nearby block and tackle. At once, Ballast ran the other end of the rope through the pulley.

"When I signal you, pull us up, and not a second before."

"Aye, sir!" the big gunner vowed. Several men gathered behind him to help lend muscle to the task.

"What if you can't get to her, Jack?" Trahern demanded. "Five minutes, and I'm pulling you in."

"Don't you dare pull me in 'til I have her."

"Jack, you'll both die—"

"That's an order! I'm coming back with her or not at all." Ignoring the unsteady bobbing and weaving of the wood beneath him, he climbed up onto the rail and dove off.

It was a long, cold drop down into the sea. The waves embraced him with a frigid clutch.

Jack shot to the surface again with a mighty gasp for air. The cold seemed to suck the breath right out of his chest, and he was painfully aware of the sea's sublime power; he was at its mercy now along with Eden.

They both could live or die as the waves saw fit.

Treading water, he turned this way and that, but he could not see her through the dividing crests of icy water.

"Eden!"

He couldn't find her.

He glanced back at his men, watching from the rails. They pointed frantically to his larboard. He turned.

"Eden!" He began swimming hard in that direction until he caught a glimpse of her.

"Jack!"

He heard her shriek his name before another frigid wave drowned out her voice.

Jack swam harder with powerful kicks, his shoulders already aching from fighting the wheel for the past hour. At least now he was going in the right direction, but if he didn't reach her momentarily, the cold would lull her struggles with its killing lethargy and he knew that she would drown.

The next glimpse of her showed him a terrified, bedraggled girl whose face held a sickly white pallor.

A girl who had tried to tell him that she loved him.

Her dark skirts were billowed around her, the heavy material that he had insisted on for her warmth threatening to pull her under.

"Hold on, Eden!" he choked out. "I'm coming!" Jack refused to admit the knowledge that he was beginning to tire. No, he was not as young as he'd once been, closer to forty than he was to twenty. The cold and power of the North Atlantic in her wrath could suck the strength right out of a man, and he had been fighting this beast of a storm since last night.

God, make me strong enough. Take me if You have to, but don't let me lose her.

The waves were not so violent if you didn't fight them, she had realized.

Their motion had become almost soothing, like swinging slowly in a big hammock made of ice. A moment ago, she had been so freezing cold that her skin hurt as if she had been burned, but it had passed and she felt much better now.

The sharp edge of the pain had begun to dull. She supposed she must be going numb, in addition to having swallowed a good deal of vile seawater. Through her shroud of sleet and snow, *The Winds of Fortune* seemed so very far away.

The last thing Eden remembered before the cold stole her senses was Jack reaching her in the icy water, his arms wrapping around her with a steely grip. Her head fell onto his massive shoulder. So warm.

Yet he was trembling, too.

"I've got you, sweet. Hold onto me. Stay awake, Eden!"

"Don't let me go, Jack," she murmured.

"I've got you."

Pulling her closer, Jack saw his men throw down a few life-rings from the very closet in which they had found their stowaway. Jack intercepted one of the floating cork rings and put it under her while Trahern quickly lowered the bosun's chair to pull them up with.

Holding on to Eden with singular determination, he looked up and waved his arm, signaling the crew. Praying that Eden remained at least marginally alert, he held her tightly with one arm around her waist while he gripped the rope with the other, one knee balanced on the wooden seat of the bosun's chair.

At his signal, the line of men up on deck heaved in unison, drawing them swiftly through the waves. Then, as the hull of *The Winds of Fortune* towered over them, the men heaved on the ropes again.

Jack tautened every muscle in his body to brace for the strain; he shifted Eden onto his shoulder and clamped her to him as the men on deck lifted them out of the freezing water into the bitter wind.

For a few precarious seconds, they ascended on the bosun's chair, swinging and twisting over the churning waves below. They flew up over the rails of *The Winds of Fortune,* past the tangled mass of rigging that had struck her, and landed heavily in a heap on deck like the blasted catch of the day.

"Eden!"

Jack laid her down, cradling her head on the deck as gently as possible as he knelt beside her. Several of the men were already bringing blankets.

"She's not breathing."

Her lips were blue. Jack gripped her bodice and tore it open, exposing her new-made corset. In their reverence for the brave girl who had won over the whole crew, the men averted their eyes. Jack wrenched the corset's lacings loose, pumped on her chest, and she coughed.

He turned her onto her side as she spit up the seawater she had ingested, hacking and coughing for air.

When it was clear that she was breathing again, and conscious, he sat back on his calves in a kneeling position. His shoulders dropped, though his chest was still heaving.

He lifted his face to the marble sky, his hand still resting on her hip. He could have wept. He closed his eyes, shaking with cold and the aftermath of pure terror.

"I'm s-sorry, Jack," she chattered, lifting her stricken gaze to his with great, green, woeful eyes. "I m-more t-trouble than I'm w-worth."

"Stop talkin' nonsense," he chided gruffly as his heart clenched. He scooped her up in his arms and hugged her to him for all he was worth. "I thought I'd lost you," he whispered. *The choice of whether or not to dare love her had nearly been taken out of his hands.*

"Oh, Jack." She started crying.

"Shh, sweeting. I've got you now." He pressed a fervent kiss to her cold forehead. A moment later, he stood up, lifting her in his arms. Holding her like the most precious treasure, he carried her back down to safety below.

CHAPTER
⚭ ELEVEN ⚭

*T*he ship had stopped its tossing; hours later, the sea was calm. A steady drizzle of rain drummed the soaked planks and speckled the bank of stern windows, but by early afternoon, it appeared they had weathered the storm.

Eden was still shaken by her brush with death, but at least she'd had the chance to dry off, change into warm clothes, and rest for a while. Jack was still on deck running things, as he was wont to do. After bringing her down here and making sure she was all right, he had simply changed his clothes and then had gone back up on deck to finish battling the storm. The man had to be perfectly exhausted.

Dressed in one of his oversized shirts, with his thick brocade dressing gown wrapped around her for added warmth, Eden endeavored to make herself useful, lighting a few candles in the day cabin to ward off the gray gloom. She gathered some things together that Jack would want when he came down, towels, dry clothes, and such. She put fresh sheets and extra blankets on the bed. As soon as the ship's cook received permission to start a fire again in the galley stoves, she ordered tea and a hot meal for them both, along with a pail of heated water to wash the sea salt off her skin after her tumble into the waves. Jack would want to wash, too, she thought.

This done, she began the wearisome task of righting the tumbled furniture and putting back in their proper places all the books and cups and random objects that had gone careening across the room with the violent rocking of the ship.

With her mind continually replaying those awful moments at the mercy of the frigid sea, her hands still trembled a bit, making her slightly clumsy as she shoved each leather-bound volume back onto the shelves. She had faced many dangers in her life, but she knew deep in her bones that that was the closest she had ever come to meeting the great Omega. If it had not been for Jack, risking his life to save her . . .

She shuddered, pausing in her task.

She still felt ridiculous for what she had said to him on deck before the storm had hit, during the St. Elmo's Fire. She had practically told him she loved him, and he had said nothing back. One could not help but feel a bit rejected.

Of course, he *had* saved her life. Actions spoke louder than words. Then again, as captain of the ship, he was responsible for everyone aboard his vessel and she knew he took this duty very seriously. He would've jumped into the waves to save anyone, she admitted, crestfallen.

Yes, he had rescued her and had carried her down here most tenderly a few hours ago, but with the crisis behind them, he was probably still angry at her for finding out about his real father. This man had more secrets than anyone she had ever met!

Frustrated, unsure how to act toward him when he returned, and still fraught with the chill of her near doom, she pulled his warm dressing gown more tightly around her and went back into the sleeping cabin.

She turned all the locks out of habit and then slid back into his berth, which, along with the extra blankets, she had already prepared with a bed warmer full of toasty coals.

She had just gotten comfortable and closed her eyes when she heard a small jangle of keys. Outside the door, she heard Jack fumbling to free the first lock. Getting up from the bed, she went to save him the trouble, quickly unlocking the rest.

When she opened the door, he was standing there with his key in hand, his face haggard with exhaustion, ice crystals on his coat and in his hair. Eden gave him a sympathetic half smile and pulled the door open wider. "Come in."

He passed an uncertain glance over her face as she turned away, gliding ahead of him into the cabin with the long brocade dressing gown sweeping behind her. Jack followed her in, taking off his black, knitted sailor's cap and raking his hand slowly through his damp, tousled hair. Eden lit the pair of candles attached to the mahogany washstand. As Jack wearily drew off his soaked gloves, she strode over to his sea chest, which was doing duty as a table at

191

the moment. Upon it sat the tray of victuals and the other things she had gotten ready for his arrival.

She poured him a cup of the fragrant Indian blend from the teapot, fortifying it with a splash of brandy to help warm him. She brought it to him, and he accepted her offering with mumbled thanks. He warmed his hands on the cup, inhaling the steam for a moment. She watched him in shrewd worry; he only drank a sip or two before setting the cup aside to pull off his coat. He threw it across the cannon to let the ice melt.

Eden went to get the towels, frowning when she returned. The man would catch his death in those wet clothes. "Let me do that," she murmured when she saw the trouble he was having trying to make his frozen, shaking fingers work well enough to unbutton his waistcoat.

He stood patiently and lowered his head while she freed him from the thick fleece vest, tugging it off his wide shoulders. "Take off your shirt," she ordered, a bit unsettled by his intense, bleary stare.

As he obeyed her order, peeling his wet shirt off over his head, she slipped off his borrowed dressing gown and held it up for him. "Quick, before the heat escapes."

"You use it—"

"I'm warm enough now."

"All right." Too tired to argue, he put his arms through the capacious sleeves, pulling the robe around him. "Oh," he said in mild surprise, a slight, weary smile breaking across his face. "You got it all nice and warm for me."

"I have my uses," she replied with an arch look as he slowly knotted the cloth belt.

Turning away to get his food for him, she eyed his lower half, now neatly concealed beneath the robe. "You might want to take off your, er, unmentionables, too."

"Yes, ma'am." He flashed a lazy grin.

Well, apparently, he wasn't *that* tired. "Incorrigible," she murmured as she went back to their makeshift table. She was glad to see him smile. Maybe he wasn't angry at her anymore about finding out his secret.

At least, perhaps he'd gotten over it.

His boots clunked to the floor and a moment later his breeches and long drawers were draped across the cannon with his coat.

"You must be starved. Cook sent up a bowl of chicken stew— it's very good." She lifted the lid and gave it a stir. "There's bread and butter, too. What else? Hot water so you can wash up. Here." She had dunked the washcloth in the basin of wonderfully warm water and turned just as he stepped up behind her.

"Eden," he murmured.

She turned around, the washcloth in one hand, the soap in the other.

He gazed cautiously into her eyes. "I owe you an apology."

"No, you don't, Jack," she said softly as her heart lurched with tremulous hope. She put the items down. "I was wrong to pry."

He touched her chin. "Nonsense. I shouldn't have yelled at you. You didn't deserve it. You were trying to help—and I pushed you away."

"It doesn't matter now. Does it?" She rested her hand tentatively on his chest, giving the black velvet lapel of his rich brocade robe a small caress. "You saved my life, and risked your own for me. Oh, Jack." She shook her head in fervent contrition. "I'm so sorry I let the boy get away from me. You were counting on me to watch over him—I hardly turned my back for two seconds, and look at what happened. You could have died!"

"A storm like that, we all could've died."

"But you didn't let that happen." Tilting her head back, she gazed at him for a moment, then reached up and stroked his rugged face softly. "Jack, my lion," she whispered. "Thank you for saving my life."

"Any time," he said quietly. Then he turned his face and grazed his lips along the heel of her hand.

She gazed lovingly at him for a long moment, a lump in her throat. She shook her head with a tender *tsk, tsk.* "Look at you, my brave man." She picked up one of the towels and reached up to blot his dark, wavy locks. "You're so tired, I know," she whispered as she smoothed the excess moisture from his hair. "I'm going to take care of you now, all right?"

Yes, please, he thought, his stomach quivering with desire as she poured out her tenderness on him. It wasn't his way to let a woman make a fuss over him, but the storm had wrung every ounce of obstinacy from him. He was stiff and sore and cold to the bone, too tired to deny his true feelings for her now, and he hadn't the will.

193

His fears still remained, but having come so close to losing her, they didn't seem to matter anymore.

"Sit," Eden whispered.

He obeyed, moving to the edge of the bed. Dressed in nothing but one of his linen shirts, which reached all the way to her knees, she came and stood between his legs, toweling his hair dry, and then gently stroking his skin with the warm, wet washcloth, wiping away the traces of the storm's abuse.

Jack watched her, entranced.

No, he had never had this before, what she gave him now. He had never sought it and if he'd found it, he probably would have distrusted it.

His pulse quickened with her every touch.

Her skin looked silken in the candlelight. All the red and golden hues in her hair burned like a sunset, or like the dancing flames of a cozy hearth fire. She stroked his face and kissed his forehead and his eyebrow, his cheekbone and his nose all the while she worked.

Her nurturing felt so bloody wonderful that he barely dared breathe for fear it might stop. He closed his eyes, absorbing her nuzzling affection in soul-deep need; ah, she was breaking him down so sweetly, kissing away his resistance, layer after layer of hardened defenses, until she reached the bare rock core of stark loneliness in him, so cold and bleak.

Jack wanted her so badly. She wrapped her softness around him, enfolding him in her tender heat.

And Eden thought *he* had saved *her*?

He dragged his eyes open again after a minute, his cock swollen beneath the robe. She hadn't even kissed him and he was nearly hard. She blushed a little when she saw his hungry stare, and lowered her gaze demurely.

"Let me get your supper," she murmured.

But it wasn't food that Jack was craving. He captured her wrist, stopping her. "All I really want is you."

She went motionless: His smoldering gaze traveled down her body as he reached out with his other hand and slipped the oversized shirt off her pearly shoulder. Her chest heaved, the deep V of the shirt falling open to expose one alabaster breast with the most exquisite pink tip he'd ever seen.

He leaned forward and pressed a reverent kiss to the curve of that silky white breast, closing his eyes. "Eden, my own lovely paradise," he whispered. "Warm me."

She caressed his head. "You need sleep, Jack."

"I need you."

"You've been up for thirty-six hours."

"One more won't hurt." When he kissed her nipple, she stopped him, backing away.

He licked his lips. "Where are you going?"

She didn't answer; her green eyes were wide and uncertain, betraying her desire when the long muzzle of the cannon behind her suddenly barred her further retreat. Jack rose and walked toward her. She turned away as though contemplating escape again.

"What is this?" he whispered, wrapping his arms around her waist. "Are you afraid of me now?"

"No." She tried to extricate herself from his hold, but he stilled her halfhearted struggles, clamping her squirming hips gently to his groin.

"Don't you want me?" he asked, letting her feel his throbbing against her sweet, bare bottom.

She let out a most intriguing whimper.

He wasn't sure if it was a yes or a no, but the shirt she was wearing rode up as she strained forward slightly over the cannon, her slim midriff pressed to the cool metal barrel. Shifting his position, he hooked his left arm around her slim waist and slid his right hand deftly under the long hem of his white shirt. He breathed a wordless sound of appreciation as he cupped her right cheek in his hand. He molded his now warm fingers around the demure, silky curve—and squeezed. She drew in her breath sharply; the sensuous arch of her back told him all that he needed to know.

His blood heated by several degrees. He curbed the roguish urge to plant a spanking on her juicy rear end—though she probably would have enjoyed it, knowing this little hellion. But rougher play could wait. For now, still gently holding her captive, he stroked her beautiful hair, pushed all her long tresses to the side, then lowered his head and again kissed the exposed stretch of delicate shoulder where his shirt was falling off her in the most distracting fashion.

She held very still, trying not to encourage him, or perhaps to deny her response, but when he let his touch wander down to the charming cleft of her backside and dipped an exploratory caress between her legs from behind, he learned the truth: Her dew immediately bathed his fingertip, and she uttered a low moan at his touch.

Jack felt his own need escalating swiftly.

He withdrew his middle finger from her wet threshold and let his hand glide around her hip to the front. He continued kissing her shoulder and her nape, while his hand played with her belly and coaxed her nipples to full arousal. Petting her creamy hips and sleek thighs, he circled her mound with a light tantalizing caress, until, at last, he grazed her hardened jewel, provoking an eager shudder.

She leaned against the cannon, braced on her hands, her body sending signals that would have shocked her virginal mind. He continued caressing her head with one hand, running his fingers through her luxurious hair; with the other, a few light strokes between her legs helped him recall exactly how she liked to be touched. And then he gave his lady just what her sweet body craved.

She was shaking, moving with him in dazed rhythm, her clit swelling, rigid and inflamed, as he gathered her teeming nectar on his fingertip and used it to lubricate each gentle, teasing stroke. After a few moments, she dropped her head back with another soft groan, driving him mad with the sinuous motion of her buttocks winding against his loins.

It soon became more than Jack could bear.

"Don't move," he whispered, his left hand still kneading the soft flesh of her left hip to make sure she didn't take it into her head to flee. He couldn't have that. "Don't be afraid," he added, untying the belt of his dressing gown with his other trembling hand. "I'm not going to take you yet. I just want you to feel me now." Letting his robe fall open down the front of him, he angled his upright cock downward, nosing into the slick, damp heat between her thighs.

"Mm," she said, riding it a bit—cautiously.

Jack swallowed hard, his chest heaving. He was panting, and as he went back to sporting with her pert little clit, he could feel his restraint beginning to splinter at the seams, like a ship coming apart in a storm.

Her wetness dripped down his cock as she writhed slowly, sliding her silken crevice along the upper surface of his pulsating shaft. He helped her, glad to be of service; he rocked his hips with a slow, careful motion, letting her get used to him between her legs. After a moment or two, she reached back and clutched his hip, pulling him closer, her teeth bared, her hazy eyes glittering.

How passionate she was, he mused as he complied, his touch quickening. Her eager panting turned to soft and high-pitched moans; she gasped his name and for a fleeting instant, her lithe body went rigid.

He realized he had just brought her to orgasm.

"Shh," he whispered at her ear, smiling to himself as he caught her, steadying her as she went limp with a groan. *Such an apt pupil.* She leaned against the cannon until he turned her around and gathered her into his arms.

He held her for a long moment, ignoring the stampede of lust inside him, for he was moved beyond words at the innocence of her release. So artless and pure. Her helpless surrender bespoke a blood-deep trust. But wasn't that what she had given to him from the start? Her words had stayed with him, haunting him from that first day in the jungle.

"I trust you, Jack."

That someone as pure as Eden Farraday could see good in him shook him to the core.

He lowered his head, cupped her delicate jaw in his hand, and kissed her. She wound her arms around his neck and returned his kiss with an earnest wholeheartedness that made him ache.

I trust you, too, Eden, he thought. *As much as I am able to trust anyone.*

She was still trembling with the aftermath of ecstasy, overwhelmed; she felt a bit thrown off balance, for she had not expected any of this to happen, at least not today, after all they had been through. Jack's rich passion flowed over her and wrapped around her, a sweetness and exquisite security.

As she kissed him slowly, savoring his mouth, she let her hand travel in a cautious exploration across the broad, warm swells of his chest, where his dressing gown had fallen open.

He quivered under her touch. She ventured further, fascinated, molding her palm against him as her hand glided down the intricate musculature of his carved belly. His velvet skin heated under her caress. He breathed out a low, needy moan against her lips, and Eden realized abruptly that although he had brought her to climax, he was still on fire.

His touch running down her sides brimmed with searing need. His hungry kiss urged her lips farther apart, and then he tasted her again with a deep, slow stroke of his tongue on hers.

She raked her fingers through his hair, caressed his stubbled jaw, and played with his neat, low sideburns.

Jack cupped her nape and drank her kisses still more deeply; Eden gladly acquiesced. She knew she was playing with fire, but she could not stop, enthralled by the firm, delicious pressure of his mouth slanting over hers with such hot, masculine greed. Her fingers dug into his powerful shoulders as though with a will of their own, clutching, claiming a man she knew she'd never tame.

His tongue swirled and danced in her mouth, thrusting in and out, as his fingertips stroked her neck and throat. The effect it had on Eden shocked her to the core: Again, he stirred the glowing embers of her desire alive with new and still hotter flame.

There was no point arguing with a six-foot wall of male muscle as he began backing her toward his bed behind her, kissing her all the while.

She stole a brief upward glance at his face from under her lashes. His aqua-blue eyes glittered harshly with the fever, his taut expression that of a man who would not be denied.

"Jack?"

"Yes, darlin'?"

"W-what are you doing?"

"Seducing you," he whispered very smoothly. "I told you I would." He lifted the borrowed shirt she was wearing off over her head, then glanced down at her naked body in starved appreciation.

He stole another kiss and kept inching her back toward the bed.

"Y-you said I would be willing."

"Aren't you?"

"I-I don't know. This is—maybe we should think about this."

"Let's not."

"But Jack." Thrill and fear and need—hesitation, distress, and longing brewed up a potent concoction of primal response in Eden as she realized he could not hold himself back any longer. She was about to be ravished.

"Yes, my sweet?"

The backs of her legs bumped up against his bed behind her. "I didn't think you wanted me."

"Oh, but I do," he vowed, slowly shaking his head. He took off the long, luxurious robe, letting it spill off his shoulders to pool behind him on the floor.

Eden gulped at his magnificent body towering before her in the candlelight.

"So very much." He pressed her down gently by her shoulders until she sat on the edge of his berth. He descended with her, sinking to his knees between her legs. "Would you like me to show you how much, Eden?"

"Um—"

His hot, wet mouth left her lips to travel down around her chin; along the side of her neck, entrancing her; and down into the valley between her breasts. *"Oh, God."* She sank back onto one elbow on his mattress, and Jack had easy access to all of her.

He stroked her body everywhere until she was breathless from his ministrations. She knew if they did this, there was no turning back, but her heart already belonged to him, and her body delighted under his hands. When he touched her like this, in long, hypnotic strokes, there could be nothing in the world to fear. Her mind felt numb and blissful, as though she had ingested one of those strange jungle plants the Waroa used in their religious ceremonies.

He cradled her head with his other hand and nuzzled her earlobe, his heavy breathing raspy by her ear. "Delicious thing," he purred in dark seduction as he glided down by her navel, "I want to eat you."

She let out a dazed laugh, thinking that he spoke metaphorically, but she soon realized her mistake when he pressed her legs apart on a wider angle and continued descending along her body, trailing thrilling kisses all down her torso and on her hips as he went. She held her breath and clenched the coverlet in her fists, throbbing with wild anticipation.

He reached beneath her and cupped her buttocks gently in his big, deft hands. Then he bent his head, nibbling at her inner thighs in teasing play, tantalizing her until she squirmed in needy impatience; his warm, manly lips hovered above her mound for a heartbeat before he slowly licked her most sacred core.

199

Eden whispered an incredulous expletive—but Jack was only getting started. The light flicking of his clever tongue duplicated the earlier motion of his fingertip; she groaned in sheer abandon. Then his mouth was upon her, claiming her, pleasuring her. She was liquid fire beneath him, like the tropical sun turning the slow-moving river to gold.

Her breath heaved as though she had run a mile. He had her writhing, arching, undulating as she sought the satisfaction of his tongue. He was ferocious in his giving. There was nowhere she could go to escape the pleasure. Starting forward, his mouth consumed her ultra-sensitized center; shrinking back, his pinky finger pressed deep into the cleft of her backside, and all the while, his two fingers glided in and out of her slick passage, working her into a lather—*again*.

Ruthless, this man. Delightfully so.

She raked her trembling hands through his thick, wavy hair, panting as she gazed down at him again. One glance revealed that all of the fierce, single-minded force of purpose in his nature was focused on giving her pleasure, nay, worshiping her body with his own.

Cupping her foot in loving play, he set her leg over his broad shoulder to drink her in more deeply. She cupped his head between her thighs, melting on his tongue like flowing honey.

"Oh, God, Jack!" she gasped out. "I could die. . . ."

A low, seductive laugh escaped him at her amazement, the deep notes vibrating against her throbbing flesh: She winced and smiled in half-drunken delight as he gave her only a moment to steady herself.

"You won't die. Trust me." He glanced up and gave her a devil's smile with eyes that burned like hot coals. He pressed a tender kiss to her belly and then returned below to finish driving her mad.

In moments, she was wild with passion, thrusting herself into his wonderful mouth. "Oh, Jack, I . . . can't take any more. Make it . . . stop . . . *please*. . . ."

Demon that he was, the exquisite torment only intensified in answer to her ragged plea. It sharpened; deepened; and then on the verge of her gasp, it suddenly ceased.

"Oh, no, you don't," he chided in knowing amusement even as she cried out at the denial.

He dragged his lips away from her teeming core and dried his mouth against her thigh. He nuzzled the lower curve of her breast as he moved upward once more.

"Jack."

"No, darling, I've got something else for you." Hooking an arm around her waist, he slid her into the center of his bed as he joined her, moving her as easily as if she weighed no more than a cat.

Eden marveled at the rock-hard arms that held her. She trailed her fingertips over the bulky swell of his left biceps, then squeezed the muscle, amazed to find it quite as solid as sun-warmed stone; laughing softly at her experiment, Jack kissed her cheek.

"You're very hard," she remarked, then looked anxiously into his eyes. "You'll hurt me!"

"No, sweet. Never." His expression softening, he reclined on his side next to her. She glanced down in worried awe at his naked body and saw that the light sprigging of brown hair of his chest matched the darker thatch from which his phallus sprung, so large and ready. Even now, it towered over her flat belly.

Good God.

Jack distracted her from staring before real fear could set in. With a gentle pressure under her chin, he tipped her head back and kissed her with slow, drugging depth. After a moment, Eden wrapped her arms around him while his roaming fingertips glided over her, connecting the dots of her occasional freckles.

He bent over her, delighting her with a little nibble on the tip of her nose, and then kissing his way down her face, rounding her chin. He licked her throat and lightly teethed her neck. She held him to her, running her fingers through his thick, silky hair.

He leaned closer and then moved atop her. "I need you," he whispered.

She searched his face, so unsure, and yet so hungry for him.

Her blood pounded like tribal drums. Her lips throbbed, swollen from his kisses. He cradled her head in his left hand but reached down between their bodies with his right and guided the throbbing tip of his hardness into her love-slicked threshold.

Her heart slammed, but Jack displayed superhuman restraint, advancing no further for a few seconds, letting her get used to him again. This was not much different than what they'd done before beside the cannon, she thought, and felt braver. Sensing her relax a bit, he began to play with her, roguishly, swirling the smooth head of his instrument all over and around her dripping core. He teased her with it until she burned for him; he skimmed her open blossom more deeply with each pass.

"You're cruel," she panted.

"I'm thorough."

"Jack," she groaned, enfolding him between her legs. She hooked her ankles against the small of his back and squirmed beneath him in wanton need, past caring about tomorrow. "Oh, . . . Jack, please."

"Easy, love. Don't move like that. You're torturing me." His voice was gruff, his angular face taut with desire, but he paused to inhale the scent of her. He glided the tip of his nose along the curve of her shoulder and her neck. "You smell so good, my orchid, my exquisite flower."

"Jack." Must she beg for him?

Her world spun like the dizzying view from the jungle's highest treetops, and her ears reechoed with her father's well-intended, scientific advice. *All animals take a mate on reaching reproductive age.* It seemed so cool and logical compared to the frenzy in her blood as his hardness slid deeper into her by delicious fractions of an inch. She drew herself down eagerly, seeking more of him.

"Are you ready for me, Eden?"

"Uhn."

Jack pressed a sweet kiss into her palm, and entered her slowly, steadily. When he reached the thin membrane of her barrier, he whispered in her ear that it would only hurt for a moment, and then he burst it with a forceful thrust of his hips.

She bit back an anguished cry, for the moment of her initiation hurt. They were meant to hurt, these ancient, bloodletting rituals. This she had learned from the timeless Waroa. Such ceremonies marked a person's entrance into a whole new phase of life.

A life with this man and all his dangerous secrets.

He was clearly determined to make the pain as small for her as possible. Except for the heaving of his chest, he remained still while she struggled to absorb the wound. He was deep inside her now: They were one.

His gentle kisses in the darkness eased her, and soon, his skillful efforts as a lover, earlier, when he had taken the time to school her in the ways of pleasure, now paid their dividends in helping her to overcome the pain.

The life she'd led, in any case, had taught her not to fear pain overmuch. Sometimes pain was a crucial part of healing, she knew, and besides, it always passed.

It passed now, moment by moment, while Jack petted her hair and stared into her eyes, offering unquestioned reassurance.

He filled her so completely that the emptiness deep inside had vanished, the hollow restless longing that had driven her from the jungle and onto this ship bound for England. Only now did she feel whole.

He held her tenderly, and with her eyes closed, Eden kissed his shoulder again and again in languid idleness; when he felt her hips relax by a few cautious degrees, he made love to her with slow, delicious eroticism. Every stroke of his pelvis brought her more keenly alive; she thrust her breasts upward into his chest. He nuzzled her brow, his breath hot against her temple. She savored the damp, humid heat of their bodies, undulating together—connected, nay, locked in lush copulation. She was shaking, no, couldn't resist him—paying tribute, body and soul, to her dark god.

She lifted her head from his pillow and kissed him, her fingers cupping his square, scruffy jaw. He growled low as he consumed her kiss; the rhythm of their elemental dance gathered speed, releasing primal powers. His sweat and his scent were all over her; she had marked him with her blood.

Eden heard the distant drumbeat of his pulse pounding fiercely in time with her own. She gripped his lean hips and helped herself to still more of his pulsating length, better able to enjoy him now. He yielded, taking as he gave.

"Come for me," he ordered in a rasping whisper, and in the next moment, helplessly, Eden obeyed.

She clutched his big shoulders and let out fairly a scream of release even as he groaned loudly by her ear, his whole frame going rigid. Triumphant their cries, uncontrollable.

His body wept within her, her shuddering passage milking his seed, while orchids burst like fireworks and pink dolphins leaped through the sparkling cloud that had once been her mind.

Sorcerer, warrior, magic man . . . come to steal her away to his golden kingdom under the sea.

Buoto. When one seduced you, you couldn't even remember how to form the word *no.*

"Oh, *Jack.*" His name on her lips faded to naught but a mesmerized whisper—her surrender unconditional.

As her shudders of ecstasy eased, Jack withdrew from her body, panting, and collapsed in the valley between her breasts. He was spent. His limbs felt as heavy as anchors.

Closing his eyes in lingering ecstasy, he pressed languid kisses to her midriff and rubbed his face back and forth against her skin, reveling in her softness, her delicate scent.

She was so different. So extraordinarily pure. When she draped her arms weakly around his shoulders, her delicate fingers against his face took Jack to heaven.

"Oh, *Jack,* you magnificent rascal," she purred at length, hugging his head to her bosom. She sounded spent, sated, richly satisfied, and that was reward enough for him.

"Are you all right?" he murmured.

"I think so. I didn't die," she added as an afterthought.

"I told you you'd survive." With a smile, he brought her dainty hand to his lips and pressed another small kiss into her palm. As soon as he released her hand, it fell limply onto the mattress, as though she were too weak from their exertions to support her own weight.

He laughed. Resting on his elbows, he studied her, marveling all over again at her beauty—doting on her, truth be told. He was gratified that she was pleased with his performance, for he'd never deflowered a virgin before in his life.

He bent his head and kissed the vulnerable notch at the base of her throat; closing his eyes, he was overcome by a deep and sudden surge of possessive devotion. "Eden," he whispered, his breath warming her skin as he made this woman a solemn vow: "I will always take care of you. I'll always be there when you need me. I will be good to you—if you'll have me."

She pushed him back by his shoulders, just far enough to stare into his eyes. Her own were wide with astonished uncertainty, as though she wasn't sure she'd heard him right.

He stared at her almost fiercely, for she must understand that he wouldn't take no for an answer. "Marry me," he commanded.

A dazzling smile broke across her face; joy beamed from her emerald eyes. Still lying beneath him, she lifted her hand to her brow and gave him a cheeky salute. "Aye-aye, Cap'n."

He laughed, relief flooding his heart, then he wiped that saucy grin off her lips with a big, wet kiss.

"Don't worry, Victor, I have the situation under control," Connor asserted as he surveyed the frigate's decks in a menacing pose. "These men won't harm you," he added, eyeing the cowering crew sharply. "They're under *my* orders now."

Dr. Farraday's spectacles had been smashed in the mutiny, leaving him half blind and helpless, but he could still hear clearly enough, and he flinched at the thump of the dead first mate's skull dropping against the planks.

Next came the dull, rough scraping of the corpses being dragged across the deck, then four loud splashes in succession, as the drunkard captain, the cruel first mate, and two other hated officers were hurled, lifeless, into the deep.

Victor doubted there was anyone to mourn them. *God help us.*

The churning undercurrent of vicious brutality aboard the death ship had exploded into blood and chaos in the blackness of the night before. The conspirators had slain their hated officers at midnight, but then Connor had overmastered the mutineers.

Now the morning sun revealed the damage and restored a shred of sanity, but the acrid smell of gunsmoke still hung upon the air, along with the metallic scent of blood and the rank body odor of too many unwashed men crowded together. Victor's nostrils protested at the vile stench. The smell of death and guilt—and fear.

Though the evil captain and his cronies were dead, along with the dangerous cutthroats who'd concocted the mutiny, now there was only one man on board who reigned supreme. Squinting to see more clearly, Victor turned and looked again at his towering assistant.

Connor stood nearby with his bloodied fists planted on his waist and a brooding expression on his face. While screeching frigate birds wheeled around the masts, five more bodies were dropped into the cold Atlantic: the rough trio who had organized the mutiny and two others who had gotten in the way.

Connor had killed them all.

It had all begun, of course, in self-defense.

Caught up in their bloodlust, the mutineers had sought to continue their rampage; after killing the officers, they had come after the captain's two guests, Connor and him. Victor still shuddered at the memory of the moment the three loathsome men had burst into their stateroom.

Perhaps it was fortunate that the darkness had been building in Connor all the while; with his preternatural senses, he seemed almost to have expected the attack.

Victor, for his part, had not. Slammed against the wall, he had caught only a glimpse of the horror, trying to see through the spiderweb cracks of his spectacles' less damaged lens.

One terrifying glimpse had been enough.

He had seen the ringleader slash at Connor with a knife and miss; Connor then ripped the man's throat out. In short order, three mangled bodies had littered the room, and with his loaded rifle in his hands, Connor had gone stalking out to restore order on deck. By the gyrating flames of the ship's lanterns, he had found the drunk and leaderless crew fighting amongst themselves.

He had only needed to shoot two of them to get the attention of the rest. After that, taking control of the ship had been easy, and Victor was glad that Connor had done it—but he could not get the image of the mauled sailor out of his mind.

It had been years since Victor had seen that bestial fury come ripping out of Connor, not since that terrible day in the jungle when the young Indian warrior had gone after Eden.

He tried not to think about it much.

The violence she had witnessed in the course of Connor's "rescue" had traumatized his daughter nearly more than the Waroa lad's advances. It had been very badly done.

Afterward, Victor had subjected Connor to a furious interrogation, but had ultimately given his assistant the benefit of the doubt. Connor had sworn the level of force he had used had been necessary, given the purse of deadly curare that the young warrior had worn dangling from the leather cord around his waist.

A mere scratch even with the milder poison could have paralyzed Eden long enough for the Indian to have done whatever he pleased to her; the stronger sort could have killed her outright. Connor had apologized if it seemed he had gotten carried away, but he vowed he could not tolerate any shadow of harm coming to the girl he had come to think of as his own sweet, young sister. Pleading with Victor not to send him away, he had sworn that such violence was a singular event, a onetime aberration, and would never, on his honor, happen again.

Not wishing to contemplate what might have happened if Connor *hadn't* come in answer to his daughter's screams, Dr. Farraday had taken the Australian at his word and, since his resilient girl had seemed more or less all right in the end, he had let the matter flow into the past.

But last night, in the bloody chaos of the mutiny, the beast within the man had reemerged, and after having been suppressed for so many years, it now showed no sign of any willingness to withdraw again into its hiding place inside Connor's savage heart.

When the final corpse fell into the sea with a careless splash, there was an uneasy silence, but then one of the lowly sailors took a small step forward and addressed their new captain in the humblest of tones: "Uh, Mr. O'Keefe, sir, w-where do we go now?"

The Australian drew himself out of his brooding. "North-north-east."

"North?" one of the others blurted out, a swarthy, piratical fellow with a gold hoop earring and a handkerchief tied around his neck. "Why not south?" He glanced at his mates as though he hoped for the others to back up his suggestion. "There's plum prizes to be taken off the trade in the West Indies shipping lanes. We'll be rich!"

"Aye!" a few started until Connor slammed the man who had spoken out of turn against the mainmast.

His hand was locked around the would-be pirate's throat; and squinting, Victor could make out several inches of air between the man's dangling toes and the planks of the deck as Connor held him aloft. The sailor's legs kicked and he grabbed Connor's wrist, to no avail, choking for air as he tried to free himself from the Australian's viselike grip.

"We are going to England," Connor ordered slowly. "Are you men or animals? Money isn't everything." He dropped the man abruptly, his point made. The sailor knelt forward on the deck, gasping and rubbing his bruised throat. "Now," Connor addressed the others, "if there are no further questions?"

The men cringed, but Victor could only stare at his friend, appalled. This brute was a stranger.

"Don't look at me that way," Connor whispered at him under his breath. "At least you're alive." He turned away once more and addressed the cowering crew in a loud bark: "Now that we've cleared away the filth, let's set this ship on a proper course!"

"Aye, sir!"

They scrambled at once to take up their usual posts, as though relieved that at least someone had taken control. Perhaps brutality was all they understood: the law of the jungle.

"Don't worry, Victor," Connor murmured, looking around at the obedience of his new servants in dark satisfaction. "We are going to rescue Eden now. We'll find her soon and bring her home safely."

You're not going anywhere near my daughter ever again, Victor thought, trembling a little as Connor pivoted and strolled away, his rifle resting over one broad shoulder.

CHAPTER
∞ TWELVE ∞

*T*hey decided to be married at sea as soon as *The Winds of Fortune* met up with the *Valiant,* captained by Jack's uncle, Lord Arthur Knight. Since they were now only about a hundred miles off the coast of Ireland, it wouldn't be long.

In the meantime, Eden threw herself into preparing for her new role in life as the wife and consort of a powerful shipping magnate. There was much to learn and, in truth, more responsibility involved than she had expected. Jack wanted her to understand how his empire was set up, how each branch ran, who his most loyal men were in each division, where the profits came from and how they were invested, and above all, where she could find the secret accounts "in case anything ever happened" to him.

She did not like the sound of that.

Yesterday, he had outlined for her the main pretense he'd be using to explain his return to England after twenty years in exile. As far as the world was concerned, Jack would only be visiting London for the purpose of buying out a competitor who had been causing trouble for his agents in various far-flung territories.

Today, it was on to reviewing the preparations needed for housing the hundreds of mercenaries that he'd soon be transporting back to South America. The vast storage spaces on the orlop and lower gun decks, now filled with timber, sugar, and all the other West Indies goods, would become, on the return trip, the living quarters of his rough-and-tumble recruits. The troops would need food, water, supplies, uniforms, boots, weapons, and other equipment ranging from canteens to bedrolls.

Trailing him at a quick pace as he marched through one of the sprawling spaces to be converted into a mess hall for the soldiers,

Eden made notes of things she was supposed to remember and hurried to keep up with the rest of the boss's present entourage: Lieutenant Trahern, the now recovered Peter Stockwell, and the purser, who was in charge of all shipboard supplies.

While the men discussed possible problems ranging from ventilation to discipline, Eden found herself musing on how easily she had slipped into the role of helper on account of all her years assisting Papa in his work. But no sooner had she thought of her sire than she suffered an acute pang of guilt.

Papa had counted on her in his quest for knowledge, and now she had gone over to helping Jack instead. One could not live for one's parents, of course—especially a parent who insisted on secluding himself in the jungle—but still, she couldn't help feeling a bit like a traitor, abandoning him. What he would say to her the next time they met, she could hardly imagine—if he would speak to her at all!

She prayed she had not lost his love, but she knew at the very least he would be furious. Not only had she run away without a by-your-leave, but the next time they met, Papa would find her married—to a decidedly controversial husband—having sought neither his blessing nor his permission. Most fathers would probably take it as a heartless slap in the face.

And the wedding . . .

She closed her eyes and cringed, sickened to think that she would be married without her papa being there at her wedding. How she wished they could have postponed the ceremony until he found them!—but she knew this was not realistic.

When she had mentioned it halfheartedly to Jack, he had been adamant that they marry without delay. He understood, he said, that Papa's absence would break her heart; but he had far more practical concerns directly impacting her best interest.

He explained that, having given him her innocence, Eden was now vulnerable to ruin until she had secured the legal protection of his name. As much as filial respect prompted her to seek her father's blessing before the marriage was a *fait accompli,* she knew Jack was right.

It might be months before Papa caught up to them. Meanwhile, the two of them had already become lovers, and a child could be conceived at any time. A baby born too soon after the wedding rather than the full nine months would be deemed by the world a product of impropriety, born in sin.

After suffering Society's harsh treatment all his life on account of his own scandalous birth, Jack refused to allow any child of his to come into the world under the slightest taint of dishonor. In his view, it was not just her that he had to protect, but their firstborn, too.

Eden couldn't argue with that, nor did she really wish to. She wanted to be married to Jack—she did not want to wait. She just wished Papa could have been there, too; but it seemed that this was the price she was going to have to pay for having given in to passion. Still, even at so high a cost, she did not regret her choice.

At least not yet.

Indeed, there was *much* to be nervous about if she were to let herself. Though she managed to thrust aside her fear of her father's reaction, there remained a deep insecurity about what the future might hold. She had given herself to the terror of the West Indies in passionate abandon and had agreed to marry him without any guarantees that she would get the kind of normal, settled life that she had stowed away on his ship to pursue in the first place.

Would they be nomads, living aboard this vessel, rootless, moving from port to port? Or would she be like a navy wife, left at home on the shore, raising her children alone while their father was on the other side of the world?

Thinking about it too much started panic boiling in her veins, so she shoved all her fears aside with a will. For now, she was going on faith. What else could she do? He had no answers for her yet. With the destiny of a nation counting on him, Jack's dangerous mission had to take precedence.

Once he had fulfilled his promise to the leaders of the revolution and got back safely, then the two of them could decide how and where they were going to live and raise their family.

Provided, of course, that he survived the mission.

Jarring herself out of the desperation that threatened, she realized Jack and Mr. Trahern were now arguing about the best solution to get more air down into the orlop deck.

"Damn it, stop questioning me and just do as I told you!" Jack barked at him.

His loyal lieutenant muttered an angry affirmative and stormed off as the captain dismissed the rest.

Eden remained, gazing at him. She leaned against the bulkhead in the dim, narrow passageway and shook her head at him after a moment. "Why are you so hard on Trahern?" she asked after the others had gone.

"Why shouldn't I be? I pay him enough."

"Jack," she chided in response to his blunt answer.

"Come, I want to check on a few more items."

"I don't see why you can't treat him a little more kindly," she remarked as she followed him down the passage. "Mr. Brody would be well advised to do the same. The old man is as hard on the poor lieutenant as you are."

"The only reason we're hard on him is because we want him to succeed in life," Jack said in a reasonable tone, opening a door for her into one of the storage areas. "Trahern's good—very good—but he came from nothing, and that means he's got to be twice as good as someone of higher birth if he's going to make men heed him."

"Well, that's not fair, if you ask me."

"No, it's not," he agreed. "But it's the way things are. For the lad to be his best, I have to hold him to high standards."

"What standards?"

"Why, the same ones I set for myself. In all honesty, I'm doing him a favor. If he didn't have the potential, I wouldn't bother. Mark this down, would you? These planks need replacing. Remind me to tell the carpenters."

She made a note of it, and then followed him back out into the tight, lamplit corridor. "Jack?"

"Hm?" He still sounded distracted, pausing to inspect some oakum caulking between the planks.

"There's something I've been wondering about."

"What's that?"

"Lady Maura."

He paused, went very still, and then sent an uneasy glance at her over his shoulder. "You know about her?"

"Papa told me she was Aunt Cecily's friend . . . and that you wanted to marry her, but her parents wouldn't allow it."

He turned to her slowly, the rugged planes and angles of his face gone tense.

"Is this true?" she asked.

"It was a long time ago."

"Yes, but if you nearly married her and now you're going to marry me, at least I'd like to know a little bit about the woman. She must have meant a lot to you."

For a moment, he seemed torn about whether or not to answer. Behind him, some distance down the cramped corridor, a shaft of sunlight pierced the gloom, arrowing in through one of the square hatches.

"What did she look like?" Eden prompted, smiling at him.

"Brunette. Dark eyes." He shrugged. "I had formed a certain attachment to her, but her parents had their sights set on my elder brother."

"Ah, Robert. The duke? Papa said that Lady Maura was the daughter of a marquess."

He nodded warily. "Marquess of Griffith. His estate borders the Hawkscliffe lands in the North Country, so they wanted to forge an alliance between our two clans. If I had been genuine issue of the ancient Hawkscliffe blood, perhaps they might have considered the suit of a mere second son. Unfortunately, the fact of my bastardy was an open secret, so any attachment between Maura and me was, shall we say, discouraged."

She furrowed her brow, studying him. "How could it have been an open secret? I mean, how did anybody find out?"

"Oh, dear," he said in a low voice, dropping his gaze as he rested his hands on his waist. "I suppose I'm going to have to tell you all the family secrets."

She arched her eyebrow in question.

He let out a huge sigh and leaned against the bulkhead. "Where to begin . . . ?"

Eden leaned across from him in the narrow passageway, intrigued. Around them, the ship creaked rhythmically in the belowdecks gloom.

Jack stared at her for a long moment. "My mother's name was Georgiana Knight, the Duchess of Hawkscliffe. As a young wife and mother of one son—Robert, named for his father—she discovered that her husband had a mistress hidden away in a quaint little love nest just outside London, and she was . . . *incensed.* Well, Hell hath no fury like a woman scorned, and so Georgiana set out to teach her duke a lesson he would never forget."

Eden listened, wide-eyed.

"She decided to cuckold him, quite publicly. She deliberately opted for a man below her station. If she had chosen another peer of the realm, a duel would have been necessary to preserve honor. I don't know how much you know about dueling, but men don't

213

duel against those who are their obvious social inferiors. Mother didn't want her duke to be killed, obviously. She wanted my brother Robert to have his father alive as he grew up. Another problem she faced was finding a man with the courage to bed the wife of a man as powerful as the Duke of Hawkscliffe. She was beautiful, but her husband was a bosom friend of the King. Well, she found her perfect specimen in the boxing champion, Sam O'Shay. The Killarney Crusher," he said wryly. "My dear old dad."

Eden's lips formed an "oh" but no sound came out.

"*I* was not supposed to happen," he explained. "I was . . . an accident. A terrible accident. A living, breathing, squalling mistake, nine pounds, four ounces."

"Goodness."

"Hawkscliffe acknowledged me as his own to try to save face. The gossips knew the truth. The amusing part, you see, is that I was not Mother's final mistake."

Her eyes widened.

"Rather than teaching her husband a lesson, her adultery simply destroyed the marriage. Their polite coexistence turned to hatred, and hatred eventually turned to apathy. At that point, Mother reunited with the man she ought to have married in the first place, Lord Carnarthen. By this time, there was no danger of a duel because Hawkscliffe no longer cared a whit what she did or with whom, as long as she was reasonably discreet. At least this time she chose a man that no one could be ashamed of. Lord Carnarthen fathered the twins, Damien and Lucien."

Eden's jaw dropped. "Oh, my!"

"Personally, I think she *wanted* to have a child with him, for love's sake. She ended up with two at one go. He was ecstatic, I hear, when the twins were born, both strong and healthy. He never married, you know. He loved her that much. He let his title go extinct, dying without legitimate issue, rather than marry another woman. To protect his sons, Carnarthen persuaded Hawkscliffe to acknowledge the twins as he had acknowledged me. One big, happy family," he said with a twinge of bitterness in his deep voice.

He paused, brooding, his dark eyebrows knitted together, his arms folded across his chest. "At least Carnarthen's high rank helped to ensure the twins' acceptance. Unlike me, they also made an effort to please Hawkscliffe. At this point, we all still thought the duke was our father and for reasons unknown, simply disliked us. It was clear that he wanted nothing to do with us. Robert was everything to him. At least the twins had each other."

"You have another brother. Alec?"

"Ah, yes. Mother and Lord Carnarthen got into a spat."

Eden winced.

"The man let his line die out for her, but she couldn't even be faithful to him, in the end. He had something to do with the Admiralty, I think, and was often away on different missions, sometimes up to a year at a time. She wanted him to quit, but he refused. Well, he sailed off again. I don't know if she was sulking or genuinely lonely, but she decided to amuse herself with Sir Phillip Preston-Lawrence, a rising actor who caught her eye treading the boards at Drury Lane Theatre in the role of Hamlet. That's how I got my baby brother, and wasn't poor Carnarthen in for a shock when he got home."

"I think I need a drink," Eden said.

Jack flashed a lazy grin. "Rum for the lady pirate?"

She just looked at him. "What about Jacinda?"

"Would you believe she, too, belongs to the duke?"

Eden absorbed this in fascination. "They . . . made up?"

He nodded. "Hawkscliffe's health began to deteriorate. Some affliction of the heart had weakened him. Well, he was sent down to Hawkscliffe Hall in the country to recuperate, and Georgiana rushed to his side like a true, devoted wife to take care of him. They finally achieved a true marriage—just in time for him to die. Jacinda was his parting gift to my mother: the only girl. So, she, like Robert, is of the true blood, but after all of Mother's escapades, you can imagine the expectations Society had about her."

"Hmm. So, all of this was the reason Lady Maura wasn't allowed to marry you?"

"Yes. Her parents would have embraced Robert, but the boxer's whelp was out of the question." He paused reflectively. "It isn't an easy world for the illegitimate, you know. Even Shakespeare casts bastards as villains in a few of his plays."

She smiled gently. "If Lady Maura grew up on the neighboring estate, then you must have known each other since childhood."

He nodded. "Yes. Her elder brother, Ian, was constantly at our house. He and Robert have always been the best of friends. Those two were more like brothers than Hawk and I ever were. Still are, I understand. Political allies, too. Of course, they've both got their titles now. Robert is the Duke of Hawkscliffe and Ian's the Marquess of Griffith. At one point, they considered finally uniting the clans by having Jacinda marry Ian, but it was not in the stars."

"I see," Eden murmured, recalling Lady Jacinda's doting rhapsodies in her letters about her beloved "Billy." After a thoughtful silence, she forced out bravely: "Did you love her?"

"I thought I did," he said with a wan smile. "In hindsight, I was just grateful somebody noticed I was alive."

She gazed at him in tender sympathy. "Did she love you?"

"Oh, of course not. I believed at the time that she did, but I soon learned that she merely enjoyed the attention and was more or less just practicing her coquetry on me before her coming-out. When her parents revealed their aspirations for her to marry a title, and ordered her to stop seeing me, I vowed they would not separate us—true love and all that—and began planning our elopement so that we could be together."

"Elopement?" Eden exclaimed.

"Please bear in mind that I was seventeen and an idiot." He took out a cheroot but did not light it. "We were too young for a legal marriage in England, but Scotland was only a few miles over the border." He shrugged. "I got everything ready and went to collect her, but she refused to come. I can't say I blame her now but I wanted to kill both of us when her protests revealed her true feelings about me. Elopement would have meant scandal, and she had no intention of being banished from the ton for my sake."

"Poor Jack," she murmured softly.

He let out a snort of a laugh. "I swore I would protect her with my life, and provide for her to the best of my ability, but she was having none of it. She wanted the rank of a fine title and the security of a fortune, ready-made. And these she soon acquired," he added. "Three months after she jilted me, she was wed to a noble marquess more than twice her age."

"Egads."

"Yes. That was the last straw for me. I kicked the dust of England off my shoes and left, swearing never to return. But now the rebels' need outweighs the angry oath of a little lovelorn Romeo," he said sardonically. "Practicality, my dear."

Eden was silent for a long moment, mulling over all that he had told her. "I suppose it will be awkward if we see Lady Maura when we get to London."

"Not for me."

"Do you think she ever regretted her choice?"

"I doubt it. She got what she wanted. She is Lady Avonworth now, a marchioness—though she has no children, which I find rather odd. Still, she became a leading hostess in the ton. On the other hand, I've got deeper pockets than her noble marquess now, and there is a certain satisfaction in that, I will admit."

"I imagine that's no accident."

"No, it's not," he admitted softly, pausing. "I swore to myself that I'd show her. I'd show them all." He lowered his lashes, veiling the deeply buried anger in his eyes. "They all said I'd never amount to anything."

"What did you mean when you spoke of becoming the villain of the family? How did that play itself out?"

Jack sighed.

One of his men hurried down the passageway on some errand. Eden and Jack squeezed against their respective walls to let the sailor go hurrying through, excusing himself as he passed.

Eden looked at her betrothed again with a questioning gaze.

"Jacinda wasn't born yet, so, apart from Robert, all of us were . . . illegitimate," he said in a low voice once the crewman had disappeared around the corner. "We didn't know that until we got to school and learned it from our classmates."

"Oh, Jack," she whispered.

He cleared his throat uneasily. "While we were younger, still at home, I eventually took it into my head that I should make the duke start treating the others like a proper father. I was used to him despising me and knew there was little hope in that vein, but I became very angry about the way he treated the younger ones. I had long since concluded that I somehow deserved the treatment I received, but there was no way Damien deserved it. Damien tried so hard to please our supposed father, all to no avail. Any other man would have gone down on his knees and thanked God for a son like Damien, but for all his striving, he was completely ignored. Lucien seemed to know better, somehow. Alec was just a three-year-old and stuck to our mother like a nettle—he was her favorite. He's been a favorite with the ladies ever since," he added wryly, "but one day, I just got fed up with the duke making us feel unwelcome in our own home. So we had a bit of a battle."

"Really?"

"Aye." He snorted. "Here I thought I was standing up for my brothers, but Damien screamed at me, telling me to stop making trouble. That I was only making everything worse for everyone. Somehow, as usual, it was all my fault."

She murmured wordless sympathy.

"But my efforts actually worked to some degree, because in contrast to me, yelling in the duke's face and standing up to him that way, the others looked like angels. Finally, Hawkscliffe noticed that he had all these young boys under his roof who believed he was their father. Well, he would've had to have been made of stone not to ease up a bit in his behavior, especially on Damien. He finally realized this lad was a born hero, just waiting for any sign of acknowledgment to point him in the right direction."

"It sounds like you really admire your brother."

"He's a bloody war-hero, Eden. The whole country admires him. Carnarthen, before he died, rallied his friends in the House of Lords to have Damien awarded a title, since truly he was Carnarthen's firstborn son, and his own title would be going extinct. They made Damien the Earl of Winterley, ostensibly as a reward for his valor in the war."

"What about Lucien?"

"Carnarthen left him a huge estate. They both did quite well by their real father," he drawled. "All I got was an old boxing trophy."

"I saw that," she murmured, shaking her head in response to his cynical smile. "Did you ever get to meet your real father?"

"Aye. After Maura ripped my poor young heart out, I went storming off to Ireland to track him down. I thought I might at least find acceptance with him. But that just goes to show you how naive a lad can be." He let out a weary sigh. "Sam O'Shay had retired from the ring by the time I was seventeen. As I said, he had returned to his native Ireland. Turned out he had gotten married to a local lass famous for her temper and her sharp tongue. The Killarney Crusher had settled down, sired a brood of children, and turned into a more or less respectable henpecked husband. When I showed up on his doorstep, the bastard son he'd fathered in a tryst with a notorious English duchess, he asked me to take a walk with him, and then explained to me that I must go away. His wife, you see, didn't know about his indiscretion, and it would have caused his *real* sons and daughters, as he put it, considerable distress and embarrassment, as well."

"Oh, God, Jack."

"He invited me to stay for supper as long as I kept my mouth shut about who I really was. So, after the meal and a polite glass of port, along with a great many lies to explain my visit, I thanked the O'Shays for supper and bid them adieu. Then I went down to a wharfside tavern and got absolutely sotted."

"Oh, darling," she murmured sympathetically.

"Ah, but you haven't heard the best part," he chided. "Got a bit belligerent at the pub. Every pint I gulped down made me ever more keen for a fight. Chip off the old block, eh? After a few too many, the landlord threw me out, and just my luck, I walked straight into the clutches of the press gang."

"The press gang!" she cried. "Jack, you were shanghaied?"

"Aye," he said, chuckling.

"But as an aristocrat—"

"I was drunk. They didn't believe me when I told them I was the Duke of Hawkscliffe's son. Ironic, don't you think?"

"So, what did you do?" she cried.

"There was nothing I could do. They carried me off and signed me up for the navy."

"Good heavens. How did you fare?"

"Oh, about as well as I had in my brief stint at Oxford, dear. For about a month, I put up as much of a fight as I could. Made a point of disobeying every order I was given. Finally, I got tired of being flogged and seized to the shrouds and thrown in the brig, so I quit fighting. I learned how to work, and I learned how to sail." He ran his hand lovingly along the stout oak planks of his ship as he leaned against the bulkhead. "I daresay it saved my life."

Eden regarded him with a tender gaze. "I'm sorry for what you went through, Jack."

"Don't be," he said with a wry smile. "Press gang was the best thing that ever happened to me. If the sun and sea can't cure a man, nothing will."

"So, what happened then?"

"By the time the question of my identity was cleared up and they saw I'd been telling the truth about my lofty connections, there were a great many apologies issued. Feeling vindicated, I chose to reenlist for another two years. His Grace of Hawkscliffe, now rather penitent in his illness, offered to buy me a handsome commission, but I refused. I didn't want any favors from him."

She studied him, trying to picture Jack all those years ago, young, alone and hurting, angry at the world. "He was awfully hard on you, wasn't he?" she asked softly.

"He was better to his hunting dogs."

"A lot of people have failed you."

He said nothing.

"I'm glad you told me, but all of that is behind you, my darling." She pushed away from the wall where she was leaning, crossed the short distance between them. "You've got me now—" She slipped her arms around his neck, kissing his cheek. "And I'm going to give you all the love you can possibly stand."

"You're very sweet," he whispered, resting his hands on her waist.

Eden stretched up on her tiptoes and gave him a kiss, offering comfort.

Jack lowered his head, happy to accept. With a firm yet gentle touch, he pressed his hand into the small of her back, bringing her closer.

When her body was flush against his—chest to chest, belly to belly, the intoxicating heat of his loins fitted snugly to hers—the reaction was mutual and instantaneous.

Desire bloomed between them there in the hull's dim twilight, like one of the jungle's night-blooming flowers.

The tender caress of his mouth upon hers deepened. A wanton sigh escaped her as she shifted restlessly between his legs. He kneaded her shoulders for a moment and then cupped her head with both hands, his fingers invading her neat chignon, and carelessly disheveling it. Eden didn't care.

Clinging to him, she ran her hands through his hair, clutching a handful of it gently to coax him down further to her. He spread his legs wider and slid his back down the wood-planked wall a few inches.

"Come here," he ordered in a husky whisper, pulling her closer still. She stepped one leg over his angled thigh, forming a closer fit between them in the place where she wished she could have him inside of her now.

He clasped her thigh through her skirts as he went on kissing her in rising passion. Her heart pounded, but the subtle motion of his hips was an invitation her body could not resist. She moved with him in scandalous simulation of the act, but Jack had become increasingly determined.

As she nibbled his lower lip in seductive teasing, he loosened her tight bodice and worked his hand down inside, cupping her breast. She let out a whimper when he gave her nipple a delicate squeeze between his thumb and middle finger.

His smell, his touch, his body against hers was driving her mad. She couldn't believe she had ever wanted a silly Town dandy in a fancy coat when there were men like this in the world—not many of them, to be sure, but this one was all hers. She stroked his face, his neck, bringing her palm slowly down his chest.

Reaching down between them, her touch sought the hefty length of him through his black trousers. He let out a low, relishing moan and she smiled lustily upon finding him already hard.

She kissed him aggressively, molding her hand along the bulging ridge that she had found.

"You'd better stop that," he whispered, panting.

"Why?" she asked innocently, squeezing him—hard.

"God." He closed his eyes and dropped his head back against the planks.

It really was the most intriguing organ. She could feel it throbbing against her palm, and the slightest homage she paid it seemed to give him so much joy.

She brought her lips to his ear: "Remember that thing you did to me?"

"What *thing*?" he asked with a wicked smile, dragging his eyes open. They smoldered with blue flame.

"When you . . . kissed me. Here." She took his hand and guided it between her legs. At once, he cupped her mound through her skirts.

"Vividly," he replied, his fingertip finding her pleasure center with unerring aim through muslin skirts and cotton petticoat. The slight touch made her shudder with bliss in response. "What about it?"

"Can—I be allowed to—do that to you?" she asked, panting.

His eyes widened briefly. "Yes!" he blurted out.

Eden smiled, her eyes flashing, but when she licked her lips in

221

anticipation and laid hold of his waistband, he shook his head with a low, chiding laugh. "Not here, little wildcat. We'll get to that some other time." He captured her wrists and moved her hands up to his neck, giving her a soft kiss. "Right now, I have to be inside you."

"Right now, Jack?" she asked breathlessly.

"Yes." He picked her up, carrying her a few feet down the corridor, out of the gloom and into the ray of sunlight beaming in from above. "We're going to have to do this quickly," he whispered as he sat her down on a rung of the companionway's tilted ladder.

Clutching the rung behind her head, she leaned back but didn't dream of protesting as he lifted her skirts, pausing to play with the ribbon garters that held up her stockings. "Very pretty, Miss Farraday," he remarked as he stood between her legs.

"Jack?"

"Yes?"

"What if we get caught?" She flinched with a little shiver of delight at his tickling touch above her knee.

"We won't. Ahh," he breathed, as his climbing touch glided up to her flowing wetness.

Eden fixed him in a sultry stare, too hot for him to bother with maidenly embarrassment when he realized just how ready for him she already was. The place between her legs was soaked with want.

"Take me," she commanded him in a whisper.

Lit up by the single golden sunbeam deep in the underworld gloom belowdecks, Jack stared into her eyes and seemed to realize in that moment how genuine her feelings for him were. Yes, she wanted him, but she was not the sort of girl ever to act on lust alone, and he knew it.

She reached out and took hold of his shirt, pulling him toward her. "I love you, Jack," she breathed. "Make me one with you again."

He leaned down to kiss her, unbuttoning the placket of his black breeches. Then he entered her with a groan. "God, Eden."

She wrapped her legs around him and savored every deep stroke of his wonderful cock. His devouring kisses ravished her mouth.

There were voices from one of the decks well overhead, but instead of deterring either of them, the risk of discovery only spurred on their stealthy lust, making them hurried, panting, frantic for each other.

When one of the voices from above them came too close, Jack lifted her off the ladder, his manhood still buried deep within her. Holding her buttocks in his hands, her skirts spilling over his arms, he carried her back into the darkness, still making love to her on the way.

She hooked her heels behind his back, dazzled and quite crazed by his virtuosity. Rippling muscle, flexing massive biceps, raised her up and down on his slick shaft with ease. His sheer physical power took her breath away, and then he had her right where he wanted her, with her back braced against the wall.

Her feet still couldn't touch the ground, so she kept her legs wrapped around him, her rear end gripped in his hands. His growl thrilled her; soon she was arching her back while Black-Jack Knight simply had his way with her deep in the lower gun deck, ramming her against the wall with the most delicious barbarity.

"Shh, sweeting," he whispered, panting. He hushed her with a soft kiss. She hadn't realized how loud her moans had become—but she noticed her lover had worked up a sweat.

"Oh Jack, you delicious beast, you're *so* good."

He smiled modestly at her moan and took a short break, breathing hard. He rested his forehead against hers, as though merely savoring the experience. The way he brushed his face against hers so lovingly reawakened her tenderness amid the storm of passion. She stroked his hair and kissed his cheek gently. She knew now how much this hard man needed her love.

Starting again, he moved much more slowly now, more deliberately, in counterpoint to his wild ferocity of a few moments ago. Eden gasped, helplessly; threw her head back and surrendered to him, going weak in his strong, strong arms. As she writhed, each breath ripping from her turned into a bewildering sob; his sweetness had burst a floodgate inside her, releasing a long-buried anguish of such piercing pain that she found herself weeping for reasons she could not begin to explain. Words sounded senseless tumbling from her lips as he kissed the tears rolling down her cheeks. "I found you. I can't believe I truly found you—Jack."

"I love you," he whispered barely audibly, and then he gave himself to her in huge pulsations of pure virility. His kiss was too fierce for her mouth—he bit her shoulder through her dress as he came, just hard enough to let her know that she was his. Shudders racked him. "Oh, Eden." After a long moment, he eased her upward a bit and then withdrew from her body, shaking.

She collapsed against the bulkhead behind her, staring at him while her chest heaved. He dragged himself two steps away, to the other side of the passageway, and leaned heavily against the wall across from her.

He let out a ragged exhalation and slowly raked both hands through his tousled hair.

She ran her hands sensuously down her belly, half imagining she could feel his potent seed sparking life in her womb.

Physically spent, her emotions also felt thoroughly wrung out as she wiped the traces of those strange tears away. "Why did I cry?" she whispered.

"Because you know now you won't be alone anymore."

His quiet answer brought fresh tears to her eyes. Maybe her heart had remembered all those times she had climbed to the jungle's highest treetops and had searched the empty horizon, praying for someone to love.

She had found him now.

"You won't be alone anymore, either."

He gave her a smile with such sadness in it, as though he was trying, but could not quite bring himself to believe.

Tra-la!

A distant sound reverberated through the silence at that moment, carrying to *The Winds of Fortune* from over the waves.

Eden turned her head with a small gasp, listening. "What was that?" She could have sworn it was a hunting horn. Two rich, mellow notes—

Tra-la! again.

When she glanced at Jack in question, his white teeth flashed in a grin as he hastily tucked in his shirt.

"Sail-ho!" the men shouted abovedecks.

Tra-la!

"What on earth is that sound?" she exclaimed, nervously tying her bodice and trying to smooth her rumpled hair.

"That," he replied, "is my uncle."

"Sail-ho!" They could hear Higgins hollering from all the way up in the crow's nest. "It's the *Valiant,* lads! Lord Arthur's come!"

224

A general cheer arose from the men.

"Sail-ho!"

Hastening to make themselves presentable after their blazing encounter, Jack and Eden hurried up on deck to greet their guest. Flying the company's colors and insignia, the frigate, *Valiant,* soon anchored at a short hailing distance off the starboard bow.

Jack gave the order for the *Winds* to drop anchor as well, coming to a full stop.

Before long, a mellifluous baritone carried across the waves as the noble old captain of the *Valiant* commanded his crew to lower one of his ship's boats.

Soon, they came across the water, the kingly, uniformed fellow standing in the lifeboat in a stately pose while a half dozen of his trusty sailors rowed.

Jack couldn't stop smiling. First Eden, and now the old fellow he simply adored. He hadn't seen Uncle Arthur in nearly seven months.

As the distinguished nabob clambered aboard *The Winds of Fortune,* at once, across the decks, everyone cheered at his arrival, for he was loved by all who made his acquaintance.

Tall and hale, gray-haired with sky-blue eyes and patrician features, Lord Arthur Knight was still handsome in his sixties, nearly as tanned as Jack after thirty years' service in India.

Arthur was the younger brother of the duke whom Jack had just finished telling Eden about; indeed, Arthur had incurred his elder brother's wrath when he had reproached Hawkscliffe for the way he treated Jack as a child. Uncle Arthur was the only person whom Jack could ever recall standing up for him.

He shook his uncle's hand warmly, received a clap on the back in return, and with a brief exchange of pleasantries, escorted Lord Arthur toward the quarterdeck.

Along the way, their distinguished guest greeted familiar faces among his crew never failing, of course, to remember Rudy. Lord Arthur reached into his pocket and tossed out a biscuit for the dog, who was leaping gleefully on him, then he rumpled the Nipper's hair.

"Ah! There you are, my brave young lad! Great Zeus, you've grown a foot since last we met!" He bent down low to the lad's eye level, bracing his hands on his thighs. "Now, boy, have you been working on your punches?"

"Yes, sir!" little Phineas cried enthusiastically.

"Show me." Lord Arthur held up his left palm. "Ow!" he exclaimed as the Nipper socked Lord Arthur's open hand as hard as he could. "Excellent, Mr. Moynahan! Well done. By Jove, you hit quite as hard as Gabriel and Derek did at your age."

"Do I really, sir?" The boy sprouted another four or five inches before their eyes at the compliment.

"Indeed so! But—not yet as hard as Jack did when he was just as big as you. Keep practicing."

"Aye-aye, sir!"

Moving on, Lord Arthur saluted Trahern with affection and bowed to old Brody, spared a nod for Martin and Peter Stockwell, and exchanged a few pleasantries with Mr. Palliser, the surgeon. Everyone beamed to see him.

Only Trahern sighed to find Lord Arthur had not brought Georgie with him, but it was just as well, Jack thought, for it would have taken ten Traherns to tame that vixen.

"And who have we here?" Lord Arthur exclaimed with a look of astonishment, as he beheld the red-headed beauty.

Eden was blushing scarlet, no doubt with the knowledge of their secret liaison belowdecks, though her gown and her hair all looked perfectly demure.

The contrast between her very proper appearance and her lusty performance of a short while ago fired Jack's interest anew. Even he was a little shocked by his appetite for her.

When Lord Arthur glanced at him expectantly, Jack lifted his bride's dainty hand to his lips and drew her nearer with gentle chivalry, presenting her to him. "This, my good uncle, is Miss Eden Farraday, and would you by chance have a chaplain on board?"

CHAPTER
⊰ THIRTEEN ⊱

*T*here *was* a chaplain on board the *Valiant,* and he married them in a simple ceremony on the quarterdeck at sunset. Afterward, a volley of celebratory cannonfire was let loose, along with cheers from the men for Cap'n Jack and Lady Jay, as the Nipper had dubbed her, now that her legal name was changed to Lady John Knight. A feast was then served in honor of their nuptials, with as fine a meal as could be made down in the galley, and plenty of grog for the men.

Now lanterns blazed and rustic tunes filled the night. Men sang ballads and played airs on a bouncy fiddle, a high-piping piccolo, and a hurdy-gurdy. Merriment filled the air, but Jack knew the occasion was tinged with sadness for his bride because of her beloved papa's absence.

It had fallen to Lord Arthur to bring her before the chaplain and to give her away in her father's stead. After the ceremony, the nabob had entertained her with amusing stories about his adventures in India, along with a few accounts of his sons' latest deeds of derring-do with the cavalry there.

She had listened, smiling, but Jack knew her heart was aching a little. When the meal was over, she let Trahern escort her up to listen to the music, leaving Jack some time to visit privately with his uncle.

They rose as she left, but sitting down at the table again, Lord Arthur beamed warmly at him. "Well done, my boy. She is a charming creature."

Jack smiled faintly in the direction she had gone. "Just being with her feeds my soul," he declared.

Lord Arthur arched an eyebrow. "Who are you and what have you done with my ill-tempered nephew?"

"Oh, leave me alone. A man's got to get heirs, don't he?" he drawled as he poured them both another drink.

"Right. That's all this is about between the two of you."

"Of course." Jack's eyes twinkled as he fought to look stern. "She was a stowaway. What else was I to do with her?"

"Ah, you may try to throw me overboard for saying it, but I know when I see a man in love."

Jack shrugged but did not protest it.

"She'll be a fine ambassador for you when you go back and face the family, I daresay. Ah—that reminds me!—speaking of ambassadors. Your brother Robert's friend, Ian, the Marquess of Griffith—"

"Yes?" he asked. He had just been telling Eden about Maura's elder brother, Ian.

"He's been sent to India to try to negotiate a treaty between our side and the rajas of the Maratha Confederation."

"Really?" Jack murmured. He knew that Ian had developed a certain expertise in diplomacy, but most of his work had taken place in Europe, according to Jacinda's letters. He had been instrumental behind the scenes at the Vienna Congress.

"He was in the region anyway, apparently purchasing tea plantations. Investment, I suppose. He remembered me from years ago and said he'd be honored to call on me in Bombay when he arrived, but of course, I haven't been home in months. Georgie wrote, telling me all of this," he added. "Her letter made its way to me being passed along by your various ships."

Jack nodded. His vessels crisscrossing the seas routinely passed along mail for him and his closest contacts, allowing urgent messages to travel from one end of the globe to the other much more quickly than they did for people who weren't lucky enough to own a shipping company. It was a service that his pretty cousin Georgie did not hesitate to use.

"Last I heard," Arthur continued, "things were coming to quite a boil between the army and the Maratha princes. Trust was so eroded on both sides that an outside negotiator was being sought—someone with whom both sides would feel comfortable—and of course Lord Griffith has developed such a sterling reputation."

"Indeed."

"It was sheer luck that a negotiator of his expertise was so near to hand. I shall be sorry to miss his visit, but Derek and Gabriel will at least get to meet him up at the frontier."

Jack arched an eyebrow. "Won't Georgie get to meet him, as well? If he's planning on calling on you at your palace in Bombay—?"

"I'm trying not to think about that," Lord Arthur said drily, "considering I'm not there to make sure my daughter behaves herself."

Jack snorted. "Even if she doesn't, Ian will. He was always so upright and serious, Arthur. You've got nothing to worry about."

"But you don't understand. To Georgie, a standoffish fellow will seem like a jolly challenge for her seductive skills. With most men, she only has to smile to make them fall in love."

"You shouldn't have named her after my mother," Jack taunted with a smile.

"I *liked* your mother," he retorted. "And admired her. After the heroic way she died, I was happy to name my daughter after her in tribute."

Jack grumbled a wordless answer and tossed back a swallow of liquor.

"In any case, the letter from Georgie wasn't the only communiqué I received on my way here to meet you. I hate to put a blot on the festivities, but—" Arthur hesitated. "Hard news from Venezuela, Jack."

He sat forward. "What news?"

"The war began in earnest shortly after you set sail, and I am sorry to say it is off to a very poor start."

"What happened?"

"A brutal defeat at La Puerta," he murmured. "General Morillo managed to ambush Bolívar's little fledgling infantry in a ravine. Chaos." Lord Arthur shook his head. "Bolívar himself was nearly killed in the retreat. The Spanish captured fifteen hundred muskets, munitions, all the baggage and supplies, even the flags."

Jack whispered an expletive.

"Paez with his cavalry of *llaneros* managed to protect the infantry from complete destruction, but in the confusion, the Spanish got hold of Bolívar's personal effects—including all of his correspondence. The mail bag apparently contained a letter from Don Eduardo Montoya confirming for Bolívar that their 'agent' had been dispatched to London to procure reinforcements as agreed."

"I see," Jack murmured. "So, now they know I'm coming."

"Well, no, they know *someone's* coming. The letter did not mention your name, of course, but the Spanish no doubt will have warned Whitehall that an agent has been sent to London for recruitment purposes. The Crown as well as the Spanish embassy in London will be on the hunt to find out who this 'agent' is."

Jack fell silent. He folded his arms across his chest and leaned back slowly in his chair, brooding on this new intelligence. The Spanish already hated him for protecting Bolivar a few years ago on Jamaica, but he did not need his uncle to explain what could happen if he failed in his quest. What was left of Bolivar's army was doomed if they did not soon get reinforcements; Angostura would be burned to the ground, and the leaders of the revolution put before the firing squad.

"I'm not going to let that happen," he said quietly.

"No, I didn't expect that you would," Lord Arthur replied. "But be careful, Jack. It's your neck on the line. You know, you mentioned your plan about taking over that rival firm in London, but it seems to me that now you've got an even better cover to help explain your presence in Town after all these years."

Jack looked at him in question.

Arthur shrugged. "It is entirely appropriate that you should bring your young bride back to England to meet the whole family."

At once, Jack shook his head. "I could never use her as a shield for my activities. I don't want her anywhere near all of this."

His uncle frowned, looking puzzled. "Well, what are you going to do with her, then?"

"I'm leaving her at the castle in Ireland," he admitted in a low tone.

"I see. And is young Lady Jay aware of this?" he asked dubiously. "Because earlier I heard her speaking with your valet about some of the sights she so looked forward to seeing in London."

Jack sent him an uneasy smile.

"Aha. You haven't told her yet."

"Not exactly."

"I see. Well. First marital spat, dead ahead."

Jack leaned closer, lowering his voice. "She's not going to like it, of course, but she's going to have to do as she's told. I'm her husband now. She has no choice but to do as I say."

Lord Arthur laughed at his assertion.

Jack frowned. "What? Why do you laugh?"

"No reason. After you've been married a month, we'll talk again. But tell me, dear lad, why haven't you told her your plans?"

He shifted warily in his chair. "I didn't want to upset her."

"Bull! It's cowardice. Not that I blame you, of course," he added as he sat back in his chair again. "I would rather fight the Grand Armada than an angry wife any day."

"Eden will do as she's told."

"Does she usually?"

Jack thought it over for a whole five seconds. "No," he announced, then he sighed. "Bloody hell."

Lord Arthur chuckled and swirled the drink in his glass. A glimmer of roguery danced in his eyes. "If you think getting your wife to mind is difficult, wait until you have children."

"You're not helping matters."

"If you ask me, she could be a great asset to you in London. Why don't you want to bring her?"

"Because it's dangerous!"

"For you, yes, but not for her. Not really."

"How so?"

"The main threat is from government agents. English lawmen, Spanish spies. Both are beholden to the rule of law. You're not dealing with thugs and criminals this time. Spain may dislike you, but we both know Spanish chivalry is such that women and children are off limits. Having Eden by your side in London would help to camouflage your activities."

"I told you, I will not use my wife as a shield. I don't need a woman's protection."

"But if she's not in danger and London makes her happy, why not bring her? I hate to see the two of you at odds, as you soon will be, I fear. Are you worried she might say something indiscreet about your mission?"

Jack considered this, then shook his head. "No," he admitted with frank honesty. "She's naive on occasion, but with my life on the line, she'd never let herself blunder. She's very loyal to me— almost protective, in her own little way." A reluctant smile tugged at his lips.

231

"I see." Lord Arthur frowned in suspicion. "Well, then. Your refusal to bring her along wouldn't have anything to do with that Maura woman, would it?"

"No, no."

"I know for a long time you wanted to make her sorry for what she did to you."

"Well, that doesn't really matter anymore."

"So, what's the problem, then?"

Jack stared at him in silence. Then he shook his head. "I don't know."

"I think you do. But, Jack, you've got to give Eden a chance to prove she will stand true by your side no matter what anyone has to say about you."

"Even if the things they say are true?" he countered, then paused. "I don't want to lose her, Arthur. I don't think I could stand it."

"Lock her up against her will the way you're planning, and you may do just that."

"It's for the best."

"For whom? For Eden or for you?"

Jack looked away impatiently.

"What are you afraid of?" his uncle asked in a low tone.

"You want to know? Fine!" he whispered angrily. "She's so damned set on London and the ton. What if we get there and people won't accept her because of me? Because she's mine? I want her to be happy. I don't want her to get hurt."

"And you don't want her to see the way they shamed you."

He lowered his head. "No. I really don't want her to see that at all. Is that so wrong? She'll lose respect for me." Head down, he looked at Arthur fiercely. "I will not permit her to be humiliated because of me."

"Oh, I don't know, Jack. She strikes me as a very strong girl, not the type to let the ton bully her. Besides, you already told her about your real father."

"Yes. But it's different when you see a thing for yourself."

"Jack, it's been a very long time since those days. You're not that angry, powerless seventeen-year-old anymore. You've got fortune. Vast power. You've got twenty years of hard experience under your belt. Use it."

The crisp tone in his uncle's voice drew his attention up sharply. He eyed him with wary interest. "What do you mean?"

"If you want the ton to accept Eden, then *make* them accept you."

"I never could before."

"You never tried. You told them all to go to hell, remember?"

"Well." His wry shrug was indeed an admission of guilt. "I don't know." He shook his head cynically. "What would you have me do, Uncle? Play the game? Bend the knee to Lady Jersey? Sue for vouchers to Almack's? Gamble at the clubs, for God's sake? Waste my afternoons driving in the park like a fop?"

"Yes, Jack. Play the game. You might surprise yourself."

"But I don't want to!"

"Why?"

"I don't know—it would seem an admission of defeat."

"How?"

"I let those people know quite clearly when I left that I didn't give a damn for their amusements or their shallow little lives."

"Ah, and to reverse yourself now though twenty years have passed would be a blow to your pride."

"Damned right! Uncle—you have no room to talk on this subject. You've been an exile even longer than me."

"Aye, I know the cost of having too much pride even better than you do, Jack. I only want you to be happy."

"Eden makes me happy."

"Then if you are wise, you will make *her* happy." Arthur watched him with a canny smile. "What you want is beside the point. What does Eden want? If you love her, that is the only question that matters."

Jack fell silent, staring down into his glass.

"It's all very simple, you see," Arthur murmured. "*Buy* the ton's affection with your gold, and give it to your beautiful young bride as a wedding gift."

Heaving a sigh, Jack leaned his cheek on his fist and scowled at him.

Many hours later, Jack awoke in the pearl-gray half light before dawn to the vision of his sweet young wife sleeping on her stomach beside him, her auburn tresses cast across her cheek, the delicate fan of her long lashes gently lowered, her expression that of sublime peace.

The soft sound of her breathing had become as familiar to him as the lulling song of the sea.

As awareness filtered back into his waking mind, luscious memories of the night before stirred his blood.

Their wedding night.

He lifted his head off his pillow, staring at her. As he came up onto his elbows, still a bit groggy with waking, it stunned him anew to remember that today he was a married man. Even more shocking, indeed, slightly terrifying was the knowledge that he was in love.

Yesterday, he had told her so. He had not expected the words to come out, but they had.

I love you.

Gazing at her now, his little Lady Jay, he knew they were the truest words he'd ever uttered.

His faint smile as he watched her was full of doting tenderness. *So, this is happiness.* The whole sensation was rather strange and new—and perhaps a bit frightening, as well. This utterly odd desire to stay with a woman made him a little uneasy; he was afraid of how much he had already come to care. His deepening passion for her was intemperate; it seemed inevitable that the rug would be pulled out from under him at any time.

Jack's smile slowly faded. He knew that the wedding had been tinged with sadness for her because of Victor's absence, but it had been bittersweet for him, as well, knowing that soon they must part.

His thoughts wandered back to his conversation with his uncle, but he would not be swayed. Already he did not like letting Eden out of his sight, and the thought of a six-month separation made him heartsick.

Beyond their separation, for him, there was nothing but grave danger and the highest of stakes.

He still hadn't told her that he'd be leaving her in Ireland for the duration. He was afraid of how she'd react—and he was perplexed that he should be afraid. Cowardice was not in his nature.

Restless with it all preying on his mind, he got up and crossed the sleeping cabin, naked. He went about his morning ablutions deep in thought, but was bemused to find that his reflection in the mirror looked the same as any other day.

Inwardly, he felt like a different man. A man, he thought grimly, who might have thought twice about risking everything to help this noble cause.

When he had accepted this mission, he had done so with single-minded determination, having no wife to worry about, no possibility of a child on the way. He had had no attachments, nothing to lose but his worldly goods and, of course, his life, but this had caused him no particular worry, considering all the brushes with death he had escaped before.

Now everything was different, and, admittedly, he was feeling torn. A part of him longed to walk away from the mission just so he could stay with her and gorge himself on this love that he had been starved for all his life. No one had ever loved him before, not like this, and he simply dreaded doing or saying one wrong thing that would take her love away from him. It was more precious to him than gold, but it felt as fragile as a flower.

This was why he could not speak to her yet about their impending separation, he thought as he got dressed. Though guilt raked him over the coals for keeping his true intentions hidden from Eden, he knew the revelation would change everything between them. Perhaps it *was* cowardice, worthy of his shame, but he had never experienced love like this before and he could not bear to ruin it with the truth.

Not yet.

He wanted to feel it, revel in it, soak it in, and make the dream last for as long as it could before he must go—possibly to his death.

Buttoning his shirtsleeves about his wrists, he returned to stand beside the bed, where he watched her sleep and brooded on his highly sensible notion of keeping her out of harm's way while he went to complete his mission.

Just off the coast of Ireland now, they would go ashore in a few hours and arrive at the castle today.

Eden must have sensed his study, for at that moment her lashes fluttered, and she began to wake. As Jack watched her with a fierce but gentle protectiveness surging in his chest, he came to a decision.

Rather than simply escorting her to the castle and dropping her off, he could surely take a few days to spend with her there while he summoned the men he intended to recruit. He could use this time to strengthen, aye, to cement the bond between them before he must sail away. After all, there was no rush to tell her what was really happening. Was there?

The right moment would present itself, he was sure of it. It was hard news but she'd take it in stride, the way she always did. At least that was what he wanted to believe.

"Good morning, husband," she greeted him in a scratchy purr. The sheet slipped down over her slim body as she indulged in a big stretch full of feline satisfaction.

"Good morning, wife," he replied in a husky tone. Jack set his knee on the edge of the bed, leaned down slowly, and kissed the valley between her bare breasts. He smiled like a drunkard as she wrapped her arms around him, and then pulled him back into bed with a mischievous laugh.

They had done it, Eden thought later that afternoon, as six of Jack's crewmen rowed her to shore through the floating mist. They had crossed the wild sea, and now, at long last, she would plant her feet on dry land again. It wasn't England—not yet—and in truth, she had come to love life aboard *The Winds of Fortune,* but Lord, she was glad to get off that ship.

Every stroke of the oars dipping rhythmically into the gray-green waves lengthened the distance between her and the mighty gunship. Behind them, greedy seagulls circled the masts, clamoring for handouts. The sound of the ship's bell and the working crew's sea chanty faded as the pounding rhythm of the surf grew louder.

Eden sat on the rocking cutter's low cross-bench, gripping the sides in nervous excitement and shivering with the cold. Phineas was wedged in against Jack's sea trunk from the sleeping cabin, now filled with Eden's newly made dresses and extra clothes for Jack. The Nipper was coming ashore, too, since his Auntie Moynahan was Jack's housekeeper, but Eden ignored the boy's eager prattle, caught up in studying this new land.

From a lush tropical paradise to the austere vastness of the ocean, she had now arrived at a whole new landscape completely unknown to her—one where the air was fresh and chill, where the breakers pounded the stark black rocks that strewed the beach. Here and there the slamming waves curled upward into tall, dramatic plumes of flying foam.

Beyond the craggy beaches, alive with all their watery motion, mysterious green hills beckoned, sculpted in smoothly undulant curves, with even more mysterious valleys between them.

The late March weather was not promising, true. Her first view of Ireland ahead was bleak and overcast, its desolate beauty whispering of grief and bloodshed, ancient heartbreak; but when the sun broke out through the heavy, piled clouds and etched everything with a glimmer of gold, she could suddenly *feel* the magic on these shores. She half expected to see mermaids twirling through the waves.

Ahead, a sturdy dock jutted forth to receive them, reminding Eden nostalgically of the rickety one in the jungle where her journey had begun; but her heart lifted higher still when she caught sight of the powerful figure waiting for her there, bathed in the sudden, fleeting sunshine.

Jack.

The mere sight of him warmed her by several degrees. He had gone ashore a few hours ahead of her to make some preparations while she packed her things: He had wished to give the servants at his estate a few miles inland at least some forewarning that he and his new bride were on their way.

He was also dispatching riders with messages for a few of his friends—Irish officers who had fought under Wellington in Spain. Eden knew of his plans because she had been given the task of copying Jack's letter five times over, asking each of the officers spread throughout the various counties of Ireland to come and meet with Jack in secret.

He had explained to Eden that if all five agreed to sign on for South America, they could rally about a hundred foot soldiers each from their local fighting units. Though the regiments had been formally disbanded at the war's end, the men who had become brothers in arms in the Peninsula certainly kept in touch. It would be easy for them to reassemble a good number of their ranks under Bolivar.

At last, they reached the dock. Higgins lashed the longboat to a post, and then Ballast handed Eden up the sturdy ladder. Jack met her with a smile, clasped her hands, and pulled her to safety. Next came the Nipper. Jack lifted the child up the ladder as if he weighed no more than a sack of flour. Finally, the men hoisted the sea trunk up onto the dock.

The sailors gave her a fond salute, which she returned. She

knew she would see them again in a few days, for as soon as Jack had finished his meeting with the Irish officers, they would get back on the ship and sail on to England.

At least that's what she thought.

Jack hefted the trunk up onto his shoulder while the Nipper ran ahead of them, barreling down the dock toward the black coach with crimson wheels that waited to carry them all to his estate. A stout old coachman took a quick nip from his flask before hopping down off the driver's box to bend and hug Phineas, who ran to him.

"Uncle Pete!"

"He knows all the servants," Jack explained when Eden looked at him in surprise. "They raised him, you see."

"Ah."

"Don't trouble yourself, Peter," Jack chided in amusement when the coachman started to set the boy aside to help his master. Jack loaded their sea chest into the boot of the coach without need of his servant's help, secured it there, and then led her over to the carriage door.

After introducing her to his trusty driver, Jack handed her up into the coach. At once, the smell of well-oiled leather and horses replaced the bracing scent of sea brine and salty oak planks.

When the Nipper had jumped up, tumbling into the seat beside her, Jack shut the door with a smile and locked it.

"Aren't you coming?" she exclaimed.

"Of course," he said, adjusting his thick black leather gauntlets. "But if you don't mind, I'd rather ride. I've been cooped up too long on that ship, and he's been too long in the stable." He nodded to the left.

Following his glance, Eden beheld a magnificent cherry-bay stallion in the nearby grove of trees, his glossy coat gleaming like burnished copper in the golden sunshine, the breeze rippling through his long, sweeping mane and tail of pure black silk.

Tall and absolutely stunning, the fiery steed pawed the ground impatiently as a liveried groom on foot held the reins, awaiting Jack's return.

"It's Fleet Apollo!" Phineas cried, rushing to the window. "He's the fastest horse in all the county!"

"The pride of my stables," Jack conceded with a smile.

Eden stared at the splendid creature as Jack gave her a farewell nod and walked away. He took the reins and mounted up with an easy swing, his dark greatcoat swirling around him; she caught a glimpse of his buff breeches spattered in mud and his shiny black riding boots. As he tugged the brim of his half-scrolled hat a bit lower over his eyes, she thought he looked for all the world like some romantic highwayman. Settling into the saddle, he leaned forward and gave his horse's neck a firm pat.

As the groom strode toward the carriage to take his post beside the driver, Eden suddenly jumped out. Jack sent her a curious glance, urging the horse forward a few steps, but when she smiled at him, understanding dawned, twinkling in his turquoise eyes.

"Lady Jay, what are you doing?" Phineas called, but Eden's stare was fixed on her beautiful man astride his beautiful horse.

Bringing the stallion to a halt beside her, Jack reached his hand down to her, smiling as he stared into her eyes, with the broad blue sky behind him.

Eden took his hand without hesitation, set her foot atop his boot, and sprang up onto the horse with him. He laughed as he hooked his arm securely around her waist; sitting sidesaddle across the horse's withers, she gripped the stallion's jet-black mane.

"Ready?" her husband whispered, wrapping his arm more tightly around her waist.

"Aye, Cap'n."

"Hey!" the Nipper shouted as they surged past the carriage.

"See you at the house, boy!" Jack boomed, his deep voice full of suppressed laughter as the coach lurched into motion behind them.

In moments, they had left the coach far behind. Jack let the mighty Irish hunter stretch out, sweeping along the muddy road at a racer's gallop. The sun shone more brightly, and Eden laughed aloud at the animal's thrilling power, his hoof beats pounding the turf like a drum. Up hills and through dales, past meadows dotted with dingy sheep, they scared a flock of blackbirds up from the stubbled corn and sent a clutch of rabbits darting off through the brambles.

Rounding a bend on the crest of a windy hill, a gust of air mussed her chignon and sent her hair tumbling down about her shoulders.

When they came upon a jaunting cart carrying four nuns back to their convent in the valley, Jack slowed his horse to greet their neighbors. The sisters knew him at once, and when Jack intro-

239

duced Eden as his wife, they looked their amazement, and then gave the two of them a fond benediction there in the road, blessing their marriage and promising their prayers for a happy and a fruitful union.

They rode on at a slower pace, and when the nuns were out of sight, Jack kissed her. "Barely ashore, and already you're winning hearts," he murmured.

"It's the red hair," she teased softly. "They probably think I'm Irish."

"Well, considering where you've come from, I think you'll be happy to hear there are no snakes in Ireland. Saint Patrick drove them out, you see."

"Ah, no snakes! What a pity. Jack?"

"Yes, love?"

"The nuns called me 'my lady.' "

"Well, of course, dear. It is your due."

"Oh." She marveled to absorb this. "I hadn't thought of that."

He laughed and urged his horse on.

Within an hour, Jack turned Fleet Apollo off the road, cantering through a pair of tall wrought-iron gates. Eden's heart beat faster as they rode up the long graveled drive, but when the "house" came into view, her jaw dropped.

"Jack—it's a castle," she blurted out, wide-eyed.

"Don't worry, you will find it very comfortable, I'm sure. Part of it is all made new, with every modern convenience."

She couldn't even find her voice to tell him she hadn't been complaining. She was simply in shock.

A real castle! There were brooding towers and formidable walls hewn from timeworn gray stone. Irregular additions jutted this way and that, made by various owners over the centuries. But the most recent bit was the main block in the center.

Through the skill of some cunning architect, a large neo-Gothic house built in front of the ancient keep somehow pulled the whole pile together, a castle-fortress fantasy with a crenellated portico above the massive front doors and matching towers framing the front face. The trim around the tall, narrow windows was fresh and white; not a weed grew out of place. It was as impeccably kept as the spotless decks of *The Winds of Fortune*.

The place was pure Jack.

Every modern convenience, indeed, she thought. As he had

pointed out, the stern Gothic fantasy was tempered by a hint of Classical ease, as if to assure the viewer that, inside, the home was graced with every luxury. She shook her head, amazed.

When they came to a halt in the sprawling courtyard, half a dozen servants came running. She couldn't tell the grooms from the footmen, though she guessed that the fellow in black was the butler, and the round lady with apple cheeks must be Mrs. Moynahan.

Eden's head was spinning. Amid a chorus of "Welcome, my lady!" Jack shooed the staff aside and helped her down from the horse. But instead of setting her on her feet, he shifted her into his arms and strode toward the front door, carrying her over the threshold.

Giving her a gentle kiss, he set her down inside. Eden nearly stumbled, staring all around her at the great hall, with its dark, carved wood, stained glass, and wondrous age-old tapestries; its gleaming flagstone diamond squares of white and bluish gray; its soaring corbeled ceiling painted white, and the cozy inglenook with a fireplace taller than she was.

"Well?" Jack murmured, watching her. "You are the lady of this house now. What do you think?"

"Shiver me timbers," she whispered, and the whole staff burst out laughing.

The next three days passed as a beautiful dream, each moment like a pearl. Three days of shining love . . . and unbridled passion.

The heat of their desire awoke the spring, melted away the gray dreary frost, and began to revive the trampled grasses back to their emerald green. They made love constantly: in the grand bedchamber; in the stable; in the curtained inglenook before a roaring fire, atop a rich fur throw; in the back stairwell, rough and quick; against a tree that overlooked the valley. They simply could not get enough of each other.

Now and then, of course, Eden sensed the shadow lurking beneath Jack's tender manner, but she attributed it to his understandable concern about his mission.

For now, however, three blissful days, all work was set aside. She had never known such joy, such pure relaxation, and above all, such love. She could hardly believe how much Jack had come to matter to her or how much she knew she had come to matter to Jack. She had never been so close to anyone before in her entire

241

life. He was more than just her husband or her lover, he had become her dearest friend.

They spent hours happily doing nothing at all but wandering the grounds hand in hand, stopping to pet the horses in the pastures. They strolled through the nearby village and Eden met the local folk, who showered them with humble wedding gifts.

On the third evening, after visiting the village shops before they closed for the day, they made love in the carriage on the way home, laughing and trying to be quiet so the driver wouldn't hear. Old Peter was no fool, though; pretending a tactful ignorance, he cleared his throat loudly upon their arrival in the torch-lit court-yard. He gave them plenty of time to make themselves decent before opening the carriage door.

Jack got out first, a trifle flushed, his dark hair tousled.

"Good man," he mumbled, tucking a fiver into the coachman's breast pocket. Then he turned back for Eden, who melted out of the carriage into his arms, feeling boneless with the aftermath of pleasure.

Wicked amusement danced in Jack's eyes as he gave her his arm, letting her lean on him. They ambled slowly back into the house. In their chamber, Eden took off her clothes and dropped into bed with the taste of his kiss still warm on her smiling lips; the moment her head hit the goose-down pillow, she sank into a deep and dreamless sleep.

The next morning, however, the dream broke off abruptly when she awoke. She opened her eyes and found Jack sitting in the arm-chair near the bed, watching her as he was wont to do.

With a drowsy smile, she stretched amid champagne-colored sheets. They smelled of sex, and so did she. "Good morning, hus-band."

A wistful half smile curved his lips.

"You're all dressed. So handsome." She sighed, admiring his tweed coat, dark green vest, and brown twill breeches. He wore knee-boots and must have been ready to walk out the door, for he even had a riding crop in his hand. He toyed with it idly. "Going out for a morning gallop?"

He didn't answer, lowering his gaze.

"Come back to bed." She closed her eyes, rolling onto her stom-ach. "It's too early."

"Eden," he said gently, "I have to go."

"Is it time for your meeting?" she mumbled against the pillow.

"Yes."

"Very well. When you come back, we can have a picnic in the old solarium—"

"Darling," he cut her off.

"What, Jack?"

He was silent for a long moment. She lifted her head again and stared at him, then noticed the quiet resolve in his rugged face.

She sat up suddenly, clutching the satin sheet to her bosom. "What is it?"

"I told you, love. It's time for me to go."

"Go—?"

He leaned closer, setting the riding crop aside. "Be calm, now," he soothed, holding her in a steady gaze. "Try to understand. I want you to stay here while I complete the mission."

"Stay here? Jack, what are you talking about? We're going next to England. . . ." Her words trailed off as the blood drained from her face. "You're going to England . . . without me?"

"Eden, my uncle told me of some bad developments in the war. I can't stay in England long. I'll only be there for a few short weeks to round up the men I need. I've got a stop at Cornwall, then at London, and then I'm sailing back straightaway to Venezuela."

"Jack!" She stared at him, scarcely comprehending. How utterly diabolical of him to do this to her first thing in the morning before she could think clearly—oh, perhaps all of this was a bad dream. She rubbed her forehead, trying to wake up. But knowing Jack, he had chosen his timing on purpose.

"I'll be back from South America in the autumn," he said in a delicate tone. "You'll be safest here until then."

"The autumn?" Eden could barely absorb what she was hearing. "You're going to leave me alone here for *six months*?"

"Darling, I can't take you with me on a ship full of mercenaries, nor Phineas, for that matter. You and the boy will both stay here, where you'll be safe."

"Jack!"

"I'm sorry, Eden. Not all the men I'm bringing back to Bolivar are simple soldiers."

"I don't care what they are! I'm not staying here by myself! That's exactly the reason why I left the jungle!" She jumped out of bed and strode toward her closet. "I need to be with you. You

243

know I do. And you need me. Especially in London. If I'm not there to smooth things over, you're going to make things worse between you and your family. You know you need me there."

"Eden," he whispered, faltering. He steeled himself visibly and stood. "I've got to go."

"Well, you can just wait because I'm getting dressed and I'm coming with you. Don't you dare walk out that door, Jack Knight."

"You're not coming with me. Eden, you've got to let me go."

She had already slipped a chemise on over her head. "Yes, I am coming with you, and do you know why? Because you promised. You promised to take me to England—just like Papa!" She reached for a gown.

"No. I never promised that." He shook his head staunchly, resting his hands on his waist.

"Well, it's what you let me believe, and that's the same thing, is it not? How long have you been planning this—all along, you blackguard? From the very start?" She was shaking and flabbergasted, scrambling to get ready to go with him. She was perfectly incensed. "I can't believe you lied to me."

"I never lied to you."

"You deceived me, didn't you? You tricked me! You had this whole plan up your sleeve from the start, admit it! Oh, all the things I let you do to me—and you were playing me false all the time! There is a snake in Ireland after all!"

"I thought you liked the things I do to you."

"That's not the point, and you know it. I trusted you!" Tears flooded her eyes. She could feel herself starting to panic, for he was implacable, and somehow she already knew the battle was lost. "How could you do this to me?" she nearly screamed at him.

"Eden, calm down—"

"No! You can't do this to me, Jack! I can't be alone here for months and months on end all by myself. Look at all I went through to go back into the world again. If you lock me up here, I might as well have stayed in the jungle with Connor!"

He bristled. "Don't compare me to him."

"I won't stay here. You can't make me."

"Actually, I can. The footmen have their orders."

"Oh? I'll drug them all with caapi leaf and make them fall asleep—I'll run away."

"You will do nothing of the kind!" he bellowed, looming over

244

her with a glower. "So help me, if you pull a stunt like that, you will know my wrath." He tore the gown out of her hands and threw it on the ground. "Stop this now! You're not coming with me. I'm leaving you here for your own safety. I will take you to England as soon as I get back. Though by that time, you may be too big with my child in your belly to travel."

"I am not pregnant," she informed him, struggling to bring her raw emotions back under control.

"No?" He eyed her skeptically. "It would explain this hysterical reaction."

She narrowed her eyes in warning. "You have not seen me hysterical yet, my lord."

"It gets better?" he mumbled under his breath.

"You add insult to injury?" she exclaimed, shocked from panic back into fury, which was no doubt his intention.

"I have to go." As he turned and walked away from her with measured paces, Eden followed, her heart pounding, knots in her stomach.

"Come back here! We need to talk about this."

He ignored her.

"This is outrageous! You can't keep me here against my will!"

He picked up his greatcoat, draped over the chair. "Good-bye, Eden. I'll be back as fast as I can. Whatever you need, simply let Mrs. Moynahan know—"

"I'll bet I know the real reason you don't want me with you!" she flung out, frantic enough to say anything to stop him now. "You just want to go and see your precious Maura in London without your wife around!"

"*Now* you're hysterical."

"Don't tell me I'm hysterical!" She threw a shoe at him. He ducked in the nick of time and spun around with a look of rage.

"You were going to leave without even saying good-bye, weren't you?" she accused him, her voice rising shrilly. "That's why you're all dressed! You nearly walked out and left me to wake up alone!"

"Right now, it rather seems a good idea."

"Did you even write me a note?" She suddenly burst into tears.

Cursing under his breath, he strode back to her and grabbed her around her waist; clutching her to him, he kissed her with rough passion, tangling his fingers in her hair.

His abrupt motion took her off balance. She clung to his shoulders to keep from falling and returned his kiss with tears coursing down her cheeks. The desperate kiss she gave him begged him to stay, though she already sensed it was futile; the man was stone. She quivered with pain in his arms to think of all those months and months of loneliness, separation, locked up here alone.

Isolation.

"I'm not ready for this," she whispered, capturing his hard face between her hands. "Please don't do this to me, Jack. Don't leave me here alone," she breathed as she kissed him. "I'll do whatever you say. Don't leave me."

"Do you think I want this?" he demanded in a harsh whisper, angrily tightening his hold around her waist.

She gazed at him in bewilderment, her eyes blurred with tears. "I don't know. You must, because you're Jack."

"What the hell is that supposed to mean?"

"It means when Jack Knight really wants something, he always finds a way. You could take me with you if you really wanted to. You just—don't," she said with a quiet sob.

He seemed exasperated. "You understand nothing."

"What's to understand?" She released him from her embrace and backed away, shaking her head. "You obviously don't love me as much as I love you."

She waited for him to say she was daft, but he stared into her eyes, emotion churning in his gaze; his face was etched with anger, indeed, with a hint of confusion. He just shook his head at her in silent, scathing reproach, then pivoted without warning, and marched away.

"Jack!"

He vanished through the doorway, the sound of his strides echoing behind him in the sharp rhythm of his boot-heels striking the flagstones.

"Jack!"

She rushed after him in her chemise and ran out to the top of the carved oak gallery.

He was below, already crossing the great hall. He didn't look back in answer to her panicked cries.

Her mind reeling with sheer disbelief, Eden flew back into their chamber and looked out the window.

In the courtyard below, he had already mounted his horse.

He looked up.

As their gazes locked from across the distance, he stared hard at her, angry torment glinting in his turquoise eyes. She rested her fingertips on the window pane as though to touch him.

Jack.

"No," she breathed, flattening her palm against the glass as he wheeled his horse around and went galloping off down the drive.

Without a backward glance.

A thousand curses poured through his mind as he raced Fleet Apollo down the muddy road, thundering on toward the bustling port town of Cork.

He refused to question his decision, locking Eden away in his castle. But he felt like utter hell.

He had been ready for her anger; he had even braced for tears. What he had not at all prepared for was her pain.

I hurt her. His mind felt numb with the realization. *I hurt my sweet girl.*

It was the most horrible feeling in the world, and he had no idea what to do. Here on the cusp of his mission, just when he most needed to have himself and everything else under perfect control, he was utterly routed, completely unsure. This was the right thing to do.

Wasn't it?

Why did she always have to be so damned much trouble? No answers came by the time he reined in his splendid thoroughbred outside the Green Anchor Pub overlooking the harbor.

As he handed the stallion off to his head groom, who had followed on a hack horse, Jack paused to survey the bustling port. Fishing boats draped in netting dotted the harbor, bringing in their morning catch; a few small sailboats scuttled about, while the daily packet ship was taking on passengers. But farther back, where the water was deeper, *there* she waited, beyond the fray—a duchess among dairy maids: *The Winds of Fortune,* right on schedule.

When he was through here in the pub, Trahern would pick him up in one of the cutters; once Jack was back onboard, they'd journey across the Irish Sea to Cornwall. There, he would meet next with a few of his past associates who would no doubt be game for a go at the Venezuelans' offer.

They were fighting men of a particularly fierce stripe, rough-and-ready adventurers from his days in the once-profitable smuggling trade.

Outlaws.

By Jack's calculation, Bolivar's army could use a bit of ruthlessness. It would take all the general's genius to control the sort of troops that he'd be sending, but he had promised to bring them devils, and now he was going to meet with the first batch.

Jack turned and trudged into the tavern to rendezvous with his Irish chums, former captains in Wellington's Peninsular Army.

The quiet local pub was as dim and cozy as a cave, with dark oak paneling on the walls, dingy ivory plaster above it, and low, heavy beams running across the ceiling. A layer of hay had been strewn across the flagstone floor for warmth and to collect the mud and wet from the men's boots. The wind moaned like a ghost under the eaves.

The dim, peaty-smelling pub was lit with whale-oil lamps, a few tallow candles, and a large, roaring fireplace. As Jack gazed briefly into the flames, an unbidden memory came, of making love to Eden in the great hall's inglenook on a pile of fur throws before a fire just like that. The vision made him quiver. He shook it off with a will. It was going to be a damn long six months.

The men he had come to meet waved at him from their table in the corner. Though no longer in uniform, they had the bearing of seasoned soldiers, ready for anything. Restless as hell on half pay, no doubt.

They grinned when they saw him coming.

"Jackie-boy!"

"The devil himself!"

Jack summoned up a thin smile. "Kirby, Torrance, O'Shaunnessy, Graves! Where's that rascal Miller?"

"Here he is now."

They exchanged hearty handshakes, rude greetings, and claps on the back. Jack gestured for a round of ale as he sat down with them. "How the hell are you, lads? Enjoying your retirement?"

"No!" they cried in roguish unison, and as soon as the first round was done, Jack got down to business.

When he left the pub a couple of hours later, an unlit cheroot dangling from his lips, the sky had clouded over and the temperature had dropped. Trahern was outside admiring Jack's horse.

"Ho, Captain! Ready to make sail?" the young lieutenant called cheerfully.

Jack gave no reply, tapping his hat restlessly against his thigh as he stalked over to join him with a disgruntled sigh.

"How was the meeting?" Trahern asked in a lower tone as Fleet Apollo nosed his pockets for something to eat.

"Quite well," he muttered. "They all agreed to the proposition." He glanced around furtively at the comings and goings around the inn yard. "We'll give them a few weeks to gather their men, then we'll be back to pick them up."

"Excellent! But why do you look so grim?"

Jack shook his head and turned away.

"It's Eden, isn't it?" Trahern murmured. "She took it hard?"

"Awful."

"Well—" Trahern took his fob watch out of his waistcoat pocket and looked at the time. "It's not too late to bring her with you. You've got just enough time to fetch her before high tide."

Shaking his head, Jack ran his hand through his hair, and then gripped the back of his neck. It throbbed with tension. "I don't know."

Trahern eyed him shrewdly. "Best decide soon."

He tossed his head with a snort and prowled away, pacing to the edge of the hillside, where he stared out over the bay.

His uncle's words preyed on his mind.

Are you really doing this for her sake or is it for yours? Buy her the ton's affection. You're not that angry seventeen-year-old anymore . . .

He looked out at the sea, the wilderness he had escaped to. Maybe not so different from her father, after all. He had always been the sort of man who, when he made a decision, seldom changed his mind. He had devised this plan entirely by his usual mode of thought: logical, precise, effective.

But so much had changed, his whole life had changed after these few days of bliss, and now the old way of thinking didn't seem to make sense anymore.

She was right, he thought. *I did deceive her. And I was wrong.* The whole point of the past few days had been to cement the bond between them so that Eden would forgive him when he sailed away, but Jack had not anticipated the effect that these days with her would have on *him*.

249

Ironically, the deepening of their love made it all but impossible for him to go, leaving her behind like this—so hurt, so angry, so alone. Surely he could find another way. . . .

Perhaps she could stay with his family while he went to South America. Then at least she wouldn't be so alone, and he could rest assured that she'd be safe.

He had never meant to hurt her in his desire to protect himself, but he still dreaded the thought of taking her to London. If they shamed him in front of her, if they swayed her to view him as a pariah, or, above all, if they dared reject her because of him, by God, he'd take a barrel of black powder and blow their precious Almack's to high heaven.

But on the other hand, Arthur was right. She was no ordinary woman, his little orchid lady. Indeed, there was an equal chance the ton might fall in love with her as he had. And how happy that would make her.

Jack pivoted, threw down his cheroot, and strode toward his horse.

"Where are you going?" Trahern called in surprise as Jack leaped up into the saddle, taking up the reins before he changed his mind.

"To get my wife," he clipped out. "I'll be back anon. We'll sail with the tide." He urged the animal into motion, and Fleet Apollo was off like a shot. Jack rode low over his neck, praying he wouldn't regret this.

CHAPTER
⟨ FOURTEEN ⟩

*J*ack had apologized—and he was sorry—Eden could tell that he wasn't just saying the words.

He had come back for her.

He had brought her to London.

He had taken the finest suite in the grand Pulteney Hotel for their lodgings, the same opulent rooms where the Czar of Russia had stayed.

But although Eden had accepted his apology, her trust in him had been shaken, and her demeanor toward him had cooled.

Every day since their arrival, he had lavished her with extravagant gifts as though she were a princess. First her clothes. The gowns Martin and she had sewn on the ship were good enough for the countryside, he said, but nowhere near fine enough for Town. Jack had dispatched his valet to discover the city's best modiste, and then gave the woman an enormous bribe and had charmed her into agreeing to put aside her usual clientele to sew a complete Town wardrobe for his young bride. Work on this massive undertaking was begun post-haste.

Jack then procured a small army of ladies' maids to wait on her and some sturdy footmen, too. A few days after that, he sent a servant up to tell her to look out the window down at the street.

When Eden had stepped out onto the wrought-iron balcony, clad in her first finished dress, a floaty thing of airy emerald silk, her husband tipped his hat to her from the driver's seat of an extravagant cream-colored barouche, which he had just bought for her at Tattersall's.

It had pink satin squabs, and surely a daintier lady's carriage had never been made: Elegant enameled flowers were painted in a garland all around the sides, while the wheel spokes were done in colors to match, gold and blue and pink. The barouche was drawn by a team of four white horses with pink plumes on their heads.

Eden had stared at it, not knowing what to say.

She did not mind the gifts, but the hurt could not be instantly forgotten.

She did not know anymore where she really stood with the man. She felt like a fool for having opened herself to him so completely, holding nothing back; she had thought he had been doing the same, but to her shock, it had turned out that he had been deceiving her.

Now she couldn't help wondering what else he wasn't telling her.

She knew that he cared about her, otherwise he wouldn't have married her, but he was a rich and powerful man of the world, and she had finally figured out that he really didn't take her all that seriously.

He didn't really respect her. Eden feared that that was her fault, for giving in to him too easily on board *The Winds of Fortune*. Now she learned the price of her weakness for him, her too willing surrender: He did not see her as an equal, the way she had believed he did, but more like a possession, an asset, a *thing*—like some porcelain doll he could bedeck in finery and place safely on a shelf until he had time to play with her again. It made her sick to realize that this might be the extent of her role in his life, when, for her part, she loved the blasted terror of the seas to distraction.

Brooding on it, and stewing in the hurt, left her bruised and unsettled inside. But, truly, he had never offered a logical explanation of *why* he had wanted to leave her in Ireland.

He had claimed on the awful morning of their fight that it had all been a question of the danger to her, but Eden still saw no evidence that she was remotely in peril. So, she was left not knowing the real reason Jack hadn't wanted to bring her to England with him. All manners of doubts and fears crept in. Maybe he was ashamed of her jungle oddball ways and feared she would embarrass him in front of his family. Maybe all these fancy trappings were being bestowed on her to try to disguise how . . . *unique* she was, she thought unhappily. For that matter, was it really love or simply guilt that had made him come back for her in the end?

As the days passed, they did their best to get along, pretending everything was normal. He took her around and showed her the sights: the Panorama, Astley's, the British Museum, the art galleries, and the parks—even to famous Gunther's for ice cream. But somehow, now that she was actually here, the glow of all her golden London fantasies had dimmed.

He said she was acting distant, but she was feeling lost and a little depressed. She didn't mean to pull back from him this way; she couldn't help it. She was afraid to let herself become open to him as she had in Ireland for fear that once again she would get hurt.

Noting her subdued response with grim resolve, her husband redoubled his efforts. Next he resorted to buying her jewels.

Eden marveled at the diamonds, but when she met his guarded stare as he waited for her verdict, the glitter could not help but make her feel suspicious.

Did he really think he could *buy* back her trust?

What the hell else am I supposed to do? Jack thought. If diamonds didn't work, there was little left to try. He knew he was wrong, and had strived to make amends, so why was she holding a grudge?

Damn it, he could not afford this distraction right now. His wife's displeasure with him preoccupied his thoughts when he most needed to focus. He was on edge with his craving for things to go back to normal between them, but that was beginning to seem downright unlikely.

Once, when he had been foolish enough to let a word of complaint about her distant manner slip past his lips, she had snapped at him.

"Shall I be cheerful just to please you, my lord?"

No, Jack didn't want that. He wanted Eden back, his saucy redhead, his smiling companion. He wanted his little orchid oddball back, not this perfectly coiffed, silk-clad stranger who was trying so hard to be a ton *élègante.*

But for all that, he knew he only had himself to blame. Eden felt the way she felt, and that was his fault. He was the one who had damaged their love, and by God, he was disgusted with himself for it, but he was doing his best to make up for it. He couldn't seem to win.

He felt alone.

She was pleasant, distant, calm. Jack feared he'd lose his mind.

What scared him most were those long, excruciating silences when neither of them could think of a single word to say to the other. They just sat there, hollow. Surely they could get back the magic they had tasted together in Ireland, but Jack didn't know how.

He thought lovemaking could have helped to heal the breach, but she wouldn't let him touch her. He could tell she wasn't denying him just to punish him—this was no game. She genuinely did not want his hands on her. It seemed the bruise he had dealt to her trust had inhibited her ability to respond to him.

When he had tried in a more determined way to coax her into passion, she had lain there, unresponsive. He had gotten up and walked away.

He was aware of other women giving him come-hither looks everywhere he went, but he was completely uninterested.

It was ironic, really. He had been so worried about the ton rejecting him in front of Eden, but maybe he should've been worried about Eden rejecting him in front of the ton.

It was now April and the Season was getting underway.

Maybe she *was* pregnant, he thought, for he had never known her to be moody. Maybe a child could help them save their love before it was too late. Oh, but that was a fine thing to do to a newborn babe, he realized cynically. Place the full burden on its tiny shoulders of saving its parents' marriage.

Jack struggled on from day to day as best he could. The spring had come, but it felt like weeks since he had seen the sun.

A peculiar side effect of his falling-out with his lady was the strange influence it had on the way he handled business. He had made his presence known to the rival company whose conquest he had plotted from across the sea.

But when he got there and saw the frail old Jewish man who had founded the firm and had spent his life building it up, Jack didn't have the heart to bring down the hammer. Instead, he caught himself musing on any possible unforeseen consequences of decisions made through his old way of thinking.

Black-Jack Knight, terror of the seas, began giving humanity quarter.

He barely knew that ruthless fellow anymore, in fact, and was no longer sure it was who he wanted to be.

Begrudgingly, and much to his own thorough bemusement,

instead of crushing his competitor, he had taken a seat across from the old man and let himself be drawn into negotiation for a more peaceable solution.

Later that night, he brought Eden some flowers and then went off to meet with the London contingent that he intended to recruit for the mission. These were not soldiers but a large gang of river rats. Smugglers. He knew them from his gun-running days.

He took Trahern with him, glad for sane male company.

The meeting went well—which was to say they did not get their throats cut—and that was a promising start.

"I'm not sure Bolivar meant for us to send him the flotsam and jetsam of the world to man his army, Jack," Trahern remarked under his breath as they stepped out of the East End tavern where Jack had just made the same overall speech that Jack had given the veterans in Ireland and the ex-smugglers in Cornwall.

"Probably not," he conceded in a murmur, "but you'll generally find that the dregs of the earth are damned tough, and make excellent fighters."

"Tell me again how you know those people?"

"Former business associates," he replied, a cigarillo dangling from his lips. He decided to splurge and lit it.

Like the Irish and Cornish, he knew these lads were desperate. The Bow Street Runners, skilled detectives, collected bounties for every thief they caught, and with the war over, the Home Office had begun beefing up the ranks of the Metropolitan Police and Thames River Police to deal with them, as well.

"I know better than anyone your situation," he had told them, realizing that if these hard lads suspected a trick, he and Trahern might not leave the pub alive. "I have stood in your shoes. But look around you, my lads. The field is bare; the walls are closing in. With the war-time trade bans lifted, proper merchants have taken over once again and have ruined your livelihood. You've got the Home Office closing the net on you, cracking down. It doesn't have to be this way," he had said, looking around at them with a cool, probing stare. "All your lives you've been treated as outcasts. Believe me, boys, I know how it goes. I'm offering you and your mates an honorable way out of all this, a chance to be something more—to be a part of something larger than yourselves, and make a new start in a profession that won't have you ending your days dangling at the end of a rope."

"You were brilliant in there," Trahern admitted.

Jack snorted. "Nice to know I can do something right."

"Nobody ever talks to such men about honor. I think you might have really gotten through to them."

"We'll see."

When he got back to the Pulteney Hotel, Eden was wrapped in a gauzy, white, translucent negligee that made Jack's mouth water the minute he stepped in the door and saw her.

"You look ravishing," he murmured.

She avoided his stare with a vague "Hm." She pointed toward the console table by the door. Jack spotted a letter on the silver tray there.

He heaved a thwarted sigh and picked up the letter. "Who's it from?"

"Their Graces of Hawkscliffe," he said wryly.

"Oh! They must have got our note."

"They did." Eden and he had sent word to his family only yesterday informing them of their arrival in Town. They had waited, he guessed, in an effort to fix things between them before complicating matters with the family.

Oh, well.

"What do they say?" she asked nervously as he opened it.

"We are cordially invited to Knight House tomorrow night. Dinner with the family."

"Gracious," she whispered, wide-eyed. "I never thought I'd ever meet a duke."

"He's just a human being," Jack replied. "He couldn't tie his shoes 'til he was nearly seven."

"Really?"

"Aye. And once when he was twelve he fell off his horse and cried like a baby."

"You're lying," she accused him, fighting not to smile.

Jack grinned and planted his hand on the wall beside her, trying not to stare too much at her nipples, visible through the wispy zephyr silk. "If it's any consolation, Robert's wife, Belinda, was no higher born than you. Her father also was some sort of gentleman scholar."

"Really?"

"So says my sister. But you already know that," he added with an ever so gently teasing smile. "You read the letters."

She succumbed reluctantly to a very small but genuine half smile. He counted that as progress.

Encouraged, and aching for her, Jack lowered his head slowly and kissed her petal-soft cheek. He lingered there, seized with a shudder of pure longing.

She had been still as his lips grazed her cheek so hungrily, but when she sensed the hot wave of his need, she took a delicate backward step, her green eyes flashing with her unspoken "no."

Jack just looked into her eyes and then lowered his gaze, flinching. "How much longer are you going to shut me out?" he rasped, but she had already vanished into her separate room.

He flexed his fist by his side, but managed not to punch the wall. *Damn it!*

She was more wary of him now than when he had first found her as a stowaway.

The next evening, they set out for Knight House at the appointed time, riding in the shiny black town coach that Jack had bought for himself at Tattersall's the same day he had bought the white barouche for her.

Eden was extremely nervous, caught up in her anxiety about finding favor with his family, while Jack sat locked in stoic silence, staring out the carriage window while the elegant environs of St. James's passed them by. After her rejection of the night before, the gulf between them seemed to have widened still more, but Eden couldn't think about that now. She was too busy privately fretting about her appearance.

She was a bit afraid to move in the glorious dinner gown that the modiste and her frantic crew of seamstresses had only finished sewing two hours ago. The fit was perfect: a half-dress evening costume of lustrous glacé silk in a pale peach shade. As for Eden's hair, her new French lady's maid, Lisette, had designed a suitable coiffure, braiding her tresses and coiling them up into a topknot, which was held in place with a great many hairpins and adorned with a string of tiny pearls that Jack had brought her a few days ago.

He had seemed pleased with the results when she had emerged from her chamber, and certainly his appearance was beyond reproach.

Stealing a furtive glance at him from beneath her lashes, her heart fluttered foolishly at the sight of her husband, all opulent, lordly elegance this night. He was awe-inspiring in formal black superfine trousers, the matching tailcoat accenting the sweeping breadth of his shoulders and his trim, flat waist. How well she knew—and missed—that powerful body beneath his snowy waist-coat of impeccable white silk grosgrain, that sweet throat enwrapped in a starched muslin cravat, superbly fashioned.

Well done, Martin, she thought ruefully. But despite his cultured evening attire, he was still Jack, with his air of ruthless danger beneath the polished veneer.

Yet he seemed a million miles away as he stared out the window, looking like he wasn't really there—as if a part of him had already sailed off across the sea.

Eden suppressed her frustration and lowered her gaze to her gloved hands, toying with her reticule. She knew he wanted sex, but what did he expect? You could not deceive a woman and then expect a welcome in her bed. Instead of expensive presents, he could try giving her answers, and then perhaps her trust could be restored.

While she stared morosely out the opposite window, they rode on in silence until the coachman turned the team of four black horses off Pall Mall.

"Here it is," Jack mumbled, nodding at the magnificent town palace that took up half the block.

"Blazes," Eden whispered, peering out the window and sud-denly feeling rather small.

With royalty for neighbors and a commanding view of Green Park, the town residence of the Dukes of Hawkscliffe was a gleam-ing monument of Palladian grandeur. Knight House had a half-moon portico supported by great columns, and a row of bronze goddesses posing here and there atop their pediments along the roof.

Her heart thumped against her ribs as their coach passed through the tall, wrought-iron gates and glided to a halt in the pri-vate courtyard. She cast Jack a questioning glance, barely noticing how it had become second nature for her to look to him for reas-surance. Instead, however, she was startled by the grim look on his face.

Long-buried anger and brooding intensity hardened the rugged lines of his jaw and brow as he stared at the mansion, and thinned his unsmiling lips into a narrow seam. His turquoise eyes were cold, and the sight of him like this jarred Eden's memory back to that day in the lower gun deck when he had told her all about his painful past.

Suddenly, she felt a flash of contrition, jarred out of her grudge.

He needs me now, she thought, and she knew then it was time to set her hurt feelings aside.

Eden understood better than anyone how difficult this night was going to be for him. Whatever troubles lay between the two of them, surely they could set all that aside for tonight and at least put up a united front.

He was already stepping out of the carriage; the groom had opened the door and banged down the metal step for them. Jack turned around again to steady her as she alighted. Eden drew her light silk wrap around her shoulders and accepted his offered hand.

She gave him a nod and they proceeded to the front door—side by side, not touching. They crossed under the grand portico, and as they waited for one brief moment for the door to be opened to them, Eden reached down and took Jack's hand.

The touch surprised him, judging by his quick, probing glance. She held his gaze, signaling her loyalty in silence.

I'm here, darling.

He said nothing, but the tension in his face eased slightly, and she caught the flicker of emotion in his eyes. Her slight smile offered reassurance: His grateful nod in answer was barely perceptible, but he lifted his chin and squared his shoulders, and then he was ready, just as the butler opened the door.

"Good Lord—old Walshie!" Jack exclaimed, lifting his eyebrows. "I'd forgotten all about you!"

"Why, thank you, sir," the stately butler intoned as he opened the door wider, admitting them with a smooth bow into the white marble magnificence of the ducal residence.

Eden gazed in awe at the sweeping, curved staircase that floated up to the main floor without visible support. A towering crystal chandelier hung overhead, as big as a waterfall.

"I trust that you are well?" Jack asked, looking genuinely pleased to see the longtime family butler.

"Persevering, sir. How kind of you to ask."

"I tell you, man, you haven't aged in twenty years. Uncanny."

Jack gave the stately servant a roguish clap on the shoulder. "Perhaps a bit more gray in the side-whiskers, is all."

"Indubitably, my lord. Madam, may I take your wrap?"

"Thank you," Eden responded, giving the dignified fellow a smile as Jack lifted the swathe of silk off her shoulders and handed it to the man, making a quick introduction between her and Mr. Walsh.

"Well, where are they, then?"

Before Mr. Walsh could answer his question, a high-pitched shriek pierced their ears.

"Jack!"

A slim figure came darting out of the room to their right in a blur of yellow satin and a flurry of bouncy gold curls.

"Jacinda?" He turned just in time as she came barreling over and leaped on him.

"Oh, my dear, dear long-lost brother!" she cried, joyfully kissing his cheeks and his brow. "Is it really you? I can't believe you're here at last!"

Jack was laughing as he hugged his exuberant sister. He swung her around in a circle and then set her down, holding her at arm's length. "Let me have a look at you now, girl!" Jacinda had big, brown eyes and rosy cheeks, and was every bit the creature of sparkle and vivacity that Eden might have expected after reading her letters.

"My baby sister," he murmured in amazement, shaking his head as he studied her, clearly marveling over the woman she had become. "Now the grand Marchioness of Truro and Saint Austell!"

"Oh, stop," she retorted.

"God's teeth, you were as big as a minute the last time I saw you," he said softly.

"I know." With a rueful smile, Jacinda brushed her tears away and then turned to Eden with a warm and heartfelt smile. "You must be Eden! Hullo!" Lady Jacinda took both of her hands, beaming at her. "I can't believe Jack's married! But I see he has excellent judgment. Welcome, my dear, new sister." Eden blushed as Jacinda hugged her, then she pulled Jack over to them and hung on his arm. "Come with me, both of you," the young marchioness ordered with a sniffle. Eden took Jack's other arm as Jacinda steered them toward the grand curved staircase. "Everyone's in the music room now. You have us all in a whirl! Oh, I can't wait for you to meet all the children, Jack, and Billy, and Beau—and Eden, everyone's dying to make your acquaintance! The lady who brought our Jack back to us! When Robert told me you were back in Town, I wanted to rush over and see you at once, but he thought it might be better to give you two a little time alone, and you know Rob, he's always right, it's really quite impossible to argue with him. . . ."

Her eager prattle continued, and Eden remained attentive, but she could tell Jack was a bit overwhelmed. He was staring all around him as though waves of pained memories were washing through him with everything he saw.

At the top of the curved staircase, Jacinda led them down a broad, formal corridor graced by alabaster statues atop chest-high pedestals. The ruckus of childish voices that echoed to them from an open doorway ahead seemed quite at odds with the pristine formality of the marble hallway.

When they arrived at the music room, Eden beheld a slew of small children tumbling about every which way amid the most impressive collection of adults she had ever laid eyes on.

Jacinda undertook the introductions, but Eden was so nervous that it was all a bit of a blur. Each of his brothers was more handsome than the next, except, of course, for the twins, who were perfectly identical, with their jet-black hair and gray eyes. Damien was every bit as impressive in his bearing as she could have expected of a bonafide war-hero, while Lucien, his twin, was more laid back, mild-mannered—but with the studied idleness of a man shrewdly noticing everything.

Robert had the same dark eyes as his sister, and, of course, golden-haired Alec stood out because he looked like an earthbound god and never seemed to stop cracking wry jokes.

Jacinda's Billy seemed a far more serious fellow than his boyish nickname had led Eden to expect. The others called him Rackford. Someone finally explained this had been his courtesy title before he had inherited the marquisate, and it had stuck. He had sandy blond hair and some fierce quality in his greenish eyes that reminded Eden of Jack.

The two hard men took each other's measure in a glance, as though identifying in each other some underlying savage quality that they shared in common—kindred spirits.

261

Beaming as her husband and her long-lost brother shook hands, Jacinda continued bouncing her beautiful son, Beau, on her hip. She told Eden the names of all the little boys, but it would be a while before she could remember who was who. There were seven of them in total, all of them under the age of eight.

Lizzie, who had been mentioned in the letters, turned out to be a sort of second sister to the family, as Eden soon learned. Except for Cousin Amelia, she did not think she had ever met a gentler or more pleasant person. Orphaned as a child and made a ward to the duke, Lizzie had functioned as lady's companion to Jacinda, and had grown up with them all. She was married now to the handsome Devlin, Lord Strathmore. He, in turn, immediately started asking Eden about her father's work, a neutral subject she was happy to discuss. Perhaps Lord Strathmore had an interest in scientific pursuits, but Eden suspected he was simply being kind and offering conversation to put the newcomer at ease.

Meanwhile, Jack greeted his brothers, in turn, and briefly met their ladies. There was some degree of awkwardness, which was, no doubt, to be expected; but whatever trace of stony defensiveness that Jack had clung to from the moment they had walked in, it was dissolved by his two-year-old niece, Lucien's daughter, Pippa.

She was the only girl-child the clan had yet produced, but despite her diminutive size, she achieved in a trice what no one else in the room could have done, not even Eden: The wee thing melted Jack completely.

Tottering over to him in a frilly little dress with a big ribbon on her head, Pippa stretched up both of her hands to him, her silvery eyes like her father's, serious and searching, needing no words to order the big man to pick her up.

Jack's tough look softened as he bent down obligingly and picked the tot up in his arms. She sat, queenlike, in the crook of his elbow and leaned against his chest, studying her new uncle at close range.

Jack returned her curious gaze, lifting one eyebrow.

Everyone watched while Pippa stared at him for a long moment. Then she began petting his cheek. "Puppy."

Taken off guard, Jack laughed. The child laughed, too, pleased with herself, while Lucien shook his head and let out a rather besotted sigh.

262

"She calls everyone a puppy."

"No, only the people she likes," Alice, the child's mother, corrected.

"Do you like your uncle Jack?" Lucien asked his little girl.

In reply, Pippa gave Jack a sloppy kiss on his cheek. A soft chorus of fond *ah*s arose from the ladies, but Pippa suddenly lost interest, flinging herself back in her father's direction.

"Where's my girl?" Lucien greeted her, holding out his arms.

Jack returned his little niece to her father and turned away with his hand on his heart and a slain look.

Alice chuckled, beaming with pride, but just then Mr. Walsh reappeared in the doorway and bowed to the duchess.

"Your Grace: Dinner is served."

"Ah," Bel responded, turning to them with an elegant gesture toward the door. "Shall we?"

Leaving their brood in the care of an army of nannies, nurses, governesses, and uniformed maids, they all went down to dine.

The opulent evening that unfolded exceeded all of Eden's golden fantasies back in the jungle, daydreaming over old copies of *La Belle Assemblée.*

From the mahogany table draped in snowy linen damask to the sterling cutlery and fine bone china with gilded edges, the formal three-course meal began with a delicate white soup, stewed cheese, and little warm exquisite shrimp loaves.

If only her stomach weren't so full of butterflies! It was hard to enjoy the gourmet meal in such a nervous state, but Jack was seated directly across from her, and gazing at him helped her to relax. The candlelight burnished the tips of his dark, wavy hair, forming a ruddy halo. He must have felt her stare, for he glanced over and met her gaze. At once, he offered her the trace of an intimate smile. She lifted her glass of white Rhine wine to him in a subtle toast meant to tell him he was doing well.

The footmen cleared the first course away in short order, and then the main course arrived, platter after platter, un-til the entire table was covered with food: Fresh-caught swordfish steaks ringed by buttered sea scallops. Steaming roast beef and marrow pudding. A golden-browned turkey with mushroom gravy. Chine of lamb. Rabbit fricassee. Jellies and syllabubs and stewed pippins. Eel pie, marinated smelts, and duck with orange sauce.

A twinge of nausea confounded Eden, but she ignored it, keeping her attention fixed on the task of protecting Jack from his siblings' friendly intrusions. When they asked him questions that she knew he didn't want to answer, she supplied a few diplomatic words before he could let slip a sarcastic reply.

She remained vigilant, changing the subject whenever he floundered, asking a question, seeking advice, or making a humorous remark now and then to shield him from any sense of attack that would put him on the defensive.

He caught her eye with a fleeting look of surprise, but his subtle nod expressed gratitude for her smooth show of charm.

Eden hadn't known she'd had it in her.

She knew she was doing a good job of helping Jack feel at ease. Because of this, he was able to relate to his family in a more relaxed and cordial way, as though there had been nothing to dread all along.

When he talked about his company or his ships, this was his strong suit, and Eden was gratified to find all of them openly admiring his achievements. They were all such affable people that, at length, she was quite mystified as to why he had not wanted to be a part of this family for all these years.

As he listened to Lord Alec entertaining them all with some risqué gossip about one of his bachelor friends, Jack seemed to be asking himself the same question.

The table was soon cleared for the third course, coffee, port, and claret served alongside apple tartlets sprinkled with raisins and brown sugar.

They separated after the meal, the women retreating to the drawing room as was customary while the men remained at table for cigars and port. They reassembled within the hour, the gentlemen joining them in the drawing room, but by that time, it was growing quite late. Eden was happy but feeling worn out. Jack suggested they take their leave, and she agreed.

After this very warm reception, they were sent on their way with the whole party's insistence that Eden and Jack accompany them to the theater tomorrow night. Jack hesitated until he saw Eden's wide-eyed look of eagerness. He accepted the invitation graciously, then they went on their way, trundling back to the Pulteney Hotel.

After a few idle remarks, they sat in silence—but it was a very different silence than the one between them on the way there.

"How are you?" Eden asked him in a soft tone after a while.

He looked at her intently and shrugged. "All right, I guess. It wasn't so bad."

She smiled faintly. "I thought you were very well behaved."

"Thank God you were there."

The acknowledgment pleased her. "Your niece seemed to like you."

"Pippa?" He chuckled in the darkness as the carriage rolled along smoothly down Pall Mall. "I may have to steal her."

"I know." Eden paused, watching the dim orange glow of the streetlamps they passed sculpting Jack's face in shifting shadows. "I worried about you when we parted."

"I worried about you, too. I'm sure the ladies grilled you for information."

"Of course."

"What did you tell them?"

"Only as much as you and I agreed upon. What about your brothers? Did they grill you?"

He smiled wryly. "Mostly they were busy praising you, and saying what a credit you were to a blackguard like me. Of course, they're right."

"Oh, Jack." Her stare intensified. "I miss you."

Sitting in the seat across from her, he leaned closer. "It doesn't have to be like this." He took her hands. "I'm trying, Eden."

"I know. You hurt me, Jack."

"I won't do it again, I swear to you."

"You say that, but you made me believe a lie before, so how can I know that you aren't deceiving me now?"

"I've told you everything," he said angrily, then checked his frustration. "Give me another chance."

She felt so fragile as he crossed the space between them, moving onto the seat beside her, and gently tucking a stray curl behind her ear.

"I miss your body," he whispered. "I need your love."

She shuddered when he bent his head and kissed her neck, but she wasn't sure she was ready to let him inside her again—in either sense.

Their coach rolled to a halt presently in front of the hotel, for the drive wasn't far.

Jack gazed hungrily at her as the groom hurried to open the carriage door for them. He got out first and handed her down, escorting her inside without another word.

They walked through the lobby, side by side, drawing glances from the other guests here and there. With her silk wrap thrown over her shoulders once more and her reticule dangling from her wrist, Eden picked up the hem of her skirts and climbed the grand stairs to their rooms. Though Jack moved in silence beside her, her physical awareness of him was keen.

When they reached their suite, Jack unlocked the door and let her in. Eden brushed past him, her heart fluttering with desire; she knew he wanted her, but she was torn. She put her reticule on the console table just inside the door and began removing her long white gloves. She heard him close and lock the door behind her, and then she pulled in her breath sharply as he came up behind her and slid her wrap off her shoulders in a very sensuous fashion. She closed her eyes when he bent his head, his silken lips nuzzling her ear.

"You look so beautiful tonight," he breathed. He ran his fingers slowly down her arm. "I can't believe you're mine."

She moaned his name in a voice that was barely a whisper.

He kissed her shoulder, molding his hands to her hips. "Let me make love to you."

She did not refuse him. She couldn't say a word. His touch commanded her full attention. She closed her eyes and licked her lips slowly as his smooth mouth nibbled at her nape.

He was too much.

"We need each other, Eden. You need me as much as I need you." Turning her gently to face him, Jack drew her into his arms and kissed her with drugging passion. She clung to him, so entranced with the deep, slow glide of his mouth on hers that she barely noticed him backing her toward the luxurious striped satin chaise over by the white fireplace.

The next thing she knew, he was easing her down onto it, and she was trembling as he cupped her breast through her bodice. Her body felt so tender all over, her skin acutely sensitized. She writhed with his caress.

"Jack."

"Come, Eden, this has gone on long enough. Let's make up, darlin'. You know I love you."

She caressed his face, at a loss; on his knees before her, he

266

turned his head and captured her finger in his mouth. In rising lust, she watched him sucking her fingertips, his eyes closed. They glittered with feverish want when he dragged them open again, and turned his attention to the task of loosening her bodice.

She withdrew her fingertip from his wet mouth and leaned forward to kiss him anew, holding his face between her hands. Within moments, his touch ran all over her, clutching her greedily under her gown. His kisses traveled up her thigh as he knelt, worshiping her body—when all of a sudden, a knock sounded at the door.

"Jack! Jack! Are you in there?" It was Trahern's voice. "I need to talk to you! Now!"

He hissed a hot curse against her skin, then lifted his head.

"What?" he yelled back none too gently.

"We've got a problem, Jack."

Eden's heart was pounding. "Oh, dear." She laid her hands on his broad shoulders, pushing him back a small space. "You'd better go see what it is," she panted.

"Give me a minute!" he called back, then looked at Eden in bitter disappointment. "One of these days—" He shook his head.

She chuckled and tousled his hair, giving him a smile full of smoldering affection.

"Hold that thought," he whispered to her.

"No, husband. I'm going to bed."

"But—"

"I need my beauty sleep," she informed him. "Especially now that I've met my sisters-in-law. I don't want to be the ugly one."

"Never."

"Besides, I don't feel so good." She'd had quite a bit of an unsteady stomach of late. Leave it to her to get seasick once they had come onto dry land.

"Are you all right?"

"Nerves, that's all."

"I could help you relax," he whispered.

"Jack?" Trahern pounded the door again.

"I'm coming! Only not in the sense that I'd hoped," he added under his breath, adjusting his hardness with a pained wince. "Look what you do to me."

Eden arched a brow in the direction of his groin, shot him a pitying smile, and then closed her chamber door.

*

267

Jack couldn't say he cared for Trahern's timing, but he soon learned the reason for his urgency. The intrepid lieutenant had taken it upon himself to do some discreet snooping around the Spanish embassy, and had discovered that the man newly assigned as attaché to the ambassador was none other than Manuel de Ruiz, head of the deadly team of assassins who had pursued Bolivar to Jack's very doorstep on Jamaica a few short years ago.

"We should have killed them when we had the chance." Trahern poured himself a drink from the liquor cabinet.

"Easier said than done," Jack murmured, declining the whisky as he rested his hands on his waist and stared at the floor, mulling over the news.

Ruiz was a man to be reckoned with, and now it appeared he had moved up the ranks despite having let the Liberator slip through his fingers. Even if Ruiz never found proof that Jack was the Venezuelans' agent in London, the former assassin would be keeping an eye on him, Jack could be sure of that.

Well, he did not expect that he could keep his presence hidden from Ruiz, nor did he care to try, for he did not hide from any man. All he could do was to cling to his pretense for being in London, remain vigilant, and in his dealings with his recruits, continue to emphasize the need for secrecy.

Trahern remained for an hour discussing various concerns pertaining to the mission. When he left, Jack checked in on Eden, but she was fast asleep.

Damn. He let her rest rather than push his luck, and closed her door with a regretful smile.

The next day, he attended to more business, visiting the Exchange with Peter Stockwell to meet with a few of his investors. He was very pleased to see his stock prices climb by twelve percent as word spread about the acquisition of Abraham Gold's company by Knight Enterprises. He accepted bids for the rare tropical hardwoods he had brought from the torrid zone, and gave a nod of approval on the price for the sugar, indigo, rum, and other goods from the West Indies.

Later that night, returning to the hotel a considerably richer man, he took his wife out to the theater.

Robert maintained one of the best-situated boxes in the house, and with Strathmore and Lizzie having bowed out on account of their newborn at home, the theater box held all twelve of them quite comfortably.

As luck would have it, Shakespeare topped the bill of fare and the Dramatis Personae inevitably listed the villain as "Edmund the Bastard."

Jack let out a disgruntled sigh to read it, shifted in his seat, and tried to comprehend why anyone would want to watch a tragedy, anyway, life being tragic enough as it was. Then again, the performance on stage was hardly the point of a Society night out at the theater. The point, of course, was to see and be seen.

The Knight ladies were up to the task, of course. All looked ravishing. Alec declared that, seated as they were along the railing, they looked like a row of posies planted in a flower box.

"Very droll," Damien's wife, Miranda, had teased him, while their sister gave him a small kick with a slippered toe and told him to behave.

During the silly pantomime on stage, meant to warm up the audience before the main play, everyone was marveling at how easily Eden had learned to tell the twins apart.

"It took me forever," Bel declared. "How did you do it?"

"Simple," Eden said with a grin. "Damien marches; Lucien glides."

Both twins had laughed aloud at that.

Before long, the pantomime players scurried off stage and it was time for *King Lear.*

The audience quieted down somewhat, but there was still muffled noise and plenty of motion throughout the theater as the ladies waved their fans and the men talked about the day's horse races in what they considered muffled tones.

Down in the pit with the lower orders, orange girls hawked their wares, so that, every now and then, a piece of orange peel went flying through the air to hit some unsuspecting playgoer in the head, much to the hilarity of the one who had thrown it.

Higher up where the rich kept their boxes, Jack noted the winking lenses of countless opera glasses trained on the Knight family's box. Oh, yes, they were being watched.

Jack watched Eden watching the stage, sweetly unaware that at this very moment, the whole ton was watching *her,* passing judgment on her—and trying to figure out what to make of him, as well.

He put the watchers out of his mind and instead savored the pleasure of looking at his wife. A true beauty. She looked wonderful in dark blue silk with the double string of pink pearls around her neck that he had brought her just today. He was glad she was feeling better this evening, and wondered when the hell she was going to sleep with him again, but just then, the soliloquizing fellow on stage—the villain, of course—spoke a line that grabbed his attention.

" 'Why bastard?' " poor Edmund demanded from center stage. " 'Wherefore base, when my dimensions are as well compact, my mind as generous, and my shape as true as honest madam's issue?' "

Jack and his brothers exchanged a wry glance.

A few of their ladies looked at them and suppressed giggles, but Eden looked shocked.

" 'Why brand they us with base? With baseness? Bastardy? Base?' " Edmund cried as if he could not comprehend it. " 'Base?' "

Jack knew exactly how he felt. Alec put his head down, laughing into his hand. His pregnant wife, Becky, elbowed him.

" 'Who, in the lusty stealth of nature, takes more composition, and fierce quality, than doth within a dull, stale, tired bed go to th' creating a whole tribe of fops, got 'tween asleep and awake?' "

"Man's got a point," Damien drawled in a low tone.

" 'Fine word, legitimate!' " Edmund the Bastard kept at it, crossing toward the limelight, so close that Eden with her fine aim could have hit him in the head with an orange peel if she'd had one.

She looked as if she might like to.

" 'Edmund the base shall top th' legitimate,' " the villain declared. " 'I grow, I prosper: Now, gods, stand up for bastards!' "

"Bravo, my lad!" Jack stood up and bellowed in a voice made to carry orders out across the waves.

Immediately, his brothers echoed the sentiment, cheering with applause and a piercing whistle of approval.

The whole theater broke into laughter, having been in on the joke for years. After all, the whole town knew who they were; their scandalous history had always been an open secret in London.

The Knight women glanced at their husbands with equal parts doting and exasperation.

Jack looked the audience over for a moment with a wry stare.

"Welcome back, Lord Jack!" somebody yelled from down in the pit, but there was no point in overdoing it.

He sat down with a look of tranquil cynicism, tugging his waist-coat into place. Lucien was still laughing and clapped him on the back.

"Perfect timing, old boy."

"Somebody had to say something," he muttered, then took a swig from his flask.

Eden shook her head at him and smiled.

In the days that followed, Jack was amused to find the invitations pouring in.

It seemed his open acknowledgment of the family scandal had quite disarmed the ton, and now Jack, the prodigal son, was being given the chance to show he wasn't such a bastard, after all.

Funny how fortune and power could make a man's sins seem mere foibles, eccentricities. At any rate, the society that had once shunned him was now offering him the olive branch.

There was a time when he would have snatched it out of their hands, snapped it in two, and thrown it on the ground, but he was not so angry anymore.

Not so full of obstinate pride.

Besides, his darling Eden wanted to belong to their world, and recalling Lord Arthur's advice, Jack deemed it an honor to make her wish come true.

CHAPTER
⟶ FIFTEEN ⟵

"*Y*ou said you wanted to put down roots," Jack murmured as she stared in shock two days later at the house he was proposing to buy.

Eden could not even answer, bedazzled by the dramatic Baroque ceiling mural in the entrance hall: blue sky and great, silvered clouds with Apollo the sun god driving his chariot across the ceiling. She had a direct view of his mighty steeds' underbellies from where she stood; one could almost hear them snorting.

The mural had a sense of vivid motion, which, when added to the rest of the entrance hall's opulent details, created an almost dizzying sense of grandeur: gilded bannisters, huge splendid door casements, decorated white pilasters, roundels with the bas-relief busts of Greek philosophers peering out like nosy onlookers, painted cherubs everywhere, expanses of gleaming Italian marble, and chandeliers above like sparkling crowns.

The house was being offered to Jack on extraordinary terms as part of the settlement finalizing matters between him and old Abraham Gold. For all its grandeur, it would need a bit of work. Jack had suggested that overseeing the improvements and refurbishing it might be an apt project for Eden while he was gone to Venezuela.

She turned rather dazedly, taking it all in, and was delighted anew by the view out the high, arched windows. The tall, spouting plume of the fountain danced in the center of the ornamental lake. The mile-long drive up to the house wound through two hundred acres of green, rolling landscape sculpted by Capability Brown.

Through the window, presently, she spotted Cousin Amelia

strolling with Lieutenant Trahern, and smiled. They had fetched her cousin on the way out to Derbyshire, where the grand house was situated, a few hours from London.

The gallant young lieutenant and her shy cousin had charmed each other from the moment they had met. Now the pair had gone out to view the grounds while Jack and Eden toured the house. When they were done here, Amelia would accompany Eden back to Town for a few days—information that seemed to please Mr. Trahern as much as it pleased the girls.

Eden quite believed a bit of matchmaking was in order.

She had never anticipated becoming her cousin's chaperone, but now that she was an old married lady, such was her privilege.

"My lord, my lady," Mr. Gold's land agent addressed them. "If you wish to come this way, I should be very pleased to show you the ballroom. It holds up to four hundred guests . . ."

Never in her wildest dreams did Eden ever contemplate owning a ballroom, let alone having four hundred friends to invite there. She looked at Jack, who was sauntering along languidly by her side.

"Can we really afford this?" she whispered.

"No worries," he murmured as the agent marched ahead. "I'll just sell off the castle in Ireland."

She gasped. "Don't you dare!"

He smiled. "I'm only teasing." The wicked sparkle in his eyes informed her he had merely wanted to see her reaction, since the castle obviously meant a great deal to them as a couple. He gave her a wink and then glanced around at the house. "If you like this place, you shall have it."

Reminded in spite of herself of those three blissful days, Eden took her husband's arm in wary affection and steered him onward to see the ballroom. They were getting along better now than they had been since that gloomy day they had left Ireland. Admittedly, Jack's cheeky outburst in the theater the other night had disarmed Eden as much as it had the ton.

The measure of amused favor that he had won from Society by his rowdy display seemed to go contrary to what Eden would have expected, but as Martin had later explained to her, true "originals" actually led fashion by breaking the rules.

Jack was an original, all right, she mused. When it came to rule-breaking, he was an expert. She surveyed the ballroom and tried to imagine the two of them hosting glittering gatherings like the ones they were now being invited to.

She glanced at her husband and found him watching her again with a soft trace of a smile on his lips and a glow in his turquoise eyes. She smiled back at him, happier than she had been in weeks; nevertheless, she still got the feeling he was up to something.

And so he was.

But his secret agenda was hardly nefarious. After his break-through with the ton, and more importantly, with his wife the other night at the theater, Jack vowed not to squander the opportunity he had gained. He was working his way back into his lady's favor, and nothing on earth would deter him.

He had taken it into his head that perhaps she needed to be wooed and courted all over again, nice and slowly.

Rushing her would only make her run from him again. All sailors had to learn extraordinary patience, waiting on the tides, waiting on the wind. If she was the moon, then he was the sea, slave to her bidding, a thrall to her mysterious pull. He mightn't like this, forced to live like a monk, but he was used to being at sea for long periods of time, foregoing the pleasures of Eros.

He always found that when he enjoyed the rites of sex again, the taste was all the sweeter, more intoxicating. And so, he had made up his mind to restrain his lust for one more week.

If she didn't give it to him by then, he had promised himself he would summon up the pirate in him and simply take the wench. He didn't want it to come to that, but damn it, he was her husband and he had his rights. He hoped instead that buying her this house might inspire her to a more amorous form of thanks.

They finished their tour a while later and left the premises with solemn assurances to the agent that, yes, they were interested and they would let him know their decision post-haste.

Then the four of them stopped about halfway through the drive back to London for a meal at a quaint coaching inn.

Jack observed the mooning looks between young Trahern and Cousin Amelia in gentle amusement, now that he knew firsthand the tender misery of falling in love. He made a few remarks to help his young friend's cause, giving Trahern openings to brag about his various feats of daring at sea.

"You should have seen him, Miss Northrop," he told the girl

while they sat at the rustic table eating roast beef sandwiches and drinking ale. "There were two feluccas full of Barbary corsairs trying to pin us in, but Lieutenant Trahern ordered the men to lower the oars and somehow managed to run the frigate right through the opening between them. Cleared it with little more than seven feet to spare on both sides."

"Oh!" she said. Amelia Northrop was a sweet thing, a pale, demure blonde with a soft, melodious voice as sweet as wind chimes. She was as harmless, biddable, and gentle as her red-haired cousin was fiery and strong-willed.

"Aye, they were ready with the grappling hooks," Tra-hern admitted, blushing modestly. "They were going to board us. Luckily Cap'n Jack was there. He fought while I sailed the ship."

"Did you . . . kill some of them, Lord Jack?" Amelia inquired in a tremulous voice. "The Barbary corsairs, I mean?"

"Ohh, I don't recall. Maybe one or two."

Trahern let out a snort of a laugh, no doubt remembering the bloodshed of that day, but when Amelia turned to him with a wondering look, he seemed to catch on that bloody butchery was not the sort of thing one discussed in the presence of a genteel and sheltered young lady—and Amelia Northrop was possibly the most genteel and sheltered creature either man had ever met.

Unsettled by the savagery beneath their attempt to conceal the reality of that day, Amelia turned to her cousin. "Edie, when do you expect Uncle Victor to arrive?"

She and Jack exchanged a subtle glance, for Eden had not told Amelia or her aunt Cecily that in fact she had run away from Papa. She shrugged. "It's difficult to say."

"Miss Northrop, you see, we're not entirely certain he'll be able to come, but if does, he should be here any day now," Jack murmured, reaching across the table to touch Eden's hand in an offering of quiet reassurance.

Eden summoned a smile and gave him a small nod of thanks. "I'm sure Jack's right. Papa will be here soon."

"And Lord Arthur, too," Jack added. "I expect we'll see my uncle any day now." He hoped so. He needed the *Valiant* to carry materièl for his recruits alongside *The Winds of Fortune* on the return trip to South America.

Arthur had needed to stop at a shipyard to have a few repairs

275

made on his vessel in preparation for the rigorous crossing back to South America.

By late afternoon, they all were back at the Pulteney Hotel.

Their sprawling six-room suite was a welcome haven, though Jack rather wished he would have insisted on one with fewer bedchambers. That way, Eden would have been forced to share a bed with him. Instead, it was much too convenient for her to keep a respectable distance, taking her own boudoir like a proper Society wife.

At any rate, Jack meant to drop the girls off, change clothes, and then go and visit the lads in the East End. He needed to verify how many of the smugglers' gang intended to join the ranks of his recruits. He had no doubt that word of the enterprise would have spread throughout the secretive rookeries by now. There was no telling how many of the city's tough street boys in need of an occupation might be interested in the adventuring life and the chance to earn the Venezuelans' silver.

Anything had to be better than those crowded, gin-soaked, tenement blocks full of squalor and treachery. Aye, he wouldn't be surprised if he scrounged up two hundred men in London alone—though, God knew, O'Shaunnessy, Graves, and his other Irish officer chums would have their hands full drilling such heathens and turning them into soldiers.

As it turned out, however, once he reached the hotel, developments occurred that altered his plans for the night's work.

Eden, Amelia, and Trahern collapsed into the elegant couches in the main sitting room, worn out from the long drive. They ordered refreshments from the hotel kitchens, but when the knock came at the door, it was one of the house under-butlers, who came hurrying to bring Jack a note—apparently urgent.

Jack lifted the small, folded note off the silver tray, tipped the servant a shilling for his pains, and opened the letter.

Meet me outside.
Manuel de Ruiz

He raised an eyebrow at the imperious command, but when dealing with a trained assassin, he supposed he preferred the direct approach rather than a length of garrotte wire around his throat in a dark alley.

He turned in the doorway and glanced back at Eden. "Stay inside. Lock the door," he ordered. He sent Trahern a sharp look, warning him to be alert; his firm nod ordered the lad to stay with the girls.

Jack went down to meet Ruiz alone.

A confrontation with the assassin-turned-diplomat had been inevitable, he supposed, but the fact that Ruiz had known where to find him meant that he'd been watching the hotel. By now, Ruiz had surely gotten a good look at Eden.

No mercy, he vowed as he walked out into the street to meet the killer in broad daylight, face to face.

Jack spotted the black-haired Spaniard leaning by the corner. He was tall and fit, well dressed. Ebony hair and aquiline features. It was no wonder he had become a killer for the king, Jack thought. The gallant pride of the Ancien Régime poured out of his every movement.

Jack marched toward him, undeterred by the traffic whizzing past. Piccadilly was as busy as usual, filled with the clatter of carriage wheels and prancing horses, people milling in and out of the fashionable shops.

Ruiz and he greeted each other with all the cordiality to be expected between two breeds of men with nearly three hundred years of sworn enmity between them: Spanish grandees and English privateers.

"Black-Jack Knight."

"Well, if it isn't my old friend," he replied, resting his hands on his waist as he joined the Spaniard across the street from the hotel.

"You're a long way from Jamaica, Lord Jack. What brings you to London?"

At least he got straight to the point. Jack smiled coolly. "What makes you think I'm going to answer anything you ask?"

"Ah, so you *do* have something to hide?"

"No," Jack said as Ruiz feigned idleness, watching a pair of women walk by. "My presence in London right now has got no remote bearing on you whatsoever."

"Are you sure about that?" The Spaniard slanted him a keen glance, trying to read Jack's closed expression.

Jack folded his arms across his chest and fixed him with a steely stare. "Well, if you are so very interested, I'm here on business and to see my kin."

"Ah, of course. Congratulations on your nuptials, my lord." Ruiz raised his glance to the window where their suite was situated.

Jack's stare turned razor sharp. "If I recall correctly, señor, your one redeeming trait was at least a shred of honor."

Ruiz flashed a wolfish smile. "Thankfully, no larger than your own."

"Women and children are off limits," Jack said softly in warning.

"Of course they are."

"Remember that. You have a family, too, I understand."

"Do I?" Ruiz looked surprised.

"After our last meeting, I thought you might become a problem one day, so I took the liberty of doing a bit of research on you, Ruiz."

"Como?"

"My spies informed me you have an old, widowed mother who lives in Sevilla."

His eyes narrowed.

"My ships are very fast, Ruiz. Seville is only a few days' sail from here." Jack stared at him ruthlessly. "We don't want any problems, do we? You stay away from my wife."

Ruiz finally succumbed with a haughty nod and then cast his casual pretense aside. "I have been sent to London to discover Bolivar's agent. Someone has been sent here to recruit soldiers to fight for the insurgents. We discovered the plot after our victory at La Puerta. I am warning you now that I am going to find out who this man is, and deal with him."

"I see," he replied. "And what's that got to do with me?"

"You tell me, Lord Jack."

"I don't know anything about it. I told you, I'm here on business and to see my kin."

Ruiz's stare could have bored a hole in him. "You protected the traitors once before."

"Aye, it was your arrogance that inspired me," Jack retorted.

"What?"

"You listen to me, Ruiz," he commanded, pointing a finger in the Spaniard's face. "Jamaica is my home turf. Half the island's in my pocket. How dare you come onto *my* island for the purpose of killing *anyone* without my permission? If you had shown respect and come to me," he said, pointing to himself, in turn, "I might have just as well handed them over to you for the asking."

Ruiz stared at him in incredulity.

Holding his shocked gaze, Jack lowered his hand to his side again, where his weapons lurked if he had need of them.

"Are you telling me you protected Bolivar and his men, and incurred the hatred of the Spanish Crown, simply out of your own . . . obstinate pride?"

"You're damned right," he said with a snort. "Call it obstinate if you want, but hell, you're Spanish—you people know about pride. If a man has no pride, he has nothing."

Ruiz arched a brow.

"Myself, I don't give a damn about politics." Jack eyed him with a cynical scowl. "Liberators, patriots—the lot of you can go hang for all I care. Profit is my creed. Ask anyone."

Ruiz appeared genuinely taken aback.

Jack stared at him, hoping he looked every inch the cutthroat privateer he had been all those years ago, raising up his empire from one ship.

Ruiz, thank God, was being slowly reeled in, probably because what Jack had just told him was a half-truth rather than a lie. He wouldn't have turned Bolivar over to the Spanish, but he had felt slighted and angry as hell that Ruiz and his men had dared come ashore without consulting him.

Pride alone had gotten him where he was in life.

The assassin studied Jack uncertainly, weighing his answer. "Do you know who the agent might be?" he asked at length. "I know you have always been well connected in this town."

He shrugged. "Haven't the foggiest, but if I did know, I can assure you, I'd make your king pay dear for the information."

"Perhaps that could be arranged. If you hear anything, let me know."

"Without delay," Jack drawled, resting his hands on his waist once more.

Ruiz's glance flicked to the window of their suite above just as Eden glided past. "She is beautiful," he said in veiled menace. "You have good taste."

"And good aim," he added softly, tapping his fingers on the butt of the pistol by his side.

"So do I," Ruiz responded.

They parted in bristling hostility, and Jack went back inside.

"Is everything all right?" Eden asked at once, straightening up over the tray of refreshments that had arrived.

He nodded. "Trahern."

His assistant sketched a bow to the ladies and withdrew, joining Jack in the other room.

"Look. Ruiz is onto me," he told him in a rather worried tone. "He's going to be watching me like a hawk. I could go after him, but it'd be too obvious. He'll have told the ambassador his suspicions about me by now. If Ruiz disappeared, I'd be the first man they'd come looking for."

"Agreed." Trahern shrugged. "I don't think it's necessary for you to get rid of him, anyway. He knows you, but I doubt he's ever noticed me. You just tell me what you want done, and I'll see to it."

"Good man." Jack clapped him on the shoulder. "Knew I could count on you."

Trahern grinned. "Always."

Jack went to pour himself a drink. "I'll need you to take a larger role in bringing everything together while I distract Ruiz and whoever else may be watching."

"Done. I have only one question."

"Aye?"

"What's in it for me?"

Jack turned to him, lifting his eyebrows. "Why, Christopher! What's this? Greed? Ambition? Self-interest? I am so pleased to see my wicked ways are rubbing off on you at last. It's about bloody time."

The lad shrugged, though his eyes danced roguishly. "I figure if I stick around long enough, you'll give me a chance to make *my* fortune, so that *I* can take a wife."

"Are you sure you want one? It's harder than it looks."

"That Amelia," he whispered, nodding fervently toward the other room. "She is an angel."

"She is very sweet," he agreed, but couldn't help chuckling. "You've known this girl all of five hours and you're already thinking of marriage?"

Trahern snorted. "I'm sure as hell not going to wait to get married 'til I'm as old as you."

"I am not *old,* ye cheeky little bastard. Ah, get going. You've got work to do."

"I've got to say good-bye to Miss Northrop first," he informed him, sauntering toward the connecting door.

Jack shook his head at him. Trahern went back into the sitting room and bid the ladies a more elaborate adieu.

A short while later, Jack took Eden aside and told her what had transpired, warning her about Ruiz and telling her that if she saw any black-haired Spaniard approaching her, she should not let him anywhere near her, but should immediately retreat to safety.

Jack believed he had stalemated any sort of threat to Eden from Ruiz, but an overabundance of caution was in order where his wife's safety was concerned. Fortunately, as wives went, his was singularly able to ward off danger far better than most ladies, thanks to her sojourn in the jungle. It comforted his mind to know the chit could throw a knife as well as Ruiz could himself.

"Well," Eden said, drawing him closer by the lapels of his waistcoat and giving him an arch smile. "If you are not going to go sneaking away tonight on your dark work, then you can have the privilege of escorting me and my cousin to a party."

"Hm," Jack said, his tone noncommittal. "What party?"

"This one." She produced an invitation from behind her back. "It's a supper and card party. Jacinda says it's bound to be quite lively."

"I see, so you're going to learn how to gamble all my money away?" he asked as he wrapped his arms around her slim waist.

"Don't worry. You'll make more."

"You are a minx," he scolded, doting on her. He lowered his head. "Give me a kiss and it's a deal."

She did, pressing her satiny lips tenderly to his.

Soft as it was, it melted him. He gazed at her, half forgetting where he was, what day it was, all of life's tiresome practicalities. But when she flashed a saucy smile as though amused by his wistful stare, he snapped out of it.

"Do you happen to know if my brothers are going tonight?"

"They are. I've already had a message from Jacinda and Her Grace, and Alice and Miranda, too. They're all going, except for Alec and Becky. Jacinda tells me Alec won't go near a card party," she said in a musing tone. "The Strathmores aren't going, either. Lizzie wants to stay at home with the baby and Lord Strathmore is hard at work on a bill he's trying to push through Parliament."

"You said the twins will be there?"

"Yes."

"Good," he murmured, nodding. He intended to enlist them as his main allies, though his sister's husband, Rackford, might also be useful as a guardian for his wife. Jacinda had shared with him in whispered tones the truth about her husband's background, and it was arguably darker than Jack's own.

"I'm so pleased that you asked if your brothers would be there, Jack," Eden said with a warm smile, sliding her arms around his neck. "I knew, deep down, you really do care about your family."

"You're my family," he whispered, "and the truth is, I have an ulterior motive."

"You? Never."

"I'm afraid I'll have to leave soon for South America, my darling." He brushed a lock of her hair gently behind her ear. "I intend to rely upon my brothers to keep watch over my most precious treasure for me while I'm gone." As he kissed her forehead, passion flared between them.

"Oh, Jack," she breathed, tilting her head back to offer her lips. But as he lowered his head to accept, they heard Cousin Amelia moving about in the other room and, pausing, they stopped themselves.

Jack heaved a sigh that came from the depths of his being, released her before she could push him away, and then set out to prove that an all-around bastard could indeed play the gentleman when the occasion called.

For the next hour or so, he sat idly on the couch opposite the ladies as tea and cakes were served on the low table between them. Privately rather tickled by their chatter, he listened in companionable silence as the two lovely cousins eagerly discussed family news and village gossip.

Later that night, he took the ladies to the party.

While Jacinda taught Eden and Amelia how to gamble at genteel whist for a penny a point, Jack took the twins and Rackford privately into a quiet side room in their host's large house, and revealed his quest, swearing them to secrecy.

He knew that Damien in particular was not going to appreciate the illegality of the mission, but out of all his brothers, it made sense to put the war-hero in charge of protecting Eden.

First, however, he had to tell his brothers where he stood.

"I realize Whitehall has recently issued a decree forbidding our veterans from enlisting in the Liberator's army. A cowardly move, in my view. I believe this cause is just," he said frankly, speaking from the heart. "The victory at Waterloo was all very well, but your idol Wellington put an incompetent king back on the Spanish throne, and the people of South America are the ones who must suffer for it. Now, I am going to get Bolivar the troops he needs to throw off the Bourbon tyranny. If our government calls this treason, so be it. I'm not asking you to get involved—I can guess how you feel about this. All I'm asking is that you keep my wife safe for me while I'm gone, for she is your sister now, and however much you may disapprove of me, none of this is her fault."

"Of course we will, Jack," Lucien said without blinking an eye.

Damien was silent for a moment, his arms folded across his chest. "I happen to know," he said slowly after a long moment, "that Wellington would happen to agree with you about your cause."

"What?"

Damien scratched his cheek and gave Jack a slight, rueful smile. "You heard me. Unintended consequences, Jack. We had to stop Napoleon. Spain going back under Bourbon rule was beyond our control. As I understand it, the Iron Duke would also like to see Bolivar win." He nodded. "I will talk to him for you.

"Oh, I don't know—" Jack looked at him in amazement. "Wellington supports the cause?"

"Not openly, of course. But we have become quite good friends over the years, and I am sure that at least he can make a few very pertinent suggestions."

"I daresay," Lucien breathed.

"Can he be trusted?"

"Jack, he's Wellington." Damien snorted. "He holds more sway in this city than the Regent does."

Lucien clapped Jack on the shoulder. "And I'll keep an ear to the ground for you in the Foreign Office. If I hear anything about your friend Ruiz or his plans, I'll let you know."

"What exactly do you do for the government, anyway, Luce?"

"Oh, it's all very dull." His silvery eyes gleamed like a blade." I wouldn't want to bore you with the details."

Rackford spoke up. "I know a few lads in the rookery who control the gangs in Seven Dials. They might be able to send more men your way."

"Excellent. My assistant, Christopher Trahern, is going to be handling that aspect of it. Make them aware of his name, will you?"

Rackford nodded.

After a round of brandy, they returned to their card-playing wives and surrounded their table, inadvertently taking over the game with all of their husbandly advice.

"Billy, do you want to play in my stead?" Jacinda finally exclaimed indignantly.

"I'm just trying to help you with your strategy," he replied.

"We're only playing for fun, not to beat each other."

"Speak for yourself," Eden drawled with a mischievous grin, and Jack laughed.

As the days passed in sunny progression to the fullness of April, Eden found her daily life transforming literally into the stuff of her former fantasies—the ones Papa had scoffed at in the jungle.

She wore fabulous clothes. She had hordes of new friends.

She had found her own little niche of quasi-celebrity in the haughty Ladies' Garden Club and Horticultural Society, thanks to her famous father's botanical exploits.

At the first meeting, which she attended with Lucien's wife, Alice, dozens of green-thumbed Englishwomen had listened with rapt attention and small sighs of envy as Eden had described her climbs into the canopy and her studies of orchids, palm species, and bromeliads.

Her informal discussions of torrid zone botany fueled a sudden craze for the building of private glass houses where tropical species could be raised under artificial conditions.

Eden was pleased to think that in her own, very small way, she had changed the face of London, for London had certainly changed her. Papa, if he had appeared then, might have wondered who the deuce she was.

She shopped, spending fortunes on frippery; she drove her dainty carriage through Hyde Park at the fashionable hour with Amelia by her side, a maid and footman to attend her. She thanked her husband with a kiss for buying her the Derbyshire mansion.

She and Jack, meanwhile, were becoming veritable social butterflies, for she dragged him around everywhere and though he was wont to complain on the way there and make a few choice, cynical remarks—at which she tried very hard not to laugh—he was obliging enough to escort her.

She did not miss the way other women looked at her husband at these events, nor did she fail to detect the ton's subtle climate of adultery. Flirting with other people's spouses seemed to be one main, unspoken purpose for all of the frantic socializing. This was an aspect of the beau monde she had not been expecting. Wasn't anyone happily married?

Ah, well. She did her best to ignore it. Nobody flirted with her, thank heavens. Nobody, that was, who knew the name of her husband.

More and more people arrived as the high Season got well underway. Her life had become a true Society whirl: She knew she had arrived when she and Jack were first mentioned in the Society page of the *Morning Post*. Like her husband, she had been pronounced an "Original."

There were horse races at Ascot next week that everyone said would be smashing, but the event Eden simply craved above all was the grand ball this Saturday night.

Her first real London ball.

She counted the hours and practiced her dancing. The gown she had ordered for the affair was sure to bedazzle all of her new friends, and her husband, too, but there was nearly a full week of pleasure to enjoy until that magical night came.

Monday had been their visit to Derbyshire and then the card party. Tuesday, she attended a lavish afternoon garden party, or "fête champetre," at Lady Madison's jewel-box villa on the Thames. Wednesday night, it was an after-theater party where London's most celebrated actors put in brief appearances, spreading their stardust as they mingled with their rich admirers, the arts' most generous patrons.

On Thursday afternoon, Jack escorted her to a polo match, after which they had to rush back and scramble to change clothes in time for the chamber music concert that evening at Holland House.

Calamity struck on Friday evening, however, when Eden realized her cunning French lady's maid, Lisette, was nowhere to be found. They had already sent in their R.S.V.P. promising to attend Lady Draxinger's at-home: They had to go.

Of course, Eden had no idea what an at-home was, but she was game to find out. All she knew at the moment was that it was time

285

to start getting dressed, and without her maid to beautify her—horrors!

Her silk dressing gown billowing behind her, she went striding through their suite to the sitting room. "Jack!"

"Hm?" He was already dressed in his black and white finery, sprawled on the chaise, and boredly reading the paper. He glanced over with a yawn.

"Have you seen Lisette? She's gone!"

He paused. "Ah, yes. Lisette."

"I cannot find her anywhere!"

"Right. Er, yes, about Lisette, dear. I'm sorry, I forgot to tell you." He sat up, lowering his feet to the floor. "She's gone."

"Gone?"

"Yes. I gave her the sack this afternoon."

"What? Why?"

He set his paper aside. "She was stealing from us."

Eden gasped.

"I caught her trying to make off with your pearls," he said.

She furrowed her brow in pure bafflement. "You caught Lisette stealing my pearls?"

"Mm."

"Oh! How horrid of her!"

"I know."

"Well, what am I to do? We have to be at the Draxingers' in an hour!"

"Darling, one of your other maids can help you with your gown, I'm sure."

"But who's going to fix my hair?" she cried.

He stared at her until Eden realized how silly she actually sounded. "Oh, you."

She walked over to him and caressed his head lightly, then bent and kissed his cheek. "What would I do without you?"

"I wonder," he murmured. "Perhaps forget who you are?"

She lowered her gaze, chastened. "It's all just been so exciting. I suppose sometimes . . . I get a bit carried away."

He took her hand, giving her an earnest look. "Let's stay home tonight," he whispered. "I just want us to be with each other."

Eden felt a jolt of longing for him. Oh, she knew that smoldering look, and the pure adoration in his gaze pierced her very heart.

How lucky she was to be loved so much. The realization reminded her of how much she missed his loving. After all these days of denial, she knew she wanted him again.

"Could we just put in an appearance?" she murmured as she petted his hair. "We already said we'd go, and it would be much too rude not to show without any explanation."

"Oh, all right. You know I can't say no to you."

She smiled. "Besides, I'm dying to find out what an 'at-home' is."

"It's boring," he called as she hurried back into her chamber, and rang the bell sharply for her other maids.

Jack heaved a sigh and picked up the paper again. God knew there was no bloody reason to tell his wife the real reason he had fired her sultry French maid.

Earlier today, when Eden had gone to her Ladies' Garden Club, Jack had been working at his desk in the sitting room, reviewing correspondence, and had not heard Lisette saunter up behind him, but he had frozen at the light female touch on his shoulder. He had assumed it was Eden reaching for him at last, and he had responded at once, turning only to find it was her attendant.

"My lady has gone out," Lisette murmured, sidling closer. "I wondered if there's anything my lord might need."

She had begun rubbing his tense shoulders before he could reply, coming up behind his chair and leaning her big breasts forward to cradle his head. "These hands can do more than make pretty coiffures," she had whispered.

Jack had sat there, motionless.

With Eden starving him for sex, he had admittedly looked at the woman—once. Unfortunately, Lisette was French and once was all it took. She knew.

But hell, Jack thought, he was married, not dead. Before Eden, Lisette was precisely the kind of shrewd, knowing female he'd have chosen to amuse himself with in some far-flung port. She was all woman, ample curves and deep, beckoning eyes, a creature of smoldering sensuality.

He knew he shouldn't have hired her.

But she had come highly recommended, having worked for several ladies of the ton, and he had been thinking of Eden, who knew nothing of Society. His wife was going to need all the help that she

287

could get, and Lisette had the air of a woman who knew her way around the world.

Her self-assured touch had told him that she also knew her way around a man's body. He had flinched at her caress.

"It is a crime that a man like you should ever be neglected," she breathed in his ear, massaging his shoulders. "She doesn't deserve you."

He had pulled away, refusing even to contemplate adultery. "Leave me. And do not speak ill of your mistress ever again."

"You love her, I know, even though she will not share your bed. But my lord, there's nothing to feel guilty for. It doesn't count, you know, if it's only your cock in my mouth."

He had stood up and lengthened the distance between them.

"You are dismissed. I don't want you anywhere near my wife. Go."

"What?"

"Get your things and go."

She had glared at him.

"We will write you a reference. Just get out of my sight."

She had hissed at him on her way out.

When she had made her haughty exit, Jack had tried to get back to work, but after a few minutes, he threw down his pen in defeat. Fairly twitching with sexual need, he had left his desk and walked out onto the balcony, struggling to rein in his ravenous lust.

He had made up his mind then that tonight was the night.

After the stupid at-home at Lord Draxinger's, he would exercise his husbandly prerogatives. It was humiliating enough that the servants were starting to notice that his wife refused to let him into her bed. He had vowed to wait a week before he took her, but five days was all that he could last.

When Eden finally figured out what to do with her hair, they went to the at-home and found it ridiculously crowded.

Hundreds of guests were packed into the grand townhouse on Hanover Square, so that it was nearly impossible to move.

The ton had many silly rituals, but Jack had always thought this business of the at-home was the biggest waste of time. It entailed a long and tedious procession through the entrance hall, up the jam-packed staircase, until it was finally their turn to pay their respects to their host and hostess. This done, the guests simply turned around and filed right back out again.

Some nights, there might be as many as three or four popular at-homes to visit at once. As far as Jack could gather, the point of it was to converse with other guests while everyone waited in line, but in his view, it was sheer torture.

This particular at-home, however, managed to hold his attention, for as crowded as it was, it meant having Eden's lithe body squashed up again him for a good half hour.

The surging motion of the crowd pressed him against her in a heated wave. It was the most contact with her that he had enjoyed in what felt like forever, and at last, he could sense her awareness of him coming to life.

As her husband, he had every right to place his hand on her waist to steady her as they inched up the overcrowded staircase.

They were thrust beside the wall, so no one but Eden noticed that his hold on her was more of a caress. She glanced at him over her shoulder, her lips parted playfully. Not enough for anyone to notice, she arched her back just a bit, with a subtle thrust of her backside into his groin.

Jack bit back a groan and slipped his fingertip into the little gap at the top of her elbow-length gloves. His heart was pounding. "Let's get out of here."

She turned her head as though to kiss him, but she knew as well as he did that two people couldn't kiss in the middle of one of these events. Not without causing a full-fledged scandal.

They were panting for each other, and the crowd was oblivious. What fun. Having an affair with his own wife.

"How can we?" she whispered.

That wasn't a no, praise God.

He looked down the stairs and cursed under his breath to see they were pinned in. There was nothing to do but to go through with the maddening ritual until they could finally escape. And then . . .

He trailed his gloved fingers up her spine, rousing a shiver. "Pretty dress," he whispered. It was off the shoulder. He liked the low curve in the back. His lips grazed her earlobe. "I can't wait to rip it off you."

She drew in her breath at his naughty whisper, but her girlish shiver spurred him on. They were only words, after all, just loud enough for his sweet pet to hear. "I'm going to lay you down and lick you from your head to your toes, every inch of your creamy skin. I'll give you so much pleasure that you'll think you've lost your mind, and then I'm going to do it all over again. And again . . . and again."

She jerked.

Jack had a few more choice ideas that he whispered to her as they made their way slowly up the stairs, but his heart was pounding, and it was all he could do to will down his growing erection.

That would be something to show to the Draxingers.

"Are you wet for me?" he wanted to know.

"Stop it," she giggled. "It's nearly our turn."

"There's got to be an extra room somewhere in this place where you and I can—"

"Shh!"

"What?" he drawled. "Drax is a friend of Alec's, so I very much doubt he's a pillar of virtue. He knows what goes on."

"And so will everyone else. Just wait until we get home."

"You promise?"

"As long as you're good."

"In that case—" He breathed the words wickedly into her ear. "I will be a perfect angel."

When they finally reached their hosts, their visit was extraordinarily brief. Eden curtsied, Jack bowed, and then they raced out, fighting the incoming tide of humanity. If she wasn't mistaken, Jack shoved a few people out of the way and flashed a smile as though it were an accident.

They hurried back to their hotel to make love, but despite the fact that he already had her wildly aroused even before they got out of the carriage—indeed, she wanted nothing but to let the delicious man do to her every sinful thing he'd promised—in the rational part of her mind, Eden was still just a tiny bit uncertain.

They made it as far as the big mahogany table in the darkened dining room, where they proceeded to have each other for dessert. His hand was up her skirts, pleasuring her, while Eden kissed his beautiful bare chest where she'd ripped his shirt open, and stroked his powerful arms, his strong back through the thin white lawn.

He smiled drunkenly between kisses as he touched the nectar dampening her inner thighs. "My pretty wife," he whispered. "I'm going to take you now."

"Jack, wait."

"Mm, no more waiting. Now." He kissed her again, filling her mouth with the velvet stroke of his tongue on hers.

"Jack—I want to give myself to you," she panted when he let her up for air. "But—"

"Oh, but what?" he teased, babying her with a doting frown.

"I-I need to know that this time, Jack, you're going to be as honest—and open with me as I've been with you. I just want to know—oh!—that my feelings are returned."

"Of course they are, sweetheart."

It was so difficult to concentrate when he sucked on her neck like that, but somehow she rallied her wits. "Then—tell me the real reason you wanted to leave me in Ireland."

He stopped. He lifted his head and looked at her in shock. "You have got to be joking."

Her chest was heaving, but her stare was dead serious. When he started to lean down for another kiss with a charming, pooh-pooh sort of smile on his lips, she planted her hand on his shoulder to show she meant business.

"Oh, come on. You're not going to start that again now?"

"Why didn't you want me with you? Just tell me."

He cast about for words. "Eden, it doesn't matter anymore."

"It matters to me."

"What I feared hasn't come to fruition, so could you please drop it?"

"What did you fear?"

"Leave it alone!" he exclaimed. "Darling, I know you were hurt but I realized my mistake and corrected it. Isn't that enough?"

"I am your wife. I have a right to know what's going on inside that head of yours."

He rolled his eyes. "Did it ever occur to you that *I* have a right to my own private thoughts? I don't want to talk about this! Especially not now. Kiss me, damn it."

She tilted her face away, shooting him a sharp look askance. "Why won't you tell me?"

He sat up. "I don't believe this."

She followed, lifting the little puff sleeve of her unbuttoned gown back up her arm. "What are you trying to hide?"

"Listen. I need you. Make love to me. Right now." He reached out and played with the little notch between her collar bones, drawing a diamond around it with his fingertip. Then he lowered

291

his hand to her thigh. "You keep brushing me off like this, you're going to lose me," he whispered.

She pulled back with a frightened look. "Jack!"

"I mean it. You've got to stop this, Eden." He grasped her shoulder lightly and gazed into her eyes. "I feel like I'm losing you. I barely know you anymore and these days, I'm not sure you know yourself. I'm worried about you. You're changing, and I liked you the way you were, my little jungle oddball, not like anybody else in the whole world," he whispered softly. "Utterly unique."

"I'm not changing."

He caught her face between his hands. "Yes, you are," he whispered urgently. "And I'm scared to death that I'm the one responsible." He squeezed her shoulder again. "Come back to me."

They stared at each other for a long moment.

Without a word, Eden reached for him. He pulled her near and hugged her. They held each other for a long moment in silence, and she thought about what he had said. She did not like the uneasy flare of guilt she felt inside. "Maybe I'm trying new things of late, but I . . . I'm happy." *I think.*

"Happy?" He pulled back and it seemed her assertion had somehow angered him. "How *can* you be, when there is this gulf between us? Happy? I'm not! But maybe you just don't care about us the way I do."

"Don't say that, Jack! You know I do," she insisted softly, cupping his nape. "You're everything to me."

"Then show me. Show me you love me. Lie with me, Eden. I love you so much it's killing me."

"But you don't understand!" She withdrew her touch. "You nearly left me in the dust once—no, twice before, if you count Venezuela. How can I trust you and give myself to you when you won't even answer one simple question?"

"How? I'll tell you how. I saved your life, for starters. I give you everything your heart desires, I love you as I've never loved before—and now you want to put conditions on whether or not you'll make love with me? I am your husband," he said with a tremor of hurt fury gathering in his deep voice. "You cannot keep turning me away!"

"But, Jack—"

"But nothing. Stop punishing me! I told you, I admit it, I was wrong. But I have been doing everything in my power to make it up to you, so quit playing games! What more do you want?"

"The truth!" she cried. "If you'd talk to me, at least then I could understand! Why must you be so evasive? What's so bad that you've got to hide, that you can't even tell me your motives?"

"You know what? Forget it," he said, sliding off the table. "This is rubbish. You let me know when you want to come back to my bed. I'm done begging for you."

He picked up his work coat in disgust and walked out the door, shutting it with a slam.

CHAPTER
∽ SIXTEEN ∾

*H*urt and furious and feeling entirely rejected, Jack dove head-long into work, just as he always did. He went straight to the office at his company warehouse beside the river, where he found Trahern in charge and the job running smoothly. He walked in, greeted his dog, glad that at least somebody appreciated him, then asked Trahern for a report on the latest progress.

"Excellent news, Captain." The higher level of responsibility seemed to sit well with the young lieutenant. He held himself straighter and possessed a new air of self-assurance. "You know those fellows your kinsman, Lord Rackford, sent me to see? Well, my visit with them produced another seventy recruits. That now makes a full three hundred from London. Provided everyone who signed on actually shows up, we'll reach Bolivar with a full brigade, exactly as we promised."

"Fine work, Trahern."

"Thank you, sir. We also received word today from Ireland and Cornwall. They're just about ready there."

"Good. How much time do we need before we can go?"

"Well, the supplies are being loaded onboard as we speak." Trahern nodded past the wide, barn-style doors toward the river, where *The Winds of Fortune* rode proudly at anchor.

Jack gazed wistfully at her, eager to be underway again and free of all this maddening Society and the exasperation of trying to get through to Eden. At least at sea he knew where he stood.

"It should take another eight to ten hours to complete the load-ing," Trahern continued. "Meanwhile, we shall have to send the word out to the men. They'll need a little notice to say their good-byes, but on the whole, these lads have nothing to keep them here.

I'd say we could probably lift anchor in forty-eight hours. The only thing still missing is Lord Arthur to load up the *Valiant* with the rest of the supplies, but he could always catch up later."

Jack agreed, nodding. "He needn't delay us. I can have Lucien tie up loose ends with him when he gets here."

"Why the sudden rush to shove off?" Trahern asked, turning to him. "Trouble with Ruiz?"

"No." He paused, lowering his gaze. "Everything's fine."

Trahern studied him. "Jack, you look like hell. What's wrong?"

He snorted and shook his head, and paced away from him, fed up. "I should've tupped the maid when I had the chance," he said under his breath.

"Fight with the wife?"

"My boy, I believe I shall spend the rest of the night in a brothel," he announced. "Pity you can't join me, but you've got work to do."

Trahern stared at him. "Do you really mean that?"

Jack looked at him for a moment then let out a weary sigh. "Let's just finish this and get out of here. Perhaps absence will make her heart grow fonder."

"Aye-aye," Trahern said warily.

As he turned away to resume his work, Jack noticed that his dog had come to attention. Rudy was staring outside at the dark in the direction of a tower of crates waiting to be loaded onto the jolly boats.

"What's the matter, boy?" Jack murmured with a faint smile. "Is it a chicken?"

Normal dogs chased cats, but his quirky bull-terrier usually went for the poultry.

All of a sudden, Rudy went tearing out of the warehouse barking viciously.

That was not the bark of a dog at play.

Rudy was on the attack, and Jack was right behind him.

Ruiz.

Leave it to Rudy to go after a trained assassin, fearless mutt. *If he shoots my dog, I'll cut his heart out.*

Too quick for a mere human to catch, Rudy had disappeared into the night, but Jack could still hear him barking. Pistol in one hand, knife in the other, Jack pounded down the long wooden quay, then turned into one of the treacherous docklands alleys between warehouses, following the sound of his dog's continued ruckus.

Down the alley, Jack spotted Rudy trying to jump over a very tall gate, bouncing as though on springs, his front paws hitting against the wooden door. Whoever it was must have slipped away behind there, he thought as he ran toward his dog to investigate.

"Down, boy. Easy, Rudy. Where'd he go, boy?"

Jack jumped up, grabbing the wooden top of the tall gate, and pulled himself up, peering over the other side. He scanned the bare, cobbled yard beyond, but there was no sign of motion and little to hide behind, other than an old wagon.

He released his hold, jumping back down again. He glanced around with his gun at the ready, but seeing no one, he bent down to make sure his brave little dog was unharmed.

"Hey, Rudy. There's a good boy. You all right?" Since the bullterrier was white with only the one black ring around his eye, Jack noticed at once that Rudy had something dark around his mouth. When he checked the dog's muzzle, he realized it was blood—and it did not appear to belong to Rudy.

"By George, you got him," he murmured. "You bit the bastard, didn't you?"

Pleased with himself but still agitated, Rudy shifted his weight from side to side, then sat down wagging his tail; he looked up at Jack with a wide, canine grin.

"You little bruiser," Jack whispered, shaking his head, but he was mystified by the obvious question. Manuel de Ruiz probably knew six ways to kill with his bare hands, and there was no way a trained assassin could have forgotten his weapons. So, why hadn't he shot the dog?

Simple answer. It couldn't have been Ruiz.

Then who . . . ?

Jack spotted a small shred of cloth on the ground. He picked it up. There was blood on it, too. He'd have bet a quid that somebody was walking around with a hole in his trousers—aye, and teethmarks in his leg.

He stood up again and glanced around uneasily. The riverside regions were famous as the haunt of cutthroats and thieves.

Perhaps Rudy had simply chased off one of the local ne'er-dowells who had come too close casing the warehouse. He was just damned glad that whoever it was hadn't killed his dog in self-defense. "Come on, boy. Let's go get you cleaned up."

Rudy trotted proudly beside him back to the warehouse until Trahern appeared, then the dog went loping ahead.

The lieutenant gasped at the sight of Rudy's bloodied muzzle. "What happened?"

"Seems we had a bit o' company."

"And Rudy's quite the host."

"Clean him up for me, would you? But give him some time. He's a little riled up."

"Was it Ruiz?"

"I really don't know. It seems unlikely. He'd have shot the dog."

"It could have been one of his underlings."

"Hmm." Jack considered for a moment then shook his head. "We spoke about limits, but I don't trust that blackguard." He nodded to himself. "I'd better get home and check on my wife."

"What about the brothel?" Trahern quirked a smile.

Jack narrowed his eyes at him in warning.

"Captain, perhaps you should stay here in London and fix things with your lady," the lieutenant ventured, arresting his attention as Jack turned to go. "I can run this mission on my own from this point on."

"The hell you can," he said idly.

"You think I can't succeed? What, that I can't get the ship past the Spanish? Then you're forgetting how many times I got our silver shipments safely through those damned hordes of pirates in the Orient."

"This is different."

"No, it's not. I know those waters like the back of my hand. The Spanish navy may have bigger guns—" Trahern paused as some passing workers nodded respectfully at them, then he continued in a lower tone. "But even they aren't as ruthless as the brigands I've faced in the Indian Ocean, the ones that prey on merchant ships. I've captained those runs, Jack. I've outrun and outmaneuvered those heathens on many occasions—quite as well as you could at my age, if I may be permitted to say so."

"Well, you're not," he muttered.

"You should stay here," his friend said emphatically. "You've got too much to lose now, and I can do this. You've got a woman

297

who loves you. You're finally back in your family's good graces—"

"Yes, but I gave the rebels my word."

"Not to fix on details, sir, but you pledged to *recruit* and *outfit* a battalion. That means making the contacts and bankrolling the effort, which you've done. There really is no need for a man in your position to have to oversee every last little detail." He grinned. "Especially when you've got *me*."

Jack raised a brow.

"Let me take the men back to South America for you," Trahern said firmly. "I'll round the troops up and get them back to Bolivar."

"No."

"Jack, I know those waters like the back of my hand."

"It isn't that."

"What then? Oh, but I already know," the younger man said impatiently. "You can't stand to give up one iota of control!"

"It's not a matter of control," he defended, though perhaps unconvincingly.

"What, then?"

Torn, Jack stared at his ship anchored out there on the water. His freedom. His safety. His means of escape.

"Never mind," he grumbled. "I've got to go check on my wife."

"Jack!"

"Let's get the hell out of here and get the whole mess over with. You said you want forty-eight hours to finish? I'm giving you thirty-six."

"You're a proper bastard, you know."

"Aye, and damned proud of it."

Eden did not know where her husband had gone. She only knew he was angry at her. It was so frustrating, this tendency of his to go storming out whenever they were in conflict. It only made everything harder to solve.

She lay awake, alone, restless, in her bed. Her desire had been awakened by his earlier caresses, but her mood remained troubled. She thought about what he had said, that she was changing, losing herself. Perhaps there was *some* truth to it. Although she had become one with her girlhood fantasies, she was feeling a bit lost. She seemed to recall Jack warning her about this back on *The Winds of Fortune*.

Very well, she admitted, *maybe I have changed a little, but I've never played games with his affection.* She turned over, worried. Did he really think that?

Oh, where had he gone? She missed him, her lover, her friend, and yearned for his loving to make her whole again. He was right. This had gone on long enough. She remembered the betrayed, angry look in his eyes and winced with pain. *I never meant to hurt him.*

In any case, he had made his point. It was plain to see he was *never* going to tell her his reasons for wanting to leave her in Ireland, so she had now officially let it go. What else could she do? It wasn't worth hurting him.

As the moments stretched out, she shifted, running her hand down her body in restless need. She was alone in her bed but it seemed she had better get used to it. Before long, Jack would be in South America, and a part of her nursed the hurt of an almost childlike sense of abandonment, an inability to understand how he could claim that he loved her so much it was killing him, and then leave her for a full half a year.

Out of sight, out of mind.

At least now she had her new family and her friends. But without Jack near to ground her in his solid strength, how much more would this life continue to change her? Would there be anything left of her by the time he returned?

Just then, she heard faintly the muffled rhythm of that swift, sure, familiar stride. Her heart skipped a beat.

Jack was back.

The faint jangle of keys and turning locks as he let himself into their suite stirred the memory of that first night she had spent in his cabin aboard *The Winds of Fortune,* after the rogue had made her strip and bathe before him.

She hadn't known that night what her fate would be. She remembered her terror, even pretending to be asleep, as if that could stop a man of Black-Jack Knight's reputation.

Instead, he had treated her with astonishing mercy. Gentleness. Consideration. Just as he always did. Thus he had won her trust. And, yes, she realized, she trusted him still.

And she wanted him more than ever.

Through the sitting room beyond her chamber, she heard his hard footsteps approaching, crossing toward her door.

"Eden?" The tone of his voice was taut, warning of danger. "Are you all right in there?"

She lifted her head from her pillow. "Fine, of course. What's wrong?"

He prowled through her room, making a sweep of the dark corners and shadowed places. His big body was tensed and bristling.

She sat up in bed. "What is it?"

"Just a minute." He stepped out onto the balcony, checked it and then glanced up at the roof. Warily satisfied, he came back inside, pulling the French doors shut and locking them.

"Has anyone been here? Any strange noises?"

"No, it's been perfectly quiet."

"Anyone come to the door?"

She shook her head. "No."

He paused, resting his hands on his waist. The movement pulled back his black leather coat, revealing the lean lines of his body. "Good."

"Trouble?" she asked softly, but he was staring at her as she sat on her bed, sensual hunger harshly carved into the angular lines of his face.

He turned away. "Perhaps." It seemed he had just remembered his sworn vow not to chase her anymore. No, he had promised that next time, she would come to him. "Don't be afraid. I'm back now. I saw no sign of anyone here. Good night."

"But, Jack, what happened?"

"Someone was spying on us down at the warehouse. I thought it might be Ruiz."

"And you came straight back here to protect me?" she murmured.

He snorted.

She sent him the trace of a pouty smile. "I thought you were miffed at me."

"I am," he said flatly, then he marched back out of her chamber to check the rest of the suite.

Eden frowned. She could hear him moving about, opening closet doors, locking windows. A pity, that, for the breezy spring night was a delicious temperature.

He didn't come back.

She climbed languidly out of her bed and went to find him.

He was not in the sitting room, not in their little dining room, either. Their fancy parlor was empty, as well.

She found him in his chamber, sitting on his bed. His boots were planted on the floor and he slumped forward, his elbows resting loosely on his knees. An unlit cheroot dangled from his lips.

His stare tracked her with a glint of insolence as she ventured warily into the room. His hungry gaze could have burned a hole in the zephyr silk of her negligée.

He had taken off his black leather work coat and had thrown it on the chair.

"It's stuffy in here. You checked already. Is it safe to open the door just a crack?"

He grunted, shrugging.

She went over and unlocked the French doors to his side of the balcony, and then opened them a few inches.

"Your maid wasn't stealing." His brusque murmur reached her while her back was turned. "She tried to seduce me."

"What?" She spun around, wide-eyed.

"Yes, it's shocking, isn't it?" he drawled. "Some women actually do find me attractive."

She took a few steps toward him, appalled. "What happened?"

"You were out with the garden ladies. She wanted to suck me off," he added, leaning back slowly on his elbows on the bed, testing her with his insolence as he always did when he most needed her to reach him.

It was a nasty little trick of his that Eden had learned to spot. When he needed her most, he tended to push her away.

Contrary beast.

"Did you let her?" she asked stiffly.

"No, I fired her," he said, then added in a cool tone: "The only one I want sucking my cock is you."

She stared at him for a long moment, knowing he was baiting her. He was trying to shock her into a reaction, but all she could think was, how dare that woman try to take her man?

"So." She sauntered closer. "You were faithful to me?"

"Aye. Even though you treat me like yesterday's slops."

"No, I don't."

"Oh, my sweet Lady Jay." He turned weary. "Do you love me or not?"

She felt a pang in her heart at the question and gazed tenderly at him. If only she had realized he'd been feeling so unloved. He shouldn't even have to ask.

Her unequivocal answer wasted no words. She walked over to him and stood between his sprawled thighs, clasped the front of his shirt, and pulled him up from his leaning position to gather him into her arms.

She captured his scruffy jaw between both of her hands and pressed a silken kiss to his lips. "I'm sorry, sweetheart."

He trembled with emotion at her soft whisper.

She climbed onto his lap and draped her arms around his shoulders, kissing him again. "I'm so sorry."

Her kiss deepened. Jack groaned. It sounded almost hopeless, as though he was sure she would set him on fire and then merely reject him again.

He was wrong.

Eden began undressing him. "I love you," she breathed against his bare throat as he dropped his head back. "I want you so much."

He seemed to be beyond words with the heat of his need. She lifted his shirt off him smoothly. His right hand moved up and down the back of her leg, taking her buttock in his grasp every few strokes and squeezing it.

"I realize I made you doubt my love," she whispered as she unbuttoned his trousers, "but now I want to take your doubt away."

She freed his cock and made him writhe with her touch as she played with it. Her heart pounded as he grasped her shoulder and pulled her down to claim her lips.

As she caressed his tongue with her own, she wrapped her hand around his member with a firm hold and stroked it, reveling in the length, the girth of him; the satin feel of his most sensitive skin; its mighty throbbing in her hand. The staff of life, she thought in rich pleasure. Below it, his pendulous sac had gone taut with the strain of his massive erection. She glided her fingertips down lightly over the dark furring at his root, to cup his big balls in loving play, and then paused in kissing him, teething his plump lower lip gently.

He moaned as she released it from her nibbling hold. "God, I want to devour you." His fingers found her nipple through her negligée. His hand was trembling.

"No, Jack," she taunted him hotly. "This time it's my turn to devour you. Would you like that?"

He groaned as she stroked his cock harder, having learned

exactly how he most yearned to be touched. He seemed as though he was ready to spend in her hand, but if her husband wanted her mouth, he would have it.

She ended the kiss and swept her gaze up to his, meeting his fevered stare in subtle question. His splendid chest heaved as he watched her, his hair tousled. She smiled at his bee-stung lips and kissed him again, lightly. Then she slid off his lap, moving down to the floor on her knees.

He grasped her arm above the elbow, stopping her. He pulled her back up again and gathered her astride his lap. "Put me in you. Now."

She obeyed with a quiver of anticipation, reaching down to guide his stiff rod to the wet lips of her passage. Jack gasped with pleasure and she held her breath as their bodies joined as one, that perfect lock-and-key fit.

It was like coming home.

"Oh, my God, Eden."

"I know, darling." Breathless, she raked her fingers through his wavy hair. "It feels so good to have you inside me." Then she wrapped her arms around his neck and moved with him in slow, tender symmetry.

"I've missed you so much," he said. "You don't know. I've been dying for you." His large, callused hands ran up and down her back through the zephyr silk negligée, molding the curves of her waist as she rode him.

She gave him an intoxicated smile, her gaze glittering, worshipful. She petted his cheek. "You're mine, you know," she whispered to him.

"God, yes. Body and soul."

"Oh, Jack—I love you."

"Sweetheart." He grasped her nape and kissed her.

A few minutes later, he clasped her hips all of a sudden, stilling her forcibly. When she looked at him, his eyes were closed, his face etched with exquisite torment. "Damn—I can't last." He laughed a little.

She thrilled to know that she had him so excited. "Don't hold back. It's all right. I want you to come."

"But I don't want it to end yet."

She nuzzled his mouth with a sultry smile. "Jack. You've got me for the rest of your life. I'm not going anywhere."

"But I am," he whispered sadly as he gazed into her eyes. "I leave the day after tomorrow."

He watched her reaction as she strove to take the news bravely. She had known this was coming sooner or later and had made a private vow to face it with courage, but a little piece of her heart died to hear it. With all her heart, she did not want him to go, but she refused to complain; she figured she had been enough of a headache for him as it was. She caressed his hair and then kissed his brow.

"Well, then," she whispered, "we'll just have to make the best of the time we have."

He nodded slowly, then they continued making love, resting their foreheads together, adoring each other, reveling in their passion. Denied as they both had been, it wasn't long before they came together, flushed and damp with sweat, gasping into each other's mouths, gazing into each other's souls. The aqua-blue of his eyes would haunt her dreams forever; this man owned a piece of her heart she could never get back.

When the storm of love had given way to the warm glow of satisfaction, they crawled under the sheets to sleep together, enjoying the feel of their naked bodies entwined, all the way down to their feet. Eden rested her head on the curve of Jack's chest. He draped his arms heavily around her shoulders.

She watched him dozing with a look of bliss.

"You know," she murmured, snuggling against him, "I just realized something about myself."

"Hm, what's that?"

She petted his chiseled stomach slowly. "I think part of the reason I pulled away from you before is that I knew you'd have to go."

"Aye?"

"I guess I was trying to protect myself from the hurt of when you go away." She looked up at him penitently. "I thought if I could hold back from loving you to such a crazed degree, then it wouldn't hurt as badly when you left."

He tipped her chin upward. "Sweeting, I don't want you to be hurt."

"I know. I'll be all right," she promised, then nestled against him once more. "You come back safe to me just as soon as you can."

"I will."

"Good. Because, Jack—" She paused and took a deep breath. "I think I'm pregnant."

The ship of the damned at last had come to rest in London. Bound and gagged in the cabin for his refusal to help Connor locate Eden, Dr. Farraday waited in terror for the deranged Australian's return.

Connor had gone off hours ago to make his foray into civilization. His stated intentions were simple: to find Eden and to kill Jack Knight.

Victor prayed for all he was worth that the man had failed on both points.

Earlier, Connor, now the self-made captain of the hell-ship, had demanded that Victor take him to the places where Eden might be found, but even if he had an inkling of where she might be, the last thing he intended to do was to lead the madman straight to his daughter.

As for Jack Knight, well, he would have to look out for himself. With his famous family, he was easy enough to track down in the heart of London. Even Connor with his terror of civilized places would be able to find *him*.

Fortunately, Jack Knight was one of the few men Victor surmised had any sort of chance against Connor, who had only grown more hardened on the voyage.

Since none of them knew where Eden might actually be, starting with Jack was the obvious route.

Still, the man deserved a warning, and Victor burned to see the possibility of help so close, yet so far away.

From where the frigate was moored in the river, he could see through the cramped cabin's porthole the warehouse painted with KNIGHT ENTERPRISES, LTD. in huge letters. It was a good thing the words were so big, for now Victor only had one lens of his spectacles left. But, blazes, seeing it alone did no good. He had no way of reaching it or warning Jack.

Who was to say that Jack would even know where Eden was, anyway? He had no reason to believe that the two of them would still be together, but somehow he prayed that they were, for he knew in his bones that Jack would keep his daughter safe.

Muffled cries of greeting from the ragged crew topside alerted

Victor that Connor had come back. His heart pounded, but he braced himself, knowing it wouldn't be long until his former assistant came down to report to him on his findings, simply out of habit.

Connor soon lurched in, cursing, bleeding from his leg, and looking a bit shaken by his expedition into the realm of men. He cupped his hand around the back of his thigh where he had incurred some sort of wound.

Victor looked at him uncertainly. Connor jerked a nod at one of his thralls. The sailor came over and untied the gag around Victor's mouth.

"What happened to you?" he asked guardedly.

"Bloody dog bit me. Jack Knight's dog," he added acidly.

"D-did you kill him?"

"The dog? Of course not. I could never kill a dog. Victor, what do you take me for?" Connor reached for some bandages in Victor's medical kit, which they had brought with them all the way from the jungle. "Which one of these salves should I use for a dog bite?"

"If you'd untie me, I could tend it for you."

Connor studied him for a long moment. "Don't try anything stupid," he ordered. Then he hobbled over on his wounded leg with a limp that very much resembled that of the drunken captain who'd been murdered in the mutiny.

Victor leaned forward so his erstwhile assistant, the ingrate, could untie his hands. "Did you see Eden?"

"Yes." He stared into space. "She is so beautiful. I saw her through the window."

He turned to him eagerly, shaking the loosened ropes off his wrists. "Was she well? Was she safe?"

"It appeared so," he admitted. "He is keeping her in a place called the Pulteney Hotel."

" 'He'? Do you mean Lord Jack?"

Connor sent him a dark look, an obvious affirmative.

"D-did you kill him?" Victor asked, holding his breath.

"No." Connor sighed and returned to where he had sat before. "I was going to. Couldn't get a clear shot. So I followed him instead, and I am so glad I did."

"Why? What do you mean? And what did you mean when you said he is 'keeping' her there at the Pulteney Hotel? Has that blackguard dishonored my daughter?"

"What do you think? I'm the one she loves. And he will pay for everything he had done to her, trust me," Connor said, then he pulled a folded newspaper out of his coat. "In here it says they are married. She couldn't possibly have wanted this. He forced her. I know it. And he's going to die."

"Connor—"

"Oh, don't worry, Father. I'm not the one who is going to kill him."

Victor flinched at the way the obsession had taken his friend over completely, addling his wits—or had they always been addled, and he had just never noticed, so wrapped up in his own pain?

What sane man ever took it into his head to go and live in a jungle, anyway?

"I was thinking back to how angry Eden was after I protected her from the warrior who tried to molest her. I don't want to go through that again by killing Lord Jack and having her find out it was me. So, luckily, I found another way."

"How?"

Connor smiled. "I'm not sure I should tell you. You're very wily, old man."

Victor said nothing as he knelt down by his medical kit and rolled up his sleeves, preparing to treat Connor's dog bite. "Well, if you don't feel you can trust me, Connor, so be it. We've only known each other, what, twelve, thirteen years? You're my daughter's true love. But I'm just her father—"

"All right," he conceded, smiling broadly to hear his fantasies affirmed. He leaned nearer. "I followed him to his warehouse. It's right over there." He pointed toward the porthole. "Did you see?"

Victor squinted. "I cannot make it out with these broken spectacles," he lied. "But I will take your word on it."

"Well, I saw what he's up to." He sat back again. "Our Lord Jack is up to some very naughty business."

"Doing what?" Victor murmured, alarmed.

"He is gathering an army for Bolivar—and won't the Spanish embassy be interested to know it? Nature is efficient, Victor. I'll let the Spanish get him for me when the time is right."

"And, er, when will the time be right, my lad?"

"Soon. Just as soon as I figure out a way to get to Eden. I know

307

she loves me, but—she is confused, you see. Like a wounded doe. She might try to fight me. I can't have that."

"Connor. You mustn't hurt our Edie."

"Of course not." Leaning forward, he reached under his cot and pulled out one of the cases containing their jungle samples.

Victor's heart pounded in trepidation as Connor opened the lid and scanned the collection of curare potions.

"This . . ." Connor murmured half to himself.

Victor paled but tried to hide his dread. "Listen to me. Those brews are deadly."

"Not this one." Connor lifted a small bamboo tube out with a placid smile. "It's very mild. I made it myself. It's quite gentle, very fast-acting. I used it to stun the little birds and creatures of the canopy for study. One tiny prick of her finger, and she'll go to sleep. When she wakes up," he crooned, "I'll have her back again, forever."

CHAPTER
∽ SEVENTEEN ∽

*T*he weather turned foul on the night of the ball, but nothing could have dampened Jack's spirits with the magic of their little secret.

If the world could have guessed it, he would not have been surprised. He walked with a strut tonight, his chest puffed out, and a lift to his chin. He felt thoroughly unconquerable, and utterly in love.

The physician had been sent for earlier that afternoon, confirming Eden's delicate condition with a fair degree of certainty.

He was going to be a dad. After all the innumerable times he had thought and spoken about his desire for an heir, having the reality of it confirmed was another matter entirely. They were going to have a child! He had not known how much he had wanted this until his wife had said it. The notion of his firstborn scheduled to join them this autumn had done something to his heart like a canary being freed from a cage.

As for his Lady Jay, she laughed and blushed and scolded him for being overprotective from the second he had heard the news. He had to remind himself this was the chit who could hurl a machete into a bull's-eye from thirty feet away. She seemed to be taking the pregnancy in stride, as she did most things.

For now, she was rapt with excitement over her first true Society ball, though getting there proved to be no mean trick.

The location was a stately manor in Richmond set in several acres of green parklands. A long line of lamplit carriages waited in the steady downpour for their turn to pull up under the porte cochere and discharge their passengers.

Rain turned the drive to mud; darkened the horses hides' and made their leather traces chafe; rain dampened the wilting grooms' wigs until white powder trickled down their matching livery coats.

Through the steady spring shower, however, the cheerful lights shining through the great arched windows of the mansion looked all the more inviting.

As they waited in the line of carriages, Jack pointed out to Eden the large, cupola-topped conservatory off the south corner of the house and asked her if she'd like one just like that to be added onto their house in Derbyshire.

"We'll go and have a look at it," she promised, her eyes shining.

Every now and then, he just shook his head and sighed as he gazed at her. She tapped his arm with her fan and gave him a kiss while they waited.

Finally, they made it inside, politely refusing a cup of belly-warming negus in the thronged entrance hall where arriving guests were milling about.

Footmen scurried back and forth with umbrellas, while cloak-room servants took the guests' endless array of hats, wraps, pelisses, and greatcoats. Ladies exclaimed over the wet as they hurried off to change out of their warm carriage shoes into their dancing slippers for the rest of the evening.

Jack and Eden exchanged a slightly overwhelmed glance. After languishing in the row of carriages, they were both daunted to find another queue to wait in, several persons deep, which snaked up the magnificent staircase into the ballroom.

Above, the majordomo was formally announcing each new arrival to the throng of guests before herding them on to be greeted by their hosts' receiving line.

The old Jack would have deemed the whole procedure damned excruciating, he reflected, but walking in with his beautiful bride on his arm and seeing how happy the whole thing made her inspired him to endure it, even the always slightly unnerving moment when one's name was shouted out to the whole throng. He was never sure which was worse, being stared at as one entered or having one's arrival completely ignored.

He needn't have worried, he realized. People everywhere turned to look, but even the bony faces of the frightening grand dames who ruled Society softened at the refined beauty of his wife. With her white-gloved hand tucked into the crook of his arm, she lifted the hem of her gown just a touch and proceeded gracefully down the entry stairs beside him.

Coming down the staircase, Jack surveyed the brilliant ballroom in reluctant pleasure. Hundreds of glittering candles lit the soaring space while a charming Mozart rondo lightened the drone of conversation with a little melody that the orchestra and pianoforte tossed back and forth playfully between them, now one, now the other.

He was glad he had listened to Martin and had worn what his valet had prescribed for the occasion. Eden had been complimentary, pronouncing him very smart in his black and white formal attire. His ebony coat of silk was double-breasted, with bright gilt buttons; his waistcoat gleamed as bright as the very cliffs of Dover.

Clean-shaved, white-gloved, and hair slicked back, he stretched his neck a bit, the starchy cravat rather more grand than what he was accustomed to, in a style with some French name he couldn't even pronounce. What did he know of such things? But Martin had declared it "all the kick" and had finished it off with a bit of sparkle from the safe: a solid gold vertical cravat pin with a sizable diamond head.

Joining the crowd, he lifted two crystal flutes of champagne off the tray of a passing waiter, but Eden declined the offered glass, casting a hungry eye over the sweets in the large, columned alcove designated as the refreshment area.

Near the wine fountain with four silver dolphins spouting Chardonnay, another liveried footman offered guests confections on a silver tray: candied ginger, licorice, chocolate drops, an array of colored bon-bons that echoed the soft, flower-garden hues of the ladies' gowns—pink and blue, green and white, lavender and yellow.

So many flowers in an English garden. But none so fair as his little orchid.

Her lithe body had only just begun to show the barest hint of her delicate condition—it hadn't been marked enough for Jack to notice it last night when she had been naked before him. Dressed in her finery now, the tautening low around her belly was not at all visible yet.

She was, of course, the loveliest female in the room, draped in a gown of lustrous shot silk, iridescent, like the wings of a dragon-

311

fly—pale green or lavender depending on which way the candle-light hit the exquisite fabric. Its shimmering quality stood in contrast to the creamy perfection of her skin, the fluid lines cascading down her figure like a secret jungle waterfall.

Her hair, the color of cinnamon, was parted in the middle, her beloved face framed by soft ringlets that fell to either side, with a high chignon on top graced with a clutch of dark pink rosebuds. He couldn't stop staring at her.

Moved by her beauty and dazzled to know their first child was now more than just a hazy fantasy, Jack had never experienced such a tug of war within him in his entire life.

How could he possibly go to South America now? How could he possibly back out? He had given Bolivar his word. Thousands of people could die if he failed.

Yet if anything went wrong to delay his journey, from uncooperative weather to violent resistance from the Spanish navy, he would miss the birth of his child—and these things did not always go smoothly.

Eden needed him, too. Her confession last night haunted him. When she had told him that she had been holding back from loving him ever since they'd left Ireland not just because of their falling out, but also because she knew he had to leave, her words had resonated with him in a troubling way, reminding him of the man he used to be and the way he had lived before she had come swinging into his world on that silly vine.

Always sailing from port to port, he had kept the world at arm's length, never allowing anyone close to him, deliberately keeping a careful detachment from others in order to protect himself. He knew how much it hurt to exist that way, and now he was about to inflict the same way of life on Eden.

Maybe I shouldn't go. Maybe I really should leave it to Trahern. But putting such a vital mission in the hands of a man barely twenty-six years old seemed insane. Thousands of people could die if he failed, their only chance at freedom crushed. Jack's wife and babe might need him, but how could he ever be selfish enough to put his private life before what he deemed right?

He found himself wondering what Uncle Arthur would have advised. Where was the old devil, anyway? Perhaps the repairs on the *Valiant* had been more involved than his uncle had expected.

At any rate, their arrival in the ballroom created a bit of a stir.

People he had never seen before greeted him with cordial nods and smiles as he and Eden sauntered past with steps perfectly fitted to each other's. Whether it was Eden or their well-matched couplehood, his wife generated an air of approval about her that he knew he could never have obtained alone.

Having been starved for human company for so long, she was genuinely pleased to see everyone, and as a result, nobody could resist her. He sensed the usual whispers behind fluttering fans, but with Eden beside him, he didn't care. Society's tireless busybodies required a constant diet of new gossip to keep their empty heads abuzz. It did not signify.

"What have you done to these people, darling?" he murmured to her at length. "Have you cast a spell on them? Put some of that what's-it leaf into the punch bowl?"

"Why do you say that?"

"They're smiling at me."

"Well, that's easy enough to explain. I haven't been merely amusing myself in all my gadding about, I'll have you know." She sent him a discreet smile askance. "I've been campaigning for you everywhere I go, as well, making a point of telling the world how wonderful you are."

"Wonderful?" he echoed. "Trying to ruin my reputation, are you?"

"As the terror of the West Indies? I'm afraid so," she replied, then greeted a pair of turbaned and jewel-covered matrons from the Garden Club who fluttered to her with an apparently earth-shattering announcement.

"Oh! Dear child, we have the most wonderful news!"

"What is it?" she asked, beaming at them very like a ray of tropical sunshine.

"We spoke to Lady Jersey and Countess Lieven on your behalf, and guess what? They've agreed!" said the first.

The second chimed in. "You are to be summoned to one of their homes to receive a voucher to Almack's! Yes, it's true—for the two of you!"

"They're letting *me* into Almack's?" Jack drawled.

"Oh, yes, my lord. It was no mean feat convincing the Patronesses—"

"But I don't wa—" he started, then shut his mouth as Eden's fingers clamped down on his arm in warning. He obeyed and merely

313

smiled. "Thank you," he responded to their frail champions. "I'm sure you're very kind."

The garden ladies warned them to secrecy. "But you can't know yet! You'll have to act surprised."

"We will," Eden promised. "Won't we, Jack?"

"Hmm."

"My dear ladies, you are so good to speak to them on my behalf! I had no idea you had taken up for me."

"Tut, tut, gel. We need more women of sense at these things."

"Amen to that," Jack muttered.

"Besides, your tips for helping to get rid of our aphids were absolutely brilliant. My prize roses owe you their lives!"

"Oh, it's just a little trick of Papa's," she said modestly.

"Ah, what's this?" The lady in white glanced in the direction of the dance floor, where the master of ceremonies had made the long-awaited announcement. "They are starting the dancing."

"You two will make such a lovely pair," the other one said, favoring them with a wreath of smiles. "Go on, then. You newly-weds run along and have a dance."

Eden turned to Jack with an eager smile. "Shall we?"

He blinked. "Uh, Eden."

The ladies bowed to them and moved on to mingle elsewhere.

Damn. He had forgotten about this dancing business. He turned to his wife in a state of extreme discomfort. "Darling, perhaps you really shouldn't, in your condition."

"Don't be silly," she whispered. "It's just a bit of dancing. It's not as if I'm going to run a marathon."

No, a marathon would have been far preferable, at least for him.

Every man had his limits, and Jack Knight didn't dance.

He had come to this silly ball, had he not? And the routs and the at-homes and the card parties and everything else? Surely he had done his duty. He hated to disappoint her, especially now, but he had made no promises about participating in this fool's art. Having come this far to gain the ton's respect, he was not about to go out there and make a horse's arse of himself.

Not even for Eden.

He could not, would not dance, never had, never would, and in point of fact would rather gouge his own eye out with a fish fork than stand up with all the other prancing idiots and march around in their daft little patterns. Dancing was a silly practice too far beneath him for words, and he was sure that most of his brothers would have backed him up on this.

Except for Alec, ever a ruling prince of Society. He spotted his youngest brother sauntering by, and was inspired to foist Eden off on him. Alec's wife, Becky, was too pregnant to dance, after all. He could see her sitting by the wall.

"Jack?" Eden persisted.

"Well, the thing of it is, dear—"

"You don't dance, do you?" she cried.

Thankfully, she looked more amused than vexed—at first.

"I can't," he said, praying she would be his angel and understand.

"Oh, you big grumpy lion. You're just being shy." She gave his face a caress. "Come on, don't be a killjoy."

"Alec!" he called as his brother drifted by.

The golden-haired youngest of the Knight brothers came bounding over with a sunny grin. "Good evening people! Don't you look beautiful, my dear lady! Fantastic gown! Let me see you." He grabbed Eden's hand and twirled her around, letting her show off her gown. "Sister, I hereby declare you a diamond of the first water."

She curtsied low to him, laughing. "Thank you, Lord Alec. Now would you please tell your great lug of a brother to dance with me? He's trying to wriggle out of it."

"What's this? Cur? Knave? Not dancing? What cruelty is this? It's her first ball."

"Yes, I know, but—" His voice broke off. *Can't* was not a word that often reared its ugly head in Jack's vocabulary.

Alec scowled at him, but picked up on his pleading look and took charge, tucking Eden's hand into the crook of his arm. "My dear, new sister, you must come and dance with me. Stand in for me in Becky's stead, won't you? You and I shall never be wallflowers."

Eden gave Jack a sulky look, but she was obviously grateful not to be left out of the dancing. "Are you sure Becky won't mind?"

"Quite the opposite. She'd wring my neck if I let you stand here frowning next to him. She quite adores you, you know."

"Likewise." She waved to her big-bellied sister-in-law, who was sitting by the wall.

Becky waved back, and Alec blew his wife a kiss.

315

"Don't worry," Alec added, patting Eden's hand. "When Jack sees how he's missing out on all the fun, he'll change his mind."

Don't hold your breath, Jack thought, but he nodded his encouragement for them to go on without him. "Enjoy."

"Humph," Eden said.

"Have a drink, old boy," his roguish brother added as he led Eden away. "It'll dull your inhibitions."

"I like my inhibitions, thank you very much."

Alec turned back to him one more time, and pointed to another quarter of the ballroom. "Damien's trying to get your attention."

Jack looked over in the direction Alec had indicated and saw the stern elder twin staring at him. Damien summoned Jack with a flick of his white-gloved fingers. Jack sent him a nod, glad for the reprieve.

As the dancing got underway, Jack struck out to go around the crowd to join the no-nonsense colonel.

Quite the opposite of Alec, with Damien, there was no such thing as small talk.

"I spoke with Wellington," Damien murmured in his ear when Jack joined him with a look of question. "His hands are tied as far as helping you recruit, but he said if you run into trouble with Whitehall, he'll do what he can to help you get out of it."

"That is encouraging. Well done, brother."

They spoke for a few minutes in greater detail about Damien's call on the Iron Duke, then Damien mentioned that everything was ready for Eden's visit. The guest apartment in the Winterleys' Town residence was waiting to receive her.

Jack was bursting to tell Damien the news about the child, but he and Eden had wanted to wait until everyone was together to announce it to the whole family at once.

Keeping the secret of his mission was easy compared to his eagerness to shout this sweeter news from the rooftops. He searched for another topic to stop himself.

He folded his arms across his chest and looked at Damien in curiosity. "What's he like, anyway?"

"Wellington?"

He nodded, curious about the mortal man behind the growing legend of England's foremost hero.

Speaking about his idol was one of the few subjects other than his twin sons, Andrew and Edward, that could inspire Damien to wax poetical. Listening to him describe the Iron Duke's unflappable nerve, dry wit, and unswerving loyalty, Jack watched his wife dancing.

He had lost sight of her in the milling throng, but when he spotted her red hair again, he was surprised that she was no longer safely paired with Alec. Instead, she was gliding through a graceful turn across from some pudgy little bald chap.

Jack frowned until he realized that the stately country dance in progress was one with a shifting pattern of figures where the participants were constantly changing partners with every new verse.

It was just a dance, but somehow this was not the sort of thing a man wanted to see when he was about to leave town for six months.

As he looked on, the weaving patterns of the dance whooshed Eden along to discard the pudgy man, and brought her around to face her next partner, a tall, lean, not unhandsome fellow with a loud red waistcoat and the sly smile of a hardened Town dandy.

Bit of a fop, this one, Jack thought, watching as a dark undercurrent of jealousy slid through his veins.

He brightened, however, when Eden's searching gaze sought him through the crowd and located him over there by Damien.

She sent him a dazzling grin, enjoying herself so much that it nearly coaxed him out to try.

Ruefully, he smiled back at her.

All but ignoring her partner, she tossed her head and gave a little twitch of her skirts in Jack's direction, as if to lure him out onto the dance floor. Ah, she was tempting.

But no, he thought, shaking his head at her.

He was rather fond of his dignity.

"My God, who is that glorious redhead?" someone murmured nearby.

Jack had almost missed the words, barely overhearing as a pair of hard-eyed London rakes strolled past him, oblivious to their peril, for they were wholly absorbed in evaluating the varied charms of all the women present in the ballroom.

They continued on, already sauntering away, though Jack could still hear their low-toned remarks.

"Damn me, never seen her before."

"Think she's married?"

"Since when does it matter?"

They snickered, unaware of Jack coming after them with a black look on his face, but a firm hand on his shoulder suddenly stopped him.

"Jack. A word, please."

He turned to find Lucien staring at him with cool intent in his silvery eyes. The younger twin was usually so laid back that Jack instantly knew from his uneasy look that there was trouble.

He let his flash of jealousy go, but still bristling, he vowed if he heard another word in that vein, he was throwing someone through a window. "What's the matter, Luce?"

"Ah, just a minor bit of, er, unpleasantness, but I thought you should know. Shall we?"

He did not know why the younger twin saw fit to shepherd him over to the wall to tell him what was afoot, but he soon realized it was merely because Lucien knew the size of Jack's temper, and could guess that his news was the sort of thing that could truly set him off.

"What's going on?" Jack waited, his arms akimbo.

"You, ah, fired a maid yesterday?" Lucien asked diplomatically.

"Yes. What of it?" Jack furrowed his brow. "Wait, how did you know about that?" He hadn't seen his brothers yesterday even to have mentioned it.

"I'm not the only one who knows, I'm afraid."

"Huh?"

"This woman, Lisette, I imagine she came to you well recommended."

"Aye, she had worked for other ladies in the ton."

"Well, she's been talking to them since you gave her the sack."

"What?"

"Jack—don't explode. She has started a rumor about you and Eden."

"Oh, bloody hell—!"

Society never changed.

"I don't know how far it's gone yet," Lucien said soothingly. "I just heard it on the other end of the ballroom. But I thought you should know. You can tell Eden as you see fit."

"What does this rumor claim? I am dying to know," he said in a jaundiced tone.

Lucien's gaze slid to the floor. "She said that, uh, the two of you

318

have a sham marriage, and that all the time she worked for your wife, you and Eden never shared a bed."

Jack's jaw dropped. He snapped it shut again, glowering. "I'll wring her neck! Of all the spiteful, petty, conniving—"

He fumed a bit at the rumor's implied slight to his manhood. What business was it of anyone if he had not been sleeping with his wife for a spell until last night? Then he realized Eden was bound to hear it soon. He had to protect her.

He looked over at her in concern. "Thanks, Luce. If you'll excuse me, I've got to go get my wife." He would rather tell her himself than have her hear it from somebody else.

He saw that the first dance had ended and blinked to spy his wife now surrounded by a swarm of elegant Town Corinthians.

The image threw him off guard. *What the—?*

Had those sly chaps heard the rumor, too?

Good God.

Some of them must have heard it, he thought, which would explain why they were buzzing about her like so many bees to a rare, delicious flower. If they believed Eden was trapped in a love-less marriage with a husband who neglected her in bed, then they would naturally assume that meant she was available, in the way that so many Society wives were—in the way, indeed, that Jack's feckless mother had been back in her day.

His anger deepened at the thought. But Eden was no sophisti-cated Georgiana Hawkscliffe, too innocent to know what was really in those scoundrels' minds—namely, bedding her the minute his back was turned.

He was already in motion, ready to start throwing people through windows.

It was not lost on him that if he had danced with her, this would not have happened.

Why was she smiling at them?

He wasn't sure what the devil to do about the rumor. Society wranglings were not his forte. He had to think. Perhaps Alec might have some ideas. Right now, he wanted out of here, and he was taking his wife with him. He didn't care anymore if it was her first ball.

They were going home.

As he marched toward her, a swarthy, splendidly uniformed stranger stepped into his path.

Jack stopped.

"Pardon me, señor." Beneath his thin, black mustache, a smile curved the man's lips, but his dark eyes were like daggers. "Lord Jack Knight, I presume?"

Jack tensed, instantly on his guard. "Aye?"

The Spaniard clicked his heels and bowed to Jack with crisp, Continental panache. "I represent the court of His Majesty, King Ferdinand of Spain. I should like very much to have a word with you—if you don't mind."

Ruiz's superior.

Jack gritted his teeth, biting back his impatience. So, there were six good-looking men flirting with his luscious, young wife, each with a blue-blood pedigree no doubt finer than his own. And at the moment, there was not a damned thing he could do about it.

Very well. Let her enjoy it, he thought with gritted teeth. He could endure it another two minutes. For now, the Spanish ambassador had his full attention. He was stuck with this mission, never mind that his beautiful—pregnant—young wife had half the House of Lords smiling at her, only biding their time.

Just waiting for him to leave for South America.

So, these were Town Corinthians in coats from Savile Row, Eden mused. The dashing gentlemen she had dreamed about, far away in the jungle.

There was something in their eyes she didn't trust; their smooth, cocksure smiles made her uneasy. Hemmed in by them and answering their polite questions in a distracted manner, she wanted Jack, but she had no sooner succeeded in extricating herself from the knot of these too-friendly men when she saw Jack being hounded by the Spaniard.

At once, she remembered his warning that if she saw a black-haired Spanish man anywhere in her vicinity, she should retreat. Jack's arms were folded across his chest as he spoke with the man; the studied way in which her husband refused even to glance in her direction served as a silent warning to Eden not to come near.

She obeyed at once, hastening away from the dance floor.

She remembered how Jack and she had admired the conservatory on the way in to the ball while waiting in the line of carriages; they had spoken of looking at it together. She decided to wait there—Jack would soon figure out where to find her.

Before anyone else could snare her in conversation, she ducked out of the ballroom and found her way through the maze of the enormous manor to the spacious conservatory.

Immediately upon stepping into the tree-filled, glassed-in world, all the trouble in her soul seemed to quiet.

Glass and lacy white ironwork were whipped upward in a froth, culminating in a beautiful center rotunda that gave the exotic trees plenty of room to grow.

There were palms and giant bamboos in huge pots and planters; their pinnate fronds reached up into the central dome. There were a few fragrant orange and lemon trees, a grapefruit tree, and several spiky pineapples, as well.

A profusion of flowers surrounded the towering Doric column at the edge of the rotunda, crowned with a graceful statue of the goddess Flora.

Fairy lights strung here and there lent an air of magic to the hothouse jungle, heated by furnaces and carefully concealed piping, a perfect, humid environment for their host's collection of tropical plants, shrubs, and trees.

With the night so dark beyond the glass, the tiny colored lanterns threw fantastic leaf-shaped shadows everywhere and etched the grids of the countless window mullions across the floor. The music from the ballroom was muffled here; louder came the rain's steady symphony drumming the glass panes of the great, arched windows.

There was a stone fountain in the middle of it all, with a wide rim that formed a circular bench; here, Eden sat down. Wistfully, she watched the large, ornamental fish swimming in the fountain. The miniature, indoor jungle reminded her so sharply of her old life. Everything was different now. How she missed Papa. Would he never come?

Taking off her right glove, she set it down beside her and leaned down to dangle her fingers in the water, reminiscing as she waited for Jack on her days in the Orinoco Delta . . . her chance meetings with the occasional pink dolphin.

That life now seemed a world away.

The rain still drummed the glass and despite the occasional flash of lightning, the setting was altogether pleasant. As she sat musing, playing with the fish, she felt a faint, instinctual prickle of warning tingling on her nape, drawing her out of her memories.

321

She lifted her head and glanced around warily, not sure why she suddenly seemed to sense someone staring at her.

She was the only person in the conservatory.

Lightning flashed, illuminating the glass house in purple and blinding silver, flickering over the statue of Flora: In that split second, as Eden scanned the trees crowding the artificial jungle, she saw him.

Connor.

He was standing outside the conservatory, watching her through the glass, as the rain plastered his blond hair to his forehead.

She gasped, but the lightning vanished and the world beyond the glass turned black again.

She pulled back, her heart pounding. She pressed her gloveless hand to her heart for a second. No.

It couldn't be.

Surely she must have imagined it. How could Connor be standing outside in the storm?

A few minutes later, another flash of lightning revealed the same spot where she thought she had seen him, and no one was there. Catching her breath again, she laughed at herself.

Her guilty conscience must have been to blame—guilty because as much as she longed to see her beloved papa, she hadn't missed Connor once since she had left the jungle. He had problems, she knew, but he had always done his best to be good to her. She hadn't been able to fall in love with him, but that didn't mean another woman could not. He was smart, handsome.

Now that she'd left and had married someone else, he'd soon forget all about her.

Footfalls echoed just then across the flagstones of the conservatory. "Somehow I suspected that I might find you here."

Expecting Jack, Eden looked over, but was jarred to find that instead of her husband, it was the dashing man in the red waistcoat who had danced with her briefly in the ballroom.

The flash of his white teeth gleamed in the twilight as he strolled toward her, his hands in his pockets. "Don't be alarmed," he said. "I saw you slip away. My dear lady, a true beauty can no sooner abscond from a ballroom unnoticed than the sun can slip behind the clouds without turning the whole world below it a dull, dull gray. I thought perhaps we could talk for a moment—oh, dear, but you seem distressed. May I be of use?"

"No. Thank you." She straightened up and flicked the water off her fingers. "Forgive me, have we met?"

"Formally, no. But we are connected."

"We are?"

"Yes."

She lifted her chin to meet his gaze as he joined her—uninvited, but too confident to care.

He propped his foot on the fountain's stone bench and posed with an elbow resting on his knee. "Just now in the ballroom, I heard someone say that you are the famed Dr. Farraday's daughter."

"Yes, I am."

He smiled broadly. "My grandfather was your father's patron for ages."

"Old Lord Pembrooke?" she exclaimed.

He laughed. "Yes! I am his heir."

"You're the new Lord Pembrooke—the rakehell earl?" she blurted out, then bit her lip and blushed.

Her foreknowledge of his nickname seemed to fill him with vain pleasure. "Ah, you know, I have simply no idea why they call me that. Do you?"

She smiled wryly. "Lord Pembrooke, would you believe that you are actually the reason that I am in London?"

"What's this?" he asked, apparently fascinated by the statement. He lowered himself slowly to sit beside her. He leaned nearer; Eden pulled back.

"You cut my father's funding," she informed him, but she had no intention of explaining all the details of her original plan—how she had set out on *The Winds of Fortune* to bring samples of her father's work to London to show the rakehell earl, so that he might be persuaded to reinstate Papa's grant.

That had been ages ago.

"Cut your father's funding . . . ?" He was feigning innocence of his misdeed. "I did? No, surely. Why should I do that?"

"You were building a new country house, I believe, and upon your inheritance instructed your solicitor to tell all the artists and scholars your grandfather commissioned to—I think your exact words were—go hang."

"Ahh, yes. Now it's coming back to me." He quit lying as he realized she was smarter than she looked. There was an awkward

323

moment as he tapped his lip. Then he gave her a smile of mild contrition and stood once more, facing her. "Perhaps we can do something to rectify this sad state of affairs, for I assure you, if I had known the naturalist's daughter was such a rare flower herself, I should have been persuaded instantly to extend Dr. Farraday's grant."

"My father doesn't throw himself on any man's mercy, my lord, and though I'm heartened to hear you'd reconsider for my sake, it won't be necessary."

"Are you sure about that?" he murmured, his rakish smile widening suggestively.

"Oh, yes, I'm sure. My husband, you see, is richer than Croesus. He'll fund Papa's research henceforth."

"Oh, really?" he asked with a haughty snort. "Anyone I know?"

"I'm not sure," Eden said sweetly, "but I can introduce you if you like. He's standing right behind you."

CHAPTER
∞ EIGHTEEN ∞

The Spanish ambassador had merely prodded him with insulting questions, but in the space of time it had taken Jack to get rid of the man and find Eden, a horrifying realization had dawned on him regarding this stupid rumor.

If Society thought that Jack wasn't bedding his luscious young wife, and his wife, in turn, was pregnant—and Jack, meanwhile, was gone away for months to South America—then the next question the ton would start asking was obvious: Who had fathered the baby?

The mere thought of this question ever being asked about his legitimate child—this baby he already loved without ever having yet laid eyes on it—made Jack utterly sick to his stomach.

The burden of bastardy had always been a sore spot for him, but to think that it would befall his innocent unborn child, too, had him shaken up, raw with emotion. He knew firsthand the suffering, loneliness, and humiliation already in store for his son or daughter if he did not find a way to repair this situation immediately.

Though the babe had barely just been conceived, it already seemed fated, through no fault of its own, to come into the world under the same dark cloud of suspicion and doubt that Jack had been cursed with himself.

Labeled a bastard. Made an outcast.

Just like him.

The injustice of it fired his sense of outrage.

It would not stand.

Better if he had locked Eden away in the highest tower of his Irish castle than allow her actions to harm their child before it was even born.

Aye, in one sense this could be viewed as her fault.

If Eden had not held a grudge for so long and denied him her bed, then Lisette would not have made a move on him; Jack wouldn't have had to dismiss the maid, and the rumor would never have started.

Bloody women and their selfish ways, he thought, too angry to care if he was being irrational.

His mother. Maura.

Now this.

It hurt to think that Eden might possess a trace of their same frailty.

His face had drained of color as he had stalked through the ballroom in search of his wife. The music had become a raucous dissonance and Jack had felt as though everyone he passed was staring at him, whispering about him.

Unwanted.

It did not help matters that his last glimpse of his wife before the ambassador had stopped him had been of Eden surrounded by smooth-talking rogues and scheming bachelors.

Did she not know she was nothing to them but fresh meat?

Where the hell had she gone?

Jack could feel himself ready to go on a rampage.

Then he had stepped into the conservatory and saw her talking alone with another man—and something inside of him snapped.

"Wonderful" Jack who had been so tame these past weeks, keeping his hands off, escorting her to all her stupid parties, was suddenly swept aside as though by a massive wave at sea.

Swept overboard.

In his place stood Black-Jack Knight in all his cutthroat pride and angry glory, and it was this side of him that the luckless Lord Pembrooke turned around to meet.

On eye level with Jack's chin, the rakehell earl gulped and looked up slowly.

Jack narrowed his eyes.

"Er, pardon," Pembrooke said in a slightly strangled tone. "I m-meant no offense, sir. Perhaps I should be going—"

The little weasel darted past him, trying to flee. Jack's hand shot out, grabbing him by the scruff of the neck.

Seizing hold of the back of the fop's coat collar and of his trouser waistband, Jack lifted him off the ground and sent him sailing into the fountain with a huge splash.

Then he dusted his hands off lightly. "None taken." Jack looked at his wife, who had leaped to her feet and stood staring at him in openmouthed shock. He grabbed her wrist and pulled her toward the doorway.

"Jack!"

Behind them, Lord Pembrooke was climbing out of the fountain, sputtering and cursing, soaked.

"What are you doing?" Eden cried. "Have you lost your mind?"

He didn't look back at her, striding ahead with single-minded purpose. "Forget him. We're leaving. You and I are going to have a little talk."

"What on earth—? Wait, my other glove—"

"Leave it. We're going home."

"Jack, y-you threw him in the fountain!"

"Yes," he said. It had felt good. At least it had made him a little less livid.

She planted her feet, refusing to budge. "What is going on?"

He turned and glared at her. "I'll tell you what's going on, love. Your dancing days are over."

"What, are you jealous?"

"Oh, I don't know. The last I saw you, you were in the ballroom surrounded by leering admirers, then you disappeared, now I find you in here having a nice, cozy tête-à-tête with another man. I think I have a right to be a little peeved, dear."

"It wasn't a tête-à-tête! I was waiting for you. It wasn't as though I invited him here—he followed me. You told me that if I ever saw you with the Spaniard, I should stay away! I was following your orders!"

"He had no right to speak to you without asking my permission."

She heaved a sigh, rolled her eyes, and seemed to strive for patience. "Do you even know who that was? He had a reason to speak to me. Remember my father's patron—"

"I don't care," he cut her off. "I'm going to tell you something. And I want you to listen well."

Her green eyes scanned his face, her expression turning slightly intimidated as he fixed her with a brooding stare. "What?"

"If any man touches you while I'm away, he's dead when I get back. Do you understand me?"

327

She gazed at him with a look of hurt at the mere suggestion that she would ever be unfaithful.

Aye, she might feel that way now, but six months was plenty of time for a beautiful young woman to begin to feel neglected and look elsewhere for company.

"Furthermore, I don't want you dancing," he ordered. I will not have another man's hands all over my wife."

Her jaw clenched, her hurt expression hardened to one of angry defiance. "Fine, master. I'll never dance again."

"Good," he said through gritted teeth. "Now, let's go home."

He turned away and continued pulling her along behind him by her hand like a wayward child. Some might argue that's all women really were. They reached the ballroom and forged on through the crowd.

"Are you going to tell me what's wrong?" she demanded.

"We'll talk in the carriage."

"My first ball, and I can't believe the night's already ruined."

"You'll live. Besides," he added, ignoring her indignant huff, "it's our last night together before I go. I've no desire to spend it with these fools. Do you?"

Eden didn't answer, too cross at him for ruining the night.

Perhaps when they were alone and he'd had a few puffs on one of his favorite cigars to help him calm down, as he sometimes did when he was in a mood, the man would listen to reason.

Never had she suspected that her husband would prove to be such a jealous man. He was as bad as Connor! After last night, how could he think she could ever have the slightest interest in anyone but him? But whatever the reason, Jack had worked himself into such a state that she knew it was pointless to argue.

As he dragged her by her gloveless hand back through the ballroom toward the exit, she noticed him watching everyone, giving the evil eye to ladies who seemed to be engaged in gossip, and shooting downright dirty looks at the men.

If she didn't know better, she would have pronounced him thoroughly paranoid. What on earth had gotten into him?

She had to lift up the hem of her skirts to keep from tripping as he pulled her along briskly toward the exit. The milling crowd parted ahead of them; Jack's fierce stare chased the other guests out of his path. Eden pasted on a hapless smile, trying to pretend everything was fine, but her husband's black scowl no doubt told the world that something was seriously amiss.

If only she knew what it was!

She got the feeling there was more to this than his ire about silly Lord Pembrooke.

They were almost to the exit when a mismatched couple stepped into their path—Eden instantly thought that the pair were father and daughter.

The little white-haired man was frail and elderly, with a cane; shepherding him along with ill-concealed impatience was a glamorous dark-eyed brunette who glittered in diamonds.

Jack stopped in his tracks so abruptly that Eden bumped her nose on his arm. "Ow."

She shot him an irritated glance at the lack of warning, only to notice the shock of recognition that flashed across his face.

Before them, the glittering lady's reaction was the same. Her rouged lips had parted in surprise; now the diamonds on her tiara twinkled as she angled her head down, looking Jack over in a slow perusal from his head to his feet, and then back up again.

"Why, mercy me!" she exclaimed in a breathy tone. "If it isn't Jack Knight!"

Well! I never, Eden thought in offense. Perhaps it was *her* turn to be jealous. She frowned at the woman's flare of interest in her stallion of a husband.

Jack was clearly put off, too. He bristled and kept his distance. "Indeed. It's been a long time. Lord Avonworth." He gave the ancient fellow a slight bow. "I hope you are in good health."

Avonworth? Eden tried to place the title.

The woman patted her doddering father's arm. "I do my best to take care of him."

"What?" the old fellow yelled, cupping his ear. "Who are you, young man?"

Jack just looked at him, as though biting his tongue to stop the reply he would have liked to have given.

Eden waited, her brow furrowed, as the woman once again trailed a decidedly lusting gaze over her husband.

"I heard you were back," she purred. "You look good, John. Life must be treating you well. I hear that you're very successful."

John? Eden looked at him, raising an eyebrow.

He glanced drily at her, as though guessing her thoughts.

"Yes, Maura, life's been very good to me—recently, in particular. For, you see, a few months ago, it sent this angel into my path."

Maura? Good Lord! His first love. Now that she knew, Eden felt much better, indeed, as Jack drew her closer, including her in the conversation.

"I just got married, and this is my bride. Isn't she gorgeous?" he added in a wicked tone.

Eden eyed him warily askance as he put his arm around her. She knew that silky, evil note in his voice; she hadn't heard it in a while, but it always meant he was up to something.

Maura bore the news of their marriage looking like somebody had punched her in the stomach; however, she managed a haughty nod. "Felicitations to you both."

"This is that person I told you about," Jack murmured in her ear, deliberately speaking just loud enough so that Maura, too, could hear his words.

Eden smiled uncomfortably at the marchioness, determined to maintain at least some semblance of tact in this exchange.

But tact was the last thing Jack wanted.

He smiled, handsome as sin, and full of treachery. "Darling, allow me to present Lord and Lady Avonworth."

Oh, dear, she thought as she bowed her head respectfully. His hand molding her waist, Jack was holding her too close for her to make a proper curtsy to the high-ranking aristocrats. In fact, if he did not release her in a moment, that voucher to Almack's might never materialize. The ton could not approve of such displays of marital affection.

He showed no intention of unhanding her. If anything, his clench tightened, turning more sensuous.

Maura's face was taut. Her hands sparkled with an array of jeweled rings as she clasped her fingers before her, looking down her nose at Eden. "Charming."

Eden began turning crimson at the lady's haughty scrutiny, but Jack seemed very glad to let Maura look her fill.

His impudent stare seemed to say: *She's younger than you, more beautiful than you, smarter than you, and she's carrying my child.* "I found her in the tropics," he told his old flame, giving Eden a smoky glance as though he could hardly wait to get his hands on her even now.

Her blush deepened. That pirate glint she had glimpsed in his

turquoise eyes when he had tossed Lord Pembrooke into the fountain was back—and it had intensified.

"It was a most . . . pleasurable voyage, wasn't it, pet?"

Eden thought she might step on his foot if he didn't knock it off.

Maura couldn't seem to resist. "She's a little young, isn't she?"

"You think?" he answered in a husky tone, pulling Eden closer.
"Come here, sweet."

Eden's eyes widened, but it was too late to flee as he captured
her face in one hand and cupped the other around her nape,
smoothly capturing her in a sensuous, inescapable hold.

He lowered his head and claimed her mouth before everyone
present, in a deep, slow, shocking kiss. Eden heard the collective
gasp from all around them, but she was paralyzed.

I am going to kill him.

Her attraction to Jack along with his expertise as a lover never
failed in their drugging effect on her senses, weakening her, but
her logical mind was appalled at the certain scandal.

Which her pagan of a husband knew perfectly well would be the
result. A scandalous display of red-hot lust.

Rallying her wits, she pressed her hands against his chest, trying
to stop him, but it only made him clench her harder.

Oh, he was the very devil! she thought furiously.

It was the exact same thing he had done that first day in the jungle, when he had kissed her for all he was worth just to enrage
Papa. Connor had wanted to kill him that day.

Eden was tempted to now.

But God, he tasted good.

Her emotions careened. The man bewildered her. She knew
exactly why he was doing this: his fit of jealousy.

If he disgraced her in Society, then he didn't have to worry
about her *dancing* while he was away.

He didn't have to leave her all the way in Ireland to make sure
she would be isolated. *Cruel, cruel . . .*

As he stroked her hair and delved his tongue into her mouth in a
way that would have driven her wild if they were in private, she
suddenly seized on a plan.

She had come too far to let him get her tossed out of Society on
her ear. He could act like a pagan pirate if he chose, but she was
not about to let him drag her down with him.

"Well!" Maura uttered in a strangled tone that strove for light-

331

ness as Jack finally ended the defiant, and admittedly delicious, kiss.

Her single syllable dropped like a penny in the excruciating silence.

With smoldering eyes and flushed skin, Jack licked his lips and looked at Eden as though he'd like to devour her on the spot.

She was glad she had been to the theater, for no words could have saved her at a time like this; she didn't even try to speak, resorting to the most melodramatic gesture a lady could call forth.

Lifting her hand to her brow, she rolled her eyes up into her head and let out a dizzy sigh of distress, then went limp, pretending to faint.

Jack caught her as another gasp erupted from all the onlookers around them—but she was fairly sure they had bought it. All, of course, but her pirate husband, who laughed—and thus made himself appear even more of a villain for his shocking lack of concern.

Eden stubbornly pretended unconsciousness as Jack swept her up into his arms. She let her head fall against his left shoulder, while his right arm hooked beneath her knees.

Her heart pounding wildly, however, she spied on the whole scene through the veil of her lashes. It was difficult to tell if Maura's shocked expression signified that she was appalled or envious of this sort of ravishment; indeed, a lot of the ladies were fanning themselves quite rapidly as they looked on, pretending to be horrified.

"Oh, that poor girl!" they whispered.

"Sweet young creature! What she must have to put up with!"

"That beast!"

"Wicked."

The garden ladies stared hungrily at Jack as he carried Eden out.

"Will you excuse us, please?" he commanded drily. "It's all right. Don't worry, I'll take good care of her," he added with a sinister smile.

Then he went swaggering out of the ballroom with her in his arms like some dark pagan god making off with his virgin sacrifice—or Hades collecting Persephone to spend half the year with him, as promised, in his underworld kingdom of hell.

Well, at least now no one could claim that there was any lack of passion between them, Jack thought in brooding satisfaction as he carried his bride down the corridor that flanked the ballroom.

332

Worried servants waved him into a tranquil and dimly lit library at the end of the hallway, but he shook his head when they asked if he wished them to send for a doctor.

They hovered about as he carried Eden in through the double doors and laid her down gently on one of the brown leather couches.

"Brandy?" he queried.

"Here, my lord." A footman quickly poured a draught for the fainted lady. "It should help to steady her nerves."

She didn't open her eyes, the little liar.

Jack took the small glass from the man and set it aside, then he chased the servants out, shutting the double doors behind them with a firm click.

There he paused, knowing he had just caused a scandal. No, wait—two. There was also the earl in the fountain, news of which was sure to travel fast. Counting the maid's rumor itself, that made three.

He was not eager to hear what Eden had to say about all this. It had been a bold move, giving her that scorching kiss in front of everyone, but it was the best that he could think of at the time. Proof positive that he had indeed known his wife in the biblical sense and was the father of the child whose existence the world would soon discover.

At least it was a start.

Combined with the lesson he had taught Lord Pembrooke in the conservatory, giving every man around a small idea of what he could expect if he came too near Jack Knight's wife, he was confident that he had dealt a crippling blow to the rumors and helped to quell any talk that could harm his child's standing in the world.

He felt a great deal better.

Kissing Eden usually had that effect on him. Truth be told, he had relished the chance to flout Society again, and to let Maura see firsthand what she was missing. He hoped she had known a pang of regret—but for his part, he felt none.

He had made himself look like a blackguard, true, but he didn't care what these people thought about *him.* He only cared what Eden thought of him. And as he flicked the brass lock on the library doors, turned around slowly, and looked across the room at his playacting wife, he knew that this was the moment of truth.

"You can open your eyes now."

333

"I don't want to," she said, "because if I see your face, I'm going to *scream.*"

She sat up swiftly like a woman waking from the dead, and swung her slippered feet down to the carpet. "How could you do that? You barbarian!" She leaned forward on the couch, her lovely face etched with ire. "What were you thinking? You don't *behave* that way!"

Jack blinked.

"Do you know what you've done? You've disgraced us! We're never going to be invited anywhere ever again!"

He paused. "Would that be so bad?"

"Oh! I've never been so mortified in all my life!"

"Mortified?" he echoed in a low tone.

"You humiliated me in front of the whole world!"

Jack could not have been more stunned if she had pulled out a pistol and shot him.

She rocketed up out of her seat, grabbed the draught of brandy, tossed back a swallow, and promptly proceeded to cough, for she never drank spirits.

Jack, meanwhile, tried to comprehend.

Mortified? Humiliated? Now she was embarrassed of their love?

She hadn't been embarrassed last night when he had made her scream with pleasure.

He lowered his head and pressed the heels of his hands into his eyes in an effort to clear his head, because he could feel his emotions fraying like a rope in a wild Atlantic gale.

Think.

He was hanging by a thread.

Eden was angry about the kiss and he could understand that.

What he was unprepared for was this talk of humiliation—as though she was actually *ashamed* of him.

Just like his mother had been.

Just like Maura had been, opting for Lord Ancient-of-Days over all of his youthful devotion.

This cut much too close to the bone.

Perhaps if he could explain to her . . .

But no. Why should he have to?

As she stopped coughing and began pacing, railing in general terms about what a very bad fellow he was—throwing the earl in the fountain, threatening to kill people who flirted with her, and half ravishing her in public—Jack could barely follow her words, let alone absorb them.

He was suddenly so depressed that he didn't think he even had the heart to try to justify himself. Couldn't she once just give him the benefit of the doubt? Trust that perhaps he knew what the hell he was doing?

He didn't deserve this, nor did he have the time to wait out another of her grudges.

One thing was clear. *She loves this world, and I just don't belong here.*

Eden might not understand his true reasons, but her anger was contagious; for when Jack saw how furious she was at him, he lost all motivation to explain himself to her.

Last night she had promised him forever, but it seemed that was only as long as he played by her rules.

With the raw emotion churning in him since the moment he had realized the rumor's implications for their child, and all the echoes of pain he was still carrying around from the trauma he had suffered on account of his own ill-starred birth, what he really needed right now was her tenderness.

Instead what he got was her rage.

He couldn't believe she was yelling at him.

It felt like a betrayal, far worse than finding her in the conservatory with some blue-blood weasel of an earl. His main ally, his beloved, was siding with the ton against him. For what?

Perhaps he was not thinking as clearly as he should right now, but he could not stand here and spell out the facts for her, the rumor and all. She was sure to hear it from someone else, he thought, so let her.

Lucien could explain it all in detail. Then maybe the genius's daughter could figure out the rest for herself.

"Don't you have anything to say for yourself?" she cried, her cheeks flushed with anger and brandy.

Head down, arms folded across his chest, Jack flicked her an insolent glance. "You could've put a bit more effort into kissing me back."

"Oh!" she gasped. "You're lucky I didn't slap you!"

"Slap me?" he echoed in a menacing murmur.

"It was a dirty trick! Just because you want no part of humanity,

335

Jack, don't drag me down with you! You can turn your back on the world if you wish, just like Papa did, but I *don't* intend to join you in your exile, too. I've already had that part of my life, thank you very much!"

He stared at her. Did it never occur to Eden that maybe it was humanity that wanted no part of him?

"Say something!" she ordered.

"Very well. Now you know why I wanted to keep you in Ireland," he uttered softly, gazing at her in reproach. "I knew that bringing you here would ruin everything sooner or later. That they would come between us, with all their artificiality, and I would end up like this—the villain, as always. But like a doting fool, I could not say no to you. I could not stand your tears."

"Jack."

"What do you want me to say? Go ahead. Side with them against me. I half expected it," he added bitterly.

"I'm not siding against you, Jack."

"Of course you are." He glanced over his shoulder in the direction of the ballroom. "These are the same people who cast me into the gutter when I was a boy. Now their approval means more to you than our love. But so be it. You got what you wanted from me. You used me and my family to get yourself into this world. Now that you're here, I've served my purpose, haven't I?"

She searched his face in disbelief. "That is not true, you cannot believe that of me. Jack—I am your family. You said it yourself a few days ago."

"Well, I was mistaken. My crew is my family. And it's with them that I belong." He paused, turning to reach for the door. "Good-bye, Eden."

"Don't you dare walk out on me now."

"I'm going to go," he said calmly, a rare note of defeat in his voice. "You do what you want. Dance to your heart's content. I'll be back in the autumn to take my child when he is born."

"What?"

"You heard me. Especially if it's a son. You know I need an heir to run the company. I'll hire a wet nurse to care for him. You don't have to come if you don't want to, but I'm not raising my child here," he said in a bleak tone. "I'm going to take him someplace far away, where people don't set so much store on how high you were born, but on what you did with your life once you got here.

336

Someplace no one can ever hurt him or make him feel like he doesn't belong. India, maybe, where Lord Arthur lives. Society's quite a bit looser there. There's always Jamaica."

"What madness is this?" she whispered, staring at him, her face gone pale. "You are not going to take my child away from me."

As her husband, it was, of course, his legal right.

"You can always have another," he said in a soft, cruel tone. "I'm sure you'll find no shortage of prospective fathers who'd be more than happy to oblige you."

"I am not like your mother, Jack, and I will not permit you to slander my honor."

He fell silent, watching her stand up to him, just like she always had. God, he'd miss her.

"Your dubious birth doesn't give you the right to *act* like a bastard," she added.

"Ah, but I am one, sweet. And that's all I'll ever be." With that, he walked out, beckoning a servant through the crowd of garden ladies who had gathered to eavesdrop outside the library door. They fled back from him when he came out, scattering like so many pecking birds. He ignored them.

"Fetch my brother, Colonel Lord Winterley, to take my wife home," he ordered the footman. The library door was still open, so he turned to steal one last glance at his beautiful wife.

She was standing as though rooted in place, her face white.

"You'll go to Damien's now," he instructed her. These flat parting words would have to serve as his farewell. With his stomach in knots, Jack closed the door on her and walked away.

Eden swayed on her feet as the shock of his departure sent a tremor through her. It took her a long moment to absorb what had just happened. He meant to leave now for South America, just like that?

No. There was no way she was letting him leave like this. She rushed to the door, only to hesitate when she heard the ladies' worried murmurs on the other side.

Would they disdain her now?

She was terrified to face them, for she was nowhere near as brazen as Jack, but she saw there was no way around this. There was only one door out, and to catch up to Jack, she'd have to meet the ladies head-on. She took a deep breath and steeled herself to face her scandal. "Right."

The minute she opened the door, they fluttered.

"Oh, my dear child, are you all right?"

"Did he hurt you?" one whispered.

"No, no," Eden assured them.

"You should lie down. Do you need the smelling salts?"

"No, thank you so much. Please, let me through. I just want my husband."

"We all want your husband, dear," a bored lady near the back remarked drily, though others tittered at her racy remark.

Eden shot a scowl in her direction. "Please, let me through! I need to talk to Lord Jack."

"But, dear, his behavior was disgraceful!"

"Yes, I know, but, you see, I need to stop him before he goes—"

"Now he is leaving you?" they cried, appalled on her behalf.

"Not if I can help it," she declared. Finally extricating herself from the knot of solicitous but nosy ladies, Eden strode down the corridor that flanked the ballroom, staring straight ahead.

She ignored the looks and kept her head high, though her cheeks flamed crimson. Their rude gawking and whispers helped her experience firsthand what Jack had gone through all his life.

A few people smiled at her, as though to assure her that they did not hold her culpable for her husband's outrageous behavior, but having their forgiveness for herself alone only made her furious.

They did not know Jack. He was no villain. He was her lion, her love. They did not understand him.

But you do, her conscience chided, *and you should have known better. You should have been gentler with him.*

In short, she should have kissed him back.

She'd had her chance to prove her loyalty and failed him. It broke her heart to see it now, but she knew the charge was true. She could have wept to know the hurt she had caused in the very place where he was most vulnerable. Outrageous as his scandalous kiss had been, now he felt betrayed. Finally, she saw that.

But how could he ever think she preferred the ton to him?

She could not live without him.

He was the rock of her life.

It was just so hard for him to believe that because no one had ever loved him before.

When it came down to it, Eden realized, her words back there in the library were empty. She would have gladly given up London for him, gone and lived in a *palafito* in the middle of a jungle swamp, rather than let her darling scoundrel ever doubt that he was everything to her, sun and moon and stars.

Aye, with Jack instead of Connor, life in the jungle might indeed have been pure paradise.

She could only pray it was not now a paradise lost.

Thanks to the garden ladies' interference, by the time Eden burst out the front door of the mansion into the night, Jack was gone.

A chill crossed her heart, for she feared that, this time, unlike at Ireland, he wasn't coming back.

The rain had stopped, but the air was warm and wet. The trees and tall bushes of the sculpted grounds still dripped, dark, hulking mounds of deep greenery in the night. A few outdoor lanterns on graceful posts threw off watery globes of orange light, barely warding off the pitch blackness.

Eden wrapped her arms around herself and walked numbly down the front path, trying to spy him. Her steps were like those of one lost in a dark forest; her feet carried her all the way to the far edge of the graveled carriage loop. Her dancing slippers were soaked through from the wet ground, ruined, but she didn't care.

Jack.

Oh, this couldn't be happening. He had left her.

He was gone. Tears filled her eyes; her mind reeled.

"Jack!" she yelled into the void, then whispered his name again as two tears spilled down her cheeks.

He was really gone—and if she had thought she was alone in the jungle, it was nothing compared to this. The whole world seemed abandoned.

She stood there trembling, still searching the darkness for him, and fighting back a sob.

They *couldn't* leave it like this. If something went wrong, she might never see him again. Never get the chance to tell him how much she loved him. To say that she was sorry—yet again. Oh, this love business was so much harder than it looked.

She drew in a jagged breath. Perhaps if she hurried, she could still catch up to him before he sailed away.

Fighting to regain her composure, she decided to ask Damien to take her down to the Knight Enterprises docks at once.

Jack might not want to see her, but she would make him listen and would not leave him alone until he finally believed her again when she told him how she felt.

Without another moment to lose, she pivoted and headed back inside.

As she started to walk back toward the house, a deep voice suddenly called her name from somewhere off to her right.

"Eden!"

She drew in her breath with sudden hope, but when she whirled around, she could not see anyone.

She scanned the area, not sure who had spoken.

Then, from among the dense greenery that flanked the mansion, a tall, powerful figure stealthily emerged from the shadows, coming out into the open. Plain clothes. A guarded posture. He walked toward her across the wet grass. As he came closer, the lamplight glimmered on his blond hair.

She narrowed her eyes, unsure if they were playing tricks on her again. *"Connor?"*

"Eden. Is it really you?"

"Connor!" She hesitated, torn between running toward him in happy reunion with one who was all but family to her, and running away, instinctively alerted to some nameless danger by the strange light burning in his eyes. Choosing neither in her hesitation, she stayed in place, but he joined her at the edge of the graveled carriage loop within a few strides, and warmly grasped her offered hands.

Her sense of this moment was surreal. Had he truly been standing outside the conservatory staring at her?

"Oh, Eden. I can't believe I finally found you. Thank God you're safe!" He leaned down and kissed her forehead.

"What are you doing here?" she cried, absently noticing the swath of dark wool cloth slung over his shoulder.

"Looking for you, of course! Let me see you now. Oh, Edie, you look so beautiful," he said reverently, gazing at her expensive gown and her elegantly coiffed hair. "Just like the ladies in your magazines! I can't believe I finally found you."

"I can't believe you've come!" she answered. "I-I thought I saw you through the window in the conservatory—Lord, you gave me such a fright! But then you were gone, and I thought I had just imagined you."

"Yes, well, I'm very sorry about that. I didn't mean to startle

340

you." He smiled. "The servants wouldn't let me in. I had to make sure I had the right place. It wasn't easy to find you. I saw Lord Jack, too," he murmured, gazing at her. "He was yelling at you."

Her face fell, then she lowered her head. "Yes, we had a bit of a disagreement tonight."

"Eden, your happiness means the world to me. I should hate to think that any man would ever raise his voice to you."

She smiled wanly at him. "Thanks, Con. So, where's Papa? Please tell me he's come, too?"

"Well, he's still on the boat moored in the Thames. Would you like to see him? I could take you there now."

"Of course I would! I was just heading to the docks myself."

"You were?"

She nodded. "Jack's brother can take us there in his carriage."

"Wait," he said as she started to pull away. "Eden." Connor's face had darkened with a look of concern. "I think I'd better warn you that your father's been through a lot since you ran away."

She paled. "Is he all right? He's safe—?" The reminder of what she must have put them through chastened her. This night would be a reckoning in more ways than one.

"Yes, he's safe," the Australian conceded.

Thank God. She lowered her head. "He's angry, isn't he?"

"Yes." Connor nodded. "A bit. He misses you—so very much. He needs you, Eden. He has often told you so. I would be lying if I said he wasn't very badly hurt by the way you left." He stared at her in his unnerving way, which she had managed to forget until just now.

She was beginning to wish he'd let go of her hands.

"But for all that, he still loves you," he said softly. "Indeed, he wouldn't want to live if he couldn't have you by his side."

The fixed intensity of his gaze led her to gather that Connor was not really speaking of Papa's sentiments at all.

She inched back from him a bit, though he still held her hands, one gloved, one not. "Well, I-I am married now, Connor, and I'd love to come to the boat to see Papa, but I have to talk to my husband first—"

"No, come now," he coaxed softly. He released her gloved hand, but possessively kept the one that was bare.

Failing to notice the way he flicked his fingers up into his sleeve like a gambler reaching for a hidden ace, Eden suddenly felt a

341

sharp prick in the flesh of her gloveless hand and let out an abrupt cry, yanking her hand away.

"Ow!"

He grabbed her hands back again with a lightning-fast movement, as though he had expected that. "Hush, now," he whispered. "It won't do you any harm. Just relax."

Confused, she looked down and saw a tiny spot of blood on her hand, as though she had just been bitten by some strange jungle insect. "Connor, what was . . . ?"

"Here. There's a chill tonight. This will keep you warm." He whipped the length of dark wool cloth off his shoulder and unfurled it.

It proved to be a capacious hooded cloak, which he draped around her shoulders with a swirling motion.

"Thank you, but's'not necess'ry." She frowned, wondering why the words came out all slurred.

"I insist."

When she looked up at him in alarm, still baffled by the dot of blood on her hand, Connor's face, staring at her, curved in a blurry wave.

Grotesque distortion.

"What have you done to me?" she whispered in horror.

"I've come to take you home, my love."

An image flashed through her mind of the animals Connor had frequently stunned in the jungle with a blow dart dipped in a tranquilizer made from a mild curare. He used to drug the animals, study them, and then free them again when they awoke.

But she knew now he'd never let *her* go.

He caught her smoothly as her legs buckled under her and the world began turning black. Connor pulled the cloak's hood up, concealing her face as he dragged her back into the shadows.

342

CHAPTER
∽ NINETEEN ∽

*T*he Knight docks were bustling as the crew prepared to put out to sea. All supplies and materials had been loaded, and now the crew were rowing the jolly boats back and forth, ferrying all their rowdy recruits out to the massive gunship.

Jack had waved down Ballast and Higgins in one of the cutters. The pair of seamen greeted their captain with hearty enthusiasm, not noticing his dark mood. They rowed him out to *The Winds of Fortune,* anchored in the middle of the deep, wide river, and he had gone aboard—to considerable fanfare, as it turned out, for Brody was already showing the newcomers the sort of discipline and order to be observed onboard this ship.

"Captain *onboard*!" the old master-at-arms bellowed. "*Sal*ute!"

The rookery boys seemed startled by this order, but they did as he said, haphazardly saluting him.

Jack gave them a dry nod and marched toward his day cabin to receive a report from Lieutenant Peabody. Within another hour or so, they could be underway. But as Jack toured his ship, making sure all was in a state of perfect readiness—which it was, nearly—he soon realized that if he had thought to escape Eden at sea, he had overlooked one small fact.

Every inch of *The Winds of Fortune* now reminded him of her.

From the depths of the very cargo hold, where she had stowed away, to the life buoy closet where he had found her; from the day cabin, where he could still picture her scowling at him from the bathtub, to the place up on deck where he had seen her get washed overboard during the storm. She was everywhere, in his head, in his heart.

He saw the stern gallery, where they had first spoken in playful flirtation about having children together. And now it was about to become a reality.

There was no place to escape her on this ship. Her presence permeated every narrow gangway. It had soaked deep into the planks and brightened every inch of canvas. But nowhere was his sense of Eden stronger than in his sleeping cabin, where she had given him her virginity, and where they had pledged each other their hearts.

It was here that Jack found the sparkly blue sea-princess gown that he had first given her to wear when she had arrived on his ship without a stitch of extra clothing or a penny to her name.

He sat down slowly on his berth, holding her dress, caressing the fabric, letting its softness slip through his fingers. He was so distracted by his tangled longing for her that he had forgotten to set all the locks on his cabin door when he'd walked in.

Or maybe he just didn't need them anymore. Maybe he was tired of locking out the world.

He closed his eyes, smelling the dress, trying to catch one last whiff of her scent. *How can I possibly go without her for six months?*

Eden.

Their love had become the living fabric of his life. And he was about to tear it irrevocably, in a way that he wasn't sure it could be sewn up again.

So, she had yelled at him back in their host's library, lost her temper. So what? Who could blame her? She had good reason to be angry. It was her first ball and Jack had ruined it. She had been looking forward to it literally for years, and the night had been one big disaster. *I didn't even dance with her.* He couldn't dance, but surely Eden was worth him making a fool of himself.

Ah, what the hell am I doing?

By all outward appearances, it looked like he was marshaling up the forces for a noble cause, but deep down, Jack knew the truth: He was merely running away.

Not because he feared that Eden didn't love him. But because he knew that she did.

It sounded a little irrational even to him, and so it was. He was out here trying to justify his bastardly existence by doing grand deeds that no one else could do, but now he finally saw what Eden had been trying to tell him all along. He didn't have to live this way anymore. *Somebody finally loves me exactly as I am.*

It was worth infinitely more to Jack than all of the gold in his coffers. He had finally laid hold of the one treasure that money could not buy. But if he went away now, he would jeopardize that.

He stood up slowly and folded the gown to give back to her. If she needed a little help these days in remembering who she was, perhaps this would jar her memory. But Jack knew he could not go. He had never been more sure of anything. If he left tonight, he knew he would regret it for the rest of his life.

He walked out of the sleeping cabin feeling half a ton lighter, and went to tell Trahern that he was giving him the mission.

The lad was right. Jack had done his part. Besides, there were practical reasons not to go, especially now, after their scandal in the ballroom.

If he hadn't attracted enough notice before simply by being Jack Knight, now, in hindsight, he saw that the triple scandal of the earl in the fountain, the titillating rumor from the maid, and above all, the very public kiss that Jack had planted on his bride tonight all would serve merely to rivet London's full attention on him and Eden.

That made it impossible for him to slip away unnoticed. The minute the ton marked his absence, everyone would be asking where he had gone.

It was going to look entirely suspicious. Eden would be left to try to explain it, and he hadn't prepared her for that.

He *had* to go back. He was now a hindrance to the mission, thanks to his angry reactions this night. His presence would draw public scrutiny like the beam of a lighthouse shining on their illegal activities—and he was not the only man whose fate hung in the balance. By Whitehall's decree, signing up to fight in South America was forbidden. If Jack drew undue attention to the mission, all of his stout-hearted recruits could face charges, as well. He had to cover for them, and the only way to do that was to stay put.

Besides, in order to return to England in time for the birth of his child, he'd have to reach South America without a snag, no storms, no calms, then resupply and immediately turn and come right back. But by then, hurricane season would have started. If he risked sailing through it, he might never look upon his firstborn's face at all.

He knew the time had come to give Trahern his chance to take the top command.

Jack simply had to trust that all his training had stuck, and that the young man was fully capable of finishing this mission without him, especially with men like Peabody, Brody, and Higgins to back him up. The lad deserved the chance to make his fortune, after all. If he was serious about courting Amelia Northrop, ten thousand pounds in the bank would go a long way to persuading the girl's barrister father to welcome the suit of such a gallant and capable young man. The job was worth at least that much to Jack.

With the start of a smile spreading across his face, Cap'n Jack went to find his right-hand man.

As for himself, he wanted nothing but to hold his darling stowaway again and beg her forgiveness for acting like an absolute boor.

Before long, he had settled with Trahern with a few final words of caution and advice; he had clasped hands with Brody, asking the old cudgel to look after the lad as a personal favor to him. His request granted, Jack had bid his men fair winds. He wasted no time in rushing back to the Pulteney Hotel, where he expected to find his wife gathering up her things under Damien's watchful eye.

He ran up the staircase, taking them two at a time, but when he burst in to their suite, it was dark.

Silent.

He stepped inside, closed the door behind him uncertainly, and took a few steps into the sitting room, hoping against hope that she might be in her chamber lying down. Well, if not, he reasoned, he'd simply go back to the ball and collect her.

"Eden?"

He felt rather than heard the whisper-soft rustle of motion a few yards behind him. From the corner of his eye, he noticed that the French doors onto the balcony had been left open.

The curtains billowed slowly on the night breeze. A servant might have committed the oversight, but Jack knew neither he nor Eden would have made a blunder like that. Not under the circumstances.

He suddenly realized the suite was not empty, and it wasn't his wife who was here. He knew the feel of her presence, aye, as well as he knew his own.

His senses narrowed in on the unseen presence he detected, and at once, he reached for his knife. "Who's there?"

Ruiz stepped out of a pool of shadows in the corner, near the curtains that draped the French doors.

Two more black silhouettes materialized out of the darkness, trained assassins from the team Ruiz had brought to Jamaica to murder Bolivar and his entourage.

Jack looked around at them, closing in on him, and prayed to God his wife was still at the ball.

He had been found out and he knew it.

Good thing he had written a will, he thought drily. Nevertheless, there was no harm in trying to play innocent. "How dare you break into my rooms?" he demanded, sounding affronted.

"Oh, what's the matter, Lord Jack? Do we fail to show you the proper respect?"

"What do you want?" he asked in a bored tone.

"Quit the games, Knight," Ruiz snarled. "We know now you're our man. I've longed for an excuse to kill you ever since Jamaica, and now at last I get my chance. We're going to take you someplace and do it slowly."

"Well, if you'll pardon, old boy, I have other plans." Jack paused, backing up slightly, though the other two were behind him. "What makes you so sure you've got the right man this time?"

"We've had a tip from an eyewitness who can place you in Venezuela at the end of February, concurring precisely with when we know the rebels dispatched their representative. Your arrival in London at just the right time was no coincidence."

"Oh, really? And who gave you this tip?" he demanded. "Who accuses me?"

"A scientist who was doing research in the jungle there."

Jack paled. If they named his father-in-law as his betrayer, it would not have surprised him, but Ruiz's answer was worse.

"O'Keefe is his name. An Australian."

When Jack heard his answer, time seemed to stop. Pure horror washed through him the likes of which he had never known, worse, even, than the day he had nearly lost Eden to the cold Atlantic.

It all came clear. Connor O'Keefe had set him up. Taking the revenge Eden had warned him about.

Jack knew the Australian's next move with a bone-deep certainty: He would go after Eden.

Aye, he might have her already.

His heart was pumping, his fingers flicking around the handle of his weapon; he had to get out of here, save her.

If O'Keefe took her away, he might drag her back into the jungle where Jack would never be able to find her again.

She had Damien looking after her of course, but his brother had been told nothing of this. Jack knew it was up to him to save his lady.

Time was of the essence.

But Ruiz and his comrades had no intention of letting him leave here alive.

Well, perhaps he need not waste his time or his blood here, getting drawn into a fight, he thought, his pulse pounding. "I'm a rich man, lads. Perhaps you'd consider a hefty bribe?"

The answer was a fist slammed into his ribs from behind—a kidney punch. Jack let out a roar as all three fell on him at once.

"Stop fighting me! We're going back to the jungle and we are going to be happy," Connor said through gritted teeth as he wrenched her up the ladder from the rowboat onto the frigate.

Perhaps the dose hadn't been large enough, for the curare had already begun to wear off. Though her head was still quite woozy, Eden fought for her life.

"Eden, you know this is right! You're the only one who's ever understood me."

"I don't understand *this*!" She was kicking, flailing, but he was so strong and so terrifyingly determined that her struggles had no effect as he lifted her toward the rails.

"Be still."

"Let me go! You're mad!" She recalled her ongoing jest with Papa that one of them was eventually going to come unhinged from being in the wilderness too long. It was clear now which one of them it had happened to.

Connor was completely delusional—and from that day in the forest with the Indian boy, Eden knew firsthand how dangerous he could be.

He hefted her over the rails and she went sprawling onto the torch-lit deck on all fours, wild-eyed, her heart pounding. She looked up through her tangled hair and saw the leering, greasy faces of his evil-looking crew.

"Stand back!" Connor barked at them as he vaulted over the rails a step behind her, and then helped her protectively to her feet.

She jerked her arm out of his possessive hold and pivoted to face him. "I want to see my father."

"And so you shall. There, there. I promised, didn't I?"

"Er, Captain," one of his henchmen spoke up gingerly.

She laughed at him. "You call yourself the captain of this leaky tub?"

Connor eyed her in warning. "If you want to see your father, you had better be a little more cooperative."

"Where is he? Where is Papa?"

"Captain!" the sailor said a bit more insistently.

"What?" Connor snapped.

The man braced himself for a blow: "Dr. Farraday escaped."

Eden's eyes widened but Connor flew into a rage. His men scrambled to and fro to escape his wrath.

"You useless bastards, get us the hell out of here! Lift the anchor and let's go! Move! He'll go for help. He's not a fool! He'll have the River Police on us any minute!"

With Connor distracted, Eden seized her chance and made a dash for the rails, ready to dive in and swim to shore, if need be, rather than let him carry her away, but Connor spun around and grabbed her by her hair.

She screamed and stopped; he gripped her arm. Releasing his brutal tug on her scalp, he swung a lantern off a nearby peg to light their way as he escorted her roughly belowdecks, his harsh face distorted with the twisting shadows.

In the lower deck, he threw her into a cabin, but when he started to close the door, she rushed at him again, determined to escape. He caught her before she could slip past him, grabbed her waist, and trapped her against the wall.

"Stop it!" he snarled. "You're not getting away from me this time! Now sit down and keep quiet. We'll be underway soon."

"Where are we going?" she cried. "I want to go home."

"I'm *taking* you home." He seemed to struggle for patience. "You're coming back to the jungle with me and we're going to be happy as we once were."

"I don't want to. I want to see Papa!"

"Your father's gone, Eden. We don't need him, anyway. He's weak."

349

"Let me out of here! I don't love you! Why can't you just accept that?"

"Because I love you, Eden, I love you so much. God, I've been waiting years to tell you so!" He ignored her clawing his face and carried her over to the bed.

She kicked and fought. "Let go of me! You're unhinged, damn you!"

"Stop it!" he barked, throwing her onto the bed and then pinning her beneath him.

Eden still struggled, but welling despair washed over her. His grip was unyielding, his steely weight impervious. He knew holds that could subdue thrashing crocodiles; now he pinned her with arms and legs. Eden went still and began to cry.

"Let me go."

"No," he whispered. "I've crossed the ocean to get you back. I'm not losing you again."

"I was never yours."

"You are now." He kissed her.

She shuddered with revulsion.

"Easy. Steady, girl," he crooned. "You're all right now."

She struggled to punch him, but couldn't move an inch. He shifted now to hold her down with one hand, petting her body with the other as if that would help to soothe her. She cringed, squeezing her eyes shut as his hand roamed reverently over her breasts. He tried to kiss her again and she turned her face away.

He kissed her neck instead as his hand traveled lower. "You're used to this, aren't you? I know he probably raped you on the voyage over the sea, but it wasn't your fault. It doesn't matter now. He'll pay. The past is gone, and I will always protect you. You and I have both learned from the Indians how to live only in the present, haven't we?"

"Leave me alone."

His roaming hand stopped on her belly. His touch changed, not lewd indulgence but a scientific sort of palpation, pressing on the cradle of her womb.

"You're pregnant."

She froze, suddenly terrified of what he might do.

He felt again. "My enemy's planted his babe in your belly." The darkening quality in his voice chilled her to the bone. He pulled

350

away abruptly, leaving her on the bed. "No matter. We have a potion that will rid your body of it."

"I won't take it."

"I will pour it down your throat."

Eden was so horrified she could not utter a word as Connor rose from the bed and picked up the lantern on his way to the door.

"Behave yourself down here, Eden. Don't make me tie you up. That's not the way I wish to treat my wife, but if you force my hand, I'll do it."

"Wife?" she echoed barely audibly.

"Yes, wife."

"I already have a husband," she whispered.

Connor paused. "He's dead."

He blew out the lantern and pulled the door shut in finality.

Eden just sat there in a state of shock as she heard the series of locks sliding home.

A great splashing sound emitted from the dark waters of the Thames across from the docks and warehouses of Knight Enterprises.

"Captain!"

"Aye, sailor?" Lord Arthur Knight intoned, hands clasped behind his back as he inspected the process of his men furling the sails now that the *Valiant* had dropped anchor.

"Man overboard, sir!"

"Oh, bother." Lord Arthur marched to the rails and peered over the side of his vessel at the source of the wild splashing from the river below.

"Ain't one of ours, sir."

"He's drownin,' he is!"

"Help!" the wretched man croaked as he clawed against the current.

"Don't just stand there. Throw him a line," Lord Arthur commanded in his great, mellifluous voice.

"Aye, Captain!"

The bosun seat was immediately lowered into the murky current. "You down there! Take hold!" Lord Arthur instructed from the rails.

The man did as he was told, and in short order he was dropped unceremoniously onto the deck in a dripping heap.

Lord Arthur frowned at the mess to his spotless gun deck. "Thought you'd go for a swim, did you?"

"Ye'll catch yer death in that sewage," a sailor muttered, at which the poor fellow retched.

"Vile!" He coughed and spat, still panting. "Oh, God bless you, sirs—I beg your help! There's no time!"

"What seems to be the trouble?" With a flick of his fingers, Lord Arthur summoned a towel, which he handed to their guest.

The man took it gratefully, dried his face, and then carefully wiped the dirty water off his broken spectacles. Lord Arthur watched him closely and decided that the half-drowned fellow had the bearing of a gentleman, though he was no youngster, perhaps in his fifties. Too old for such nonsense as moonlight swims, he thought with a humph.

"I have just escaped," the fellow blurted out, sounding quite frantic and still struggling to catch his breath. "I-I managed to elude them undetected. I was held, you see, held against my will on that frigate!" He pointed to a worm-eaten craft moored about a quarter mile upriver.

"I say!" Lord Arthur murmured. He lifted his spyglass to his eye and frowned. "Most suspicious. I shall go and have a closer look—"

"No, no, never mind them! There are too many of them, nearly sixty men, and cutthroats all!"

"Well, what do you wish us to do, sir? Let me alert the River Police—"

"No time! I beg you, sir. I have to see Lord Jack Knight, who owns these docks—a brother of the Du ke of Hawkscliffe."

"And what would you want with him?" Lord Arthur inquired, peering down his nose at the man in suspicion.

"I must find him! My daughter is with him—she is in dire peril!"

The plea of parental distress commanded Arthur's immediate attention—and his complete sympathy.

He would have been here sooner himself if he had not been delayed by a most distressing, cryptic message from his middle son, Derek.

That young rogue never wrote to his father, always too busy chasing about on some adventure.

The moment Arthur had seen Derek's scrawly handwriting, he had known something serious had happened.

The short note had reached him in Portsmouth while waiting for the minor repairs on his ship to be completed. Arthur had read it so many times now he had it by heart.

Dear Father,

Stay in London. We will come to you. Afraid we've had a spot of trouble here and must egress. Gabriel and I have been asked to resign our commands in the cavalry, but rest assured we kept our sister safe. Georgie will be arriving first. We sent her on one of Jack's ships. I've got to stay with Gabriel. He was hurt holding off the palace guards of the maharaja. Pray for us. Will explain all soon.

Your devoted son,
D.

Post-Script: Would be dead if not for that quick-thinking chap, Lord Griffith. Capital fellow. Fancies Georgie, I think. Don't they all?

The half-drowned fellow's pleadings roused Arthur from his own fatherly woes.

"I beg you, Captain, will you not help me save my child? Both she and Lord Jack are in grave danger. Let your men row me to shore so I can go to the Pulteney Hotel and warn Jack he must protect Eden! O'Keefe is here and he's coming after both of them. He is dangerous," he whispered. "Unstable. He must be stopped!"

Lord Arthur lifted his chin and narrowed his eyes in fascination. "Would you by chance be Dr. Farraday?"

"Yes! How ever did you know?" He looked amazed.

"Long story. I'll tell you on the way. Come with me. Lower a boat!" he bellowed at his eavesdropping men.

"Aye, Captain!"

The sailors leaped to attention and scrambled to obey.

The two seasoned gentlemen rushed to the Pulteney Motel with all due haste.

When they arrived and located Jack's suite, they banged on the door, but it was locked and there was no answer. Lord Arthur took charge.

"Stand aside, my good fellow!" he commanded.

Farraday, still sopping wet, got out of the way. He went and fetched a candle from the wall sconce in the corridor while Arthur kicked the door in with a few repeated blows.

When it finally banged open and the light from the candle poured in, both men gasped to find the room littered with the bodies of four dead men.

It was a scene of pure destruction.

There was blood on the carpet, blood on the furniture. Even a splash of it up on the ceiling.

"Good God," the naturalist whispered.

Speechless, he and Farraday walked in.

Then one of the corpses showed a flicker of movement and let out a groan.

"Jack!"

Lord Arthur spotted his nephew sprawled facedown on the ground, over by the French doors.

The other three swarthy chaps were dead.

Farraday rushed to Jack's side and touched him, feeling his pulse. "He's alive."

Somehow Arthur wasn't surprised, but he had never been gladder to have a doctor in the house. Now it was Victor's turn to give orders. He told Arthur to fetch cold water and find some clean cloths to use as bandages while he turned Jack over and checked the extent of his injuries.

Fury boiled in Arthur's veins when he saw the injuries done to his proud nephew. His face was swollen and bloodied. He had been stabbed in several places, and they had even tried to cut his throat, but thank God, they had only managed to nick it.

His color was terrible and his skin was covered in a clammy sweat after his savage battle, but he was alive. Arthur marveled at his nephew's bloody victory. He must have fought like a lion.

After a few minutes, their efforts managed to revive him.

"There, lad." Accepting a drink of water from his uncle, Jack finally found his voice. "Eden," he rasped. "O'Keefe—set me up."

"Then that means he may already have her," Farraday whispered.

Jack's stare homed in on his father-in-law's face. His aqua-blue eyes were feverish with pure savagery.

Even Arthur had never seen Jack like this before.

Slowly, Jack dragged the back of his hand across his mouth, and then rolled forward, resting his weight on his hands. With a sudden, painful heave of effort, he began climbing to his feet.

Arthur stared at him. Magnificent to behold—a beaten, battered man, pulling himself up from the brink of death and despair, like a half-dead gladiator dragging himself up from the sands of the Colosseum to fight again.

Jack was on his feet, though his balance was off. He wove a bit after too many blows to the head, but he stopped the motion by a visible clamping down of his will. His jaw was clenched.

His chest rose as he steadied himself with a deep, noisy inhalation, his nostrils flaring. Rage burned in his eyes.

"Where is he?" he ground out.

Farraday took a step backward, equally awed. "I will show you."

It was hard to say how much time passed in her lightless cage. An hour? Maybe two? Eden refused to believe that Jack was dead. Quite reversing herself, she now prayed he was on his way to South America to complete his mission. But with every moment she grew more frantic. She could not figure out what to do. The cabin door was hopelessly sealed and banging on it only brought threats of being bound and gagged, so she left off, knowing that would only make her chances of escape even slimmer.

She had pulled over the three-legged stool that went with the writing desk and stood on it, trying to squeeze herself through the porthole, but the opening was little bigger than a supper plate. It was no use.

Peering out of the small round window, though, Eden noticed that there was no flicker of ship's lamps reflecting on the water, nor did she hear any sound of orders given, or sailors' calls coming from the deck above. The frigate cut through the water in darkness and silence, predatorlike: She realized Connor meant to slip away by stealth.

Accustomed as he was to the inky nights in the deep jungle, she knew he could see very well without the light. She did not know how long it would be before they reached the ocean. But she knew if she didn't get away from this madman soon, her hope was doomed. Connor might take her anywhere, and if he managed to drag her back to the Orinoco, she was as good as lost to the outer world—and to Jack.

Holding back terror, Eden felt her way blindly through the cabin, seeking anything that might help her plight. It was too dark to make sense of most of the objects her hands discovered, but then, in a drawer of the writing desk, she unearthed a small stump of candle with a tinderbox built into the bottom of its pewter holder.

She struck the flint without success time after time, losing patience with her shaking hands, and then cursing with frustration when she scraped the knuckle of her thumb with the flint's sharp corner. She gripped it harder, focused entirely on the simple task, when, all of a sudden, a deep, reverberant sound reached her from the dark distance.

Tra-la!

She lifted her head and turned slightly toward the sound, holding her breath.

Again: *Tra-la!*

A flicker of memory stirred. She had heard that sound before. . .

The deep echo of the ship's horn blew across miles of river.

She flew to the porthole and stood on the stool again to peer out the little round window. Then she drew in her breath at the sight of the large vessel gliding slowly into view from around a great broad meander some distance behind them—it was difficult to judge how far, in the dark.

But Eden made out one detail that made her heart suddenly lift and begin to soar.

The ship's huge whale-oil lamps illuminated the bold red mark on the mainsail proclaiming it the property of Knight Enterprises.

The Valiant!

Rescue was on the way! Connor had been right, then—Papa had escaped and gone for help! Her hope reborn, she found herself fiercely roused to action. She could not say if it was Lord Arthur alone come to rescue her, or Papa, as well, or Damien and the rest of the formidable Knight brothers; she only knew that, first off, she had to let them know where she was.

This time, when she struck the flint, she managed to capture the spark at once on the bit of linen rag, which she transferred at once to the candle wick. A small flame rose.

Why, if Connor thought that they were going to steal away under cover of darkness, then he was sorely mistaken. One paltry stump of candle, however, was not going to be enough to draw her rescuers' attention, providing little more than a firefly's glow.

Hurrying to search the contents of the jumbled, messy cabin, she held the candle up, trailing its flickering illumination slowly across the array of odds and ends the cabin offered. The small, light frigate did not have the luxury of the *Winds'* capacious cargo holds, but the wheels in her mind turned swiftly.

She saw fisherman's netting.

Some extra wood planking in case of damage to the boat.

Black tar for sealing the deck.

Tra-la!

Her smile grew as a plan crystallized in her mind. Several minutes later, the stump of candle still burning nearby, she began trying to kick down the cabin door.

"Let me out of here, you blackguards!"

Each kick jarred all the way up to her hip, but with less than ten blows, she had the thing half off its hinges in her determination to get out.

When Connor sent one of his lackeys scurrying belowdecks to deal with her, she was ready for him, fisherman's netting in hand.

"Scurvy wench, quiet down!" The moment the sailor yanked the mangled door open, Eden threw a wide length of fishing net over him and pushed him backward hard.

The sailor stumbled over his heels fighting the net and then fell back onto his rear end in the cramped passageway. Eden paused to light her makeshift torch of pitch and wood from the stump of candle, and then went dashing out of the cabin. Just as the sailor got free of the net, she bent with an apologetic look and set the passageway on fire, barring him from coming after her. Then, still carrying her torch, she strode up the companionway and burst out onto the deck.

As the crew's shouts erupted, she set it all on fire, everything in arm's reach—the rails, the helmsman's wheel, and the shirt of a man who tried to grab her.

He dove overboard with a shriek to douse the flames that licked at his clothes.

"Eden!" Connor came marching toward her with wrath carved across his stony face.

She swung the torch in an arc at Connor to hold him at bay, but he grabbed her shoulder.

Transferring the torch to her other hand, she threw it as hard as she could, straight at the mainsail. The largest stretch of canvas on which the frigate relied burst into flames.

Now the Knights would know just where to find her!

There was only one small problem.

The next step of her plan was to dive overboard, but she could not get away, for Connor held her fast by her shoulders.

And this time, he was angry.

"There! What is that fire?" one of Arthur's men cried, pointing.

Jack's heart pounded as he stared through the folding telescope. His gaze swept the deck of the frigate, homing in on Eden just in time to see her throw her torch into the canvas.

Good girl, he thought with surging pride in his little lioness. Then Connor O'Keefe grabbed her by her shoulders, and Jack tensed, starting forward at the sight of their struggle.

"Come on, girl, shake him off. Get out of there," he urged her under his breath. O'Keefe's men were working fast to put out the fire. Jack did not intend to let them get away. "Send a ball across the bow," he ordered. "That ought to get his attention."

"Aye, sir!"

Jack joined the gunner beside the carronade on the fo'c'sle, every inch of his body aching, but he ignored it. He adjusted the trajectory, and after the crew had loaded the cannonball, he took a torch and personally lit the fuse.

The warning shot went screaming through the night in a rain of fire, arcing across the frigate's bow.

It plunged into the river, sending up a plume of water where it landed. Lifting the spyglass again, Jack watched the reaction on deck.

Confusion broke out. Taken off guard, O'Keefe half turned to see if the cannonball had hit his vessel, and Eden used the opportunity to wrench free of his hold.

A pirate smile curved Jack's lips as his lady dashed to the rails, climbed up on them, as quick as a cat, and made a perfect dive into the deep river, leaping free of the ship.

Fearless.

God, I love her. The river swallowed her into its blackness as O'Keefe ran to the rails, bellowing her name.

"Lower a longboat," Jack commanded. "I'm going after her. Uncle?"

"Aye, Jack?"

"The minute she's out of the way, you blow that bastard out of the water."

"With pleasure, my lad."

"Let me go with you!" Dr. Farraday implored him. "Jack, I can't bear to lose her—"

"Neither can I." He moved the scientist gently aside. "I will bring your daughter back."

Farraday watched him in anguish as Jack descended into the longboat. In moments, he was rowing swiftly with the current, fighting the pull of the river as it tried to drag him toward the burning frigate. O'Keefe's vessel had caught in earnest now, towering flames reaching toward the night sky.

Jack had to look continually over his shoulder as he rowed to make sure that he cleared the burning debris and fiery streamers of the sails falling from above as the frigate slowly disintegrated.

Smoke drifted across the scene, making it hard to see. Putting all of his muscle into the oars and pouring on the speed, he noted grimly that instead of muddy riverbanks, this section of the Thames had been contained by high smooth walls to stave off the tidal river's occasional flooding.

Eden was in the water somewhere but there was no place for her to go to land. Until he could find her in the dark current and scoop her up into his longboat, she had no choice but to keep swimming in this filth.

Speeding toward the levy wall, Jack heard a sound that made his blood run cold.

Bang!

The crack of a rifle.

He whipped his head around and stared, aghast, over his shoulder. By the blaze's glow, he saw O'Keefe standing at the rails of the burning frigate with his rifle in his hands. He took aim and shot again into the water, pausing to reload.

Good God, he is trying to kill her. Jack drew breath to scream to draw the madman's attention to himself, scarcely minding that he would make an easy target, exposed as he was in the longboat.

But his scream was drowned out by the barrage that went slamming into the frigate as the *Valiant* unleashed hell.

Boom!

Boom!

The mainmast cracked and crashed earthward, tearing down lines, yards, and rigging as it fell. Where O'Keefe had gone to, Jack did not know.

He had rounded the crippled vessel and now spotted a small, pale face in the cold, dark river. She was treading water as hard as she could and fighting to keep her head above the swirling current.

"Eden!" He roared her name and threw his all his might into the oars.

"Jack!" she sputtered. Through the smoke and chaos, she heard him calling to her and answered frantically. "Jack! Jack! I'm here!"

She was weakening. The cold, slimy river continued dragging her away in its powerful current, the high retaining wall leaving her no place to crawl ashore.

It was all she could do not to gag on the smell and taste of the vile water—she tried not to think about the refuse of a million people, horses, fish markets, potteries and worse, all of which got dumped into the Thames and had done, since the time of the Romans.

She would have preferred piranhas.

She was so cold, treading water with dwindling hope as the river continued whisking her through the darkness as it wound toward the sea. Her wet clothes were weighing her down, but none of this posed much concern compared to the island of burning debris that was drifting straight toward her as the frigate broke apart. She couldn't swim fast enough to get out of the way.

"Eden, talk to me! Where are you?"

"Jack!" She realized he couldn't see her because of the smoke. "Jack! Jack! Here!" she shouted with the last of her strength.

He emerged at that moment from the darkness and the gray, choking billows, his beloved face etched with grim rage as he maneuvered the longboat swiftly toward her.

Rising to his feet aboard the small approaching craft, Jack knelt at its side and thrust an oar in her direction.

"Grab hold!"

When she did so, clinging to it with all her strength, Jack pulled her toward the boat. He leaned down and grasped her hand. "I've got you." Then, using his own body as a counterweight to steady the wobbly craft, he hauled her up into the longboat.

While she collapsed on the boat's damp wooden bottom, panting heavily, Jack grabbed the oars again and in the nick of time sped them out of the way of the mountain of burning debris heading right for them.

Eden looked up at him and thought she had never beheld a more beautiful sight.

When Jack leaned toward her, she threw her arms around his neck. "You came back," she choked out.

"Oh, Eden," he whispered, holding her close. "I couldn't leave you." He cupped her head against the crook of his neck. "Shh, I've got you now. Are you all right? Did he hurt you?"

"I'm fine, as long as I've got you. He said you were dead!"

"Almost," Jack said ruefully.

She pulled back to gaze at him and then cried out when she saw how battered he was. "You look terrible! What happened to you?"

"Ruiz. It's over now."

But it wasn't.

At that moment, the longboat rocked violently. Eden gasped and Jack tensed as O'Keefe sprang into the boat with one swift, powerful heave of his muscular body.

"You son of a bitch," he said to Jack, glaring at him as dirty water dripped down his face. "She's mine."

Jack pushed Eden behind him as Connor unsheathed the jungle machete at his side with an evil metal hiss.

"Stay down!"

Eden shrieked as Connor swung the knife at Jack in a savage sideward arc, but Jack blocked it with the oar and then took a swing at Connor with it. Connor ducked and slashed out again at Jack; Jack grabbed his arm and twisted it, wrenching it up hard behind him.

Connor looked momentarily astonished to experience an enemy equal to him in sheer brute strength.

"Release the weapon," Jack ordered.

"Go to hell!"

"Have it your way," Jack muttered.

Eden dodged aside with a cry as they twisted around. Jack slammed Connor's hand against one of the chunky metal hooks that held the oars. With a loud bellow, Connor dropped the knife. It fell into the river, lost. He kicked Jack off him, thrusting his heel into his stomach, but Jack soon recovered, and a full-out brawl ensued.

As the two big men exchanged shattering blows, Eden continually threw her weight this way and that to keep the longboat from capsizing.

All the while, the boat was rushing sideways down the river, one oar lost in the fray, the other dangling. She looked on in distress, her heart banging behind her ribs.

Then Connor was strangling Jack, his powerful fingers squeezing, viselike, stopping Jack's air. At first Jack tried to pry Connor's hands off his throat, but when a few seconds passed without success, he slammed his fist into Connor's ribs.

The Australian's grip slipped. Jack took a gulp of air and then punched Connor in the face with the force of a flying cannonball, spinning the man around so that he fell facedown, sprawling on the bottom of the longboat.

Before the stunned Connor could recover from the blow, Jack swooped down and grabbed his arms, pulled them up hard behind him, and planted his foot squarely on Connor's spine, no words needed to warn the man he'd break his back if he made one false move.

Eden was unutterably grateful Jack did not kill Connor, at least not right in front of her. Apparently, he'd already had enough killing for one night.

With flames in his eyes and blood trickling down the side of his rugged face, Jack held him subjugated in that position as the Thames River Police glided up alongside them and placed Connor under arrest.

*   *   *

Back on the *Valiant,* Jack did not remember much of the fight in the Pulteney Hotel. Victor told him he had a mild concussion.

His injuries were extensive, though he was walking around; he was only just beginning to feel them as the pumping rush of violence began to wear off. He'd been stabbed three times—leg, arm, shoulder. His jaw felt a bit off, his ribs were bruised, he had a black eye, a ghastly cut on his neck where Ruiz had nearly succeeded in slitting his throat, and he'd probably be pissing blood for the next few days from the kidney punch, but all things considered, he had never been happier in his life.

Eden was safe.

That was all that mattered.

Meanwhile, the River Police were rowing around picking up the remainder of Connor's sailors who had jumped into the Thames to escape the burning ship. All of the miscreants were being placed under arrest.

Victor and Lord Arthur were being questioned separately by Bow Street Runners and men from the River Police to give information about everything they had witnessed that night.

Jack hoped Wellington really was as influential as he claimed, with his promise to keep Jack out of legal trouble insofar as his mission was concerned. Ruiz and two of his underlings, after all, lay dead in Jack's suite back in the Pulteney Hotel.

He was still shaking all over with the aftermath of violence, but Eden's small, delicate hand on him helped to calm him down. She wasn't much better off, in truth—bedraggled, exhausted, and soaked to the skin with the river's unhealthy water.

But they stood together at the taffrail, refusing to let any power under heaven part them ever again.

"Jack," Eden whispered, turning to him. "I want to say I'm sorry."

He looked over at her and felt a lump in his throat at her earnest gaze. *So pure.* He shook his head. "I'm the one who should apologize for the awful things I said."

"No. I knew you were only speaking out of pain, my love." She started to cup his face, but it was all so swollen and sore that she stopped herself. "I don't want you *ever* to think that I care more for the ton's silly at-homes and such than I do about you. I love you. You are the center of my life. I can see how you would have wondered if I was really on your side, the way I've been acting—but I *am,* and I'm going to stop all that now. I promise you that. And if I hurt you, my lion, I'm so sorry. We can leave London if you want to, Jack. I'll go anywhere you can be happy."

He hadn't imagined he could've fallen any more deeply in love with her than he already was, but her artless pledge positively enslaved him. He took her hands in his own as he gazed at her. "Sweetheart. I have to be honest. The truth of it is, I have always wanted to belong here. You know, this is my home, London. I was born here. My family's here. I've been running from all of this for a very long time. But you helped me see that it wasn't just them judging me, I was pushing them away, too. But you gave me a reason to at least *try* to participate, be a part of the world. You gave me a reason to stay."

363

Then he briefly told her about the rumor Lisette had started about them, since no one had had a chance to explain it to her yet, and how that had made him fear for their unborn child's future standing.

"But Jack," she chided with a tender smile. "We're going to be together now, and we're not going to let anybody treat our child the way they treated you. Besides,"—with a very delicate touch, she smoothed his hair back—"there is nothing to worry about. When they see my baby and he's the spitting image of you, they'll *know* who his papa is."

It hurt to smile, but her words slowly coaxed a big grin across his face.

She hugged him, clinging around his neck and trying to find one spot that she could kiss without causing more pain.

"Edie! Edie! Halloo? Enough, man, let me see my daughter!"

"Papa?" she breathed, turning in answer to the call, though she did not release Jack from her embrace. He smiled tenderly, watching how she lit up before his eyes. "Papa!" she cried. She had been waiting for her sire to come out from the room with the lawmen and interrogators.

"Edie, my darling child! I'm here!" Waving frantically, her father came running across the decks to her.

Jack let her go and stood at a respectful distance while she ran into her father's arms.

She laughed with tears in her eyes. "Papa!"

The two bedraggled Farradays held each other tightly.

"Oh, Papa, I'm so sorry for all I put you through."

"No, my darling. You were right to go. I broke my promise and I've been a fool! I should have listened to you better, about so many things." He caught her lovely face between his hands and kissed her forehead. "My brave girl. You make me so proud, Edie. Don't be sorry one jot. You had a dream for your life and you had the courage to pursue it, my darling."

She hugged him again. "Well, I found my dream, Papa," she said after a long moment, wiping away a tear. She turned and pointed to Jack. "He's standing right over there."

Jack gazed at her with eyes that glowed as blue as the St. Elmo's fire, and a heart ablaze with love so fierce and tender.

"He doesn't dance," she said softly, "but I can live with that."

Holding her stare, he spoke up barely audibly: "I could learn."

❧ EPILOGUE ❧

Jamaica, a year later

*T*he elegant white-stuccoed villa sat on a sun-drenched cliff overlooking the sea. The lush tropical hillside below it plunged down to white powder beaches, turquoise waters, and the whispering surf.

It was the hour of siesta, and Eden sat on a wicker chair on the red-tiled terrace, writing a letter to Cousin Amelia.

> *Your mother is quite right, you'll forget all about the pain once you hold your child in your arms. Besides, you have your dear, gallant Trahern by your side, and I thoroughly trust that he'll take wonderful care of you both.*

The cries of seagulls carried to her on the breeze, but she paid no mind to the tiny green lizard that darted along the curve of the wall. Above the terrace, palm trees waved against the azure sky, while all around her graceful mounds of red bougainvillea and delicate frangipani rustled in the ocean breezes.

> *Grandpa—by which of course I mean Papa—has made a most interesting acquaintance recently. Cousin, I think there may be romance in the air. Miss Jane Rossiter is a local spinster lady with distinct bluestocking leanings and a great interest in Papa's work. Why, just last week, he could not come to see us because he was escorting her to the theater! Is that not civilized of him? Wonders never cease.*
>
> *Well, now you have my gossip, so don't deprive me of yours. What's this I hear about the Knights of India being seen about*

Town of late, and Miss (Georgie) Knight bringing the great Lord Griffith to heel? Do send whatever intelligence you may unearth, dear cousin.

But I am not all idle gossip today. There is serious business to report, as well, not the least of which was the Liberator's establishment only two months ago of the Congress of Angostura.

Indeed, the war seems to have turned a corner. There have been some victories over the past few months, and it would seem we have reason to be proud of our husbands. The Englishmen who came over to fight are helping Bolivar turn the tide against the Spanish Crown. Jack thinks that in another year or two, Venezuela will be free.

She paused in thought, watching white sails travel along the distant horizon for a moment. A smile played about her lips. Then she dipped her quill pen in the ink one last time.

Well, my dearest cousin, that is all the news that I can think of at the moment. We are all fine here, no, I should say we are ridiculously happy, and cannot wait to see you both in London next spring. When little Johnny gets a wee bit older, we intend to live half the year here in the tropics and the other half in London so we can be near you and all our family. (Don't tell Jack, but I am becoming entirely spoiled.) As always, thanks for sending the magazines. With all my love, Eden.

As she signed off and put her writing things away inside the portable lap desk, the massive diamond on her finger caught the sunlight and broke it into a twinkling rainbow. Her mood was relaxed and contemplative as she rose and drifted back inside.

She walked slowly through the house, reveling in its easy tropical luxury, until she came to the morning room and found her handsome husband sprawled out on the couch, his arm draped protectively over their five-month-old son.

Her lion and his cub. Little Johnny was fast asleep on his doting papa's chest.

Eden's heart clenched with tender adoration. She leaned in the wide, rounded doorway and folded her arms across her waist, gazing at them with quiet joy beaming from her eyes. Curled below the pair, Rudy thumped the floor with his tail in greeting, but Eden lifted her finger to her lips and hushed the dog before he woke the baby.

Jack, however, must have sensed her presence. He stirred, though not enough to disturb their son's slumber. He turned his head to face her as his aqua-blue eyes swept open.

He smiled at her in drowsy contentment, so much love in his deep, serene gaze.

Love, and gratitude—and a wicked glint of a promise in his eyes of something a bit naughtier for later tonight.

Eden blew him a kiss and smiled back.

She could hardly wait.

Turn the page for a sneak preview of another title from the
Knight Miscellany series. Available now. . .

The Duke

⚔ CHAPTER ⚔
ONE

London, 1814

Many years ago, as a curly-headed youth on grand tour, he had fallen madly in love with beauty and so had stopped in Florence to take drafting lessons from a bonafide Italian master. Starry-eyed and romantical, he had followed the light-winged muses south to the Bay of Sorrento, where he had first heard the ancient Italian proverb "Revenge is a dish best served cold." He was an old man now, without illusions, cold and canny as a scheming pope. Beauty had betrayed him, but decades later, oddly enough, here on this gray English day, the Sicilian proverb held true.

A neat, slight-framed man, James Breckinridge, the earl of Coldfell, gripped the ivory head of his walking stick in gnarled fingers that ached with the needling April rain. He permitted his footman to assist him down from his luxurious black town coach while another held an umbrella over him.

The slumbrous quiet in this place was like a church, but for the pattering of the rain. He turned slowly, looked past the servants' blanked faces, past the jagged wrought-iron fence, into St. George's Burying Ground on the Uxbridge Road, just north of Hyde Park. Three weeks ago, he had buried his young bride here. Under a chilly gray drizzle, where the hill curved green, her marble monument rose like an angry needle to the smoke-colored sky. Beneath it, just where Coldfell had expected to find him, stood the tall, powerful, brooding silhouette of a man; wind-blown and lost, the wide shoulders slumped as the gusty rain blew his black greatcoat around him.

Hawkscliffe.

Coldfell's mouth flattened into a thin line. He took the umbrella from the footman. "I shan't be long."

"Yes, my lord."

Leaning on his walking stick, he began the slow ascent up the graveled path.

The thirty-five-year-old Robert Knight, ninth duke of Hawkscliffe, appeared unaware of his approach, stony and immobile as the monument. He stood in bleak granite stillness, the rain plastering his wavy black hair to his forehead, running in chilly rivulets down the stark planes of his cheeks, and dripping off his rugged profile as he stared down at the yellow daffodils that had been planted on her grave.

Coldfell winced at the ungentlemanly intrusion he was about to make on the other man's grief. Hawkscliffe was, after all, the only one of the younger generation he respected. Some of the old-school pigtail Tories found the young magnate's views alarmingly Whiggish, but none could deny that Hawkscliffe was twice the man his weak-willed father had been.

Why, Coldfell reflected as he hobbled up the path, he had seen Robert become a duke at the age of seventeen, managing three vast estates and raising four wild younger brothers and a little sister practically single-handedly. More recently, he had heard him deliver speeches in the Lords with a cool force and eloquence that had brought the whole house to its feet. Hawkscliffe's integrity was unquestioned; his honor rang true as a bell of finest sterling. Many of the younger set, like Coldfell's own idiot nephew and heir, Sir Dolph Breckinridge, considered the so-called paragon duke a rigid high stickler, but to wiser heads, Hawkscliffe was, in a word, impeccable.

It was pitiful to see what Lucy's death had done to him.

Ah, well. Men would see in a woman what they wanted to see.

Coldfell cleared his throat. Startled, Hawkscliffe jerked at the noise and spun around. Tumultuous emotion blazed in his dark eyes. Seeing Coldfell, his dazed expression of pain took on a stab of guilt. With his honorable nature, it had no doubt tormented the duke to have wanted an old friend's wife. Himself, he had never been that chivalrous. James nodded to him. "Hawkscliffe."

"Beg your pardon, my lord, I was just leaving," he mumbled, lowering his head.

"Stay, Your Grace, by all means," Coldfell answered, waving off the awkwardness. "Keep an old man company on this dreary day."

"As you wish, sir." Narrowing his eyes against the rain, Hawkscliffe looked away uncomfortably, surveying the jagged horizon of tombstones.

Coldfell hobbled to the brim of the grave, cursing his aching joints. When the weather was fine, he could hunt all day without tiring. But he had not been energetic enough for Lucy, had he?

Well, she had had her fashionable London burial, just as she would have liked. Having died at his house just outside London, she had a spot in the most exclusive cemetery in the city, complete with a Flaxman funerary monument, the height of good taste, sparing no expense. And well he should have to pay for this most expensive mistake—an old man's folly, he thought bitterly. Beauty indeed was his weakness. With nothing to recommend her but a magnificent mane of flame-colored hair and the most luscious thighs in Christendom, the twenty-six-year-old Lucy O'Malley had been an artist's model in Sheffield before she had bewitched him into making her his second countess. He had sworn her to keep quiet about her background, devising a false one for her. At least she had given *that* pledge sincerely, eager as she had been to join the ton.

Coldfell was merely glad he had not been forced to bury Lucy next to Margaret, his first wife, who was reverently enshrined at Seven Oaks, the ancestral pile in Leicestershire. Ah, wise Margaret, his heart's mate, whose only fault had been her failure to give him a son.

"I am—very sorry for your loss, my lord," Hawkscliffe said stiffly, avoiding his gaze.

Coldfell slid a furtive glance at the duke, then sighed, nodding. "It's hard to believe she's really gone. So young. So full of life."

"What will you do now?"

"I leave for Leicestershire tomorrow. A few weeks in the country will help, I warrant." A visit to Seven Oaks would also take him out of the way of suspicion when this man carried out the deed for him.

"I'm sure you will find it soothing," Hawkscliffe said—polite, automatic.

They were both silent for a long moment, Hawkscliffe brooding, Coldfell reflecting on the uneasiness of living anymore in his elegant villa in South Kensington with its four pretty acres of sculpted gardens—the site of Lucy's death.

" 'Lay her in the earth. And from her fair and unpolluted flesh may violets spring,' " Hawkscliffe quoted barely audibly.

Coldfell looked at him in pity. "Laertes' speech on Ophelia's grave."

The duke said nothing, merely stared at the carven letters on the monument: Lucy's name, her date of birth and death.

"I never touched her," he choked out abruptly, turning

to Coldfell in impetuous anguish. "You have my word as a gentleman. She never betrayed you."

Evenly, Coldfell held his gaze, then nodded as though satisfied, but of course he had already known.

"Ah, Robert," he said heavily after a long moment, "it is so strange, the way they found her. She went out to our pond every day to sketch the swans. How could she have slipped? Perhaps my brain is muddled with grief, but it makes no sense to me."

"She could never slip," he said vehemently. "She was graceful . . . so graceful."

Coldfell was taken aback by his ferocity. This was going to be easier than he'd hoped.

"Did your servants report anything strange that day, my lord, if I may presume to ask?" pursued the duke.

"Nothing."

"Did anyone see anything? Hear anything? She was in earshot of the house. Could they not hear her cries for help?"

"Perhaps she had no time to cry out before she fell beneath the water."

Hawkscliffe turned away again, his firm mouth grimly pursed. "My lord, I have the blackest suspicions."

Coldfell paused, watching him. "I wish that I could put your mind at ease, but I'm afraid that I, too, am haunted by severe doubts."

Hawkscliffe turned and stared penetratingly at him. His dark eyes glowed like hellfire. "Go on."

"It doesn't add up. There was no blood on the rock where they said she . . . struck her head. What am I to do? I am an old man. These sore limbs are weak. I haven't the strength," he said slowly, emphatically, "to do what a husband should."

"I do," vowed Hawkscliffe.

The earl felt his dry soul thrill to the resolve in the fiery young man's eyes.

"Whom do you suspect?" Hawkscliffe asked in tautly leashed savagery.

Coldfell had never seen the man look so wild and fierce. He had to hide his glee. All he need do was utter the name, provide a target for all that churning wrath, then Hawkscliffe would duel and the viper who had turned on him would be struck down. He was not above playing Lucy's devotees against each other to save himself and his sweet, flawed daughter, Juliet. What else could he do? He was nearly seventy, a little weaker every day. Dolph was in his prime, a brutally skilled hunter who had been blooded at the tender age of nine with his first stag.

The tremor that moved through his limbs was real. "May God forgive me," Coldfell said under his breath with a look of distress.

"Whom, Coldfell? Do you know something? I know this was no accident, even if the coroner said it was. You and I are not fools," he said hotly. "She was in that pond for four days before they found her. There is no telling what else might have been done to her before she was killed."

"I see our fears run a similar course, Robert. To think that she might have been . . . violated. Oh, God." He leaned on Hawkscliffe, who steadied him. "It's almost worse than her death itself."

Hawkscliffe's chiseled jaw tautened. "My lord, I beg of you. Tell me what you know."

"I don't *know*, Robert. I only suspect. Lucy said to me once—"

"Yes?"

Coldfell paused. So hungry for someone to punish, someone to blame, he thought, passing a shrewd glance over Robert's face, assessing his features like an artist preparing to sketch his portrait. It was the hard, noble face of a warrior. His raven hair flowed back richly from his broad forehead; beneath his wide, flared, charcoal black eyebrows, his piercing eyes burned with iron will; his hooked nose was aquiline, hawklike, his mouth, firm and clamped, yet there was a sensitivity about his lips that captivated women.

"She said there was a man who . . . frightened her."

"Who was he?" Hawkscliffe demanded.

Coldfell drew a breath and looked away, knowing he was handing down a death sentence.

He was glad of it.

"My nephew, Your Grace," he said, cool as a consummate Italian. "My heir, Dolph Breckinridge."

E. LE JOLY

WE DO IT
FOR JESUS

*Mother Teresa
and her Missionaries of Charity*

Darton, Longman and Todd

TER

First published in Great Britain in 1977
by Darton, Longman and Todd Ltd
89 Lillie Road, London SW6 1UD

Reprinted 1980

ISBN 0 232 51387 2

Imprimi Potest N. D'Souza, SJ
        Calcutta Provincial, the Society of Jesus
        12th February 1977
Imprimatur Lawrence Cardinal Picachy, SJ
        Archbishop of Calcutta
        15th February 1977

Printed in Great Britain by The Anchor Press Ltd
and bound by Wm. Brendon & Son Ltd, both of Tiptree, Essex

GIFT

Contents

Foreword

This book is not a complete biography of Mother Teresa – she does not want one to be written; neither is it a full history of the Missionaries of Charity, the religious congregation God inspired her to found – which can only be written at a later stage, when all the relevant documents are made available.

This book tries to depict the beginnings, aim and spirit of the Missionaries of Charity, as seen by one who was connected during many years with Mother Teresa's foundation.

'We do it for Jesus' owes its inspiration and title to Mother herself; it is the only book she has asked to be written to explain her objectives to her numerous friends and helpers all over the world.

This narrative is based on Mother Teresa's own words, in public or in private conversation, her letters, the Constitutions she framed for her Congregation, and the testimonies of eye witnesses who worked with her, especially during the heroic first years.

I wish to express my gratitude to Father Céleste Van Exem, Father Julien Henry, Mr Michael Gomes, Monsignor H. Eric Barber, Brother Andrew, and several of the Senior Sisters, who may not like to be singled out by name from among their Sisters. I owe much to the spoken testimonies of these witnesses, who all took an active part in the establishment of the Missionaries of Charity.

I also wish to thank Mrs Ann Blaikie, Miss Jacqueline de Decker, Father Gorrée and Mr John J. McGee, for sending me precious data and information.

To Mother Teresa I cannot express adequately my gratitude for being privileged to collaborate with her, even if in an humble manner, in the spiritual formation of hundreds of devoted Sisters who daily spread God's love in the six continents.

When I told Mother Teresa that I had finished writing this book, she made a single comment which sums up her spirit and attitude: 'If this book causes a single person to make one act of love for God, it was worth all the trouble and labour of writing it'.

Thank you, Mother.

Sacred Heart Church
3 Lenin Sarani
Calcutta — 700 013

1. Father, Tell Them

'I heard a voice behind me shouting like a trumpet; 'Write down all that
you see in a book, and send it to the seven churches.'

(*Rev. 1, 10–11*)

'I want to see you', said Mother Teresa. 'I must talk to you.'

She was just back from Mexico where, as a Vatican Delegate at
the International Women's Conference, she had spoken on
woman's role in society. She led some eighty American tourists
into the courtyard of the mother-house. I was delighted at the
prospect of meeting her again.

We entered the courtyard, followed by the tourists. The Indian lady serving as official guide to the tourists approached
Mother Teresa and asked her: 'Would you kindly address them,
they would like to hear a few words about your work.' Mother
agreed.

First she was made to pay the price of celebrity: as she stood
before the crowd, cameras clicked. After this Mother sat down
on the cement floor of the courtyard. Some tourists followed her
example; others stood in a semi-circle. In a corner of the courtyard, Sisters were filling buckets of water from a hand pump. In
a class-room others were studying. From the chapel came the
sound of voices singing psalms to the praise of the Lord. Mother
very simply spoke of the work of the Sisters and of the love for
Jesus that prompted them; of the poor who were so patient and
kind and joyful; of crippled children whom she had befriended
and knew by name. She spoke of God and of the happiness of serving him in the poor, with simplicity, humility, homeliness. This
was an echo of the Sermon on the Mount. The Gospel came
alive: Blessed are you the poor, and you the patient, and you,
eager to listen to one who speaks of God.

When she was free, Mother Teresa returned to the tiny parlour

9

where ministers, cardinals and bishops have sat on simple wooden chairs before a small table, talking to one of our generation's great spiritual energizers. On the wall, charts spelled out the aims, activities and location of the Missionaries of Charity, the religious congregation she founded.

'How was Mexico, Mother?' I asked.

'Too much politics,' she answered. 'Disappointing. They did not mention God.'

She added, for fear of being unfair to anyone: 'Maybe someone did, but I did not hear the name of God mentioned.' No doubt, God's name would have rung a bell in her heart.

'This is rather strange,' I said, 'considering that many important Moslem ladies were present at the meeting.'

'I spoke of the dignity of women,' she continued, 'of their God-given functions and prerogatives. As mothers, as wives, they are called to be the heart of the home, to make a happy home for their husbands and children. What a noble calling, to be the mothers of the human race. I told them it was their privilege to give generously, as God himself gives to his children.'

'Did the President of Mexico call you to the Palace?'

'Yes, he wants us to start a house in Mexico itself. At the Palace I met the President, his wife and three of their eight children. I spoke of our work and of the love of Jesus. When I spoke of Jesus, his wife was crying.'

'Yes, of course, women are more sensitive to religion than men.'

'No, it is not so. The President is deep. He gave me the impression of being very deep. He insisted on our coming without delay. He said he would give us a house and see to the travel expenses of the Sisters. I must send him some of my best Sisters. I told him that as religious we require the permission of the Cardinal to establish a house in his archdiocese. This should not be difficult, since the Cardinal had already asked us to come to Mexico.

'I think the civil and religious powers do not collaborate much there. I had an excellent occasion of bringing them together. The President himself contacted the Cardinal and gave me his authorisation to start a house in Mexico. I hope to return there in October with some Sisters and to start work without delay.'

Speed is typical of Mother Teresa. At times she opens a house a few weeks after the official request has been made. As Superior General, she has to refer to no one, to ask nobody's permission. Later that will change, as the Institute continues to increase in numbers.

'From Mexico I went to Lima, Peru, where we have recently opened a house; then to New York, to London, Rome, and back here.'

'What was Lima like?'

'Latin America offers tremendous opportunities for religious work. It is mainly religious help that is asked of us there. The people are short of priests and nuns. My Sisters must do all that priests normally do, except say Mass and hear confessions. In practice they are like deacons. Take the case of marriages: the Sisters make all preparatory arrangements and have the marriages celebrated. In one place they had thirty marriages celebrated together. In another village they regularized the unions of three generations of couples living together: grandparents, parents and children. A lawyer works with them to arrange for the civil marriages – he gives his time free. When they have received the sacrament of matrimony, the couples are so happy.'

'Splendid, Mother. You require more Sisters to do God's work over there. I hear you have received a large number of applications from girls wanting to join the Institute?'

'Yes, I have received of late fifty applications from girls who wish to join us, from America, Australia, England, Africa. We have some very good postulants in Africa. One Japanese girl has applied, though we have as yet no house in Japan.'

'We have three novitiates: in Calcutta, Melbourne, Rome. Altogether at present we have two hundred and nine novices. Most of them are in Calcutta.'

'Why do they join you, what brings them to you?'

'I have received a sheaf of beautiful letters from candidates from Europe and America. The girls say they want a life of prayer, a life of poverty, humility, in the following of Jesus. Is that not wonderful? And this happens at a time when others complain of a lack of vocations and say that the youth of today are not ready for a life of humility, poverty, and obedience. I find nothing of the sort. Ask them to do something hard for Jesus, and they will come forward.

'We require many more Sisters. I have fifty-eight applications for new houses. I cannot take them all. The Archbishop of Trinidad asked me for a house. We have recently opened one in Papua. The Sisters had to look on the map to find out where that country is. The Bishop is extremely poor; he cannot help much. But I thought it was one more reason for us to go to his help.'

Fifty-eight houses asked for: as Mother puts seven or eight Sisters in each house, that would mean about 450 Sisters just to start these houses. She has 209 novices in the two years novitiate, which allows her to dispose of about a hundred Sisters a year at present. The Congregation is young, and the mortality rate is very low; few die, and not many leave after their first vows. Still, it would require about five years to comply with all the requests; and many more will be coming meanwhile. The backlog of applications will go on increasing, unless the recruitment can be much accelerated, which seems highly probable.

Then I presented my own request:

'Mother, I have to ask you a favour; may I write a book on you and the Missionaries of Charity? Will you allow me to do so? We have worked many years together. I intend to write from the spiritual angle, to show your motivation, the hand of God directing and protecting your Congregations.'

'Yes, Father, write about us, You have known us well, you have been with us from the beginning. We have the same ideas.'

'You must have our Constitutions. But mainly, you must tell people what brings us here. Tell them,' said Mother, and she became eloquent, pleading, passionately involved – 'tell them that we are not here for the work, we are here for Jesus. All we do is for Him. We are first of all religious; we are not social workers, not teachers, not nurses or doctors, we are religious Sisters. We serve Jesus in the poor. We nurse Him, feed Him, clothe Him, visit Him, comfort Him in the poor, the abandoned, the sick, the orphans, the dying. But all we do, our prayer, our work, our suffering is for Jesus. Our life has no other reason or motivation. This is a point many people do not understand. I serve Jesus twenty-four hours a day, whatever I do is for Him. And He gives me strength. I love Him in the poor and the poor in Him. But always the Lord comes first.

'Whenever a visitor comes to this house, I take him to the chapel to pray for a while. I tell him: "Let us first greet the

Master of the house. Jesus is here; it is for Him we work, to Him we devote ourselves. He gives us the strength to carry on this life and to do so with happiness. Without Him we could not do what we do; we certainly could not continue doing it for a whole life-time. One year, two years, perhaps; but not during a whole life, without thought of reward, without expectation of anything good except to suffer with Him who loved us so much that He gave His life for us. Without Jesus our life would be meaningless, incomprehensible; Jesus explains our life.'

Mother Teresa took a deep breath, then summed up her briefing with a strong command: 'Father, tell them, WE DO IT FOR JESUS.'

As I walked home, the thought struck me: She is Paul writing to the Colossians: 'There is only Christ: He is everything and he is in everything.' (*Col. 1, 11*) And Mother Teresa's command rang in my ears: 'Tell them: we do it for Jesus.'

2. The Call

'One day ... the Holy Spirit said, 'I want Barnabas and Saul set apart for the work to which I have called them.'

(Acts 13, 2–3)

Father Henry Speaks

Father Julien Henry received me in his small office at St Teresa's church presbytery. This room was so crowded with boxes, books, gadgets and instruments that there was not even a chair in it and we both had to stand for one hour. He usually writes at a high desk, standing. I asked him:

'Father Henry, you have known Mother Teresa longer and better than anyone else. What struck you most in her? What would you say is her main quality? Why did she succeed to such an extent?'

Father Henry reflected silently, as if lost in prayer. Then he answered slowly, with deep feeling and emotion.

'What is most extraordinary is the enormous amount of good Almighty God has worked through this humble instrument. God has used this woman with all her qualities and defects, yes, her great qualities and her defects, with her weak training, to do His work, because she is completely subservient to Him. She obeys His promptings, His direction, without questioning. She does not think of herself, she does everything for Him. And she does it with such complete trust in His power that nothing seems impossible to her. It is all done for God.

'In all her interviews, even with unbelievers, even with non-Christians, she insists that what she and the Sisters do is for God, for our Lord Jesus Christ. All they do is for Christ; and they find in their love for Jesus, in prayer and in adoration of the Blessed Eucharist the strength to serve the poor.

'She comes from peasant stock and from a community of hill

people. An Albanian from Yugoslavia, she is tough and a revolutionary. If the structures stand in the way of fulfilling your ideas, change them, destroy them, ignore them – that is what happened in her case.

'God made use of her spiritual and human qualities and weaknesses to producé extraordinary fruits. In His hands she has been supple. He guides her. Her ideas came gradually, her aim became clearer and clearer, until one day it was concretised in a deep spiritual experience in the train taking her to Darjeeling.

'In those days she was educating Bengali girls at St Mary's High School, Entally. She was very insistant about their spiritual training, as was also Mother Cenacle, her companion.

'We must remember what had brought Mother Teresa to India. As a school-girl, Agnes, as she was then called, was caught in the wave of enthusiasm for the missions and for the expansion of the Kingdom of Christ, a truly spiritual Kingdom "not of this world", and for the work of spreading the Gospel in the missions, an enthusiasm generated by the writings of Pope Pius XI and highlighted by the institution of the Feast of Christ the King.'

In the Sodality she prayed and meditated on these ideas; she became aflame with the desire of spending herself for the cause of Christ, for the Gospel that was to be preached to all men.

'And so,' continued Father Henry, 'through the paper of the Sodality of Our Lady, Agnes learnt about the Indian Missions. Some Yugoslav Jesuits who had recently come to Bengal worked in the Ganges Delta, South of Calcutta.

Anthony, whilst studying theology at St Mary's College at Kurseong, in the Himalayas, regularly despatched news of the Bengal mission and of the work among the Nepalis of the Darjeeling District. He sent hundreds of letters to friends in Yugoslavia and elsewhere.

'So,' continued Father Henry, 'Agnes learned of the religious, educational and charitable work carried on by missionaries in Bengal. She decided to consecrate her life to this apostolate and enquired about the means of going to India. She was advised to seek admission into the Congregation of the Loreto Nuns who worked in Bengal. Their headquarters were in Dublin. Agnes would have to join them, learn English, and ask to be sent to the missions. She did so.'

When she arrived in India in January 1929 she was sent to the
novitiate at Darjeeling, in the Himalayas, where the very scenery
speaks of God's majesty, power and beauty.

'At the end of her two years of novitiate she took her first
vows of religion. She was then attached to the High School for
Bengali girls run by the Loreto nuns at Entally, on Calcutta's
Eastern side. There for some twenty years she taught geography
and history; later she became Headmistress. She was also put in
charge of the Daughters of St Anne, a diocesan Congregation of
Indian Sisters, who wore a blue saree and taught in the Bengali
secondary school.

'The Loreto nuns at Entally occupy a large property purchased
with the money bequeathed to them by a wealthy Protestant
planter. In this spacious property the Sisters run an English high
school for over five hundred girls, boarders, including a large
number of orphans who pay no fees whatever. In the same
property the Bengali high school houses two to three hundred
boarders and some day scholars, mostly from families of modest
means.

'The Loreto nuns are well known for their college and six high
schools in Calcutta. They are generally esteemed and respected as
hard working religious and as first rate educators. At Entally,
Mother Teresa devoted herself whole-heartedly to the intellectual and spiritual formation of Bengali girls under the direction
of Mother Cenacle, a Loreto nun from Mauritius, a saintly person.

'At Entally there was a Sodality of the Blessed Virgin for the
girls, where they imbibed the same ideas that had brought
Mother Teresa to India.'

'You were the spiritual director of that Sodality, Father
Henry?'

'Yes. Besides the spiritual meetings there was a study club to
which Hindu girls also asked to be admitted. Then we had
various activities. Every week a group visited the Nilratan Sarkar
Hospital. We rotated the girls so as to have some continuity in
the apostolate. We first sent numbers one, two, three; the next
week numbers two, three, four; then numbers three, four, five
and so on. The girls grew enthusiastic about this work, which
was mainly religious: consoling the patients, cheering them up,
rendering them small services, writing letters for them. Another

group went to visit the slums. Behind the wall of the school there was the slum of Motijhil. The girls went to do service there. Mother herself never went with them.

'Mother saw the dire poverty of many people in and around Calcutta. She felt an inner prompting to do something to relieve the hardships of the very poor, and to lead them to God. Spiritually they were completely neglected – truly sheep without a shepherd. She realized that within the structures of organized education, aimed mainly at the middle classes, in which she worked, it would be impossible to achieve this aim. She had to get out of the system and start something quite different.

'At the same time, some of the girls she was teaching and who visited the poor in the slums and the sick in hospital, expressed to her the desire of becoming nuns so that they could devote themselves fully to the apostolate among the very poor.'

Then came God's call. 'It was,' Mother Teresa told me 'on the tenth of September, 1946, in the train that took me to Darjeeling, the hill station in the Himalayas, that I heard the call of God.' In quiet, intimate prayer with her Lord, she heard distinctly what she says was for her, 'a call within a call.' 'The message,' she explains, 'was quite clear: I was to leave the convent and help the poor whilst living among them. It was an order. I knew where I belonged, but I did not know how to get there.'

She had already been called by God to the religious life and there was never any question of abandoning it. God was calling her to another kind of work and service in the religious life.

Mother felt intensely that Jesus wanted her to serve him in the poorest of the poor, the uncared for, the slum-dwellers, the abandoned, the homeless. Jesus invited her to serve him and follow him in actual poverty, material poverty, to practise a style of life that would make her similar to the needy in whom he was present, suffered and loved.

As at the Annunciation Mary Immaculate had answered 'Yes, be it done to me according to your word, according to God's will,' so, whole-heartedly, to this call of God she heard in her heart, Mother Mary Teresa answered 'Yes.' She did not know how it would be done, but she surrendered to God in unlimited faith.

It was a flash of light on the road to Damascus, a meeting with

Jesus, injecting a new spirit and direction to her apostolic life. This light did not blind her – she was prepared for it, accustomed as she was to follow God's inspiration and having reflected as she had on the unfortunate lot of so many who had little chance of knowing God's infinite love for them. Mother accepted. There was no encounter, no struggle, no compulsion: obediently, lovingly, she accepted. Was she not wedded to Jesus, ready to follow him in utter poverty? Did she not always trust him and do His will fully

The Missionaries of Charity keep this day as 'Inspiration Day,' for truly it was the start of their Institute.

As the Apostles had been prepared by Christ for the final call, not only to discipleship, but to be apostles, so, says Father Henry, 'Mother Teresa had been prepared.'

In the train, the inspiration or call was crystallized, became a clear and definite expression of God's will. This 'call within a call' originating from God resembled that of Barnabas and Paul.

'One day,' say the *Acts*, 'while they were offering worship to the Lord and keeping a fast, the Holy Spirit said, "I want Barnabas and Saul set apart for the work to which I have called them." So it was that after fasting and prayer they laid their hands on them and sent them off.' (*Acts 13, 2–3*) The Christian community, aware that the call came from the Holy Spirit, sent them off cheerfully, with prayers and their blessing. In these days, more distant from Pentecost, the Holy Spirit's call came to a nun who would have to reveal it to the authorities of the Church, the Archbishop of Calcutta and her Superiors, and obtain their approval and blessing.

On her return to Calcutta, Mother Teresa made her desires known to some members of her community, who listened to her, as may be expected, with mixed feelings.

'When he had become very old and retired to St Xaviers' College, Archbishop Périer said to me,' recalled Father Henry, ' "One day, as I was making the visit of Entally Convent, someone told me that a young nun of the community had some queer ideas. Now, whenever anyone tried to put me on my guard in this way, I always asked myself whether the Hand of God might not be there, and gave full freedom to the person to explain his or her case. If the religious is humble, obedient, dutiful, the impulse may come from God." '

The Archbishop applied St Paul's advice to test the various spirits to find out if they come from God. He gave the young nun with strange ideas a sympathetic hearing as she outlined her plan to work among the poorest and most needy. Of course, to realize her plans she would have to leave her religious Congregation and start a new one.

After speaking to the Archbishop of her plans, she was transferred to Asansol for reasons of health. But the Archbishop insisted with her Superior that she be brought back to Calcutta, since she had applied to him for permission to leave the convent for a time. Meanwhile, trouble arose in the school, fanned by the political situation of the day. The school authorities could not settle the dispute with the girls. When Mother Teresa returned to Entally, she called the girl leaders and within half an hour the trouble was over. They could not resist her appeals to sanity.

The magnetic influence she exerted was to be the trump card which helped her to fulfill her desire to start her new congregation.

Many years later, I asked Mother:
'Did the Archbishop ever ask you for a sign from God?'
'No, he did not ask me for a sign.'
'Did you give him one?'
'No, I did not give him any.'
Had the Archbishop done so, he would have set the matter immediately in a spiritual and supernatural context. A superior may do this. A religious who seems specially able to perform a task at home, when he requests to be sent to the missions, may be told by his superior: 'Give me a sign that God wants you to go to the missions.' The religious then convinces his superior somehow.

But in the case of Mother Teresa things did not go so far. The religious authority tried to discover whether Mother's vocation to a special work was not an illusion, but was true and had chances of success. Some indications convinced the Archbishop that the Finger of God might be there.

The first difficulty was political, and arose from the atmosphere and the mentality prevailing in the days preceding and following the Independence of India.

'One day,' said Father Henry, 'the Archbishop asked me

"What would you think of a European woman who dressed in Indian style and went out to work among the very poor in the slums, at the head of a group of Bengali girls? Would she succeed? Would she be accepted?" ' The point was: in those days of acute nationalistic feelings, what would be the reaction of the thinking public? This was before India became independent, when under the inspiration of Gandhiji groups of congressmen went out to do social service among the poorer classes.

'I answered the Archbishop: "Undoubtedly this is a gamble: there is a real risk of arousing opposition. But it could be tried, especially if you have the right person. She will have to make herself acceptable to the civic and political leaders. With the poor, the matter presents less difficulty – they will be won over by the charity of the person who bends over their misery, whatever her nationality.

'And so, the Archbishop agreed to try the gamble and give Mother Teresa a chance.'

The second difficulty was that Rome did not favour an unnecessary multiplication of religious institutes of women. There existed already too many small ones. A bishop who applied for the approbation of a new religious institute in his diocese had to show that none of the existing ones could do the particular work for which the new one was established. Now, Calcutta Archdiocese already had a religious congregation, the Daughters of St Anne, under the jurisdiction of the Archbishop. They devoted themselves to the care and education of the poor in the villages and in Calcutta. They dressed in Indian style, slept in a dormitory, ate very simple food, lived in the Indian manner, spoke Bengali, worked among the poor and unsophisticated.

The Archbishop would have liked Mother Teresa to first try to work out her plans with their help and collaboration. But Mother quickly found that she could not. The sisters had their tradition, their own activities, their ways of proceeding. She wanted a group that would be highly mobile, that would visit the people, that would work not only among the poor, but among the poorest of the poor. She could not simply follow in others' footsteps. She wanted to start from scratch, train her novices in her own way, make them imbibe her own spirit. The future was to prove her right.

The Daughters of St Anne lived in the same compound as

Mother and worked in the school of St Mary's where Mother Teresa had been headmistress. They were understandably worried about their future prospects and asked me, as I was then their spiritual adviser, to speak to them on the consequences of this new religious institute that would compete with them for the few Bengali girls who wished to enter the religious life. I told them that this was a challenge to them. . . .

Indeed they have multiplied, and their Congregation has increased in strength, initiative, the variety of works undertaken, in self-reliance. They now have their own Mother General; they run their own schools and orphanages very successfully. Competition has proved to be an excellent stimulus.

It took some time and much discussion and prayer for light before the Archbishop was ready to apply to Rome for permission to start in his archdiocese a new religious Congregation for women. At least ten novices had to join Mother. Constitutions would have to be drafted and sent to Rome for approval. The first step was to obtain from Rome exclaustration or permission for a religious, bound by perpetual vows, to live for a time outside a convent and to be no longer under religious Superiors, but directly under the authority of the Bishop.

Mother Teresa's request for exclaustration was duly despatched to Rome, in February 1948. When the permission arrived, Mother prepared to leave.

'Did you have any difficulties with your religious Superiors before you left?' I asked her at the time of the Jubilee.

'None whatever.' she answered, 'they were most understanding and cooperative.'

And so Mother Teresa, in response to God's call, on the 16th of August 1948 walked out of the convent, closed the door behind her and found herself on a Calcutta street, alone, in the dark.

God had called her to himself in a very special way. Twenty-seven years later, Mother confided to me:

'To leave Loreto was my greatest sacrifice, the most difficult thing I have ever done. It was much more difficult than to leave my family and country to enter religious life. Loreto meant everything to me.

'In Loreto I had received my spiritual training; I had become a

religious there. I had given myself to Jesus in the Institute. I liked
the work, teaching the girls.'

As an adolescent Agnes had been called by God and had turned
to him. Following His call, she left her family, her father's house,
her culture, her country, all she had been accustomed to see, to
hear and to love, to go to a foreign land. In the first flush of
youthful enthusiasm and generosity it was not too difficult. But
the first period of training would exact more self-denial.

Then, gradually God was to invite her to a more complete
donation of herself, a second turning towards Him in deeper faith
and a more intense yearning to do only what pleases Him. This
grace must have come after some years of religious life, when she
had acquired the habit of doing the difficult thing for God, of
choosing to carry the Cross with Jesus, of thinking only of the
Beloved, until she saw the world in God and God in the world.
This grace is given or offered to many a person faithful to God's
grace and ready for great sacrifices.

One day, she received from God a special invitation. Some
chosen souls are granted a great grace, which may be offered
once or twice only; if they accept it, they start on the road to
holiness.

God bestows this grace upon those He finds sufficiently
generous, and on whom He had special designs, whom He wishes to entrust with a special mission or task, who have the mettle
and the will to accept suffering in His service and for His glory.

Masters of spirituality describe the soul's progress: it turns to
God in a more intense, complete, thorough manner, after a
heroic self-surrender, in response to a powerful grace, which invites and strengthens the soul.

Mother went through this spiritual experience.

'It was much more difficult than leaving my family when I
entered the convent. Yes, when I left the convent I did not run
away from it to obtain more freedom.'

She left the security of the convent, its friendliness, its way of
life, its spiritual help, in order to throw herself blindly into God's
hands, in pure faith, not asking, not knowing, not questioning,
but blindly surrendering to God's guidance.

She was on the street, with no shelter, no company, no helper
no money, no employment, no promise, no guarantee, no security.

'My God, you, only you. I trust in your call, your inspiration; you will not let me down.' Now, she was His.

Patna

After the break with her past way of life, a period of training afforded a welcome period of transition and reflection. Mother Teresa left Calcutta and proceeded to Patna for a short course in nursing and outdoor dispensary work under the guidance of the Medical Missionary Sisters of Mother Dengel. To be of service to the poor, she had to know, therefore she had to learn.

At Patna, on the bank of the Ganges, the medical Missionary Sisters run an efficient hospital to which is attached a popular and well attended outdoor department. The Sisters also direct an excellent nurses' training course.

In July 1969, as a patient in the hospital's surgical department, I enquired about the Calcutta student Sister. She was still remembered as a keen student who had packed as much knowledge and experience into her three or four month's stay as anyone could acquire in so short a time.

At Patna Mother Teresa also sustained the first shock and upset to her plans and ideas concerning the way of life she and the girls she expected to join her would embrace. She had intended to live in utter poverty — they would live, dress and eat like the very poor among whom they would work, in an effort to bring them to God, and whom they would serve as the suffering members of Christ.

Mother Dengel, an Austrian-born woman of unlimited zeal and energy, had obtained from the Holy See the permission for her nuns to practise both surgery and midwifery in hospitals run by them, something new in the Catholic Church. Thus, she could understand and sympathize with a nun wishing to start new ways and activities in religious life.

Mother Teresa explained to Mother Dengel and her Sisters that she planned to start a congregation whose members would live like the poor in India. The nuns' diet would not even consist of simple rice and pulses, which is modest enough, but would be just 'rice and salt' a diet considered to be below the poverty line, the humblest of Bengali diets.

'We shall eat rice and salt,' said Mother Teresa with determination.

'If you make your Sisters do that,' retorted Mother Dengel, emphatically, 'you will commit a serious sin. Within a short time those young girls will fall a prey to tuberculosis and die. How do you want your Sisters to work, if their bodies receive no sustenance? The very poor work very little, become sick and die young. Do you want your nuns to suffer that fate? Or do you wish them to be strong and able to labour for Christ?'

Mother Teresa accepted this expert advice. She could not tempt God, could not ask His divine Providence to go continually against the laws of nature He had established, and work a continual miracle for the health of her Sisters, when food was available. Humbly she changed her plans. The Sisters would receive the sustenance their bodies required, their food would be simple, without luxury; obediently they would eat the portion they were given.'

Years later, Mother told me: 'The Medical Missionaries of Patna said I was to feed my Sisters well; I have followed their advice.'

Indeed, years ago several Indian Bishops had trouble with poorly fed nuns and seminarians who suffered from tuberculosis and other diseases. The Bishops took adequate measures and among the younger generation the trouble is over.

The good Lord was training His loving spouse, correcting here and there, moderating where need be what might have been otherwise excessive zeal. Mother's Sisters could not all be expected to receive the same charisms and grace God had granted her with such lavishness.

At Patna Holy Family Hospital, Mother met Miss Jacqueline de Decker to whom she revealed her plans. This young Belgian woman would have liked to join the future Institute. But her physical condition would not allow it. She was later to become one of Mother's 'Second Selves' and to organize the wing of the Sick and Suffering who would pray and suffer for the success of the Institute and its apostolate.

And in this hospital Mother later lost her first religious, who left earth for heaven. One of her novices died there, after taking her religious vows on her death-bed, the first fruits the Congregation offered to its Lord.

The short stay at Patna was soon over – an interlude in the

drama. Like her Master coming out of the wilderness after preparing Himself for His public life by prayer and fasting, Mother Teresa was ready to begin the task the Father had appointed her to perform for the glory of His Son. She returned to Calcutta, where she found a temporary shelter with the Little Sisters of the poor.

First Beginnings
'One day in December 1948,' said Father Henry, 'on her return from Patna, Mother appeared at St Teresa's presbytery dressed in a white saree with a blue border.'

'Do you recognize me?' she asked me.

'Of course, Mother Teresa.'

'Where is Motijhil?'

'What? You don't know? Just behind the wall of the school where you were teaching.'

I asked a woman to show her the way. They went together. Soon I heard that Mother had found a vacant room in the slum.

'What rent?' she asked.

'Five rupees per month,' said the owner.

'I'll take it,' she said.

'The next day,' continued Father Henry, 'as I was passing through Motijhil, a very poor slum area, where we had some Catholics, I heard a voice repeating the first letters of the Bengali alphabet. I looked inside the room and what do I see? Mother Teresa teaching a few children. No table, no chair, no blackboard, no chalk. With a stick she drew figures on the earth.'

After that she went to see the Corporation scavengers in their quarters, enquiring about their families, the sick, the children.

At night she stayed at St Joseph's Home, run by the Little Sisters of the Poor for Aged Persons without means or relatives able to support them. It is one hour's walk from Motijhil.

Jeanne Jugan, the French nun who started the Congregation of the Little Sisters of the Poor had much in common with Mother Teresa. She insisted on absolute poverty – the houses of the Institute were to have no foundations, no regular income, not even a bank account. The Sisters went out and still go out daily on a begging mission to obtain the support needed for their inmates.

The spirituality of the Little Sisters is centred on humility and charity, a delicate, refined, exquisite, perfect charity. There lived in the house a Sister who for forty years remained in charge of the kitchen – a wonderful soul, a true mystic who would tell her confessor 'I love Our Lord to the point of madness.' To Him she had given everything, and Our Lord as usual had asked her much.

The Sisters looked after some two hundred old people who had no resources. Mother Teresa lived in that holy house for a short time. God, who had called her, would soon show that she was His chosen one.

Motijhil, the first small school

Right at the beginning, when she was still alone, Mother took me round to show me her work, as she would do with many visitors later on.

We went along by the dwellings of the Corporation sweepers, crossed some railway lines, walked through a slum area. No one seemed to notice her, no one greeted her or gave any sign of recognition. She was not yet part of their life. We looked inside a mud hut.

'This is our school room,' said Mother Teresa.

'How many pupils do you have?'

'Thirty-five,' I think she said, 'when they are all present. But usually some are sick or absent for some reason or other.

'I teach them the alphabet; and also how to wash and comb their hair. I give them a cake of soap as prize for regularity, attention and cleanliness.'

I thought they would prefer sweets, but made no comment.

'Then they receive milk at midday.'

She was taking the wrong person round; as a professor of economics, who knew how to obtain the maximum results from our limited resources, I could not be impressed. The whole thing was rather pathetic and inefficient. Here was the headmistress of a fairly good high school trying to teach the alphabet to children who would never become literate, and teaching the use of soap to children who would not be able to afford to buy it.

She was making a desperate effort to uplift the very poor, to give them a sense of respectability and teach them that God loves them. Unless she could gather a team around her, these efforts would produce no fruits. But would anyone join her for this task? Or would she find some other means of helping the sufferers of mankind?

'This is not much,' she commented.

But we, who were doing more pleasant work, gave her all encouragement.

These were the pathetic days of the small entries in the diary she then kept. Years later she showed it to me. There were no special secrets, no revelations, just small notes on the persons she had met or on some particular happening. Some of them remained embedded in my memory twenty-five years later.

'Met N., who said there was nothing to eat at home. I gave him the fare for my tram, all the money I had, and walked home.'

At the time of the Jubilee, I reminded Mother of the small notebook and asked if she still had it. She shrugged her shoulders and said: 'No, I think I threw it away.' The right thing to do.

Meanwhile God was training her – she had to feel utterly useless, inadequate to the task. She had to cling to Him, throw herself entirely on Him: 'You, Lord, only you, all for you; make use of me.

'You pulled me out of my convent where I was useful. Now guide me, as you wish.'

The Lord heard; He took over. He got her a house, He sent her helpers. She was to become the leader of a team that would extend her in time and space, as she extended Christ Himself. Her first great task would be to build and train her team.

3. The Upper Room

'Listen, said Jesus, as you go into the city you will meet a man carrying a pitcher of water. Follow him into the house he enters and tell the owner of the house, 'The Master asks: Where is the dining room in which I can eat the passover with my disciples? The man will show you a large upper room furnished with couches. Make the preparations there.'

(*Luke 22, 10–12*)

Michael Gomes speaks

'Brother Michael, tell me all you remember about Mother Teresa during her stay in your house.'

I called him Brother, because for many years we had worked together in the Legion of Mary. We were sitting in one of the rooms occupied by Mother Teresa in his family's three-storeyed house.

'Willingly, Father. But first I must repeat what I said some time ago. The Chairman of a group of Co-Workers of the Missionaries of Charity praised me saying "We are happy to have today in our midst the man who did so much for Mother Teresa, by putting her up free of charge in his own house and giving her his time and all possible help." I answered:

'Friends, it is we who have been benefited. If we have given much, we have received much more in return. Mother Teresa's presence in our family house has been a wonderful source of blessing.

'Mother,' he continued, 'occupied the second floor. From the ground floor the staircase leads to the top floor directly into the room the Sisters used as chapel. The wooden altar and wooden candlesticks and furnishings were made by Father Henry with the help of his boys. Above the altar hung the picture of the Immaculate Heart of Mary given by Father Van Exem, who was then the rector of the church of Our Lady of Dolours. It is now in the chapel of the Mother-house.

'Archbishop Périer came several times to say Mass for the Sisters during the first years. Cardinal Spellman also came to see Mother in this house.'

'How did it happen that she came to your house?'

'Well, Father, we were four brothers living in this house. At the time of the partition of India, two of my brothers opted for East Pakistan, now Bangladesh. Two of us stayed in Calcutta.

'One day Father Van Exem came to our house and asked me "Could you find some place for Mother Teresa to stay; a mud house, a hut, something simple, anything, but close by. Can you find something?"

'Then came the voice of a child. My daughter, aged eight, said: "Daddy, the rooms upstairs are empty; there is nobody. Mother could come here."

"No," said Father Van Exem "that is far too good, it is not what she wants. She wants something much more humble."

'But we insisted, "Father, send her here. She is a nun, she must be treated well. She does the work of God." And so in February 1949 Mother came and occupied the second floor.

'Was she alone?'

'No, she came with a woman who served at St Mary's School, Charur Ma, a widow.'

'Mother took my eight-year-old daughter to visit the slums with her. Then, she needed medicines. So I went out to beg for medicines with her.

'Once we went to a big shop with a list of medicines she required. The manager was very busy. Mother showed her written list and asked for them all free.

' "You come to the wrong place, lady" answered the manager. "Let me finish my work in peace."

'Mother and I sat down. She said her rosary. When she had finished, the manager said: "All right, here are three parcels with the medicines you need. You may have them as a gift from the Company." '

In March 1949, on the Feast of St Joseph, there was a knock at Mother's door. She opened it and stood motionless, whilst her heart beat faster, faster, as she looked at the frail figure facing her, and heard her say: 'Mother, I have come to join you.'

'It will be a hard life; are you prepared for it?'

'I know it will be hard; I am prepared for it.' And the girl stepped in.

Mother turned to her Lord, in gratitude: 'Dear Jesus, how good You are. So You are sending them! You keep the promise You made me. Lord Jesus, thank You for your goodness.'

The first candidate to join Mother Teresa became Sister Agnes, taking Mother's baptismal name.

At her evening prayers Mother Teresa poured out her heart in thanksgiving and expressed her joy and confidence in God who protected her and blessed her in this manner. Now, they would start work.

I did not ask Mother what her reaction had been; I did not need to. I experienced the same feelings when the first of my ex-students told me: 'I want to become a Christian.' I also asked him: 'Do you realize that it will be terribly hard for you? Have you the courage to do it?'

'I have the courage' he answered.

'Dear Lord, thank You' I prayed. So, in spite of all they told me – that I had false hopes and was wasting my time, that educated people were not ready to embrace Christianity – you have heard my prayers and those of my parents and friends.'

Mother never forgot that Sister Agnes had been the first to believe in 'the Cause' and to trust her inspiration as coming from God. A special relationship was established between the two of them, which everyone respected and understood. They were like Paul and Timothy. Paul had brought Timothy to the·faith and appointed him as a Church leader. A special friendship would unite them until death; together they would work for the glory of the Lord Jesus, even when separated physically.

Sister Agnes became Mother's second self; for a time she replaced her as Mistress of Novices; then she was put in charge of the Mother-house and replaced Mother during her frequent absences when new foundations were being established.

Some weeks later, a second candidate appeared, and then a third. With joy Mother could say and write that their numbers were increasing.

In May 1949 Mother writes to a friend in Europe:

'You will be glad to hear that at present I have got three companions – great and zealous workers. We have five different slums where we go for a few hours. What suffering; what want of God. And yet, we are so few to carry Our Lord among them. You should see their eager faces, how they brighten up when the Sisters come. Dirty and naked though they be, their hearts are full of affection. I trust in your prayers. Ask Our Lady also to give more Sisters. In Calcutta itself, we could have full work even if we were twenty.'

And so they were four. Six months later Mother could report that they were five: a slow increase. As for work, what were even twenty Sisters among Calcutta's six or seven million people? Mother did not seem to foresee that one day they would be not twenty, but two hundred, and still unable to cope with the task.

In November 1941 she writes:

'Pray much that the little Society may grow in sanctity and members if it is the will of God. Yes, there is so much to be done; at present we are five. But, please God, more will join, and then we will be able to make a ring of charity round Calcutta, using our centres in the different slums as points from whence the love of Our Lord may freely radiate on the great city of Calcutta.'

Here she expresses her aim clearly to a person able to understand and share her life's goal to make Jesus known and loved by the poorest of the poor.

She succeeds in bringing children to church on Sundays; she writes:

'You will be glad to know that at Boitakhana we have a Sunday Mass for poor slum children. We bring the poor children and their mothers to church. We have up to 120 mothers and 300 children. We started last May with twenty-six children only.'

Already Mother has obtained the active collaboration of many lay people whose devotion she praises:

'At the dispensary the Catholic doctors and nurses are wonderful. The way they look after the people, you would think they were the princes of the country. Their charity is most wonderful.'

Mother adds a charming note: 'In the slums you can now hear the children sing. Their little faces smile when the Sisters come. And their parents too do not ill-treat their children. This is just what I have been longing to see among the poor. Thank God for all.'

A year after she had found a haven of peace and love at 14 Creek Lane, Mother could rejoice that the Lord had sent her six disciples. In 1950 she writes to her friend in Europe:

'You will be glad to know that we are now seven, and in a few days we shall be eight. Our little chapel was blessed on the 18th December. The work is slowly forming. Ask our Lord to help me to realize His plan.'

Michael Gomes recalls how the group increased and multiplied according to the promise God had made Abraham, the Man of Faith, whom Mother Teresa had imitated in his trust in God:

'The Sisters started coming after a few months. First Sister Agnes. She had been in the school under Mother and she believed in her. Mother never forgot it, Sister Agnes imbibed Mother's spirit. Though very simple and humble, she has always been the second in command, replacing Mother whenever she is out of Calcutta.

'Then came Sister Gertrude, then others, Dorothy, Margaret Mary. This one came from Bangledesh; when she heard Mother had started, nothing could stop her. She knew no English at the time. Many years later she returned to Bangladesh as Superior of the foundation there. She had to organize relief work. She had been well trained. A consignment of good French blankets arrived for distribution to the poor and the refugees. A minister sent his bearer, a bishop sent his driver for a blanket. Sister sent them back empty-handed, saying: "They are for the poor; you are not poor people; you are working men with a decent salary."

'How many Sisters were there when they left?' I asked.

'Thirty or thirty-two.'

Mrs Gomes interposed:

'No, they were exactly twenty-eight.' She was positive about it. She remembered better.

Michael Gomes continued:

'Mother took first one room, then another for the Sisters. Then some got ill, they had to be isolated; Mother asked for a room for the Sisters who were infectious. As the numbers increased, she took the whole floor, and even the annexe.'

'Yes, it has always been like that, she takes all she can get.'

'At first there were only two bathing rooms on their floor. As the number of Sisters started to increase, this created some difficulties, as they had to get ready early. So, Father Henry with some of his boys built some bathing rooms on top of the annexe.

'By eight a.m. the Sisters were all out. They came home for lunch. In the afternoon there was perfect silence in the house. The Sisters had classes, studies and instructions. But after dinner, the house was filled with laughter and singing. The Sisters ran on the terrace; they had tugs-of-war, played and made the whole house tremble. It was good to hear them laugh. After recreation, it was time for prayer and again there was complete silence. They were truly God's children.'

Father Henry recalls that when Mother's first disciples arrived, they expected that the life would be terribly hard and that the food would be insufficient. At their first meal, as Mother put before them a plate well filled with food, they looked at it with astonishment. 'Eat it' said Mother, 'that is your portion.' They were to learn that God wants 'obedience rather than victims'. They had come here to do not their will according to the flesh, but the will of the One who had called them and would send them out – as Christ, who was sent by the Father, said: 'I came to do not my will, but the will of the Father who sent me.'

Father Henry adds: 'In one of my instructions right at the beginning, I told them: "Yes, you have plenty to eat now; food is not lacking. But it may happen that one day on coming home from work you find that there is nothing to eat. . . ." Sister Dorothy interrupted me and said "That day will never come." She had already acquired Mother's trust in God's providence, who looks after his own.'

The house of the Gomes brothers proved to be truly a replica of the Cenacle, the Upper Room in a disciple's house, where Jesus took the Last Supper with His apostles. It was a cenacle hallowed by the presence of the Lord; daily the Last Supper was re-enacted in it and the place remained full of His spirit during the rest of the day.

In this cenacle, the Sisters were, as Jesus had prayed, closely united and acutely conscious of their oneness in the Lord. There they worshipped, prayed, studied, ate, slept, talked, sang and relaxed. There they cooked, washed clothes, scrubbed floors,

prepared bandages, mended clothes, There, mainly, they learned
the principles and the practice of the spiritual life, of life
dedicated to God in union with Jesus. As more novices were admitted, the group grew, took shape, gathered strength.

Mother was Christ in their midst, instructing them, demonstra-
ting to them the purpose of the Institute. They listened, rapt in
admiration, full of the desire of giving themselves completely to
Jesus. Then, at the end of a full day's work and prayer, they
retired to take their rest. Within a few minutes most of the Sisters
were fast asleep.

Mother remained working at a small table, writing. She wrote
to candidates who wished to join her Institute, to inform them
that it would be a hard life; she wrote to priests and to helpers in
India and abroad. She drafted some articles of the Constitutions.
For a long time she wrote; then, when the task was ended, she
joined her hands and slowly fell on her knees to pray to her
Lord.

In this atmosphere, close to the living Presence of Christ in the
Eucharist, responsible to God for the disciples He had sent her,
she summed up the purpose of her coming here as Jesus in His
Sacerdotal prayer had summed up the purpose of His coming on
earth. With Him she consecrated herself to the Father for the full
and perfect sacrifice He wanted of her. With total faith in God's
help, protection and goodness, she prayed;

'Father, glorify Your Son that Your Son may return the glory
to You; Father, glorify Your Son, let Him be glorified through
Your unworthy instruments, for it is for Him, for His glory that
we are here, that we work and suffer and pray; all we do is for
Jesus; our life has no meaning if it is not all for Him. Let men
know Him, and thus come to possess the eternal life He brought
us.

'Eternal life, Father, is to know You, the one true God and
Jesus Christ, whom You have sent.

'May we bring this eternal life to the poor, deprived as they are
of all comfort, of material possessions; may they come to know
You, love You, possess You, share in Your life, You who are the
God and Father of men and of my Lord Jesus Christ, Source of all
truth and goodness and happiness.

'May we bring to You those we meet, those for whom we
work, those who help us, those who die in our hands, those we

receive as Jesus received the children He blessed, the sick He cured, the sufferers He befriended.

'Father, I pray You for these Sisters, whom You have chosen to serve You and belong to You; they were Yours, and You gave them to me; You want me to lead them to You; You wish them to be an image of Your Son, Your own perfect Image, that men may believe that You have sent Him; that seeing their works, men may acknowledge that Christ was sent by You;

'You gave them to me, and I bring them to You;

'You took them away from the world and its spirit, that they may live in the world as the brides of Jesus, neither belonging to the world nor following its corrupt ways;

'Holy Father, I pray for them that they may be dedicated to Your holy Name, sanctified to You, reserved for Your service, immolated to You in sacrifice. To this end I consecrate myself to You, I dedicate myself as Your victim with Jesus Christ, the Victim of the Sacrifice.'

Father so good, I pray not only for these my Sisters, but for all those who will come to join them and those who through them will be drawn to You and believe in You.

'Father, grant that my Sisters may all be one, as You and Jesus are one; that they may live through Your Spirit.

'That the love with which You loved us may be in them and that Jesus may be in them.'

Mother Teresa let the Spirit pray in her, and asked Him to love her divine Spouse Jesus in her.

Slowly her head fell on her hands. She needed some sleep; tomorrow or perhaps already today there was much work to do for Jesus. She lay down and slept, God's Angel close to the Sisters she was to mould for his service.

They were in the world, but not of the world – they were to keep away from its spirit of greed, pride and sensuality. They wore humble sarees of coarse material, like the poor; from their left shoulder hung a small crucifix. The cross was to be in their life, the cross on their arm, the cross in their heart; the cross calling, teaching, a constant reminder of the cross Christ had carried out of love for men, out of love for them. They were to be for the whole of their life on earth like Paul 'crucified to the world and to whom the world is crucified,' brides of Christ, similar to their divine Spouse.

Mother trained her young Sisters by word and example, as Jesus had done with His apostles at the Last Supper. She told them how they were to treat the poorest of the poor, in whom they were to see Jesus, their Lord and Master, the Son of God become man.

The Gospel recalls how Jesus taught His disciples humble charity.

'Ar they were at supper, Jesus got up from table, removed His outer garments and, taking a towel, wrapped it round His waist; he then poured water into a basin and began to wash the disciples' feet and to wipe them with the towel He was wearing.' (*John 13, 2–5*) Jesus thus assumes the dress and performs the work of a slave. A Jew could not ask a Jewish servant to wash his fee, he could only ask a slave.

After He had washed his disciples' feet Jesus told them: 'Do you understand what I have done to you You call me Master and Lord, and rightly; so I am. If I, your Lord and Master, have washed your feet, you should wash each other's feet. I have given you an example so that you may imitate what I have done to you.' And Jesus added: 'Now that you know this, happiness will be yours if you behave accordingly.'

This took place as Jesus was about to institute the Eucharist and give to the world the greatest proof of His love for men. He would not give them spiritual food once only but thousands of times, if they so wished. Similarly He wanted His disciples to perform acts of love and humility not once but many times.

Mother Teresa was teaching her young Sisters to wash the bodies of those in need, to clean their sores and bandage their wounds. They were to do this not a few times, but thousands of times. Their service of love was to last not a few days, not even a year or two, but a whole life, as long as the Lord God wanted them to serve Him in their brothers.

The poor would come to them, emaciated, covered with sores and ulcers, suffering from elephantiasis, venereal disease, cancer, leprosy.

'At times' Mother told me, 'they arrive in a terrible state, filthy, covered with sores, eaten up by syphilis. We wash them all. Of course when a case is really too bad, I do it myself.'

'Of course, Mother.'

Every religious Superior worthy of the name would do so. But it was good to hear it said in all simplicity.

Seeing their Mother doing this, the Sisters also understood what they would be expected to do later, when they would be in charge of a community in some near or distant land.

The sick and the dying would be brought to them. Knowing neither their names, nor their place of origin, nor their antecedents, the Sisters were to treat them all in a loving way. 'It is Christ you tend in the poor,' explained Mother. 'It is His wounds you bathe, His sores you clean, His limbs you bandage. See beyond appearances, hear the words Jesus pronounced long ago; they are still operative today: "What you do to the least of mine you do it to me." When you serve the poor you serve Our Lord Jesus Christ.'

And in the morning, on the way to the slums, the dispensaries, the homes for the dying, the children's homes, the Sisters remembered that it was the Lord they had received in the Eucharist at Mass that they were going to attend, nurse, serve lovingly in His suffering brothers and sisters. They would see Him with the eyes of faith and perform their task with utter respect for Christ present in the poor.

Was it pleasant? It was not; except perhaps for a few who were granted an extraordinary grace. But they did it with faith; they believed in the words of the Lord; 'Now that you know this, happiness will be yours if you behave accordingly.'

They performed their various tasks with cheerfulness, as Mother asked them to. On their way home they might experience the joy the Holy Spirit pours into the hearts of those who belong to God and serve Him only.

Meanwhile Mother was busy writing the Constitutions of the Congregation she wished to found; they were to be sent to Rome for approval.

The structure of the new Institute, its aims and rules had to be determined and approved before the Congregation could start to exist. For this difficult work Father Van Exem's help proved invaluable. He helped Mother to present her case, and defended her plans before the Archbishop.

At the time of the Jubilee, as she remembered the difficult first years, Mother said 'God was good to me, He gave me good

priests to help me in my work: Father Henry, Father Van Exem,'
and she named two others.

Father Celeste Van Exem proved a great help to Mother. He
was a Belgian Jesuit who had been prepared to establish contacts
with Moslems. He had learned Arabic and lived for some time
with the Arab bedouin to imbibe their spirit, assimilate their
language and culture, become acquainted with their religious
life. He came to know Mother Teresa; he espoused her cause and
lent it his support. He greatly helped to frame the Constitutions
of the Missionaries of Charity. He knew Canon Law and could
foresee what might be introduced into the Constitutions and
what would not be allowed by Rome.

Though he supported Mother's ideas, he had to oppose certain
provisions which could not or would not be accepted by the
Roman Congregation for Religious. He spoke for Mother before
the Archbishop; the weight of his knowledge, experience and
perseverance helped her to such an extent that some Sisters called
him 'The Co-Founder' or 'The Cardinal'. Priests would say
jokingly, 'the Cardinal Protector.'

The other priest who helped Mother most was Father Julien
Henry. Father Moyersoen, the Jesuit Superior in Calcutta, had
asked the Belgian Provincial to give him some priests ready to
start work in Bengal immediately. Father Julien Henry offered
his services. Soon he was in Calcutta where he worked for many
years at St Teresa's parish. He may be the man who best knows
Mother, as her spiritual adviser, and who helped most in the
training of her Sisters. He is well informed about the wonderful
saga of love of God and Christian charity for the most needy
enacted by the Missionaries of Charity.

The Constitutions
'Father Henry, who wrote the Constitutions?' I asked him.

'That is a good question,' he answered. 'The first draft of the
constitutions was entirely due to Mother Teresa herself. Her
spiritual background and aspirations are expressed in the
Constitutions she gave to the Missionaries of Charity. You find
in them her passion for the Kingdom of Christ, for preaching the
Gospel and making Christ known and loved by all men; also her
devotion to the Sacred Heart, to Our Lady, to the Blessed

Eucharist and her faithfulness to the Church and to the Pope.

'Father Van Exem helped her, especially with the juridical and organizational aspects of the Constitutions. As a canonist and theologian, he knew what would be acceptable to Rome and what would not. Mother wanted to introduce some measures that were impossible: for example, she did not wish them to own any property, even their own houses. The ownership would have been vested in the Church, which was not possible since the Church of Rome or the Vatican is a foreign body in India.'

St Francis of Assisi had wanted something similar. He did not want to own the houses in which the Friars would live and work, in order to be perfectly poor. But Rome would not allow it for practical reasons.

There were some points on which Mother and Father Van Exem disagreed. The healthy tensions that ensued between these two strong characters, each wanting to have his or her own way, resulted in a remarkable equilibrium.

The first draft of the Constitutions, drawn up by Mother Teresa, was given to Father de Gheldere for eventual correction. He improved the wording here and there, but otherwise made no changes. 'The Finger of God is here' he said, and respected the work he considered to be inspired by the Holy Spirit.

Christ, who lived in her, must have inspired, guided and sustained Mother as she wrote the Constitutions of the Institute that was to work entirely for His glory.

The Constitutions were the work of a woman who knows by personal experience 'the length and breadth, the height and depth of the love of Christ.' That love excels all human understanding, proceeding as it does from the Saviour's heart; that love the Spirit of Jesus pours into the hearts of those who eagerly open themselves to receive it.

Mother begins by stating the goal of those who will join the Institute, as revealed on the day of her inspiration:

'Our aim is to quench the infinite thirst of Jesus Christ for love by the profession of the evangelical counsels and by whole-hearted free service to the poorest of the poor, according to the teaching and life of Our Lord in the Gospel, revealing in a unique way the Kingdom of God.

'Our particular mission is to labour at the salvation and sanctification of the poorest of the poor.

'As Jesus Christ was sent by His Father so He sends us too, filled
with His Spirit to preach His Gospel of love and compassion to
the poorest of the poor all over the world.

'It shall be our utmost endeavour to proclaim Jesus Christ to
men of all nations, especially to those who are under our care.'

Then Mother states the fundamental duty of the Sisters, which
flows from God's nature, His purpose in creating, the reason for
His calling the Sisters to the religious life as expressed in the very
name of the Congregation:

'We are called the MISSIONARIES OF CHARITY.

' "God is love." A Missionary of Charity must be a missionary
of love. She must be full of charity in her own soul and spread
that same charity to the souls of others, Christians and non-
Christians.'

Mother's vision encircles the world in a passionate desire to
make it answer the love of God and of Jesus Christ. It recalls to
mind the great Rules of Benedict, Bernard, Francis, Ignatius.

The Constitutions charm by the kindness and gentleness, the
balance and moderation they display, which do not weaken their
passionate outburst of love for God and for his children. Tact and
sensitiveness are apparent: the author is a woman.

In October 1950, on the Feast of the Most Holy Rosary,
Mother received from Rome permission to start a new
Congregation of Sisters destined to work among the poorest of
the poor. Archbishop Périer came to celebrate Mass in their
little chapel. Father Van Exem, who assisted him, read the
bull received from Rome, sanctioning the existence of the
Congregation of the Missionaries of Charity, approving and confirming the aim for which they were established. This gave great
happiness to Mother and her young team of generous apostles.
They sang the praises of the Lord in thanksgiving for his kind
protection.

From this moment onwards the recruitment to the Congregation never slowed down. Candidates came in increasing
numbers, from Bengal and Chota Nagpur, from the East Coast
and South India, and also from foreign countries.

Sister Eugene speaks

The first candidate from Kerala to join the Missionaries of Charity came by way of Shillong, a hill station in the North-East. In June 1976 I met her at Darjeeling; she was the Superior of the house there; and asked her to tell me her recollections of the early days.

'Tell me, Sister, what struck you most when you were in the Upper Room right at the beginning?'

'I was number twenty-one. We all received a number in the order in which we joined. I was only fifteen years old, still at school at Shillong. I had come to work with the Sisters during the holidays. But I got to like the work and stayed. At first I had no idea of what the religious life meant; I was serving the poor and found it stimulating. Only when I took my profession did I really realize what it meant to be a religious.

'What struck me most was the spirit of faith, the tremendous faith shown by Mother; we lived in that atmosphere. We depended fully on God for everything. I remember two instances when essential things were missing in the community. There was no food for the evening meal; but Mother said 'Do not worry, it will come.' And by the evening, someone, unexpectedly, brought what was required.

'During the day I went to work in the dispensaries or the slum schools.

'How many were you when you left Creek Lane?'

'Twenty-six.'

'And with Mother that would mean twenty-seven. Were you not twenty-eight?'

'Perhaps. But before we left, we started praying very instantly to obtain the Home of Kalighat and a new house for the novitiate. During about three months, we went in the evenings in procession to Fatima Chapel. Father Henry had erected an open chapel.'

'Yes, about two kilometres from St Teresa's Church, where the church dedicated to Our Lady of Fatima stands now.'

'Well, Father Henry organized a procession every evening. He accompanied the Sisters as we went through the Calcutta streets saying the rosary aloud. Some lay people came to join us. And from six to about nine, we went on the road from our house to the Church of St Teresa's and thence to Fatima chapel, praying

there and again on our way home. We were asking Our Lady of
Fatima to obtain for us the new house we needed to expand our
novitiate, and also the refuge for the dying of Kalighat.

'After a full day of work we were on our feet walking and
praying. We truly stormed Heaven to obtain these two houses.
We forgot that we were tired, so caught were we by enthusiasm
for our work. God had to give it; Our Lady was to help us obtain it. And God granted our prayer. Kalighat was turned over to
us. Immediately we went to work there. As I was not yet a
novice, I went every day.'

'Did Mother go with you daily?'

'Yes, she came with us and worked with us; but not daily. The
Sisters took turns; sometimes Sister Dorothy, sometimes Sister
Gertrude and some others. We received much help from Mrs
Chater, a Chinese lady.'

'Yes, I knew her well. She was devoted, generous, and a good
organizer. Business-like, efficient, she would certainly fit in with
Mother's style of work.'

'She took us in her car daily, at the beginning, when we did
not know Calcutta well and the trams and buses we would have
had to take to reach Kalighat, which was very far from our
house. Mrs Chater took us at eight in the morning and brought
us back at three in the afternoon. We ate something there. I fed
the patients, sponged them, and so on. Mrs Chater often sent the
food for the inmates. Then her cook came and prepared things on
the premises. He was a Moslem; he became so attached to the
place that he stayed at night, and after some time worked only
there. He died still in harness. He had a deep devotion to Our
Lady and decorated her altar for her feast days.'

'Did you experience any opposition?'

'From where?'

'From people of the locality or other groups?'

I was told by Mother that there had been difficulties at the
beginning.

'Mother did not tell us anything. We did our work and then
returned to Creek Lane. We continued going there from th
new house. We shifted to the new novitiate only after some time.
I remained there and became a novice. Kalighat became our first
big work.'

'It was something quite distinctive. Before that you only had dispensaries and small schools as other religious institutes also have.'

'Yes, Kalighat was the result of Mother's faith and the prayers of all.'

'Truly it was Our Lady's gift to the Missionaries of Charity, that you might devote yourselves there to the glory of Jesus, her Son.'

The second floor at 14 Creek Lane was now full. Mother had taken every available room, and also the annexe. Applications from candidates came in increasing numbers. The works were developing and becoming more diversified. The Holy Spirit indicated that it was time to give up the friendliness and intimacy of the Upper Room, to 'launch into the deep', and to prepare to spread out the apostolic endeavours of the Sisters throughout the world.

Mother Teresa could repeat after St Paul, with full strength, and the Senior Sisters could gently echo her words: 'I have been through my initiation, and now I am ready for anything, anywhere. There is nothing I cannot master with the help of the One who gives me strength.' (*Phil. 4, 12–13*)

4. Pentecost

'When Pentecost day came around they heard what sounded like a powerful wind from heaven, the noise of which filled the entire house. . . . They were all filled with the Holy Spirit and began to speak foreign languages as the Spirit gave them the gift of speech.'

(Acts 2, 1–4)

In February 1953 Mother Teresa, her novices and postulants moved to larger premises, to what is still the Mother-house of the Congregation. Mother brought with her the picture of the Immaculate Heart of Mary which had stood above the altar in their chapel.

The spirit of Pentecost soon invaded the new house. Like the apostles, the Sisters were united in prayer around Mary the Mother of Jesus. Full of confidence, they rejoiced because the Lord is risen, has appeared to Peter and has shown himself alive to his disciples. Gloriously risen he now manifests his power to us.

God our Father who accepted the sacrifice of Christ, and raised him from the dead, had also rewarded the sacrifice of Mother Teresa and her Sisters. Their Institute and Constitutions had been approved by the Authorities of the Church. In April 1953, at the Cathedral of the Most Holy Rosary, the first group of Sisters took their first vows and Mother Teresa her final vows in the Congregation.

Now the Sisters had a house of their own to receive and train postulants and novices. The new house, at 54A Lower Circular Road stood some ten minutes from the parish church of St Teresa where Mother had opened a dispensary, and twenty minutes from the 'Cenacle' in the house of the Gomes family.

The Sisters were able to occupy a three-storeyed house which was part of a small complex of buildings erected around a courtyard. The Sisters erected a statue of Our Lady in a conspicuous place. Since Mother did not have the money to buy the property, Archbishop Périer advanced her the sum. By shouldering the risk he proved his sympathy and effective support for the Missionaries of Charity. The age of large generous donations had not yet arrived. The Sisters lived in the years of pure faith and uncertainty of the morrow, but Mother says that the thought of having to repay debts contracted in the name of Almighty God, never troubled her, it was for His glory and the service of His children.

When the house was bought for her, Mother objected: 'What shall we do with such a large house?' But the Lord God soon sent her postulants and novices to fill it.

Vocations came in increasing numbers. It was as at the beginning of the Church when the disciples rejoiced, seeing God's power call more and more members to be added to the glory of the Lord.

With more members they could expand and diversify their works of charity: visits to the slums, slum schools, dispensaries, home for the dying, soon a home for abandoned and crippled children, work among tuberculosis patients, work among leprosy patients, training for poor girls, adoption plans for orphaned children.

God's visible protection and the infusion of his Spirit filled them with optimism; they were a dynamic group, contagiously enthusiastic.

As at Pentecost, the Holy Spirit gave them a character of *universality*, as participates in the universal mission of the Church. Sisters from different parts of India, speaking various languages, came to join their ranks.

Support came from all sides: from the Archbishop of Calcutta and many priests; from the Chief Minister of West Bengal, and later from the Prime Minister of India; from scores of Indian friends – Christian and non-Christian – from groups of American and British ladies.

Charitable Agencies sent supplies of foodstuffs and medicines; the local and national press praised the work, whilst international reviews also became interested in the young Congregation.

Like the apostles, the Sisters are witnesses to Christ's death and resurrection and to His glorious exaltation in heaven; their lives, their works proclaim Him as the Lord, who, after redeeming mankind on the cross and rising up to a glorious life, has sent the Holy Spirit upon them. Through His power they perform their service to God and men. (*Acts 2, 22 ff*) The Sisters could also say:

'All of us are witnesses that God raised Jesus to life ... what you see and hear is the outpouring of that Spirit.'

They are witnesses to the nations. Many see it, and, perturbed by this fact, ask us: 'How can they go on with this life among the down-trodden?' The answer is:

'They do it by the power of Jesus.'

Like the first disciples of Jesus, the Sisters 'remained faithful to the teaching of the apostles, to the brotherhood, to the breaking of bread and to the prayers. They all lived together and owned everything in common. They shared their food gladly and generously; they praised God and were looked up to by everyone.' (*Acts, 2, 42–47*)

This 'brotherhood' or 'fellowship' implies a united purpose and also concern for the poorer members, so that everything is pooled in common; which shows perfect charity.

Thus, the young Missionaries of Charity relived the first years of the Christian Church, by their faith, by their optimism, their joy, strong in their belief that they belong to Jesus who sends them to bring to all men the Good News of God's love and redemption.

The Holy Spirit filled them with charity, an active charity manifesting itself in an unquenchable desire to help their neighbours to God.

The group was animated by a healthy enthusiasm, resulting from the belief that theirs was God's work and from the certainty that the Lord Himself had inspired and still animated their young Congregation. His protection was evident as they went forth, progressing in numbers.

We see among them the same happiness at the growth of their community that had possessed the members of the early Church: 'day by day the Lord added to their community'. It was his call; he supplied the grace. Mother repeated to them the words of Christ: 'I chose you, you did not choose Me.' It kept the young novices and soon the young professed in humility: the merit was not theirs, the call came from God. It gave them great confidence, for the Lord who calls also gives the grace necessary to obey His call.

Joy was manifested by their singing of hymns and canticles; by their prayer in common and in private. By the dedication they made of themselves daily to the Lord as they repeated together: 'Lord make me an instrument of your peace. . . .'

Yes, an instrument: I wish to be supple, obedient, docile in Your Hand. Mother put before them the three virtues she wished would characterize them: total surrender − trust − cheerfulness.

There were other similarities between the young Church and the young Institute which was now part of the great Catholic Church.

At the beginning of the Church, a man called Simon Magus was struck by the power the Apostles had of giving the Holy Spirit to the believers and by the extraordinary works they did; he asked them to give them that power, even for a consideration, which of course the Apostles did not do. Peter rebuked him, saying 'May your silver be lost for ever, and you with it, for thinking that money could buy what God gave for nothing.' In a similar way, the influence the Sisters acquired over people through the good works they performed by the grace of the Holy Spirit, and their example of brotherly love moved some Communist workers to approach them and ask them to share with them the secret of their attraction and power.

Mother told me: 'Communist workers in Calcutta, especially in the Entally area, want to know the secret of the Sisters' influence. Why do poor people listen to the Sisters and not to the Communists who promise them comfort on earth' There is no secret; the Sisters preach and practise love.

Some time later Mother told me: 'I met in Delhi an official of the Ministry of Relief and Rehabilitation who is very much impressed by our work. He gives us all the help he can. Now he has written to me, asking if I could train some of his officers. He would send a batch of some twenty to be trained by us for three months and would pay all their expenses. He hopes that thus they would imbibe our spirit and follow our methods. Do you think I should accept? And would you give them lectures if they came here? I cannot do the whole work myself.'

We discussed the matter. The gentleman seemed to be mistaken about the reason for the Sisters' success and influence on the people. He thought they had evolved some new technique and used some method not described in the textbooks of sociology. How could their approach to the people be assimilated and emulated? Other official agencies had also asked her how she succeeded in getting the confidence of the poor; why did people trust her; and what made her Sisters devote themselves to such an extent?

'Mother, I would suggest that you inform this gentleman that what activates your Sisters is their motivation, which cannot be passed on to professional people who do not believe in Christ. We can at most deal with ten persons at a time. Send them by batches of two to accompany your Sisters every morning, see how they work, and give them one or two talks in the evening. But they will not relish this programme. They cannot imitate your Sisters.'

I tried to draft a programme, and devise a system of motivation that might agree with the beliefs and feelings of the officials. Of course, if they had the spirit of devotedness, if they believed in a humanitarian cause, we could help them in some way. But without a firm belief in God and in man as God's child, in the dignity of every man, the poor, the lepers, the slow-witted, the abandoned, how could they enter into our spirit?

A week later we discussed the matter again. Mother informed the Officer in Delhi of the difficulties of the project and what we were prepared to do. Nothing came out of the proposal, as we had expected.

A cause of deep frustration and disappointment was the provision of Canon Law forbidding new Institutes to open houses outside the diocese during ten years after their inception. On that point the Archbishop was adamant: 'Mother, you may not start any house outside the diocese before ten years are completed.'

Mother felt an irresistible urge to go forward to spread, develop, occupy new territory, start new houses, new ventures. Her active temperament was coupled with an unquenched zeal. Needs were great, whilst time was short; why these delays?

This meant that between forty and fifty years of age, when a person's activity is normally at its peak, while she was burning with the desire to produce, to start new ventures, during those strong creative years, she was to sit still and wait.

She was told to concentrate on training her personnel, especially future superiors. She was to learn later the wisdom of the Church's law; ten years to build up a team and fill it with a new spirit, pattern it on the simplicity of the Gospel, and to mould women of character, capable of taking charge of new foundations, was not excessive.

Once Mother saw a chance of opening a house outside the diocese of Calcutta. The offer, the call even, came from Father Harrison, who had sent her many candidates from Chota Nagpur. As the parish priest of Mahuadan he had a house ready for Mother Teresa at Daltonganj in his parish, with a garden, a well, and all that the Sisters might need. He invited her to come and work there.

Mother asked Archbishop Périer for permission to accept this offer, but he could not grant this. Father Harrison was disappointed, but both from Mahuadan and from Noatoli, where he was moved, he sent girls to join the Missionaries of Charity in Calcutta; at times he sent as many as ten in one batch. He thus helped to give to the new Institute an all-India dimension and the possibility of opening houses in Hindi speaking areas.

The day the ten years probation period ended, Mother started houses in the archdioceses of Ranchi and Delhi and the diocese of Jhansi. Nothing would stop her now. Her pent-up energy and zeal poured themselves out with the full power the Spirit gave her.

In all fairness to the delay caused by the Church's prescription it should be said that when in 1976 she was asked:

'Mother, what is your greatest difficulty' she answered:

'Superiors, Father. To find suitable superiors and keep them zealous when they are in charge. Once they exercise authority, they may lose the sense of poverty and do things independently.' In fact, several of the perpetual professed who left were or had been superiors.

The Novitiate
When I was appointed confessor and spiritual director of the novices and the postulants, Mother asked me: 'Please, Father, do not interfere in the running of the house. You know, some

Fathers want me to change certain things. For instance, they tell me that the Sisters should have fans in the common room or in the chapel. I do not want them to have fans. The poor whom they are to serve have no fans. Most of the girls come from village homes where they had no fans. They should not be more comfortable here than at home. The same for the routine of the house. Please do not interfere.'

I told her 'Mother, I shall not interfere in material things; I have been appointed spiritual adviser; that is my province; I shall not go beyond that.' She trusted me, since she had asked the Archbishop to appoint me. We always had the best of relations. I respected her judgement, admired her zeal and spirit of faith, envied her humility and charity.

Mother had much experience of the spiritual life, its problems and requirements. She gave stimulating spiritual conferences to her Sisters, speaking four or even five times a day, to different groups.

The novices were 'hand tooled' receiving personal attention from Mother. When the number of new foundations started growing she had to leave the Mother-house more often, and the burden of forming the novices fell on the shoulders of Sister Agnes, the Mistress of novices, of Sister Frederick, her assistant, and of other Sisters, later put in charge of groups of novices.

When I started, there were about thirty-five novices and postulants. After a year or two there were fifty, later sixty-five, then eighty-five, then the number reached one hundred. It was wonderful to see how the Lord blessed the young Institute. Candidates arrived from various parts of India and also from abroad. Twice a year some novices took their vows; they were soon replaced by others. Larger numbers meant more work for the confessor. My weekly task started with a spiritual instruction; then there was a holy hour during which I began hearing confessions and the exercise went on, from three o'clock till five, six and seven p.m., as the number of novices increased. It even became necessary to devote two afternoons to them to have more time for the spiritual direction of the Sisters.

For some months the novitiate was shifted to a house on Park Street. But later the novices returned to the Mother-house and junior Sisters were lodged in the house in Park Street.

For many years I went every week to the Mother-house. No one ever brought me tea or anything else; there was a glass of water in the sacristy. I felt that was normal; since the Sisters did not take any refreshments, why should their confessor have a more comfortable life than theirs? The material side of life, creature comforts, seemed to count for nothing. I had been allowed to join an expedition, difficult and thrilling; hardships were part of the game, real practical poverty had to be experienced. I felt indeed grateful that the Sisters accepted me, who came from a more comfortable house, as a part of the team, and let me live their life for a while.

Now things have changed. The heroic days are over. More consideration is shown for the poor human body, aging and suffering. After a talk, the Sisters may request you to stay for a while and take some refreshments.

When of late, Mother saw me removing my shoes and walking on the cold cement floor, she came to me and insisted:

'Father, please keep your shoes on, otherwise you will catch cold.'

'But Mother, you walk barefooted, can I not do it also?'

'We are accustomed, Father, and you are not.'

This was like Paul writing to Timothy, the old fighter showing his concern for a fellow worker: 'Timothy, take a glass of wine; it will help your weak stomach.' To crown heroic detachment and the mortification of all human affections and desires, there is kindness and gentlenees.

The novices were very similar to the novices of other religious congregations. They exhibited the same desire for holiness, generosity in making sacrifices, eagerness to progress on the way to perfection. They belonged to the same race as their sisters, friends and neighbours who joined other Institutes, without knowing them very well.

But one sensed − or was it only imagination − a definite spiritual quality, that particular brand of enthusiasm, joy and submission to the guidance of the Holy Spirit, which are found specially in all new religious ventures relying on deep faith and trust in God.

The community lived in circumstances that brought it close to the original Pentecost. They could see God's hand in their foundation. They needed more faith in God's day to day protection than the well established Institutes; they needed more simplicity, the 'one step enough for me' process and progress, which brought its own reward: simplicity, trust, joy.

The few novices or Sisters with intellectual problems or complicated minds, those worried by the inadequacy of present political and social structures, did not persevere very long in the Institute. Partly on this account, and partly for reasons of the material conditions of life, the few foreign candidates and novices presented their confessor with as many problems as the Indian Sisters who were ten or fifteen times as numerous.

Obviously for a novice from Germany, the U.K. or Malta, climate and living conditions at the Mother-house were a challenge requiring an unusual dose of courage and self-denial. And so some went home. A fair number remained, went through the training and became excellent professed nuns. Indian novices hailing from comfortable homes and arriving with a university degree found the way of life no less uncomfortable, but could better foresee what their life would be than those who came to India for the first time.

I did my best to foster in the generous young recruits to the religious life, love for God and total surrender to his guidance, in a joyful offering of their service. Mother often came to listen to the instructions, sitting on the floor like the novices. When it was time for the sacrament of penance, she took her place among the Sisters.

Often Mother would come to the parlour, when confessions and adoration were over, to talk of spiritual matters and appraise me of the progress of the Institute and its works. The praise of God was always on her lips; she never complained of any hardship. We never disagreed or had any argument. She wanted a serious, solid spiritual formation to be given to her Sisters, and it was her responsibility to see that they received it.

It was good at times to hear a senior Sister remark: 'Mother doesn't see; she can't understand. . . .' They were fully obedient to their Superior, but showed mature judgement and ability to think for themselves, as also interest in the well-being and progress of the Congregation. These Sisters had to prepare themselves to shoulder responsibilities and take decisions – even if at times they would be blamed for them. A Superior must be able to decide for herself, after due consultation, and cannot be expected to be always right.

They had special problems. Food was one of them, but not in the manner we would have expected.

'At the Holy Family Hospital at Patna,' said Mother, 'the Superior told me: 'You must feed your Sisters well. They will have much work, and move among the sick in unhealthy localities; to resist disease they must be well fed.'

'And so the penance of the Sisters is to eat what they are given; they should not deprive themselves of what they need to be good workers. Their penance is not to choose, but to eat their portion and obey.'

This posed a problem for the spiritual director. Several times young novices asked 'What must I do? I cannot eat what is put on my plate. I have made frantic efforts to eat it and swallow it. They give me four chappattis, which is too much for me. What should I do?'

The rule was for their good; they required strong nourishment, being out much of the day, visiting homes, nursing the sick, often performing hard work.

Once the Sisters discussed together the matter of food. So many people are going hungry; should the Sisters not reduce their own consumption? They might perhaps do with only three chappattis per head for one of their meals? The question was considered by those in charge. Mother argued from the standpoint of her Sisters' health. Some nuns in other congregations and also in her own suffered from tuberculosis. She did not want this to happen to her Sisters if it could be prevented.

A few days later, one of the Sisters announced smilingly: 'The question of the chappattis has been decided. Instead of four, we are to get five per head and eat them with obedience.'

From the start, Mother Teresa received much encouragement from Dr B. C. Roy, the eminent statesman who for many years presided over the fortunes of West Bengal as its Chief Minister. A giant of a man, in more senses than one, who seldom appeared at public functions or political rallies, he administered what Nehru once called 'the problem State' with remarkable ability, competence and assiduity.

To meet him, Mother, at the beginning of her career, went at six o'clock in the morning to the free medical consultation he gave every day for an hour at his residence. A medical practitioner of repute who attended on celebrities like Gandhi, Nehru and the King of Nepal, he kept in touch with the medical art by giving daily free consultations to those who approached him. A few persons seized this occasiono to present him with their petitions.

The scene was worth seeing. Admitted by his secretary, the patients sit on benches or chairs along the walls of the hall near the entrance. Doctor Roy goes round, looks at a patient's face, his eyes, his tongue, puts his stethoscope to his chest, feels his stomach and asks a few questions. He quickly sizes up the situation, and has an extraordinary gift of diagnosis; prescribes, advises, passes on to the next patient. The whole thing is done in public, without wasting a moment. All feel members of a great family and trust the famous doctor.

Mother does not come to consult him about her health but to put forward the case of some poor people who need help or redress. Could she obtain a water connection for a slum? Electric light for another? The Chief Minister signs a memo addressed to the Officer-in-charge. It is as good as an order. 'Please enquire into the matter.' – 'Please look into this complaint.' After a few such requests, he has noticed the little nun who cares only for others; and they are not people of influence, but always poor.

Soon Doctor Roy tells Mother to call on him at his office. Later he will tell her that she need not make an appointment but just come in whilst he is at his desk, where he works most of the day. Thus began a real partnership, with the two of them trusting one another, working together for the good of the poor. He a man of immense experience, wielding powers in the whole State; she a fledgling in the work of uplift and organization, but strong with the power of her divine Lord. Doctor Roy was a member of the Brahmo Samaj, a believer in one God, excluding all image worship, deeply respecting Jesus Christ and his teachings.

Soon it was he who urged Mother on.

'Dr Roy wants me to expand Sishu Bhavan,' he told Mother. He said 'Bigger, Mother, bigger. We have so much misery here. Our problems are enormous.'

Another time, she said; 'Dr Roy asked me if we would take charge of the government-run Vagrancy Homes in Calcutta.'

'How many are there?' I asked.

'Four. He told me "I trust you. I shall not ask you for any accounts. You will have no financial problem. Just put your nuns in charge of these houses." But I had to refuse. I do not have enough Sisters. I do not want to put too many of them into the same work. There is too much to be done.'

It was true at the time. But also I suspect that she did not want to take over other people's work. In this case she would certainly have made enemies among the officials, which she always tried to avoid. 'Dr Roy never gave me money,' said Mother, 'but his protection, his recommendation to an official department was worth much more than money.'

At times they differed, even strongly disagreed. Both of them had too much character to bow down easily. Mother argued for the Leper Asylum Dr Roy wanted to remove from Calcutta's neighbourhood, since the town was expanding. I think he was right. He saw the good of the local population; Mother fought for the lepers who were finally moved to some other place. At least she got them a decent home.

Doctor Roy paid Mother this greatest tribute on his eightieth birthday. On that memorable anniversary, he went to work as usual at his office. Reporters called on him and enquired 'How do you feel on your eightieth birthday, still being Chief Minister?' He did not answer 'I thought of Mahatma Gandhi, with whom I fought for Independence, or of Jawaharlal Nehru, my friend and India's Prime Minister,' or make any other personal recollection. He said simply; 'As I climbed the steps leading to my office, I thought of Mother Teresa who devotes her life to the welfare of the poor'. The next day it was front-page news in the papers. No one could any longer ignore the humble nun in a blue-bordered white saree, who saw Christ in the poorest of the poor.

5. Service of Love

'I was hungry and you gave me food; I was thirsty and you gave me drink; I was naked and you clothed me; I was sick or in prison and you visited me. Whenever you did this to the least of my brothers you did it to me.'

(*Matt. 25, 35–40*)

'In the choice of the works of the apostolate,' said Mother, 'there was neither planning nor preconceived ideas. We started work as needs and opportunities arose. God showed what he wanted us to do.'

So they began schools for the poorest children of the slums, dispensaries, Sunday schools to teach the children prayer, craft schools that the poor might learn how to earn a living.

The first big work of the Missionaries of Charity was the Kalighat Home for the Dying, began whilst they still lived at 14 Creek Lane. Michael Gomes remembers vividly how the search for a place to house the dying destitute started.

'One day, we saw alongside the Campbell Hospital (now the Nilratan Sarkar Hospital) close to our house, a man dying on the roadside. Mother enquired; the hospital authorities could not accommodate him. We went to a chemist to get some medicine for him; when we returned with the medicines, the man was dead on the street. Mother did not hide her feelings. "They look after a dog or a cat better than a fellow-man," she said. They would not allow that to happen to their pets.' She went to the Commissioner of Police to complain about this state of affairs. That was the origin of the Kalighat Home for the Dying.

'Are you positive on this point? The story as written by journalists is usually that Mother saw a woman on a pavement, full of sores, with maggots in her wounds. She stayed with her the whole night, keeping the rats away from her, and in the morning the woman died in her arms.'

'That is not the truth. First, Mother never stayed out at night whilst she was in our house, not a single night. And Kalighat Home was started from our house. I was with her when the man died on the street, in front of the hospital where he had not been admitted.'

Such occurrences were not exceptional; Mother must have seen more than once destitute persons lying on the pavements, sick or at death's door. She herself narrated that one day she came across a dying woman on a pavement close to a hospital, who had festering wounds and was lying on a piece of sackcloth. Mother succeeded in getting the woman admitted into a hospital. Something had to be done about it; she moved heaven and earth to this end. It is no exaggeration to say that she moved heaven since the young Missionaries of Charity went for several weeks to pray to the Shrine of our Lady of Fatima. That she moved earth at the same time is evident: she approached the Commissioner of Police who was most happy to help her to find a place and remove this blot on Calcutta's reputation. Mother also approached Dr Ahmed, the Health Officer of the Corporation, for a place to receive the more hopeless cases, the persons dying on the street; 'Give me at least a room' she pleaded.

Calcutta has excellent doctors and very good hospitals and nursing homes. There are free beds in the hospitals. But the city's population was swollen by an influx of refugees at the time of partition, and of villagers in periods of scarcity. Thus the number of beds to receive the huge number of sick people proves insufficient. Naturally the hospitals prefer to admit patients who have a hope of recovery rather than those dying of old age or malnutrition.

Mother Teresa offered to take care of the homeless destitute, sick, starving, those dying on the streets. She needed a house, but had neither the funds nor credit. An empty wing in a rest house for pilgrims was found; it was attached to the famous temple of the Goddess Kali in South Calcutta. Mother Teresa was allowed to use the building 'provisionally'. From this day one of the headaches of the Police Commissioner was removed. The city's social-minded citizens felt relieved. No one could write any more to newspapers lamenting the state of affairs in a city in which some people were allowed to die without a roof, without food, without medical care.

The help of the police proved useful in another way. Mother knew that to open a house where food and shelter can be had for the asking in Calcutta is to invite an endless rush of candidates. Hence it was decided that only persons brought by the police would be admitted.

The home, or hospital, Mother called Nirmal Hriday: the Immaculate Heart of Mary. It can accommodate about sixty men and sixty women inmates in two wards. Over thirty thousand destitute have been admitted. Half of them died in the home, decently, peacefully, prayerfully. The Sisters and their co-workers washed them, fed them, consoled them, cheered their spirits, prepared their souls so that, rejoicing in the hope of a happy life in heaven, each one of them might 'die with God'.

Some opposition was to be expected. The Home stood on sacred temple ground. The Kalighat temple, which enjoys tremendous popularity and a considerable income, is served by four hundred priests. Recalling the first days of that new venture, Michael Gomes says: 'At first there was opposition. A group of young people said that Mother was coming to convert people to Christianity here in the centre of Hinduism.

'A political leader told the young men that he would get her out. He came to see the place. Mother offered to take him round. He answered he could see things by himself and needed nobody to take him round. As he went round, he saw the miserable emaciated bodies, the sunken eyes, the Sisters washing the sores, feeding the hungry, distributing medicines, giving injections, all in a gentle, loving manner.

'When he came out he met some of the young men. He told them: "I promised I would get that woman out of here, and I shall. But, listen to me, I shall not get her out of this place before you get your mothers and sisters to do the work these nuns are doing. In the temple you have a Goddess in stone; here you have a living Goddess." That was the end of the opposition organized by this group.

'The Sisters went on caring for sick bodies and drooping spirits with a holy unconcern for outside murmurs. They had God's approval, that was enough for them, But their charity could not fail to impress many visitors. It happened one day that a priest of the temple, who suffered from tuberculosis, sought and found a welcoming haven in the Sisters' hospital. The service rendered to one of theirs made a deep impression on several of his brethren.'

Mother told me at the time:

'One morning, as I was washing the patients, a priest of the temple entered the ward. He prostrated himself before me, touched my feet with his.hands which he then laid on his head. Then he stood up and said "For thirty years I have served the Goddess Kali in her temple. Now, the Goddess Mother stands before me in human form. It is my privilege today to worship the Mother present to my eyes." '

Later, Mother said:

'The question of the Kalighat Home for the Dying is to come up at a Corporation meeting. Some people object to destitute persons being brought there to die, on religious grounds; they say it defiles the place.'

'Mother, you know how these things are decided. It will be one item on a crowded agenda. The chairman will announce; Item No. 67, Mother Teresa runs a Home for the Dying in a building belonging to the Kalighat temple. Are there any objections? Should she be allowed to continue or asked to vacate the place? So, Mother, you need an influential Councillor to fight your battle and another one to support him. Then you will be allowed to remain until a more suitable place can be found – which means that you stay for good.'

And so it was. Some days later Mother was happy to report:

'At the Corporation meeting only two members objected on religious grounds. Nobody offered to provide a better place. So the resolution was passed that we are allowed to remain at Kalighat until a suitable place is found to accommodate the dying. My friends told me: "Do not worry. The objection has been duly registered and put into cold storage." '

The Calcutta Corporation supported the Kalighat Home for the Dying with a monthly subsidy. One day Mother informed the Corporation that she was no more in need of their help, and the subsidy was stopped.

A new house, Prem Dan, was given to the Missionaries of Charity by I.C.I. in 1975. After the inauguration ceremony, I asked Mother: 'Will you shift Nirmal Hriday of Kalighat to Prem Dan? She replied: 'I shall never give up Kalighat, unless they eject me forcibly.' Soon she had filled the new house with needy persons. In Calcutta there was no difficulty in doing this. As for Kalighat's Nirmal Hriday, the Home for the Dying has become a hallowed place. Its very ground has been made holy by the countless acts of love, of devotion, of those who nurse the sick with limitless patience; a place sanctified by the total surrender to God of so many who from there left earth for heaven – a sacred place which all believers enter as respectfully and silently as they enter a temple – because as Mother put it tersely: 'God is here.'

Prem Dan is used as a home for those who have a better chance to recover and survive; they can be kept there longer if need be, until they are back on their feet. It serves also for other classes of needy persons. Kalighat remains as a home for the dying destitute who have little chance of surviving.

With the inception of the Kalighat Home for the Dying it was hoped that destitute persons would no longer die on the Calcutta pavements. Well, not quite. It was impossible to completely stop this scandal in a city officially numbering one hundred thousand pavement dwellers with no other abode, and unofficially a good few thousands more.

The children's homes
The care of orphans, of abandoned or crippled children, has always been a preferred work of religious institutes.

Most Catholic centres in India and other countries have one or more orphanages, and facilities to receive orphans in their boarding schools.

Jesus himself gave us the example of love for children, who are naturally trustful, simple, loving.

'Jesus then took a little child, set him in front of the Twelve, put His arms around him, and said to them, "Anyone who welcomes one of these children in My name, welcomes Me; and anyone who welcomes Me welcomes not Me but the one who sent Me." ' (*Mar 9, 36–37*)

Later, adds St Mark, 'people were bringing little children to Him, for Him to touch them. The disciples turned them away, but when Jesus saw this he was indignant and said to them, "Let the little children come to Me; do not stop them; for it is to such as these that the kingdom of God belongs. I tell you solemnly, anyone who does not welcome the kingdom of God like a child will never enter it." Then he put His arms around them, laid His hands on them and gave His blessings.' (Mark 10, 13–16)

So it is a duty and a source of joy to minister to the children Jesus loves, and to serve Our Lord in the person of the child.

'How did the first Children's Home start, Brother Michael?'

'Well,' he answered, 'Mother had been looking for some time for a house where she could receive and care for unwanted children. One day as she came home she told me: "Mrs X. asked me to pray for her husband that he may stop drinking. He drinks a full bottle of whisky every day, and the market price of imported whisky is ninety rupees per bottle. Well, if Mr X can pay ninety rupees per day for his drinks, I can pay five hundred rupees a month for that house on Lower Circular Road which is to let. I shall take it and start a children's home." '

I remarked to a Sister: 'I cannot see the logic of arguing from the cost of a bottle of whisky.'

'No,' she replied, 'you men go by logic. We women follow our intuition, and we are more often right than you.'

'Here, you are correct, Sister. Your intuition is based on love and it is more often right than our dry reasonings.'

This was another case requiring trust in God. Was the work really needed for His glory? If so, His Providence would see that the means did not fail. He would take care of the work started for Him.

And so the house was rented.

There were so many problems, so many needs: unwanted children, unwedded mothers who could not have their baby at home nor take him back there, orphans, crippled children, mentally retarded children to be looked after.

Catholic charity was already active in the field: the Franciscan Missionaries of Mary had a creche where the police would bring abandoned infants. There were other orphanages. But the needs of Calcutta seemed inexhaustible.

And so Sishu Bhavan, the Children's Home, was started.

Abandoned infants were brought by the police and by private parties. Some of them were found in dustbins – not many, let us be fair. Some were left at the doors of convents. Others were brought by people who did not want to reveal their names.

One infant was found lying before the altar of the Blessed Sacrament in my own Church of the Sacred Heart, by the sacristan when he opened the church doors in the morning. The child was crying. The sacristan fetched some milk, made the child drink it, and soon the baby fell asleep, happy. The police were informed, and the baby duly taken to Mother Teresa's Sishu Bhavan. He was adopted by a Catholic family and is doing well.

Some infants are sickly or crippled. Some die soon, but many recover, become strong and healthy.

In 1976 a picture of Mother Teresa fondling a smiling child appeared in Calcutta papers. She had just accepted to take charge of five babies abandoned by their mothers in the maternity ward of one of Calcutta's main hospitals. Later it was announced that the authorities of the hospital had another hundred and two babies or infants who had been similarly left behind by their mothers after their delivery. Mother Teresa declared that she would take charge of all the abandoned babies.

After showing such willingness to help the civil and medical authorities to solve their human problems, it is not astonishing that she obtained their full co-operation for schemes for the betterment of the lot of the poor. She assumes the duty of charity whether or not she has the means. God will provide, she says.

In most localities where the Missionaries of Charity are established they receive unwanted or crippled children.

Sishu Bhavan in Calcutta has been for many years the centre of varied activities. Apart from receiving abandoned children and cripples, it is a place where some unwedded mothers stay whilst expecting their child. There also are stored food supplies to be distributed free to the poor.

Walking past the house on an afternoon, you may see fifty or eighty women with small children, waiting for the distribution to start. No distribution means for some of them no food for that day.

There are hazards and dangers in the free distribution of food.

'Mother has been seen,' says Michael Gomes, 'pushing back with unexpected physical strength a whole line of women rushing forward to receive rations.'

1. Mother Teresa in prayer. A church in Germany 1976.
In the background stands Miss Jacqueline de Decker.

2. Treating a leper on the roadside from the back of a mobile clinic.

God Bless you

M. Teresa MC

4. Novices at prayer.

5. Professed sisters—brides of Christ.

The Sisters also have experienced some unpleasant moments when serving the poor. At Sishu Bhavan one day there was no stock to distribute rations to card-holders. The agency supplying the Sisters for this project had stopped sending foodstuffs to Calcutta to divert them to another area they considered more urgently in need. The Sisters were unable to give anything to the crowd standing at the gate. Some people manifested their anger by shouts and even tried to set fire to the house, whilst they abused the Sisters and accused them of robbing their food for their own benefit. But the police and the Fire Brigade appeared on the scene in a matter of minutes, thus saving the house, the children and the crippled living there.

The Sisters had other moments of danger. Close to Calcutta two Sisters were confronted by a group of lepers, displeased with the arrangements which had been made for them, who locked them inside their van, and started pushing it towards a canal. Fortunately another Sister called the police, who arrived in time to save the two Sisters from an enforced bath or worse. Such things are part of the work of charity.

The Sisters narrate their disagreeable adventures during the evening recreation.

Mother defends her policy.

'At a meeting in Bangalore', recalled Mother, 'a Sister attacked me for distributing food freely to the poor. She said that I spoiled the poor by my acts of charity. I answered her: "If I spoil the poor, you and the other Sisters spoil the rich in your select schools. And Almighty God is the first to spoil us. Does He not give freely to all of us? Then why should I not imitate my God and give freely to the poor what I have received freely" They had nothing to answer.'

Mother could have quoted St Paul's words to Timothy, 'God who, out of his riches, gives us all we need for our happiness.' (*Tim. 16, 17*)

Work among lepers

Mother Teresa was led to start working for the welfare of leprosy patients in an indirect way. It was again the force of circumstances, or to look at it with the eyes of faith, the Hand of God working through human instruments, that brought her into that particular field of charitable work.

For many years the Sisters of Charity had run a leper asylum at Gobra, on the outskirts of Calcutta. In this leper asylum lived one hundred and fifty inmates, well cared for by the Sisters. It happened that plans for the development of Calcutta covered the area of Gobra. The large compound including the houses occupied by the lepers was to be expropriated, to allow the locality to be developed in a planned manner. People would never accept housing close to an area they thought infected by germs of the dreaded disease. And so it was decided to take over the property occupied by the Sisters; the lepers would have to find some other shelter.

Mother Teresa, informed of the project, was indignant. What would happen to the poor sufferers? Where would they go? Who would provide them with a suitable place to live? Mother took up their cause and went to plead it before the Chief Minister. Dr Roy, her patron, listened to her; but he would not reverse the decision. Calcutta had to expand. The city was bursting at the seams; the housing problem defied solution. Suitable lodgings were to be provided for hundreds of thousands of people. A development project in an area contiguous to the city could not be stopped on account of a hundred and fifty lepers living in a colony with little contact with the outside world. They would be displaced.

At least Mother obtained that the lepers would not be removed before some alternative accommodation had been found for them.

The Chief Minister offered a place in Bankura District. Mother, not finding the place suitable, complained to him: 'You told me you would give the lepers a good place to live in, but the place you offer us lacks a good supply of water, which is essential for leprosy patients.'

Thus Mother became active in leper work. She started a Leprosy Collection Day. Collection tins were taken around Calcutta for Mother Teresa's Leprosy Fund, bearing the words: 'Touch the Leper with your kindness.' Money poured in from all sources.

'At the time of our Leprosy Day,' said the Sister in charge of finance, 'we just throw the cheques into a basket, so numerous are they.

'One can only admire Calcutta people, so anxious to help the lepers. Leper asylums and villages are needed in India, but they are not enough.'

'You missionaries do not seem to understand,' a high Government Official told me several years ago, 'that our problems are of a magnitude the developed countries do not suspect, certainly do not experience. Take the case of leprosy; in a leprosarium you can look after two or three hundred patients. But we have two million sufferers from leprosy in this country, out of the world figure of four million. So you do not offer any workable solution to the problem; you do not even scratch the surface. We need an approach to the masses, a method that will reach hundreds of thousands of people.'

He was right: and this could now be done. Dr Hemeryckx, a Belgian who had worked for several years in Central Africa, had come to India, and had introduced a method of treating lepers on a mass scale. He favoured leaving them at home, from where they could regularly attend mobile clinics. In this manner he reached a considerable number of sufferers; many who were ashamed of showing themselves would come to the clinic. Parents could remain with their children, at least when they were not dangerously contagious.

It may be mentioned that before leaving India Dr Hemeryckx was received by the then Prime Minister, Mr Nehru, who thanked him for his services and for showing the way to mass treatment of leprosy.

Mother Teresa went to see the centre established by Dr Hemeryckx, near Madras. Then she offered to collaborate with government agencies and doctors. And so the Sisters started medical assistance to the lepers in a big way. This work became one of their main activities in India.

There would still be a need for some institutions or villages where infectious cases, or lepers with no one to look after them, or unable to take care of themselves, could be received.

To this end Shanti Nagar, the 'Town of Peace', was founded as a colony and rehabilitation centre for lepers in the district of Burdwan.

The same grace that blessed Father Damian, a modern hero of

charity, may bless those who today devote their whole life to the apostolate among lepers.

Two or three Sisters at different times confided to me 'I think I have contracted the disease. What must I do?' They were still young and slightly afraid, though ready to accept; that may have been all God asked from them.

The doctors are rightly cautious, and give the Sisters and Brothers who work with them strict instructions.

'The doctor forbade me to touch some patients because they are actively contagious. What should I do?' a Sister asked.

'Obey the doctor, Sister. You should not run any unreasonable risk of contracting the disease. You must take all the precautions ordered by the doctor. Thus you will be able to serve the patients better and for a longer time.'

But these devoted brides of Christ know that if the Institute assumes this apostolate on a large scale, some Sisters may experience what it means to be attacked by leprosy. Thus a religious may be able to give witness to the lepers in a specially convincing manner, by carrying a leper's cross behind the Saviour. Nuns of other Congregations have suffered and are still suffering from the disease they caught whilst ministering to leprosy patients. And they bless the Lord for this grace.

Mother Teresa knows that the poor need belief in God more than other people. The poor need hope, they need God. Those who would deprive them of hope, their only solace, commit a crime against humanity. If these others wish to be self-sufficient, not to tend to an infinity of truth, goodness and beauty, let them be self-sufficient alone — but let them not rob others of their hope.

Mother and her Sisters bring the poor hope, eternal hope and belief in God's goodness. The Sisters, young and educated, bend over them, wash their sores, smile to them and cheer them whilst never uttering a rough word or losing their temper. Why do they treat unknown people as true brothers and sisters? And they do it, not for two or three years, but for a whole life time. Simple people are neither fools nor easily fooled; they are not blinded by sophiscation; their simple minds discover the truth; those women miiror God's love. Thus through their sufferings they come to God.

6. Witnesses of Christ to the Nations

'You will receive power when the Holy Spirit comes on you, and then you will be my witnesses not only in Jerusalem, but throughout Judaea and Samaria, and indeed to the ends of the earth.'

(*Acts 1, 8*)

Ten years had elapsed since the Congregation of the Missionaries of Charity had been approved by Rome. The Sisters had been trained. Together Mother and the Sisters had prayed, worked, studied. The Spirit of God had lavished His gifts on them.

Conforming to their Lord Jesus Christ, they lived His life, shared His passion for the salvation of men. They had heard from Him secret words of friendship, they had learnt His intimate thoughts and desires. Like the Apostles they had the promise of Jesus, that he would send them the Holy Spirit, and His command to make Him known to the world.

'I shall send you the Spirit of truth; he will be my witness. And you too will be witnesses, because you have been with me from the beginning.' (*John 15, 26–27*)

The Sisters were ready to go out and bear witness to their Lord. Calcutta was their Jerusalem, the starting point of their apostolate, which had its roots there; but the tree was to spread its branches and bear fruit in many parts of the world.

They had the same purpose as the Apostles: to bear witness to the Father's love for men, who loved us so much that He sent His only begotten Son; to Christ's love for us, who died for our sins, that we might become the Father's children of adoption, in and through Him; to the love of the Spirit who pours into our hearts His choice gifts; love for God and for all men.

Their Constitutions told them to bring the Good News to the poor, to the poorest of the poor. This had been given as a sign of the coming of the Saviour; a sign that the Kingdom of God had

67

appeared among the people: 'the Good News is preached to the poor.'

The third phase of the life of the young Congregation was beginning. Mother did not waste a single day. Some bishops, aware of the Sisters' work in Calcutta, wished to obtain their services; they requested Mother Teresa to establish houses in their dioceses.

India

The Sisters went first to Ranchi, then to Delhi, then to Jhansi. The Ranchi or Chota Nagpur Mission had previously belonged to the Calcutta Archdiocese. The Church now fully established in the region was the most lively young church in North India. From Ranchi Archdiocese many candidates had joined the Missionaries of Charity. It was only fair that the archdiocese should be rewarded for its generous gift of personnel. At the Archbishop's invitation Mother opened a house in Ranchi.

Next came Delhi. Archbishop Joseph Fernandes had known Mother Teresa during his many years in Calcutta as Vicar General and Auxiliary Bishop. Archbishop Knox, the Pro-Nuncio, was also interested in Mother Teresa's work. Since the number of local Catholics in Delhi was small, to strengthen the Catholic presence in the capital, the policy was to bring religious congregations from other parts of the country, to open schools and institutions that would benefit the people.

Mother found it useful to be close to the centre of government, to the ministries, to the offices of agencies providing help for social and charitable work. So she went to Delhi, which was said to be the fastest growing city in India, receiving as it did one hundred thousand immigrants a year.

Ranchi, Delhi, Jhansi became for the Sisters new fields of apostolate and the sign that the Lord wanted them to spread out through the whole of India. The work pattern for the new houses had been tested in Calcutta. The Sisters would bring the dying destitute to a haven of rest; they would take care of orphans, of crippled children. They would teach people to pray to God, organize Sunday schools, prepare children for the reception of the sacraments; they would visit the slums, teach poor girls crafts and prepare them for marriage and family life.

Mother was only too happy to start work in the capital. She soon received help from many quarters. Mr Cuttat, the Swiss Ambassador to New Delhi, an eminent scholar and devoted Catholic, was instrumental in obtaining his country's financial help for the foundation of a children's home.

Mother, who was generally considered to be a social worker interested mostly in bodies, in health and material well-being, took advantage of this occasion to show the Prime Minister that her primary concern was the spiritual welfare of the poor. A few days after this memorable occasion, she reported:

'The inauguration of our new Children's Home in Delhi was attended by Mr Nehru and the Swiss Ambassador. When the Prime Minister arrived, accompanied by Mr Krishna Menon, I said to them 'Let us first go and salute the Master of the house.'

'Then I led them into the chapel where I knelt in prayer. Mr Nehru, standing at the back, made a *pranam* with folded hands. Mr Krishna Menon went up to the altar to read an inscription and asked me its meaning. Then we went to sit on the grounds for the inaugural ceremony. The children garlanded the Prime Minister and offered him a spiritual bouquet. I explained that it meant that they had offered prayers and small sacrifices to God to obtain His graces for the Prime Minister. Then I asked 'Sir, shall I tell you about our work?' Mr Nehru answered me 'No, Mother, you need not tell me about your work, I know about it. That is why I have come.'

This simple, absolute word of praise was the finest acknowledgement of the services rendered to the poor of the country by Mother Teresa and the Missionaries of Charity. It came from the man who for seventeen years had spoken the mind of the people of India.

Bombay

Mother wished to open a house in Bombay, where she hoped to find good vocations among the large, fervent, well-educated Catholic community. This manufacturing city possessed many mills whose labour force lived in tenements, *chawls*; there would be plenty of work for the Sisters.

Bombay prides itself on being the premier city of India, the main centre of the country's trade and banking, the glamour city of cinema; it has a wonderful marine drive, rich villas and palatial mansions on Cumbala Hill. It is also the Indian town with the largest number of Catholics and the See of the first Indian Cardinal. The city has developed a large network of Catholic schools, colleges, social and charitable institutions.

'I have received invitations from several bishops,' Mother said, one, 'but no call has come from Bombay, though the Cardinal knows what we do.'

'Well, Mother,' I replied, 'you should not wait to be called. The Cardinal is an important person, a Prince of the Church; do not wait till he requests you. Offer him your services, he will accept, you will see.

Two weeks later, Mother was radiant:

'Father, I wrote to the Cardinal, just two lines to ask him if he would welcome us in his archdiocese. By return of post he answered that he would be very pleased for us to work in Bombay.'

Soon she was there, and Cardinal Gracias provided a house for the Sisters.

'He is very kind,' she said. 'He told me: I shall give you one of my best priests as a spiritual director for your Sisters.'

Mother soon returned to Bombay with a batch of Sisters and the work started.

At first, the people of Bombay frowned on Mother Teresa. She provoked their displeasure by remarking bluntly at the end of a short visit of inspection of the town: 'The slums of Bombay are worse even than the slums of Calcutta.'

The Press was indignant, the people shocked by this quasi-blasphemy. Of course, Calcutta was known as dirty, rowdy, unkempt; but Bombay was the pride of India. How could this nun, after a few days in their city, pass such a sweeping and injurious judgement?

Mother silenced her critics. It did not take her long to size up a slum. She knew the criteria: light, water, garbage disposal, ventilation, air pollution, proximity to the market. In a matter of minutes she saw, weighed, compared, judged.

'The Calcutta slums', she replied, 'are mainly single-storied: fresh air enters into the dwellings, there is less congestion, more space for children to move about. Bombay is an island – its *chawls*, built close to the factories on scarce and expensive land, are three or four-storied; water has to be carried up several narrow flights of steps; ventilation is poor, the children have no open spaces for fresh air and games.'

The press soon réalised that Mother knew more about poverty than they did. Criticism gave way to respect. Still, the atmosphere would not be as friendly as that of Calcutta, at least for some time.

In November 1963 I was in Bombay to preach retreats to the diocesan clergy at the Bandra Retreat House. One morning, looking at the papers on the news-stands, a title struck my eyes: 'Woman found dead on Queen's Road'. A photo of the corpse which lay on the road for several hours was also published. The daily went on to deplore the shame of a city where a person could die on the street and remain there for hours before anyone came to remove the body.

During the retreats I spoke to the priests of apostolic charity and mentioned the wonderful work Mother Teresa's Missionaries of Charity were doing. At least in Calcutta the papers no longer reported cases of neglected destitute dying on the streets. The Church of Christ was showing to all what service of the Lord in his Brethren meant. The priests were visibly impressed. One of them came to me afterwards and said, 'I am in charge of a large parish. We have a house that is not used. Perhaps the Cardinal might allow me to offer it to Mother Teresa to open a home for the dying.'

Two weeks later, Mother said happily: 'Thank you, Father, you have helped us to obtain a house in Bombay. A parish priest has offered us a property where we can open a house for the dying.' It was quickly established, and became, as in Calcutta, one of the Sisters' most characteristic works.

The next year, the Eucharistic Congress took place in Bombay. The President of India, Dr Radhakrishnan, was there to receive the Holy Father. Pope Paul VI drove in triumph through the Bombay streets in a white Lincoln open car presented to him by an American benefactor. The popular enthusiasm cannot be described. Not thousands, but truly millions of people lined the fourteen mile route from the airport to the congress grounds; never in any country had such a crowd gathered for a reception to a Pope or for an Eucharistic Congress. In this very religious country, people belonging to all religions wanted to have a 'darshan' or spiritual glimpse of the great Holy Man of Christendom. They wished to see, listen to, come in contact with the most influential religious leader in the world. Wherever the Pope went, a huge mass of humanity surged forward to receive his blessings. Even among the organizers, no one had expected such demonstrations of respect and friendship.

The Pope had expressed a wish to visit some of the poorer quarters of Bombay, to meet at least a few slum-dwellers. It should not be said that he had come only for the well-to-do, in the land that had produced Mahatma Gandhi, the Father of the Nation, who travelled third class and journeyed extensively on foot. The Pope wished to show his interest in the poor and to approach them in their own houses. But the Civil Authorities quite rightly would not allow the Holy Father to move among the slum dwellers, followed by hundreds of reporters and photographers, of journalists and cameramen, who would have exposed to the eyes of the world the least attractive side of the country's life.

The Congress organizers solved the problem by taking the Pope to visit some charitable institutions. The Pope mixed freely with the children of an orphanage and delighted them by sharing their breakfast of buns and fruit; he showed his appreciation of the devoted work of those running this and similar houses.

Before leaving, the Pope donated his open white Lincoln car to Mother Teresa to be sold for her works. The occasion was acclaimed in the world press, which displayed photos of the Pope and Mother Teresa. Some of Mother's friends decided to raffle the car for her; they sold raffle tickets at one hundred rupees each, with the one single prize the car donated by the Pope. The sale of the tickets brought about four hundred and fifty thousand rupees for her charities. A non-Christian was the lucky winner.

Venezuela

Mother appeared to be thrilled as she said:

'We have been invited by a Bishop to go to Venezuela. Is that not wonderful?'

'Splendid, Mother. Where? Caracas?'

'No, not Caracas, a smaller place, not far away. This will be our first foundation in Latin America.'

We surveyed the great opportunities offered by the great continent which comprises nearly one half of the baptized Catholics of the whole world. There the Sisters would have real spiritual work, as much as they could cope with, among the millions of baptized Catholics who hardly practised their religion for lack of priests and nuns to instruct them and nourish their faith.

'Mother, you must make a big effort in that direction. Do accept every offer made by the bishops. Much can still be saved, preserved for Christ, but speed is essential. The Church loses adherents in South America every day, due to lack of spiritual care.'

Mother agreed: 'I shall send my best Sisters to start the new house.' She hoped to get vocations from the country itself, so that from Venezuela they could move into other South American countries. Soon, Mother was on her way to Venezuela. She would see her Sisters established, meet the Bishop, obtain help and collaboration from authorities and lay friends. In July 1965 the first foundation outside India was started. Mother came back delighted. The people were friendly, the Sisters had been well received.

This was only a start. Two more houses were established later in Venezuela. Then one in Lima, Peru. But the spread of the Congregation was slower than we had hoped. There was not the same enthusiasm as in India, though ten years later, at the beginning of 1975, she had requests from several bishops and made plans to open houses in Colombia, Bolivia and Brazil. The bishops were to discover what great help the Missionaries of Charity would bring them for the spiritual uplift of their poor.

Sister Dorothy, who had been Superior there and returned to Calcutta, reported: 'We were like deacons there. Generally the people are baptized; but many have never seen a priest or a Sister, due to the scarcity of priests and nuns in the country. So many people know nothing about Jesus. We had to teach them. We took communion to the sick. Eventually we administered Baptism. The poor live in *favelas*. We live in their midst. At first I could not understand them, as they only speak Spanish. But within two months I could manage. I learnt the language with the children's help. And some local girls joined us.'

'In Latin America,' sid another Sister, 'we do much spiritual work. We do all that a priest here does, except hearing confession and consecrating the holy Eucharist. It is really wonderful work.'

Still, we had to acknowledge that the Missionaries of Charity had not spread there as fast as in India, as fast as we had hoped. Bishops and priests may not have realized their potentialities for the life of the Church. Their spirit and method, their personal, loving approach are well adapted to the needs of the downtrodden and spiritually neglected poor of Latin America.

The Sisters do not come with intellectual notions of conscientization, they do not worry about changing structures, or about opposing policies in the church. They go to the poor with the charity of Christ, with open hearts and hands. They speak to them a language they can understand. Their action is contagious and challenging – they obtain co-operation with the people among whom they work for their work. They bring a sense of respectability, of decency and self-respect to people who did not know them, did not realize that they count in God's eyes, have value for Christ.

Rome

Mother was radiant as she greeted me:

'Father, we have been invited to go to Rome. The Pope himself asked us to open a house there.'

A rare note of victory rang in her voice.

To Rome at the Holy Father's request; what an honour for a young Congregation. To Rome, like Peter and Paul. To her strong ecclesial sense Rome meant much; it was the heart and centre of Christianity, the See of the successor of St Peter, the Vicar of Christ on earth.

In a voice more subdued and thoughtful, Mother added: 'There is much work to be done, much poverty in Rome's suburbs; many people are in need of the Sacraments; many children do not learn their prayers; and there is much anti-God influence and propaganda. But we shall be close to the Holy Father; we shall work in the shadow of St Peter's.'

Mother did not need to reflect on this invitation nor to compare it with other possibilities. This was a sacred duty imposed by the Holy Father, who had befriended the community openly in Bombay. The Sisters would get ready as soon as possible, as soon as arrangements could be made.

To Rome the Sisters went, thrilled and joyful. They needed to show that they were not afraid of shouldering the cross of Christ. Romans knew more about virtue and vice, through centuries of experience, than any other city existing today.

To Rome had come countless saints – more were buried in Rome than in any other town; in Rome saints were officially proclaimed by the Catholic Church. But the Romans do not wait for any official proclamation to establish the fact of holiness. They discovered holiness behind appearances. When Benedict Labre, the Frenchman, who had come to Rome and for years lived in the porches of churches, neither washing much nor changing his clothes, eating whatever people gave him, passing his days in prayer to God, died, immediately the rumour spread through the whole of Rome: ' "Il Santo" is dead.'

When the Sisters were well established and fully at work Mother spoke with special warmth of her Roman community.

'The Sisters are in a slum area; they live among the poor. They go to the market to beg for them. Everywhere they are well received. "The Indian Sisters" as the people call them, even though several of them are European, get chicken every day; at the market, the stall-holders give them, free, the less good portions which hotels and restaurants do not want.

'The Sisters teach the children their prayers and prepare them for the Sacraments. They visit the sick and old people in their houses.'

Thus the good work of the Sisters, backed by the prayers of many co-workers and of the sick and suffering, produces acts of love for God in Rome.

'The good works are links forming a chain of love around the world,' as Mother had prophetically written to her Belgian friend during the first days in the Upper Room.

To increase their Roman presence, Mother shifted the novitiate she had established in London to Rome. It was to receive the candidates from Europe and America, and also some from Africa. The postulants remained in London.

Australia

In June 1969, after holy Mass, a tall man introduced himself to me and asked: 'Could you do me a favour; I would like to meet Mother Teresa.' I introduced Mr McGee to Mother Teresa, who welcomed him.

He opened his briefcase, and pulled out a large bundle of notes, which he pushed across the table saying:

'Mother, this is to begin with.' Mother Teresa took the bundle, made no comment and started talking of the possibilities of apostolate among the poor in Australia.

Mother had paid her first visit to Australia in April 1969 at the invitation of Bishop Warren of Broken Hill, who wished her to start work among the aboriginals. So Mother and Mr McGee now made plans for this work. Knowing Ministers and officials as he did, he could help to get the required authorisation for the Sisters to establish themselves in his motherland.

John J. McGee's first visit to Mother laid the foundation for a most fruitful apostolate in Australia. He became a faithful friend of the Institute.

In the middle of September 1969, Mother went to Bourke with five Sisters to start their first foundation in Australia and to work among the aboriginals.

Mother was invited to Melbourne by Archbishop Knox who had known her in India. Some objected; in a country as rich as Australia, enjoying an advanced social legislation, surely there would be no work for her. There were no slums, no destitute, no people dying on the streets. Mother retorted: 'What, no work for us? And what about the habitual offenders when they come out of prison, what about their wives and children? What about the drug addicts, the alcoholics, are they not God's children in need of guidance and help?'

On the 26th April 1970 Mother Teresa and five Sisters left Madras by plane for Melbourne. They reached there the next day. Sister Monica was the Superior. The very first day, Mother, accompanied by the Provincial of the Loreto Sisters, found a house, and entered it. With the help of co-workers and students they cleaned the place. They started work immediately.

Sister Monica directed the Sisters to go on to the streets and discover the needy people. The Sisters came back, saying there were none on the streets. 'Then knock at the doors of houses' said the Superior. They did so, asking if there were any old person or persons in need in the house. At first people found them strange in their Indian dress. Also, they would not believe that they were nuns, wearing those strange habits. But the Sisters, by their kindness, gradually won their trust. They prepared the people for the sacraments and for the consecration of the families to the Sacred Heart of Jesus. They were helped and encouraged by some priests, and later by civic leaders who reported cases to them.

Their first big venture was to be a Home for the Rehabilitation of Alcoholics and Drug Addicts. In 1972 a plot of land was purchased in Greenvale and building started on the Convent and the Rehabilitation Centre.

Mother was invited to attend the Eucharistic Congress at Melbourne. There were three speakers only at the main session and Mother Teresa was one of them. She spoke on her favourite topic: her mission to serve Christ in the poor, to see the suffering Lord in his brethren in pain. Her words and her conviction moved the hearts of her listeners.

The Convent was blessed by Cardinal Knox in February, 1973.

Before departing in April, Mother Teresa left her Sisters with advice they remembered: 'I do not want you to perform miracles with unkindness, rather I prefer you to make mistakes in kindness.'

The Middle East

Mother was happy:

'Father, we are going to Jordan, in the Middle East; close to the birthplace of our Lord. The Sisters will be walking where our Lord walked and preached and worked miracles. Where our Lord died out of love for men. Is it not wonderful'

Yes, this was truly good news. The Middle East was the cradle of the three great monotheistic religions: Judaism, Christianity and Islam, the religions followed by more than half the believers of the world. They were born in that rugged country, where man senses God's might and holiness. Abraham, Moses, were men of faith, as Mother was a woman of faith.

Christianity, starting from Jerusalem, had spread over the world in ever widening concentric circles; now it returned to its starting point through these nuns from the East.

In July 1970 the Sisters started work in Jordan.

In March 1973 they settled in the Gaza strip to alleviate the sufferings of the hundreds of thousands of refugees from Palestine. They were thus on both sides of the political frontiers.

Some time later, Mother expressed her happiness at spreading farther into the Middle East:

'We are going to Yemen, Father. We have been invited by the Prime Minister himself. After six centuries of Christian absence, with no priests in the country, no Mass, no Sacraments, there will be Mass again for the Sisters. After six hundred years! Is that not wonderful?

'The Prime Minister promised to do everything for the Sisters. He said, they should have no fear. He holds himself personally responsible for their safety. He guarantees that no one will cause them harm. His Government will give them every needed help and support. As a sign of good will be presented me with a "Sword of Honour" ' She laughed: 'A sword to me!'

'Yes, Mother, they are a martial race and good fighters, that is why they present you with a sword of honour.'

I thought too late of 'the double edge sword' that is the Word of God. That one the Sisters would have to wield – whilst bringing to all the peace so much esteemed in the East, the Peace of Christ.

Jordan
At the Mother-house, February 1976.

'Where do you come from, Sister?'

'I arrived from Jordan a few days ago. I am from Kerala, from the diocese of Trichur.'

'One of the best in the world for priestly and religious vocations. There is a wonderful spirit in your country. But now tell me about Jordan.'

'I was five years in Jordan, Father. I was sent there immediately after my first vows, at the end of the novitiate.'

'Did you come into contact with ministers or high officials of the Government?'

'No, we met only the poor.'

Here all glamour is absent, any feeling of being important and acknowledged as such. There is only the daily, humble, hard work, the contact with the very poor.

'What are your works there, Sister? Do you follow the same pattern as in Calcutta?'

'First, we work among the Catholics. Jordan has eight per cent Christians out of which two per cent are Catholics. We find them, teach the catechism, prepare the children for their first Communion. Then we visit the poor families, both Christian and Moslem. We give medicine to the sick. We have a home for the "unwanted", old people, mentally retarded, handicapped, abandoned children.

'We also go to the Jordan in a van given us by Caritas, and there we visit the sick.'

'What reception do you get?'

'The Moslems are quite friendly. They call us *Hajis*, because we wear white as they do when they go on pilgrimage to Mecca.'

'Do the women go to Mecca?'

'Yes, some go on pilgrimage. Of course the Moslems do not know what it is to be a nun; so they do not understand our kind of life. But they respect us.'

'At the beginning, how did you solve the language problem?'

'We had to learn Arabic. We were six Sisters; there are only five whilst I am absent. First we had a paid teacher. Then some local Sisters in Amman kindly volunteered to teach us.'

'Did you find the language difficult?'

'No. It is much easier than some of our Indian languages, say Tamil or Hindi. It has hardly any grammar. We learnt enough Arabic to be understood by the people.

'Our house is some distance from the capital. We hope to open a house in Amman itself soon. Then things will be easier; we shall not have to move about as much as we do now.

'You must one day have a Middle East Province or Region; can you hope to find vocations there?'

'Hardly; unless it be from among the girls we educate.'

'Did you receive the spiritual help you required?

'There are very few Catholic priests in Jordan. In Amman, only two or three ministered to us. We could not find a priest for our annual retreat. Finally, we joined other groups of Sisters, and made our retreat with them.'

'And books? Do you have the spiritual books you need?'

'No, we are very short of religious books, especially good meditation books. Do send us some.'

'Yes, I shall try to help you. As you know, our Catholic Charitable Agencies provide food for the bodies of men, but less sustenance for their souls. That strikes many people in the much more spiritually-inclined East.'

'Your benefactors should also remember the spiritual needs of the Sisters.'

Yemen
At the Mother-house, February, 1976.

Two tertians have just arrived one is from Kerala, one from Ranchi district. They have been in Yemen more than two years.

'What works do you do there, Sister?'

'We have a home for the unwanted, with 120 inmates. We have a handicraft class with a hundred students who learn sewing and various crafts. We have a dispensary.

'You should see the long queue of patients who come, often from far away. There have been up to six hundred in a single day. Now a hospital has been built close by, so we have fewer, but still two or three hundred a day. Sister Gertrude attends to them. They have a tremendous faith in her.'

'She was one of the first to join Mother.'

'Yes, the second, I think. She came from what is now Bangladesh. She is a doctor. She is very spiritual and has a wonderful way with the people. People come even from the Communist part of Yemen to consult her.'

'How are the officials? Do they help?'

'The Prime Minister is very sympathetic. He helps us in all ways. The Government officials also. They built our house. They asked us to give them a plan of a Catholic church, as they did not know how it should be built. They wanted to put up a church for our use. But we told them that we would use a room of our house as a chapel. If we used a big building, some might take it as a provocation. Many people are still very anti-Christian.

'The Prime Minister and the officials send us supplies. Twice a week they send us a pair of goats, so that the children and poor people may have good meat. They help us in every way. We had to open a second house, and they ask for a third.'

'Where are you established?'

'In Hodeida.'

'Can you go to the Communist part of Yemen?'

'People cross from one side to the other without difficulty. But we cannot go to Amman.'

'What about the work among the lepers?'

'It is wonderfully successful. At first I was frightened to go to the leper village. Have you seen Ben Hur? It was just like that. As in the days of Our Lord. We could hardly enter the village, because of the accumulated filth and rubbish blocking the way. We had to wade knee-deep through the filth. Then there were no houses. Only some sort of caverns cut out in the hills, into which people ran when they saw us approach. The women, completely covered by their *burkas*, hid themselves. Children ran for safety. The men were dishevelled, the children filthy. We called and waved to them, but they would not come. Slowly Sister Gertrude succeeded in establishing a few contacts. Gradually the people became accustomed to us and showed friendliness.

'For me, to go through the filth to reach the village proved an awful experience. But we had to change the ways of life of these people. With the help of Government officials we cleared the way, and removed the rubbish. Houses were built, gardens developed, flowers grown. We taught the women and children cleanliness, introduced some crafts for those able to work, to bring them respectability and make them feel useful.'

'Do you manage to prevent the children from contracting the disease?'

'When we arrived, nearly all of them were affected. Now, mainly through cleanliness and by isolating some cases, we hope to be able to protect the children.

'But the village has completely changed. Within two years, from a filthy spot it has become a garden village. The children sing the whole time. It is a real joy to go there. They love us and sing for joy.'

We remained silent for a while, thanking the Lord for the wonderful things He had deigned to do through His humble servants.

Seeing the spiritual results of their labours, the Sisters felt truly enthusiastic about their vocation. They did not mention the hardships of life, the harsh climate, the difficulty of adapting oneself to a difficult tradition, culture, language, attitude to life. They did it all for Jesus.

'Mother mentioned that a number of girls from the country wanted to join you; what do you do about it?'

'Yes. You know, their parents arrange their marriage with boys they have never met. Some of the girls do not like that. Then, after coming in contact with us and seeing our religious life, they want to live like us for God and for their neighbour. Several girls told their parents they would not marry, but follow our way of life. They would become Christians if they could and enter religious life. But of course we have to be cautious, for there might be a strong reaction from the families, endangering our presence and work. So we let them come during the day and work with us. For the night we send them home. They prove most useful to us, for there is so much to do we could never achieve it alone. We are only five Sisters.'

'Do you have a priest to minister to you spiritually? I believe there are White Sisters and a couple of White Fathers.'

'Yes, the White Sisters reached Yemen a little before us. They have opened a very good hospital. Now there is also a third congregation. Three White Fathers reside in the country; one, who is a doctor, works in the hospital. Now we have Mass every day; we did not have Mass daily at the beginning.'

'Do you hope to return to Yemen at the end of this year of tertianship?'

'Most certainly. I long to be back there and work again among the lepers and hear the children sing and praise God.'

India: Coimbatore

This is a town in South India, which developed in an orderly fashion, where some fifty middle size mills, most of them well laid out, give employment to the local people. The place looks prosperous and confident. The Bishop says he is invited and welcomed everywhere, at every function organized by different groups. An open society, unbigoted, forward looking. Also, a centre of excellent coffee.

The Franciscan Missionaries of Mary, whose host I am, run three well patronized high schools. Their very well kept orphanage is a model of devoted and efficient medical care. The diocesan congregation of Sisters, fully active, also looks after the poor. This town does not seem to be a place where Mother Teresa's Sisters are specially needed. Still, the Bishop has invited them.

On the road I meet two Sisters in blue-bordered saree.

'Father, you do not recognize us?'

'Of course, I do. Can I come to say Mass for you?'

'Yes, the day after tomorrow. We shall come to fetch you.'

Two Sisters arrive at six a.m. We walk down the road.

'We shall take a bus. Let us wait here,' proposes one of the Sisters.

'But there is no bus stop,' I object.

'Never mind,' she replies. 'The drivers all know us and they stop anywhere to take us.'

And so it happens. A bus arrives, they wave to the driver. He stops to take us. He does not do this for anyone else on the way.

This makes me reflect: so these recently arrived Sisters have already struck the mind of the non-Christian drivers. They are not from the district. do not speak the language fluently, have no big institution; yet already it is accepted: they are for us, they work for us. The Sisters have established a personal relationship with these simple folk. They are closer to the people than other religious, who also spend their lives in work of charity.

'It is the same at the market,' says the Sister. 'Everyone knows us and helps us.'

We reach their house. In a verandah I see the emaciated faces of four persons lying on cots or mats, each covered with a blanket.

'They are close to death,' says a Sister.

Against the chapel wall stands the crucifix, and the call of Jesus dying is written: "I thirst!" I offer a Mass for the Sisters and a few children. I also tell them of the work God deigned to do through Mother Teresa, and of His love the Sisters must bring to the world.

After Mass, a Sister tells me: one of the old persons has died during the Mass.

We say a prayer, asking God to receive his soul in His love.

The Sisters then explained how they were gradually settling down, evaluating needs, finding out the possibilities for action. One typical problem; water was not easily available in sufficient quantity. It rains only five or six days a year in the area. For the children and the dispensary a good supply of fresh, clean water was absolutely needed and had to be found.

On my return to Calcutta, I told Mother that I had been to the new house at Coimbatore, and that this district gave many vocations to the Church.

'Yes, Father, that is why we opened a house there,' she answered.

Three years later one of the Sisters I had met at Coimbatore could report that their hopes were being fulfilled.

Already five novices and ten postulants had come from the district, who would be able later to work in places where there were few or no Catholics.

India: Mariapolli

'Mother, you are opening a house at Mariapolli?'

'Yes, Father. It is not a town and there are no slums, but to work in the villages is not against our Constitutions.'

She sounded apologetic.

'There are so many poor people in the area. We are also established at Takdah, which is not a town, and in Andhra Pradesh in some villages. We shall start with a dispensary; then see what the poor need most.'

On the Feast of Our Lady, Mother accompanied the first batch of Sisters to Mary's village, 'Mariapolli' in Bengali. Father Gabric had three buildings ready for them in the new mission station he had just started. It was truly pioneering work. For the sisters a chapel, a dispensary, a convent built with bricks were ready. The priest would live in a mud hut, for the present.

There was a nice teak wood *almirah*.

'Will this be for our medicines' asked the Sister in charge.

'No, Sister,' replied Father Gabric, 'this is for your library of spiritual books, to protect them from the white ants.'

Father Gabric, who hails from Yugoslavia, is a priest after Mother's heart. He is the kind of person to whom Mother can refuse nothing; spiritual, austere, dynamic, habitually on the move,

Father Gabric is the kind of person to whom Mother can refuse nothing; spiritual, austere, dynamic, habitually on the move, always ready to give something, visiting the villages, knowing every one of his parishioners and all the officials of the region. He exhorts his Catholics to pray and fast. He is often seen moving about with his beads in his hand. This helped him when he called on a Bishop in Australia.

'I went to visit a Bishop in Australia,' he recalled, 'and as I entered the room he was addressing a clergy meeting. "Look, Fathers," he exclaimed, "here is an old missionary from India who still believes in saying the Rosary. See, he prays to Our Lady even as he goes about." After that the bishop was ready to sign any cheque to pay for my new mission station.'

The Sisters started by opening a dispensary which proved to be an immediate success. Two hundred patients attended it daily. After a few weeks there were five hundred, and on some days even close to one thousand. People said: 'We come for the Sisters' prayers more than for medicine.'

Expansion goes on with increased momentum, in a cheerful, optimistic manner. The dynamic spirit of Pentecost continues to animate the Missionaries of Charity. New foundations were at first founded three a year, then five a year, and reached the number of twelve a year at the time of the Silver Jubilee.

'I wish to put seven or eight Sisters in each house,' confided Mother. 'This helps to keep up a cheerful spirit. Variety is good; more work can also be taken up.'

The new constitutions stipulate that each house should have at least six Sisters. In practice the initial number may be reduced to five or even four Sisters. Once needs have been estimated, activities can be diversified and expanded.

The geographical diffusion, helped by modern facilities, is probably unparalleled in the history of religious institutes. Starting from Calcutta, as their Jerusalem, the sisters went to five, ten, twenty different countries. They will soon be in fifty countries, and the novices who join now may one day be thrilled to count on the map one hundred cotntries where their society is at work for the glory of God. They will be happy, but not astonished; expansion is a fact of life for them. Often they have seen on the notice board: pray for our Sisters who leave tomorrow to open a house in Peru, Tanzania, Trinidad, Papua, Fiji.

A year after the Jubilee, even a book of five hundred pages could not describe adequately the genesis, preparation, establishment and first developments of all the new foundations. The few mentioned here indicate the main areas of development and tell of a few typical foundations in which the sisters work, and show God's hand guiding the Foundress and her Sisters.

In October 1976 a large map of the world was placed at the foot of the Crucifix standing in the staircase of the Mother-house, showing the various places where the members of the Congregation work for the poorest of the poor. Mother's dream has been realized; her Sisters form a chain of love for Christ and men, truly encircling the world.

7. In His Footsteps

'Take me for your model as I take Christ': St Paul's advice to the Corinthians.

First witness

'Sister Dorothy, you were one of the first to join Mother, you have known her well, what would you say is her main virtue? What struck you most in Mother's character?'

She thought for a while, and answered unhesitatingly:

'Her faith.'

'Sister, I would say exactly the same. The rock on which she has built her Institute and her whole organization is her faith in God. She is a woman of faith. She deserves the praise Elizabeth, moved by the Holy Spirit, bestowed on the Blessed Virgin Mary: "Happy are you because you believed." '

Like Abraham, the man of faith, Mother committed herself fully to God, accepted obedience to His order; sacrificed all she had, her religious congregation, her security, to put herself blindly in God's hands, not knowing what her fate would be. For her obedience in faith, God rewarded her as He promised to reward Abraham, saying:

'Because you have done this, I will shower blessings on you, I will make your descendants as many as the stars of heaven and the grains of sand on the seashore.' (*Gen. 22, 17*)

Her posterity on earth will be great, her posterity in heaven will be innumerable: the Sisters who came to her and all their spiritual children, those they helped 'to die with God', the children and adults they taught to know and love God.

Mother's faith and trust in God were never found wanting, being always alive and active.

'I take our Lord at his word,' she likes to say.

His word she finds in the Gospel, which she respects and obeys

as the inspired Word of God. 'Our Lord said it' is for her a final
argument. Thus she shows her faith in His person, His power,
His concern for her.

When Jesus said 'It is written', the argument was final; so
Mother says 'Jesus said', and holds fast to His word.

Second witness

'Father Van Exem, ynu have helped Mother from the very start;
tell me, what struck you most in her?'

'Besides her littleness, her trust in God.'

'Yes, the words of the Prophet Isaiah have proved fully true in
her case; "Those who trust in the Lord will renew their strength.
They will soar as with eagles' wings." ' (*Is. 40, 31*)

Her spiritual strength has gone on increasing with the years,
whilst her physical forces were renewed in a remarkable manner,
notwithstanding a hard life, repeated journeys on foot and by
train, lack of sleep, fever, trials, the care of a thousand Sisters.

Truly, she can say 'God has never let me down; my trust in
Him has never been misplaced.'

Yes, God knows his own and takes good care of them.

Once as we were talking in the small parlour, I said:

'Mother, you remember what our Lord told St Catherine of
Siena: "Take care of me and I shall take care of you." Well, you
have taken good care of Jesus and he has taken good care of you.'

'If it is for God's glory, Father, he will give us the means.'

She practices perfectly the advice of Jesus in the Sermon on the
Mount: 'Do not fret and worry about tomorrow. Your Father
knows what you need. If he feeds the sparrows, will he not much
more willingly give you good things if you ask him for them?'

Mother does not plan ahead; she allows God to guide her and
show what he wants her to do.

Her littleness, her sense of nothingness, strikes all who approach her and work with her. Perhaps it can be said that it
follows on her faith and trust in God.

She echoes the great mystics speaking of God and themselves as
'the Double Abyss', God's abyss of greatness, majesty and power,
man's abyss of littleness, misery and weakness.

By herself she can do nothing, but with Him she has power.
Power because she is His instrument. Her sense of being God's

instrument is extremely acute. Repeatedly she has said quite spontaneously:

'I am nothing. He is all. I do nothing of my own. He does it.'

One day, in 1975, she took a small pencil, about five cen-
timetres long and holding it between her thumb and index
finger, she said:

'See, that is what I am, God's pencil. A tiny bit of pencil with
which he writes what he likes.'

Third witness

'Brother Michael, you have seen Mother at close quarters, tell me
what struck you most in her character?'

'Two things I found remarkable in her, first her activity, then
her smallness. Her activity is amazing. While others talk, she
works. While others put questions, she solves problems. She has a
sense of the real, of the urgent. She sees a need and fills it on the
spot. An extremely practical person, she can take trouble to get
things done.

'Then her littleness. She feels so humble, so insignificant in the
hand of God. That is why it does not trouble her to be continually in the news, as she is now. She returns the glory to our Lord.
All the good she does she attributes to Him."

Her activity, her dynamism are of an exceptional richness and
intensity. All her projects started to fill a need she had found. A
man dies before a hospital, on the street: she seeks and opens a
house for the dying. She sees abandoned children, she starts her
Sishu Bhavan. A colony of lepers is expropriated, she goes into
leprosy work in a big way. There is a famine somewhere, there
are refugees to be looked after, immediately she arrives there
with her personnel. She has a scheme, a programme; she
organizes relief, begs for supplies, distributes help. Whether it be
during the Bihar famine, the Bengal famine, the flight of nine or
ten million refugees from Bangladesh, or later the earthquake in
Guatemala, she is prepared to help. She must open a house in
Papua because the people are very poor and the Bishop has no
money – never mind, she will find the means.

She trains boys of the slums to make very simple pieces of furniture and sell them in the market. The Calcutta streets are

littered in places with green cocoanut shells, she will organize people to gather them and make ropes our of the fibres. She has heard of an organization that rehabilitates lepers, trains them for some useful work; she too will open a house for that purpose.

She works fast; she is ready in a matter of weeks or months, not the years which some other religious societies may take to discuss conditions before opening new houses.

Essentially active by temperament, Mother Teresa cannot understand the long sessions at meetings where nothing or little happens.

'I was at a meeting of Superiors General in Europe,' she said. 'They talked only of changing the structures of society, organizing things in a different way. It all came to nothing; it did not do something for the poor, or preach Christ to those without religion, to those totally ignorant of God. I was happy when it was all over. They had insisted on my going there, but I felt like a fish out of water.'

Fourth witness

Brother Andrew, on his return from Saigon, stopped at Hazaribagh to meet the Australian Jesuits. I asked him:

'Brother Andrew, you have worked several years with Mother Teresa. You were caught by her ideal and you have successfully established the Missionary Brothers of Charity; may I ask you what impressed you most in Mother, during your long association with her?'

He remained thoughtful for a while. Then he answered:

'I suppose it is her single-mindedness. She has only one purpose.

'Mother also has a sense of humour; I think no one can be a Catholic if he takes himself too seriously. We must be aware of our inadequacy, our weakness, our nothingness before God.

'Mother works hard,' he continued. 'She sleeps little. Not more than two or three hours each night. I think she goes on writing letters till one or two in the morning. She always gets up at half past four.'

'Thank you, I shall remember that and try to imitate her singlemindedness.' Yes, she has one idea, one consuming passion. When we talk it is usually of Jesus and of 'the work'; for her the work is all to the glory of her Lord; she cares for nothing else.

Spiritually Mother Teresa resembles St Paul. Like Paul she is conscious of having been chosen by God the Father to work for the glory of Christ; to this end she founded her Society.

She has St Paul's passionate love for Christ and the Gospel. Like him she is Christ-intoxicated, entirely surrendered to Jesus and completely taken over by Him. With St Paul she can affirm 'Christ lives in me'. This presence of Christ acting in their souls has become for them a fact of experience. The truth, believed in faith, that by grace we become partakers of the divinity of Christ, who lives in the soul consecrated to Him, has become a matter of experience.

'Christ acts in me; he acts through me; he inspires me, directs me as his instrument.'

'I do nothing,' Mother likes to repeat. 'He does it all.'

When she speaks to non-Christians, *He* means God; when to Catholics, *He* means Jesus, to us she usually says Jesus, more intimate, more personal than the word Christ and showing her attachment to the person of Jesus. She likes to repeat that all is due to God who acts through her, inspires and sustains her. Thus she accepts no credit for any good effected through her. With St Paul, she can affirm without boasting: 'I live no more of my own life; Christ lives in me.' She knows it is not her weak frame, her limited capacity which turned the little headmistress of an obscure high school into the Superior General of a rapidly expanding religious congregation, and a world organizer of charitable works, hailed by the world press, praised by Pope and bishops, presidents and cabinet ministers.

Mother Terera mirrors St Paul in her faith, her reliance on God, her burning activity.

She shares his zeal, fearlessness, restlessness.

Both say, 'Preach only Christ and Christ crucified,' both are ready to suffer with him for the progress of the Church. Both are urged on by one thought and one passion; 'Christ crucified and risen'.

As St Paul says 'I rejoice in my suffering', so Mother asserts: 'We are happy to do this work'.

St Paul's vision embraced the whole world; he wished to proclaim the Gospel as far as possible. Mother from the start wished for a universal society that would work in every country, building a chain of love around the world. She has travelled more extensively than any religious founder ever before. She has opened houses in every continent, and sends her Sisters to as many countries as possible.

St Paul advises 'Treat everyone with equal kindness; never be condescending, but make real friends with the poor.' (*Rom. 12, 16*) Mother echoes: 'The poor make us the honour of allowing us to serve them.'

Like St Paul, Mother is shocked that Christ was not received by his own and is not received in the modern world. 'When I see how the poor remain neglected and unrecognized all around us,' she says, 'I understand the sadness of Christ at not being accepted by His own. Today those who ignore or reject the poor, ignore or reject Christ.'

When addressing the rich, Mother follows St Paul's advice to Timothy: 'Tell them that they are to do good, and be rich in good works, to be generous and willing to share – thus they will save up riches for the future if they want to make sure of the only real life.' (*Tim. 6, 18–19*)

And to the poor she says: 'Be satisfied with your condition, seek the better things, those that do not perish, are not eaten by moth or by rust, seek the Kingdom of God.'

To those completely surrendered to Him, Christ sends His Spirit in abundance; and the divine Spirit, says St Paul, brings them: 'love, joy, peace, patience, goodness, trustfulness, gentleness and self-control.' (*Col. 5, 22*) What a shower of wonderful gifts the Holy Spirit brings us. Love for God and men: true divine love animates those in whom the Spirit of love dwells. From love, joy blossoms as God, perfect bliss, brings joy to the soul in which He lives. Peace and harmony follow – we are united to God and friendly to all men. Joy and peace produce serenity, confidence that all God does is well done and that what He sends is for our greater good; as Mother tells her Sisters: 'Be happy, God loves you, especially when the work you do for Him is hard'.

Gentleness should lie in our relations with men, seeing in all of them God's image; kindness to all, treating them as we would Christ.

This requires self-control, since the spirit of Christ is opposed to the spirit of the world. And so St Paul adds 'You cannot belong to Christ unless you crucify all self-indulgent passions and desires.' (Col. 5, 24). Crucify; a harsh word – nail to the cross your selfishness, your vanity, your sensuality.

I found Mother habitually smiling, kind and increasingly serene, as the years went by. No doubt, the Spirit at times pours spiritual joy in her soul. But she has paid, she still pays the price of the souls she wants to save with Christ. The Spirit pours love, joy and peace into our hearts proportionately to our emptying ourselves of all self-indulgence, vanity, anger, ambition, and to our willingness to shoulder the cross of Christ. This is the price we must pay for spiritual happiness.

The Eucharist is the centre of the spiritual life of the Missionaries of Charity. The Eucharist as sacrifice, as food, as presence. In the Eucharist the Sisters find the strength, the inspiration and consolation that make their life both possible and meaningful.

With Christ they offer themselves as victims of the sacrifice of redemption to glorify God the Father. In Christ, received as a spiritual food, they find the strength to devote themselves unceasingly to all sufferers. To Christ, present in their midst, they come for advice, light, consolation. They keep Him company in his dereliction, quench His thirst for love.

The Cross of Christ and the words: 'I thirst' face the Sisters as they enter the chapel – Jesus calls them, asks for their love, their service, their attention. They go down on their knees to adore Him, and then stay with their Lord, whether they are consoled or not; often they will feel like dry, parched land; they will suffer, as their Lord did at Gethsemane or on Calvary. 'I thirst,' says Jesus, and they understand His pleading: if they do not allay their beloved Lord's thirst, who will?

He is the Master, the Lord, the Friend, the Bridegroom, the divine Spouse to whom every one of them belongs body and soul.

They start the day by coming to the chapel for morning prayers, followed by meditation and Holy Mass. In the afternoon, the Sisters remain a whole hour in adoration of the Blessed Sacrament.

'I have no difficulty in believing in the real presence of our Lord in the Blessed Eucharist,' said Mother.

'Neither do most priests have any difficulty in that respect, Mother. What really tests our faith is the slow progress of the faith in Christ, the slow progress of His Church, the huge amount of sin and unbelief that remains in the world after nineteen centuries of redemptive grace, of the presence of Christ, of the heroic holiness of countless saints.'

Christ affirmed that He was present in the Eucharist when He said: 'Take and eat, this is my Body that will be given up for you; take and drink of this chalice of my blood that will be shed for you; do this in memory of me.'

The Fathers of the Church unanimously teach the reality of the presence of Christ. The Council of Trent declares most forcefully: 'Christ is present truly, really and substantially in the Eucharist.'

'Why then,' asked Mother, 'do some young priests shake the belief of our people by saying that, after the Mass, there is no real Presence in the Tabernacle? What do they teach them in some seminaries, nowadays? A newly ordained priest was sent here to give an instruction to the Sisters. I was present. The priest laughed at a number of our traditional beliefs; he said there was no need to genuflect before the Blessed Sacrament when you come to the chapel outside the time of Mass, for the presence of Christ was limited to the time of Mass and Communion. He also attacked the idea of religious obedience and ridiculed our traditional devotions. He spoke in that vein for a whole hour. When he had finished I led him to the door, thanked him and told him he need not come here any more.

'Then I returned to the hall and told the Sisters: "You have just heard what a young priest without experience said; they are his ideas and those of a small group. Now I shall tell you what is the traditional teaching of the Church." And for one hour I refuted all he had said.

'Mother, you did well. The Second Vatican Council reiterated the Christian belief, both Catholic and Orthodox, that Christ remains present under the Eucharistic species after the Mass, and that Christians should worship Him and visit their Lord present in the Eucharist in our churches and chapels.'

Mother firmly believes in the teaching of the Church, as entrusted by Jesus Christ to the supreme Magisterium: the Pope, and the Bishops united to him.

She obeys the precept of St Paul who said:

'You must live your whole life according to the Christ you have received – Jesus the Lord; you must be rooted in him and built on him and held firm by the faith you have been taught, and full of thanksgiving. Make sure that no one traps you and deprives you of your freedom by some second-hand, empty, rational philosophy based on the principles of this world instead of on Christ.' (Col. 2, 6–8)

Mother strongly believes that the Sacraments give us God's grace. They also indicate the proximity of Christ, who today acts in the world. The Gospel of St John, 'the spiritual Gospel' advocates worship in spirit and truth, giving little importance to structures and external rites, yet proves to be the most 'sacramental' of the four Gospels. Similarly, Mother's independent outlook and her dislike for structures do not affect her belief in the efficacy of the Sacraments instituted by Christ, nor her desire that as many as possible be helped to receive them.

This conviction fits in perfectly with her strong sense of instrumentality. We are God's instruments of sanctification for our brethren, whilst the Sacraments give grace, instruments used by Christ. She has also a peasant's respect for nature and matter which makes it easy for her to accept the signs established by Christ as signs of grace that all men can understand.

Mother strongly believes in the need for and efficacy of baptism; Christ told the apostles: 'Go and baptize in the name of the Father and of the Son and of the Holy Spirit.' For anyone who believes in God and his dispensation, baptism is neither a luxury, nor an optional practice.

'Father,' she said, 'I believe in the need for and efficacy of baptism. Some priests, imbued with modern ideas, tell me I am wrong; I answer them "Let's not argue. You will not convince me and I shall not convince you." So, we shall continue to baptize those who want to receive that Sacrament.

'Our best helpers,' she often says, 'are all the baptized poor who died and went straight to Heaven. Our best helpers are the forty thousand inmates of our homes for the dying who "died with God" after making an act of perfect love for him, surrendering fully to His holy will. They now pray for us and for our work; that is what brings so much grace to our apostolate.

'In Latin America many people have not seen a priest for several years, and so they ask the Sisters to baptize their young children; what a cause of happiness for the Sisters.'

Mother recalls with joy that tens of thousand Catholic children belonging to poor families have been prepared by the Sisters for their first confession and first Communion. They received their Lord in their simple and pure hearts. Some may not persevere in the practice of the faith, but at least they have received the good Lord in their childhood and that grace will always remain with them.

The new Constitutions stipulate: 'We take special care of the older children. We do our utmost to find out those who have not received the Sacraments and instruct them without delay.' Thus they will be prepared to receive the Sacraments of penance and the Eucharist; also baptism and confirmation if they have not received them.

Mother and her Sisters rejoice in seeing many marriages regularised and celebrated according to the rite of the Church. In Latin America especially, the Sisters have helped to sanctify thousands of unions of people who had not sought out or perhaps not found a priest to bless their union.

In one simple ceremony, said Mother, thirty marriages were celebrated by a Sister. In one case three successive generations received the grace of the Sacrament of Matrimony together, grandparents, parents and their children, a young couple.

Mother narrated with real happiness:

'In Rome, the Sisters are doing a wonderful job. They visit the houses of the poor; they wash and sweep, tidy, mend and cook for those unable to do so. They found an old man who must have been well off in earlier days. He lived all alone. As he was sick, the Sisters did all the work for him. One day he told them "Sisters, you have brought God here; now, bring the priest also." They brought a priest who heard his confession. The old man had not confessed his sins for sixty years. The next day he died in the peace of the Lord.'

Mother added:

'I told this story in the United States at a meeting they had asked me to address. After the meeting a priest came to me and said: 'I had decided to leave the priesthood and sent my letter of resignation to my Bishop. After hearing what you said, I shall cancel my resignation and remain at the service of souls as a priest of Christ.'

God's merciful ways proved too beautiful for words; we both kept quiet; this was truly the beginning of the joy of heaven: to behold God's splendour in His own light whilst bathing in His love. Mother's trust in God's divine providence never falters. Twice or thrice, with fifteen years' interval in between Mother described her attitude regarding money problems in exactly the same words.

'Money, Father, I never think of it. It always comes. The Lord sends it. We do His work; he provides the means. If He does not give us the means that shows that He does not want the work. So why worry?'

When Mr Thomas, the chairman of Hindustan Lever came to see Mother Teresa, to offer her a property in Bombay, he first asked her:

'Mother, how is your work financed?'

She answered him very gently:

'Mr Thomas, who sent you here?'

'I felt an urge inside me. . . .'

'Well, other people like you come to see me and say the same; that is my budget.'

It was clear: God sent you, Mr Thomas, as he sends Mr X., Mrs Y., Miss Z., and they provide the material means we need for our work. The grace of God is what moved you. God sees to our needs, as Jesus promised.

Her trust is as complete as ever. But it requires less of a foundation of faith, of belief in the words of Christ, than it did at the beginning. Faith was more needed, faith, namely belief in unseen things, as hope is the expectation of things not yet possessed, was more needed in the first dark years. After twenty-five years of the Institute, God's protection and help had become a thing of experience, a fact of life. It astonished no more, since it was always there. But it continued to warm and comfort the heart, whilst it called for never-ending gratitude. Mother could not possibly budget, that is, put down on paper her receipts and her spending for the year in advance. She could not foresee how many Mr Thomases would appear during the year. It was God's secret.

The Missionaries of Charity had benefited from the fact that some multi-national companies had disposed of their unwanted properties. These had shown the way to other companies. In Calcutta, there was the *Prem Dan* of I.C.I., in Bombay there was the *Asha Dan* of Hindustan Lever. Mother called them respectively Gift of Love and Gift of Hope. Another Company might provide later a *Viswas Dan*, a Gift of Faith; then the three theological virtues would be represented. And one could foresee a Gift of Grace, a Gift of Joy, a Gift of Friendship. As needs arose, God would move the donors interiorly. They would be the first beneficiaries of the gifts they made to God, by entrusting them to the Sisters.

Mother has sparked off many acts of generosity. Various organizations collect for her works. People want to donate.

'Where does Mother Teresa live?' people asked several times after church service, or by telephone, or even on the street.

'I want to donate some money. How can I meet her?'

Of course, there may be the pleasant feeling of sharing in a noble enterprise, of taking part in a great adventure. One jumps on the bandwagon of a true pioneer of a new era of practical charity. One enters into partnership with 'a living Saint'.

Mother is not affected by this psychology. If it helps the cause of God and the welfare of the poor, good. But she considers before all the spiritual value of the act of giving.

'I hope you are not giving of your surplus,' she tells a group of rich businessmen who offer her a purse at the end of an excellent dinner. 'You must give what costs you, make a sacrifice, go without something you like, that your gift may have value before God; then you will be truly brothers to the poor who are deprived of even the things they need.'

The value of the act before God, not the amount of money given her, that is her main concern. As a girl soldalist she learned to make sacrifices for the missions, for the cause of Christ; to go without a meal, to do without sweets or a new dress. She had taught her Bengali pupils at St Mary's High School the same: forgo a picture, an outing, a meal and give the money to the poor. They did it, trained in self-giving until it hurts, and thus they were prepared to assume the hardships of religious life on a permanent basis, to love without limit the Lord Jesus and to take up the Cross with Him.

Money did not matter much; still, as good administrators of God's property, as stewards of God's gifts, they had to be faithful.

People who sent donations to the Missionaries of Charity knew that everything would be spent on the welfare of the poor.

At times it was the donors who were not sufficiently prudent. 'They steal my cheques,' Mother complained.

'Yes, such things happen. Foreign cheques, sent by post, are stolen and cashed in Hong Kong or in the Middle East. Have you lost many in that way?'

'I have informed my benefactors to send money only through bank drafts. But they do not always take this precaution.'

It was found that at least one hundred and fifty thousand rupees had been stolen from her; a man had even opened an account in her name and was signing for her in a bank located in Calcutta. But that fraud was discovered by the Security Department and the racket was stopped.

Money comes in from everywhere. Nineteen thousand pounds after the B.B.C. programme in 1975. The different prizes and awards were spent immediately on new foundations.

New foundations were started without debt, were paid for even before they were occupied. Benefactors have shown themselves extremely generous.

'We are opening a house at Nagpur,' says Mother. 'This is a town of a million inhabitants, with many cotton mills. The children's home and the house for the sisters are paid for by an Australian friend, fifty thousand in his currency. How many rupees does that make?'

'Five hundred and fifty thousand rupees, Mother.'

'Well, that is too much; the buildings cost only four hundred and fifty thousand rupees. May we use the rest of the money for another foundation, where the Bishop is very poor.'

At times the inviting Bishop provides the property and buildings. At times the Government makes all the arrangements. In Orissa, India, the Chief Minister, Mrs Satpathi, complained 'Why do you neglect our State, have you anything against us?' And soon the Missionaries of Charity opened a house there.

Once, on the feast-day of St Teresa of Avila, as I wished Mother a happy feast, she laughed:

'I am not the great Teresa, I am the little Therese,' she said; 'she is my patron.'

'No, I retorted, you are not the little Therese, who called herself "the plaything of Jesus, the football of Jesus," you are not the charming little Saint, who never left the four walls of her convent and died courageously at the age of twenty-four. You are Mother Teresa, a follower of the great Saint of Avila, always ready to go out to start new foundations. For your Sisters you are Mother; for us priests you are La Madre: a woman with an iron will, dynamic and efficient.'

Spiritually, Mother is not a Carmelite, She follows St Francis, the poor man of Assisi, and also St Vincent de Paul.

'In the plane from Madras to Calcutta,' she recalled: 'I spoke of God to my neighbour, a gentleman I had never met. It was just like meditating for the two hours of the journey.'

According to Indian spiritual usage the holy person, when travelling, usually keeps quiet to apply himself to the contemplation of the divine Presence. Everyone respects his silence and his communion with God. Nor is there a better way to remind ordinary folk of the divine Reality to whom we are all going, whom some know to be close to themselves. But for St Francis, the joy of loving God and being loved by him deserved to be told to the neighbouring traveller, who otherwise might remain ignorant of it. So, when you travel, make your choice, edify by your words, or by your silence. But I know what I would recommend to the young nuns who have not yet reached the sphere of perfect detachment from earthly things.

To imitate the perfect joy of St Francis in complete surrender to God and full trust in his divine Majesty, such is the programme of life Mother proposes to her Sisters.

Her spirituality owes much to St Francis. She emulates him in the cult and practice of evangelical poverty, the love of the Cross and the suffering Saviour, as also in obedience to God's guidance expressed in the Scriptures. Like him she adopts a simple, unsophisticated approach to life and its problems.

Every day the Sisters recite St Francis' prayer, to obtain from God kindness, gentleness, devotion, love and joy. They pray

'Lord, make me an instrument of your peace'. The prayer fits in with Mother's idea of instrumentality. We are just 'God's pencil' to write in the hearts of men what He wants. Like the Lord's Prayer, this prayer has the advantage that it can be said by all believers in God to whatever religion or denomination they belong; they can pray it together, making a ring of love around the world. It provides those who say it with a complete programme of life.

The kind of works the sisters perform and their style of life also recall to mind the Daughters of Charity of St Vincent de Paul and St Louise de Marillac. Vincent de Paul wished his Daughters to visit the poor in their houses, at a time when nuns were restricted to their enclosure and worked in their convents. He sent out his Daughters of Charity to nurse the poor and sick at home, carry food to the hungry, take care of orphans. They dressed at first like French peasant women, and lived poorly and austerely.

At times, Mother looked rather sad. Several times she remarked:

'Father, we do so little. They praise us for our actions, but what we do is not more than a drop of water in the ocean. It hardly affects the immensity of human suffering.'

'You are right, Mother, but we are not divine providence. You do all you can with the means and the personnel at your disposal. God does not ask you to do more.'

Indeed, the magnitude of human problems in several Asian countries might discourage, if not appall. The Sisters may work in twenty Calcutta slums, but an official estimate speaks of three thousand slums in Calcutta. Then there are at least a hundred thousand pavement dwellers. If the Sisters reach one hundred thousand lepers, there are another two million in the country, and also two million blind persons; and, according to an official declaration of May 1976, three quarter of a million regular beggars and vagrants.

Still, the work of the Sisters amounts to much. The Sisters work, the Co-Workers are active, and a stimulus has been given to the cause of charity all over the world among the millions who read or heard about the Missionaries of Charity. We have all become better for hearing of Mother and her Sisters and Brothers' love and devotion.

Again, Mother remarked:

'Father, our work among the slum children seems hopeless. When we succeed in educating a child, he goes to live in better surroundings and the slum people remain without any leader able to uplift them.'

On another occasion, Mother said somewhat sadly:

'Father, I do not build the Church.'

'No, Mother, perhaps not, but you are its best advertisement. You show the charity of Christ to all who come into contact with your institutions. And you have brought many children and adults to know Christ and receive the Sacraments they otherwise would not have received.'

'You see,' she said, 'we may not preach Christ as we would like to, because we receive help from the Government and from various agencies. So our hands are tied. You may preach because you receive no help from anybody. A government official told me: "Tell the truth, you would like me to become a Christian, you are praying for that?" I answered him: "When you possess something really good you wish your friends to share it with you. Now, I think that Christ is the best thing in the world and I would like all men to know Him and love Him as I do. But faith in Christ is a gift of God, who gives it to whom He likes." The gentleman went away satisfied.'

Mother has ever been a woman of action, indefatigable, always practical, concrete, quick to decide and implement her decisions. She brooks no delays, believes in today – yesterday, she says, is past, tomorrow is not under our control, it may never come, we have only today to be up and doing, to work for the glory of God.

She is a dynamo, an energizer, getting everybody to work. Whilst discussing matters of property with a government official, a Sister comes in and interrupts:

'An American tourist wants to see you; he is the person who came the other day.'

'Tell him to go and work in Kalighat.'

'But he says he went there yesterday.'

'Yes, he can go again today; the poor are still there.'

Another day I tell Mother:

'A lady would like to meet you.'

'No need. She can go and help. What can she do?'

'Well she runs a restaurant. I suppose she knows about catering.'

'We have no need of a caterer. Our meals are simple. Tell her to go and help at the dispensary. How many days a week can she spare?'

'I shall ask her.'

Many years ago Mother suggested:

'Father, you should write a book of meditations for my nuns.'

'No, Mother,' I replied, 'I cannot do it. I am not good enough.'

Some years later, she comes charging in again:

'Father, write a book of meditations for the Sisters. There are so few books of meditations adapted to the spiritual needs of the Sisters.'

'Mother, I cannot do it.'

Again, a few years later:

'Father, what about the book of meditations I asked you to write?'

'All right, Mother, I shall try.'

When my publisher a little later made the same request:

'No, I said. I cannot do it.'

But a week later I started writing meditations on the Gospel of St John. Inspiration came, and during a whole year I worked on this book – it was sheer delight. When the book was published, I sent one of the first copies to Mother.

She phoned me up a few days later:

'Father, thank you for writing "Remain in My Love". I use the book every day.'

I was repaid for all my efforts.

Mother's spiritual outlook has naturally progressed since the inception of her Congregation. Those of her generation who have remained in touch with her have noticed how her spirituality evolved during these thirty years, which was to be expected. She progressed in her understanding of the faith, of the ways of God's providence.

In Mother, with the passing of time and prayer, work, self-sacrifice, and a continual outpouring of love, the fruit of the Spirit has ripened and mellowed. In many of us, with age, as our physical arteries become sclerosed, so do our spiritual arteries. But this does not happen to those fully open to God's grace. The sap of divine life renews the arteries and the fruit of kindness becomes more fragrant and delicious.

Mother's faith and trust increased during the years; they gained in strength, naturalness, spontaneity, surfacing easily in conversation. Ingrained in the soul, they showed the reality of God's protection, his love always present.

At the Kalighat Home for the Dying, as a visitor wondered at the peace reigning in the last rest-house for the poor before their final departure, Mother said simply: 'God is here.' A concise, terse, perfect summing up of the situation. In earlier years she would have given a more elaborate explanation; now one word suffices: 'God' present, active, loving. In all matters, life's pattern appears simpler to her in God's increasingly stronger light.

Mother sees God active in these people as he prepares them for an eternity of happiness with Him. The ugliness of poverty and misery recedes into the background, as God's hand comes forward to receive His children whom the Sisters help to 'die with God'.

Serenity increases with age. Looking at the world from a greater height, we discover things those closer to earth cannot behold. We see how events fall in place to fit in God's plan; we realize that God is powerful enough to bring good even out of evil, if we let him do so. All serves to lead us to God, especially our sufferings, if we love Him. Suffering unites us to Christ, renders us similar to Him, brings merits, obtains grace.

Seen in the light of eternity, poverty, hunger and sickness shed their ugliness; they are seen as means helping us to reach God. Only sin is to be shunned — a worse evil than all the human suffering not caused by man. But to lighten man's burden on earth remains a sacred duty — to imitate the compassion of Christ for the multitudes that were as sheep without a shepherd, waiting to be led to good pastures.

Mother now would perhaps no more regret: 'We do so little; we do not build the Church, our action is like a drop of water in

the ocean.' She appreciates fully the sisters' call to collaborate
with God, to serve him in the poor, in a simple, humble way.

'Father, this is wonderful. . . .' Often she repeats this word of
praise of the Lord God who guides her. 'Wonderful' is the
qualification she uses most frequently when relating some event
or mentioning a favour received from God. In the spirit of St
Luke's Gospel she extols God's goodness, His providence caring
for His children, the grace and happiness of knowing and serving
Christ.

'They went away praising God' is Luke's usual comment after
narrating a miracle of Jesus. The ways of God really are wonderful; every spiritual person discovers the divine guidance in the
events of his life.

'How good God is', Mother likes to say, 'His guiding hand is
here'. It is. This renders her habitually optimistic.

Coming daily in contact with physical and mental suffering,
with misery, injustice, trampled-down human dignity, she suffers
from it, and tries to remedy the situation in a practical manner.
But she also sees all the good there is in the world: devotion, service, love, sharing, compassion, mercy, acceptance, gratitude,
good-will.

Camus, the author of *The Plague*, though an agnostic, thought
that in the world the sum total of goodness exceeds that of evil.
He could not give the reason for this. But a believer in God's
Providence and a disciple of Christ our Saviour can explain why
it is so.

8. Sharing His Cross

'Follow Christ by loving as he loved you, giving himself up in our place as a fragrant offering and a sacrifice to God.'

(Eph. 5, 2)

Mother knows suffering. She has shared in the Cross of Christ. Like every loving soul she would not wish it to be otherwise. 'We always find;' says St Teresa of Avila, who knew by personal experience, 'that those who are closest to Jesus have most to suffer.'

Mother puts before her nuns this ideal: to quench the thirst of Jesus crucified for souls. To do this they should be ready to suffer with Christ and even wish to be similar to Him and to suffer for the redemption of souls.

'The wounds I bear in my body are those of Christ' writes Paul; indeed, they are the wounds he suffered because he belonged to Christ. The Sisters, when they enter the chapel for their morning prayers, see the picture of the crucified Saviour, calling to them 'I thirst', They will soon receive in communion the Victim of the sacrifice, who will give them strength to serve Him in the poor and suffering.

With Jesus they are to bring the world back to God our Father. This call brings them joy as they ponder Paul's words expressing the mystery of Christian love. 'It makes me happy to suffer for you, as I am suffering now, and in my own body to do what I can do to make up all that is lacking from the suffering of Christ for the sake of His body, the Church' *(Col. 1, 24)*. In this process of redemption, as in everything connected with the existence and well-being of men, God wants our collaboration. We are to be His active instruments, sharing in His work.

Mother knows the suffering of men. How could she have true compassion without a sharing of experience, a 'symbiosis,' between those she cares for and herself. The sick understand the sick; the bereaved those who lose a loved one.

Mother has known fatigue, hard work, tiring walks, long waits; she has travelled in crowded trams and buses, she has sat up whole nights in cheap compartments; she has eaten rough food, and squatted on the floor with the poor in unfurnished dwellings.

'God made me a great gift: good health.' Mother told me. She has the hands of a peasant woman: strong, active, energetic, working and praying hands. She looks frail, increasingly so, as the years go by, but she is a bundle of energy. Her power comes from above: Christ is her spiritual power-house.

Like Paul she can be compared to an athlete perpetually in training, wishing to obtain the crown. With him she can say 'I treat my body hard and make it obey me' (*Cor. I, 9, 27*). Up at four-thirty every morning, she soon comes to the chapel for prayer. She goes to sleep late at night or even in the early morning. Sister Fabienne, who lives in the Mother-house, tells me: 'She works habitually till midnight or one in the morning.'

I always saw her sitting on the edge of her chair, her back erect, even when dog-tired, even when visibly feverish. When she is sick, it is difficult to get Mother to take some rest, still more so to keep her in bed. At times, Sister Agnes or a doctor has succeeded in forcing her to rest a little.

'I cannot ask Mother to come down today,' Sister Agnes said one day. 'She is not well. If I told her you were here, she would come down the two floors from her room and then climb up again. People come the whole day to see her. I must keep them away.'

'You are right, Sister Agnes. Look after Mother, protect her, give her the short rest she badly needs.'

She usually travels by train, in the lower class; she enjoys a free pass on the Indian Railways granted her by the Railway Minister. To spare her much time and fatigue, Indira Gandhi gave Mother a free pass for the Indian Airlines, in 1973. She can thus travel to all the important towns in India by plane.

Trials

Mother was deeply affected when some of the Sisters she had patiently formed and led to Jesus decided to leave the Congrega-

tion. Years ago, when she was asked: 'Do you lose many Sisters?'
she replied: 'Very few. In fact you could count those who have
left on the fingers of a single hand, and you would not even need
all the fingers.' It is so no more. With the considerable increase in
number of the Sisters, it must be expected that more will leave
the Congregation.

'Do you lose many Sisters?' I asked Mother after the Jubilee.
'No,' she answered, 'not many. Last year three left. The
Superior of one of our houses went away with the parish priest
who was the spiritual director of the convent. I went to see the
Archbishop of the place who told me he knew this priest had his
own ways. I answered him "Your Grace, if you knew he was not
reliable, why did you put him in charge of our Sisters?" '

But, if Adam proved weak, Eve was not altogether blameless.
She had been advised not to go alone to the parish house in the
evenings. As the Superior, she had not listened to her Sisters.

A senior Sister gave me a more complete picture of the losses
the Congregation had sustained during the previous year. 'Three
Sisters,' she said, 'left after their final profession. Nine more
Sisters left after their first profession.' These were free to leave at
the expiry of the period for which they had bound themselves by
vows. 'Danger,' added this Sister, 'comes from priests, drivers,
lepers, and co-workers. One Sister left to marry a leper she had
attended to; another left to marry the driver of the community's
van; still another left with a co-worker who had come to help
us.'

After the Jubilee Mother suffered a hard blow, when a Sister in
London who had been one of the pillars of the Congregation expressed the intention of leaving. Mother was so distressed that she
took the plane for London when she heard that this Sister, a
trusted and efficient helper on whom she had much relied, had
decided to leave the Congregation – perhaps on account of ill
health. Mother tried to make her change her mind, but failed.
Her magnetic power did not work. There remained only to
thank God for the good effected through this Sister, and to pray
for the spiritual well-being of those who had left the Congregation, as the Constitutions recommend in Mother's own
words:

'Pray for all those who have been in the Society that God may
protect them and keep them in His love.'

'We remain very human; we have our ups and downs,' Mother confessed several times.

'Yes, Mother, they keep us humble and make us feel the need of God's grace.'

Mother feels intense pain and immense sorrow when someone who has committed himself for life proves unfaithful to God's call and to his promise to live with Christ and to die for Him. 'How is it,' she asked, 'that nowadays all over the world so many priests and nuns abandon their calling? Were they not chosen by Christ? Did they not commit themselves to follow him after long and mature reflection? How then can a nun pronounce perpetual vows, and some years later give up the religious life? Are married people not bound to remain faithful to each other until death? Then, why should the same rule not apply to priests and nuns?

Mother suffers for her Lord, treated as an unwanted person, whilst His love is despised. Yes, someone will have to offer Him reparation for the faithlessness of those He had favoured with his call and His love, and who turned away after first following Him.

Mother has personally experienced that the Lord purifies us interiorly, in a subtle manner, depriving us of all spiritual consolations. Every loving soul must expect at times to be tried and deprived of all sensible consolation, of every feeling of God's sacred presence, as it is made to pass through the tunnel of the dark night.

In that *noche oscura*, as St John of the Cross calls it, that Dark Night known by all mystics and by many others, the marriage between God and the soul is being prepared.

Then those who out of a passionate love for God have left everything for Him, – or perhaps not yet everything, since He asks still more from them – are heard to complain 'I have no faith; I work without faith, without feeling. Do I still believe? I see nothing.' They suffer with Christ in the Garden, with Christ on the Cross, sharing His apparent abandon by His Father, and exclaim: 'My God, my God, why have you abandoned me?'

To His chosen disciples Jesus says at some stage of life: 'From now on you must keep constantly before your mind: the Son of Man is to suffer. . . .' And with him they set their face determinedly towards Jerusalem. Their pace does not slacken, their faith in him does not weaken, as they show him their love by sharing in the great act of redemption.

That grief and pain will also give way to the joy and serenity of the Resurrection. Then perhaps, right at the end, or close to the end of the road, the Lord will make the soul pass through a final purification.

Setbacks

The Missionaries of Charity have experienced a few failures, which is all to the good. Mother certainly thanks the good Lord for them. Failures render us more similar to our Blessed Lord, who failed with Judas; failed with the rich young man he invited to walk in his footsteps; failed to attract and convert most of the priests and Pharisees of his nation. We should also experience that aspect of our Master's life: his disappointment at the treatment meted out to God's prophets and even to His chosen One. Still, the failures of the Missionaries of Charity have been remarkably few.

There was Simla. The Sisters opened a house in that hill station. They came from the hot plains, the hills were very cold in the winter; their clothing and style of life was not adapted to cold days and nights; there being few Catholics in the area, the opportunities for spiritual work were slender. The Sisters lost heart, found their work useless and left the place. Yet they remained at Darjeeling, which has a similar cold climate in the winter, and flourished there; they went to Takda, as cold as Darjeeling, and more isolated. Such disappointments may depend on the grit, determination, spirit of penance, enterprise and enthusiasm of the first group.

Then there was Colombo. When Mother told me that the Sisters had been invited to Sri Lanka, I asked her; 'Why is it that other foreign religious have been asked to leave, whereas you are invited by the Prime Minister to open a house?' Mother answered: 'Ah, that is because we do what others don't do.' But later the Missionaries of Charity were also asked to leave, and they returned to India.

Belfast proved a more humiliating failure. Mother took four

Sisters there to open a house in 1972. The place offered a challenge: Protestants oppressed the Catholic minority, economically weak. Hatred was preached even from the church pulpits. Some Catholics in desperation retaliated with acts of terrorism. Mother was told: Here is a place for you, go and practise Catholic charity in Ulster; try to unite Protestants and Catholics through deeds of charity. Mother took up the challenge, in the spirit of St Francis going to the Holy Land occupied by the Moslems. Francis did get away with it, but the friars he sent a little later were soon despatched to enjoy the Beatific Vision in heaven. Their time of trial on earth ended with martyrdom.

The Missionaries of Charity did not die martyrs in Ulster, which would have covered them with glory and might have awakened world opinion. The Indian Sisters in their sarees had to pack and go home; they were not wanted.

What happened at Ranchi sounds less believable. As Mother arrived with some Sisters to open a new house, she was met with cries of 'Go back, Mother Teresa!'; she found a barricade erected on the road to prevent her going farther. Mother tried to argue, but in vain. The people were determined not to allow her to occupy the land bought for her new foundation. Mother told them 'By refusing entrance to the sisters you refuse entrance to God.' But this proved of no avail, and they had to turn back.

This was due to a misunderstanding, but also to a wrong choice of location. When doing good to the poor, we should respect the local people's interest and susceptibilities. Rumour had it that the new foundation was to be a home for lepers. The Sisters said it was not. It would be a house for the old and destitute. But the local people, who had built decent houses with their savings feared that a home for destitute would diminish the value of their properties and spoil the name of the locality.

A peaceful solution was found; the children's home established in another part of the town was shifted to the new property and the home for the dying destitute was moved to the old children's home.

Mother suffered a personal failure when she tried to settle a quarrel between the laity, some priests and the hierarchy. At Cuttack, Mother went to speak to the Catholics who opposed the appointment of a bishop; she spoke of the love of God, of faithfulness to mother Church, of our duties as Catholics, and of obedience to Our Lord, and they said they would stop their protest. The peace lasted a few days. Mother went back to her other duties, and soon the fight broke out again.

All this, and a little more, does not add up to much in the way of failures. Other religious founders have known much greater disappointments than this.

Other problems

Like St Paul Mother experienced some trials on her journeys. One memorable incident happened on a hill-road. A terrible landslide had shocked Darjeeling, affecting a whole section of this hill station; the whole of Bhutia Basti had been destroyed, scores of houses had collapsed, some people had died, others, many of them, had been rendered homeless. It was the beginning of the monsoon and heavy rains had caused large chunks of earth to run down into the valley.

As soon as she heard of the plight of the people, Mother Teresa was on her way to Darjeeling to organize relief operations.

Then an accident happened. 'We were in the jeep,' recalled Bishop Eric Benjamin, 'the driver, myself and Mother Teresa, sitting on the front seats, and travelling on the old military road – for the regular road was blocked by several landslides. Suddenly, at a bend of the road, we were met by a lorry, and there was a head-on collision. The driver and myself, seeing the lorry come straight on us, steadied ourselves in order not to fall forward, and we escaped injury. Mother Teresa fell forward, her head went violently against a steel fixture attached to the windscreen, and she was badly cut. I noticed that she was bleeding under the saree that covered her head. She said it was nothing. But we returned immediately to Darjeeling and I took her to the Planters' Hospital where the doctor attended to her and put in nineteen stitches. Had the wound been a little lower she would have lost an eye.

'That very evening Indira Gandhi, who was in Darjeeling, hearing of Mother's accident, called on her at the hospital to express her sympathy and to convey her good wishes for a speedy recovery.'

A few days later Mother was back in Calcutta. When I met her at the Mother-house, she still appeared bruised and shaken. She smiled and said only: 'I am all right, Father.'

The Sisters also encountered dangerous animals. Dogs were not always friendly: A Sister at Raipur was bitten by an unknown small dog. She did not take the injections against rabies. For several weeks nothing happened to her. Then one day she was attacked by the dreaded disease. When she was brought to a Pasteur Institute and received anti-rabies injections, it was too late. She died; the Lord rest her soul and reward her for her good works.

At the Mother-house there was a terrible animal, a barker and a biter, aptly nicknamed by the Sisters 'Kala Shaitan', Black Devil. It was as fierce as a dog can be. It disturbed the classes and the study. Whilst I spoke on the Gospel of St John, the Black Devil would bark so loudly from its lair next to the hall that I had repeatedly to interrupt my instruction. One day, as I was leaving, it tried desperately to bite me, but I managed to escape its threatening jaws. A little later, it broke its chain and attacked Sister Camillus whom it bit in the leg, the arm and two other places. It had previously bitten Sister Fabienne who was in charge of the choir and a Sister in charge of novices. Then it bit a little novice in charge of nothing.

I suggested to some professed Sisters that the dog might be dispensed with; but they objected that Mother would be very sad; she loved Shaitan, who behaved like an angel towards her.

The Sisters also argued that Shaitan was to protect them against thieves. But a novice then told me, 'I live in fear and trembling of that dog, because I must cross the courtyard for my work in the evening, when Shaitan is let loose, and I am too small and weak to fight him back.'

It seemed to me that Shaitan had not right to disturb the peace and recollection of the novices, so I told this Sister: 'There is only one way out, we must pray the Lord to deliver us from this Black Devil.' Our prayers were heard sooner than we had expected.

A few days later two thieves came at night, and threw poisoned meat to the Black Devil. It ate the meat and became sick. The Sisters tried to save the animal, but their efforts failed. Kala

Shaitan had to be given an injection by the veterinary a few days later. The novices could now cross the courtyard without fear, even after dark.

9. Training the Sisters

'What do you think is our pride and our joy? You are; and you will be
the crown of which we are proudest in the presence of our Lord Jesus
when he comes; you are our pride and our joy.'

(1 Thess. II, 19–20)

Soon after the Jubilee, Michael Gomes said, 'Mother asked me
lately, "Michael, do you know what is my most important
work?" '

' "I suppose to work for the poor," ' I answered.

' "No," she said, "try again." '

'I tried to find the answer, and proposed several things. Each
time she said "No, that is not the most important thing for me."
Then she said: "Well, I shall tell you: my most important work is
to train my Sisters." '

'Of course, Brother Michael,' I said, 'what could she do
without the Sisters?'

'And what could they do without Mother?' he retorted.

'True, but she needs a team. She cannot run a single institution
without the Sisters, who multiply and extend her influence.
Mother knows that the Society will live after her only if the
Sisters are fervent religious; she has told me so repeatedly.'

At first it was her main occupation. Now, due to her society's
growth and expansion, Mother can devote less time to the essential work of formation, which she must entrust to the Sisters she
trained.

Mother has to form Christ in the young candidates who come
to join her Congregation. Like St Paul she can say 'My children!
I must go through the pain of giving birth to you all over again,
until Christ is formed in you.' (Gal. 4, 19).

For two years she watched over each new batch of novices,
preparing them to become the chosen brides of Christ. She introduced them to spiritual life, abnegation, humility, service,

115

love of God and of their neighbour, and trained them to find
God in prayer.

Mother carefully prepares her young Sisters to become worthy
of their bridgegroom Jesus, so that their Lord may say when they
take their vows and pledge themselves to live only for him, to
serve only Him, to love only Him, to follow Him even unto
death on the Cross, in the words of the bridegroom of the *Song of
Songs*:

'You are wholly beautiful, my love, and without a blemish.'
These words the Catholic tradition applies to Our Lady. They
are an ideal we can aim at, an ideal put before the young
religious.

'If the Sisters are not to be faithful,' Mother told me, 'let the
Lord suppress the Institute. He can do without it, the Church can
do without it. They must be faithful to Him who has called
them, who is the ever faithful One.'

'Mother, they will be faithful.'

Having spared herself no pains for their training, to each of her
Sisters Mother can say with rightful pride 'I have betrothed you,
a chaste virgin, to Christ.'

'Father, I tell them: "You are the brides of Christ. He deserves
all your love. None of you must love Jesus less than a wife loves
her husband."'

'Yes, Mother, Jesus is the perfect Bridegroom, always faithful,
thoughtful, attentive to their needs, seeing to their spiritual
progress. But as a true lover, He is exacting. "I am a jealous
God" said Yahweh.'

'If they start seeking consolation in human things,' she added,
'if they divide their hearts between God and men, He may let
them fall.'

Mother teaches her Sisters by her example, and her words; she
guides them by her letters, and her visits to the various houses.

St Paul wrote to his disciples at Corinth, 'Take me for your
model, as I take Christ.' (*I Cor. 11, 1*) Mother can say the same to
her Sisters in all truth, without ostentation or self-praise. Indeed,
the Holy Spirit inspires the founders of approved religious
Institutes, whose members are expected to live according to the
ideal expressed in their Constitutions and their founders' life.

Mother can ask much because she has given much. She does

not ask the Sisters to do anything she has not done herself. She has washed feet, like Jesus; she has bathed sores and bandaged wounds like the good Samaritan; she has pressed babies to her heart as Christ did; she has lifted up the cripple. She has visited the slums; she has begged for the hungry and the sick. She has experienced hunger, thirst, tiredness: she has passed sleepless nights; she has had fever but still attended to her duties as Superior.

Mother constantly teaches the Sisters by her example. She arrived with five Sisters in Melbourne in April 1970. The same day, helped by the Provincial of the Loreto Nuns, she found a house which had been deserted after the death of the previous owner. It had been badly neglected, the roof was leaking, the floor covered with dirt. Mother announced: 'Well, we can start cleaning.' Immediately the front room was cleaned, prepared for Mass, and the beds were made ready. Since there was room for only five beds, one Sister slept under the table. Mother's arm had been fractured, and so the Sisters, to make her comfortable, disposed some blankets on one side of her bed that she might rest her arm.

When the night came, the Sisters soon fell into a sound sleep. On waking up, they discovered that the blankets had been spread over them to keep them warm during the cold night. Mother had seen to it; she could live in discomfort, like her Lord. No doubt, her action impressed the Sisters more than any instruction on charity could have done.

At the very beginning, the Sisters were hand-tooled; a carefully finished product coming from the hand of Mother, who spoke frequently to the several groups of Sisters.

'I give four of five instructions a day,' she could say at the time of the first foundations, 'and I meet personally every one of the Sisters.'

Gradually, as the number of houses increased, she had to rely more on her first companions. They were becoming seasoned and experienced; having imbibed Mother's thoughts, they transmitted her ideals and ideas, even using her favourite expressions. They were rightly exacting; candidates and novices had to be ready for a hard life under strict discipline. As Mother became more and more frequently absent, due to the opening of

new houses, the senior Sisters shouldered an increasing share of
the work of forming the postulants and novices.

From the start several priests also helped. Father Van Exem
contributed much to the Sisters' training, as the confessor and
spiritual director of the community in Calcttta. He helped to
mould the character of the Sisters in the spirit of the
Constitutions he explained to them.

Father Julien Henry also helped Mother in the spiritual formation of the novices and professed Sisters. He exerted a considerable influence on Mother and on the Sisters, stressing the
need for prayer, insisting on devotion to the Sacred Heart, the
Blessed Eucharist and to Our Lady. After twenty-eight years of
service to the Institute, he still gives an instruction daily to one or
another group of the Sisters.

'Father Henry,' said Mother with an impish smile, 'tells them
things no one else would dare tell them. He knows all their
defects and points them out in his instructions. When novices
spot him on the road, if they are not praying the rosary as they
are expected to do, they quickly reach for their beads and start
praying. But Father Henry has seen their gesture, and in his next
instruction he is certain to make them a remark. Nothing escapes
him, even though he himself, when alone on the road, usually
says his rosary.'

When they have left the Mother-house, Mother continues to
teach her Sisters through her letters. She directs, reproaches,
redresses, advices, suggests. She solves problems, encourages and
stimulates.

'I keep in touch with all the houses and all the Sisters,' she says.
'I visit them as often as I can; of course my visits become less frequent as the number of foundations increases. I also write often to
the Sisters.'

They are always present to her mind. Their problems are hers
to solve, their difficulties she must help to settle. She sends them
in the name of Christ whom she represents for them; hence she
must know whom to send where, whom to appoint as Superior of
the local community, what apostolate the Sisters should undertake in a particular place. She goes to inspect the site of every
new foundation, by herself or with her counsellors. Once the
Sisters are established, she continues to guide them through her
letters and visits. She directs, encourages, reminds, corrects,

stimulates them in all religious and apostolic matters.

Sister Letitia, who later became the first Superior in Papua, when she was in charge of the house at Amravati wrote to Mother that the Bishop was giving the house two hundred rupees a month. Mother replied: 'Next month return the money to the Bishop and tell him you need this contribution no more. You must get the local people to help and support the work.'

At times she adds a note of humour to her advice, as when the Sisters from Dorunda, Ranchi, wrote to Mother that they could not sleep at night because thieves climbed the pipes along the walls of the house and tried to enter into the rooms were they slept.

'I wrote back,' chuckled Mother: 'since none of you is so pretty that a thief would want to take her away, they can be coming only for money and supplies. Well, allow them to take these things they need, and let the Sisters enjoy the sleep of the just. God will look after you.'

St Paul directed that his letters be read publicly to the assembled Christians, and then passed on to other communities. Mother's letters are also read in the community and travel from house to house. Many quotations from these letters have found their way into the second redaction of the Constitutions written in 1975.

A Belgian journal requested Father Van Exem to interview Mother, among other questions asked her was: 'What would you consider to be most important in the formation of nuns today?'

'What is most important,' Mother answered, 'is to train the Sisters to a deep, personal love for the Blessed Sacrament, so that they may find Jesus in the Eucharist; then they will go out and find Jesus in their neighbour, and they will serve him in the poor.'

This stress on the presence of Christ in the Eucharist and in one's neighbour as a key to spiritual training shows how concrete and incarnational her spirituality is: Christ is to be found on earth today, in definite conditions of time and space, in a truly tangible manner.

Thus the key-note of the training she imparts to her Sisters is Jesus found in the Eucharist, Jesus found in the neighbour.

The Eucharist is the Victim of the sacrifice to which the Sisters unite themselves, the sustaining Food that gives them the strength to carry out their apostolate and the sacred Presence of their Lord and Saviour, to whom they come to offer consolation and love, and to receive inspiration and comfort.

Mother insists on prayer before the Blessed Sacrament, on faithfulness to the hour of adoration every evening, which the new Constitutions prescribe. Mother takes visitors to the chapel and invites them to greet the Master of the house. She rejoices when she learns that groups of her Co-Workers organize hours of adoration.

This devotion to the Blessed Eucharist, fully in the tradition of the Church, was again recommended by Vatican II.

Popular Indian tradition favours a concrete religion. But the deeper current of Indian spirituality seeks God's presence in the world and especially in the soul. The Sisters pass much time away from their houses, since their work is largely outside. They spend much time on the road or travelling. Thus, they must learn to converse constantly with their Lord and to find God present everywhere.

When speaking to the Tertians, I insisted on the divine Presence within. Some of the Sisters understood this; some did find God present in their soul and this discovery rendered their prayer personal, intimate, habitual.

The one who loves Jesus will keep the two great commandments: Love for God and for one's neighbour. Thus the Sisters by their vocation are called to love, in a thorough and at times a heroic manner. They discover God's presence, wonderful inspiring, drawing the soul to Himself. With utter respect they serve Him in their neighbour, as they tend the wounds of Christ's suffering brothers and sisters.

Then the soul is itself a tabernacle. My Lord dwells always with me, in me. Once as I spoke to Mother of the Presence of God in the soul, she said: 'The indwelling? Yes, we have too long neglected it.'

Like St Paul, Mother likes to feel close to the One she loves. She sees the Eucharist as a continued Incarnation; she finds Christ in the tabernacle and in His brethren; He is the Head, and they and she constitute his Body. Christ in the tabernacle and in the suffering poor expects the Sisters; they can visit Him and attend on Him. Devotion to the Blessed Eucharist appeals to affective souls, to those with a vivid imagination, to persons who like concrete things and situations. Several Sisters report that they find strength to perform the day's work and shoulder its crosses in their prayer before the Blessed Sacrament, telling Jesus in effect: 'Lord, take everything, all is for you.'

For her Sisters Mother has a high ideal.

'Father, I want to give saints to the Church.'

'Yes, you are right, Mother; to produce saints is the task of the Church.'

And so she asks much and obtains much. She trains her Sisters· to perfect obedience.

For Mother obedience means complete disponibility to Christ's service, wherever and in whatever capacity he calls us. Like St Francis of Assisi she asks from her religious perfect submission to God's will as known through the order of the Superior, in a spirit of love, and prompt execution of that will.

In the summer of 1968 there took place at Darjeeling the blessing and inauguration of a new building at the home for orphaned, crippled and handicapped children. The Bishop blessed the new premises; the Governor of West Bengal praised the wonderful work performed by the Sisters. The Superior, who had brought a difficult task to completion, might have thought of relaxing for a while, but no – Mother Teresa, just back from America and Europe, had news for her:

'Sister, I want you to go to Africa and start a new house there.'

'When, Mother?'

'As soon as you can obtain your passport. There is plenty of work for us in Africa.'

Indeed after starting a first house in Tanzania, the Sister was appointed to establish a second foundation in the same country. This was a true acknowledgement of her pioneering ability.

To another Mother says:

'Sister, you leave for South India.'

'When, Mother?'

'This evening, Sister, by the first train that goes there.'

The Sisters are usually told of their assignment on the day they take their vows, except for a few who require passports or visas to go to their destination. When Mother is absent, they must wait till she comes back.

'There is no problem of packing for us,' said a Sister. 'Since we have nothing, we are ready in ten minutes.'

The Sisters' training in poverty proceeds in a rigorous manner. They must not only know and esteem, but also experience practical poverty during their period of probation and during their whole religious life.

Poverty in dress which comprises:

A simple and modest white habit, covering them from neck to ankle and wrist.

A white saree with blue border to cover their head and most of their habit.

A crucifix hanging from the left shoulder.

Sandals.

They are allowed three habits: one to wear, one to wash, one to dry; and two sarees of coarse material, such as the poor would wear, one to wear and one to wash or dry.

The houses must exhibit poverty in style, in furniture; the manner of travelling must be the cheapest available: much is done on foot; when trams, buses or trains must be used, they choose the cheapest class.

Food should be of the most simple, yet sufficient to keep up the Sisters' health so that they can work strenuously for the good of the poor.

The Sisters sleep in dormitories, without any privacy, like the poor who live in crowded slums or tenements.

Cleanliness should be observed so as to give an example to the poor, who should be taught to work and not to be lazy.

The reason for the practice of poverty is love. Mother writes:

'Our people are poor by force, but our poverty is of our own choice. We want to be poor like Christ who, being rich, chose to be born and live and work among the poor.'

The Constitutions state: 'We and our poor will rely entirely on divine Providence. We are not ashamed to beg from door to door as members of Christ, who himself lived on alms during the public life and whom we serve in the sick and the poor.'

St Francis of Assisi was not ashamed to beg for the poor and to receive the scraps of food he would share with them. Similarly the Sisters are not to be ashamed to ask for the poor, even if begging represents a form of poverty that has come to be despised in the modern world.

The Sisters must learn to ask; they start doing it during their novitiate.

Two young novices come to the parish house, all smiles, and ask:

'Have you any candle drippings, Father?' Then both novices burst out laughing. They laugh and laugh heartily as only young girls can laugh. Who could refuse them?

'What do you need them for, Sisters?'

'To make a paschal candle.'

This is Passion Sunday. The two young novices went out early, gathered the children of a parish for the Sunday Mass and catechism class. On their way home they ask from other churches if there are drippings of wax with which they can make a paschal candle.

Another batch of novices went to ask for biscuits from a factory to prepare a treat for the children that they may share in the joy of the Resurrection of the Lord.

Bishops and government officials who invite Mother want her spirit, her approach to the poor and the abandoned, her way of work. Through the Sisters she has trained she can multiply her presence and her influence, her activity and her apostolate; they are the spirit and presence, the influence and work of Christ, living in his humble, docile, indomitable instrument.

Like Paul writing to the Corinthians he had nursed and formed into images of Christ, Mother can tell her Sisters: 'You are yourselves our letter that anybody can see and read, and it is plain that you are a letter from Christ, drawn up by us.' (*II Cor. 3, 1–3*)

The Sisters are to be a small replica of the foundress, modelled on her. In their behaviour and their work all men must see and read what Mother thinks and teaches and does. And because her spirit is truly the Spirit of Christ living in her, the Sisters are a letter from Christ, speaking to the world of His mercy, His goodness, His kindness, His power, His concern for every individual person.

Since Christ lives in them and acts through them, they should not fear to let the world see their good deeds.

'I tell them, Father, not to be ashamed when people praise them for what they do. They must let people see what Christ does through us, His humble instruments. It is all to His glory.'

'Yes, Mother; that is what Jesus told us: "Let your light shine before men that seeing your good works they may glorify your Father who is in heaven." Christ is the supreme Light, "the light that comes into the world to enlighten all men." He wishes us to be small lights, reflecting his truth, his splendour and glory.'

The Spirit of God grants the Sisters various charisms; it is for Mother to discover them, to help to develop them and to allow them to be used to the full.

At the Mother-house, I often saw a particular Sister speak to women and children on religious matters. As I mentioned this to Mother, she answered:

'Yes, this Sister has a special gift for contacting people and getting them interested in religion. She speaks to them of God with simplicity and conviction. Yet she only studied up to the eighth standard.'

'Well, Mother, if she has that God-given charism, use her entirely for that work. It is most important.'

'I shall,' said Mother.

Mother can ask much from her Sisters; but she also knows the limitations of human nature.

'I find it difficult to appoint a good mistress of novices,' she told me one day.'

'You might try Sister X.; She is a woman of God, given to prayer.'

'No, she would be too strict. She exacts much for God and might break some of the young, weaker novices.'

In 1975, I asked Mother:

'Do you still know all the Sisters?'

'I know personally and individually every professed Sister of the Congregation,' she answered. 'But not all the novices and postulants.'

She judges them quickly. With correct insight, it would seem. Once, to test her knowledge of her Sisters, I asked her about a recently professed Sister.

'Where is Sister Y. at present?' If she knows the state of her soul, she will comment, I thought.

Mother answered: 'At our house at Z.' She added: 'she is a very spiritual person.'

'Yes,' I said, 'a very spiritual person.' We understood one

another. She knew that I knew, and I knew that she was aware of the treasure the Lord had given her.

Mother does not want mass production. There are nine separate groups of novices for the two years' novitiate at the Mother-house, with a Sister-in-charge to guide each group. Mother naturally puts her best Sisters to train the young candidates.

The novices do some field work, thus receiving in-training in the kinds of work they will have to perform later. The first year novices go out for work on Thursdays and Sundays. The second year novices go out for work every day except Thursdays.

Three points Mother stresses especially in the training of the sisters are:

Total surrender to God.

Loving trust.

Cheerfulness.

These three virtues must enable them to go through their religious life, coming closer and closer to the Lord Jesus whom they serve in the poor.

Each renovation of vows is preceded by a triduum of prayer during which the preacher is asked to take one of these subjects each day. Thus the nuns are prepared to give themselves again to God, to renew and perfect their offering to the divine Majesty in the spirit of the Congregation.

Cheerfulness in the fulfilment of the most unattractive task is a characteristic of the Institute. Mother teaches, and her words are inscribed in the Constitutions:

'Never let anything so fill you with pain or sorrow as to make you forget the joy of the risen Christ.' This is written at the top of the chapter on bearing the Cross of Christ, which is the proof of the greatness of His love and of ours in return for His.

Mother's faith has carried her through all the trials of the beginning of the Institute. Faith in the power of the Risen Christ and of the Holy Spirit He sent us will see the Sisters through all the difficulties of their life of service to the poorest of the poor.

Twice a year, on a feast day of Our Lady, takes place the ceremony of the vows. Those who have just finished their novitiate or are still juniors take temporary vows for a period of one year; those who end their tertianship, after six years of temporary vows, take their final profession, binding themselves for life to serve Christ in the Congregation. On these days Mother brings to Jesus the best offering she can make, the young religious she has carefully trained.

For the Sisters these are solemn occasions.

In December 1975, in crowded St Mary's Church, twelve Sisters were ranged in a single row before the altar; the Archbishop was going to concelebrate with twenty priests the holy Mass during which the Sisters would offer themselves for ever to Christ.

They were living the words of Hosea:

'I will betroth you to myself for ever, with integrity and justice, with tenderness and love;

'I will betroth you to myself with faithfulness and you will come to know Yahweh, your God.' (*Hosea 2, 21–22*)

It was their great day, long expected, long desired, long prepared. The day of their exchange of gifts with their bridegroom, Christ. They were coming forth in total surrender, joyful trust, perfect love.

The King who had called them to leave their families and every human attachment to serve him, had told them:

'Set me as a seal on your heart,
     as a seal on your arm.'

A seal to attest its owner's will – the seal that will guide and inspire her for ever, since 'Love is strong as death'.

After the Gospel and the homily, the deacon calls those to be professed, each one by her name:

'Sister Mary Edward.'

'Lord, you have called me,' answers the bride, acknowledging that her vocation is from God, not from men.

The celebrant asks:

'My dear Sister, what do you ask of God and his Church?'

'I ask that I may follow Christ my spouse and persevere in this religious community until death.'

The celebrant explains that this religious profession aims at the holiness of the nun who promises to follow Christ and work for the good of souls. By baptism they have already been consecrated to Christ; now they wish to be more closely united to him so that all they do and say, think and desire may be only for His glory.

6. 'Immersed in God' – Mother Teresa in the chapel of
the mother house.

7. Food distribution in the courtyard of the mother house in Calcutta.

8. Clothing distribution outside a clinic in Calcutta.

9. Devotion and love – the young generation of
Missionaries of Charity.

10. June 1977 – Mother Teresa receives an honorary doctorate
from the University of Cambridge. Behind her walks
Mrs Ann Blaikie, Chairman in Britain of the Co-Workers of
Mother Teresa.

'Dear Sister, are you resolved to unite yourself more closely to Christ by the bond of perpetual profession'

'I am so resolved.'

'Are you resolved with the help of God's grace to follow the life of perfect Chastity, Obedience and Poverty which Christ our Lord and his Virgin Mother chose for themselves and to persevere in it for, ever?'

'I am so resolved.'

'Are you resolved, by the grace of the Holy Spirit, to spend your life in whole-hearted free service to God's poor?'

'I am so resolved.'

'Are you resolved to strive constantly for perfect love of God and your neighbour by zealously following the Gospel and the rule of this religious community?

'I am so resolved.'

The whole congregation then prays that they may be faithful to God's calling and to their vows.

The Sister reads the formula of the vows, in which she says:

'I, Sister Mary Edward, vow for life Chastity, Poverty, Obedience and whole-hearted free service to the poorest of the poor according to the Constitutions of the Missionaries of Charity. I give myself with my whole heart to this religious community so that by the grace of the Holy Spirit and the help of the Blessed Virgin Mary I may seek to practise perfect charity in the service of God and the Church.'

The person who receives the vows then tells the Sister:

'By the authority entrusted to me, I accept your vows in the name of the Church for the community of the Missionaries of Charity. I commend you earnestly to God that you may fulfil your dedication which is united to his Eucharistic Sacrifice.'

The newly professed goes to the altar, places on it the document of her profession which she has just read, and leaves it there to be united to the offering of the Body and Blood of Christ.

She is to be a victim and a witness of God's love.

The celebrant proceeds to offer the Holy Sacrifice.

At the time of Communion, the words of Paul to the Galatians, expressing his proud profession of faith are sung:

'I am nailed with Christ on the Cross; I live, not by my own life, but Christ Lives in me!'

(II Gal. 19–20)

They belong entirely to Christ, they are ready to be sent out to any part of the world to do His work. They will go and integrate themselves into a community of the Missionaries of Charity, which, as their Constitutions direct, should by its fervour and active devotedness, radiate peace, joy and love.

10.   The Brothers

*After this the Lord appointed seventy – two others and sent them out
ahead of him, in pairs, to all the towns and places he himself was to visit.*

(Luke 10, 1)

'Behind Bishop's College in Ahiripukur Second Lane,' Mother
said one day, 'the Sisters have discovered a group of Catholics
who do not seem to be known by the parish. Nobody goes to
Church and the children have not made their first Communion.
Several unions are irregular. The Sisters would like to regularize
a few marriages. The same happens in other slum areas; we discover people who were not married in the church and yet live
together. The Sisters try to obtain the information and
documents required to regularize the situation of these people.
When dispensations are required, parish priests do not always
prove very helpful. I need one or two sympathetic priests to
work with the Sisters; they would visit the slums and co-operate
with them. Then we could do more spiritual good.'

I quite understood their predicament. The prescriptions of
Canon Law had to be followed. Some matrimonial situations
were intricate. As happens in every large city, people came to
Calcutta in search of a job, leaving a wife or husband at home,
and then settled down with another person to cook and keep
house for them. Children were born out of wedlock. We all tried
to help these innocent children. Mother said she needed sympathetic priests to help her Sisters, visit families with them and
settle cases. She seemed to throw out an invitation.

But I told her I was not her man, as I had a full time job as
Professor of Economics. Mother foresaw many difficulties in the
way of a man visiting the slums when the menfolk were out at
work, and only the women and children were at home. That
would hardly be tolerated. The man would be suspected and unwelcome.

129

One or two priests did try the experiment of slum work with
the Sisters. But Mother had larger plans. She was considering a
new foundation: a Congregation of Brothers, similar to that of
her Sisters, trained in the same spirit, working together with
them.

The beginnings of the Missionary Brothers of Charity proved
more laborious and less successful than that of the Sisters. But
Mother's perseverance prevailed. The Church does not favour,
even does not allow a woman to be the head of a religious congregation of men. So Mother Teresa had to find a suitable priest
or brother to direct the new Institute and launch it into being.
Divine providence sent her the required person, a Jesuit, author
of several books and booklets presenting the Catholic faith to
non-Christians, and destined to work at the Catholic Enquiry
Centre of Poona and the Institute for Home Studies. He was
Father Ian Travers-Ball, an Australian Jesuit, then making his tertianship.

The tertianship brings to an end and crowns the long religious,
philosophical and theological training of a Jesuit, with ten or at
least several months of prayer, study, reflection and experiments
conducive to spiritual development and to discovering the will of
God for his religious. Father Travers-Ball made it with zest and
zeal. He felt the call of God to work with Mother Teresa, in the
same spirit, to work among the poorest of the poor in the slums,
among the most needy and abandoned. He received all encouragement from his religious Superiors and from his brother
Jesuits. All rejoiced at seeing one of their own help to develop
the family of the Missionaries of Charity by opening its male
branch.

Mother Teresa was delighted, as she saw God truly bless her
work. She could not expect better than a fully trained religious
priest, young and dynamic, experienced in the religious life.

Some years later the Congregation of Brothers had grown, and
I had a chance to learn more of their work.

In September 1975, I chanced to meet Brother Andrew, the
bearded Superior General of the Missionary Brothers of Charity,
who had just arrived in India from Saigon.

'I was not exactly expelled from Vietnam,' he said, 'but the
Communists took away the three houses we had and occupied

them. With no possibility of work, of starting anything, and no place wherein to reside, I took the plane for Bangkok and India.'

He had previously sent home to the United States four American Brothers and also a Brother from the Netherlands; the Americans would have been in danger at the time the Communists troops entered Saigon.

Three Indian Brothers had already returned to India from Cambodia. One American postulant refused to leave when the Khmer Rouges entered the city where he was working. The last that was seen of him — and that was five months before we spoke — was that he was marched away by soldiers from the Cathedral Square.

'I am going to write a book on Mother Teresa and the Missionaries of Charity,' I told Brother Andrew.

'Yes,' he answered, 'by all means do it. Tell them that we are very ordinary people, that God does everything. You must "demythologize" what has been written about us, and what many people think of us.'

He hesitated before pronouncing the word 'demythologize'; as a theologian, he knew its ugly undertones. He was aware of the harm some religious theories had done to the faith of many, by tearing off and discarding all the miraculous elements in the Gospels. But he used the word, and repeated it without any sign of regret.

'You must demythologize what has been written about us and our work. No doubt much good has been done to a large number of readers by what has appeared. But we have to spend at least six months trying to correct the wrong ideas of the candidates who come to join our Congregation after reading some of the things published about us.

'You must say that we are very ordinary people, all of us. We have our defects, our foibles, our shortcomings, the Sisters as well as the Brothers, even Mother Teresa. She and I do disagree and at times we quarrel. We are instruments inadequate to the task. But the marvellous thing is that God uses us for his work and has produced through the Institute a tremendous amount of good.'

Brother Andrew spoke in the true Christian spirit, as Scripture says: 'To you, Lord, not to us, to you be the glory.' And when we labour for him in that spirit, the Lord does work marvels through his grace.

Brother Andrew stressed the point, as he must have done often when speaking to his young Brothers: the glamour of being in the public eye is dangerous and may do us harm. He had just experienced true poverty and had been forced into complete detachment: of his three years of exertions in Cambodia and Vietnam to establish his Congregation, what remained? Of the Brothers' work, of their efforts to help people, what were the results? Nothing visible – only a few acts of love of God made in faith, which had value for eternity.

Then we spoke of the very beginnings of the Missionary Brothers of Charity. I asked him:

'What influence did Mother exercise on you and your decision? Did she ask you to join her?'

'No, the decision was entirely my own. It just happened. It took very little time. It was during my tertianship at Sitagarha, near Hazaribagh. I had always been interested in the poor and wondered what I could do for them. During my tertianship, I was sent as an experiment to work with the Brothers residing at Sishu Bhavan for a few weeks. When I returned to Sitagarha, I spoke to Father Schillebeeckx, our instructor. I told him I wanted to join the Brothers. He immediately agreed. The Calcutta Jesuit Provincial approved the plan. Permission was asked from Rome to allow me temporary exclaustration. Within weeks this permission was granted, and I left immediately for Calcutta to join the Brothers. All the Jesuits were most encouraging and co-operative.'

'Was the Brother's Congregation already established then.'

'No. There were a few candidates: but Rome did not approve the foundation, though the approbation was requested by Archbishop Albert D'Souza and by Mother. Rome answered: 'First get more candidates, then we shall approve you.' This was a vicious circle; no approbation meant few candidates, since priests would not send us candidates as long as we were not a recognised Institute, but recognition by Rome depended on larger numbers. We explained the matter and finally Rome granted us recognition.'

'Who was in charge when you joined?'

'When I joined them, the few candidates were being trained by Mother and Father Julien Henry. I am afraid did not relish being under a woman Superior.'

'Neither does Rome allow congregations of priests and brothers to be ruled by women.'

'Soon we got a house in Kidderpore and we started on our own.'

'Did Mother have much influence on the training of the Brothers?'

'Well, we disagreed on some points. We had some arguments.'

He hid his face behind his hands, and added: 'There is a letter not to be published as long as one of us is alive.'

Out of discretion I did not enquire further about the cause of their disagreement. Had not St Paul quarrelled with John Mark who refused to follow him? When later Barnabas proposed that they take Mark with them, Paul refused and 'after a violent quarrel they parted company, and Barnabas sailed off with John Mark.' (*Acts 15, 39*) This quarrel puts in the shade the disagreement between Mother and Brother Andrew.

Of course the Brotherhood was first Mother's brain child, the product of her efforts, her prayers and her financial backing. For many years the brothers would be known by the public as 'Mother Teresa's Brothers'. Indeed, they are the Missionary Brothers of Charity, having the same name as the Sisters.

'How many Brothers do you have at present?' I asked.

'The Brothers number about one hundred and fifty. We have already opened fourteen houses, in Calcutta, Titaghur, Noorpur, Midnapore, Bokaro, etc. They started in Los Angeles, where two of the four American Brothers speak Spanish. The Cardinal gave them a house which serves as a novitiate.

'In India vocations have come mainly from Chota Nagpur and Kerala; a few came from Bengal, Tamil Nadu, Bombay and other regions. Some candidates joined us from the U.S. and other Western countries.'

'It will be more difficult to recruit and train the Brothers than the Sisters,' I commented.

'I am glad you recognize the fact,' said Brother Andrew.

The life of the Brothers is not easy; it asks for much self-denial and a deep spirit of prayer.

The percentage of Brothers dropping out during their training is much higher than that of the Sisters. As Brother Ferdinand stated: 'We were thirteen in my year of novitiate in 1967; at the end of two years training seven remained to take their vows. In 1975, for our final profession, we were only four to bind ourselves for life to the Institute.'

'What are your main works, Brother Andrew?' I asked.

'We try not to go where the Sisters are working. But we collaborate with them wherever it is useful. We share the work with them at the Kalighat Home for the Dying. We look after the men whilst they take the women's ward. The Brothers also take care of some destitute sick who are not too ill or weak, in one of our houses. We look after orphaned, abandoned and crippled boys. Many of the Brothers work among lepers. In villages and small towns the lepers are much neglected. The Brothers have assumed this apostolate in earnest; they render very valuable service in this field.'

'Yes, you have here a rich field of apostolic service, calling for genuine Christian self-denial, devotion and true love.'

The Brothers took charge of the Titaghur hospital for lepers after the Sisters had experienced some difficulties in dealing with the men. This specialization should attract to the Brothers good vocations and rich blessings from heaven. Indeed, several Brothers, including Brother Sebastian, the Master of Novices, who is a priest, felt attracted by this apostolate and applied to join the Missionary Brothers of Charity.

Whilst Brother Andrew, the Superior General, was away in Vietnam, Brother Ferdinand was chosen to be his Vicar in India, and he still occupies this post. This allows Brother Andrew to travel about more freely and organize new foundations abroad. He does not intend to bring to India candidates and novices from Western countries to train them in the Indian manner. He thinks that living conditions are too different, whereas Mother at first brought to Calcutta all her foreign candidates. She started novitiates in Melbourne and Rome only when she found it difficult or impossible to obtain visas for her foreign candidates.

Girls may be more resilient and adaptable than boys. Still, Brother Andrew may be right in adapting the Brothers' training and life style to local conditions. His Jesuit formation prepared him to follow the example of St Ignatius, a founder of genius, who told his religious to adopt the language, culture, and style of life of the people to whom they ministered. The Brothers have no distinctive habit; they dress simply and wear a cross pinned to their shirt or coat as a sign of their religious consecration.

The Society counts five priests among its members. Some joined it as priests. As a rule no candidate is admitted specially for the priesthood; it is left to the Society to decide who will be sent to study for the priesthood. It does help the Brothers to have priests among their own members, since this allows them to open houses in mission areas without priests or church.

The Missionary Brothers of Charity, who share Mother Teresa's universal outlook and concern for the souls of poor and suffering children and adults, at present look eastward and plan to open houses in Taiwan, Hongkong, South Korea. They will expand as much as their resources in personnel allow. In this they depend on God's providence; but prospects for recruitment seem fairly good. The future progress of the Congregation will depend mostly on the solidity and depth of the spiritual formation of the young Brothers.

11. The Helpers

'You are God's chosen race, his saints; he loves you, and you should be clothed in sincere compassion, in kindness and humility, gentleness and patience.'

(Col. 3, 12)

'I have three Second Selves,' said Mother.

Indeed she has her own, inalienable self, then she considers as her Second Self in the Congregation Sister Agnes, who replaces her when she is out of Calcutta. She has of course, her spiritual Self, her innermost Self, the Lord Jesus living in her by his grace. Completely surrendered to Jesus, she allows him to take over her direction and act through her.

'I have three Second Selves directing groups of helpers, who work on behalf of our Institute. These form three branches: the Co-Workers or Coadjutors, the Sick and Suffering and the Contemplatives.

'The co-workers are directed by Mrs Ann Blaikie in England. They are forty thousand lay persons. Fourteen thousand in the U.K., six thousand in the U.S., some in Belgium, France, Australia, and so on. They meet regularly; they pray for us; they also prepare bandages and clothes, and other things we need for the dispensaries, for poor children. What matters is that they work for God. In several places they have started organizing holy hours for our work; they have meditation, prayer.'

The material aspect had little importance for Mother; it was only a way of showing one's love for God in action. That they prayed for her work delighted Mother's heart. For this woman of God, money counted little and material services were unimportant, if they did not proceed from love of God.

For a while we remained silent, thanking the Lord for this auspicious development.

'Then,' Mother continued, 'there are the Sick and Suffering, seven hundred of them, I think, organized by Miss Jacqueline de Decker, my Second Self. She worked for some time in India. Now she is in Belgium. She underwent seventeen operations. Some time ago she wrote to me:

' "You are going to receive a great favour from our Lord, because of late my pains have increased." She offers her sufferings for the work of the Missionaries of Charity. Miss de Decker has organized several hundred sick persons who also offer their pains for the success of the Sisters' work.'

'My third Second Self,' said Mother, 'is a French priest, Father Georges Gorrée, who organizes the wing of the Contemplatives who support the Missionaries of Charity by their prayers and penances.'

'Have you houses in France?'

'No,' she said sadly. 'We have not been asked.'

'I quite understand. The present French attitude, mainly among priests and religious, may be too sophisticated for your simple approach to religious and charitable work. But some bishop will probably call you before long.'

'Do write to my three Second Selves,' concluded Mother, 'they will provide you with information for your book on our Institute.'

The Sick and Suffering

The Sick and Suffering was the first link to be organized and connected with the Missionaries of Charity. The idea and initiative came from Mother herself and in the first years of the Institute. She felt acutely that prayer and sacrifices were needed to obtain graces for the apostolate of the Sisters. She felt like St Paul, writing: 'I beg you, brothers, by our Lord Jesus Christ and the love of the Spirit, to help me through my dangers by praying to God for me,' (*Rom. 15, 30*) and repeatedly asking for prayers in his letters to his new converts.

Mother had met Jacqueline de Decker at the Patna Holy Family Hospital where she stayed after leaving her Loreto Convent. Miss de Decker wished to work with Mother and join her religious Institute, but her ill health would not permit it and she was forced to return to Belgium after a stay of two years in India.

Miss de Decker kindly sent me copies of letters Mother wrote to her during the heroic first years, the years of blind faith and trust in God. These hitherto unpublished letters, written with complete openness to a kindred soul, reveal Mother Teresa's ideals, aims, and feelings at the start of her new vocation as no other document does. The letters were written in the Upper Room, in the spirit of the Cenacle. For the history of the beginnings of the Missionaries of Charity they provide an invaluable source of information.

Mother asks the support of Miss de Decker's prayers and suffering. Very early she wished to organize a 'wing' of Sick and Suffering persons to help her fledgling Institute.

In October 1952 Mother Teresa wrote from the Upper Room at Creek Lane to Jacqueline de Decker:

'Today I am going to tell you something which I am sure will make you very happy. . . . Why not become spiritually bound to our Society? While we work in the slums, etc, you share in the merit, the prayers and the work with your sufferings and prayers. The work is tremendous and I need workers, it is true, but I need souls like yours to pray and suffer for the work. Would you like to become my sister' – Mother had first written 'child' but crossed out the word and wrote above it 'sister' – 'and become a Missionary of Charity, in Belgium in body, but in soul in India, in the world, where there are souls longing for Our Lord; but for want of someone to pay the debt for them, they cannot move towards Him. You will be a true Missionary of Charity and you will pay their debt, while the Sisters – your sisters – help them to come to God, in body.' Here Mother echoes the words of St Paul: 'I fulfil in my body what is lacking in the sufferings of Christ for His Body, the Church.'

Mother continues: 'Pray over this and let me know what is your desire. I need many people like you – who would join the Society like this – for I want to have:

1. 'A Glorious Society in heaven.
2. 'The Suffering Society on earth – the Spiritual children.
3. 'And the Militant Society; the Sisters on the battle-field.

'I am sure you would be very happy to see the Sisters – fighting the devil in the field of souls. They count nothing as too hard when there is a question of souls.'

Then Mother adds a remark that will comfort all those who suffer with peace and joy: 'Our Lord must love you much to give you so great a part in his suffering. You are the happy one, for you are His chosen one. Be brave and cheerful and offer much for me – that I may bring many souls to God. Once you come in touch with souls, the thirst grows daily.' Mother again stresses that what moves her to action is the welfare of souls she wants to help to know, love and serve God.

In January 1953 Mother writes and explains further the function of the Sick and Suffering: 'I am happy you are willing to join the Suffering members of the Missionaries of Charity; you and all the sick and suffering will share in all our prayers and works and whatever we do for souls, and you do the same with us your prayers and sufferings.

'You see, the aim of the Society is to satiate the thirst of Jesus on the Cross for the love of souls, by working for the salvation and sanctification of the poor in the slums. Who could do better than you and the others who suffer like you Your suffering and prayers will be the chalice in which we the working members will pour the love of souls we gather around. Therefore you are just as important and necessary as we are for the fulfilment of our aim – to satiate the thirst of Jesus we must be a chalice, and you and the others, men, women, children, old and young, poor and rich are welcome to make the chalice.' Mother does not discriminate between persons; everyone is invited to help, to contribute whatever he can in the matter of love for Christ.

But there must be unity of purpose among all the members, who should be animated by a common spirit. Mother specifies that they should show forth the three characteristic virtues of the Missionaries of Charity:

'One thing we must have in common is the spirit of our Society: total surrender to God, loving trust and perfect cheerfulness.

'Everyone and anyone who wishes to become a Missionary of Charity is welcome, but I want especially the paralysed, the crippled, the incurables to join, for they will bring many souls to the feet of Jesus.' Again Mother stresses that her aim is to lead souls to Jesus; to achieve this end prayer, work, suffering offered to God are needed. Thus started the link of the Sick and Suffering that was to help the work of the Missionaries of Charity.

In March 1955 Mother writes to the Sick and Suffering: 'Every day we offer you or rather offer each other to Christ for souls.

We, the Missionaries of Charity, how grateful we must be – you suffer and we work. We finish in each other what is wanting in Christ.' Here Mother again refers to the Paulinian idea of our collaboration with Christ in his Passion for the good of souls. She adds:

'What a beautiful vocation is ours: to be carriers of Christ's love in the slums. . . . We stand together holding the same chalice and so with the adoring Angels satiate Christ's thirst for souls.

'My very dear children, let us love Jesus with our whole heart and soul. Let us bring Him many souls.' Mother indicates again her main purpose, namely to bring souls to Christ who thirsts for them, who offered himself as a sacrificial Victim to reconcile them to his Father.

She ends with her usual advice: 'Keep smiling. Smile at Jesus in your suffering – for to be a real M.C. you must be a cheerful victim.' She echoes the words of St Paul: 'God likes a cheerful giver,' and 'I rejoice in my sufferings.'

Mother ends with words reminiscent of the Last Supper: 'How happy I am to have you all. You belong to me as much as every Sister belongs to me here.' The Father to whom the Sick and Suffering belong has entrusted them to Mother that she may offer them to Christ for whose glory they were created and now labour. 'Often when the work is very hard, I think of each one of you, and tell God "Look at my suffering children and for their love bless this work" and it works immediately. So you see you are our treasure house.'

In another letter Mother explains what is for her 'the Way of Love': 'Very often I come to you in my thoughts and offer your great sufferings when my own are small or nothing. When it is very hard for you, just hide yourself in the Sacred Heart, and there my heart with you will find all the strength and love which He chooses for you.

'What a beautiful vocation is yours: a Missionary of Charity – a carrier of God's love; we carry on our body and soul the love of an infinite, thirsty God; and we – you and I and all our dear Sisters and the Sick and Suffering will satiate that burning thirst – you with your untold suffering, we with hard labour; but are we not all the same — one "As you Father in me and I in you" said Jesus. You have learned much, you have tasted the chalice of His agony . . . and what will be your reward More and more suffering and a deeper likeness to Him on the Cross. When you pray, ask Jesus to draw me closer to himself on the cross that there we may be one.'

Mother shares St Francis' idea of the 'perfect joy' on earth: the soul reaches this fullness of joy when she accepts to suffer for Christ, and even asks to be united to his Passion, so that the Master and his loving disciple may be more perfectly similar.

Mother feels specially attached to her Sick and Suffering Brothers and Sisters, similar as they are to Christ their Head who suffered for the redemption of mankind. She considers their help to her work invaluable.

The Co-Workers

'The organisation of the Co-Workers,' writes Mrs Ann Blaikie, 'started in a haphazard way when I approached a friend in 1954 to find out if she knew whether Mother Teresa could be approached, as I thought that among our European friends we could collect enough toys for her annual Christmas party, about which we had read in the Calcutta press. (I was living in Calcutta at the time.) Without delay we met Mother Teresa and proposed our plan. She was delighted, and asked us whether we could raise enough money for her to buy dresses or shirts and shoes for her Christian children at Christmas. This we were able to do. After Christmas, Mother came and saw us and asked if we were able to raise sufficient money for the Muslim children's annual festival! After this, of course, we realized that she would be asking us for the Hindu children's party, and so we were, as they say, "hooked".

'We called our small group of women the Marian Society, as it had been started in the Marian Year, and we did, of course, also work for many of the Catholic missions. Soon we spread out and were joined by Indian ladies and other non-Europeans.

'Mother Teresa then asked us to take over the money-raising for her leprosy work, and this we also did. Then gradually groups of women formed small working parties to roll bandages and to make paper bags for the lepers' pills.

'In 1960 several of us who had belonged to the original group left India and returned to England. The good Lord saw to it that we settled within ten miles of each other and it was only a week after my arrival in England that I was caught up again in the work of Mother Teresa by John Southworth, the chairman of a leprosy relief charity. He had been sending money to Mother Teresa and she told him to contact me as I could give him first hand information on the work. About six months later Mother Teresa passed through London and appeared on television, and from that small beginning the U.K. branch of the Co-Workers was born. John Southworth was its chairman, I was its vice-chairman and our other ex-India friends in Surrey formed the committee.

'We based our work on prayer and on giving our members an opportunity for service; people knitted or rolled bandages, collected old clothes and either sent them to India, or sold them and sent the money. But always we emphasised that it was the love that was put into the doing that was important rather than the amount of money raised.

'Some four or five years later Mother Teresa saw the poverty in London and asked her Co-Workers to help those in need in their own neighbourhoods; this is the development which is spreading through the country. Co-Workers now work in geriatric hospitals, with the mentally handicapped, with lonely old people and with others.

'Our prayer life, too, has developed, and hours of prayer among the Co-Workers are now held in very many towns and villages. The one is this village is held in the home of a Co-Worker who is a link with the Sick and Suffering. She is an arthritic in a wheelchair, and her husband is an epileptic. We meet with them once a month and pray with them, and meditate on the prayer of the Co-Workers. Day and week-end retreats are also held around the country. All our prayer activities are on an ecumenical basis, as Co-Workers are of all denominations and religions.

'Similar work is being carried on in other countries where there are branches of Co-Workers. Some countries started when nationals returned to their countries and formed groups. Others started spontaneously, as for example, in Ireland.

'Some have started because a Sister from the country joined the Order, and her friends supported her, and still others have been moved by the publicity about Mother and the Missionaries of Charity to write in and ask what they could do to help. Then after a year or so they have become branches of the International Association. We have Co-Workers also where there is no official association, and these we keep in touch with through our International Newsletters. We have Co-Workers in Poland and Hungary, and as far as Japan and with the Eskimos in the Arctic Circle.'

Thus the Co-Workers have penetrated where the Sisters have not yet entered.

'Our Co-Workers' way of life,' Mrs Blaikie explained, 'is a way of love, seeing Christ in everyone and ministering to Christ in that person. The Missionaries of Charity take a fourth vow, that of wholehearted free service to Christ in His most distressing disguise and it is this which we as Co-Workers must carry on in our lives. Mother Teresa bases the life of the Co-Workers on prayer. The daily prayer of the Co-Workers is the daily prayer of the Brothers and Sisters. Our meetings start with the prayer and then two or three minutes of meditation. She also asks her Co-Workers to join together for an hour of prayer once a month.

'The Co-Worker then goes to show his love for his family, for those in his street and in his neighbourhood, in his country, and in the whole world, seeking out the lonely, the handicapped, the sick and the old, the bereaved and the abandoned, bringing the love of Christ to them.'

On the 26th of March 1969 the International Association of Co-Workers of Mother Teresa was affiliated to the Congregation of the Missionaries of Charity, and their constitutions were blessed by Pope Paul VI.

The link with the Contemplatives
Father Gorrée writes from France: 'In September 1974, as she travelled through France, Mother Teresa expressed her wish that all the houses of her Missionaries of Charity be adopted spiritually by one or several convents of contemplative nuns. Mother asked me to organize this spiritual twinning on an international level.'

Father Gorrée willingly accepted responsibility for this 'linking up' of active Sisters and contemplative nuns in various countries. He approached a large number of contemplative congregations and found a ready response among many of them. Soon he could contact the houses of the Missionaries of Charity and inform them that 'Contemplative nuns have accepted to offer to God the Father their prayers and sacrifices in union with those of His Son Jesus Christ, to obtain the graces that will render their apostolate fruitful.'

The twin communities were asked to send news of their respective work, apostolate, and spiritual experience to one another, so that by knowing each other better they might both be stimulated to serve God more generously.

The result has been remarkable. Within a year, close to four hundred monasteries in Belgium, Canada, France, Germany, Italy, Luxemburg, England and some other countries had with joy and enthusiasm accepted to be linked spiritually to a house of the Missionaries of Charity. An exchange of news and letters started; prayers, sacrifices and work were offered reciprocally for one another.

What struck the organizer of this spiritual twinning most is the joy that it caused among the Sisters of both communities. This feeling for Co-Workers we have never seen nor spoken to is a manifestation of the charity the Holy Spirit pours into our souls.

The Spirit Christ sent us brings joy in abundance. This is the joy Christ promised his disciples at the Last Supper, when he said: 'Remain in my Love ... so that my joy may be in you and your joy may be complete.' (John 15, 9–11). This is the joy of the Risen Christ, the joy of the messianic era that has begun, the joy that the Spirit of Love, the Spirit of Holiness pours into the souls of the disciples inasmuch as they are surrendered to Christ who lives in them.

The Contemplatives are on the mountain with Christ alone in prayer to His Father, sometimes in the morning, sometimes in the evening, at times even the whole night. They are reserved entirely for the service of God, interceding for the needs of the Church and the sanctification of men, whilst the Missionaries of Charity, in the field, work for the salvation and sanctification of the very poor, those cherished children of God.

Thus Christian charity stretches out over the oceans, beyond all barriers, all frontiers of language, culture, nationality. United two by two, each team a link of a strong chain encircling the world to the praise and honour of the infinite God.

12. Publicity

Mother Teresa's success owes much to her remarkable ability to obtain collaboration from every side. She enlisted the help of the Pope, of prime ministers, chief ministers, presidents of various states, and a considerable number of laymen.

She also used all the modern means of mass communication. The media made her known and thus rendered her work possible. They made her first a state, then a national, and finally a world figure. Without the help of the press, the radio and television, her activities would have developed only slowly and would probably have remained confined to India.

'The Statesman,' a leading Calcutta daily, was the first to throw a spotlight on her by mentioning her in its columns. 'The Amrita Bazar Patrika,' another leading daily, followed suit.

English and American ladies spread her fame abroad: *Time* mentioned her several times and carried her photo.

In 1975, *The Illustrated Weekly*, the weekly magazine most widely read by the middle and upper classes in India, displayed Mother Teresa's picture on the cover. In the main story the editor, Kushwant Singh, praised the work of the Missionaries of Charity.

Some months later, in August, Mother told me: 'Mr Kushwant Singh's article has changed the people's attitude towards us. I notice the difference: there are no more misgivings or frowns when we are mentioned. All show sympathy and appreciation for our work. This is really marvellous.'

Mother added: 'Kushwant Singh wrote to me – he wished to make me meet other newspaper editors when I go to Bombay, so that I may talk to them of the poor and of their responsibilities to the weaker members of society. He ends with the words 'God bless you,' she added with a chuckle, 'though I think he is not a believer.'

'I gave a B.B.C. interview,' recalled Mother. 'Malcolm Muggeridge had asked me to appear on one of his programmes. That was the first time I appeared on T.V. They received me at the studio and led me into a small room with a table and two chairs. I sat on one of the chairs and started saying my rosary. After some time, Mr Muggeridge arrived, sat down in front of me, and started asking me questions. He had a paper with a list of questions before him. He read two of them which I answered; then I went on talking about what I wanted to say.'

Naturally, his prepared questions dealt with her and the history of her work. As usual, Mother did not want to speak of herself, but of God. It was all God's work. He did it, not she. Malcolm Muggeridge, a good journalist and interviewer, was conquered by the personality, the dynamism, the energy, the faith of the woman sitting before him. Still, it was unusual to see a Catholic nun in religious habit lead an experienced writer and producer to the subject she wanted to develop. She would make the public hear about God, his love and power. They would be told of the love of Christ which alone motivated these Sisters to devote their whole lives to the service of their Lord in his suffering brothers and sisters.

'Whilst I spoke,' continued Mother, 'they were taking pictures of me. But I did not care; I just went on talking, looking straight in front of me, without moving my head.'

She was a good subject for the cameraman, who must have shifted his camera from her wrinkled face to her sandalled feet, the white saree with a blue border covering her head and forehead right down to her eyebrows, her right hand holding her prayer beads, the cross in evidence on her left shoulder; then back to the expressive mouth, the straight looking eyes of a woman with a single purpose and an iron will. She spoke simply, without show; a deep conviction rang in her voice as she appealed to the viewers to understand and love those around them who feel lonely or unwanted or who lack proper care. She made no mention of money, issued no call for help in favour of her institutions. She stressed that even in well-to-do countries, boasting an elaborate social welfare service, there were legions of persons who looked in vain for love in their own homes, who craved recognition or attention. Further, true love should also embrace those people who belonged to other countries, races and cultures.

Many viewers of the T.V. interview were impressed. Donations for Mother's works poured in.

Malcolm Muggeridge was perhaps the person most impressed. Promoter and organizer of the drama, he had taken an active part in it. He brought a camera crew to Calcutta to make a film depicting the daily life and work of Mother and her Sisters. He stayed three days at the Mother-house, enjoying the freedom of the place. The crew filmed the Mass and the Sisters at prayer; the dormitories; the classrooms; the Sisters taking their meal; the clothes drying; the Sisters filling water buckets and carrying them up the stairs.

He visited the dispensaries, the Kalighat Home for the dying, the Children's Home, the leprosy clinics.

He made Mother talk – she spoke of God's action and goodness, and of the Sisters who worked as his instruments.

Muggeridge interviewed the Sisters. The faith of the nuns struck him and their devotion deeply moved him.

But for the Sisters it is a hard life of· faith, the uneventful repetition of the same humble task day after day. Mother sees the beauty of their life, not with human eyes, but with the vision of faith God gives her. She has nearly reached perfect Christian joy and serenity, since, as she says 'We do it for Jesus,' it is all beautiful. And when she tells us in the Home for the dying 'God is here': her intuition sees him present as simply and obviously as she does the destitute.

But the Sisters, the Sick and Suffering, the Co-Workers and all of us, her friends, we have still to discover God's presence the hard way and work in pure faith as we carry the Cross after Christ. Mother knows it well when she speaks to her Sisters. Her great duty is to train them to constant self-denial, humility, service of the poor, love of God. Close to the great crucifix alongside the staircase of the Mother-house, I read the words: 'The miracle is not that we do this work, but that we are happy to do it.' This conviction Mother drills into the minds of the young novices. 'Be happy to do this work for God,' this disposition, which is neither natural nor easy, requires God's grace and help.

Mother Teresa was the first living Catholic nun privileged to appear on the cover of *Time* in 1975. The caption was 'Living Saints' and the sub-title called them 'Messengers of Love and Hope'. The cover bore her portrait. The artist made the portrait on the basis of photos taken at the Mother-house. Mother Teresa confessed that during this ordeal she asked the Lord to deliver a soul from purgatory for every picture taken. On the cover she certainly looked like a sufferer and not at all as we are accustomed to see her, smiling, kind, serene in the certitude that the world moves constantly, if slowly, towards God. She seemed to bear the suffering of the world. It is one aspect of her personality: she knows suffering; but her faith makes her see the love of God calling men to himself. She brings joy wherever she goes and wants her Missionaries of Charity to do the same. The leading article depicted her correctly, as it stressed that her charity was fostered and sustained by an intense spiritual life.

The various awards and distinctions Mother Teresa has received also helped to make her work and that of her sisters more universally known, appreciated and supported.

In September 1962 Mother received the Padmashree Award from the President of India. Although this is not the highest Indian honour it was a remarkable sign of appreciation shown for the Mother's work.

This was the first time Mother was singled out in this way and the honour caused some difficulties. Archbishop Dyer asked whether he should let Mother Teresa go to Delhi to receive her Padmashree, as some priests feared she might feel some vanity at being thus noticed.

But others, who knew Mother well answered: 'Your Grace, have no fear, Mother does not know what vanity is. Just tell her that by honouring her the Preshdent means to honour all the religious who devote themselves to the service of the poor.'

On her side Mother was reluctant to be thus honoured and she asked the Archbishop 'I suppose I should not go to Delhi?' He answered her 'You must go, Mother.'

The Indian honour was followed by an international recognition: the Magsaysay Award given Mother by the President of the Philippines, who invited her to dine with him and his wife. This Award helped her to establish a Home at Agra and contributed to the knowledge of her as a well known international symbol of Christian charity.

In 1971, there was a flood of prizes:
The Pope John XXIII Peace Prize given to Mother by Pope Paul VI; the Good Samaritan Award in Boston; the John F. Kennedy International Award; a Doctorate of Humane Letters in Washington.

In 1973 Mother went to the U.K. to receive the Templeton Award; the substantial sum of money it carries was immediately spent by her on a foundation for lepers. The Award was given her at a ceremony presided over by Prince Philip. At lunch she was seated next to Prince Philip: a slight nun in a coarse cotton saree next to the tall and smart Prince Consort. Both had at least one thing in common: like Mother, the Prince knows his own mind and speaks it publicly.

'Prince Philip was charming,' said Mother some days later. 'He had kind words to say about our Institute. During the meal he enquired about our work and I told him what we do and why we do it. They served only one course; I suppose it was out of consideration for me, and my work among the poor.' This was a thoughtful and tactful gesture in the best British tradition.

Here stood, in this modern world of comfort and luxury, a living replica of John the Baptist. Her cheap dress, her sandalled feet, her hands fingering the rosary, her direct speech, her single-mindedness reminded all of the Kingdom of God she was announcing. She stood as an index finger raised up high, pointing to heaven. Her smallness and humility raised her above the powerful of the world, whom she lifted up spiritually. Her very example made them cut down their pleasures and comfort, that they might share their wealth with the poor. In the breast of many arose a clearer consciousness of the needs of their brethren, as Mother reminded them of the words of Christ which were the cause of her service to the poor: 'What you have done to the least of my brethren, you did it unto me.'

13.   Mother Teresa Speaks

On the fifteenth of October, eight days after the Missionaries of Charity had celebrated their Silver Jubilee, I had an hour long talk with Mother, a very personal, spiritual, intimate talk. She was perfectly relaxed, serene. It is extraordinary how quickly she had recovered after the heavy exertions of the Jubilee, when she looked pathetically tired and physically exhausted. Now she was fresh and smiling as she spoke.

She was to deliver a speech at the U.N.O. Temple of Religions on the 24th October. She wanted to describe the essential characters of the Christian religion. Her speech was to begin: 'God is Love'. Love in himself, a wonderful process of life, of giving and receiving, of sharing the divine Essence. God creates us out of love; the Father sends His Son to save the world out of love, 'God so loved the world that He gave His only Son that the world might live' (*John 3, 16*).

The Son gives his life and dies for us out of love for mankind. The Spirit Jesus sends us is the Spirit of Love, the Bond of Love between the Father and the Son; He comes to unite us to Jesus and to one another in love. Then, Christ commands us to love one another; and our service to our brethren, who are first the brothers and sisters of Jesus, is a service of love. We serve Christ especially in the needy and the poor, but also in all men, out of love for Him. That love will be all the more perfect if we allow the Lord to live in us and love in us with the perfection of His love.

Mother could close her eyes or look straight before her at nothing or nobody in particular, let the Lord speak and explain this Catholic vision of brotherly love, and the great need men have of it today. That was what the public expected from her. But we agreed that the theological foundation of her vision of love had to be clearly expressed.

Mother took notes, adding to her outline. Then she closed her file.

'When are you leaving?' I asked her.

'Tomorrow I leave for Rome, where a Jubilee Mass is to be celebrated by a Cardinal.'

'Will you go to see the Holy Father?'

'If he calls for me; otherwise I shall not go. After that I fly to New York. I shall stay with the Sisters in our house in Harlem.

'There are times,' she said suddenly, 'when I feel absolutely empty; an empty shell; a thing without consistence, with nothing in me to support me; I feel so lonely and miserable.'

'Yes, and still you go on working for God's glory. It is as St Paul said: "By myself I can do nothing; but I can do all things through him who strengthens me." '

I said this to console her. But I thought of St John of the Cross, and understood what she meant. At times God tries us; at times He gives us a share in the dereliction of Christ at Gethsemane. God seems absent; He withdraws from the soul all consolations and all feeling of His Presence. We must plod on in sheer faith; a faith no more felt, dumb, cold and lifeless.

'Yes, Mother, whoever loves God must pass through the dark tunnel – sometimes more than once; perhaps often and for a long time.'

The fact is well known; the details, the frequency and intensity of the trial vary according to God's plan.

We remained silent for a while, before the mystery of God's work in souls.

Then I asked her:

'When I speak to the Tertians, Mother, on what point do you want me to insist especially?'

'Insist on prayer,' she said. 'In prayer they must find God, find strength to live their vocation and be faithful to it.'

'Yes, in all your chapels on the wall is inscribed the call of our Lord "I Thirst".'

In Yemen 'I THIRST' in English and Arabic.

In Gaza 'I THIRST' in English and Hebrew.

In Rome 'I THIRST' in English and Italian.

'In every house of ours, you enter the chapel and you see "I THIRST!" The call of Jesus. We exist to console Jesus, to quench His thirst for love. It is our function, our aim.

'I pray to our Lord that if the Sisters are not to be faithful to their vocation, he may let the Institute die. God can do without us. The Church would go on existing without us. If the Sisters are not faithful to their religious calling, our Lord may suppress our Congregation.'

'They will be faithful, Mother, I assure you. Our Lord will keep them close to His heart; He will not let them go astray. Your prayers and your blessings will help them.'

'Yes, the Sacred Heart. In Latin America, we consecrate families to the Sacred Heart of Jesus. The Sisters prepare groups of forty or fifty families, regularise marriages, prepare the children for their first Communion. Then, when all are ready, they solemnly enthrone a picture of the Sacred Heart in the house. Is that not wonderful! Our Lord comes to reign over those families, to sanctify them. He brings love in their midst. But first, they must be religiously married, otherwise there is no enthronement. The family must be established on a firm basis to receive God's blessing.'

'Latin America, what a field for your apostolate – such poverty, misery, ignorance, but also such good will, and desire for spiritual values. Mother, do all in your power to spread there. I wish the bishops would call you more earnestly. Your Sisters have the right approach to many of those who live in material and spiritual need in Latin America. Will you open a house in Mexico, now?'

'No, later. Things are not ready as yet.'

'I shall come back via Africa. We have already nineteen African novices and postulants. Excellent vocations. They are keen to devote their lives to our Lord.

'You should open a novitiate there and train your African Sisters in their own environment, culture and tradition. Later you can bring some of them here that they may have the genuine spirit of your Society.'

'We have already two African novices in India. Three are in Rome, and the postulants remain in Africa. Travelling is expensive; it costs much to bring them by air from another continent.'

'Have you any financial problems?'

'Money? I never give it a thought. It always comes. We do all our work for our Lord; He must look after us. If He wants something to be done, He must give us the means. If He does not provide us with the means, then it shows that He does not want that particular work. I forget about it.'

To the same question put to her some fifteen years earlier, she had given exactly the same answer. So that was truly a part of her attitude in life, her trust in God, her assurance that he looked after this small Society. She took our Lord at His word in this matter of material means. Thus a great source of worry and anxiety was removed from her mind, allowing her perfect freedom of thought and action. Having put her full trust in God, she abandoned herself to His holy guidance in all she did, thought, said and taught.

'Mother, do you still personally know all the Sisters and novices?'

'Not the novices. But I know all the professed Sisters.

'I write to them all. Last year one hundred and fifty three took their vows. I wrote a personal letter to each one of them, giving them advice on spiritual matters. They also write to me.'

'So, that is what you do in the evenings! You must write a huge number of letters.'

She smiled.

I thought of the one hundred and fifty-three fish caught in the apostles' nets after the Resurrection of our Lord, as recorded by St John: 'Simon Peter went abroad and dragged the net to the shore, full of big fish, one hundred and fifty-three of them; and in spite of there being so many the net was not broken.' (*John 21, 11*) This was of course an image of Peter's future work, which was to bring men into the Kingdom of God, as followers of Christ. Mother would also catch both women and men and bring them into the Kingdom of God.

January 1976: Mother was back from America, Europe, Africa.

'Each time I go to Europe and America,' she said, 'I am struck by the unhappiness of so many people living in those rich countries: so many broken homes, children not looked after by their parents. Their first duty is to work among their own people, bring together separated couples, build good homes where the children may receive their parents' love.

'They have material wealth; they lack spiritual values.

'Then there are the mentally handicapped. Have you met Jean

Vanier You must meet him. A fine man. He established *l'Arche*, a home for mentally retarded persons. We must work with him, start a home for these people in Calcutta.'

'His organization is completely different from yours, he works with volunteers, free to come and go when the wish.'

'I met some of them and this is what I understood. But their aim and spirit resemble ours: both manifestations of Christian charity.'

'Did you meet them in Canada?'

'Yes, earlier they invited me to Toronto and I spoke to them there. I came back via Africa to visit our house in Ethiopia and the two houses in Tanzania. Africa is a land of promise. There is much poverty there, but also a large field of apostolate. We have excellent prospects. We are going to open a novitiate in Africa, at Tabora. Some twenty African girls want to join us. Four are on their way, to join the novitiate here. After a year I shall send them back with four Indian Sisters and start a house of formation there. They are very keen to work with us.

'In London seven postulants have joined. One Belgian girl has joined; she is the first from that country. Others are from the U.K., France, the U.S. In Melbourne, we have three Chinese novices, and already some candidates from Papua. In Yemen, thirty Moslem girls have refused to marry, and want to work with our Sisters. As Moslems of course, otherwise it would not be tolerated.'

'Where are you opening new houses?'

'I am going to the Philippines to open a house in Manila. The Archbishop is very keen on our settling there.'

'You will have plenty of spiritual work in the Philippines. The people are in the majority Catholic, but the number of priests is very small. There are more than 5000 Catholics to each priest.'

'Why is that?' she asked.

'Well, there is a scarcity of vocations, as in South America. People are baptized but many do not attend Mass or receive the sacraments. Perhaps your Sisters will be able to improve matters, at least in a small manner.'

'We have also been invited to South Korea.'

'Go to Korea, Mother. Go by all means. The Church is growing fast in that country and has a tremendous future. But we must not delay.'

She did not know this. I wondered how then she could decide where to open new houses to the best advantage. Was she sure of the guidance of the Holy Spirit in every case? She did ask advice from some priests. She had her counsellors, but mistakes had been made in the choice of locations.

'Why do you do so much for Darjeeling diocese, a relatively small diocese, as far as population and the number of Catholics are concerned, with a high ratio of priests and nuns to the population?'

'We are going to open a new house in the diocese, at Gangtok, the capital of Sikkim. The Bishop is very keen on our going there. The Church is not represented in this small town.'

'I know many people are well disposed towards the Catholic Church and some are asking for instruction. I said Mass in the palace of the Chogyal of Sikkim some years ago. But we have no church there as yet. Tell me, have you a soft corner in your heart for Darjeeling? Is it because you made your novitiate there or because you got your inspiration in the train on the way to that hill station?'

'No,' she said, brushing away the idea with a gesture of her hand.

'Then has the Bishop mesmerised you?'

She laughed. 'Go to see Takdah,' she said, 'a new house has been given to us there.'

That was a cogent argument. When a property suitable for her work is presented to her, then Mother is inclined to accept the gift. She sees the hand of God in the offering of the property for the Sisters' work.

'Mother, what do you consider most important in the training of your Sisters?'

'Silence. Interior and exterior silence. Silence is essential in a religious house. The silence of humility, of charity, the silence of the eyes, of the ears, of the tongue. There is no life of prayer without silence.'

'Yes, Mother, we need silence to find God, and hear him speak to the soul.'

'Silence,' she said, 'and then kindness, charity; silence leads to charity, charity to humility. Charity among themselves, accepting one another when they are different; charity for union in a community. Charity leads to humility. We must be humble.

'It strikes me how God is humble. He humbled Himself; He who possessed the fullness of the Godhead took the form of a servant. Even today God shows His humility by making use of instruments as deficient as we are, weak, imperfect, inadequate instruments.

'Then, there must be joy in the heart, the joy of serving God, the joy of doing His work. That is not incompatible with humility.'

'Indeed, in her Magnificat, Mary exclaimed that she rejoiced "because He who is mighty has done great things to me!" '

'Yes, I tell the Sisters not to fear to do good before the eyes of men. Our Lord said "Let your light shine before men, that seeing your good deeds they may praise your Father in heaven!" So, let men see your good deeds: it is Christ who does them through you.'

'Father, when they praise us for what we are doing, I do not mind it at all; rather, I rejoice because it all leads to the glory of God.'

'You have just returned from Kerala, Mother. Did you visit all your houses?'

Mother did not answer for a moment. She frowned slightly. I thought I sensed some diffidence or disappointment in her voice, as she answered:

'We have five houses there. People used to look down upon the Sisters because we work for the poor. Now we start to be accepted.'

'You are getting plenty of vocations from that State.'

'Yes. But I want to keep a good mixture. Many novices come from Bihar and Orissa. Vocations also come from Tamil Nadu. We were invited to go to a place where there are eleven hundred temples. A real citadel of Hinduism, very orthodox, with no Christian influence. The Archbishop was very happy when he heard it and he requested me to accept.

'I have to go to Santiniketan to receive a degree. I don't know why universities and colleges are conferring titles upon me. I never know whether I should accept or not; it means nothing to me. But it gives me a chance to speak of Christ to people who otherwise may not hear of him.'

In fact, universities or institutions, especially perhaps the less
known ones, sometimes make use of the world-famous Mother
Teresa to get into the news. At the start Mother may have been
helped by this publicity; but not any more.

'I have also been asked to speak at the Philadelphia Eucharistic
Congress in July.'

'That is a reward for your deep devotion to the Blessed
Eucharist. You already spoke at the Eucharistic Congress in
Melbourne.'

'Yes, but this time it will be more complicated. This is an eight
day affair, and they want me to speak every day on all kinds of
subjects.'

'Well, the Lord will come to your help as usual.'

'Here is Sister Dorothy, who is leaving for Australia to take
over the office of regional Superior.

I felt very unworthy to give a blessing to these two women
whose prayers I needed more than they needed mine, but they
trusted in the priestly power conferred by Christ. Still, I
suggested that we first pray together. We fell on our knees and I
prayed aloud; 'Lord bless the Missionaries of Charity at work in
Australia, make them holy, send them chosen candidates, bless
those to whom they minister, and bless us all.' Then I blessed
Sister Dorothy, and Mother Teresa kneeling by her side.

February 1976: 'I have just come from a meeting of the Calcutta
Co-Workers, said Mother. I told them: "Holiness is not a luxury
– you are all invited to it." I said this to Hindus, Moslems, Jains,
Parsees, Christians.

'They seemed pleased to hear it. I developed the theme in this
way. Holiness is to love God and love men. It is therefore not a
luxury reserved for a few favoured persons. All are invited to be
holy. I told them also that the Sisters need their prayers to be able
to do their work; that the poor need their help, their understanding, their love. We all have much to give, to share, to contribute wherever we find ourselves to be living. Holiness starts in
the home, by loving God and those around us for His sake.'

'Yes, Mother, you spoke rightly; holiness is not a luxury

reserved for a few chosen ones. Still, in practice, real holiness is fairly rare.'

I groped for the text of St Peter which so well applies to the Sisters Mother must train and to all the Co-Workers she inspires and encourages on the way to holiness: 'Be holy in all you do, since it is the Holy One who has called you, and Scripture says: "Be holy because I am holy." These are the words of God, since he is holy, he wishes those who belong to him to be like him.' (*I Pet. 1, 15*)

Mother still felt the pain caused by one of the Sisters who had left the Institute.

'Happily the cross is still there in your life, otherwise Jesus might not recognize you,' I said.

'Yes, we follow Christ, we hear his words "I thirst." So many people still misunderstand us; they take us for what we are not, for social workers.'

'You are certainly not at fault when this happens; you tell them clearly enough that you are first religious women consecrated to the service of God.'

February 1976: Bishop James Toppo of Jalpaiguri was in the parlour with us.

'We are preparing new foundations,' said Mother.

'We are opening a house at Jalpaiguri, where his Lordship has a property ready for us.

'I am just back from Gangtok, the capital of Sikkim. We intend to open a house there shortly.

'And yesterday three Sisters left for Mexico.'

'As a result of your meeting with the President last year?'

'Yes. They have a house ready for us. Later on I shall send a few more Sisters. Some Sisters are also going to . . . what is the name of that country which was recently badly shaken by an earthquake?'

'Guatemala,' I volunteered. 'The people are practically all Catholics, but there are few priests in the country.'

I was happy to hear that the Sisters were broadening their bases in Latin America. And their experience and efficiency in organizing relief in areas afflicted by natural calamities would serve them well.

'Then,' Mother went on, 'we are starting in Manila. Already several girls from the Philippines have asked to join us.'

'Wonderful. You really have the Lord's blessing. I hope you weill soon have a network of houses there. The Philippines suffer from a great scarcity of priests.'

'Why is that?'

'It is due to political and other reasons. The people have a solid Catholic tradition and a deep devotion to Our Lord and to his Blessed Mother. You can build on that foundation. You should get many good vocations from that country.'

March 1976: As I enter the parlour, Mother is talking to an elderly gentleman.

'Father, meet Dr Gupta.'

As we exchange greetings,. Dr Gupta tells me that his son was my student in the Economics Honours class. So we are no strangers.

'Carry on, Mother. I do not want to interrupt your conversation with Dr Gupta.'

'Sit down, Father.'

'Mother,' says Dr Gupta, 'I own a property which I would like to donate to you for your work. I cannot put up a large building, but I shall get some friends to contribute to the expenses. The property is situated on a road near DumDum.'

'Wonderful, Dr Gupta. We have a house at DumDum. The Sisters could go and work in your property. We might establish there an Asha Niketan – a House of Hope – for mentally retarded people.'

I give Dr Gupta my address and invite him to call; then I take leave, as it is time for my talk to the Tertians.

Two days later Dr Gupta comes to see me.

'How did you come into contact with Mother, Doctor?'

'Well, it happened like this. A young woman belonging to a respectable family was brought to me for delivery. Since she was not married, the family would not accept the child. Her parents asked me to find a suitable place for the baby. I had heard of Mother; so I called at her convent. She was absent, but the Sister-

-in-charge was very kind. She immediately said that this was their work; they would take the child any day I chose to bring him. They would look after the baby and eventually get him adopted. This act of kindness struck me much. Since then I try to help the Sisters in whatever way I can.'

This was wonderful. Good people were coming spontaneously to offer their help, to share their property with the poor.

March 1976: 'More and more often,' says Mother, 'I am requested to speak in public. This is an ordeal for me; I wish I did not have to do it.

'How do you manage to speak, Mother.'

'I close my eyes and I do this,' she answered, making with her right thumb a small cross on her lips. 'Then I let him speak. I follow his inspiration.'

'Do you look at your audience?'

'No. I look straight in front of me, above their heads. I look at no one. I deliver my message.'

She remembers what Christ promised 'When you stand before kings and judges, do not worry about what you are to say.'

Still, when she has been warned that she will have to address a gathering, it would be tempting God to go completely un-prepared – that would not be trust but presumption. Her listeners today are not judges and enemies, but friends and sympathizers, who appreciate this opportunity to hear the Word of God. Mother always speaks of God and Christ.

She goes forth in the power of the Lord, as the young David faced Goliath, without embarrassing himself in armour not made for him; he took his sling and five pebbles. God guided his arm and gave him strength. Mother does the same; her words, like pebbles, strike men's minds and shake them out of their ig-norance and complacency. They do not kill; they vivify, awaken, stimulate good impulses and generous actions. She can say, like Paul to the Corinthians, that she does not appeal to human wisdom, but only to knowledge of Christ Jesus. 'As for me, when I came to you, brothers, it was not with any show of oratory or philosophy, but simply to tell you the testimony of God. The only knowledge I claimed to have was about Jesus, and only about him as the crucified Christ.'

As Paul confesses: 'Far from relying on any power of my own, I came to you in great fear and trembling'; (*I Cor. 2, 1–5*) so does Mother, who finds public speaking a most painful and trying exercise; yet for God's honour, she accepts to do it. Like Paul she strikes the minds of her audience because she is filled with Christ.

She talks in a homely, simple, but forceful way. Her speech elevates, yet remains always practical and adapted to the audience.

After my instruction to the Tertians, Mother said:

'We shall take you home, Father. The van is going to the station with the Sisters who take the night train for Kalimpong. We are opening a house there.'

The Sisters sang a hymn in honour of those leaving for Kalimpong. Then the latter went into the van waiting outside, full of luggage; somehow they all managed to squeeze in. I sat next to the driver; Mother sat just behind me.

'We always sing when Sisters leave,' she said.

As the van started Mother led the prayers for a safe journey, and we all answered. The last invocation was as usual 'Immaculate Heart of Mary, cause of our joy, pray for us.' Mary brings joy to the world in the person of Jesus, her child. And now serving Christ in the poorest of the poor, the Sisters put the accent on 'joy'.

We made for the station. On the way Mother spoke of the new foundations she was preparing.

'God,' she said, 'is good to the Institute. The Sisters are invited in many places; we cannot accept all the requests. More Sisters are needed. We must pray for vocations.'

When we reached Sealdah station, the Sisters unloaded the mattresses, blankets, buckets, bags of foodstuffs and all that they were taking with them for the poor.

'We carry all our goods ourselves,' said Mother, laughing. 'They call us the coolie-sisters, because we always do without porters.

'I shall go up to Kalimpong in a few days, when the Sisters have settled down and I can see better what their needs are. They will have discovered what kind of work is more urgent.'

Thus Mother goes from one foundation to another, spreading her work of love always farther into new cities and new countries.

But even in its vast extension this work remains centered on the human person, as Mother shows her concern for the spiritual and material welfare of the individual.

Every human being counts for her; she sees not crowds but faces revealing human souls to her.

14. The Jubilee

'First I thank my God through Jesus Christ for all of you and for the way
in which your faith is spoken of all over the world.'

(Rom. 1, 8)

On a Sunday in October 1976 at the Cathedral of the Most Holy
Rosary, the Archbishop concelebrated Mass with a large number
of priests in thanksgiving to God for the blessings He had
bestowed on Mother Teresa and her Missionaries of Charity and
through them on such large numbers of Christians and non-
Christians.

Members of many religious institutes united their prayers to
those of the Sisters; children and adults, instructed by the Sisters,
benefactors, helpers, all thanked God for the Congregation and
the good it had effected.

On Monday, Mother Teresa and one of her Sisters came to the
Sacred Heart Church, to invite Monsignor Barber and myself to
concelebrate the Mass of the next day, a Mass to mark the Silver
Jubilee of the Missionaries of Charity, a great day of joy and
thanksgiving. As she sat upright in her chair, as usual, I noticed
how tired she looked. Yet she talked cheerfully with us for an
hour and a half.

'I am so grateful to you and to your father,' Mother told Monsignor Barber. 'Your father was the first to help me when I left
Loreto and started this work.'

'You must be very tired, Mother?'

'Yes, but it was all wonderful. People prayed for us and with
us; thanked God for what he had done through the Missionaries
of Charity. These last days, we went every day to pray in some
temple or church. The Archbishop gave us permission to do so.
We prayed with the Jews, the Armenians, the Anglicans, the
Jains, the Sikhs, the Buddhists, the Hindus. It was extraordinary.

All hearts united in prayer to the one true God, thanking Him for the great things He has done through his servants.'

'Yes, this is the spirit of the Magnificat in which Mary exclaimed 'My soul praises the Lord and my spirit rejoices in God my Saviour: because He has done great things to me and holy is his name.'

'Yes. We did nothing; He did everything. All glory must be returned to Him.

Today we were with the Jains in one of their temples. There were four Jain priests who wore no clothes. They sat behind a table.'

'You have been so long in India and you do not know the habits of the Jain priests of the Digambara sect?'

'No. Whilst they were reading from their Scriptures and praying to God, a woman clad in white, a nun, I think, was pulling out some of her hair. In a spirit of penance, I suppose. I tried also to pull out some hairs from my head. It is painful, you know.'

We all laughed. Mother's head is usually so well covered by the border of her saree, that I have never seen her hair.

After some more reminiscences, she spoke of the work. Truly she was indefatigable.

In October, on the feast of the Most Holy Rosary, on which the Congregation of the Missionaries of Charity had been approved by Rome Twenty-five years earlier, a simple, intimate ceremony took place at the Mother-house. All over the world, in some eighty houses of the Congregation, in every continent, in Rome, Harlem, Tabora, Melbourne, London, Lima, Mauritius, Yemen, Jordan, Calcutta, Bombay, Madras, Delhi, Ranchi, among other places too numerous to name, prayers ascended to God in thanksgiving. The Sick and Suffering, the nuns in cloistered monasteries, the Co-Workers of many countries, joyfully sang their gratitude to God and asked him to bless abundantly the Missionaries of Charity during the next twenty-five years.

At six a.m., as I approached the Mother-house, I looked up; there were no clothes hanging to dry on the roof, as there usually were. On the street a milk distributor went on his rounds. People slept peacefully on the pavements. Before the house a discreet police service indicated that the Governor of West Bengal was coming to assist at the Mass at this early hour.

Some twenty priests prepared to concelebrate the thanksgiving Mass with the Archbishop of Calcutta. Father Van Exem was present; Father Henry did not come – he was praying in the church of St Teresa, not far away. Father Gorée had arrived from France for the occasion.

The small chapel was filled to capacity. As the priests entered the chapel for Mass, they could see the crucifix hanging from the wall, and the inscription next to it, 'I THIRST'.

There were pews for the special guests. Mother and the Sisters knelt or sat on mats.

Archbishop Picachy expressed the gratitude of all present for twenty-five years of grace. He expressed the wish that the Sisters be holy and fully dedicated to the service of Christ their Lord.

As the Mass proceeded, words and songs of praise of God and gratitude were on all lips whilst peace, joy, serenity filled all hearts. The promise Jesus expressed in the Upper Room: 'I have told you this so that my joy may be in you and your joy be complete' (John: 15, 11) was realized. The Holy Spirit had come at Pentecost to fill the minds and hearts of all present, bringing his gifts: love for God and men, joy in the service of Jesus and his brethren.

The universality of the Society was manifest: Sisters coming from the six continents were present, eager to return to their posts for work.

In the afternoon, Mother went to Creek Lane, where she had received such heart-warming hospitality from Michael Gomes and his family, and climbed the stairs leading to the Upper Room. Mother brought the picture of Our Lady which had adorned the altar during the years of pure faith. She wished to thank their first helpers and hosts. She stayed ten minutes and left.

The next day, Mother was off to Cuttack, in Orissa, to start a new house there. It was again work as usual, and expansion throughout the world continued.

The Jubilee provided a fit occasion to sum up the results of twenty-five years of work under the direction of the Holy Spirit, of twenty-five years of extraordinary graces and blessings.

In India the Missionaries of Charity have been an unqualified success. The results have been beyond all expectations.

Mother Teresa is the best known and most loved, most widely respected disciple of Christ in the country. She personifies selfless love and service.

Before Mother and her Sisters appeared, the Catholic Church was mainly known as an educational organization; Mother has made the Church known as a charitable organization and as a force for social progress. It still requires a contemplative leader, inspired by the Spirit, to establish the Church before the public as a spiritual and mystical force, leading to the knowledge and experience of God.

During the years, Mother Teresa's fame in India has grown steadily. She was always professed to be first a religious, completely devoted to God's service, receiving her inspiration and strength from God. She has proved to be a model of Christian charity, selfless, caring for all, devoted, asking for and ready to accept the collaboration of others whatever their beliefs.

She has been noted for her quick decision, prompt action, and forceful implementation; and for her readiness to start difficult tasks even without the necessary means, in the certitude that God will provide them when the work is for his glory.

The Sisters, trained by her, imitate her simple, efficient, practical style; they constitute a highly mobile force always ready to render service in time of emergency or calamity.

Mother has worked in the Gandhian tradition – living simply, poor and frugal in her ways, keeping out of politics, working for the destitute, teaching self-help, making use of local resources. Joining prayer to work she proved always ready to assume the most unpleasant tasks.

In Latin America, a continent in many respects similar to India, a few outposts have been established. The Congregation started with great hopes, which have not yet materialized. Valuable spiritual help has been given; but this is still very little compared to the needs and possibilities of this vast area.

The Institute has half a dozen houses and plans to open a few more. But it has not yet taken roots there.

Latin America, with close on half the Catholic population of the world, suffers from a great scarcity of priests and nuns. Its peoples are hungry for religious teaching, leadership and manifestations. In most Latin American countries there is much poverty, a great inequality in the distribution of wealth, large families, numerous slums and terrible poverty in the cities. But there is also a deep Christian tradition on which to build. There are many people who are responsive to the right approach, devoted to *La Madre de Dios* and Jesus crucified.

In such circumstances the Missionaries of Charity could have been expected to succeed as well, or nearly as well as in India. Yet the response has been weak. Calls from bishops came slowly, and are not the numerous, earnest appeals we expected.

When reminded of this, Mother, always optimistic answered: 'We have two novices. Some girls are applying to join us.'

'Yes, Mother, but what is that among three hundred million people of Catholic tradition and belief, with enormous needs?

'You have struck no roots as yet. You have three houses in Venezuela, all right; one in Peru, one in Colombia, one or two elsewhere. But how does that compare with the multitudes, the needs, the possibilities?'

By the end of 1974 the Co-Workers were organized in only one country, Venezuela.

'Why did you fail to effect a real start there, as you did in India?'

The Holy Father himself asked Mother Teresa, in a private audience, to make a big effort to multiply her activities in Latin America. Why did the Sisters not succeed better?

A reason may be the present efforts of some young priests to unite Jesus and Marx; the stress put on economic well-being and social justice rather than on faith in Christ and in the sacramental life; the bent towards political action and revolution, sometimes through violent means; the capitalistic structures which are considered the root of the evil, rather than the sin, pride, greed and sensuality which create them; the move towards Communism.

The Missionaries of Charity are outside politics and care not at all for these preoccupations. When in the United States Mother Teresa was asked 'Do you and your Sisters go in for politics?' she answered 'We have no time for them.'

This attitude in many countries is an advantage: the Sisters are suspected by none; they are concerned only with spiritual and charitable work. The Sisters' outlook is pragmatic; they are saying, in effect: 'We do the work appointed to us; others may, discuss and prepare blue-prints for the society of the future.'

But perhaps people expect from the Sisters a greater degree of adaptation to their life, culture, language. Can the 'Indian Sisters' in Indian sarees catch the imagination of simple folk elsewhere? Should the effort to become adapted to local conditions and the mentality of the people Mother made so successfully in India, not be repeated in Latin America? Various countries have distinctive cultural features that affect their religious life and style.

The adoption of English as their common language has given the Missionaries of Charity a certain universality: it has helped them to spread smoothly in all the countries where English is the language of the people or at least of the educated class. But in non-English speaking countries progress was modest. Should English remain the Society's usual language in Spanish or French-speaking countries?

'A bishop asked me,' said one of the Sisters who came back from Venezuela, 'Why do you not adopt Spanish as your community language?'

In Africa, a good start has been effected. Prospects are bright, possibilities of work enormous, whilst many vocations can be expected from the English-speaking countries of Africa.

The numerical increase of the Missionaries of Charity, though very remarkable, should not be considered exceptional. On the day of the Jubilee, the Sisters numbered 1133, including more than 200 novices.

The progress of the Franciscan Missionaries of Mary, whose Mother-house is at Ootacamund in South India and whose story resembles that of the Missionaries of Charity, was still more spectacular. When they celebrated their silver jubilee, the institute, founded in 1877 by Mother Mary of the Passion, numbered about 3000 members.

Both Congregations wish to offer signal service to God. The Franciscan Missionaries of Mary add to the religious vows of poverty, chastity and obedience a promise to offer themselves as victims of love to Christ. the Missionaries of Charity take a fourth vow to dedicate themselves to the service of the poorest of the poor.

St Paul wished to go to the ends of the world, at least to one end. He planned to visit Spain, considered as it was one extremity of the inhabited world by the ancient Greeks and Latins. He may not have succeeded in reaching Spain, though he saw many countries and preached the faith in more places than anyone in his time.

Mother Teresa was more fortunate; with the same desire, to spread the message of Christ, His work, His influence, as far as possible, she went to the extremities of the world. How otherwise would one explain her keenness and happiness to open a house in Papua, to go to places as widely appart as Fiji, Mauritius, New York?

Still, like Paul she would have to suffer some setbacks. Even after a spectacular development, half the world remained beyond her reach. She had not penetrated behind the Iron and Bamboo Curtains. The Chinese Communist world and the Soviet Communist world, close to one half of the earth's population, were out of bounds.

China, with her eight hundred million people, all God's children, looked like a dream country. Would she ever enter that Promised Land? Would the men in power really object to the Missionaries of Charity, unassuming, unsophisticated, unattached to any political system or ideology? The Sisters were certainly no spies, no revolutionaries, nor did they forward the interest of any foreign country.

Two Chinese Sisters had joined in Calcutta, three more elsewhere. Houses were opened in Taiwan, Macao, Hong Kong, perhaps as stepping stones; one day the Sisters might cross into the mainland of the Celestial Land.

To China, yes, some day, they will go. Francis Xavier died facing the mainland, on Sancian Island, from where his body was brought back to Goa. The Sisters might go one step further; reach the mainland and enter it.

Would the second quarter of a century not see the Missionaries of Charity expand towards the East? Mother had gone East from her native land. Her Sisters had gone mainly West, when they left India.

I asked Mother:

'Are you in Japan?'

'No; but we have a girl who applied to join us.'

'Are you in South Korea?'

'No, but we may go there.'

Now, with a footing in the Philippines, the Sisters can spread eastwards. The Philippines offer a solid Catholic basis and a promise of many vocations. From there they will be able to go to Taiwan, Hong Kong, Indonesia, Japan, South Korea, and even China, in God's own time.

The most admirable result of Mother and her Sisters' apostolic activity is the tremendous number of acts of love for God and the neighbour they have caused to be produced. Acts of love originating from poor and rich, young and old. Acts of love – many of them of heroic quality, coming from the dying destitute whose last words had been 'My God I love you,' or 'Thank you, Sister.'

The acts of love and evotion of children all over the world who went without a meal, an ice-cream or a picture to help some poor brother or sister in some unknown town or village.

The acts of love of viewers of a T.V. programme, of listeners at a meeting, of readers of newspapers and magazines, shown and told the beautiful example of a life-long commitment to the service of Jesus in the poor, and responding to it.

The acts of love of Co-Workers, Sufferers, Helpers, many of them performed in an humble and unobtrusive way.

Countless acts of love of God, forming an uninterrupted chain and encircling the world, as Mother had envisioned in an early letter, when her whole community could still fit within a single room. But could even she foresee the wonders God would work through his weak instruments?

The Future

'After Mother Teresa, what next?' Many asked the question after the glorious days of the Silver Jubilee.

Mother seems to be so indispensable; the whole edifice she has built up appears to rest on her shoulders. She is Atlas carrying the world. The public and the officials know of her above all. Near-

ly everyone speaks of 'the Sisters of Mother Teresa,' whilst
acknowledging her unique charism. This God-given charism is
granted to an individual, not to a group. She believed, remained
faithful, divested herself of all human self-love to belong to God,
entirely; in her Christ lives and acts in a special manner.

What will happen after her? Charisms are not inherited; God
dwells in the individual soul; mystical graces are personal. Then,
in the world we know, hero-worship is directed to a person,
though influence may belong to a group. After Mother Teresa,
what will happen to her Institute?

'If the Society is God's work, it will endure,' said Mother. 'But
if the Sisters are not to be faithful, if they are not to work for
God's glory, then God may as well suppress the Society,' she
added with determination.

Mother does not wish to see her own particular work extended
and continued, but the name of the Lord proclaimed and glorified. This concern should obtain the graces necessary for her Society to continue after her.

Mother said: 'If the Society is God's work.' Is it presumptuous
to affirm that the Society *is* God's work? The Institute has been
officially approved by the Church; it has been blessed and com-
mended repeatedly by the Holy Father, and by many cardinals
and bishops; it is daily praised by the voice of the people, which
is certainly in this case the Voice of God.

Men of all nationalities, social classes and religions are united in
admiration for the works of charity performed by the Sisters.

'After Mother Teresa, what next?' ask many of her friends and
collaborators. 'Will all this good work come to a standstill? Will
the Sisters be able to carry on their apostolate without her
leadership, guidance and support?'

To dispel all lingering doubts concerning this matter, I went to
the Darjeeling Children's Home run by the Missionaries of
Charity. It dominates the town, standing on a hill, two thousand
metres above sea level. As I climbed up, I waved my hand to
children playing on the roof. One of them ran down to open the
door for me, then went to call a Sister.

'This building is new,' said the Sister who took us round.
'Two years ago we had here a shed that was destroyed by a
violent storm. So we rebuilt this part of the building. The people
helped us; the District Magistrate also.'

We went through the different rooms, which housed about a hundred inmates.

'All these children suffer from malnutrition. We feed them, give them vitamins and injections to make them strong. Many have wounds.

'This girl is sixteen years old; when she arrived she had a large sore on her leg. Now the wound is closed and healing. It was due to malnutrition. This girl has a stunted arm; this one is mentally retarded.

'We have ten orphan boys I sent as boarders to the Pedong High School; we must pay eighty rupees per month for each boy. We have also twenty orphan girls studying at the Bethany and St Teresa's Convent Schools close by; these come home for the night.

'Here is an old lady who is close to death.'

The lady, who was not a Christian, recognized me as a priest and asked for a blessing. I blessed her. The other ten or twelve inmates also asked for a blessing. We said a short prayer together and I blessed them.

'One person died the other day,' said Sister. 'Come this side; there are more children. Some are total orphans, others have one parent living. Either the father is at work and cannot look after the small children or the mother is too poor to feed them. One woman has four children here; a widow, working for a very small salary; she could not keep her four children. They all suffered from T.B. and malnutrition. Now they are picking up. This boy here seems to have no intelligence; he does not react to anything you say. We are trying to find out if he really is mentally deficient. With better food he may improve.

'Many of these cases come from the villages. We have a van and go down to the valley for dispensary work once a week. We brought here some of the more needy children.'

As we reach the chapel, Sister tells me:

'You know this place, you gave us some instructions two years ago.'

'Yes, I remember the chapel. Let us say a prayer for these good people and for the Sisters who look after them.'

The chapel is the source of strength and the oasis of consolation in the midst of all this misery, and among the poor of the Lord.

The visitor who stays one hour in the Home, smiles at the

children, says a kind word, pats a cheek, gives a blessing, finds this pleasant. But for the Sisters it is the same hard task from morning till evening, and sometimes at night, caring for sick children and the dying destitute, not for one or two years, but for their whole life, with never a break.

The only spot of beauty and intimacy in the house is the chapel. It is as beautiful as they can make it; for the Lord dwells there. I see two vases holding lovely white lilies, lilies for Jesus present in the tabernacle, present in these suffering brothers and sisters. Against the wall stands a large crucifix; above it are written the words of Christ 'I Thirst'. The Sisters are daily reminded of the call of Jesus that brought them here.

As we leave the chapel, I put to Sister the question for which I had come to see her:

'Sister, does Mother Teresa come here often'

'No, she has not come to Darjeeling for a long time.'

'Does she write to you often?'

'No, she is too busy. She writes very seldom.'

'Do you receive any supplies from Calcutta?'

'We receive some supplies from Catholic Relief Services, as other charitable institutions do. Once a year I go to Calcutta to get a supply of medicines.'

'Do you ask the Bishop for any help?'

'No, we do not ask the Bishop for any financial help. He sends a priest from Bishop's house to say Mass for us daily.'

'Of course, he must look after your spiritual welfare. And did you contract any debt on account of this new building?'

'No, we have no debt. We manage things by ourselves.'

'I see that you do it very well.' I took her leave and came back singing on the road. I had the answer to the question so many people were asking: 'After Mother Teresa, what next?' The answer was simple:

'After Mother Teresa the Missionaries of Charity.' This house of the Sisters and many others like it were being run quite smoothly without Mother's intervention or help. The Foundress had succeeded in her main task. The well trained Sisters could stand on their own feet and take over.

There remained to answer the question: 'After Mother Teresa, who? Who will take the reins and guide the Society in its progress?' The answer lay in the Constitutions that specified how the Society was to be governed.

Mother and Father Van Exem had created the pattern of government in conformity with church rules for religious congregations.

In 1975 the General Congregation of the Institute had appointed Mother as Superior General for six years. All the ballot papers, except one, bore Mother Teresa's name as their choice to direct the Institute for the next six years.

Father Van Exem, the presiding officer, destroyed the only differing ballot paper, so that only he knows for whom Mother voted.

When Mother Teresa becomes unable or unwilling to carry on as Superior General, the Sisters elect a new Superior according to the rules laid down in their Constitutions. This Superior will not inherit the personal charisms of the Foundress; but she will receive from God the graces necessary to carry out her duties of Superior General of the Millionaries of Charity.

15. It was Thirty Years Ago . . .

September 1976
'How was the Eucharistic Congress in Philadelphia, Mother'
  'Very fine.'
'Did you have to speak many times?'
'Yes, they wanted me to speak everywhere. I went about with
eight policemen around me the whole time. The people would
have crushed me. . . . I am so small. It was my worst penance to
be thus guarded all the time.'
'Was there much pomp? or did you feel in a real religious atmosphere?'
'There was no show of pomp, no display. It was simpler than
the Congress at Melbourne. The great procession with four hundred thousand participants was very religious. Cardinal Knox
knelt on a priedieu behind the monstrance of the Blessed
Eucharist, carried on a float. The American people are very
pious. There were groups of other, how do you call them?'
'Denominations, they say nowadays.'
'Yes, denominations, present at some of the functions. We
washed each other's feet, exchanged the kiss of peace, broke
bread and ate it together, but then when it came to the
Eucharistic sacrifice, they fell back. This was very painful. At
Mass they would not join us. When there was Communion to
the Body and Blood of Christ they were not with us. That was
painful.'
'Yes, the Eucharist is the sign and touchstone of unity. We are
truly one around the altar where the Lord becomes sacramentally
present. We must pray for unity, complete unity that we may
truly form one body of Christ.'
'Your General made a beautiful speech at the Congress. I must
quote it when I meet some of your Jesuits,' she chuckled, 'I must
tell them to live more poorly and go to the poor.'

Soon she was back to her great preoccupation.:

'We must work for souls; it is really souls that matter. I feel so happy when I can do good to souls.'

She had written this in her intimate letters to Jacqueline de Decker, thirty years earlier. Her hunger for souls had not abated; it had grown with the passing of the years.

'I think the Sisters also feel happy when they can do good to the souls. After all that is why we started looking after the dying, that we might help them think of God at their last moments and made an act of love of God before dying; we want them to die with God.

'I think the Sisters also see the souls behind the bodies and rejoice when they can do spiritual good.'

She said 'I think' with imperfect conviction.

'The work does not distract me from God,' she continued.

'I went to Mexico. We have opened a house there. When the Sisters go round, the poor do not ask them for clothes, do not ask them for food, they ask them:

' "Teach us the Word of God." '

'So the people ask to hear the Word of God. . . .'

'No, they don't ask to *hear*, they ask the Sisters to *teach* them the Word of God.

'The President himself made arrangements for our house there, not the government. Everything is well arranged.

'Mexico is a huge city. On the outskirts where they gather all the garbage brought by the conservancy department, some five hundred families live on the picking and sorting of refuse, as many people do here. I told the President to leave them to that work, that is what they can do. Make the surroundings better and improve the houses and let them go on with that work. Already the Sisters have started instructing the children for their first Communion.

'We shall buy five hundred New Testaments and distribute them to these families. The whole Bible is too expensive. Also it is too difficult for them. Is this not wonderful that the people are hungry for the Word of God? Of course, in Mexico Catholics have been persecuted; this may be the result. Even now priests and nuns are not allowed to wear clerical or religious dress. Our Sisters go about in their habit – nobody knows what the saree is. But they wear their cross.'

'But, Mother, it is such a pity. In many places God's children are hungry for spiritual food and no one is found to give it to them.'

'Things are better in Mexico than in South America.'

'You are not doing too well there?'

'We have only two vocations. Lima, Peru seems more promising than Venezuela. The poor hanker for spiritual things. Why must so many priests and nuns busy themselves with politics when their primary work is to teach the faith?

'Everywhere people tell us: speak to us of Jesus.'

'Did you not start a new congregation? The news came out in the papers.'

'Yes, the Sisters of the Word. They are a contemplative branch. They have three hours of prayer at home and one hour in the church. Then daily two hours to go out and speak of Jesus. Not public speaking in the squares or street corners, just to speak of Jesus to people who want to listen. People are eager to listen to those who speak of our Lord.

'I wish I could retire there among the Sisters and just live a contemplative life, just be with Jesus.'

'Not yet, Mother; you have still much work to do. Why did you start that branch in the U.S. and not here?'

'Because they are ready for it. Sister Nirmala is in charge. She will do very well. She has already seven candidates.'

'Is the aim to receive nuns who left their convent and wish to come back?'

'There may be some such cases, of people who wish to do penance and to join the Institute.'

'I suppose the Congregation will develop under the inspiration of the Holy Spirit.'

'Yes, And speaking of inspiration, today is 'Inspiration Day' the 10th of September. It was thirty years ago, in the train taking me to Darjeeling that I heard His call.'

'The call to serve Jesus in the poorest of the poor. And you obeyed his call. When did you come to this house?'

'I do not recollect.'

'Was it in February 1954?'

'Yes, about that time.'

'Did you go to pray to the Fatima Shrine to obtain the house?'

'Yes, I went at times with the Sisters, praying on the way.

'They had first told me about another house, which was to cost us eighty-five thousand rupees. As I did not have the money, I decided to offer the sum in Memorares to Our Lady. So we all started saying Memorares. Every Sister one thousand Memorares. I said the prayer thousands of times. But we did not get the house. Instead a person told me "there is a gentleman who has a suitable house; I shall take you to him." He did so, introduced me and then left. The proprietor was astonished. "I don't know that person, neither did I tell anyone that I wanted to sell the house. But I was contemplating doing so." The house came to one hundred and twenty-five thousand rupees. Monsignor Barber paid it out of the diocesan funds.'

'And you paid them back slowly.'

'Yes, I paid back two or three hundreds at a time.

'I did not pay Our Lady again in Memorares, I had paid her once.'

'And now, it has become too small. You should look for another house for another novitiate. The place is too crowded.'

'No,' she said.

'But then you will have to refuse candidates, since the numbers are always increasing and you really cannot accommodate more in this house.'

'Why not? The Sisters can sleep on the floor; the poor do it.'

'They require more space; you cannot train them properly in this manner.'

'I shall remove the postulants who are here and send them to Park Street. And the candidates can be first received in various houses to see our kind of work and life.'

'That will lighten the burden on this house. Even so, you may have to open another novitiate in India.

'No. They must all come to Calcutta.'

She thought that only in the historical Mother-house would they imbibe the real spirit of the Congregation.

'You should open a novitiate in the Philippines,' I suggested. 'Transfer there the one from Melbourne. And from the Philippines you can spread towards the Far East; Hong Kong, if you find a property, Taiwan, Indonesia, Korea, Japan.'

'There is plenty of scope there. And one day, China.'

'Yes, the Philippines would be better than Australia. We have only two girls from that country, and do not expect to recruit many.'

'In the Philippines you will have plenty of candidates. For the training of the sisters in poverty and in work for the very poor, Australia is not the place – the country is too rich.'

'You should see our work among the aboriginals; they are terribly backward; it is incredible the way they live.'

'But the style of life will be more similar in the Philippines to what the novices meet in the East and Far East, except perhaps in Japan, which has become a rich country. But of course you require the good will and support of the Bishops of the Philippines.'

'Yes, in the course of time we can open a novitiate in the Philippines, and of course one in Africa.'

'And how was Rome, Mother?'

'Wonderful. I saw the Holy Father, in private.'

'I had told you he would call for you.'

'There was nobody else. I talked to him as I talk now to you, just facing him and quite simply.'

'Did he enquire about your work?'

'He knows about it already. I spoke of the new Congregation, the Sisters of the Word. He sent a blessing to all the Missionaries of Charity, to all the Co-Workers, he gave a special blessing for the Sisters of the Word.'

'You had a meeting of the Co-Workers in Germany?'

'Yes, it was wonderful. There are eighty thousand Co-Workers now, twelve thousand in the U.S.'

'Did you meet Jacqueline de Decker? was she able to travel to Germany?'

'Yes, she runs the Sick and Suffering. Only the national Vice-Chairmen came to Germany. They had to pay their own passages. The organization did not pay for them. I had told them to save the money during the year, that it be not a burden on their family budget. The Germans were marvellous; no one had to go to a hotel; they were all received in families. When we met they insisted on prayer; prayer meetings every week, or every second or third or fourth week.

'I told them to practise charity first in the home, then among neighbours, then in their locality, in their country and finally in the world. But first have a home where there is love and understanding. Love between the members of the family will bring happiness.'

The Angelus bell rang in the convent. We said the Angelus. Mother then said:

'In many places the poor are happy to hear the Angelus bell. In New York the poor complained to the Sisters: 'Why is it that we don't hear the Angelus now? We were happy to pray to Our Lady when we heard the bell rung, the announcement of the good news of the coming of the Saviour.' The Sisters asked the priest, who said he had no time to ring the bell three times a day, and the parish could not afford to pay a person to come and ring it. So the Sisters took up the duty 'We shall come and ring, Father' they said. And now the poor of that very difficult locality are happy that they can again pray the Angelus.

'The poor are hungry for God; they want to hear about Our Lord. They do not worry so much about material things; they want to hear that they have a Father in heaven who loves them.

'About the book, I must ask you, nothing personal, that is, no personality, no personal credit. He did it all. It is all His work.'

'Yes, you do not want any praise; all praise is reserved for God. But you may say with Our Lady in her Magnificat 'He has done great things to me and holy is his Name.' What the Virgin Mary said you may say also.'

She was right; she had no merit in the whole thing except that of having allowed God to work through her. Humility is truth, said St Teresa of Avila. All good comes from God. But looking back to the moment of her call on the Road to Damascus — rather, to Darjeeling — she could say with St Paul 'I have kept the faith God had reposed in me, I remained ever faithful to Him.' Then he did great things through His humble handmaid

'We are not channels,' I added, 'we are instruments. Channels give nothing of their own, they just let the water run through them. In our action we are instruments in God's hand.'

'Yes,' she said, 'I like the comparison. I feel like a pencil in God's hand.'

She looked for a stub of pencil on the table, but there was none. She made a gesture with her fingers: 'God writes through us, and however imperfect instruments we may be, he writes beautifully.

'In God,' she continued, 'I find two things admirable: His goodness and His humility. His love and His humility are striking. God is truly humble; He comes down and uses instruments as weak and imperfect as we are. He deigns to work through us. Is that not marvellous?'

'Yes, it all starts with the idea of the Incarnation. The Son of God assumes our human condition; He walks among us and works with us; He even accepts to die on a cross to atone for men's sins.'

I knew well that Mother did not want any praise. I had recorded as objectively as possible what I had seen and heard and felt during these years with her and her Sisters. I took my clue from St John writing to the second or third generation Christians: 'What we have seen and heard and touched of the Word of Life, that we make known to you, that you also may share in our fellowship;' yes, share our experience, and rejoice at the coming of the Lord, at his manifestation to men, at the wonderful works he performed and still performs for our spiritual good, to save us and sanctify us.

I had an obligation to my readers who wanted to know how this page of Church history had been written, how this spiritual saga, this wonderful story had started and developed under the guidance of the Holy Spirit. A senior Sister had suggested: 'Father, please write especially about the beginnings. Say how the Missionaries of Charity started, give us a book that may inspire the younger members, the future novices who have not known the first years....'

'Yes, Sister, the years of pure faith, the heroic years. Those who will join you later on have the right to know how the Congregation started. There are two trunks full of documents still with Father Van Exem. They may perhaps be opened at the next Jubilee. They will reveal details of juridical proceedings, correspondence dealing with the establishment, the constitutions, the rules of the Missionaries of Charity. That is for the historians who will sift the material, when all those connected with the foundation are gone to their reward.'

I had written at Mother Teresa's request to tell those who wanted to hear the simple and beautiful truth about the origins and the purpose of the Missionaries of Charity. I tried to write soberly, critically, constructively. As the spiritual director and confessor of the Mother-house for many years, I had felt that the Spirit of God guided the young Congregation. I had spoken with Mother on spiritual matters; we had discussed various aspects of the work and new foundations.

And now, to crown it all, the Lord had been good to me. In ninety minutes, on the thirtieth anniversary of the Day of Inspiration when Jesus had called Mother Teresa to be more closely united to his divine Majesty, we had gone over the different phases of the Institute, and summed up one by one the chapters of this book. Mother had followed the lead and confirmed what was written. She had always remained single-minded in pursuing her aim; neither the substance nor the emphasis had changed over these thirty years. God had been good to her, he had been good to me.

The bell went for the community supper. I got up and took Mother's leave. She accompanied me to the door; we both folded our hands in parting in the Indian manner. Then she bent down low, very low, out of respect for the priestly character of the man who makes Christ present on the altar. Mother Teresa is a woman of faith.

'Be careful,' she said gently, as she opened the door leading to the narrow lane and remembered that I am half-blind, 'there are two steps.'